DAUGHTER OF FIRE & STORM

K.C. PRESTON

Book Cover by Etheric Designs

Illustrations by Etheric Designs

Edited by Starweather Press

ISBN 979-8-9893621-0-3 Hardback

ISBN 979-8-9893621-1-0 Paperback

ALSO BY K.C. PRESTON

Daughter of Fire & Storm Series:

Daughter of Fire & Storm
Throne of Blood & Lies

To the person who never let me give up and who stopped me from throwing my entire novel in the fire pit on more than one occasion. To the one who begrudgingly hauled all my notebooks all over the world so I could write on vacation, and the one who put up with me being "absent" when I had words to get down. I love you and I promise one day Morgan Freeman will tuck you in and read my book to you.

ONE
ABRAHAM

THE AIR WAS CRISP, the clouds above Howling Cove loomed ominous as thunder sounded in the distance. Icing from my sweet roll coated my lips. I moved through the crowd of patrons who bustled among booths and shops in the market district. Carriages rushed by with people bundled up inside against the cold. Pausing for a moment to let one such carriage pass, I crossed the road to the tavern. The Hidden Gem. Pulling the door open, a wall of heat hit me, and I coughed.

It reminded me of the Abyss. Hot. The stench of smoke, stifling. I looked around the room, catching three men sitting in the corner—Sam, Bones, and Lucas—Soul Collectors like me.

Making my way toward them, I pulled out a chair and sat down.

"Abe," Bones said, nodding at me. His voice rasped. He was lanky; his skin clinging to his bones, making him look skeletal.

Sam shuffled a deck of cards and dealt. Locks of his brown hair fell into his dark eyes. I looked at my hand.

Four knights and a serpent.

Chuckling under my breath, I threw several coins into the pot. I didn't even look at my wager. Lucas discarded two cards and picked up two more. Smiling, he tossed in enough coin to meet my bet. It didn't matter what he drew. I had the Luck of the Fallen One with me. I always won.

"Been slow lately. Doesn't seem like many are looking to sell their souls," Sam said, brushing a lock of his hair from his wide forehead.

"The Fallen One is none too happy about it." His silver eyes glanced at all of us in turn. There was the usual edge to his gaze.

I knew all too well of Themesis' displeasure. Out of all of us, I was the closest to him, being a Soul Collector for longer than I could count. And I was the one who bore the brunt of his disappointment on the regular. Service to Themesis went without perks, though the other Soul Collectors might not agree with my sentiment. They did not know any better.

"I'm out," Sam sighed, tossing his cards down. I glanced at Lucas, then Bones.

"Show them," Bones said.

I put down my cards, showing the four knights and a serpent. The three men groaned, and I chuckled as I pulled the pile of money toward me. It wasn't much, but I knew the loss hit them hard, and I was happy to make their purses lighter.

As I put their coin into my pouch, my vision grew hazy. Through it, I saw a man lying on the floor of a bedroom, a dagger embedded in his chest. A woman loomed over him. My companions looked up as I rose to my feet. "There's a soul in need of some attention," I said.

"Why do you get it?" Sam grumbled.

I said nothing. Nodding my goodbye, I slipped out of the tavern. It was dark now, which meant it was easier for me to call the shadows. The demons closed in, and I slipped away. I sent tendrils of my magic out, feeling the darkness, and I found the Abyss.

The shadows slunk across the road to the corner where I stood. Red-eyed demons with white teeth, and maws dripping saliva, loped over the cobblestone.

No one but me saw. Good thing. If anyone else had seen them, it would have stricken horror into the strongest hearts and minds. I beckoned the shadows. The demons gathered, hissing and snarling, eager to take a soul to Themesis, the Fallen One.

I felt a rustle in my beard and heard a purr. Sighing, I reached up and pulled out a demon. He was tiny at the moment, fitting in the palm of my hand. Silver scales covered his body. Wings flapped, his back arched, and his barbed tail wrapped around my arm. Pointed ears turned, listening. A forked tongue flicked out, tasting the air, and red eyes looked up at me. He was my protection. My familiar. Though he was small at the moment, if provoked, or when protecting me, he could grow to the size of two draft horses.

"Bel," I said, bringing him to eye level. "This is an easy one."

And it was. Damiyun Rayne's soul was dark as soot. With every deed he'd done, it drew him closer to the Abyss. I could feel the blackness in his soul.

Bel let out a series of chirps and growls. "You are a curious one," I chuckled as I tucked him back beneath my beard and let the demons and darkness carry me to my destination.

When I entered the room, the stench from Damiyun's wound and the blood filled my nose. Bel hissed at the dagger in his chest. The woman looked down on him, a smile quirked her lips, and her eyes danced with delight. The floor was soaked in his blood. His skin had grown paler than usual, deathly still. Cold had come in place of life's warmth.

Damiyun didn't look surprised when I appeared between the plains of the living and the dead. I pulled out the contract, a typical form with Themesis' seal promising to spare his life for now for eternal servitude later. I glanced at it, wishing to tuck it away and leave this place, but Damiyun had called out on some level, or rather his soul had called. It was his choice. Still, I would not wish such a fate upon anyone. Not even Damiyun Rayne.

"My name is Abraham, and I am a Soul Collector. You called to me. I want to make sure you understand what this is. What you have asked for with your last breath." I unrolled the contract and read. "Damiyun Rayne, you have died and your soul has summoned an Agent of the Fallen One. This contract, should you choose to sign, will bind your soul—"

"I know all of this," he said.

I raised an eyebrow. "There is no turning back, Damiyun. Once your name is signed, I will own you. He will own you." Most think they know the terms. Think they understand what they are getting into, but when the time comes, when the contract is called, it is always nothing but surprise. Nothing but tears and begging.

He laughed. "Do you think signing this contract makes any difference? My soul is his, regardless."

I shook my head. "Perhaps, but signing this will secure your Eternal Rest. Think long and hard about what you will agree to."

His eyes flicked to the woman, his wife Zenith, who loomed above his dying body, and I followed his gaze. She shook her head, her lips moved, and I could read the words she spoke. *Goodbye, Damiyun Rayne, you pathetic excuse for a man. I only wish this had happened earlier.*

Damiyun looked back at me. "I understand the terms and I wish to put my name on the contract."

"For that?"

"I love her."

I laughed. Ice ran through that woman's veins. Her words proved she never loved him. She had tried to kill him. And Damiyun? A pretty face and a warm body is what he loved, though I could hardly blame him for being captivated by the fairer sex, as most men are wont to be.

"Are you sure?" I didn't care. Not truly, but I did want him to think about his choice. I wanted to make absolutely sure this is what he wanted. While it was true his soul, his eternity, resided in the Abyss, what he would have suffered if he just let himself go would pale in comparison to what would await him once he signs his name. Once the contract was called, Themesis would own him and he would inflict unspeakable horrors. Torture beyond anything anyone could endure would twist him into a monstrous being whose thirst was blood and pain.

"I am."

"This is a binding contract. Once you put your name—"

"I told you. I am aware of how this works."

"Have it your way," I said, pulling out my golden quill. Grasping his index finger, I stabbed the nib into the tender flesh, drawing his blood into it. Handing the quill out to him, I held the contract up. "Sign."

Taking a deep breath, he signed his name.

"It is done. Themesis holds your soul, and when the contract is up?" I shrugged.

Dark mists surrounded him. Demon claws reached out, pulling him nearer. Damiyun's eyes widened in panic. A look of regret flickered across his face, but there was nothing I could do. I watched as he was brought to the plains of the living; his soul returned to his body. His eyes opened, and Zenith drew back in surprise and disgust.

Sighing, I rolled the parchment up and again stepped into the shadows with the demons who escorted me to the Abyss.

TWO

I DETESTED THIS PLACE. The scorching heat was oppressive and the obsidian tomb suffocating. Demons loped about, once men and women who had sold their souls. In the Abyss, their suffering twisted them into demonic monsters, not only enslaved but willing to do The Fallen One's bidding. None deserved pity. They chose this existence. Unlike me, I was born to it.

I always warned them. I always gave them a few moments to think about what they were about to do. Always their reasons were selfish, love and riches being the most popular. The only ones I pitied were the living who called out to me. The ones whose reasons were selfless, to save a life, to assist a friend. It was not for me to question their damnation. My job was to heed their call and get their contract.

Shaking the thoughts, I pushed the doors to Themesis' drawing room open. It was richly furnished. Plush couches and comfortable wing-backed chairs with deep cushions upholstered in rich, blood-red brocade. Tables chiseled from the tomb's obsidian rock with intricate designs of demons and ivy carved into them. Plush rugs dotted the floor and tapestries depicting Themesis lined the walls, and a large portrait of him hung on the wall above the fireplace behind the chair where he casually lounged. As always, he was smartly dressed, wearing a royal blue tailcoat over a black shirt, blue pants, and polished boots, black hair flowing about his shoulders. His feet were propped on the table in front of him. One hand holding a glass of wine dangled off an armrest, the other held open a book on his lap.

The sound of my shoes scraping on the black obsidian floor drew his attention. A smile curled his lips and his blue eyes met mine.

"What do you have?" He set his book aside. Holding his hand out, I strode forward and handed him the contract. Unrolling it, his smile widened. "Damiyun Rayne. Excellent. While I always appreciate another slave, this one in particular matters," he said, handing the parchment back to me. Draining the contents of his glass, he snapped his fingers. "Jaylynn," he called out, and I stiffened. The door opened, and I couldn't stop myself from turning. I watched a young woman enter the room. Black hair tumbled down her back in soft waves. She wore a silver dress, sheer, low-cut with slits on the sides up to the hip. The low lamp light glinted off the hundreds of diamonds that made up the collar she wore.

Jaylynn. My daughter and Themesis' mindless slave.

Her chocolate eyes met Themesis' blue ones, and she smiled.

"Refill my glass and pour one for him," he said, holding his glass out. Jaylynn hurried to grab the empty glass, returning moments later with fresh drinks. My stomach roiled as I watched her kneel beside him, his free hand idly scratching her head. She smiled up at him, and I had to stop myself from vomiting on the floor at the look. Stop myself from running him through with my dagger, though I knew it wouldn't kill him. It would only infuriate him.

I pulled my eyes from my daughter and turned my attention to Themesis. "Why does Damiyun matter?"

"He will have what I want." He leaned forward in his chair. "The Goddess of Nature will task him with bringing her daughter here to destroy me." He chuckled low, lips curled into a snarl.

I took a sip of my drink, choking down the sickeningly sweet wine. "How do you know this?"

Themesis eyes narrowed, and his hand curled around his glass. "I have ways. You know this." He sat back in his chair.

I was sure those ways had to do with inviting Felicity, the Goddess of Nature, to his bed. She was as conniving and narcissistic as he, possibly more so. It wouldn't take much convincing for her to say yes. She spread her legs for any man she thought she could easily manipulate, though Themesis wasn't a fool. He was calculating and cunning, and I have often wondered if the coup he orchestrated thousands of years ago was for this purpose. His magic pulled from the Abyss, and the longer he resided here, the stronger he became. If he were freed and unleashed upon the world, everything would turn to darkness. People would become his slaves, eventually turned into disfigured and demented demons. Women would be used and abused. Devilish children, Themesis' children, born to them.

None would be safe from his grip.

I shook my head. "Why should that matter to me?"

"Because you will guide Damiyun and Nature's daughter," he said, a smile curling his lips. "I have other plans for both of them."

Clenching my jaw, I dropped to a knee. "Of course, my lord. Whatever you want." The words felt like bile on my tongue. "I will bring them both here." *But first, I'd bind Damiyun to me. That man had many uses, and I planned to get mine.* "Are we done?" I rose from my position.

Themesis waved his hand in dismissal as he rose to his feet. "Jaylynn, dear. I'm tired. Prepare my bath and room for sleep," he said with a yawn, holding his hand out to her.

My blood boiled as I watched her jump to her feet, taking his hand and leading him out of the room. Bel let out a soft growl. I reached up and patted his head, calming him.

"Don't worry, Bel. He will get everything he fucking deserves."

Pulling the shadows around, I made my way back to the plain of the living and to Howling Cove. I had to make sure Damiyun never found the girl. Though I didn't know exactly what Themesis' plans were, his words sent a chill down my spine.

His words spoke of something ominous and evil. Something that would destroy humanity and possibly the world itself.

THREE
DAMIYUN

S LIPPING OUT OF BED, I padded down the hall to Zenith's room. While I did not agree with her having a separate room, I understood her want for privacy and, as I always did, I gave into her wants.

And, as always, I found myself outside her bedroom filled with lust and desire, but this time, I vowed to take what was rightfully mine. What she had denied me since that night that felt so long ago in the garden when we met. I raised my hand to knock, but thought better of it. She would only tell me no. Tell me to go away or that she didn't feel well, but I was done with her excuses. Pushing the door open, I stepped inside her room. Her scent—lavender and lilies—filled my nostrils, sparking my desire further. I looked around the dark room, my Sight of the Fallen One allowing me to see clearly, and I saw her. I saw my Zenith standing in the moonlight, naked, in the embrace of another man.

Vinset Abernathy. A man who was a partner in my shipping company. A man who was once a close friend.

"What the fuck is going on here?" I clenched my fists and pulled my magic close, ready to unleash it. Ready to send this room, and Pine Crest Manor, up in flames.

"Damiyun," Vinset chuckled. "My apologies for leaving you with a wet deck, though I'm sure that won't bother you."

My heart pounded in my ears, my chest constricted, and I saw red. I lunged, the flash of metal—a dagger tumbling through the air—caught my eye, and I leaped to the right. But I was too late. Too slow.

Pain radiated through my chest. My breath hitched, and my hands curled around the hilt of the blade embedded there. Stumbling, my feet were caught in the throw rug, and I crashed to the floor, my head smacking painfully against the marble. My eyes caught movement, Vinset slipping out onto the balcony and disappearing into the night. Zenith grabbed a blanket and wrapped it around herself before making her way to where I lay. My hands gripped the dagger. The warmth of my blood poured down my chest and pooled on the floor. Chills racked my body and my vision wavered. I was dying, I knew, and though I had longed for my Eternal Rest, I wasn't ready. Not yet. I had a life and a woman I loved and though she betrayed me, I knew it was my fault and all I wanted was to fix what was wrong with us.

As I drifted along the plain between the living and the dead, a black mist crept in. Red-eyed demons with sharp teeth and even sharper talons drifted toward me. I knew they were coming to take me to the Abyss. I looked at Zenith, who squatted beside me, and though I longed to go back to her, I accepted my fate. My death. But instead of being dragged to the fiery pits, a man dressed in black appeared.

Tall and broad, with black hair that just brushed his shoulders. Red eyes peered out from his well-kept beard. When he told me his name and what he was, I knew that my plea, my want to live, had been heard. Though it was Themesis that had answered and though I knew all about the terms, I signed my name in blood, sealing my fate. Giving my soul over to the one who had owned it, regardless. As soon as it was done, a dark mist poured off Abraham. Demons crawled across the floor to me. Claws grabbed and scratched, tearing skin. They wrapped themselves around me. Sharp teeth glinted in the ethereal light in the plain between the living and dead. Panic seized me. My chest constricted and I couldn't breathe. Perhaps I had made a terrible mistake. I shouldn't have been so rash, so quick to give up my soul, but then I opened my eyes and saw her above me. Her blond hair, luminous in the moonlight. Her face goddess-like and I only saw the woman I loved.

Zenith jumped when I took a breath and sat up. A snarl curled her ruby lips, twisting her beautiful face into something ugly and mean.

"What did you do?"

"I was offered another chance." I reached for her hand. She quickly snatched it away. "We can fix this. I can fix this. I love you, Zenith. Tell me what you want. Tell me what I can do."

She rose gracefully to her feet, a snarl fixed on her face. "You should have stayed dead. All of this would have been mine," she gestured around with her hand. "Do you think I want you?" She laughed, and I slowly stood up. Coldness washed over me at her words. "I only want what you have. You're just a boy playing at being a man with your dead father's money. The mere thought of you touching me..." she shuddered and rubbed her bare arms. "Every one of my lovers is far better than you will ever be. I am glad you can't give me a child. Even if you could, I would rid myself of the evil bastard."

I stumbled at her words. At the anger.

I went after her. Clutching the dagger, I had pulled from my chest, I stabbed her. Over and over and over again, ignoring her cries.

Her pleas for me to stop until she was silent.

Until her body slid to the floor, sightless eyes staring up at me. A massive pool of blood soaked the floor and rug. I should have left her there. Let Vinset see what he had done, but I feared the servants finding her body, discovering what had happened and sending the Enforcers after me, so I wrapped her body in blankets and buried her in the woods, leaving Levin a note that we were leaving for a while. I paid what I owed the household servants plus a whole Grand Passage and fled, like the coward I am, out of this place. Away from Pine Crest Manor. Away from L'Ochal.

Away from home, never to return.

FOUR

THOUGH THE BODY WAS buried, the blood cleaned, and my clothes changed, the metallic scent of blood lingered in my nose and the taste cloyed my tongue. I gave two hoots out to Xander, who trotted to where I stood, his silver hair shining in the moonlight.

"Hello, boy," I said. He stepped forward, nuzzling my neck. Swinging up on his back, I nudged his sides, urging him out, though he felt my haste. His silver mane shifted with each step, his gait increasing, feeling my need to be on. I was not superstitious; I still offered a prayer of protection to the gods. If they heard me, I doubted they'd oblige me my boons. I had no offerings to give.

Dusk fell and with it, the coldness of autumn. I pulled my cloak close and my magic closer, letting the heat flow through my veins, giving me warmth. We traveled on, a light snow beginning to fall. Xander snorted his displeasure.

"I know, boy," I said, patting his neck. He tossed his head with another snort, and I laughed. "I promise we will stop at the next village. You will have a warm stable, hay, and feed," I said in a soothing tone. No sooner had I spoken the words, than I saw a sign at a crossroads. I pulled Xander to a halt.

"Hmmm...Howling Cove or...," I squinted at the other sign. "Rangers Pass." I dropped the reins. "The choice is yours, Xander."

He swung his head to the left, toward Rangers Pass, and then looked at the road ahead. Pawing the ground and tossing his head, he moved forward.

"Howling Cove, it is," I chuckled, taking the reins again.

We walked down the road, over a small bridge, and into the village. It was bustling despite the time and the snow. Swinging down from Xander, I guided him through the town. My eyes darted around, catching the black and white uniform of the Enforcers, and the all black of the Suppressors.

Fuck.

Releasing my magic, I pulled the hood of my cloak over my head and urged Xander on. I was on high alert. The Suppressors would have a Feeler. They often did on raids. I kept to the shadows. Arden's face surfaced in my mind, and I quickened my pace. I had no desire to see my brother.

My body trembled. The bite of his whip left a deep impression on my body's memory, but worse, his magic scarred the depths of my soul. My bladder nearly loosened a stream of piss.

With my head down, I hurried through the people, ignoring the angry curses of those I bumped into. Lifting my gaze, I saw a sign hanging on a rusty chain. Hidden Gem Tavern and Inn. Guiding Xander around back, I gave the stable hand two coppers.

"Warmth and food. Just like I promised," I said, scratching his nose. Handing the reins to the young boy, I made my way to the front of the building. Pulling open the door, a wall of heat hit me, along with the stench of stale liquor, smoke, and body odor.

The tavern was crowded. Serving wenches, hands filled with tankards, splashed ale on the floor as patrons brushed by them. Some balanced trays on their heads, expertly weaving through the crowd, dodging groping hands without dropping a plate. An ax thudded into the wall over in the corner for a game of axes. Folks gathered around a table where people played cards, tossing coins in the middle. A bard strummed a lute in another corner, but peals of laughter and voices muted the song.

Finding an empty table in the back, I settled in, sitting with my back against the wall. Folding my arms, I observed the crowd of revelers. A pretty serving wench stopped by my table. She had long, auburn hair pulled back in a braid and big, brown eyes. The corset she wore pushed her breasts up invitingly, and her small waist gave way to generous hips. I put in my order of food and a bottle of Serpent's Venom.

"You're not from around here, are you?"

I cocked my head to the side. "What makes you say that?"

She gestured with her hand. "Your finery and weapons." Her eyes swept over me, tongue flicking out to lick her lips. "And I would surely remember a man as handsome as you. Just passing by?"

I scratched my chin. "I don't rightly know." It wasn't a lie. I had left with no direction, no clear idea of what I was going to do once I was out of L'Ochal.

She smiled. "Well, if you stay, you know where I am."

Reaching into my pocket, I pulled out my pouch, flipped through, and I slid a silver across the table. "I'll be here all night."

Her smile widened, as did her eyes, at the sight of the coin. Palming it, she dropped it down the front of her dress. "I will be back with your food and spirits," she said, turning and walking away, hips swaying provocatively. She came back moments later with a bowl of stew, a hunk of bread, and two bottles of Serpent's Venom.

I knew she would be in my bed later this eve.

The smell of the stew, root vegetables, beef, and gravy made my mouth water and stomach growl. Pulling off a piece of bread, I dug in. I was halfway through my meal and a quarter of the way through my second bottle when a commotion erupted on the other side of the tavern. Pushing my bowl away, and curiosity getting the better of me, I trained my attention across the room. My eyes went to the woman who had served me. A soft look crossed her face as she looked at a young woman standing at the counter. The look quickly turned to a snarl, and she disappeared into the back. I turned my attention to the young woman with fiery red hair who stood at the bar. She wore black trousers and sturdy boots. A blue cloak was flung about her shoulders. She was young, about seventeen Grand Passages, petite and thin. Almost painfully so.

She gestured to the man behind the counter, lips moving as she spoke. Turning my head, I trained my keen ears in their direction.

"...think we're fucking charity?"

"I'm not asking for you to serve me a meal. I know you toss most of your food away." She crossed her arms. Her chin jutted defiantly as she challenged the man. "Give me what's not eaten. Give me scraps, I don't care." She pleaded.

The man made a shooing motion with his hands. "Off with you, beggar. How many times do I have to tell you, we don't even give scraps for free?"

She reached into her pocket. "I have a few coppers."

The man laughed. "That won't even get you a crust of bread. Get the fuck out of here before I call the Enforcers."

Anger roiled in my body. Pushing back from the table, I strode across the room. The young woman, face dejected, was turning to leave.

"No," I said, grasping her arm. Green eyes looked up at me in question. And fear.

"What will this get me?" I slid a silver and four coppers across the counter.

The man snatched it up. I grabbed his wrist and twisted.

"What will that get me?"

His jaw clenched. "A bowl of stew, bread, cheese, and a flagon of ale."

"Get it."

He jerked his wrist out of my grasp. "If you feed the strays, they only come back for more," he said, voice dripping with disgust. Turning, he stalked to the kitchen.

"Why?" The young woman's voice pulled my attention. I looked down into her emerald eyes.

Because I am trying to repent for my sins. Perhaps this might forgive what I have done.

The man came back with the food and placed it on the counter.

"Because you're hungry. No one should have to beg for food. No one should eat scraps from rubbish bins."

Her gaze dropped to the floor, and she bit her lip. "I—I can't repay you." Her voice was so soft I almost didn't hear it.

I tipped her chin up. Her eyes swam with tears and my heart broke. "That's not what this is about. It's about giving a starving young woman a meal." I looked down at her. "Do you have a place to stay?"

She nodded.

I handed her the food and drink. She hesitated a second, as though I were going to snatch it back. A cruel joke at her expense.

"Thank you," she said, grabbing the plate and flagon from my grasp.

I chuckled and watched her sit at the nearest table and dig into the hot food and went back to my table. A fresh bottle of Serpent's Venom sat in front of my seat. My eyes went to the serving wench who stood against the wall. She looked at me, a smile curling her lips, and jerked her head toward the stairs that led to what, I assumed, were the rooms.

Grabbing the bottle, I rose and followed her swinging hips up the stairs.

Perhaps the gods had forgiven me this day.

Pulling out a key, she opened a door halfway down the hall. Swinging it open, she stepped inside, with me following not far behind. Kicking the door shut, I grabbed her from behind, pulling her against me. She smelled of elderberry and lilacs, a pungent, feminine scent. She pressed her ass against my swelling cock, and I groaned.

"Eager, are we?" she purred.

"It's been a while," I growled, teeth nipping her neck.

That was an understatement. It had been six Moon Cycles since Zenith had let me in her bed. I was turned away time and again. Left with a burning desire and an aching groin. I never stepped out on her, rather, I took care of my needs myself.

Vinset's face flashed in my mind, as did Zenith's, her lips pulled back in a cruel smile as she looked down at me. I saw her bloody body on the floor.

Shaking the thoughts from my mind, I brought my attention back to the woman I held. Turning her around, I forced her to her knees and undid the laces on my trousers.

"Aggressive too," she said, licking her lips as she grasped my length.

I closed my eyes with a groan as her mouth enveloped me, soft and hot. Grabbing the back of her head, I thrust deeper, losing myself in the way she felt. Pulling her to her feet, I pushed her onto the bed, lifting her skirts. She gasped as I roughly entered her. Placing my hands on either side of her head, I thrust harder and faster.

This was for me, not her. I didn't care if she got any pleasure from it, or if she just laid there. I needed my release. She gripped me tight, wrapping her legs around my waist, lifting her hips, and meeting my furious thrusts. Biting down on her neck, I let myself go, a growl rumbling in my chest as I spent myself.

The sound of my ragged breathing filled the silence. Pulling myself off her, I laced my trousers. She pushed her skirts back down and sat up, a smile on her lips.

"Well, that was hardly the session Damiyun Rayne is noted for."

I frowned. I didn't recall telling her my name. "How do you know who I am?"

"I know the name of every person who has prayed to me."

Prayed to her? What was she talking about?

"And those who have forsaken me, such as yourself," she said.

I shook my head. She laughed, and the air shimmered about her. I watched as the brown-haired woman transformed into someone with long, blond hair. Blue eyes looked up at me, mischief dancing in them. She was stunning. Painfully so.

I stumbled backward as pictures of her floated in my mind. Paintings in the temples that had been erected, now long gone to ruin.

The woman, who I now gazed upon, who I had just fucked, was Felicity, the Goddess of Nature. No. This had to be some magic at work. Had someone slipped something into my spirits?

"I can see you're shocked," she said, tone amused.

"This is a trick." I finally managed to speak.

She cocked her head. "No trick, Damiyun."

I shook my head and laughed. "Right. How did you know I was here?" Clearly this had been planned. But why?

"I didn't. It was a mere coincidence that you fell into my lap." She laughed. "Though I would have found you, anyway. Your current deeds... let's just say your favorability among us has plummeted. But that doesn't matter. You can still redeem yourself."

I snorted. "I have never been in your favor." Crossing my arms, I leveled my gaze on her. "What do you want?" I knew I was going to regret the question that hung in the air.

She smiled up at me. "I want you, Damiyun darling, to look after my daughter."

I knew I shouldn't have asked. "No. I am not a nanny."

She waved her hand. "You will watch her from afar."

"Why?"

"I need her kept safe. If the Suppressors got her..." she shook her head.

My nostrils flared. "You are her mother. Take care of her yourself."

She sighed, a dramatic sound. "I am closing in on my one Grand Passage and a day and cannot stay. I came here looking for you, and I have found you. My time here is done."

I shook my head. She was a piece of work. "No," I said again. "Surely, you can find someone else for this task."

Standing, she crossed the room to where I stood. "I could," she purred, running a gold lacquered nail down my cheek. "But this could be your redemption. Do this for me, and I will see what I can do about your predicament. Surely, you don't wish to spend eternity in torment."

I laughed. "My entire life has been torment. What difference would an eternity make?"

Felicity clucked her tongue. "So much despair in you," she said. "I have watched you, Damiyun. You have intrigued me from the moment you were born. Everything you have been through, the torture at the hands of your brother, the whippings from your father, all the innocent lives you have taken. A river of blood flows from your hands." She pushed a lock of my hair out of my eyes. Her soft touch felt like fire upon my skin. "I can help you, Damiyun. This can help your damned soul."

Her tone was soft. Hypnotic. The urge to say yes was strong but... "At what price?" I pulled away from her. Broke whatever spell she had cast.

"Eternity in bliss. Whatever you desire," her voice dropped to a low and husky tone, "will be at your fingertips."

Oh, but how tempting those words were. To not spend my eternity in torment and horror. To be in a place I never thought I would go. But I know the gods never did something for nothing.

"What's the catch?"

A smile curled her lips again, and my blood ran cold. I knew there was more, and I knew I wasn't going to like it.

"You will bring Lillyanna to Kraagswell Mountain to defeat Themesis. Her blood is the key to keeping him locked beneath the mountain for eternity."

I laughed. "I can't travel to the Abyss."

"Damiyun, darling. Always so negative. Abraham, the one who holds the contract on your soul, will take you."

Shit. What I thought was a clear out, wasn't. She had an answer for everything.

"I trust you, Damiyun. You are a man of your word. I know you will protect her with your life."

I rubbed my eyes. Though I hadn't said yes, clearly there was no way out of this. "Who is she?"

"The young woman you bought the food for," she said.

And with those words, I knew I had no simple task ahead of me. I felt trouble, the kind to tear a person apart, the kind to ruin a soul, only I had already damned mine. There was nothing in it for me then, though, why did I feel there was something more to this task? Something ominous. Nothing was ever easy for me, and I knew this task to be a test of my will and strength.

I knew it to be a test I wasn't sure I would pass.

FIVE
ABRAHAM

The streets were almost silent when I returned from the Abyss, back to Howling Cove. I had to find Damiyun. I had to make sure he didn't find the girl. Though I did not know what Themesis' plans were, his revelation sent chills down my spine.

Reaching into my beard, my hand closed gently around Bel. I pulled him out, raising him to meet my eyes. He yawned, eyes blinking in sleep. I chuckled. "You're so lazy." He let out a hiss, and I laughed. "I need you to find Damiyun Rayne," I said. He perked up, cocking his head to the side. I pulled out the contract and opened it. Bel sniffed it, his forked tongue flicking out to lick the paper where Damiyun had signed his name in blood. "Come back to me and tell me where he is."

Bel jumped to the ground and scampered off, invisible in the darkness.

Finding a spot to wait, I leaned against the wall, watching the few people who hurried about. Curfew must be coming. It was a time when people were encouraged to go home and stay inside until the light of day. They enacted it to keep the people safe from the cutpurses and murderers. And from the demons who roamed when night fell. In reality, it was a way to control the masses. My eyes caught a movement close to the ground.

Bel.

He scampered to me, taking a flying leap and landing on my shoulder, letting out a series of chirps and growls.

He had found him. Pushing off the wall, I made my way quickly through the village to where Damiyun was, a plan forming in my head as I walked.

Themesis would get what he wanted. And a whole lot more.

I T DIDN'T TAKE LONG for me to find him. He stood with his foot propped against a wall, the hood of his cloak pulled up, arms crossed. His eyes scanned the people who hurried to their homes.

"Damiyun," I said, standing beside him.

Recognition crossed his countenance. "Come to call the contract already?"

"No."

He turned to look at me. "So, what then? I hardly think you check up on all the contracts."

"I don't." *Only yours.*

He rubbed his eyes. "You're here because of the girl."

It wasn't a question, and his voice held no surprise. So, he had met with Felicity already.

"Yes."

His eyes scanned the crowd. "I haven't seen her yet, though I know she's here. The man at the tavern spoke to her as though she were familiar."

I scratched my beard. "Then we keep searching the village until she shows."

"What's in it for you?" Damiyun's eyes flicked to me. "Clearly, you're not here on Felicity's bidding. What does he want with her?"

Nothing that you need to concern yourself about. "I can't be around all the time," I said, avoiding his question. "I'm going to bind you to me. This allows me to know where you are, and we can communicate through it as well."

"Why do you need to know where I am?"

"How will you get to the Abyss if I'm not here to guide you? Surely, Felicity told you who would be taking you there."

He sighed. "She did," he said. "Do what you must."

I called the shadows, the darkness turning to demons as they moved across the cobblestone, wrapping themselves around Damiyun. His eyes closed and his teeth clenched. Pain flashed across his face, he stumbled with a grunt, catching himself on the wall, and then opened his eyes. I felt a heaviness in the back of my mind. The feeling of another presence and I knew I had bound him to me.

"It's done. Now let's go see if we can find the girl," I said, striding off down the empty street. Glancing over my shoulder, I saw Damiyun push off the wall and follow behind.

We walked through the streets, retiring when the bell for curfew tolled.

I knew this would be a tough job. I knew when we found her, when she was finally with us, I would have to do everything in my power to keep Damiyun on the right path. She was, after all, a beautiful young woman and that was Damiyun's downfall.

Something told me I had a long road ahead of me.

FIVE GRAND PASSAGES LATER

*G*ET SOME FOOD AND *go home, and for the love of the gods, don't get caught stealing.* Every time my coin ran low, forcing me to visit the village of Howling Cove, I repeated the mantra. It kept me safe.

The town bustled with foot traffic until curfew. But when the bell on the tower rang for the second time, you had best secure yourself inside your home. Those still out and about were taken for thieves or murderers and imprisoned within the Enforcer Compound without trial. That is, if they weren't taken by the demons first.

Curfew, of course, was meant to keep the crime down. To keep those nefarious people, the cutthroats and thieves, from harming the helpless townsfolk, as though it made a difference. And yet, curfew did nothing to stop the starving from snatching coin or food. It was a useless law set in place to make the wealthy feel safe. Those whose affluence encroached further and further out into the areas where the less privileged lived.

Where I lived.

I shoved my icy hands deep into the warmth of my cloak pockets and shouldered my way through the crowd, ignoring the snarls and nasty remarks from the finely dressed. I headed deeper into the market. The fresh scent of meat and fish taunted me, making my stomach growl. A harsh reminder, I had spent my last coin the day prior. The sounds of merchants hawking their wares drummed in my ears, drowning out all other noise. But beside all the market stalls stood dozens of men and women wearing black clothing, others in white, deliberately standing out with stern faces and watchful eyes. The weapons strapped to their waists looked dangerous. I didn't have to see their emblems—two crossed swords piercing the letters S and E—to know they were Suppressors and Enforcers.

While I expected to pass by Enforcers patrolling the village, keeping peace and order, seeing the Suppressors gave me pause. They rarely patrolled at this time of day. It was the only reason I came so late.

I pulled my hood over my head and stared at the ground.

Vel warned me about them. I remember standing with him in the shadows, watching them violently drag a man with magic away from his family.

"This is why you must be careful, Lillyanna. You must avoid the Suppressors at all costs," he said, kissing the top of my head.

And I listened to my father, doing my best to avoid them, and seeing them here now... I held my breath. Keeping my head down, I continued through the crowd.

Get some food and go home.

"Sorry," I said as a man bumped into my shoulder, sending me stumbling.

"You." The man pointed at me; lips pulled back in a snarl. My eyes darted around, noting a few people had stopped to stare at us. "I know what you are."

I froze. My heart hammered, as sweat formed in the palms of my hands.

"You're coming with me." His giant hand closed around my arm.

I jerked my arm, but he held fast. I had not spent ten Grand Passages of my life avoiding the Suppressors only to get caught now. I would not let *them* take me.

"Not likely." I drew on my magic, feeling it flutter around inside me like a bird. Laughter threatened to bubble up from inside, as it always did when I touched the power. I pulsed out a stream of tingling magic through my body into his hand. He snatched it back and clutched it, eyes narrowing on me.

"Fucking bitch." He lunged at me.

I leaped back, just barely escaping his grasp. Fury marked his face, his lips pulled back in a snarl, spittle flew from his mouth. His fists clenched as he advanced. I backed away step by step, looking frantically around for a way out. People scattered away from me, muttering and pointing.

"Suppressors. I got a Wielding bitch here." The man's loud voice echoed off the buildings.

Shit.

Six men in black pushed their way through the crowd. My breath caught in my throat. Spinning around, I pushed through the throng and fled down the cobblestone street.

"After her!" someone yelled.

"Get back here, Wielder!"

I raced through the streets, dodging carts and people who yelled and swore as I crashed through. The sound of pounding feet closed in, and I ran harder, my lungs burning with each step. I risked a glance over my shoulder. Two Suppressors loomed behind me. I had gained some distance, but they started catching up.

Streets flew by as I ran, my legs ached, and a fire scorched my lungs. I would not make it.

Then a man stepped out of the shadows, cutting me off. I skidded to a halt, slamming into the tall stranger.

He cocked an eyebrow, glancing toward my pursuers, and then he grabbed my arm and pulled me a few yards into an alley. I hardly had time to get a look at him, his face, or his clothes. All I noticed was the massive broadsword strapped to his back. But as he whisked me further into the alley, the filthy old walls around us shimmered and brightened like moonlit water. The Suppressors ran past, somehow not seeing us. When their footsteps faded, he let me go. The darkness of the alley closed in again.

The man was a Wielder, and whatever magic he used had kept us hidden from the Suppressors.

"Follow me." He pushed past me and strode away.

"Why?"

He paused, turned his head, and looked at me. I gasped at his glowing yellow eyes.

"Because if you do not, the Suppressors will take you." He moved down the alley without waiting for my response.

"Rayne," a voice snapped from the alley's entrance.

I whirled around, my eyes going to two Suppressors who had appeared behind me. Their hands gripped swords, and sneers graced their faces. The Wielder they had called Rayne sauntered casually past me, an amused smile on his lips. His hand rested on the hilt of a long dagger tucked into his belt. He exuded an air of deadly confidence. Wind rustled the white hair framing his chiseled features. He shifted on his feet; his well-polished boots glinted in the darkness as he stepped forward.

"Get out of the way," one of the Suppressors said, gripping his sword tighter.

"Or what?" Rayne reached behind and grasped the hilt of the broadsword strapped to his back.

"You know she's a Wielder. She is ours."

Rayne laughed and drew his sword with one hand, while the other pulled his dagger. "Is she now?"

"You know she is. You're breaking your agreement with the Elder by not giving her over."

Rolling his shoulders, he brandished the weapons and widened his stance. "I grow tired of talking. Shall we dance?"

I blinked. Who was this man, and why was he defending me? *Was* he defending me? An awful thought entered my mind. That he might just be putting on a show before turning me in. I eyed my exit, the faint light at the far end of the alley. The sound of steel on steel pierced the evening, and I glanced back at Rayne, watching his blades flash in the fading light as he cut the men back.

I made a run for it, bolting down the dark corridor, skirting around an overturned cart, and leaping a knocked-over barrel. Footsteps echoed off the walls as I neared the end. As I looked over my shoulder, I glimpsed a pair of golden eyes, a mane of billowing, white hair. He was closing in!

No.

Digging in deep, I willed my legs to move faster.

It didn't help. In mere moments, he caught my arm and pulled me to a halt.

"Let me go!"

"Calm," he said, his voice soothing, his breath a light puff of mist in the cold air. "They know you're here. If you flee, they'll catch you. Let me help you. My home is just around the corner. I can give you shelter, food, and a warm bed for the night. You'll be safe there."

"Safe? That's the first place they'll look. It's clear they know you."

"My home is shielded. They won't feel you."

I chewed my lip and stared back into the alley.

"I'm the only choice you have."

"No, you're not." I wrenched my arm from his grasp and backed away.

"Lillyanna…"

My eyes widened. Fear washed over me. How did this man, this stranger, know my name? I had to get out of here. If I could make it home, I would be safe. I lunged, shoving him in the chest. He stumbled back, and I bolted back in the direction I had come.

"Damn it," I said as feet pounded on the ground behind me.

I didn't risk a glance. I couldn't. So, I surged on, ducking and weaving between people and carts, ignoring the curses that followed. Men shouted in the distance, footsteps thundered, and the ringing sound of steel sliced through the night. I risked a look over my shoulder, seeing the man called Rayne pulling his blade from the body of a Suppressor. His eyes met mine as he wiped it off on the body, sheathed his weapons, and raced after me again.

I was exhausted, my legs felt weak, but I kept running. The edge of the village was near. I was almost on the road home. Almost to safety. Almost…

No.

I skidded to a halt. Dozens of Suppressors blocked the road ahead.

"There she is," a blond man shouted, pointing in my direction.

I looked around and darted into the woods on the left. It was too dark to see. A hand clamped down on my arm, another around my mouth to stop me from screaming. Even still, I fought to break free.

"Stop resisting me," Rayne hissed in my ear, removing the hand from my mouth.

"Let me go!"

"So they can take you? Not a chance."

"Who—"

"Quiet." He shoved me away. I stumbled and landed hard on my backside in the brush. "Don't move." Coldness washed over me, and I gasped. The woods shimmered in the same way the alley had. Muted voices and muffled footsteps on dry leaves echoed all around. My eyes went to Rayne, who casually drew his sword.

"Where is she?" A tall, lanky man with short brown hair growled, storming right up to Rayne.

"Where is who?" Rayne said, his tone casual.

"You know who I'm talking about. We saw her go this way."

Rayne glanced around. "Apparently she didn't."

The man growled and leaped at Rayne, who deftly stepped to the left as another man burst through the forest and slashed at him with a curved sword. Horrified, I watched him fight the two men from my spot on the ground. He was a thing of beauty and grace. Light on his feet and nimble. His sword moved like a blade of grass in the wind as he cut the two men down. I blinked, and the woods returned to normal. The muffling effect dissipated, and all the sounds of blowing leaves and cawing crows returned to their normal volume as he released whatever magic he had used on me. I looked around the clearing, my eyes settling on the bodies of the dead men. My stomach lurched, and I emptied what little contents were in it onto the ground.

"Now, will you go with me?" Rayne sheathed his weapons and crossed his arms.

I stood up, brushing twigs and dirt off my trousers. "I want to go home."

"You won't get out of the village."

Gritting my teeth, I peered back at the road. "The men are dead. You killed them," I said, gesturing to the dead bodies.

"And you think there won't be more, further up the road? I'm the only chance you have, if you wish not to be caught. My house is warm. I have food and a place to sleep."

My stomach clenched at the thought of a meal. "Fine. I'll go with you—for now." I would take the meal and bed he offered, though I doubted I would do much sleeping. Upon first light, I would run as far away from him as possible.

Nodding, he effortlessly slipped through the woods with me in tow. The moonlight shone through the leaves of the trees, casting its silver rays upon the brush on the ground. I looked at Rayne's back. He walked with confident, long strides that ate up the distance. He looked about, eyes scanning the darkness, stopping every now and then to listen. After a while, we came out at the edge of the road.

"Wait here," he whispered. He slipped out into the road and disappeared. I stood in the dark, hoping the Suppressors had stopped searching the woods. Drawing energy from the world around me, I thought of an invisible barrier in my mind. Soon, the energy shifted around me, unseen but felt to my very core. It masked my scent and form.

Rayne returned a few moments later. "No sign of Suppressors. Follow me."

I let the magic go and trailed behind as he walked out into the street, hand on the hilt of his dagger, eyes alert, casting glances over his shoulder now and then. Presumably he felt the need to make sure I was still following. I buried my annoyance and rolled my eyes at his back when he turned away. We hurried on, taking a left down another alley and then another left at the end, where he stopped at the base of a short staircase that led up to a door. He ascended it, opening the wooden door at the top, and stepped aside. I hesitated, though the cozy warmth of the interior and the savory scent of cooking stew lured me inside.

He closed the door and brushed past me. I followed him a short distance into a sitting room that opened to a kitchen, where a well-worn oaken table sat with four chairs tucked beneath it. Intricate patterns of vines and flowers were carved into its legs. Just across from the table on the far side of the dwelling sat the living room. I longed to sink into the plush cushions of the couch, but my eyes instead drifted up a ladder to my left, which led up to a cozy loft. The furnishings made my own home feel shabby and rundown.

The blazing fire beckoned to my frozen toes and fingers. I made my way closer to the flames, the warmth making my cold limbs tingle.

"Come. Take your cloak off and sit," Rayne said.

Pulling my cloak tight, I shook my head. I wasn't about to take it off. What if I had to flee? "Who are you?" I asked, turning in his direction.

"Damiyun Rayne. Are you hungry?"

My stomach growled, and he laughed.

"I guess that's a yes. Please. Sit down," he said.

I watched him go to the pot sitting on the cook stove. My mouth watered at the sight of stewing meat and vegetables. I made my way back to the kitchen and settled into a chair.

He filled a bowl and set it down in front of me. After pouring two glasses of amber liquid, he handed one to me, removed his scabbard, and then sat in a chair across the table. Lounging back, he pulled his sword free and nodded at the food as he cleaned and sharpened his blade.

Without a moment's hesitation, I dug into the steaming bowl. The tender meat and vegetables filled the painful void in my stomach. As I ate the stew, I felt his eyes on me. I took a sip of the liquid he had poured, and then sputtered as fire burned its way down my throat.

Damiyun chuckled. "Serpent's Venom takes some getting used to if you've never had it," he said, tipping back his glass, then refilling it.

"When having to choose between drinking spirits or eating food, I choose food," I said, taking another drink of the unfamiliar spirit. Warmth spread through me, making my face flush, and my skin tingle. A sad look crossed Damiyun's face as he reached for my bowl and refilled it.

I studied Damiyun as I consumed my meal. While he looked to be in his late twenties, the fine lines around his mouth and eyes made him appear much older. He was tall, probably around six feet. Six feet of lean muscle and pale beauty. The odd, white hair flowed about his shoulders, and his eyes were a gray so light they looked white. Though his clothes were spattered with blood, I could tell they were made of expensive cloth. The fine furnishings in his home gave the impression of wealth, though his attitude and demeanor did not. What did he do for a living? The way he used his sword—and the hordes of men he killed—kept me from asking.

"You're fortunate I heard the commotion and saw you," he said, pulling me from my thoughts.

Much to my chagrin, he seemed to read me, or at least see parts of me likely hidden to myself. I waved the spoon in the air. "I can take care of myself. I am certainly not a child. I have been on my own for ten Grand Passages. I know how to survive." I scooped another bite. Of course, I knew how to take care of myself.

"They had Feelers with them. They can feel magic. It makes it difficult to hide from them." He paused and took a deep breath. "I know this because I am one. How do you think I found you? Why do you think that man called for the Suppressors?"

I finished my food and placed the spoon in the bowl.

"How did those Suppressors know your name? Why haven't they caught you?"

His face remained neutral. "Dead men can't catch me."

"Why did you help me?"

"Would you rather I didn't?" He quirked an eyebrow. "I was just at the right place at the right time."

"I don't believe you," I said, narrowing my eyes. He had spoken my name, and I hadn't forgotten. When he shrugged, I tried another tactic.

"Won't their Feelers find us here?"

"I told you. My home is shielded. We should be safe," he said, rising to his feet. He picked up my bowl and placed it in the sink. "There's a bed in the loft up there." He gestured toward the ladder with his head. "Get some rest."

"How long will I be here?"

He glanced over his shoulder. "It's getting dark, and the town is teeming with Suppressors. We can't move tonight. We leave at daybreak."

I made my way up the ladder into the small loft. A large, thin mattress and an old dresser sat in opposite corners. The shabbiness of the furniture in this room was a stark contrast to the expensive arrangement below. Moonlight spilled in from a single window. Removing my cloak, I made my way over to the window, and threw it open wide. A light breeze drifted in, cooling my warm skin. I shivered. Pulling away, I sat on the mattress. Though I was exhausted, I couldn't rest. I had entered a strange house with an even stranger man, with intentions of which I had no certainty. I glanced out the window again. Daybreak wouldn't be for some time, though I knew there was no way I would sleep. I settled in to spend a long night waiting for the sun to rise.

Waiting for my chance to escape and go home.

SEVEN

"**W**HAT DID YOU TELL her about Vel?" an unknown man's deep voice rumbled from below.

I jumped at the sound, heart pounding as I realized I had accidentally fallen asleep. Then, coldness washed over me at the sound of my father's name. I crept to the edge of the loft to peer down at Damiyun and the stranger.

"Nothing yet. She was being chased by the Suppressors, and I offered her safety, food, and a bed to sleep in. I will tell her in time."

"Time is something we lack." The unknown man moved out of the shadows. He was large, a head or so taller than Damiyun, with a thick neck, broad frame and a set of veiny muscles bulging through his shirt. His black hair brushed past his shoulders, and his close-cut beard lent him a menacing appearance.

Damiyun sighed. "It was a tiring evening for her. I didn't think it's necessary to overwhelm her."

The other man snorted. "How touching. I dare say you're growing soft."

Damiyun laughed bitterly. "Soft is one thing I have never been. Is that not why you own me?"

"I saved you." The man shrugged.

They fell silent, and I crept away from the edge and sat back on my haunches. My head spun. I gripped the mattress to steady myself.

They knew my father. What else weren't they telling me?

I'm not safe. I need to get out of here.

After taking a deep breath, I crawled across the bed to the window. Sticking my head out, I looked down, my palms clamming at the sight of the roof below. It stretched out on both sides, connecting the long row of houses together. I glanced over my shoulder, fear gripping me at the sight of shifting shadows in the distance.

I slipped through the window onto the roof just as Damiyun ascended the ladder.

"Damn it." Damiyun cursed. I glanced over my shoulder, seeing him pull his long frame out behind me.

Shit. I bolted toward the edge, but something black moved in the corner of my eye. Dread cinched my stomach. A Suppressor met my eyes, snarling.

"Get over here, girl."

I glanced at the man approaching me, then behind at Damiyun.

Shit, shit, shit.

Damiyun lunged, taking me off guard, and shoved me off the roof. The ground came up fast, and I slammed into it, the bare cobblestones knocking the wind out of me. I lay there, trying to catch my breath, but the sound of feet on cobblestone urged me to get up and keep running. Voices yelled, and boots pounded all around me. I risked a glance over my shoulder. It was Damiyun, nearly on top of me.

There was no way to outrun him. My legs burned already, shaking with effort. He grabbed my arm as he sprinted past and dragged me along. We staggered, bolting for an alley nearby. Skidding to a halt, he steadied me with his other hand.

"Why did you run?"

"Why in the Abyss do you think—?"

He silenced me with his hand, eyes scanning the darkness.

"Shit. More of them." He pushed me against the wall. The same cloak of magic he used earlier fell upon me. Damiyun's glowing eyes locked on mine.

His hard body tensed, and his heart pounded against me. Warmth radiated off him. He smelled of cloves, cinnamon, and pine. The closeness made me uncomfortable and breathless at the same time. I started pulling away, but his arms slipped around me, and he pulled me even closer.

"Don't move," he whispered, his breath warm in my ear.

The muted voices of the Suppressors drew closer.

"Are you sure they came down here?" One said.

"Yes. I was following them closely." This one had a deeper voice, sinister.

"It's black as pitch. How could you see anything? How could he?" The first one responded.

"They say he has the Sight of the Fallen One." The Suppressors stopped right next to us.

Damiyun pressed himself closer, and I closed my eyes and willed my breaths to slow. After a few heartbeats that felt like a few eternal heartbeats, our pursuers moved on. I only let myself breathe when their footsteps faded. We stood against the wall for a few more moments, and then he pulled away and released the cloak shielding us.

"Where are we going?"

"There is a place just at the end of this alley."

I took a deep breath, still shaking. For a moment, I hesitated. He had saved me once more. Still, I didn't trust him. He had known my name, my father. However, he had not explained himself either.

He glanced over his shoulder at me. "Come on," he said, voice soft.

Sighing, and knowing he could catch me again if I ran, I followed him down the alley. The only thing I could see in the dark was his white hair. He took a right onto the street, but he stopped abruptly, and I walked right into him. He glanced down at me, and then looked to the wall beside us. Without a sound, he pushed open a large door that blended in with the building's brick facade. We stepped inside a pitch-black room. I shivered, teeth chattering, and rubbed my arms against the chill.

"Where are you?" I reached out a hand, blindly feeling around.

"Right here," he said from my right. A warm weight fell on my shoulders and wrapped me in spicy pine scents. I pulled his cloak tightly, absorbing the warmth left from his body. As a host of lanterns and candles came to life, I blinked my eyes to adjust to the darkness. I looked at Damiyun who stood beside me.

"How did you do that?"

"I'm a Fire Wielder," he said, his tone casual.

A Fire Wielder. From what I knew of Wielders, they were a rare kind. "Where are we?"

"A friend's home. We'll be safe here. At least for now," he said. He propped his sword against the wall, then headed toward a stone and brick fireplace. Furniture was arranged around another table, the plush cushions begging me to sit. On the sideboard, four glittering glasses were arranged around a decanter.

He knelt, stacking pieces of wood and parchment. I watched him strike a flint, the paper coming to life on the fifth try.

"Why didn't you use your magic to make the fire?" I found it curious a Fire Wielder would rely on a Non method for starting a fire.

He blinked, then laughed. "I suppose I could, though there is something primal and satisfying—no—normal, about making a fire by hand," he said, sitting back on his heels. "You shouldn't have fled, Lillyanna. I told you, I am the only one keeping you safe and out of their hands."

"How can I be certain?"

His gray eyes penetrated my soul. "I didn't hand you over in the street. Three times by my count."

I tried to think back at how many times I'd run from him so far. I wasn't sure, but perhaps he was not either. *Three times.* I rolled my eyes. "You also haven't answered my questions. I don't know you from the gods, let alone what you are going to do with me," I said, drawing a bit of magic and holding it close.

"I wouldn't do that," he said, rising to his feet.

"What are you going to do?" I goaded, pulling my magic even closer.

"Lil—"

"Answer my questions, Damiyun. What are you going to do with me? How did you know my father?"

"I will tell you. Now is not the time," he said, taking a step in my direction.

"Now is precisely the time." Clenching my fists, I released the magic I held, pulsing it out at him. The wave sent him backward, crashing into the wall behind.

"Damn it." He cursed, pulling himself to his feet. He took a step in my direction. I backed up and drew more magic. He stopped and held up his hands. "I am not the enemy, Lillyanna."

"Then answer my questions." I narrowed my eyes at him. He had said my name again. "How do you know my name?" Racking my memory, I tried to figure out if I knew him. Images flashed in my mind of a man peering beneath his hood, eyes glowing faintly in the shadows. I took another step back. "You've been following me. Why?"

He sighed. "I—" His head snapped up as the door burst open. In the blink of an eye, he had pulled his dagger, eyes trained on the door.

Before I even had time to turn around, Damiyun was already relaxing. "Hello, Abraham," he said, sheathing his weapon as the door closed and the man I had seen earlier stepped into the room.

Black eyes sized me up. "This her?"

"Yes. This is Lillyanna." Damiyun nodded in my direction and crossed his arms.

I backed slowly away from them, pressing myself against the wall. Frantically, I searched for a way out. Defeat filled me upon seeing the only exit—the door we had entered—was across the room. There would be no way to reach it without them seeing me. I glanced back at the two men. They weren't speaking, though their expressions and nods told me they'd begun communicating in some way I couldn't hear. The possibility they were talking about me made me want to flee even more.

I can make it.

Inch by excruciatingly slow inch, I sidled down the wall, monitoring the men, who were focused intently on their silent conversation more than on what I was doing. When I reached the end, I bolted toward the door. As I touched the handle, a hand closed on mine and squeezed. I winced at the pain.

"You are not going anywhere," Abraham jerked me backward, growling. I twisted in his grasp, but his fingers tightened, biting into my skin. I swung my free arm around and struck him across the cheek. Those black eyes of his narrowed on me. His grip tightened like a vice.

"Let her go, Abraham," Damiyun's jaw clenched.

Abraham ignored him. I clenched my fists, and heat flushed my skin. My magic bubbled beneath the surface again and let a little trickle out. Just enough to make Abraham release my arm in surprise. He glared at me as he shook the hand holding me, then lifted the other.

A gray cloud-like mist swirled in my direction and circled me. Fear pricked my skin at the sight of it. An oppressive pressure fell upon me like a blanket. Pain pulsed through my body. I couldn't breathe. I collapsed to my knees, trying to get air, as the world grew dim. Was I dying? Was this the fate Damiyun had brought me to? Thoughts rushed through my head. I never should have gone to town tonight. I should have trusted my instincts about Damiyun. I should have tried harder to get away. I should have...

And then the feeling fled.

I took a deep breath and gasped as my lungs filled with air. Glaring at Abraham, I rose to my feet and reached for my power.

It was gone. "What—?"

"I blocked your magic." He narrowed his dark eyes on me while directing his next words to Damiyun. "She shocked me."

I crossed my arms and looked up at Abraham. "You asked for it. You're the one who grabbed me."

His scowl deepened. "That was only a small fraction of her power. If she'd used anymore, we would not be here right now."

"She used some on me earlier," Damiyun said.

"The block will remain until she can control herself." His words were again directed to Damiyun while his eyes remained on me.

I clenched my fists and glared at him. "I would appreciate it if you would speak as though I were here. It's not as though I don't understand what you're saying. And I didn't annihilate you. I'd say I showed control," I growled, fists clenched. "I don't know either of you. I don't know that you're any safer than those Suppressors."

Abraham clicked his tongue. "No, you don't." His voice came as a whisper.

I snarled, my magic just out of reach.

Damiyun snorted. "Come sit down," he said, touching my arm as he passed by me. Grabbing two glasses and a decanter of amber liquid, he poured drinks, motioning toward the chairs. Abraham's eyes bored into me. The hair on the back of my neck rose at his intense gaze. Backing slowly away from him, I crossed the room to where Damiyun sat. Abraham sat down at the table and took an orange from a bowl in the center.

"You knew my father," I accused, taking the glass, and tossing it back. The fiery liquid burned down my throat, making me cough. Damiyun's eyes studied me, his face devoid of expression. "Where is he? What happened to him?"

"I can't... now is not the time for that." He rubbed his eyes, his face weary.

I settled back in my chair, grabbed the decanter, and took a healthy sip from it, a warm tingling sensation filling my limbs. "I'm not going anywhere. It's curfew, remember? And the town is teeming with Suppressors." I took another healthy drink.

"Do you know why the Suppressors are after you?"

I rolled my eyes. "Obviously because I'm a Wielder."

"What do you know of them?"

I chewed my lip. "They hate us. They take Wielders and either kill them or force them to join. But... I'm not exactly sure why. My father never really explained it to me. He only told me to be watchful and stay away from them."

Damiyun took the decanter from me and took a drink. "Solid advice," he said.

"Why do they hate us?"

"Jealousy. Wielders live far longer than Nons. Our aging slows dramatically upon our eighteenth Name Day, and though the Grand Passages advance, and our age increases each Name Day, we remain the same, physically, and mentally. For that, they despise us. It's another thing which makes us different. Makes us evil—according to them." He glanced at me. "What they don't understand is the reason we live longer. Our magic holds the binds on the Fallen One's tomb in place. But they have rejected this belief. They see us as his agents. And as they assume we are protecting him, they feel the need to eliminate us."

"Why would they think this?"

"Ignorance begets fear," Abraham spoke from across the room. We both looked up at him. He slowly ate his orange, eyes on Damiyun, who turned his attention back to me.

"A man named Zachariah Farnsworth founded the Order. He gathered a group of Nons and went after known Wielders. Captured them. Locked them up. They called themselves Suppressors, and after a while, the cells became full. That's when he offered the choice to join or die. Though with magic blocked, we do not differ from the Nons, and the Fallen One's binds weakened more."

"If all Wielders know this, why would they join?"

"People have many reasons for joining."

No. I didn't completely understand what Damiyun was saying. Still, each Wielder had a choice. Reaching forward, I grabbed the decanter back and took another long drink. Warmth spread through me. My fingers tingled and my head spun.

"Easy, Lillyanna," he said.

I kept my eyes on him and took another long pull.

"I said, take it easy." He snatched the bottle from my hand and put it on the table. I rose and tried to grab it back. The room swayed, and I stumbled. Damiyun's warm hands closed around mine, keeping me from falling down.

"I'm going to have my hands full with you," he said, his breath a warm caress against my face. Abraham looked up from his orange. I took a step away, my face heating from his closeness or the spirits I consumed, I wasn't sure which.

"I think I should go to bed." My head was swimming, and I stumbled back a few steps.

"Up the stairs and the door on the left," he said, nodding toward a staircase to the right. "Can you make it on your own?"

"I... Yes." I placed my hand on the wall and made my way toward the stairs, his voice stopping me.

"You will have answers, Lil. You have my word. I promise I will reveal all to you."

"Lillyanna," I corrected. The shortening of my name felt far too intimate a gesture for my comfort.

Ascending the stairs, I entered the dark bedroom. Weariness took over, and I removed the cloak, kicked off my boots, then crawled into the soft bed, drawing the blankets up to my chin. It had been a long and tiring night, and I had hoped I was done running from the Suppressors. And though I didn't know or trust Abraham and Damiyun, they knew my father and that was enough to convince me to stay.

For now, anyway.

EIGHT
ABRAHAM

ONE NIGHT PRIOR

I DIDN'T LIKE THIS part of my job. This part of my existence, but it was something I had to do. It was never my choice to be a Soul Collector. Themesis made me who I am. He had taken my soul, and now I was forced to serve him. I was forced to find the desperate, the hopeless, the greedy. And I did. I presented them the choice to move on into eternity, or to give me their soul.

There was always a price, and they always forgot. They always had a story, always begged for me to look the other way. To forget what they owed. I held no pity for most who chose to sell their souls. Chose to give themselves over to the Fallen One for eternity. Their decisions were selfish, and they deserved to suffer in torment and despair.

But then there was the living. The ones who sold their souls not for riches or material goods, but for someone else, a sick spouse or for a child that they dearly wanted. Those souls were the hardest for me to take.

Those souls made me hate my job even more.

I raised my hand to knock, a pointless gesture, really. The darkness that trailed me alerted those whose time had come. The door opened slowly, hinges groaning in protest. A pair of brown eyes met mine. Fright locked onto me, realization dawning in the man I had come to take. His legs shook and he gripped the door frame.

"It's time."

He licked his lips, eyes searching frantically over his shoulder. "Must you? My wife is with child. She is due any day. If you could—"

"What? Let you remain until the child is born? And then what? Let you watch her grow up? Watch the binding ceremony as she pledges her love? Watch her offspring steal your heart? No. You knew the terms when you gave over your soul. It is time to pay."

He glanced over his shoulder again. "My wife—"

"Will only think you passed peacefully in your sleep. There is no more bargaining. Your contract is up." I shrugged, palms up, letting him know there were no options.

He sighed. His shoulders slumped in defeat as he stepped out onto the porch. I stepped off onto the overgrown walk, fearful the rotting structure would collapse, sending the porch and house down upon us.

"How does this happen?" Hesitation colored his voice.

I pulled out the contract and my golden quill. Stabbing my finger, I drew in my blood, and then wrote "Contract Fulfilled" across the parchment, rolled it up and tucked it away. Reaching into my cloak, I pulled out a box made from obsidian found in the Abyss.

The obsidian from Themesis' tomb.

I opened it up and held my hand out to the man. Magic pulsed through me. It was magic born from the Abyss. Dark and evil. Demons crawled from the shadows, snarling, and snapping their jaws. Fire glowed where eyes should have been. Blood and saliva dripped from sharp teeth. Claws reached out toward the man who cowered in fear. Skeletal arms reached out, wrapping themselves around him. His mouth opened in a silent scream. Body convulsed and eyes rolled to the back of his head as his soul was ripped from him. I drew the demons driving his soul into the box to contain it, the obsidian binding him to the Abyss, until I brought him to serve his master. Slamming the lid shut, I picked up the corpse crumpled at my feet and strode into his house, placing him on the couch, for his wife to find in the morning.

The vile deed done, I rubbed my eyes and made my way back to the village to the tavern, where a high-stakes card game awaited me. There was a kind of solace in betting, the game made it seem like there were choices and chance involved. Nothing orchestrated, nothing controlled. The illusion soothed for a time. I found it particularly just to play against my fellow Soul Collectors.

"I WON AGAIN," I smiled as I dragged the pile of coins toward me.

"Damn it, Abe," the three men at the table moaned and cursed.

"One more?" I raised an eyebrow as I separated and stacked my winnings.

"You've cleaned me out. My wife is going to have a fit." Sam shook his head and drained his tankard of ale.

"It's no fun playing against you. You never lose." Lucas sat back with a huff and crossed his arms.

I laughed. "So, same time tomorrow?" The men rose to their feet.

"Just because we haven't won yet doesn't mean we won't," Bones chuckled. One after the next, the three men bid me farewell as they left the tavern.

I shook my head as I scooped the money into my purse, eyes going to a fair-haired whore with an ample bosom and generous hips. I reached into my pouch and tossed her a coin. Her eyes widened at the gold, and I knew she would thank me proper for it in a bed with her legs locked around my waist.

I felt a presence behind me. "Hello, Damiyun."

"Fleecing your mates again, I see." He slid into the chair across the table. I picked up the cards and started dealing. "Aren't you the least bit bothered about cheating them the way you do?"

My eyes widened at the accusation. "Cheating? I play quite fair."

"I would hardly call having the Luck of the Fallen One fair," Damiyun chuckled as he picked up his cards and studied them.

I shrugged. "You know, I hate losing."

Damiyun snorted as he placed two cards face down and took two more. "I doubt losing your head over a game would be worth it."

If only my death were that easy. Placing two cards down and selecting another, I focused on the man across the table.

Damiyun Rayne.

A man with a heart as black as his soul. He played the part of a righteous hero well, but he was as pure as a muddy gutter. I knew him. I knew him better than he knew himself. It was why I appeared to him that night.

Why I owned his soul.

He turned his back on all things good the night he had killed his father, and he lost a piece of himself with every dark deed he did.

And his deeds were very dark.

I knew when he completed this task, he would only wish for rest. To spend eternity serving his master, but I would not let that happen. Death would be a release from his painful life. But that pain paled in comparison to his future in the Abyss. Better to delay it as much as possible, even if it meant he served me.

"You didn't come here to lose at cards. What's on your mind?" I displayed my hand: four serpents and a knight. Damiyun laughed. Tossing his cards down, he took a long drink from the mug in front of him.

"It's the girl. She is the only thing occupying my thoughts of late," he said. "I'm thinking of making my move and collecting her. The Suppressors' presence is increasing. I have seen patrols when there should be none. I am concerned about her safety. If they were to capture her..." His voice trailed off. He didn't need to continue. I was well aware of the consequences if they caught her.

"I agree with you. The sooner we start our journey, the better."

The sound of a bell ringing in the town square broke through the low din in the tavern. It was the first bell warning that curfew was upon us. I watched as the patrons paid their tabs and dutifully shuffled out to go to their homes. Damiyun drained his mug, then rose to his feet, tossing coins on the table.

"I will gather her tomorrow eve. She seems to have the same schedule. It is clear her father has taught her how to stay clear of the Suppressors, when they traveled," he said. "Not that it matters, of late. Their numbers have increased and their patrols." He gave a short nod goodbye and left.

I sipped my ale as the reverberation of the bell died, and the night turned quiet once again. I stayed where I was. Suppressors left us Soul Collectors alone, but I hardly enjoyed crossing paths with them. They wanted magic abolished. Rejected the fact that magic alone kept Themesis locked away in his tomb in the Abyss.

That was where the girl came in. If the Suppressors found her, they wouldn't only seal their fates, but the world's.

The soft swish of skirts pulled me from my thoughts. Glancing up, I saw the whore standing next to the table. She held up a key. I rose to my feet and followed her to a room backstairs where she obliged me, properly thanking me for my generosity.

I WOKE AS THE sun crested the horizon, painting the sky in brilliant reds and oranges. I carefully extracted myself from the woman whose name I could not recall. She was a wildcat between the sheets, and I was more than happy to tame her. Not that she was unhappy to lend me control. I quietly pulled on my discarded clothing, securing my sword about my waist, and slipping a dagger in my boot. Another one went in my waistband against my back. I heard the stirrings of sheets and glanced over to the bed where the woman lay, pulling herself up onto her elbows. The blanket slid down, revealing an expanse of flesh, pink nipples standing erect in the chilly room. Her heavy-lidded eyes gave me a sultry glance, and I had to stop myself from disrobing and taking her again.

"Leaving so soon?" Her voice was husky with sleep. I said nothing as I grabbed my cloak and headed for the door.

"Don't be a stranger. I would very much enjoy another toss with you," she said, voice rising as I slipped out of the room.

As much as I enjoyed her company, I knew this was a onetime deal. Remaining with the same woman often proved quite a bore. Only one had captivated me. Claimed my heart and caused me to bind myself to her, joining in blood as I pledged my love and faith.

Now was not the time for nostalgia.

I hastened through the town. The sun poked just above the horizon, a new day dawned, merchants readied their wares for the day. Wagons piled with goods lined the streets. Shouts and curses punctuated the relative quiet of the new morning.

Ducking into an alley, I reached out to the shadows and pulled them around me; icy fingers of blackness caressed my body. Contorted demons embraced, and I shivered at their touch, slipping from the world of the living to the world of the dead. Releasing the darkness, I returned to my human form. I heard a soft hiss and felt a movement in my beard. Sighing, I reached in and pulled out the demon buried in the warmth.

"You again?" I chastised lightly, holding him in my hand. His little wings flapped, and he wrapped his tail around my arm. Red eyes looked up at me.

"Alright, Bel. You can come. I suppose I could use some support," I said. The demon unwrapped himself and climbed my arm, wrapping his tail around my neck and resting his head on my shoulder. Taking a deep breath, I made my way down the hall.

I despised this place.

The cavern closed in on me. My shoulders brushed the rock walls, and the mountain felt as though it were pressing down on me. The air stifled, oppressive and stagnant. Sweat trickled down my back, making my shirt stick to my skin. I made my way through the small corridor, past the jagged rocks and molten rivers flowing toward the looming structure.

Themesis' tomb.

The black as pitch castle of obsidian rose high into the rock ceiling above. Striding past the demon guards, I continued through the doors and down the long, cold hall to where Themesis sat upon his obsidian throne. As always, he was dressed smartly. He wore a velvet coat of deep-blue over a white shirt. Black leather trousers sheathed his legs, and black boots reached to his knees, the lamplight reflecting on the polished bronze buckles. His jet-black hair was loose, and his ice-blue eyes watched as I crossed the room.

Carved griffins made up the legs and armrests of the monstrosity. Delicate flowers curled around the base, the purple petals bright against the black. The flowers inspired the throne's name, Nightshade. His fingers curled around the heads of the griffins; neat nails tapped a bored rhythm. He leaned forward as I approached. I sighed in relief at not seeing Jaylynn kneeling at his side like she usually was, her naked body, usually covered with gold paint woven into an intricate design. Diamond-encrusted collar around her neck, with a golden leash held in Themesis' hand. The collar forced her to obey, to adore.

I knew he brought her out to show me whenever I returned to the Abyss. It was a torment and not seeing her adoring eyes upon him, well...it was a small boon.

I had lost everything the day I lost my Jaylynn. I saw no clear way out of the job. Themesis owned my soul as much as he owned Jaylynn's. It twisted more than my gut, it twisted my heart and soul. Still, I remained stone faced as much as possible.

Themesis smiled at seeing where my eyes went. "Jaylynn is busy. I can summon her when she is done entertaining," he laughed, then brought his attention back to the box I held. "Who have you brought me?"

I opened the lid. A swirl of black smoke poured out, whirling around like a tornado. The smoke dissipated, leaving behind the form of a man who shook as his eyes went to Themesis.

"Ah," Themesis smiled as he sat back, fingers still drumming on the griffin's head. "The child lover. The one who was killed for what he did to a boy. He pleaded for his life. Yes... I remember." He paused, eyes on the soul coalescing into a solid being. "Tell me. What would you have done to the girl your wife is to bear?"

I stood behind the man, watching. It was all the same when they came here. Disbelief. Fear. Terror. Then the tears.

This man fell to his knees weeping, and crawled to Themesis, grabbing at his ankles, something which both angered and humored him.

"I didn't mean to. I couldn't help myself. Please?"

Themesis laughed. "I can forgive your sins. Give me your daughter."

The man grew silent, and I knew what he was thinking.

I knew he was considering the offer. I could almost see the thoughts running through his head. He opened his mouth, and I grabbed his arm and jerked him back.

"Think long and hard on what you are about to say," I said. "Give your daughter over, and I can assure you her fate will be even more horrific than yours."

He looked from me to Themesis and back. "No," the man finally said.

"You have chosen your fate. Let it be so." He turned his ice-blue eyes to me. "Come see me when you are through." Then, he waved his hand in dismissal, and settled back against the plush throne. I sighed. The last thing I wanted was to return. Grabbing the man's arm, I hauled him away. He dug in his feet and tried to jerk his arm from my firm grasp as I dragged him, his pathetic screams and pleas grating on my last nerve. The terms of the contract were clearly stated.

Every one of them knew once they signed their name, it was binding, yet it always went the same way. Time made them forget, or at the least hope Themesis had forgotten. But he never forgot. This man wouldn't have been spared even if he had given up his daughter. Themesis always kept what was his.

"You knew the outcome. You knew what would happen."

"But..." His terrified eyes met mine, and I shoved him into a cell.

The place where he would become the child enduring the same horrors he inflicted on the innocent.

Rubbing my eyes, I made my way through the dark and cold halls back to Themesis' throne room. The light from the torches and lamps reflected on the smooth black stone, the walls danced as if on fire. He stood with his back to me, filling two glasses with red wine. Handing me one, he sat back upon Nightshade. The garish monstrosity of his throne loomed above the room on a dais so he could look down upon who came before him. I stood in front of the throne, eyes on him as I sipped the drink he offered.

"The time is drawing near," he said. "Soon I will be free of this insufferable tomb. Free to walk the lands. Free to lord over man, who will cower in fear as they grovel on hands and knees before me."

I wanted to laugh at his delusional lunacy but thought better of it. "Did you forget about the girl?"

"Do you think me afraid of a child?"

"You know who she is born of."

He waved his hand. "She is still a child. She will be my queen. She will kneel before me and serve me like the rest." He smiled over the rim of his glass.

Not if I can help it.

Blue eyes turned to me again. "You will be by my side. You will be there when I take over the pathetic humans. When I become their lord and master."

"And if I'm not?"

His eyes narrowed to slits. "Do not disobey me." He leaned forward on Nightshade. "You had best remember your place. Remember who you serve and who made you."

"Are we through here?" I drained my glass and slammed it down onto a table. Not waiting for an answer, I reached out toward the darkness, pulling it around me like a blanket, and slipped from his tomb. From the Abyss. Back to the world of the living.

T HE DARKNESS OF NIGHT cloaked the town. Time moved differently in the Abyss. What had seemed like a few hours, there was an entire day above. The market teemed with armed Suppressors. My muscles tensed, seeing them running about, and I frowned. Curfew was still a bit away. My pulse quickened upon catching fragments of conversations as men rushed about.

"... almost had the little bitch. She's with Rayne," a Suppressor yelled at his comrades as he ran by. Something must have happened, and the Suppressors had moved in on Lillyanna. I made my way quickly through the crowded streets to my home, where I knew he waited. As I entered my home, I looked around, and my eyes lighted on the petite girl. She was a pretty young thing. Long red curls spilled down her back, bright emerald eyes darted around in fright, and I knew her to be a curse.

At least, where Damiyun was concerned.

She was mouthy and insolent, and she cringed every time she laid eyes on me. Not that I cared. My job wasn't to be her friend. It was to keep Damiyun on track and make sure she made it to Kraagswell Mountain.

I looked at Damiyun, frowning as his feelings slipped through the bond. A pretty face easily swayed him. His wife Zenith, long dead and rotting in a grave, was a testament to that. She was the reason I came to him. I couldn't fault him for his feelings, as I too had once become enchanted by one from the fairer sex. But to call what he had felt love... no, he was a slave to her. He gave in to her requests, spending coin like a drunken sailor might with a whore. He was blind to see her for who she was. Even when she revealed herself, he still turned a blind eye to her deceit. Traded his soul for a chance to salvage what she destroyed in one fateful moment. All to win back a woman whose deceit ran through her veins like blood.

Sitting down at the table, I listened to Damiyun and Lillyanna talk, noting the lies rolling easily off his tongue. How he managed to convince so many women to trust him was beyond my ken. They paused in their discussion, and he sent her off to bed. I followed, making my way up to my room.

Raising my left arm, I unclasped the bracelet I always wore. As I held it, I caressed the words engraved on the back. Words I knew by heart:

To my Abe. Forever into eternity, Lenore.

I clutched the gold band, and, like every night, my mind went to the woman I had loved.

The only one who knew me. The real me. She alone knew who I truly was and even then, she gave herself to me. She would often shake her head and laugh. "I know you're lying, Abe. You cannot possibly be who you say you are." She would say as she settled into my arms, head resting upon my chest.

But I never lied to her. I clutched the bracelet she had given me. It was the very last anniversary of our Blood-Binding. A time shortly before our lives fell apart, and she left me. Pressing my lips to the metal, I gave it a soft kiss.

"I'm sorry, Lenore. I never stopped loving you," I said to the woman whose bones were dust in a grave. Placing the bracelet on the night table, I slipped beneath the covers and closed my eyes to tortured sleep.

NINE
LILLYANNA

I WOKE UP THE next morning exhausted, a dull ache pulsing in my head. Gods, how could I have been so stupid last night, getting drunk in a house with two men I didn't even know? My cheeks heated with embarrassment at the thought of how I almost fell on my face after drinking the Serpent's Venom. Done is done. I threw the blankets off and shivered from the cold. After I slipped out of bed, I laced up my boots, picked up the cloak Damiyun loaned me and opened the door. I made my way quietly down the stairs, Abraham and Damiyun's voices grew as I did. The words "Vel" and "Suppressors" came up a few times.

"... a price on your head. A hefty one, I might add."

"What was I supposed to do? You cannot think I'd hand her over."

I looked around the corner at Damiyun, who leaned casually against the wall. He wore a white shirt, tucked into dark-brown trousers. Black boots reached just below the knee, and loose hair brushed his shoulders. Abraham sat at the table toying with a glass, disapproving eyes on Damiyun.

"I understand. I broke the agreement." Damiyun shook his head. "I can give anyone to them—and curse the gods I have—but they cannot take her."

Abraham shrugged. "I'm just telling you to watch your back."

Damiyun waved a hand in dismissal. "I always do. This isn't the first time I have pissed someone off, and it won't be my last." He flashed the other man a brief smile that better resembled a grimace.

Abraham grunted as he placed the glass on the table. "I ask you, try not to have your head taken. At least until you have completed your task."

Damiyun looked up and caught my eyes. "Good morning, Lil. I didn't hear you come in."

Abraham cast a glare in my direction. "No doubt she snuck down to eavesdrop," he turned back to Damiyun. "We should have left hours ago."

"We will leave at midday." Shrugging, Damiyun pulled out a chair for me.

I sat down on the edge and studied Abraham as he and Damiyun talked idly about a journey we were apparently embarking on. I didn't know what magic Abraham had. I shuddered in fear every time I saw him, so I kept my distance.

Sensing my gaze, he turned his black, soulless eyes in my direction. A chill came over me and I tore my eyes away.

"Where are we going?" I looked at Damiyun.

"Someplace safe."

I rolled my eyes with a sigh. "Still cryptic, I see."

Damiyun said nothing.

Abraham rose to his feet. "We leave now. I will check for Suppressors." The sound of his boots echoed down the short entryway, followed by the slam of the door.

"Does he have to go with us?"

Damiyun sighed. He pulled out the chair next to me and straddled it, resting his chin on his arms, light-gray eyes burrowing into me.

"Yes, he does. I am bound to him by magic. The only way to break the bond is if I die, and even then..." He shook his head and laughed wryly. "If I could go back, I never would have agreed." He stood up. "Nothing good comes from love," he said.

Baffled, I sat still for a moment, unsure of what to say. I opened my mouth to speak, but the door slammed open. We both jumped at the sound. Damiyun's hand went for his dagger.

"There are a few Suppressors around, but nothing too concerning," Abraham said as he stalked into the room. "Gather whatever provisions you may need." He turned and walked back outside.

"What crawled up his backside?"

Damiyun said nothing, but his shoulders loosened. The corner of his mouth twitched. He turned and quickly made his way upstairs, returning a moment later with a bundle of bedrolls, a leather bag and his sword strapped to his back. He filled the bag with hard cheeses, stale rolls, dried fruits and cured meats along with two water skins. He hoisted the bag and tucked the bedrolls under his arm.

"Let's go," he said, striding in the door's direction.

"Not until you answer my questions," I said, sitting back in my chair and crossing my arms.

Damiyun stopped. "We don't have time for this."

"You should have thought about that last night."

"You will get your answers, just not right now. Suppressors are in the village. It's only a matter of time before they figure out, we're still here."

"Why should I go with you? Why should I even trust you?"

Damiyun rubbed his eyes. "Because you have no choice, Lillyanna. You could take your chances in the village. Go home, like you said you would, but they will find you and when they do, when they capture you... let's just say it would be the most unpleasant thing you will ever experience."

"I told you last night, I am well aware of what the Suppressors do. I have seen them take Wielders. Why do you think my father told me when they patrolled?" I said, crossing my arms. "And speaking of my father..."

"We need to go," he said, continuing for the door.

"No."

"For the love of the gods," he muttered, facing me. "I will answer them. I promise. I will tell you what you need to know when we are out of here and away from the Suppressors."

I shook my head and stood up, throwing Damiyun's cloak around my shoulders. I followed him outside, my eyes flicking to Abraham, who sat astride a humongous, black horse, two others beside him. Damiyun grabbed the reins of a stallion whose coat shone silver and secured his bundles to the saddlebags.

"We will only take two mounts," he stated, patting the horse's neck. "The Suppressors are looking for Lillyanna. I can't cloak her from afar. She will ride with me."

Abraham pursed his lips, eyes narrowed dangerously on Damiyun before nodding his agreement.

Damiyun pulled his hood over his head and motioned for me to get up onto the horse. I'd never ridden, and I hesitated as I looked at the massive beast, who tossed his head in irritation. Damiyun's hands closed around my waist, and he hoisted me up onto its back, then swung up behind, securing me with one arm around my midsection. My breath hitched at the closeness. Taking the reins, he heeled the horse into motion, following Abraham.

"Quiet now. We're entering the village." Damiyun kept his voice low, pretending I wasn't there.

The sounds of the village became muted and wavered for a moment as the cloaking spell, ability, took effect. We made our way slowly through the town, passing a few Suppressors as they milled about, carefully observing those who walked about the market. I remembered what Damiyun had said about Feelers and felt a sliver of panic.

"Won't their Feelers spot us?" I whispered.

"They know you're here. Chances are high they'll send more Suppressors. Possibly toss the entire village in their search."

His breath came as a caress, so close to my ear as he spoke. I shivered at his words. At the thought of people being hurt because of my presence.

"It's alright, Lil. You're safe."

As we continued through the town, I held my breath. Soon enough, we made it through the village without detection, and I sighed in relief. When we were quite a distance away, Damiyun released his magic and he and Abraham heeled the horses into a distance-eating canter. We rode for at least an hour through the woods, the sunlight filtering through the leaves above us. I shifted in the saddle, my backside and inner thighs aching from the constant bumping up and down. My midsection burned from keeping myself stable as much as Damiyun held me in place. A horse required a bit more physical exertion than I had ever realized.

Abraham slowed his horse to a walk, guiding us through the forest to a small clearing. "We can rest for a bit. Let the horses cool down," Abraham said as he climbed off his horse.

Damiyun released his hold on me and dismounted. I attempted to follow suit, but I winced at the pain radiating through my body, my left leg cramping up. Damiyun chuckled, then reached up and helped me off the horse.

"It will hurt less with practice," he said, his voice light.

I glowered.

A river rushed just past the edge of the clearing, and I made my way toward it. After splashing my face with water and taking a long, hearty drink, I sat by the bank to rest my legs. The sun danced brightly in the sky, and I lifted my face toward the warm rays. Spring's fresh scent filled the air, hinting of flowers and leaves and clean water. I preferred the openness of nature to the cramped confines of the town.

Abraham and Damiyun's voices drifted as they spoke, the sound carried on the light breeze. I looked back to where they stood by the grazing horses and back to the river. The water flowed rapidly, small white caps forming as it raced by. The current was powerful, but I was a strong swimmer and even if I were swept away, at least it would carry me far from these two men. As if sensing my thoughts, Damiyun looked my way and walked toward the river's edge to fill the water skins.

"I don't suggest running again." He paused for a moment, his eyes on mine. "I understand this is difficult for you, Lillyanna. You have no idea what's going on, but I promise I will tell you. You just need to trust me."

"And Abraham?"

"You can trust me, Lil. I have sworn to protect you, and I will until my dying breath. Abraham is no concern of yours."

"He blocked my magic."

"He did it to protect you and everyone else. You are powerful. Until you can learn how to harness and control your magic, you're a danger. You could kill everyone, including yourself."

"Yes. I'm sure, Abraham is very concerned for my welfare." I snorted. "Who did you swear to?"

"I promise I will tell you. Later."

Rubbing my eyes, I changed the subject when it was clear he wouldn't answer my questions.

"Who was she?"

"Who was who?"

"The one who didn't care."

He looked away. "My wife."

Interesting. "What happened?"

Damiyun looked at me, his gray eyes empty. A soft breeze blew a lock of hair in my eyes. He lifted his hand to brush it back, and I took a step away. Dropping his hand, he looked back out across the river.

"I was a fool. I loved her and she—"

"Time to move," Abraham said, standing a few yards away. His hands were on his hips, and his lips pursed. We made our way back to the horses. I looked up at Damiyun's stallion, who didn't look as scary as he did earlier. He was quite majestic with a silver coat which seemed to glimmer in the sunlight. The beast tossed his head, and Damiyun patted his neck.

"Don't worry, Xander. We're moving." His voice was low and soothing. "He gets annoyed when we stop moving."

I reached up and tentatively stroked the horse's nose. He took a step forward, nuzzling my neck with a snort. I couldn't help but laugh.

"I think he likes you," Damiyun said, as we mounted up.

"What's your horse's name?" I asked Abraham who rode beside us.

"He doesn't have one."

"So, how do you address him?"

"I don't."

I glanced at Abraham's horse. The black coat shone in the sun, and ripples of purple ran through its mane.

"Violet."

He turned dark eyes on me. "What?"

"Your horse's name is Violet."

"Violet?"

"Yes."

He tightened his lips and sat higher in the saddle. "It's a male."

"And his name is Violet."

He scowled down at me. "If you think I'm going to call my horse Violet—"

"How will you get him to come to you if he doesn't have a name?"

Damiyun laughed. "She has a point, Abraham."

"Fucking ridiculous," Abraham muttered, turning back to the road ahead.

I laughed. "Where are we going?" I turned my attention back to Damiyun.

"There is a place a few days' ride away from here. I will teach you there," Damiyun said.

"Teach me? Teach me what?"

"How to use your magic. You've never really let it loose. You need to know what you can do."

"And you somehow know how my magic works?"

"While magic comes in different forms, the general principle on how to use it is often similar."

"And why do you need to do this?"

Silence.

I gritted my teeth. "What is this place you're taking me?" A horrible thought crossed my mind. He was a slaver. He wanted to bring me to a ship and sell me somewhere across the Calgonian Sea.

"A secluded place, so if something goes wrong, you won't hurt anyone."

That didn't help. "Except you and me." For a moment, I glanced at Abraham. I really couldn't have cared less if I inadvertently obliterated him.

"Don't worry about me. I'm difficult to kill. Right, Abraham?"

Abraham looked over at Damiyun but said nothing. The secrecy between them infuriated me to no end.

"Is he going to remove the block, or do I need to ask his permission first?" I asked. Abraham glared at me.

"How did you survive all this time?" Damiyun asked, changing the subject.

"Why does it matter?"

"Ten Grand Passages is a long time to be on your own. Especially at such a young age."

I tossed my head. "I managed."

Damiyun shifted in the saddle behind me. "Clearly." His tone dripped with sarcasm.

"I'll tell you later," I said. If he would rather not tell me anything, then why should I?

"We have time." His tone was amused as he adjusted himself.

I clenched my teeth. "It was difficult. There were times I had to eat out of waste heaps. Times I stole things, praying the Enforcers didn't catch me. I wasn't left with much in the way of coin."

"Surely, you weren't eating trash and stealing the entire time?"

"No. I did odd jobs, ran errands for neighbors, but they didn't always pay enough," I said, fidgeting in the saddle. Gods, my backside hurt. "I worked the most for a healer. He taught me how to treat wounds, make elixirs for different ailments. I took the knowledge and began making my own to sell. It was hard. I was turned away more often than not. I suppose I could understand why. I was a child selling potions. But I didn't give up though, and some bought them, most likely out of pity. When people discovered they actually worked, I sold more. Still, there were far too many times I went without food."

"I'm sorry, Lil."

"The thing I found most curious was a few times every Moon Cycle, someone would leave me packages of food, even coin, on my porch." I thought back to those nights after my coin had run out. Long after my food was gone, and my stomach was empty. So painfully empty.

"Someone was looking out for you."

"I don't know of anyone who would have known I lived alone. I did my best to keep it a secret. If anyone inquired about my father, I always had a lie ready."

"Perhaps it was a neighbor."

I shrugged. "Possibly. I just wish I knew who had done it. I was grateful whenever I saw the sack on my porch. I wish I could thank whoever it was."

Damiyun shifted behind me. "Well, maybe the time will come for that one day."

"It just would have been nice to meet whoever it was. I... I was lonely. The only people I spoke to were the ones I did errands and odd jobs for. I was afraid to make myself known. Terrified of what would happen to me if people knew I was alone. I didn't know if the Enforcers would take me, so I laid low. Stayed home, only ventured out for food and coins."

"I'm sorry, Lil." Damiyun's voice was low. "It must have been tough for you. You were young and I'm sure scared."

"I managed."

"I'm sorry," he said again.

I leaned against him. Heat radiated from his body, wrapping me in warmth. "I just don't understand why he left me," I murmured.

Damiyun shifted behind me again but said nothing.

I thought about my father. The memories I had of him before he left me still felt so vivid. His face, those blue eyes that danced with amusement and love. The warmth of his arms holding me close as he read me a story. And then, one day, he left without a goodbye, leaving a sack with a small number of coins. I waited for him to come back. Days. Weeks. And when he didn't, I had to accept he was truly gone. I didn't—I couldn't—understand why he abandoned me. The confusion, and the pain, ran deep. Eventually, it boiled into anger. And then hatred. And finally, a numbing nothingness.

I yawned, weariness washing over me, and settled back against Damiyun. His earthy scent enveloped me. The sound of his heartbeat soothed me, and I closed my eyes, letting the gentle sway of the horse and the rhythmic rise and fall of Damiyun's chest lull me to sleep.

TEN

BLACKNESS, THICK AND SUFFOCATING, *blanketed the world. I stood with Damiyun and Abraham on a hill. Below, fires blazed all around. Bodies littered the ground and screams pierced the night. The scent of burning flesh drifted on the breeze. Oppressive heat scorched me. A river of molten rock flowed, melting and consuming all in its path. Trees, brush, and people burst into mist and evaporated from the intense heat.*

Then I saw him.

A tall man with jet-black hair flowing about his shoulders. Piercing blue eyes turned toward me. He smiled. A look that stole the warmth from my blood.

"You did this, Lillyanna. You did all of this. You set me free," the man's voice whispered in my ear.

"No," I gasped as I gazed out at the death and destruction below.

"W AKE UP." DAMIYUN'S VOICE drifted toward me, and he shook me lightly. "We're setting up camp."

I jumped. My eyes snapped open at the sound of his voice. We had reached a small clearing in the woods and the sun was going down. I climbed down from the horse first, and Damiyun followed. He shook his arm like it had gone numb.

"Sorry," I muttered.

"It's fine. I didn't have the heart to move you."

"Start a fire. I will go see if I can catch some food." Abraham gestured to the center of camp, before stalking off.

I helped Damiyun gather sticks and branches, then sat back and watched absently as he built the fire, my mind on the nightmare I just had.

"Are you alright?" His gray eyes filled with concern.

"Bad dream."

"What about?" Damiyun sat next to me, propping an arm on his knee.

I shook my head. The searing heat of the dream ripped through me again. The stench of burned flesh and the screams of so many people being burned and tortured. It all clung to me, and I shook my head, trying to clear it from my mind. It had felt so real.

We sat in silence waiting for Abraham, who returned sometime later carrying a large rabbit. He tossed it to Damiyun, who pulled out a dagger and began skinning the carcass.

"Lillyanna rides with me tomorrow," he stated as he settled his bulk on the ground.

"I am not riding with you."

"You will ride with me, or you will walk."

"Then I'll walk."

Damiyun paused in his work and glanced at me, giving an almost imperceptible shake of his head, eyes silently telling me to stop pushing the issue. I jumped to my feet and stalked away, taking a seat on the ground a few yards from where they sat. Their voices drifted on the breeze, and I turned my head in their direction, straining my ears to listen.

"... being difficult?" Damiyun hissed as he skewered the rabbit meat on a spit and secured it over the fire.

"... too close to her."

Damiyun replied something unintelligible, his next words were just barely audible. "... Keeper... close to her."

Abraham mumbled, and Damiyun laughed.

"... have a weakness for attractive women."

Damiyun glanced over at me, his words drifting clearly in my direction. "Don't we all?"

I felt myself heat at his words. At his intense gaze. "She is slowly trusting me. If you push her, she will become even more willful. No. She rides with me tomorrow."

Abraham's voice rose. "Remember your place. You are her Keeper. Not her friend."

Keeper? What does that mean?

Damiyun cooked the meat, cutting off two hefty pieces and placing them on a piece of tree bark. He stood and walked over to where I sat, placing the food on the ground between us.

"Thank you," I mumbled.

With a grunt, he glanced at me. "Do you always listen in on other people's conversations?" He chewed a piece of meat as he spoke.

"You can hardly fault me when the two of you are sitting right there."

"No, I suppose your nosiness is neither mine nor Abraham's fault."

"Nosiness? The two of you could wake the dead with how loud you talk."

The corner of Damiyun's mouth twitched up. "I'll give you that."

I trained my attention on him as he ate. "Tell me what happened to my father. Tell me how you knew him."

Damiyun sighed, a long and sorrowful sound. "Your father is dead, Lillyanna. I'm sorry."

Somehow, I knew, but hearing the actual words spoken was something entirely different. It felt like someone had punched me in the stomach. Nausea washed over me. My chest tightened, and I rubbed it with a shaking hand as I struggled to breathe. Tears poured from my eyes. Somewhere around me, there was a whine like a wounded puppy crying.

Me. It was me.

I shrugged off the hand he placed on my back.

"How?" I whispered when I had semi-composed myself, turning my watery gaze to him.

"I heard the Suppressors tortured him to get information on your whereabouts. Eventually, they killed him. I'm sorry."

I brushed the tears from my cheeks with a shaking hand. My father had sacrificed himself to protect me. "How did you know him?"

Damiyun ran his hand through his hair and let out a puff of air. His face looked haggard. The lines around his eyes and mouth were more pronounced, and he looked decades older.

"You have to understand that what happens to us is predetermined by the gods," he said, folding his legs. He looked down, his finger absently digging a hole in the dirt as he gathered his thoughts. "Ah shit, Lil. This isn't easy for me." He took a deep breath and raised his eyes to mine. "I was a Suppressor and Vel... Vel was an Elder, the highest rank in the Order."

"You lie," I leaped up.

"Lil—" he glided to his feet. I slapped his hand away as he reached for me.

"You lying bastard. You told me last night you weren't one of them. I should have known," I spat, taking a step away from him. "How dare you try to soil the memory of my father by telling me he was a Suppressor? An Elder. I knew I wasn't safe with you."

"Lil—" He took a step in my direction.

Looking over my shoulder, I peered into the woods behind. They loomed over me, dark and ghostly, and though I feared what lay beyond, I now feared Damiyun more.

He took another step, and I turned and bolted into the forest.

"Damn it." he cursed, and I heard footsteps pounding on the ground as he gave chase. The branches scratched my face and snagged my cloak, slowing me down. Twice I stumbled and almost fell, but I kept running.

I didn't know where I was going. I needed to get as far away from Damiyun and Abraham as possible. His footsteps drew closer. Arms grabbed my waist, dragging me to the ground. We rolled on the forest floor for a few feet before coming to a stop. I kicked and clawed at Damiyun, who straddled me, pinning my wrists to the ground above my head. He was lithe, and it surprised me how heavy and strong he was, his grip tight and painful. His face was inches from mine, his ragged breath warm on my face, his gray eyes glowing with gold light.

"Get off me."

When he released my wrists, I slapped him hard across the face. His head snapped to the right.

"I deserved that." He sat back and rubbed his cheek. "If I release you, will you promise not to run?"

"No."

"Lil—"

"You lied to me."

"No, I didn't. I'm not one of them anymore," he said.

"Do you really expect me to believe your bullshit?"

"My brother sent the Suppressors after me. They beat me, then tossed me in a cell. They left me in a small, dark place with no food. Pitiful rations of water. No human contact for weeks. Finally, Vel came and gave me a choice. Die or join them. I didn't betray my kind. I did what I had to do to live and survive. Many choose the same. When faced with the thought of dying alone in a small, dark cell, what would you have chosen?"

I sniffed. "Death is far more honorable. So, what now, Damiyun? Are you and Abraham bringing me to them?"

"No, I'm not," he sighed. "Your father chose the same fate as I did."

My eyes narrowed. "Bullshit. There is no way my father would have joined. He abhorred the Suppressors. He told me all about them and how evil they were. He told me when they patrolled, so I wouldn't get caught. You're nothing more than a lying piece of garbage."

"How else do you think I knew him if not for him being a Suppressor? He joined for your sake. He didn't want his daughter growing up without a father."

I snorted. "Which I did anyway."

He rubbed his face. "He had no choice. If he had stayed... if he had stayed, you would have been in danger. They would have taken you. Your father did a good job of keeping you hidden. He used a spell to hide your magic from the

Suppressors." His eyes met mine. "And from yourself. He couldn't risk you using it and hurting people."

That explained why I didn't know about the magic I wielded until four Grand Passages ago.

"When did he die?"

"I heard it was a few Grand Passages ago." He paused. "I made him a promise. I promised I would find you and watch you and when the time came, I'd keep you safe and out of the hands of the Suppressors. We struck a deal. He let me walk away with the promise I wouldn't be harassed, wouldn't be hauled in, by any Suppressor, as long as I kept up my end of the bargain."

"Which was?"

He sighed. "I became an informant. When a Wielder joins the Suppressors, they're forced to wear a bracelet called the Sigaa'Lean. It blocks a Wielder's ability to use their power. If they try, the pain is excruciating. Being a Feeler, I didn't have to wear the bracelet. I would find Wielders and tell the Suppressors where they were. In exchange for my information, they paid me in coin."

"You betrayed your kind?" No surprise there. I scoffed. Unbelievable. To find myself with a man who knew my father, who betrayed my...our kind. My father too. I froze. My father was a Wielder.

"I only did it to keep my head. I promise I'm not taking you to them," he said. "Your father loved you. His only wish was to keep you safe."

"If you would betray your own kind to keep your head, you would certainly go back on a deal with a dead man when it no longer suited you." I roughly pushed him off me.

Damiyun rolled with my push gracefully, making me even angrier. "He suppressed your magic, though when you turned eighteen it broke through the block, he put in." He offered a hand down to me. Ignoring it, I stood and began walking toward camp. Silence stretched as he fell in step beside me. I couldn't say I believed what he said, though I was unable to say I didn't. My father had always deflected my questions. Either way, I obviously couldn't escape on foot. I'd need to have a horse, and control of my own magic to get away. I decided to stay with them until I had both, and then I would leave and find my own answers about my father.

We walked on toward camp, neither one of us saying a word. I grabbed my discarded blanket, then made my way to the cookfire. What Damiyun had told me about my father—and himself—made me feel nauseous.

Turning my back to both men, I lay down, pulling my cloak and blanket around me. My mind churned over what Damiyun had told me. I couldn't believe my father was an Elder. Yet, looking back, the signs that he was a Suppressor were there. There were times he would leave for several hours, even a day. He would tell me to stay inside, giving me toys to play with and paper to draw on. Other times he would hide me in the root cellar. Those times I would hear footsteps and voices above. I would often silently creep up the stairs, pressing my ear to the door to listen to the muffled voices beyond. I never understood what was being said. Or why I had to hide. And then one day, shortly after my twelfth Name Day, he sat me down on his lap.

"I have to leave, Lillyanna," he had said, eyes sad. Why did he look so sad? His words weren't anything new. "I won't be coming back."

I frowned. "What do you mean?"

He pushed a lock of hair behind my ear. "There's something I have to do. Some place I have to go and I... I can't come back."

I bit my lip; tears stung my eyes. "Was it something I did?"

He pulled me into his arms, crushing me in his embrace. "Gods, Lillyanna, my sweet girl. No." He pulled back and looked down at me, eyes shining with tears. "I love you, Lillyanna and if I could stay, I would, but..." he shook his head with a sigh. "This is for your own good. If I stay...this will keep you safe."

I frowned. "I don't understand."

He smiled sadly. "Someday you will, and I hope that when that day comes, you forgive me."

When I woke the next morning, he was gone.

I was only twelve. Unless you were born on the streets, what child of that age knows anything about survival or even the harshness of life? I admit prior to being left on my own, my life was anything but harsh. My father loved me and looking back, I realize he shielded me from much of the surrounding unpleasantness. He never raised a hand to me, and while I can't say I was the model child, his punishments weren't severe. I only knew love and patience when I was small.

My father's leaving hit me hard because I was forced to figure out how to survive on my own. He had told me about the Suppressors, explaining the evilness of their ways. It wasn't until I discovered my abilities did I understand why he had warned me about them. I had watched dozens of them march into my tiny village and violently take Magic Wielders, dragging them away from their families. After seeing that, I realized I needed to keep my head low and avoid any confrontation.

I knew the magic I wielded was strong, and I struggled to keep it under control.

It was always there.

Pulsing through my veins.

The deliciousness of it.

I kept to myself, doing my best to keep my head down and my anger in check. I won't pretend it wasn't difficult. I hardly knew anything, yet here I was on my own. I didn't know who my mother was or *where* she was. And now my father had left me. He told me the approximate times the Suppressors would patrol. At the time, it meant nothing to me. After what Damiyun unrevealed, I realized he wanted me to be aware so they didn't take me.

I did my best to avoid the Suppressors as well as others. It wasn't easy being a girl as young as I was and on her own. I had to watch myself when I was at the market lest someone robbed me or worse. Some store owners looked out for me. They made sure no one hassled me and in a dire situation brought me into the back of their shop for safety. I can't say those who protected me were my friends. No, I can't say they were my enemy either. I had no doubt that if any knew of the power that pulsed inside me, they wouldn't have hesitated to turn me in.

I wasn't ignorant. I knew the only person I could trust was myself, and when my coin ran out, I did minor jobs for the people in the village. I ran errands for some shops. I mucked stalls for those who were my neighbors. While I could have earned coin by robbing to put food in my belly, I didn't. I knew the Enforcers would take me, and the thought of sitting in a cell for a week—or however long they felt they could keep me—was unappealing.

And then, one fateful evening when I was out on my usual run in the market, someone marked me.

I don't know who the man was that called me out. I didn't understand why there were so many Suppressors there. The only safe place I saw was Damiyun.

And now I found out he was a Suppressor. Someone my father told me to stay away from.

And my father was part of the Order.

Finally, hours before the sun rose, I succumbed to sleep.

ELEVEN
DAMIYUN

Tossing a log onto the fire, I settled back against a pine tree, the pungent musk of sap drifting down on the light breeze.

I would not sleep. I wasn't about to risk her fleeing while Abraham and I rested.

Telling her about myself, about her father, brought up a wave of memories I had long since buried. I admit I was not truthful with her at first, and I offer no apologies for my deception. She was in a fragile state and telling her the truth was not something I felt she could handle. Her reaction to it told me I was right. The hate in her eyes, the mistrust when I told her I was part of the Order... well, I can't rightly say I blamed her for her feelings.

But she didn't understand. She had never been in the position I had been in. She didn't understand it wasn't a betrayal. It was a need to survive. Many joined for their own reasons. Some to protect their family. Some because death isn't an option. As a Regulator with the Order, Vel and I became close, though I would never have called him a friend. One night, he'd revealed the truth about his daughter. Much like her mother, he had demands. Find her, he had commanded, protect her and when she came into her magic, I was to bring her to the Order. Vel's direction did not sit well with me. He had abandoned his daughter to protect her from the Order and after all these Grand Passages, he wanted her brought to the Compound. I'd protect her to my last breath. She'd never step foot there. And when Felicity had set me to my task, to take Lillyanna to Kraagswell Mountain...she was the Goddess of Nature. Who was I to argue?

Fuck, but I would rather not do this. Felicity was a curse, I knew. I could admit Lillyanna was a beautiful woman. At twenty-two Grand Passages, she was petite with fair skin as smooth as river stone, large, wideset emerald eyes and fiery red hair that cascaded down her back in soft curls. And perhaps that was precisely why she chose me for the task. Perhaps it was a test of my strength.

And my will.

I rubbed my eyes. Keeping her safe—and with me—was going to be harder than I had bargained. She was tenacious, I had to give her that, with how many times she's tried to flee. I couldn't rightly say I blamed her for it, either.

I watched the sun rise, yellow, purple, and orange streaking the sky. I tossed dirt on the campfire's dying embers, strapped my weapon to my back and made my way to Xander, and checked his straps. A movement out of the corner of my eye caught my attention, and I saw Abraham not far from Lil who crawled out of her bedroll. She sat up, stretching her arms above her head, working the kinks out of her body. Her eyes were heavy with sleep, her hair a mass of tangles. I smiled as she walked over to me, and handed over her blanket, which I secured on Xander.

"Good morning, Lillyanna." I reached out and plucked a twig out of her hair, and she self-consciously ran a hand over her head. "Let's go." I stepped back and gestured to Xander.

"I think I'll walk," she said.

"Lil—"

"I will not ride with a Suppressor."

For the love of... "I told you. I'm not one of them anymore. Please. Just... just get on Xander. We can't afford to take any more time, and your walking will slow us down."

"Then I'll jog."

"Why are you being difficult?"

She raised an eyebrow. "Am I? Abraham asked me to walk last night."

"Abraham is an ass. Now, get on the horse."

Her lip quirked up, and she swung up onto Xander's back. As I mounted behind her, I let my shoulders loosen a bit and dug my heels into Xander's sides to catch up with Abraham. I slipped my arm around her waist and held her close. She smelled of the earth. Her body was warm against mine, and I couldn't say I disliked the feel of her pressed up against me. We rode in silence as the sunrise painted the sky in a brilliant display.

"I know what I told you last night was a shock. I have done plenty of things I'm not proud of. Hurt countless innocent people to save my skin. I am not a good man by any stretch of the imagination. I am sure that's why Abraham sought me," I said. "I wanted to spare you the pain. Vel did what he did because he loved you." I felt the need to explain—to apologize—for not being upfront with her the first night.

"And you?"

"To save myself. I only do what is beneficial to me."

"And how do I benefit you?"

"You don't. I have been thrown into something I don't understand. What I told you last night was the truth. I'm sorry. You have my word I will be forthcoming with you no matter what." I gave her hand a gentle squeeze, hoping she felt the truth behind my words.

"Why did you join?" She turned her head and looked up at me.

I sighed. "I had no choice. My brother Arden sent them on my fourteenth Name Day. It was a gift, he said. I never wanted to be a part of that."

Six men had come on my Name Day, six with Arden at their heels. They dragged me from our family home, bound me to a horse, and brought me to the Suppressors' Compound. The smell of blood and urine still haunted me on my bad days. I remember the crack of the whips, the hot metal against my skin. Sweat. Blood. It wasn't much of a choice.

"How long were you one?"

"Five Grand Passages the first time."

"What do you mean the first time?"

"Like I said, being a Feeler, I never wore the bracelet. My brother, though, would block me so he could torture me, just like when I was a child. Even then, he would come to my quarters at night and use his magic. He had this game he liked to play. He would release the block and tell me to kill him, and then he'd always put it back before I had a chance to call the flame. Once he forgot and I escaped." I shifted in the saddle. "I was out for fifteen Grand Passages before he caught up with me."

"Why didn't your brother have to wear the bracelet?"

"He is the Master Torturer. He needs his magic to cause pain."

"Why didn't you try to escape before if you didn't have to wear the bracelet?"

"Because he blocked my magic. The only time I had access was when I headed the parties to find Wielders. I'm useless without it." I shrugged. And it was true. My magic was a part of me. Whenever I was cut from it, I felt hollow. It was much like living with a missing limb, one might adapt, but I did not feel whole during those days. It wore on me.

"And the second time? How long were you one when you betrayed your kind?" Her voice was terse.

"Ten more Grand Passages before I defected and disappeared," I said.

"But they still found you."

No. They found you. "I'm not proud of what I did, but it kept me alive and that's all that mattered."

"And how can I be certain you're not taking me to them?"

I sighed, weariness consuming me. "You can't, though I would hope my actions two nights prior have convinced you I am on your side."

"That remains to be seen." She sniffed.

"I am not the enemy. You needn't fear me. I need you to trust me, Lillyanna. At least give me that," I whispered.

"Prove yourself worthy. Show me you can be trusted, and perhaps I will."

I closed my eyes and released the breath I held.

Her answer wasn't an outright no.

For now, I would take it as a victory, however small.

TWELVE

W E RODE DAY AND night, only stopping to rest the horses and refill our water skins. The following morning, as beams of light announced a new day, for the first time I second-guessed my decision to come to L'Ochal.

I heeled Xander into a gallop and raced toward the large house that came into view.

"What is this place?" Lil said, as she looked around.

"Home sweet home," I muttered. My chest constricted as my eyes swept over the property. The once emerald splendor of grass was now brown in patches and choked with weeds. Flower beds, once blooming in vibrant colors, were empty. Pine Crest Manor looked shabby with the chipped paint and crumbling stone. Weed-choked walkways and undergrowth grew through a rotten and collapsed deck. My heart hurt to see my home in such a depressing state. Though I no longer lived here, I should have had someone taking care of it.

Keeping alive the memory of the brief time when I was happy.

Shaking the thoughts, I pulled Xander to a halt. Swinging down, I marched up the crumbling steps, Lil and Abraham followed. I reached up to the shelf above the door and fished for the key I hoped was still there. My fingers brushed by it and I used it to unlock the door, hesitating before throwing it open and striding through.

The place smelled of must, and hardly any light breached the windows. Sheets covered the furniture, giving the impression of black, shapeless creatures ready to waken. Waiting to claim whoever dared disturb their peace.

I strode across the room, pushing open heavy curtains. The bright daylight made me blink. I opened the double doors leading outside. Dust sparkled and swirled in the sun, an ethereal display, and I briefly wondered if they were specters of my past. I moved about the room, opening drapes and windows, pulling the coverings off furniture, the dust burning my eyes and making them water.

Or perhaps that's what I wanted to believe.

Being here again weighed heavily on me. Nothing had changed since I left. No one had crossed the threshold since that night. My eyes swung to the grandfather clock, pendulum still, hands frozen in place.

Two forty-five in the morning. A moment that forever changed my life. I could not recall what stopped the clock at the exact same time.

When I finished tidying up, I showed Lil to her room. I was unable to say why, with all the other bedrooms, I gave her Zenith's. Perhaps it was an unconscious form of self-punishment. A reminder of what could happen if I allowed myself to care. I opened the door and stepped inside, my eyes flicking to the spot where the fateful event played out.

Where I sold my soul to Abraham.

I could almost smell the musky scent of perfume. Her presence was everywhere, and I wondered if her spirit roamed the halls seeking revenge. Memories assaulted me as I tidied the room.

There, by the wardrobe, I saw myself behind her, ready to button up her dress. I slid my hands around front, cupping her breasts, my thumbs caressing her nipples as I pressed my lips to her neck. She turned and pushed me away in what I had thought a playful manner.

I knew better now.

My eyes swung to the bed I was rarely allowed in.

To the place she revealed her deceit.

I sighed as I slipped out of the room, leaving Lil to rest, pretending I didn't see her questioning eyes.

I made my way down the hall, boots silent on the carpet that ran down the center, to my room at the end. After readying my room, I drew myself a bath, heated the water with my magic and lowered myself into the tub, the warmth enveloping me and easing my tension. I closed my eyes and leaned back, sinking deep into the depths, my thoughts going to Lillyanna.

Lil. I rubbed my eyes. She had stoked a fire in me, I had thought long dead. No. Perhaps it was this place. Returning here made the past come alive. The old wounds opened, and I thought to seek solace in the one flesh and blood available to me. Lil. No. She had nothing to do with my desire.

Pushing the thoughts out of my mind, I quickly bathed, pulled on clean clothes and prepared a bath for Lil. When I finished, I ventured downstairs. Abraham lounged casually on the couch, and I sank into a musty old chair.

"I find it curious you would give her Zenith's room," he said, lowering his book onto his lap.

I should have known he would have something to say. He always did.

"Would you rather I put her in my bed?"

"I fear you will."

"I am her Keeper and nothing more."

"I'm not a fool, Damiyun."

"Nor am I."

"When it comes to a pretty face, you lose your senses. I have felt your feelings through the bond."

I said nothing as I rose from my chair, glancing at Abraham, who returned to his book. It was a light-hearted tale that didn't suit the man.

"*The Prince's Promise*?" I laughed, reading the title. It was a story about a young prince who vowed to slay the dragon who kept his beloved as a pet.

"Your bookshelves lack adequate reading material," he said, burying his head back in the book.

Shaking my head with a chuckle, I crossed the room to the doors and stepped outside into the warm sun. I made my way up a slight hill to a mossy knoll, where I surveyed the disheveled estate below, vowing to rehire my servants and return it to its original splendor. My eyes lit on Lil, as she stepped through the doors. She looked around briefly before seeing me and making her way up to me. Her hair was damp, and I caught the faint scent of lilac wafting off her on the breeze.

"Zenith's wardrobe is full of dresses if you need a change of clothes," I said. "I'm sure they'll fit."

"I prefer trousers, thanks."

"I'll send Abraham out to buy you new clothes."

She gazed down at the land below and then looked at the fields and forests behind.

"The Suppressors paid you well."

"Lil—"

"I'm sorry. I didn't mean it," she said, glancing off.

"Yes, you did." With a choked chuckle, I squared my shoulders. "They paid me handsomely. I'm not proud of what I did. I—"

"Did what you had to, to survive," she finished.

We stood in silence, our eyes on the manor. The afternoon warmed our backs, a soft breeze bringing the scents of flowers and damp earth, a promise of an early spring. The silence stretched, but it wasn't uncomfortable.

"What do you do for coin now?" Her voice startled me.

Not expecting the question, I answered truthfully. "My father was quite wealthy. He was in the business of trading and made a good deal of coin. When he... passed, I took it over. I have since put someone else in charge and pay them a small fee, while I collect the rest."

She raised an eyebrow, glancing at the disheveled state of things.

I waved my hand, dismissing the conversation. "Let's get to it, then. I am going to teach you hand-to-hand combat. I suppose you've never been in a fight?"

She shook her head. "I did my best to lie low and obey the law. I preferred to avoid spending the night in a cell. I've heard the Enforcers don't provide very luxurious accommodations. Still, I'm sure I could hold my own," she said with a sniff, tossing her hair.

We'll see about that. "Come at me."

"What?"

"Come at me," I repeated.

Her face screwed up in confusion. "I don't—"

I pushed her, and she stumbled backward. Glaring at me, she tried to shove me back. I grabbed her wrists and swept her legs out from beneath her. She thumped onto the grass, flat on her back.

"Why aren't you teaching me how to use my magic?"

"What would you do if someone blocked you like Abraham did?" I crossed my arms and looked down at her. "We can't always rely on our magic. The more a Wielder uses, the weaker they become. Now get up."

She glared at me as she rose, wiping dirt and grass off her already soiled clothes.

"Is it possible to deplete your magic?"

"There are those who burn out, yes."

"How does that happen?"

"If a Wielder uses a great amount of magic at once, they can burn out. Even die."

"Do all Wielders burn out?" Her eyes widened. Clearly there were things she hadn't considered about having too much power.

"Not typically. As we age, the power wanes. It's still there, just not as strong."

"What happens to the person if they burn out? If they don't die?"

I shrugged. "They're a Non. Many have taken their lives when that happens. Magic is a part of us. It's who we are and without it..." I shook my head, knowing full well what it was like to have that part of yourself ripped away. "Enough stalling. Let's continue."

Time and time again I commanded her to swing at me, and every time I easily defeated her with light blows or by knocking her to the ground. I instructed her on different approaches and ways to hurt me, but always she hesitated at the worst possible moment.

As the sun rose higher in the sky, the day grew warm, and I removed my shirt, the light breeze cooling my sweaty skin. Lil had pulled her hair back in a messy knot, sweaty strands sticking to her neck. Her soaked shirt clung to her. The thin fabric showed the outline of her body, which was quite distracting.

She was messy, dirty, and undeniably beautiful. The gods be damned, but I wanted her. Shaking myself of that dangerous thought, I continued.

"You hesitated again," I said when, once again, she ended up with a mouth full of dirt.

As she spat dirt out, she shot me a death glare. I couldn't help but laugh. "I'm glad you find this amusing," she said.

"Get up."

She rose to her feet, green eyes on me, and swung a right hook. My head snapped to the right when her fist painfully connected with my cheek.

"Nice one, Lil," I praised, rubbing my face.

She smiled, confidence bolstered, and lunged at me again. I caught her wrist mid-strike. Spinning her around, I twisted her arm behind her. My left hand encircled her neck, and my right leg captured hers in a lock. She struggled in my grasp, and I laughed. I released her for a moment, and she gasped for breath.

I wasn't about to let her off that easily, though. I swept her legs out from beneath her, and she landed hard on her back, wheezing as the wind rushed from her lungs. I pounced on her, grabbing her wrists, and pinning them above her head.

"Never assume you've won until you're sure," I said. Her eyes traveled down my naked torso. She licked her lips, and I stifled a groan. For a moment, she struggled beneath me, trying to buck me off with her hips, and I couldn't say I disliked the feeling. My mind began to conjure images of the dozens of things I could do to her at that moment.

"Get off me," she hissed.

I released her, knowing if I remained longer, I was likely to do something I wouldn't regret. Slowly standing, I reached my hand down to her.

"Can't we take a break? I'm hot and tired," she said, sitting up and resting back on her hands.

I couldn't have agreed more. Her clinging shirt and the feel of her beneath me made my mind and body go in a very dangerous direction. I stretched out beside her on the grass, resting my head on my arms. I closed my eyes, calming my breath and trying not to think about the woman sitting painfully close to me. I just reveled in the sun's warmth upon my face. The silence stretched, the only sounds those of the soft rustle of leaves on the gentle breeze and the chittering of birds.

"What's that on your chest?"

I jumped at the sound of her voice, which pulled me from my doze. I sat up, propping my arm on my leg, and looked down at the ugly brand: a large "S" on the left side of my chest.

"Every Suppressor is branded. It's a reminder of who we are and who we serve." And a reminder that one could never truly leave the Order. It was a life sentence. Though they had once allowed me to leave—and later I defected—I still belonged to them. I had no intentions of going back.

"Who do the Suppressors serve?"

I glanced at her. It was a perceptive question. "Well, the Suppressors and Enforcers report to the Task Masters. They compile the list of the daily duties, where to patrol, where Feelers have found Wielders. The Task Master reports to the Regulator. My brother Arden currently holds the position. He also operates as Master Torturer thanks to his particular... abilities. The Regulator, who takes direction from the Elder, oversees operations and hands down orders. He is also an adviser and confidant to the Elder. And because of that, the Regulator is always next in line to be an Elder."

"When does that happen?"

"Whenever the Elder chooses. I... I was next in line to be an Elder before I left."

"Would you have accepted the position?"

"There's really no choice in the matter. There's never a choice when you're a Suppressor." I glanced at Lil whose eyes drilled into me, face intent.

"The marks on your back. Are those from the Suppressors? Did you get the tattoo to cover them up?" Her fingers traced the tattoo of the serpent entwined around the broadsword that covered my back. I shivered at her light touch.

"No. The sword is for strength and protection, and the serpent is a symbol of transformation. As for the marks?" I looked away. In truth, I did get the tattoo to cover up the marks, but not the ones from the Suppressors. No, those marks—like the brand—would never leave me. As much as I tried to cover them up, I would never forget the marks inflicted by my father.

I took a deep breath. This wasn't a story I wanted to tell, but I had promised her honesty, and so I told it, anyway. "Some are from the Suppressors, yes, though my father inflicted the majority. He was a Non. And he despised me."

"Why? You were his son."

"He thought I was evil. A spawn of Themesis—and I can't completely say he was mistaken. Why else was I cursed with the ability to call and control fire? To see clearly in the darkness? He whipped me... almost daily. Tried to... beat the evil out of me. He let me know he hated me. That I was an abomination and should have never been born." The mantra stayed with me.

"How horrible, Damiyun," she said. "I'm so sorry."

I took a deep breath and continued. If I didn't let it rush out of me, I would probably never talk about it again. "When I was a child, I took the beatings in silence. As I grew up, they became more and more brutal, and my hatred for him festered and swelled in kind. One eve, he came into my room wielding the whip. 'Get up, boy,' he commanded. I slipped out of my bed, removed my shirt, and turned around. I heard the whip fly, but I had enough. That night, I was going to get my pound of flesh." I paused for a moment. "I ducked before it hit, then spun around to face him. He jerked back. Tried to raise the whip again, but I grabbed it, wrapped the leather around my hand, and forcefully yanked it from his grasp. I told him he would never hurt me again."

"What did he do?"

"He all but soiled himself. He apologized. Begged me to not hurt him. He had the nerve to call me son. Not boy. Not spawn or evil bastard. *Son*." I laughed bitterly at the memory. Taking a deep breath, I continued. "I'd had enough of his cruelty and... I..." I ran my hand through my hair and licked my lips. Turning my head, I locked eyes with Lil. I needed to see her reaction. "After telling him to send Themesis my regards, I... used my magic and burned him to death. His screams were like sweet music. The smell of his burning flesh was so beautiful, so final," I whispered.

Lil's eyes widened in shock and her legs shook as she rose to her feet and stumbled back a step.

"Y-You killed your father?"

"He beat me, Lillyanna. Almost every single day I was beaten."

"And killing him makes it right? You could have just left."

I clenched my fists. "I suppose the answer would seem simple to you. You, whose father never raised a hand in anger. You couldn't possibly understand. Just—to be frightened all the time. To know you could never hide because if you did... the punishment would only be worse," I said, my words tight and clipped.

She glared at me. "You know nothing about me."

"I know your father loved you."

"Right. He loved me so much, he recruited for the Suppressors and left me all alone. You didn't have to stay," she said. "You're a murderer."

I rose slowly to my feet. "Of course I am, Lillyanna. I told you I wasn't a good man. What do you think the work I did for the Suppressors was? Rocking infants to sleep? I am a murderer—but the only person I have killed who deserved it was that abhorrent excuse of a father."

I realized I was shouting and stopped, taking ragged breaths. I had hoped she would understand. That she would have sympathized with the helpless child abused by a tyrant. Instead, she looked at me with fear and disgust.

"Lillyanna—" I reached out to apologize to her, dropping my hand when she recoiled.

She backed away, then hurried back to the house.

I rubbed my eyes, thudding back down on the ground. A dull ache formed behind them, and weariness washed over me. I should never have told her my story. I should have kept it locked away. I should have known she wouldn't understand. Damn it, but we were having an enjoyable afternoon. She was being civil. I could have lied.

I stared at the manor, debating going down to speak with her. To make her understand, I wasn't the monster here. Then Abraham stepped out the door and began wandering toward me.

"What was that about?" He stopped a few feet in front of me.

"I told her about my father and what I did. She's... quite unsettled." Enraged may have been a more accurate description.

And now she fears me and more than likely hates me.

"Perhaps this is a blessing from the gods," Abraham said. "Maybe now you'll keep your hands—and your cock—to yourself."

I ignored the comment. "What news from town?"

"I bought food and provisions. While there, I noticed an increasing number of Suppressors. There's a hefty price on your head, Damiyun. If I wasn't in the position I am, I dare say I'd turn you in myself."

Had I not made the biggest mistake of my life, you wouldn't be in this position.

I laughed. "That much, eh?"

"This isn't funny."

I waved my hand. "There are always patrols in the villages. This isn't anything new."

"Yes, but not ones inquiring about a defector and his female companion."

"I'm not concerned."

"Perhaps you should be."

I locked eyes with Abraham. "I won't let her get caught. I would die before that happened."

Abraham grunted. "We both know I won't let that happen. Not yet anyway." He turned to leave, then stopped. "We need firewood." He gestured to the tool shed and continued back to the house.

Sighing, I grabbed my old ax from its hook on the wall and began chopping firewood.

THIRTEEN
LILLYANNA

DAMIYUN'S WORDS ROLLED OVER me like a boulder. I knew he said he wasn't a good man. That he'd done things he wasn't proud of, but... he killed his father. I wanted to be anywhere but near him. I ran to the house and smack into Abraham's broad chest as I entered.

"Finding out Rayne isn't the virtuous white knight who saved you from the Suppressors?" his deep voice rumbled as his big hands steadied me. "Listen and remember well, Lillyanna. Damiyun hurts everyone he gets close to. You are no exception. And you...You he will hurt far worse than anyone else." He stepped around me and strode out, crossing the yard to Damiyun.

I didn't understand what he meant. Not that it mattered. I planned to stay as far away from Damiyun as I could. I needed time to comprehend what he had said. Yes, I understood the horrible situation he was in, but why wouldn't he have tried to flee?

Why did he think killing his father was his only option? The fact he did and rejoiced in it—I shuddered thinking about how cold someone would have to be to kill family.

I locked myself in my room, then stepped through the double doors out onto the balcony. My view faced directly above where Abraham and Damiyun stood. Abraham turned, saying one last thing before making his way back to the house. Damiyun ran his hand through his long hair as he made his way to a small shed, coming out carrying an ax. He looked up, eyes briefly meeting mine, then walked over to a fallen tree. He swung the ax, the blade thudding as it hit the trunk. He wrenched it out and struck again. I watched him work, studying the muscles rippling beneath his skin as he chopped. My mind drifted to the combat training we did earlier. The feeling of his body on mine. His warm, powerful hands that held my wrists above my head. His heat radiating from his hard, muscular chest. At that moment, he could have done whatever he wanted to me, and I wouldn't have said no.

I have had relationships, but nothing so solid. Nothing I cared to keep. I flushed thinking of Damiyun's touch, his heat. I had been on my own for ten Grand Passages, abandoned by both my parents without anyone who cared. Thoughts of Damiyun had me feeling like love and stability were possible. He'd married before. He was clearly capable of commitment. My body warmed at the thought.

I rubbed my eyes, a sudden tiredness falling over me, and made my way back into the room. Stripping out of my soiled clothes, I crawled into bed, slipping beneath the blankets, the silk sheets cool against my skin. My head sank into the down pillow, and I closed my eyes for a brief rest.

I WOKE SEVERAL HOURS later, the soft gray light telling me dusk had descended. Throwing the covers off, I slipped out of bed. The steady thud of the ax had stopped. Damiyun must have finished up for the day. My stomach growled, and I opened the doors to the wardrobe. Damiyun had said it held his wife's dresses, but I didn't think she would own so many. I ran my hand across them, feeling the soft silks, satins, and velvets. I had never felt anything so fine. And the colors—bright-green, blue, deep purple and yellow. She had every color and shade imaginable.

On the floor, lined up in a neat row, were dozens of delicate shoes. My stomach growled again, and I pulled out a cornflower blue dress. The sleeves drifted past my wrists, and small white flowers decorated the low bodice. I slipped the garment on, the soft satin caressing my skin, and tied the laces securing the bodice. Then, I perused the row of shoes, chose a silver pair, and slipped them on. The soft leather sheathed my feet, and it felt as though they were still bare. I turned to appraise my appearance in the mirror. My red hair tumbled about my shoulders in soft waves. The dress fit as though it were made for me.

Though I looked lovely, a pang of resentment fell over me at the thought of the luxuries this woman was afforded while I barely had enough money to buy food.

I slipped out of the room, shoes silent against the carpet, and descended the stairs. As I walked toward the kitchen, the aroma of meat and vegetables hit me, and my mouth watered. I slipped through the door, stopping short at the sight of Abraham and Damiyun sitting at the informal wooden table used for prepping food. My slipper scuffed on the tile, and they looked my way. Both men appraised me, though Damiyun's eyes slowly swept over every inch of me. I squirmed under such scrutiny. Something soft flickered in his eyes, his lip twitched a moment, then the look was gone.

"Please, Lillyanna. Come and sit down," he said, rising and pulling out the chair next to him.

I grabbed a plate and piled it with meat, vegetables, and a hot, buttered hunk of bread. Picking up the carafe of wine and a glass, I made my way back to the door.

"Please, join us," Damiyun all but begged.

I hesitated. "I think I will take my meal in my room." After retracing my steps back to my room, I ate my meal in solitude.

Finished with my food, I refilled my drink, and walked outside, drawn by the repetitive thudding sound of Damiyun's ax hitting wood again. As before, muscles rippled beneath his skin, making the serpent entwined around the sword blade on his back appear to move. I padded back into the room and sat down in a chair, resting my head on the back.

You're being childish, a voice hissed in the back of my head. And while he wasn't someone I cared to listen to, Abraham's voice rang in my mind as well, repeating, his warning of how Damiyun hurt anyone close to him. How he would hurt me far worse than anyone else. I didn't know what those words meant, and I was sure I would receive no answers should I ask.

His words made me wonder if perhaps I should continue distancing myself. Perhaps I should keep our relationship neutral. End any friendship that might be forming and keep it more of a teacher and student. There was no denying he invoked feelings of desire whenever he was around, and I didn't dislike it...

I took a sip of my wine and sighed. Maybe coming here with him wasn't such a good idea after all.

For the next few days, Abraham took up the training. At first, I was relieved. With him teaching me, I wouldn't have to sort out how to behave around Damiyun. However, after a few moments with Abraham, I realized how much I would have preferred for Damiyun to be the one training me, no matter how awkward it was, but he had all but disappeared. Compared to Abraham, Damiyun's blows had been nothing more than a kiss.

"Is it necessary to hit me so hard?" I pulled myself up on all fours, gasping for breath from the blow he delivered to my midsection.

"Hard? I barely touched you. Get up."

"Can we take a break?" I pulled my aching body up.

"There are no breaks in fighting, Lillyanna. The longer you stay on your feet, the better the chance you have of winning. Now. Get into your stance."

Rolling my shoulders, I stood with my left foot forward, right foot back, and my fists below my chin. Abraham assumed a similar position. We slowly circled each other. I watched him, looking for tells of when he was going to strike. He lunged forward, left arm poised, and I ducked right, only to be hit with a right uppercut. It was a bit lighter than the previous blows, but not by much. Rubbing my chin, I glared at him. He stepped back with a chuckle and relaxed his position. I saw the perfect opportunity. Smiling to myself, I bent my head and ran straight at him, leading with my shoulder, intent on getting him in the gut and hopefully pushing him over onto his ass.

Strong hands grabbed me, flipped me in the air and tossed me onto the ground. The breath rushed out of my lungs, and I gasped, trying to get in air. I lay in the grass looking up at the sun. Abraham's big form came into view. He held out a hand and hauled me to my feet.

"I'm impressed," he said. "You seized an opportunity that was wide open."

"And still landed on my ass." I grumbled.

"It will take practice to become good. Even I was humbled when I was first learning to fight."

I raised an eyebrow. Abraham? Humbled? It was almost laughable.

"Where's Damiyun?"

"That's not your concern. Now continue."

Sighing, I took my stance again, facing off with him. Not waiting for him to throw the first blow, I feinted right, a move I knew he wouldn't go for, something I counted on. A smirk played on his lips as he went to attack my left. Blocking his blow, though just barely, I swung a wide right hook. Pain vibrated up my arm as my fist connected with his chin. It was like hitting a wall of stone, and he barely moved. He rubbed his chin, a look of surprise and appreciation flickered in his eyes.

"Well done, Lillyanna," he praised, and I beamed at the words.

Abraham worked me until the sun dipped below the horizon. I was sweaty, and exhausted, and every inch of my body screamed in agony. I dragged myself up to my room, pleasantly surprised to see a hot bath awaiting me. I stripped out of my dirty clothes and sank into the water, the warmth enveloping me and soothing my aching muscles. When I was through, I dried off and applied the poultice Abraham provided to lessen the bruising and sent up a silent prayer to the gods, Damiyun would return on the morrow.

THE HOUSE WAS QUIET the next morning, the lack of heavy footsteps on the floor told me I was alone, and I couldn't help but thank the gods Abraham was not there. There was no one to force me to endure another round of training. I flipped through the assorted clothes in the wardrobe, choosing a short-sleeved dress in a soft green satin and a pair of matching shoes, then made my way downstairs.

I slipped out of the doors into the warm morning sun, and my eyes swept about the yard. There wasn't much to do here, and I was itching to do something. Stepping out onto the grass, I wandered to the right, to the edge of the woods, curious about what lay on the other side. I stepped beneath the canopy of trees and picked my way through, careful to avoid snagging my dress and muddying my shoes. I walked in as straight a line as possible to make it easier to find my way back should I get in too deep.

The forest was peaceful. Only the sounds of birds chirping above, the soft rustle of leaves, and the clacking of branches in the light breeze, kept me company. I walked, breathing in the natural perfume of earth, leaves and pine, the scent calming.

I was about to turn back when I saw the other side of the woods come into view. Curious about what lay beyond, I continued walking, coming out into a large yard. A lake lay to my left, while to my right sat a decent-sized house. It appeared to be abandoned and in the same state of disrepair as the manor. I wandered down to the lake's edge and rested on the grass. Who had owned this place, and why had they abandoned it? The area was tranquil, the soft slap of the gentle wave hitting the shore soothed and the cool breeze off the lake refreshed.

I leaned back on my hands and let the serenity wash over me. For a moment, I could almost pretend I wasn't being hunted by Suppressors. That I wasn't sharing a house with two strange and dangerous men. I could almost pretend this estate belonged to me.

The snapping of a twig pulled me from my daydream, and I whipped my head around to see who—or what—had made the noise. Body tense and alert, I scanned the woods, panic rising as a figure stepped out of the shadows.

Damiyun.

I let out the breath I had been holding. Relief bloomed in me. He was no wild beast or Suppressor. Well...not anymore.

He crossed the yard and sat down beside me, placing a small burlap sack between us. The wind shifted, and I caught the pungent scent of spices mixed in with his earthy, manly scent. My skin tingled at the smell of him, warmth spreading through me, and I cursed myself and shifted my position.

"I'm sorry, Lillyanna," he said. "I never intended to tell you that story."

I hugged my knees to my chest and rested my chin on them. "So why did you?"

I risked a sidelong glance at him. His hair was pulled back, and I studied his profile. His sharp features. High cheekbones, firm jawline and a sharp nose that had a slight bump on the bridge, the small imperfection somehow made him look even more perfect. Flushing, I turned my eyes back to the lake.

"Because you asked me about the marks on my back, and I promised to be honest with you." He paused. "I'm not sorry for what I did."

I could feel the heat of his eyes on me, and I turned to meet them.

"I was a child, Lillyanna. My father used a whip on me, a child, for no reason other than I was a Wielder. For ten Grand Passages, until the age of fourteen, I endured his punishment. I took the beatings he gave me. My father... My father deserved what he got."

"And you have the right to deal out justice based on how you feel about a person?"

He looked down at the grass. "I didn't leave because I was a child. Where would I have gone? And eventually, I believed him and his hateful words. I believed I was evil, and I deserved the punishment. And then one day I met someone." A ghost of a smile formed on his lips. "She helped me realize I wasn't evil. That I didn't deserve the whippings. She helped me to see what I have is a gift. Wielders are special. Once I came to realize—to believe that truth—I knew my father no longer had any power over me. He no longer owned or controlled me. That was when I truly freed myself of him. I'm sorry, Lillyanna." He raised his eyes and I couldn't see anything other but pain within them.

"Where was your mother?"

"It was a hard birth. They couldn't stop the bleeding. She died days after I was born."

"I'm sorry."

"It's alright, Lil," he said, a small smile touching his lips. "I came bearing a gift of peace, just in case." He picked up the sack. Reaching inside, he pulled something out and handed it to me. I looked down at the item I held.

A dried fig. A treat I hadn't had since I was on my own. I popped the fruit in my mouth, my mind going back to the time when I would find food and coin on my doorstep, and always—no matter what—my anonymous benefactor left me with dried figs.

I stopped chewing. The coincidence was too much.

A peace offering of dried figs. My heart raced, and I couldn't stop my jaw from dropping.

"You. It was you," I breathed, raising my eyes to look at him. "You left me food and—and coin, even."

Perhaps it was because the day was warm, or it was from cutting wood in the sun, I didn't know, but I saw a touch of pink on his cheeks.

"Of course, I did. I couldn't stand by and watch you starve."

"But I struggled."

"I kept the Suppressors away. I did what I could."

"You could have done more."

He looked at me. "You're right. I could have."

I popped another fig in my mouth and slowly chewed the sweet fruit. "Why didn't you tell me when you asked me how I survived? Why didn't you reveal yourself to me then? Why be so secret about it?"

He shrugged. "I don't know why I didn't admit it," he said, glancing at me. "As to why I didn't reveal myself? What would you have done if I showed up on your doorstep and told you I was there to take care of you? Your father had sent me to care for you." He shook his head. "You would have been stupid to let me in, and even more so if you went with me." He ran a hand through his hair. "I was trying to figure out how to talk to you. There were many times I saw you at the market. Many times, I was going to reveal myself then, but..." He sighed. "It was hard, Lil. I didn't know—still don't know—why I was asked to find you. Why I was given this task."

"But how come I never saw you before this? We live in the same village. Surely, we would have come across each other at some point."

"I used my magic to hide myself, like I did with you in the alley."

I said nothing, letting my mind digest his words as I ate my figs.

"Take one." I offered him the bag, feeling bad I was eating them all.

He shook his head and smiled. "Those are for you."

I reached in, fished one out, and held it out to him. He leaned forward, taking the fig in his mouth. He pulled back slowly, his tongue flicking over the tips of my fingers, cleaning the stickiness off. My breath caught in my throat. His lips were soft, mouth and tongue warm, and I wondered what they would feel like on other parts of my body.

"Delicious," he said, sitting back, his eyes on me. I looked away, my face heating from his intense gaze and my thoughts.

"Where have you been?" I hoped a distraction would calm me.

"I had an errand to do for Abraham," he said, his eyes on the lake, jaw hard.

"Well, I'm glad you're back. He's not exactly gentle."

He turned to look at me, concern marking his face. "Did he hurt you?" He pushed a lock of hair behind my ear, fingers brushing my cheek. I winced. "Fucking bastard."

I pulled away from the warmth of his touch and his penetrating gaze. "Whose house is that?" I nodded in the building's direction.

"Mine."

"What do you need two homes for?"

He laughed, eyes drifting to the structure. "It housed my servants. While I could have given them their own wing, I didn't want them feeling as though they needed to cater to me all the time, though Zenith gave her maids the room adjacent to hers. She had no issue rousing them at all hours for petty things," he said, his tone bitter. "I built the building for them to live. To give them privacy and not feel like I was lording over them."

"Where is Zenith now?" Despite how often he referenced his wife, I had no idea who she was, where she went, and whether she'd come back. A pit formed in my stomach at the thought she might.

"She died."

"I'm sorry," I said in complete shock.

"Let's go back to the manor." He leaped to his feet. He held a hand down and pulled me up. We stood so close I could feel the warm caress of his breath on my face. I took a step back from him. His eyes swept over me from head to toe and back.

"You look lovely, Lil. Zenith never looked so lovely in those clothes." I warmed at his words. We picked our way through the woods back to the manor. The chirps of squirrels and the sound of birds twittering broke the silence that stretched between us.

"Damiyun, I—"

"Quiet," he hissed, pulling me back to the edge of the woods.

"What's wrong?" I frowned.

"Hush." He said, grasping my hand.

"Someone's here," he said, pulling me closer.

"Abraham?"

"No," his voice was low, breath a warm caress on my face. "Shit." He cursed.

I turned back to the house, panic filling me as half a dozen Suppressors spilled out the door.

FOURTEEN
DAMIYUN

I GRIPPED LIL'S HAND and pulled her closer, letting my magic flow to hide us.

"Fan out and search the property." One man gestured with his sword, and the other five scattered. Two strode up the incline, painfully close to where we stood. Lil stiffened against me, and I squeezed her hand in reassurance.

"That bastard thinks he can hide from us," one man said. "We found him."

"We found where he might be. He's not here now."

"He'll be back. His horse is missing. He probably just went to town," the first man said as they made their way past us again.

"Then why didn't we see him?"

"Curse the Fallen One if I know."

They strode down the hill and reconvened outside the manor.

"The place is empty. He's not here."

"He'll come back."

"Should we stay?"

"No. We go back to town and send word to Regulator Rayne and await orders," the one in charge said.

"But if he comes back, we can catch him."

"We go back to town. That's an order, now move."

Coldness washed over me at the sound of my brother's name. I hadn't seen him in three Grand Passages. And for all that time, I had hoped it would stay that way.

I watched as they dispersed, listening until the sound of horse hooves faded. When I was sure they were truly gone, I released my magic. No doubt they were hoping to surprise me.

"They're gone. It's ok, Lil."

"What do we do when they come back?" she whispered, her wide, green eyes searching mine.

"It will take a while before word gets to my brother, and I plan to be gone by then." I pushed a lock of hair out of her eyes and cupped her chin. "I won't let them take you."

I looked down at her. Her frightened eyes locked on mine. The warmth of her hand as I held it. The close call with the Suppressors heightened my senses, and her scent—sweat and woman—drifted on the breeze, arousing me.

I softly caressed her bottom lip. Her eyes closed, lips parted, and I bent my head and brushed my lips against hers. She gasped, eyes snapping open to search my face, and I pulled away. She wrapped her arms around my neck, our lips coming together again, tongues dancing. Her fingers entwined in my hair, and I gripped her as the kiss deepened. I slid my hands beneath her shirt, her skin soft and warm. My hands slid to cup her breasts, my thumbs caressing her nipples. She sighed and arched against me. My desire mounted.

I wanted her.

I wanted to feel her skin beneath me. I wanted to touch and taste every inch of her.

I pulled away for a moment and saw the smoldering desire reflected in the green pools of her eyes. She pulled me close again, mouth, and tongues meeting once more. Fingers danced lightly on the waistband of my trousers. I groaned as they softly brushed skin, her touch sending jolts of desire through my body. Her hands grasped my belt, fingers fumbling as she tried desperately to get it undone.

"Interesting form of combat training. What do you call that move?" Abraham growled from behind.

I tore my mouth from Lil's and checked my belt, then calmly turned around. Abraham scowled at Lillyanna, who glared back defiantly.

"I see you decided to cash in on the bounty on us," she said, crossing her arms. "How much was I worth? It must be a lot since six of them came here."

Abraham laughed. "That question is more suitable for Damiyun. He knows how much whores are worth." He turned his eyes to me. "After all, you sampled her wares. How was she, Damiyun?"

I clenched my fists and glared at him. "Fuck off, Abraham."

"What did you say?"

I ignored him and turned my attention to Lil. "Let's go."

"You're just going to be another notch on his bedpost, Lillyanna. You're just another body to warm his bed until he tires of you, which won't take too long."

Fiery anger surged within me. "Fuck off, Abraham."

"Does the truth hurt?"

I took a step toward him. "You know nothing about any of this."

"I know enough. Shall I tell her how you'll hurt her? Besides using her like a whore?"

I swung at him, fist connecting with his chin. He rolled with the blow and rubbed his face, glaring at me.

"Watch yourself. Remember who owns you." His voice was low and dangerous.

"I wish I could forget." I reached for my magic. The air rushed out of me as I did so, pain radiating through my body.

"You son of a bitch."

He took another step, eyes furious, and lifted his hand. My body went rigid. Pain exploded in my chest. It felt as though someone had reached inside and pulled out my lungs. I couldn't move.

I could barely breathe.

My knees buckled, and searing pain tore through my body. I fell to the ground. The throbbing intensified, and I screamed. My body convulsed. I had no control over myself.

"What are you doing? Stop it." a voice cried from far away.

Lil. Shit, the voice belonged to Lil. I tried turning my head to look at her, to beg her to leave, but I couldn't.

I could only scream.

"He didn't tell you?" Abraham's voice cut through the pain.

My screams.

"Tell me what?"

Abraham laughed. The pain intensified, and I howled like a dying man.

"Stop it. You're killing him."

"Not yet, I'm not. Who owns you, Damiyun?"

I wouldn't answer. I refused to humiliate myself further, though I wasn't sure I could even speak as I writhed in unbearable agony.

"Who owns you, Damiyun?"

No. I wouldn't answer.

A feeling like a metal whip slammed across my back, spine and ribs breaking beneath. A memory of my father whipping me flashed in my mind. The torture was unbearable. I knew all of this was only in my mind but the pain... The pain was real.

I couldn't take it anymore.

"You do," I gasped.

"I didn't hear you."

"You do," I spat between clenched teeth.

My chest constricted and I couldn't breathe. I could feel my Life Force leaving my body.

"Who owns you?" He stood above me, stance wide. Cold, black eyes stared down at me.

"You do."

Pain shot through my head, and an explosion of lights and stars flashed behind my eyes. I clenched my head, screaming as an invisible force closed in and crushed my skull.

"Who. Owns. You. Damiyun?"

"Abraham. Abraham owns me," I sobbed, forehead pressed to the ground, fists clenched.

"Never forget that."

He released me; the pain slowly retreated. Sickness rose inside and I retched. Clutching the grass, I sobbed as I vomited.

"Damiyun," Lil cried, placing a hand on my back. I winced at the pain that shot through me.

"Don't touch me. Leave me, Lil." My shaking voice was barely above a whisper. I heard the rustle of her clothing as she stood, but she didn't leave.

"Please, Lil. Leave me." I let myself breathe when I heard her retreating footsteps. I let her see me in this broken and vulnerable state. See me lying in my vomit, sobbing.

Damn Abraham. Damn me for selling my soul to him. For binding myself to him forever.

Not for the first time, I wished for the chance to go back and undo the horror I had inflicted on myself.

I lay on the ground until the sun dipped below the horizon and cold seeped through my clothes. In the distance, I heard what sounded like a child being torn limb from limb. Wraiths. To my left, I heard a deep growl. Turning my head, I saw a pair of red eyes peering out at me from the forest. My blood ran cold, and I pulled my aching body up and hurried back to the house, ignoring the grunt and snarl that came from behind, ever so close. Seeing the manor come into view, I broke into a run, flying up the steps, slamming and locking the door. I peered out the windows, seeing four pairs of red eyes in the yard. An eerie howl pierced the night air. Not that of a wolf, something worse. Something evil. The sound, coupled with the screech of the wraiths, sent chills down my spine. Closing the curtains, I crossed the room to the couch and stretched out.

The manor was quiet and felt empty, but I knew Lil was in her room waiting for me.

Waiting for an explanation of what she had just witnessed. But I would rather not tell her.

Not yet.

Thoughts of Zenith invaded my mind, but I brushed them away. I sure knew how to pick them. I thought of Lil. She never behaved so entitled. Bratty and pushy but not entitled. The aches from the beating I had taken throbbed. I needed a bath, though a drink for now wouldn't hurt.

Prying my body off the couch, I poured myself a hefty glass of Serpent's Venom. Knocking it back, I poured another, and risked a look outside. There were no signs of the demon eyes. No shrieks and wails. Only the high-pitched screech of tree frogs and the haunting hoot of an owl. The stars glittering like diamonds against the blanket of black. Soft clouds floated in the sky, occasionally hiding the moon that glowed above.

I needed to forget the things I had done. The lessons on what happens when I love. I mess it up every damn time. Lil's face grew clearer in my mind, and I took another sip of the venom.

I finished my drink and crossed the room, stretching my weary and aching body out on the soft couch again, and locked the memory of my wife back up, never to be called forth again.

FIFTEEN

I WOKE THE NEXT morning as dawn broke, the sound and vibration of Abraham's boots against the floor pulling me from my always dreamless rest. I pulled my stiff and aching body up as he entered the room and took a chair.

"They will send more," he said. I didn't have to ask who they were.

"We will be gone before that happens."

Abraham's nostrils flared. "We will leave now."

Crossing my arms, I leveled my gaze at him. "She doesn't know how to control or use her magic."

"You can teach her while we travel."

I shook my head. "No."

"You know you are not safe here. They came here looking for her," he reminded again.

"They were looking for me," I said.

He exhaled sharply. "Because she is with you. They would not have come here otherwise. They want her, Damiyun, though why, I don't know."

I laughed. "Because she's a Wielder. In case you've forgotten, that's what the Suppressors do. They hunt Wielders."

Abraham glared at me. "There is more to it than that, Damiyun, and you know it."

I rolled my eyes and rose from the couch. "She is safe with me. We will stay here a week at the most."

"You are allowing yet another pretty face to dictate your actions. It appears she cares nothing about my warning."

My head snapped around, and I narrowed my eyes at him. "What warning would that be?"

"The truth. That you hurt anyone who gets close to you. You know you will hurt her in the worst way possible."

I clenched my fists. "How dare you—"

"It is for her own good. Leave her alone, Damiyun. Seek your pleasure from your whores." Abraham stood and glared down at me.

I kept my mouth shut, not wanting another painful lesson, then turned and left the room. After all these nights alone, I was full of pent-up anger and lust. Abraham's suggestion was just what I needed. Saddling Xander, I heeled him toward L'Ochal. As I drew near, I pulled the hood of my cloak up and peered about, noting the Enforcers and Suppressors milling about.

They looked casual, but I knew they were anything but. Hands never left hilts, eyes never stopped looking about. There were far too many of them in the village. The hair on the back of my neck pricked up in concern. For once, I was glad Abraham had blocked my magic. Perhaps he was right. Perhaps we should leave this place sooner than I anticipated, though I admit that I was loath to. Though the memories were thick, being back in L'Ochal, back to Pine Crest Manor, made me realize how much I missed my home. If I were to be truly honest, I didn't want to leave, but I knew we had to. I knew that despite my ability to keep Lil safe, she wasn't.

Slipping off Xander, I guided him to the stables behind the inn. Not many people had a horse with a coat as unique as his, and I definitely didn't want to get caught. Walking by the tavern, the door swung open for a moment, the sound of a bard singing, and laughter rose and then fell as the door closed. Though I was tempted to go in and drown myself in drink, I needed to know what the Suppressors were up to. Tucking my hair beneath my hood, I wandered casually through the busy streets. I trained my keen ears on the surrounding chatter, listening for any signs that the Suppressors were looking for Lillyanna and me.

I followed a crowd that moved toward the square. Finding a spot in the shadows and that offered me a view, I leaned against the wall of a building. Folding my arms, I watched the chaos unfold. Shouts rose above the noise of the Nons who cheered as Wielders were dragged to the square. Men, women, and children, Wielders who were unfortunate enough to be at the right place at the wrong time.

The crowd grew even louder and rowdier as Wielders were forced to their knees, hands bound behind their backs.

"Kill the evil bastards," someone yelled, fist punching in the air.

"Hang 'em!"

"Torture 'em!"

"Make them pay!"

The crowd was causing a ruckus. Townspeople made their way to where the defenseless, innocent people knelt. Some spat on them. Some kicked them. Others urinated on them. One man undid his trousers and forced his cock into the mouth of a young woman. Cheers erupted, and with it, unbridled mayhem. Women were violated, their screams, and those of their spouses, rose above the cheers.

I clenched my fists, my heart pounding in my ears at the sight before me. I pulled my hood lower to block my eyes. I wished I could block my ears. And I wished I had my magic, though unleashing it would kill the innocent Wielders, though death would be a mercy.

"Enough." Someone called out.

Silence fell across the crowd. The crude activity in the center stopped, the men adjusted their clothing and returned to the throng. Ice chilled my veins at the sound of the voice. Lifting my head, I watched a man saunter through the crowd that parted before him. Tall and muscular, his black hair was pulled back in a low ponytail. He had chiseled features, a strong jaw, high cheekbones, and a prominent nose. I would have thought him handsome if I didn't know who he was. If I didn't know what he was capable of. His fingers stroked his close-cut goatee, and ice-blue eyes looked about the crowd. More Wielders were dragged to the square.

"Excellent job, Suppressors," my brother, Arden, praised as he walked around the captured Wielders. He placed his finger under the chin of a young man and tipped his head up. "You thought you could hide from us?" Arden snarled. "We know where every one of you resides. We will hunt every last one of you."

The young man spat at him, which earned him a sharp backhand to his cheek.

Arden's eyes scanned the hushed crowd. "We are the Suppressors. Our job is to eradicate the world of evil, of filth. Of Wielders." He spat the word.

I clenched my jaw at his words. Lillyanna might have thought I betrayed my own kind, but I had no choice. Arden, on the other hand, joined the Order willingly. He reveled in going after Wielders. Reveled in causing them pain and more so in killing them. I didn't know what caused him to despise and betray his kind. Perhaps I was the one who made it happen. My birth killed our mother, and he never let me forget how much he hated me for it. Perhaps I had unknowingly caused him to hate himself.

Hate his own kind.

"You all will be given a choice."

Arden's voice pulled me back from my thoughts. He turned from the crowd to face the two dozen Wielders that had been rounded up. I looked at the men, who glared at him in stubborn defiance. The women who cowered and the children who wailed.

Shut up. I willed the wee ones whose cries of terror rose.

Arden stalked over to a crying child. Grabbing a fistful of hair, he pulled him up. The child's feet dangled in the air.

"Shut the fuck up," Arden growled.

The child whimpered.

Sunlight glinted off a dagger blade. My body coiled like a spring, ready to explode in a second. Arden held the dagger in front of the whimpering child. Piss ran down his legs, pooling on the ground.

"Stop your crying, or I will cut your tongue out. Do you want that?"

The child's cries came to an abrupt stop, as did that of the others. Arden dropped the boy to the ground and sheathed his weapon. I relaxed, but only slightly.

"I will give you all a choice," he said again as he paced back and forth, hands clasped behind him. "Join the Order or die."

"I would rather die than join," a man called out.

"Fuck you and your fucking Order," a woman yelled.

"I will never betray my kind," another called. Other voices joined in, and I sighed, wishing I could do something, but that would put Lillyanna in jeopardy.

"So be it," Arden said.

Screams made me wince, and my stomach turned as heads were removed from body. As people were eviscerated. At least he left the children alone. For now. The stench of blood and death filled the air. Onlookers retched, the smell of vomit almost made me retch too.

"Stop. Please, stop. We will join," a man cried as a Suppressor held his sword aloft, ready to strike. Arden held up his hand, and the Suppressor lowered his weapon.

"I knew you'd see it my way," he said, lips curling into a smile.

Those that remained were hauled to their feet and marched over to where a group of horses were tethered. The crowd began to disperse, and Arden strode over to where the Wielders were being tied to a long rope tethered to a horse.

Pushing off the wall, I began making my way through the crowd toward the tavern to gather Xander and go home. A massive shadow raced across the street. A screech that knocked my teeth and made my ears ring echoed off the walls. I looked up, shielding my eyes from the sun. A large, winged mass circled in the sky. The size of a small house, its wings were torn, bone and sinew protruded from leathery skin. Eyes of fire peered out of a rotting head. Smoke streamed from where its nose should have been, and a forked tongue flicked out, tasting the air.

It circled lower and lower, sending the townsfolk screaming and scattering. The beast landed on all fours in the square. Its barbed tail flicked, taking out a dozen fleeing citizens. It sniffed the air, letting a breath out in a puff of smoke.

"Wielders," it said in a low voice that made my chest vibrate.

It loped toward the group tethered to the horse, its long talons clicking on the cobblestone. The people yanked against the ties that bound, screaming and whimpering as the beast came closer.

And I was powerless to do anything but watch. My eyes flicked to the Suppressors who stood about, and I frowned. They didn't appear terrified. None reached for a weapon to strike the beast down. None did anything but stand there.

The beast's tongue flicked out, licking its ragged lips.

"Mine." It said.

"Yours," I heard Arden answer.

What the fuck?

The beast lunged, its large maw opening and within seconds, the people, the Wielders who were to be taken to the Compound, were gone.

What in the Abyss just happened? What did I witness?

The beast's huge head swung around, its fiery eyes locking on me.

"Wielder," it hissed.

Its gaze penetrated me. My heart stopped, and I about pissed myself. Heads turned, trying to see where the beast looked. Suppressors pulled their swords. The beast took a step. Sweat trickled down my back. It took a deep breath, sniffing the air. A snarl curled its lips.

"His," it hissed. Turning around, it took two giant steps then leaped into the air, flying away. With everyone occupied by watching the beast, I took the opportunity to dart down an alley. Standing against the wall, I took deep, cleansing breaths in an attempt to stop the shaking in my limbs.

I didn't know what I had just witnessed, but I knew it wasn't good. I needed to tell Abraham. I needed to figure out what was going on, and I had to do it fast.

The fate of the Wielders depended on it.

I made it back to the manor unseen. I couldn't get the vision of the beast out of my head. I needed a distraction. I needed something to help block it out. I entered the manor looking for Lil. The house had a quiet and empty feel to it. I stepped outside and though Lil wasn't there, I knew where she was. I picked my way through the forest and found her lying in the grass at the edge of the lake, eyes closed. I silently made my way to where she lay and stretched out beside her, propping myself up on an elbow, and gazed at her sleeping form. She looked beautiful lying there. The sunlight dappled her fair skin and set her red hair aflame. Face relaxed and peaceful. I brushed a curl from her brow, and she stirred, a soft sigh escaping. I felt my body relax as I looked at her. The tension, the fright from what I had witnessed, eased out of my body, almost becoming a memory of a bad dream.

I rubbed my face. She had gotten under my skin, and I let her. I let her make me feel.

After a while, she woke up, stretching her arms above her head. She jumped at seeing me lying beside her, and I laughed.

"Remind me to never share a room with you," I said. "I almost lost my hearing, you snore so loud."

"I don't snore." She sniffed.

"Hm. How would you know if you're sleeping?" I raised an eyebrow.

She swung at me, and I grabbed her wrist, flipped her on her back, and pinned her to the ground.

"It seems like we are always in this position," I mused.

"Get off me," she growled, bucking against my weight.

"I'd stop that if I were you, lest I do something I won't readily regret," I murmured, face inches from hers.

She stopped struggling and looked at me. "What was Abraham doing to you?"

Sighing, I let her go and sat down next to her as she sat up. "Teaching me a painful lesson."

A frown pulled her lips down. Gods, but it made her look alluring. "I don't understand."

Propping my arm on my knee, I looked out across the lake. "Abraham owns my soul."

"What? How?" She barely hid the shock in her voice.

"I made a horrible and irreversible mistake."

"Is there any way out of it? A loophole?" Lil's sad eyes looked at me.

"No. Once you sign your name... there's nothing you can do. Abraham owns me and when the contract is called... I'll belong to Themesis." I sighed and flashed a false smile. "I always knew where I would rest long before I sealed my fate. Like I said, Abraham came to me for a reason."

"I'm sorry, Damiyun."

I reached out and pushed a lock of hair from her eye. "As am I."

"I thought you were going to train her." For once, I was grateful for Abraham's interruption.

"Why don't you go change?" I said to Lillyanna, who wore a pale rose-colored dress. She looked ready to protest, but she must have seen the strain in my eyes, and so she acquiesced. She raised her chin imperiously as she passed by Abraham, and I smirked.

"I thought I told you to leave her be?" he said after Lil had slipped through the woods.

"We were only talking."

He slipped his hands in his pockets. "I know what you're feeling, Damiyun. You care for her."

"She's gotten under my skin."

"As they all do. You're letting your cock dictate your judgment. I fear your feelings will impede on your ability to complete your task."

I sighed, shoulders sagging at the weight of his words. "I can do it, Abraham."

"I am sure you can. The question is whether you will."

Ignoring his comment, I took a deep breath. "There were Suppressors in the town when I was there. They were rounding up Wielders."

"Why do you sound surprised? I told you there were."

"That's not all, Abraham." I said and told him about what I saw. "What does it mean?"

"I don't know, but I'm sure Themesis is behind it," Abraham said. "I'll see if I can find anything out about it, though it's not likely he'll tell me anything."

I nodded, my attention drawn to Lil who made her way toward us. She had changed into her training clothes. I felt the rush of flame pulse through my veins, and joy spread through me. I stumbled at the sudden onslaught of my magic returning. I looked at Abraham and saw Lil stumble backward with a gasp. He had given us our magic back.

"Teach her how to use her magic," Abraham said as he brushed past us and headed in the manor's direction.

I turned to Lil, who scowled at his retreating figure. "Why does Abraham hate me?"

I glanced at her. "I wouldn't say he hates you." Stopping next to a tree, I turned to her.

While I didn't think he hated her, I couldn't say with certainty he didn't. For him, she was too strong-willed, stubborn. Abraham couldn't control her, and it was something he despised.

"Don't concern yourself with Abraham," I said, waving my hand in dismissal. "First, you need to learn how to control your magic. What do you feel right now?"

"I can feel it pulsing. Thrumming and vibrating beneath my skin. I itch to let it loose. I feel like it wants to be let loose."

I knew what she felt. When I had discovered my magic, it pulsed within my veins. Being around fire made it worse. I could feel the heat racing through my body. It felt as though it was going to burst from my skin.

I nodded. "Close your eyes and relax your breathing. Focus on something that brings you peace."

"What is that going to do?"

"Right now, your body is fighting against it. If you relax, it will calm it. Magic... Magic is a part of us. It's like a being living inside our bodies. Pulsing through our veins like our blood. It's constantly battling to be let out. Relaxing yourself, it makes you more one with it."

"Do you battle with yours?"

I shook my head. "It settles down after practice, though when I am around fire... that's when it's difficult to control. It fights to be let loose, to join in with the flames. Now, close your eyes and relax."

I studied her as she stood still. A sad smile formed on her face, and I saw her relax, tension easing from her body, and I knew she had her magic somewhat under control.

I thought about what I could have her start with. I didn't want to do anything complicated, lest she hurt or exhaust herself completely. I looked around, walking toward a large oak.

"Put your hand on the tree and tell me what you feel."

She stepped forward and did as I instructed, her eyes widening in awe. "I can feel her. It's like she's breathing." She looked at me. "She feels me, too."

"It's your connection with nature. Now, I want you to change the color of the leaves," I said. "Focus your energy—your magic—into the tree. Visualize what you want to happen, then pulse your energy through and wrap it around the tree. When I call the flame, it feels like a warmth that wraps around me and flows through me." I smiled at the feel of my magic pulsing within and held my hand out, watching the dancing flame. "What are you feeling right now?"

"I—it's difficult to describe," she said, chewing her lip. "I can feel the tree. The energy within. The life." She looked at me, a smile curling her lips. "I can feel nature. The animals... gods, Damiyun. It feels wonderful. And... terrifying."

I laughed. "You'll get used to it. Now, change the color of the leaves. Pulse your magic through. Think of it as throwing out a line connecting the tree to you."

She closed her eyes, her brow wrinkling in concentration. "She doesn't like it," she said, opening her eyes. "I'm hurting her."

"Keep going."

"But—"

"Keep going. Change the leaves."

She took a deep breath and closed her eyes again. I looked up at the branches, smiling when the leaves turned from green to a vibrant orange.

"Excellent, Lil. Look at what you did."

She looked up, her smile fading as the leaves withered and fell, the tree turning a ghostly white.

"I killed her." She turned horrified and angry eyes on me. "I told you I was hurting her."

"Calm, Lil," I said. "It's only a tree."

"I felt her, Damiyun. She was a living thing."

"Let's try something else." My eyes fell on a sapling a few feet away. "Make it grow into a mature tree."

"No."

"Lil—"

"No, Damiyun. I don't want to do it."

"I don't know what happened, Lil. I don't know why the tree died, but I know it wasn't your fault."

"It was. My magic killed her."

I took her chin and tipped her head up. "You can't let a mistake affect you. Perhaps in turning the leaves, you were taking some of the tree's Life Force, I don't know, but you can't let it bother you. Your magic comes from nature. You can give life and take it away."

"I don't want to use my magic if taking a life is what it can do. I want Abraham to block me for eternity."

"No one wants to take a life," I said, ignoring her raised eyebrow and crossed arms. "Now. Make the tree grow."

"How do you know my magic works?"

I sighed. "It's all basically the same. It comes from deep inside you. It runs through your veins." I lightly traced the blue webs streaking up her arm. "It's a part of you, and you need to know how to control it. Yours came out in the market because you were scared, and with Abraham, it was because you were scared and angry. You can't rely on your emotions. You need to learn how to call upon it at will. As I said, mine came out when I was angry. I didn't have anyone to show me how to learn control. I had to teach myself."

Lillyanna chewed her lip. "But what if I can't control it?"

I crossed my arms. "That's why we're doing these exercises. Now. Make the tree grow."

She hesitated a moment, then pulled away and placed her hand on the tree. She closed her eyes, and her face screwed up in concentration. The tree shuddered, and I watched, awestruck, as it shot up into the sky. She opened her eyes, taking a step back, a proud smile crossing her face as she looked at what she did.

"I knew you could do it."

Her smile widened.

For the rest of the afternoon, we explored all facets of her magic. I only had her do small things to start—make and animate a small rock figure, turn a puddle into ice—nothing that would backfire were she to lose control.

Feeling her confidence and feeling she had a good grasp of how to handle her magic, I looked around for something else—something more—for her to do. I looked out over the calm waters of the lake.

"Make a waterspout."

She frowned. "What?"

I gestured to the lake. "Make a waterspout over the lake."

I followed her to the water's edge. She stood with hands on her hips, looking out. "I don't know if I can."

"You can," I assured her. "You've got a good grasp of how to use your magic. You're a quick study. With this, anyway."

She looked at me. "What if something goes wrong?"

"Then we get wet."

Her lips quirked into a smile, and she turned back toward the water. Taking a deep breath, she closed her eyes and held her hands out in front of her. Her face screwed up in concentration. The wind picked up a little, and leaves spun about like a tornado on the ground. The water in the lake rippled.

She dropped her hands and shook her head. "I can't."

"You can, Lil."

"Why are you so confident in my abilities?"

I pushed a lock of hair behind her ear. "Because I know what you can do. I feel the power within you, remember? You're strong, Lil, and you're going to need to learn how to do more than just change leaves and make a tree grow."

"But—"

"You can do it."

Sighing, she turned back to the lake and assumed her position. She steadied her breathing, inhaling, and exhaling slowly. The wind picked up again, and leaves rustled in the trees and scattered about the ground. Clouds moved quickly across the sky. Flickers of lightning lit up our surroundings, and the faint sound of rumbling thunder followed.

I frowned as I watched the darkness grow. The wind kicked up more, and the thunder and lightning grew closer. I glanced at Lil who stood with palms out in front of her. I thought I saw her veins light up at the next flash of lightning, but it was gone as soon as it happened, and I couldn't rightly be sure of what I had seen.

"Lil, maybe you should stop."

"I've got this, Damiyun."

My hair whipped in the wind and dirt stung my eyes. A light rain began to fall, clouding my vision as I looked out at the middle of the lake. Water churned and rose into the air, spinning in a tube, meeting the dark clouds above. Wind whipped Lillyanna's hair around her head. She opened her eyes, which had a slight glow to them, and looked out across the water, a small and terrifying smile crossing her lips.

"That's enough, Lil," I said, placing a hand on her arm.

She turned and looked at me, face blank as though she didn't recognize me, her eyes bright. I stepped back, coldness creeping through my veins at the sight of her.

"Release your magic."

A frown crossed her face, and she looked back out at the water. At the long, twisting waterspout moving across the lake. Lightning and thunder still flashed in the distance, and the light rain was becoming heavier.

"Lil..."

She glanced at me again, then released her magic. The spout splashed back down. The clouds rushed away, and the rain stopped. As did the thunder and lightning.

She was breathing hard as she dropped to the ground. When she looked up at me, I sighed with relief to see the recognition in her face.

"You did well, Lillyanna," I said carefully, dropping to the ground beside her.

It wasn't a lie. She did do well. It was the magic she started to use—magic she was calling—that concerned me.

"Are you alright?"

She yawned. "I feel like I could sleep for a week."

"Unfortunately, that is one price of using magic. It exhausts the Wielder. That's why I started with hand-to-hand fighting."

She lay down, placing her head in my lap, and I softly stroked her hair. "What's the other price?"

"Parts of magic pull from a dark place and draw you closer to evil. To the Fallen One." I lowered my voice. I was all too aware of this, having used my magic in unimaginably horrible ways. "I suspect that's why I am bound to Abraham."

Evil to the core.

A shadow fell over us and I looked up to see Abraham looming above.

"I see training is going well."

"Just taking a break."

He laughed. "It seems I always happen upon you when you're just taking a break. What have you taught her?"

I told him what we had worked on. He crossed his arms over his broad chest.

"Child's play."

"I didn't think the waterspout was child's play."

Nor was the magic she was using.

Lil sat up and rose to her feet, eyes locked on Abraham, whose face held a hint of amusement.

"What would you wish me to do?"

Abraham smiled, a look that chilled me to the bone. "Call the lightning."

"No." I jumped to my feet. I didn't want to tell him that was what she had started doing. While it was remarkable, it was frightening as well. "That's too much for her."

"Do you think her incapable?"

"It could kill her."

"Then I will bring her back."

"No." I clenched my fists and took a step in Abraham's direction. "I will not allow this." I turned to Lil. "Come on, Lil. Let's go back to the manor. We're through here."

"No, we're not," she said, eyes locked on Abraham.

"Lil—"

"Call the lightning, Lillyanna." He challenged her. I might as well not have been there for all the attention they paid me. Knowing she would not listen, I moved to the edge of the lake and stared out across it.

"I'm waiting." Abraham crossed his arms.

There was a distant rumble of thunder. The air was charged, and the hairs on my arms raised up as the lightning sizzled, forks streaking the sky. I looked at Lil, who stood with her hands outstretched, palms up.

I watched as the lightning snapped around her.

"It's too much, Abraham. Tell her to stop."

He ignored my plea, so I moved toward her. The raw, fierce energy of the lightning loomed all around. I was afraid to reach for her. Afraid of what would happen to me.

To her.

I stood back and watched, helpless to do anything to stop it. The sky flashed; forks hit the ground, igniting trees in the woods. Lil bent her head, her shadowed face illuminated with each flash, making her look menacing.

Evil.

I shuddered at the look. At the twisted smile on her face. That wasn't the Lil I was used to. It was someone—something—else, and it frightened me to my core.

The wind picked up, blowing her hair about her head in a swirl of red, and the lightning drew closer. The air thickened and pulsed with her magic and energy as she drew more and more and more. The lightning danced around her, circling her, becoming her. She drew it into herself, veins lighting up, pulsing as it moved through her body. She lifted her head and regarded me, eyes glowing, a slow smile forming on her face.

And then she released it, an outstanding pulse of power bursting from her body. She screamed as the magic exited. Wind and light rushed across the lake, ripping trees from the earth and frothing the water into a roiling fury. The concussive power threw me to the ground. When she had expelled it all, she collapsed. I jumped up and ran to her, my heart pounding in my chest. Her breathing was ragged and shallow, but she was alive. I snarled wordlessly at Abraham as I picked her up, cradling her limp body in my arms. Turning my back on his blank face, I slipped through the woods, back to the manor where I tucked her into her bed, and then went downstairs to confront Abraham.

"What the fuck were you thinking? She could have killed herself."

"She didn't, though."

I clenched my fists and glared at him. "I told you it was too much. She has completely spent herself. We will be fortunate if she didn't burn herself out as well."

"I told you to only teach her what will be beneficial for defense. What you had her do does nothing to help," he said, sitting in a chair and propping his feet on the table.

"She had to start somewhere. You know, calling lightning is a dark power. As it was..." I shook my head.

"What, Damiyun?" He crossed his arms.

I looked at him. "When I asked her to make the waterspout, she started to call the lightning. I don't know how but... I felt it. I saw it."

"Good."

"I know she tapped into the darkness with this. Before... I felt as though she didn't know me. Didn't know where she was and with this, with what you made her do... she looked evil."

"It is that power that will help her against Themesis." He said, a satisfied look on his face.

I glanced at him. "Will it? Or will it only bring her closer to him?" I rubbed my eyes. "I don't know if she's strong enough."

Or if I am.

Abraham sighed. "That's why I have chastised you, chastised her, against letting feelings dictate actions."

"I have no feelings for her."

Abraham laughed. "Even I can see that for the lie it is."

I said nothing. His words turned over in my mind, and I couldn't rightly deny what he said.

I was lying to myself.

Running a hand through my hair, I made my way back upstairs to Lil's room, where I kept vigil over her sleeping body.

SIXTEEN

ABRAHAM

I FELT A TUG inside my mind as I watched Damiyun lope up the stairs, probably to Lillyanna's room. The call in my mind grew insistent. Themesis, calling for another soul. Gritting my teeth, I saddled Violet, and made my way in the direction of town. The village of L'Ochal was a quiet and sleepy one on the shores of a mighty river that emptied into the Calgonian Sea.

It was also a land of opulence. Finely dressed people walked the streets. The storefronts lining the road boasted fine wares. Silk and satin dresses, fine cloaks and suits hung in the window of one shop. Cured meats dangled from the ceiling of another, a large boar slowly roasted on a spit just outside. The clang of hammer striking metal rang out as a man pounded an intricate blade, while a finely dressed patron assessed the work.

It did not surprise me Zenith would have wanted to live in such an affluent town, though I was sure she did not appreciate the manor being so far away. She reveled in attracting attention, always dragging Damiyun to events or making him host his own. A house full of people was the perfect place for her to hold court and show off what she had. What Damiyun had foolishly provided her with.

I walked the streets, eyes noting the groups of Suppressors who milled about, hands on swords and eyes searching. Their presence concerned me. While the manor was far enough away so as not to harm anyone should Lillyanna's magic go awry, I did not agree it was safe. The Suppressors in the village proved I was correct, but Damiyun had a tendency of being stubborn and an even worse habit of thinking he was right. Sighing, I pulled the door to the tavern open and stepped inside. Scanning the throng, I found the one I was looking for. His eyes met mine as I crossed the room and drew near. Blood drained from his face, and he jumped to his feet, bolting for the door. I followed him outside, catching him ducking down an alley. Striding in the direction he fled, I laughed when I saw the passage led to a dead-end.

"Please," he begged, holding out his hands, wide eyes on me. "I'll do anything you ask. Just please let me live."

"I have no doubt you will do what you are asked when you serve the Fallen One."

I pulled out the obsidian box and opened it. A black mist drifted out, taking the form of a demon. It stood in front of the man, who cowered in fear. Piss wet his pants and shoes. The demon grasped his head. Opening its mouth, he inhaled. The man's eyes rolled to the back of his head. A light mist drifted out of his mouth and into the demon. His body fell to the ground, sightless eyes staring at the sky. The demon drifted back to the box. I shut the lid and pulled the shadows around me before descending into the Abyss.

As I entered the tomb, my attention went to Sam. His back was to me, Jaylynn on her knees in front of him. I heard him grunt, his body shuddered, and then he pushed her away, lacing his trousers up. I tried to control my anger as Themesis patted her head. The look she gave him was one of a child who had pleased a parent.

No one knew Jaylynn was my daughter.

No one except Themesis.

The thing that hurt the most about all of this was she didn't know who I was. He had wiped her memories—everything she had known—to make her a mindless and obedient servant. A slave who did whatever it was he asked. All for a smile or a pat on the head.

"Abe." Sam said with a smile. "That girl has quite the mouth. I have never felt anything like it. I am sure she wouldn't mind letting you have a go."

"Yes. Why don't you have my Jaylynn give you pleasure?" Themesis said, laughing as he idly scratched her head. "Bring me the one you have."

I crossed the room to where he sat on the throne. Pulling out the box, I opened it, the man flowing out in a dark mass. His eyes were wide and frightened as he looked upon Themesis.

"Kneel before your master." I snapped, kicking him behind the knees. His legs buckled, and he fell to the floor.

He sobbed as he looked up at Themesis. "Please," he begged. "Give me another contract."

I snorted. "Last I checked, you only had one soul, and it now belongs to the Fallen One."

This man was a slave trader. He kidnapped and sold women to rich men looking for playthings. His pleasure was torture. For days, he would abuse and torture them into submission before handing them off to the buyers. His death came when one woman fought back, turning his weapon on him. He hadn't thought twice before he sold his soul for riches. Endless money so he could buy more women, building a harem which he could torture and abuse.

Themesis rubbed his chin and looked down at him. The man shook beneath his icy gaze.

"You are all so confident when you put your name on the contract. When what you are promised is yours. Your lust for what you desire makes you forget what you agreed to. It's all the same with you pathetic humans. Crying. Groveling. As if I would show kindness and pity." Themesis spat. "Yours was not a heinous crime. All women need to know their place, be it with a firm hand or whip. They need to obey us. Serve us as we see fit. Still..." He paused; his look thoughtful. After a moment, his lips pulled back in a cruel smile, and he leaned forward. "I will make you a eunuch. You will obey and serve me as I see fit, much like the women you used. You will submit to me, and if you don't? Rest assured, the torture I inflict will be like nothing you have ever seen or done." He waved his hand in dismissal, sitting back in his chair. I hauled the weeping man to his feet, marching him to the cell to await his castration.

I didn't pity those who sold their souls for worthless mortal pleasures. Love. Time. Riches. Youth. Escaping disease or famine. None of it was worth an eternity of torment in the Abyss. None of it was worth the torture by the most expert hands—Themesis. The pain, the agony he inflicted, was debilitating. Bones crushed beneath hammers, barbed whips biting and tearing flesh, only to be healed to relive the torture again. And then there were his demons that used and abused those brought to the Abyss for their own carnal pleasures. All the torture, all the abuse turned those souls into twisted versions of themselves. Turned them into the demons that did Themesis' bidding.

No. I didn't pity these people. They made their choice when they signed their name. I, on the other hand, was given no choice. I made my way back to the throne room, where Themesis spoke to Sam.

"—man will cower. They will hail you a god," he was saying.

Sam smiled. I could tell he was buying into what Themesis had said. I knew better. There was only one deemed worthy to stand beside him and rule. The rest would become his slaves. Mindless servants who would grovel at his feet, happy with whatever scraps of praise he threw at them.

Mindless like my Jaylynn. Shaking my head, I strode across the room. "Are we through here?"

"You are free to go," he said, waving his hand, fingers idly scratching Jaylynn's head. The look of happiness on her face made me sick, and I turned away.

"Fancy a drink?" Sam said.

"Sorry, no. I have something I must tend to." I drew the darkness around and drifted back to the world of the living.

I SLOWED VIOLET DOWN when the manor came into view and looked down at the shambles of Damiyun's home as I guided my horse to the stables. I unsaddled and brushed Violet, then gave him food and water before I made my way inside.

I knew we shouldn't be here. The Suppressors showing up was proof I was correct in my assumption, but far be it for Damiyun to actually listen and heed my advice. I knew he had feelings for the girl. He could deny it all he wanted, but I saw the truth, and the more he denied it, the more insolent he became. I didn't want to hurt him, not really. But he needed a lesson to remember who owned him.

I would not take his soul. No, I hadn't written the words to seal his fate on his contract. I had still needed to let him know I was in charge, but when he answered me sufficiently, I let him go. I didn't think he wouldn't forget himself anytime soon. I strode up the stairs of the manor and slipped into a bedroom. Closing the door, I removed my weapons and stretched out on the bed.

My mind went to what I had seen. Once again, he had succumbed to a pretty face. Not that I could fault him for it. I too had once fallen under the same spell.

A pretty face and a soft voice. Light-brown eyes hauntingly sad. Eyes beseeching me. Eyes I vowed to make shine with happiness. Lenore. The only one who claimed my heart. The only one who had ever truly owned my soul.

I WOULD NEVER FORGET the day I met my Lenore. It was in the market where I lived, in Saldon. She was examining fruit at a booth. She wore a white dress, the color accenting her bronze skin. Amber hair spilled down her back. Long, delicate fingers picked up pieces of produce.

I sidled up beside her, making as though I were looking to purchase. She was beautiful. Her features were soft. Eyes wideset, small, delicate nose and a sensuous mouth. She examined an exotic-looking fruit, inquiring on the price. When the merchant revealed the cost, she placed it back down with a sigh and began to leave. I quickly bought the item, touching her arm as she turned away.

"Here," I said, holding the fruit out to her. Brown eyes went from the item back to my face.

"Thank you, but no." She sniffed, lifting her skirts, and striding away.

I chuckled as I bit into the fruit, sweet juice running down my beard.

She would be a challenge, but it was one I was willing to accept.

I watched her day after day as she shopped. Twice I made my way to a booth she perused. Twice she rebuffed me, the blatant snub making her more intriguing.

Then one day she was gone. I went there like always, scanning the crowd, but she was nowhere to be seen. Finally, when I was about to give up, she appeared. She wore a cloak, hood pulled up over her head, and I watched her make her way slowly through the booths.

I frowned. It was far too warm to wear a cloak, let alone with the hood up.

I drew up alongside her at one of the stands. The scent of freshly baked bread, a warm yeast smell, made my stomach growl.

"Go away." Her voice was low.

"I am just buying bread," I said, pointing to a loaf. The shopkeeper grabbed it, and wrapped it up in paper, and I tossed him some coin.

"No. You have been following me," she hissed, and I couldn't deny her words. The wind kicked up, blowing her hood back. She quickly grabbed it and threw it over her head.

But not before I saw the bruises on her face.

"Who did this?"

She spun away, and I grabbed her sleeve.

"Leave me alone." She pulled her arm free, knocking over a tray of bread.

"See what you made me do?" Her voice cracked as she squatted down to pick up the loaves. "I can't afford this."

"Easy," I said with the softest voice as I could muster. "Let me." I nodded to the shopkeeper, tossing him more coin for the bread, which he packaged up.

"Take it," I said, holding out the bundle.

She shook her head. "I can't. He... He knows we can't afford it. He'll think I stole it and..." She turned away.

"What's your name?" I asked as she began to leave.

She paused. "Lenore," she said, rushing away. I hollered out my name to her as she retreated, hoping she heard it through the raised voices of the crowd.

I shook myself from my thoughts and returned to the present, my thumb idly stroking the words on the bracelet I didn't realize I had removed.

Lenore was the only woman I had loved, Jaylynn the only child I would father.

Closing my eyes, I allowed darkness to take me. The darkness that never left.

Darkness that, in sleep, brought me to my home.

The place I had rejected, yet... I always knew it was where I belonged.

SEVENTEEN

LILLYANNA

MY EYES SNAPPED OPEN. Someone had put me in my bed. It was dark, and shadows danced on the walls from the lantern light. Out on the balcony stood Damiyun, his outline illuminated by moonlight. Why was I in my bedroom?

Then the reality of what I'd done hit me. My head spun, and nausea bubbled in my throat. Stumbling out of bed, I padded outside and stood beside him.

"Why?" he asked, eyes focused on the dark night beyond.

I was unsure of what to say. Of how to answer one simple question.

I thought about how it felt, the pulsing magic, the raw power as it snapped around and flowed through me. I had felt more power, a supremacy had come over me like never before. The destruction I wielded. Even now, just thinking about it, I craved it again. My body buzzed, and I felt a pulsing beneath my skin. I saw a faint flicker in the sky, and I clenched my fists as the buzzing, the pulsing, pushed harder against the block on my magic. Clearly, Abraham didn't trust me, just as I had trouble trusting him and Damiyun to a lesser degree. The danger in them seemed less so, knowing I had a trick or two of my own now, if I could just remove the block on my own.

I closed my eyes, the temptation. No. I was glad to have the block. The energy behind the invisible wall made me itch to draw it. To call the lightning once again.

"I wanted to see if I could," I said. "I know nothing about the magic I wield. I don't know what I can do with it. This... What I did..." I laughed. "It was incredible. The power I held. It felt amazing. Terrifying. I didn't want to stop. I wanted more." And I still felt drunk with the power that vibrated within.

Thunder rumbled in the distance. The air smelled of rain and felt charged with lightning. Or perhaps it was me who was charged, the soft, thrumming buzz more persistent as the sky flashed in the distance.

"You should be scared." Damiyun's voice was quiet. Feeling his eyes on me, I turned and looked up at him.

"What Abraham had you do is a dark and dangerous magic. It's seductive. By the gods, I have let it seduce me before. I have used my magic in destructive ways. I have traveled down a path I cannot return, and you—." He paused. Face grim.

"Every time you use magic to destroy, a part of yourself dies. It brings you closer to the darkness. I will do what I can to keep you from it. I won't lose you to it. To him," he said, cupping my chin.

The vibration inside intensified at his touch.

Thrum, thrum, thrum.

It pulsed through me. It heightened my senses. The softness of my shirt against my skin. The smell of the rain gently falling. The sound of Damiyun's breath.

His scent—earth mixed with primal maleness. I was aware of everything. It filled me with desire and need.

I needed to have Damiyun. To feel his skin, mouth, and hands on me. Snaking my arms around his neck, I pulled him close, my mouth devouring his. He pulled back a moment, muscular arms lifting me as though I weighed nothing, and he strode into the bedroom, gently placing me on the bed. He stretched out beside me, propping himself up on his elbow.

"You're so beautiful," he breathed. I reached up and pulled his face closer, lips meeting again. He slipped his hand beneath my shirt, warm fingers brushing against my skin. Rough, calloused palms gently cupped my breast. He pushed my shirt up and pulled it over my head. Eyes dark with desire raked over my naked torso. He dipped his head, mouth capturing my breast, teeth grazing my nipple in a delightful and painful way.

I moaned as he trailed kisses down my stomach, hands fumbling with the binds on my trousers, finally getting them undone and off after what felt like an eternity. He stood at the end of the bed, lust-filled eyes sweeping over me.

Crawling across the bed, I knelt in front of him, pushing up his shirt and removing it. I ran my hands up his chest, feeling his warm, smooth skin. The hard muscles beneath. I pressed my lips to his chest, tongue licking his salty skin, hands roaming about to undo his trousers and easing them over his hips. He stepped out of his trousers, then grabbed a fistful of my hair. He yanked my head back, teeth nipping at my neck. I hissed in pleasure at the feel. At the primal action. He pushed me onto my back, hands capturing my wrists and pinning them above my head. He dipped his head, trailing slow and lazy kisses down my body, tongue tasting my skin. He held my wrists in one hand, while the other slipped between my legs, fingers gently exploring. I pressed against his hand, moving to his rhythm, moaning as his mouth returned to my breasts.

"Damiyun, please," I gasped.

"Please what?" His voice was soft in my ear, breath hot. His teeth grazed my earlobe, and I struggled beneath him, groaning. I was close. So close to exploding. His mouth captured mine, teeth biting my lower lip, tongue filling my mouth, his kiss hard and demanding.

"Please what?" he asked again, stopping what he was doing. My eyes snapped open. He loomed above me, hand holding my wrists, eyes boring into me.

"Don't stop. Please, Damiyun. I need you," I desperately tried to free myself, so I could have him.

He dipped his head, lips nibbling my ear, neck, and collarbone. He ground his pelvis against mine and I bucked my hips, desperate to have him inside me.

"Mmm. I do like it when you struggle. But I like it more when you beg." His voice softened, warm breath caressing my skin. "Tell me what you want."

"I want you."

"You have me."

He stopped moving and slowly and deliberately began pleasing me, stopping just short of my climax before starting again. Over and over, he teased and tormented me, the wicked smile he wore never leaving his face. I grit my teeth and writhed against him, frustration and desire washing over me.

"Tell me what you want."

"You," I gasped again. "Please, Damiyun, now."

His mouth ravaged mine as he clutched my wrists and roughly entered me. Pulling back, his eyes locked on mine as he moved slowly inside me. I lifted my hips and met his slow and deliberate thrusts. He planted his hands on either side of my head, and I raked my nails down his back. He groaned, grabbing my hips, and driving himself deeper inside me. I clutched the bedsheets, rising to meet him, my body exploding as waves of pleasure washed over me. Damiyun thrust hard, fingers digging into the tender flesh of my hips, his body shuddering as he spent himself inside me.

He leaned down and softly kissed me, then flopped onto his back, arm resting across his eyes. I propped myself up and softly ran my hand up his chest, feeling the solid muscle beneath my fingers. He shuddered at my light touch, and then pulled me down next to him, lips brushing my forehead. I rested my head on his chest, the steady thump of his heart and the rise and fall of his chest soothing.

The room lit up with the flickering of lightning. The rumble of thunder and the patter of rain against the windows split the silence.

That vibration—the constant thrumming I had felt earlier—was subdued. I still itched to feel the power, but the need—the desire—had lessened.

"I'm sorry. About what I did. Calling the lightning."

Damiyun shifted his position and looked down at me. "There is no reason to apologize, Lil. Abraham should never have had you do that."

"But—"

My words cut off as his mouth captured mine again and his hands roamed down my body.

I lost count of how many times he claimed me before we collapsed in a mass of sweaty, tangled limbs, our bodies spent, our desire satiated for now. Damiyun's arms tightened around me, and I closed my eyes, the steady beating of his heart lulling me to sleep.

THE SUN WAS HIGH in the sky when I woke. Light poured through the windows. I sat up and stretched my arms above my head, wincing at the discomfort between my legs. My thoughts went to the night prior, and I flushed, a feeling of want and lust rolling through me again. I washed up, dressed, and slipped downstairs. The house was quiet, though out front I heard Damiyun and Abraham's low voices. Following the sound, I stepped outside, my eyes taking in the two men and horses. Damiyun was securing bulging saddlebags to Xander's sides. He turned in my direction, a smile lighting his face.

"Good morning, Lil," he said, coming over and kissing me softly. I turned my head and cleared my throat, and my eyes flicked to Abraham, who scowled.

"What's going on?"

"We're leaving," Abraham jerked the strap on Violet's saddle. I looked up at Damiyun, who turned back to his horse. Why did we have to go? I had become comfortable in Damiyun's home.

"Now?"

He glanced at me over his shoulder as he finished securing the bags and checking straps. "It's no longer safe here. What you did, it raised some attention," he said.

I frowned. "But the Suppressors were already here. How could what I did raise any more attention? They already know where we are," I said.

"Gather whatever you think you'll need," Damiyun said, ignoring me.

I retraced my steps back into the house. I only came with the clothes I had on my back, though I went to my room and took one last longing look at the dresses in the wardrobe. Glancing at the row of shoes, I took a silver pair and then grabbed a long cloak of red velvet with gold stitching. I made my way back outside. Abraham sat astride Violet, face impatient, and Damiyun stood next to Xander with his arms folded. I handed him the cloak and shoes, then climbed up into the saddle. Damiyun swung up behind and took the reins, heeling Xander after Abraham.

"You could have taken more," he said, slipping an arm around my waist.

I had thought about taking a few dresses. "I didn't want to ruin the fabric." Which was true. I had no idea where we were going or how long we would travel.

The thought of the beautiful silks, satins and velvet being crammed into our damp saddlebags made me want to cry.

I leaned back against Damiyun, resting my head on his chest. His lips brushed the top of my head and I settled into his warmth, a pulsating heat radiating off him.

"Where are we going?"

Damiyun stiffened. "Kraagswell Mountain." His reaction to my question felt a bit odd, so I vowed to ask Damiyun more when we stopped to make camp.

"Which we would have been a Moon Cycle closer to if you had not made your foolish stop at home," Abraham growled.

"And had you not had her call the lightning, we would have been ahead by two days."

"Two days?" I sat up, alarmed. "I was out for that long?"

"Yes, Lil. You scared me." Damiyun's voice was low.

It scared me, too, now that I knew. I began to wonder if the cost to feel that power could get too high. If perhaps I would burn myself out if I tried again. Or die.

We traveled through the day, alternating between the road and paths through the woods, stopping for quick meals and to rest the horses. As dusk descended, Abraham called the journey to a halt, and we made camp. He stalked off into the dark woods as I helped Damiyun make a fire.

I watched the flames undulate and dance, watched Damiyun's eyes follow the snaking blaze.

"You had asked me what happened to Zenith. How she died." His voice was soft. His eyes met mine, sad and haunted. "I wasn't honest with you. I promised I would be, and I wasn't."

"It's alright, Damiyun. You don't have to—"

"I do, Lil." He took a deep breath. "I loved my wife. When we met, the attraction was instant. She was beautiful. Perfect. If I didn't know better, I would have thought her to be a siren with how she entrapped me. One flash of that beguiling smile, and I... I would do anything. I was devoted to her. I did whatever I could to make her happy. I gave in to her every whim and fancy, lavishing her with whatever she desired. She was a Non. My magic frightened her, so I promised her I would never use it in her presence."

"If she was so scared, why would she have been Blood-Bound to a Wielder?"

"Because she loved me," he said. "Or at least I thought she did. It appears I was a blind fool. Blind to her deceit. To her betrayal. I discovered far too late she didn't care about me. Or even love me." He tossed a log on the fire and took a deep breath.

"We had separate rooms. Zenith insisted on such, said, she needed her privacy. Of course, I believed her. But one night, like most nights, I desired her. So I went to her quarters. When I entered her room, I saw the reason she had turned me away. Why she had insisted on her own bed chambers. I saw her silhouetted by the moon, sharing a passionate kiss with another man."

"How horrible."

Damiyun laughed, a hollow sound. "I was shocked. Furious. I couldn't think. He pulled a dagger and mortally wounded me." His hand absently rubbed his chest. "That's when Abraham came to me."

"And you sold your soul."

"Yes."

"Why?"

"Because I loved her. I wanted to understand her. I wanted to fix whatever was wrong between us."

"What did Zenith do?"

"She laughed when I came back. Said I was weak. Pathetic. I was an abomination and the thought of me touching her... of taking her... made her sick." His eyes met mine. "She had a slew of lovers, and the only reason she was with me was for what I afforded her. She was only playing a part. The night we met, she planned it. She knew who I was and what I had. Long ago, she had set her designs on me."

"She told me just how inferior I was. She was glad I couldn't give her a child. Even if I could, she would have rid herself of it." He took a deep, shaking breath. "Her..." he shook his head. "I wanted her to shut up. To just stop saying those things. I lunged at her. We struggled and... I don't know where the dagger came from. I don't remember picking it up. Perhaps it was already in my hand. I wasn't thinking clearly. I'd just caught her with another man. Her words, those hateful, ugly words—"

"How long were you Blood-Bound?"

"Six Moon Cycles. I was young and foolish. I thought I loved her, Lil."

I stared into the fire, letting his words sink in. Letting the fact he killed his wife sink in. I should have been shocked and outraged over it yet... I wasn't. I was beginning to learn what sort of man Damiyun was. Killing his wife didn't surprise me, and I had to wonder if he would do the same to me someday. I wondered if I cared. The thought should have astounded me and yet, I felt a sort of calm as if I had always known this kind of man and his many revelations.

"I'm sorry, Lil," he said. I turned and looked at him. "I regret what I did every day of my life. If I had the chance to go back... I would have let her go. She only had to ask." His voice softened. "I can't blame you if you hate me."

I said nothing, my mind turning over his confession, and the silence stretched. The sound of a branch snapping sliced through the quiet, making me jump. Damiyun swiftly rose, blade in hand, eyes scanning the dark woods. I stood slowly up.

"It's got to be Abraham." I said.

"No. He's off hunting. He wouldn't have caught food that fast." Damiyun took a step in the noise's direction.

"Animal?" I offered. My eyes widened as a man stepped out into the clearing, dressed in black. My eyes went to the insignia on his left breast of his shirt: two swords crossed over a scarlet "S."

A Suppressor.

He was as tall as Damiyun, with more bulk. Black hair spilled over his shoulders and ice-blue eyes glared at him. He waved his hand and Damiyun stumbled back with a grunt.

He'd blocked Damiyun's magic.

"Arden," Damiyun growled.

Arden?

The tall, black-haired man who had stepped out of the forest was Damiyun's brother.

EIGHTEEN

"**I** DARE SAY YOU are a difficult one to find." He stroked his goatee and folded his arms across his chest. "Had you given the girl over from the start, all would have been forgiven, but as always, you prove to be stubborn."

"And that surprises you?" Damiyun scowled.

Arden chuckled. "No. Nothing surprises me where you are concerned. I will be more lenient on you if you give her over, or I can pretend I never saw you. It is not you the Elder wants."

"You know I cannot do that," Damiyun's voice had gone low and threatening.

Arden sighed. "So be it." He nodded, and four Suppressors stepped out of the shadows.

Damiyun sliced the air with his blade and stood with his feet apart, arms out. "Shall we dance then?" He leaped toward the men, cutting them down with little effort. I stood frozen, watching his subtle movements. He lunged, darted, his footwork, truly seemed to flow as if he were at a monarch's court. He was a thing of beauty. I looked around, heart dropping and mouth going dry at the sight of more Suppressors pouring out of the woods. As good as Damiyun was, I knew he couldn't win. There were just too many of them, and my intuition proved true when Arden nodded, and they descended on him at once.

"Don't get any ideas, bitch," a voice growled in my ear, and someone wrenched my arms behind me. I struggled in the man's grasp, jerking my head back, slamming it into his face. He released me with a curse, and I bolted, stopping short when hands clamped down on my hair and jerked me back. Spinning around, I kneed the man in the groin, and he released me. I turned to flee once more, my hopes dashed as two men advanced on me, and my arms were once again wrenched behind by the one I had fought. The men in front drew their blades, tips poised and ready to kill.

"Try that again, little girl, and you'll find yourself on the end of those swords." He growled. My heart fell. I had no choice but to watch helplessly as six men pounced on Damiyun. He did his best to cut them back, but they overtook him. One Suppressor brought his foot up and kicked him in the stomach. I heard an audible grunt, and he bent over in pain and surprise, which proved to be the end for him.

"Enough." Arden sauntered over, hands clasped behind his back. They stopped immediately and stepped back in unison. I pulled from the man's grasp and bolted to where Damiyun was on his hands and knees, coughing up blood.

He sat back on his haunches and looked at me, eyes filled with shame and defeat. "I failed you." His breathing was labored, his voice barely above a whisper.

I opened my mouth to respond when rough hands grabbed me again. I twisted my arm free, my eyes going to the dagger secured in Damiyun's belt. I reached forward and pulled it free. Unsheathing the weapon, I spun around, my eyes taking in the Suppressors who milled about.

"What are you going to do, little girl?" the man who grabbed me snarled. He took a step forward, and I slashed the knife across, slicing his arm. Blood dripped from his wound. He pulled back and glared at me. Springing forward, I buried the blade deep in his chest. My stomach lurched as the warm blood spilled over my hand when I pulled it out. The sound of swords clearing scabbards rang through the air as a handful of Suppressors drew their weapons, casually brandishing them as they stepped in my direction.

Damn you, Abraham, for blocking my magic.

I knew I couldn't fight them with a dagger, and I wished I had picked up Damiyun's sword instead.

"Hand over the weapon. You're only going to hurt yourself," a voice to my right said.

I heard a grunt and glanced over my shoulder to see Damiyun standing up, one hand holding his side, the other clutching his sword.

"You are far outnumbered. I suggest surrendering," someone snarled.

"No." Amusement colored Arden's voice as he stepped forward. "Let them play their little game. I need a bit of entertainment."

Despite the brief flash of pain on his face, Damiyun sprang forward, still swift, and agile even while injured. He brandished his blade, slicing through men, and I followed behind, stabbing, and slashing with the dagger. A hand grabbed my wrist, twisting my arm around. I cried; the dagger slipped from my fingers. I swung around with my free hand, fist connecting with the man's face. His head snapped to the side, but his grip never wavered. Grabbing my other arm, he yanked my arms painfully behind my back. Damiyun turned in my direction, his head snapping to the side as a fist slammed into his cheek, a grunt escaping as another hit him in the stomach. His sword fell from his hand, and he fell to his knees, head snapping back as a boot connected with his chin.

I closed my eyes, unable to watch him get beaten.

"Enough." Arden's lips curled into a smile. Two Suppressors grabbed Damiyun under his arms and hauled him to his feet. Spitting out blood, he glared at his brother, who sauntered over and stood in front of him. "You could have made this so much easier on yourself." He tsked. "I can't wait to hear you scream."

He turned in my direction, ice-blue eyes piercing me. "And you. I have something special planned for you, love." He ran a finger down my cheek. I jerked my head away and spat at him, which earned me a sharp backhand to the cheek.

"I strongly advise against making Regulator Rayne angry." The man who held my arms growled in my ear.

"And I strongly advise you bathe more often." I growled back, stomping on his foot, taking great satisfaction in his yelp of pain.

"Bind them. We travel now." Arden tossed lines of rope to our captors, who quickly bound our wrists in front of us. Arden stood in front of Damiyun and tied another rope around his wrists.

"He walks behind the horse," Arden said to Damiyun's captor. He was a tall, thin man, and I dubbed him Giant. He barked orders to the crowd of Suppressors, who dispersed in different directions. Arden strode toward the woods, Damiyun, our captors, and me following behind. We walked in silence for about half an hour before, finally, coming upon a small clearing where three horses were grazing. Arden hopped astride a large, black stallion. My captor, who I called Surly on account of his crooked angry smile, boosted me up onto his horse, then swung up into the saddle behind. I watched as they tethered Damiyun behind the third horse. As soon as the third man hopped in his saddle, Arden heeled his mount, and we began our journey.

As we traveled, Arden occasionally commanded Giant to speed up, causing Damiyun to run lest he fall and be dragged, a stunt which seemed to please Arden. He was a vile man, and I hated him more with every passing mile. The full moon split the dark, casting its silver rays on the road ahead, creating long silhouettes of the men. The trees made an eerie and foreboding sight.

Arden declared we stop and set up camp, and Giant untethered Damiyun from the horse, leading him by the rope to a tree where he threw the length of cord up over a branch. He pulled it so Damiyun hung suspended in the air, the toes of his boots barely touching the ground. I started toward where he hung, but Surly grabbed my arm and stopped me.

"He is being punished. No food, no water, no contact." His voice held a hint of amusement.

I tried to force my way over to him, but Surly held me fast. I turned my head toward where Damiyun hung. Arden leaned up against the tree, a smirk on his face.

"Is he going to kill him?" My eyes refused to leave Damiyun. I watched Arden step forward and place a hand on him. Damiyun's body jerked as his face contorted with pain, and he cried out in agony. Arden said something to him, then laughed.

"There were many times he could have killed his brother," Surly said after a while. "He prefers to torture him. It gives him satisfaction, causing him pain."

"Why?" Damiyun had told me what his brother did to him when they were young, and I balled my fist at the thought of Arden torturing him again for the sake of his own pleasure.

Surly said nothing, just grabbed my arm and dragged me to where Giant sat. For a moment, he rummaged through a canvas bag by Giant's side. Pulling his dagger from his belt, he cut the ropes binding me. I rubbed my wrists as he handed me some bread and cheese to eat, then sat down next to me, chatting idly with the other man. I placed the food on the ground. I couldn't eat. The sound of Damiyun's screams—the agony he was in—made me sick. I pushed the food away. Damiyun screamed again. I winced, tears stinging my eyes at the sound. Surly picked up my discarded food and put it back in the bag.

"Perhaps you'll be hungry later," he said, not unkindly. I glared at him.

I looked back toward where Damiyun hung, watching as Arden again put his hands on him, and Damiyun's body went rigid beneath his touch. His screams tore through the night. I wouldn't look away. I would watch whatever torture—whatever horrors—he endured at the hand of his brother. He was willing to die to protect me and, in turn, I would suffer the pain with him. His eyes met mine, and I offered a silent message.

I'm here. I will endure the agony with you.

He smiled briefly as though he understood and, with his eyes locked on mine, he continued to bear the pain and humiliation.

After what felt like hours, they stopped, and Arden came over to where we sat.

"Keep him awake." He pointed to Giant, who jumped to his feet with a nod and trotted over to where Damiyun hung. I turned my head and looked at him, his angry eyes fixed on Arden, who sat down in front of me.

Arden trailed a finger down my cheek. "Has my brother made you his yet? He has a weakness for pretty faces." I jerked away, and he laughed. He glanced over to where Damiyun hung, then leaned forward, his lips close to my ear. "Perhaps I should make him watch as I take you," he murmured, slipping a hand between my legs, his lips brushing my cheek. I pulled away, and he grabbed me, his mouth coming down on mine, his tongue forcing its way inside. I bit down hard on it, and he pulled back with a cry. He glared at me and raised his hand, my cheek exploded in pain at the sting of his slap, my head snapped back with the force of it.

"Leave her alone, Arden," Surly stood between us. "You made a promise to the Elder that we would not harm her."

Arden licked the blood from his lip and glared at me. "I will hurt her in ways the Elder will never see." He grabbed a fistful of my hair and yanked my head back. "Make no mistake, love. I will have what is mine." He released me, then sprang to his feet and stalked back over to continue torturing Damiyun.

After what seemed like an eternity, Arden stopped and went to sleep. I stretched out on the cold ground. I looked at Damiyun, whose eyes met mine, a brief smile of reassurance crossing his face. I lay awake for a long time watching Giant, who roughly shook Damiyun whenever his eyes closed. And after a while, I forced myself to sleep, knowing Damiyun wouldn't get any shut-eye and at least one of us needed to be alert in the morning.

T HE NEXT DAY WAS the same, with Damiyun walking behind the horse. I could see his exhaustion, his feet tripping over stumps. Occasionally Giant heeled his horse into a brief trot, forcing him to run, much to the amusement of the Suppressors.

I swallowed over the lump that formed in my throat, pity flooding me at his humiliation. I looked away, unable to take it anymore.

We rode through the afternoon, our procession traveling through small towns. People scattered at our approach, soon a tall wall loomed before us. We made our way through the gate, and Arden nodded to the men who kept watch. I scanned the streets as we passed through the courtyard, before we stopped in front of a large stone and brick building.

Arden swung down, snapping orders for Giant to untether Damiyun. I dismounted and Surly gripped my arm, guiding me through the door Arden had entered. The hall was dim despite the candles and lanterns. Sallow light cast eerie shadows on the walls.

We walked down the hall, our footsteps echoing through the empty chamber. Finally, we stopped at a set of closed, oaken doors. Arden knocked once, then pushed the doors open, and we slipped through. The room was large and bright, a row of windows letting the late afternoon sun in. A large ornate desk sat across the room in front of a fireplace and brightly colored rugs were scattered on the stone floor. A tall man with brown hair peppered with gray stood in front of the windows, hands clasped behind his back. His profile was strong, with a sharp nose and a chiseled jaw. There was something familiar about him, though I couldn't put my finger on what it was.

Arden strode forward, standing a few paces next to him. "Elder Castille," he said. I stumbled, unsure if I had heard him correctly. I glanced at Damiyun, who frowned. The man at the window turned his head.

No.

I froze, my mind not comprehending what I saw.

"Father?" My voice was barely above a whisper.

"Vel?" Damiyun's tone was incredulous.

A soft smile formed as his blue eyes set upon me. "Lillyanna. Daughter," he said, voice soft.

I clenched my fists and shook myself.

He was alive. My father was alive. My chest constricted, taking my breath. I should have been thrilled. I should have wept with joy, but I strode across the room, raised my hand, and struck him hard across the cheek.

"You son of a bitch." My hands shook as I stood in front of my father. Anger flowed through me, and along with it came a shift deep inside. The block Abraham had put in place wavered. As I let my rage fill me, the block shifted more, cracking, and a stream of magic pulsed through.

"Lillyanna—"

"Shut up, Vel." I pushed him in the chest. He stumbled backward, catching himself on the desk behind. Arden strode over and struck me hard across the cheek.

"You will show respect to Elder Castille."

I rubbed my face, eyes never leaving my father. "He doesn't deserve my respect."

Arden raised his hand again, but my father caught his wrist.

"Enough, Arden." He turned his attention back to me. "My daughter has had a shock. It is natural she would be upset."

I laughed. "Upset doesn't describe what I am feeling."

"There is a room ready and a hot bath waiting. Marcus will take you there," he said, glancing at Surly. "Clean up and rest. I will send for you when it is time to eat." He turned to Arden and nodded in Damiyun's direction. "You know where to take him. Teach him a lesson."

Arden grinned and grabbed the rope.

"No. You will not torture Damiyun anymore," I said.

Arden's eyes narrowed to slits. "I don't take orders from a woman. If you do not watch yourself, love, I will have your tongue and I will torture you far worse than anything Damiyun has ever felt." He smiled. "I look forward to hearing you scream."

I risked a quick glance at Damiyun, who was slowly moving in our direction, rope held in his hands. "You will not hurt me, or Damiyun." I turned my attention back to my father. "You will not torture Damiyun," I said again. "He protected me. If you ever cared about me, you would let him be." I drew on the little magic I felt pulsing through my veins and clenched my fists.

Damiyun pounced. He wrapped the rope around his brother's neck and pulled. Arden's eyes widened in surprise. Hands grappled for the rope while his feet kicked out on the slippery floor.

"Not smart, Lillyanna," my father said.

I let the anger I felt flow over me, feeling my magic pulse more. "What's not smart, Vel, is making me think you were dead." I leaped forward. The movement took him off guard and he stumbled. Placing my hands upon him, I set forth a pulse of magic, which tossed him into the wall with a loud crash. Something slammed into my back, and I fell to the floor. I looked up to see Marcus standing over me, grasping his sheathed sword. Breath left my body as his boot slammed into my midsection. Gasping, I placed my hands on the floor and let out another pulse, intending to send a surge through the stone to where Arden and Damiyun fought, the action cut short when someone grabbed me by the hair and hauled me to my feet. I yelped, hands clawing at father's wrists.

"Foolish little girl." My father's spittle hit my face. "You will not win this game." He forced me around and my heart dropped as I looked upon Damiyun, who Arden had by the throat, while Marcus beat him. I clenched my fists, ready to use my magic again. My father's hand tightened further in my hair.

"I would think twice before doing that again. Everything you do will have a direct impact on Damiyun. And you. If you wish to see him again, alive, and, if you wish not to be hurt as well, I suggest you stop this foolishness. The choice is yours."

My body sagged, and I released my magic. "You win, Vel."

This time.

"That's quite enough, Marcus. Arden. My daughter has come to her senses."

Arden and Marcus stopped, and I rushed to Damiyun, who collapsed to all fours. His face was battered and bruised, and blood dripped from his mouth. I dropped to my knees in front of him.

"I had to try something," I said.

He looked at me. A small smile lit his lips for a moment. "You did good, Lil." He reached out and smoothed my hair back.

"He's all yours, Arden," my father said. Scrambling to my feet, I stepped away, watching Arden haul Damiyun up.

"I have something special in store for you. You can thank your bitch for it later." He snapped, dragging Damiyun out of the room.

"Take my daughter to her room."

"Let's go, Lillyanna," Marcus grabbed my arm. His fingers dug into my skin as he steered me out.

My anger mounted over what had happened. Over the fact my father was alive. That he had turned into a cruel man, willing to have his own daughter tortured.

He clearly didn't die trying to protect me. I caught myself questioning everything I had known about him. Had he ever loved me?

I shook my head of the thoughts as we stopped in front of a door.

"Clean up and rest. I will get you when Elder Castille is ready for his meal."

I glanced around the room. A fire blazed and a claw foot copper tub sat in the corner, steam rising into the air. A bed lay directly in front of me, flanked by an extensive wardrobe whose open doors revealed an array of dresses, cloaks, and shoes to my right. Large windows looked out onto the sprawling grounds, the sky lit in deep purples and pinks as dusk descended.

My eyes scanned the room again, and a crisp chill fell over me. My father knew I would be coming here. The icy fingers of terror gripped me, and I struggled to breathe. *He* had sent the Suppressors after me.

My mind spun, and I rubbed my temples where a dull ache was forming. Stripping out of my clothes, I lowered myself into the hot water, the warmth blanketing me and making me feel wearier than I was. I sat in the tub until the water went cold, my mind and body exhausted. I dried off, wrapped myself in the luxurious robe, and then perused the wardrobe, choosing a long-sleeved, high-necked dress in a dark gray, the color best suiting my current mood.

Crossing the room, I sat down on the bed and waited for Marcus to fetch me, like Vel's pretty little pet.

MARCUS CAME SEVERAL HOURS later, and I followed him back through the halls to a dining room where my father waited, seated at the head of a long table piled with food. He stood when I entered, hands grasping two glasses filled with wine, and crossed the room to me.

"Tell Arden to bring Damiyun here," he instructed Marcus, as he handed me a glass. "Now. Are you through acting like a child?"

"How did you expect me to act? Did you think I would run to you with open arms? Weep with joy at seeing you? I thought you were dead. Damiyun told me you were tortured and killed." I spat as I took a sip of wine. "Why did you leave me?"

"I knew you would survive."

"I was twelve."

"You are of powerful blood."

"There were several days I didn't have food. Days I was eating scraps out of trash bins. I was eating garbage while you—," I gestured in the table's direction, "—you have enough food to feed our entire village. You probably throw most of it away."

"I'm sorry, Lillyanna. I did what I did to protect you. I have been a Suppressor for a long time. If they had found out about you..." He shook his head. "I couldn't risk it. I couldn't risk you being caught."

Realization dawned on me. "You mean you couldn't risk your career for having a Wielder for a daughter," I said, finishing the wine. "Did you send them after me?"

"What do you know about Damiyun?"

I frowned at the change in subject. "I know he kept me from getting caught in the market."

"Did he?"

"Yes. He has protected me. On your order."

Vel laughed. I clenched my fists. "Is that what he told you? The lies flow so easily off his tongue, I doubt he even knows how to tell the truth."

I folded my arms and narrowed my eyes at him. "Why would he lie to me? What does he have to gain by not giving me to the Suppressors? He did his job these past few weeks, and you had him tortured for it." He said nothing as I pointed out his hypocrisy, so I continued to try nudging some semblance of a conscience within him.

He opened his mouth. Whatever he intended to say was stopped by a sharp knock. The door opened, and Arden shoved Damiyun through. His shirt was dirty, spatters of red staining the white. Blood dripped down his fingers. My stomach roiled, and I clenched my fists at the thought of them whipping him. At the thought of whatever else his brother had done to him, and I felt the crack on the block shatter some more. Did Abraham feel the block breaking?

"Welcome home, Damiyun," Vel said as he offered him a glass of wine, waving his hand in dismissal of Arden.

Damiyun snorted into his glass. "I would hardly call this place home."

"Once you did."

"This was never my home. What is your agenda, Vel?" Damiyun's eyes narrowed.

"I have no agenda. You are simply back where you belong. You know this. Now let's eat before the food gets cold." He motioned to the table, and we took seats. Me, reluctantly, Damiyun because he couldn't possibly stand for any longer. We passed around food, and I filled my plate, though I wasn't hungry, and went through the motions of eating, half-listening to Damiyun, and my father have a forced conversation.

"—defected. You're a traitor."

I heard Damiyun chuckle. "—never wanted—to betray my kind."

"—your time in a cell." Vel said.

"No." Damiyun's sharp voice drew my attention. "I will not be locked in a cell. I will not leave Lillyanna alone. You, of all people, should know how dangerous it is for her here."

My father pursed his lips, but said nothing.

I turned my thoughts back inward. This was wrong. Everything was wrong. I knew without a doubt he sent them, though I didn't know why. All this time I was able to avoid the Suppressors, only to have my father send them.

"Why were the Suppressors suddenly after me?" I interrupted Damiyun and Vel's conversation.

"They were after Damiyun."

I laughed. "And I just conveniently happened to be with him? Bullshit, Vel. You knew I was with him. You can't pretend you didn't. You're the fucking one who told him to find me."

"Lil—" Damiyun started.

I ignored him. "Why did you leave me?"

Vel sighed. "I told you. I did it to protect you. If you had any inkling I was alive, you would have searched for me. Word would have gotten back to the Suppressors, there was a child looking for me. A child claiming to be mine. They would have known you were a Wielder. They would have captured you."

"Spare me your lies."

He sighed. "Do you think I wanted to leave you?"

"Yes." Though it pained me to admit it. Seeing his daughter for the first time in ten Grand Passages didn't seem to be his highest priority once I had arrived.

"Lillyanna—"

"Fuck you, Vel." I leaped to my feet. Vel jumped to his, and Damiyun slowly rose as well.

"I would strongly suggest you reconsider whatever it is you're thinking of doing," my father said slowly. "You may be my daughter, but I will not hesitate to have you punished for your insolence. Your shock has worn off. Everything you do from now on will impact what happens to you. And to Damiyun."

I stalked across the room and left him at his sham of a family dinner. The sound of Damiyun's boots echoed off the walls as he followed and fell in step beside me. He said nothing, his presence a comfort, and my anger dissipated a bit. The corridors were quiet, only a handful of Suppressors coming and going, our steps silent as we walked to my room. We slipped inside and Damiyun sat on the edge of the bed and removed his shirt, wincing as the fabric pulled away and opened his wounds again. I inhaled sharply at the sight of dozens of bloody welts crisscrossing his back. At such a gruesome sight, I couldn't hold on to my rage.

"It looks worse than it is." He glanced over his shoulder at me, flashing a smile that looked more like a painful grimace. I knew he was lying. Pouring water into the washbasin, I brought it to the bed. After dipping a cloth in, I pressed it to his back. His body tensed, and he exhaled hard as I gingerly cleaned his wounds. My magic pulsed deep inside as I worked, pushing against the cracked block. I felt a few tendrils slip through, felt the pulsating hum, my fingertips vibrating. I placed a hand on his bare back and concentrated on sending a few tendrils through, picturing them weaving and wrapping around the wounds. Damiyun gasped, his body shuddering.

"What—?"

"I... I'm healing you." I watched the angry, bloody welts fade to light scars. I ran my hand over his back, shaking my head. He slipped off the bed and looked over his shoulder at his reflection in the mirror.

"How? Abraham blocked you. How?"

I shook my head. "I'm not sure. When the Suppressors came, when they were beating you, I felt the block crack with my anger. When I saw my father... it fractured more."

Damiyun sat back down on the bed.

"I felt something while I probed. I... I think I can break through the block Arden put on you."

I couldn't explain it, but I felt something. A barrier and a pulsing feeling trapped behind it. I had to at least try. If it didn't work, it didn't matter, but if it did...

"Give me your hands," I said as I held mine out. He placed his in mine and our fingers entwined. I locked eyes with him, sending a tendril of magic through and into him. I probed, coming up against the solid wall. Taking a deep breath, I pulsed more through. His eyes widened in shock, a grimace contorting his face.

"Wait—" he grunted.

I sent more through, poking the tendrils at the invisible barrier, sending more magic, pushing harder. Damiyun gripped my hands so hard I thought he would break them, but I didn't stop.

I continued to push, to probe, to wrap my magic around the unseen wall.

Until finally, it cracked, a spider web fracture forming, small waves of magic slipping through the breach. Damiyun released my hands, and I collapsed onto the bed, wiping the beads of sweat from my brow. I looked at Damiyun, whose eyes glowed faintly in the dim light, and watched the small flame dancing on his palm.

"How did you do that?" His eyes met mine.

"I don't know. It was like my magic was guiding me. I don't know how much I gave you."

"You gave me enough," he said, stretching out next to me. He pulled me into his arms and pressed his lips to my head.

"I think my father sent the Suppressors," I said, breaking the silence. "It did not surprise him to see us. There was a hot bath and a wardrobe full of clothes waiting."

"I agree. Something isn't right."

"I will find out what's going on," I said, yawning. "Why he would have hidden me, sent you to protect me, only to send them."

"If he'll even be forthcoming," Damiyun said.

"If he'll be forthcoming." I settled into his embrace, the nagging feeling something wasn't right, the thought my father was still lying to me about a great many things, weighing upon my shoulders.

NINETEEN
ABRAHAM

I HEARD VOICES AS I made my way back toward camp. Not just Lillyanna and Damiyun's voices.

I pulled the shadows, they darted to obscure me and I crept quietly forward, closer to the camp. There I saw Damiyun, and Lillyanna surrounded by Suppressors.

Sighing, I watched as he tried to cut them back. I admittedly felt a bit victorious when one kicked him in the stomach, and the mass descended on him. Chuckling, I sat back and watched him get beaten.

While I did not want Lillyanna taken, I knew this would serve as a lesson. I would gather them, but not before I let him spend some time with them. With his brother. I watched the Suppressors lead them off, then washed up and left camp. I had a high-stakes bargain I couldn't ignore.

THE TAVERN WAS BUSY. A bard played in the corner, and I scanned the room, my eyes going to Bones, Sam, and Lucas, who sat around a table in the corner.

"Abe," Lucas smiled as I pulled out a chair.

"Are you ready to lose?" I pulled out my pouch of coin and tossed it on the table.

Bones laughed. Pulling out a deck of cards, he began shuffling.

I raised an eyebrow. "Don't trust me?"

He shook his head as he dealt. "You always seem to win with your deck. I figured this would even the odds."

I laughed as I picked up my hand: four serpents and a knight.

It was far too early to win.

I tossed some coins in the pot, discarded all but one card and chose four new ones and looked at my hand: three banshees and two knights. Still a winning hand.

"You interested in a job, Abe?" Lucas said.

"How much does it pay?"

I tossed more coins into the pot and grabbed new cards.

Four serpents and a knight again.

"I fold," I said, tossing my cards down. Six eyes looked at me. "Fine. If you wish to see…" I revealed my hand and the three men groaned, tossing their cards down. I pulled the coin toward me and, feeling generous, divided the winnings between us.

"So, how much does this job pay?" I folded my arms on the table, eyes on Lucas.

"More than this pitiful pot." Lucas laughed.

"I'm listening."

"There's a shopkeeper who has been having trouble with some kids trying to shake him down for money."

I waved my hand. "That's nothing unusual. Why would this be our problem?"

"It's not," Lucas said, taking a long pull from the ale placed in front of him. "But I could use a bit more coin, since you keep wiping me out."

I looked at Bones and Sam. "And you?"

The two men shook their heads. "That's not our thing," Sam said. They both rose and bid us farewell.

I turned my attention back to Lucas. "And it's yours?"

Lucas sighed. "Maybe I'm tired of collecting souls. Perhaps for once, I want to do some good."

I laughed.

Lucas sat back and crossed his arms. "Why is that so difficult to believe?"

"You just said you wanted the coin." I pointed my tankard at him.

"True, but there's more. The man has a wife, and they threatened to kill her if he doesn't pay."

I sighed. Draining my ale, I stood up. "Where is this shopkeeper?"

Lucas smiled, and I followed him out of the tavern.

"MASTER RICTOR," LUCAS SAID as a gray-haired man opened the door. "I have someone who might be able to help you."

The man's eyes went to me, and I shouldered my way past him and into his house. It was a small dwelling. The eating area and living space commingled all in one room, along with what I presumed to be sleeping quarters blocked by a curtain. I looked around his poor and meager abode, doubting the coin earned would be as much as Lucas said, but I was here and willing to help. Or at least listen to his plight.

"Are you behind on your rent or taxes?" I got right to the point.

"I pay the Enforcers what they request."

"Hmmph. Lucas said they threatened harm to your wife. Sounds to me like you're behind," I said, moving in the door's direction.

I knew how the Enforcers worked. They were no different from the Suppressors. Threatening and killing to elicit cooperation was nothing new.

"Pay them what they require, and your wife won't be harmed," I said.

"Please." The man wrung his hands. I paused, glancing at Lucas, who stood off to the side. "I have a receipt that shows I am in good standing. These young'uns...the money they are demanding... it's more than I would make in a week. And my wife..."

I rubbed my eyes.

"I don't think they're truly Enforcers, either."

I frowned. "What makes you think that?"

He motioned to the couches and chairs, and we sat down. "They just don't seem like they are. Their uniforms look wrong, and I have never been bothered by the Enforcers."

I sighed. "Thank you for the information. Go to bed. Lucas and I will figure something out."

Rictor's shoulders relaxed. Nodding, he got up and disappeared behind the curtain. I scanned the room and, seeing a bottle of Serpent's Venom sitting on a sideboard, I got up and grabbed it. Pulling the cork out, I took a long drink, then passed the bottle to Lucas.

"So, you'll help?" Lucas held the bottle out to me.

I scratched my beard. "I suppose," I said, taking the bottle back. "Make a branding iron."

"What?" Lucas said.

I took another drink, wiping my mouth on my sleeve. "Make a branding iron. If these boys turn out to not be Enforcers, I will make them into real ones."

Lucas grinned as he rose from the chair. "You got it, chief," he said, crossing the small home and exiting into the night.

I sat back in my chair and sipped from the bottle. The low voices of Rictor and his wife in the bedroom behind the curtain punctuated the silence. I would accompany him to his shop and confront these children. If words would not sway them, I knew the iron would.

I WATCHED AS THE sun lit the sky, and I pulled myself out of the chair. Lucas had come back much later the evening prior with the branding iron he had made.

"Let's go," I said as Rictor stepped into the room.

We followed him out of his house and into the sleepy town. Stopping at the door of a bakery shop, Rictor inserted a key and led us inside the small establishment.

"Did they say when they would return?" I moved out of the way as two young women entered and slipped behind the counter. Tying aprons around their waists, they began the laborious task of lighting the ovens and making breads and pastries to sell. Lucas followed them into the back to place the branding iron in the fire, then settled back beside me.

Rictor shrugged. "One of them said late morning."

I glanced at Lucas, and we took a seat at a small table in front of the window. I scanned the road, which began filling with foot and horse traffic as the sun rose higher. As the hours passed, I began doubting the boys would come today, until I saw two youths dressed in white storming toward the shop. Yanking the door open, they stepped inside, glaring eyes searching the confined space.

They were young. One boy had blond hair and was thin, while the other was taller and dark-haired. They looked to be around twenty.

"Rictor." The tall boy swaggered further inside, hand resting on the hilt of his sword. Rictor appeared from in back, wiping his hands on his apron. I glanced at Lucas, and we rose to our feet.

"Do you have our coin?"

Rictor licked his lips, eyes flicking nervously to us, then back. "No," he said. The tall boy snarled.

"What you're asking for is more than I make in a week," Rictor said.

The two boys took a threatening step forward. "Did we not tell you the fate that will befall your most lovely wife if you refuse to pay?"

"I strongly advise you rethink your actions," I said, folding my arms.

His head whipped around, and his eyes narrowed on me. "Mind your business, old man." He placed his hand on the hilt of his sword, his accomplice mimicking him.

"This is my business," I said. I looked at both of them. They weren't Enforcers; their badly made uniforms confirmed as much.

"I wonder what the real Enforcers would do if they knew two boys were going around impersonating them," I said. "Extorting shop owners for money. Threatening harm to women. My guess, they will not take too kindly to it."

His eyes narrowed. "We are not impostors. We are a part of the Order."

I laughed. "Are you now? That's not even their insignia. And it's on the wrong side." I poked the right side of his chest, where a scarlet "E" was drawn. Grabbing him by his collar, I pulled him toward me and yanked up his shirt. "Where is your brand?" The boy struggled, taken aback at my strength.

Lucas rushed into the back and grabbed the red-hot branding iron from its spot, handing it to me. I held it inches from the boy's chest. His eyes widened, and he struggled in my grip.

"If you wish to play at being an Enforcer, at least make it believable," I whispered, bringing the iron close, touching it to his skin for a brief moment. He howled in pain and thrashed around, desperate to free himself.

"Please," he begged in a pathetic tone. "Don't hurt us. We didn't mean nothing by it. We just wanted money. We weren't going to hurt no one." Tears ran down his cheeks.

"Pathetic children," I shoved him away. "If I again hear word of two boys playing Enforcer and threatening shopkeepers, not only will I brand you, but I will deliver you both personally to the Compound. Believe me when I say they do not take kindly to impostors."

The color drained from both boys' faces, and they shook at my words.

"Get out and pray we do not cross paths again." I barked.

They nodded, then bolted out the door, sprinting as fast as they could up the road and out of sight.

Lucas's laughter broke the momentary silence. "Damn, Abe," he snorted. "Those boys all but shit themselves."

I chuckled.

"Thank you for your help," Rictor said. "I—I don't have coin yet, but I could give you the day's earnings tomorrow."

I sighed. I knew this man to not have the coin for payment, and I wasn't about to take his day's wages. "Don't worry about coin," I said. Lucas opened his mouth, and I cut him off with a shake of my head.

"If it wouldn't be too much trouble, you can pay us in some pastries. It's been a long time since I've had a decent one, and I do admit I have a bit of a sweet tooth."

Rictor smiled and nodded, running to the back of the shop, and coming out with a bag of day-old sweets. I grabbed the payment and Lucas, and I left the shop, bidding each other farewell.

I walked back to the tavern to spend a blessedly quiet and serene day to myself with a bag full of sweets and a tankard full of ale.

I CROSSED THE TAVERN that was slowly filling with patrons, finding a table in a corner. Ordering a flagon of ale, I settled back in the chair. Opening the bag of sweets, I pulled out a chocolate pastry and took a bite, delighted to find out it was filled with a sweet, buttery cream. I watched people file into the tavern, taking up tables, ordering food and drink. The sounds competed. Voices louder, the clink of mugs, and then feet stomping.

Abraham. A voice hissed in my mind. It was Damiyun.

Yes, Damiyun? I said. Fishing around in the bag, I pulled out another treat. A powdered pastry filled with a tart jam. Rictor did not disappoint with his selection.

Where the fuck are you? Lil and I, we were taken by the Suppressors.

I chuckled. *How surprising.*

Anger rolled through the bond. *Come get us. We can't stay here, we have a task to fulfill.*

I snorted as I licked the powder and sticky jam off my fingers. *That didn't concern you when you decided to take your ridiculous detour and go home.* I said, taking a sip of ale.

Abraham—

I'll get you, I said, then closed the connection.

While it is true, time is of the essence with our task and the ridiculous stop Damiyun insisted on taking had wasted precious time, I had warned him about the Suppressors. I knew it was only a matter of time before they captured them, but he was pigheaded and refused to see reason or danger. Though I did not want the girl in that place, I knew Damiyun would protect her still, even there. I would let them sit. Let them squirm for a bit, if only to make my point clear to him.

Flagging the serving wench over, I ordered another ale and bit into my last pastry. The voices in the tavern rose, snippets of conversation reaching my ears. Most were about mundane things like farming and trade, though my ears perked up at some interesting chatter at a table in front of me. Sitting back in my chair, I crossed my ankles and settled in to listen.

"—resurrecting the temple to the gods," a deep voice said. The man was graying. Brown spots dotted his sun weathered skin. His companion was younger, brown, curly hair and sun-kissed skin.

The other man laughed. "Whatever for? No one has worshipped that lot in hundreds of Grand Passages."

The gray-haired man took a sip of his drink. "Fenter said Samanka came to him in his dreams. Told him to resurrect the temple. If he did, he would be blessed with a long life and bounty."

I lowered my drink. Samanka? Why would she be meddling in mortal affairs? What were they up to?

The brown-haired man choked on his drink. "The Goddess of Dreams came to him?" He threw his head back and laughed. "You know as well as I that Fenter is a drunk. Why would any god visit him?"

The white-haired man leveled his gaze on the other. "He was a High Devout."

"Whose faith left him when the temples were desecrated."

"As did everyone's. Once the temple is resurrected, people will come back around. They will worship the gods again. Samanka said as much." The gray-haired man took a drink. "I left an offering to Felicity, hoping she would do something about my failing crops. The offering was gone and since then, my crops have been growing. Better than any I've ever planted. They're coming back."

I shook my head. What in the Abyss did any of this mean? Were others resurrecting the temples in the hopes to bring the gods' favor back? If they were to be worshipped again... My blood ran cold. That would mean Themesis would be worshipped by some. Those whose hearts and souls were dark and evil. Their words, their love and devotion, would weaken his binds further.

Fuck.

I hoped the words of the person named Fenter were that of a rambling drunkard. Draining my mug, I reached for the fresh drink that was placed before me. I gazed around the busy tavern, watching the serving wenches with trays balanced on their heads and tankards of ale in hands, weave their way through the crowd. Laughter echoed off the wall, as did some angry curses.

"...cattle slaughtered in my field."

My ears picked up another conversation to my right. Three men sat at a table drinking ale and eating stew.

"Aye," a redheaded man said around a mouthful of food. "My chickens too. A hundred of them found stone dead."

A blond hair man nodded as he took a long drink. "My animals would rather not be left out at night. Soon as the sun begins to go down, it's a stampede to the barn. Not that it keeps them safe. Two kids and my best workhorse were torn wide open. They were bled dry, too."

"Aye," the redhead said. "Mine as well."

"And mine." The first man nodded.

I frowned. This news was disturbing to say the least. The only thing that would do that was—

"Demons, I say," the first man said, pushing his black hair off his forehead. "I hear them at night wailing and screaming. It's enough to loosen your bowels."

I hadn't heard any demons at night, though that's not to say these men were wrong. The decimation of the animals, the lack of blood, was enough to make me believe and cause me much concern. Finishing my ale, I tossed coin on the table and rose.

The conversations I heard rankled me. I needed to digest their words and unravel the mystery of the gods, and the demons that are coming forth.

TWENTY
DAMIYUN

THE SOUND OF POUNDING on the door startled me. Hearing a noise outside our chamber the night prior made me realize I had to be extra vigilant and alert. I had placed a chair against it and holed up for the night. I had made it clear to Vel I was not going to leave Lillyanna alone. Not in this place.

He wasn't pleased, though I reminded him I was her Keeper, and my duties would not end, no matter where she was. I got up from the chair and opened the door to Marcus.

"Elder Castille would like his daughter to join him for the morning meal," he said, then held out a bundle of clothes. "Your uniform. Be sure to wear it," he said, backing away and moving down the hall. I closed the door and turned, seeing Lil propping herself up on her elbow with a yawn. The blanket slipped down, and I took in the glimpse of creamy white flesh, desire flowing through me. I crossed over to the bed, crawling across it to where she lay, and pushed her back and pulled the covers completely off. I slid my hands down her body, my lips, and tongue tasting her. She writhed beneath me.

"I need you, Damiyun," she panted, hands fumbling with my belt. I groaned, flicking my tongue over her nipples, slipping a hand between her legs, feeling her soft wetness as she gently stroked me.

Someone knocked again, and I cursed, pulling away from her. Wrenching the door open, I glared at Marcus, who again stood on the other side.

"Elder Castille grows impatient. Hurry."

I slammed the door, glancing at Lil, who gave a frustrated sigh before padding over to the wardrobe to select a dress. I stripped out of my clothes and pulled on the uniform. I could tell she wasn't happy with it, and neither was I, but I had to play the part until we could leave. I knew Abraham would come for us. What I didn't know, however, was when.

W E ENTERED THE DINING room and Lil took a seat at the table. I took a chair across the room to give them some privacy. I looked around the area, a place where I had shared many a meal with Vel.

I had been a Regulator, and he was grooming me to be an Elder. An honor I did not want. I was relieved whenever he allowed me to leave. Allowed me the freedom of not being tied to the Compound. Of not having to wear the Sigaa'Lean.

And, while I had turned informant, I vowed I would do whatever necessary to never come back here again. As it were, I found myself in the place I despised most with the woman I had tried my best to protect. Hardly a rousing success story. Lil drew my attention as she rose from her seat. Pulling myself out of the chair, I followed her as she brushed past me. We walked in silence, her brow furrowed and eyes dark and troubled.

"Are you alright?"

She looked up at me, her eyes sad. Taking her arm, I guided her to a door and pushed it open. Crossing the empty room, I pulled out two chairs from beneath a table. Straddling one, I motioned to the second. She sat with a sigh.

"Talk to me, Lillyanna. What did Vel say to you?"

She chewed her bottom lip. "That your intentions aren't so altruistic. That trusting you was a mistake."

I shook my head. I didn't know what game Vel was playing. His lack of surprise made me wonder...

"What?"

I inhaled. "This wasn't an accident. You were meant to come here," I said slowly, realization washing over me like an icy wave. "Your father sent me to keep an eye on you so... So when he sent the Suppressors, it was under the pretense of capturing me, when in reality it was you he wanted."

She frowned. "He said they didn't know who I was. The Suppressors didn't know he had a daughter."

"Of course, he would have told you that. He wants you to think I was the one who put you in danger. He's throwing mud on my face and telling you to bathe in it." My eyes met hers. "And it appears it's working." Vel must have another plan going. Between her mother and father, while I didn't know the whole of it, they had designs on Lillyanna. The Suppressors hunted Wielders. Some they convinced with the most unpleasant means to join their ranks in hunting other Wielders and others, they tortured and kill.

"Let's go. I'll show you around a bit," I said, rising from the chair. Reaching down, I grasped her hands and pulled her to her feet. I showed her around the Compound, which was littered with Suppressors. The place was a stone fortress. High walls enclosed the grounds, tall gates manned by guards in the front, turrets at the four corners and a high tower with a bell graced the entrance.

The foyer was grand. High, domed ceiling, a statue of Zachariah Farnsworth sat in the middle. Paintings of past Elders and Council Members lined the walls. Smaller busts of descendants of Zachariah sat on rich, oak tables throughout the building. The black marble floor present throughout the Compound was always polished to a mirror shine.

As we walked through the halls, some Suppressors snarled at me. Others spat on me. Most called me a deserter. I shook off the jeers, wiped the spit off my clothes and continued down the hall. We walked on, the sound of our boots on the black marble floor echoed in the silence. Portraits of past Elders and Eminences, battles with Wielders and with the gods hung on the walls. Lillyanna slowed down as we passed, her eyes appraising each painting. Had I not defected, my portrait would have hung on the wall with the past Elders.

I showed her various rooms in the Compound. One room we stopped at had desks lined up in neat rows with a large oak desk at the front.

"Is this a classroom?"

I nodded. "It's where the recruits are indoctrinated, forced to listen to the instructor preach about the goodness of the Order for twelve to fifteen hours a day." I walked into the room where I too once sat. Memories flooded my mind, and I quickly pushed them away. "Recruits are forced to repeat over and over the Five Principles of the Order and the one hundred articles until they knew it by heart, and if you stumbled or forgot?" I shook my head and looked at Lil. "You were beaten with a willow switch and forced to stand in the corner with a stack of heavy books on your arms for the duration of class. And don't you dare drop a book. If you did, you were sent to my brother for further punishment." I winced at the memory of being beaten for the minor infraction.

"That's horrible," Lil whispered. She looked up at me. "Do you remember them?"

"Unfortunately, yes. Much like the brand, it is something that will never leave me."

"I'm sorry."

I squeezed her hand. "Don't be. It's part of who I am," I said, pulling her away from the room and down the hall. "Let's get some air."

"Wait," she said, coming to a stop at a door. Dropping my hand, she went inside the room. I followed behind, chuckling when I saw what brought her to an abrupt halt. We had passed the library.

It was a large, round room. The high ceiling made of stained-glass, the panels depicting a violent battle. On one side were the gods and an army of Wielders. On the other, the Suppressors. The vision was dark and bloody. A depiction of a time past.

I looked around the room. High bookshelves lined the walls, with a ladder on rails to help reach the uppermost shelves. A black marble fireplace sat to the right of the room with an overstuffed couch, chairs and tables arranged in front. Other chairs and couches were scattered about the room, a comfortable place to sit and read.

Lil turned in circles, her eyes wide in awe as she looked about the room. "My father liked to read," she said, crossing to a shelf, her fingers caressing the leather-bound books. "He taught me at a very early age, and I devoured books. Once a week, he'd take me to the bookstore and let me buy two books, but that was never enough. I always finished them before it was time to go again. He never let me read any of his. He claimed they were too adult for me. Do you enjoy reading?" She turned and looked at me.

I crossed the room to where she stood, pulling a book off the shelf, and flipping through the pages. "Yes. It was my only way to escape my life," I said, putting the book back. Lillyanna smiled sadly, then made her way down the aisle, tilting her head to read titles, occasionally taking books off the shelf and looking through them.

"What's this?" She hefted a thick book in her hands. Reaching out, I took it from her, my fingers tracing the two swords crossed over a scarlet "S" on the front.

"It's the History of the Suppressors," I said, crossing the room to the chairs in front of the cold hearth. Settling down on the couch, I propped the book on my lap and opened it.

"Who's that?" She pointed to a picture of a man with flowing blond hair. He stood with his back straight, hand curled around the hilt of his sword. His dark eyes peered out at the artist, his black uniform a stark contrast against the sterile background.

"Zachariah Farnsworth. He's the founder of the Order."

"He looks surly."

I laughed. "You could say that."

I turned the page which listed the Five Principles of the Order, the next ones, I knew, listed the one hundred articles. The sound of voices chanting them in unison filled my head. My arms ached as though I were standing in the corner holding a stack of books. I quickly shut the cover and placed the book on the table. Silence stretched between us.

"Is that what I was born to do? Lead an army of death and destruction?" Her voice startled me. I followed her eyes as she looked up at the ceiling. I studied the images. Suppressors fought against the gods and Wielders. The Order opposed the gods or had at one time. How had a Suppressor mated with a goddess? I felt her eyes on me, and I looked away like the coward I am. I couldn't tell her the truth. Tell her she had to die to seal Themesis' binds. Nor could I tell her that her death would be by my hand.

Laughter echoed in my head. *You will fail, Damiyun. You will hesitate and fail. You will grovel at my feet. Serve me and do my bidding. She will be my queen,* Themesis purred. *You will watch as she pleases me in every way.*

"What's wrong?"

I looked at Lil and shook my head, forcing a smile. "Headache."

Lies. They keep stacking up. She will hate you. She will fear you. She will be mine.

Her eyes searched mine for a moment. She glanced up at the ceiling again. "I want to find my mother," she said, eyes coming back to me.

I blinked. "Whatever for?"

"She has answers."

"What could she possibly say to make things different?"

The truth.

She shrugged. "I don't know."

"I'm not sure if that's a good idea, Lil. I don't know she has the answers you need."

"But she has answers."

I rubbed my face, weariness settling in. "Lil—"

"Please, Damiyun. I need to find her."

I sighed. "That won't be difficult. I know who—and where—she is."

"What do you mean, you know who she is? How do you know? What's going on, Damiyun?"

Weariness settled in my body. "Your mother is Felicity, the Goddess of Nature."

Her eyebrows furrowed for a moment, her stunned expression turning to one of amusement, and she laughed. "Come on, Damiyun. You can do better than that. You can't expect me to believe you." She laughed again.

"It's the truth, Lillyanna."

"Hmm. So what? She just popped down into the mortal world looking for someone to father her child and just happened to meet Vel?"

"A rather simple way of putting it, but in a sense yes."

"Why wouldn't she just have a child with one of her own?"

"Because the gods can't meddle in the affairs of mortals. While what is happening—what will happen—affects them, the biggest impact will be on mankind."

She shook her head. "You're speaking in riddles, Damiyun."

I ran a hand through my hair with a sigh. Rising from my chair, I made my way to the shelves at the back of the room. It didn't take me long to find the book I wanted. The Suppressors were an orderly bunch. I pulled the book off the shelf and looked at the cover. There was no title, though I knew what it was. It was a book about the gods. I ran my hand over the figures on the cover. Sarlay, the

God of War. Leoatle, the God of the Sea. Valtra, the God of Fire. Euphina, the Goddess of Healing. Dhala, the Goddess of Fertility. Samanka, the Goddess of Dreams. All the gods surrounded a picture of Felicity, the Goddess of Nature. The only one missing was Themesis, the God of Knowledge, now ruler of the Abyss. Tucking the book beneath my arm, I crossed the room and settled back in my chair. Propping the book on my lap, I opened it and flipped through the pages until I found a series of pictures depicting the gods and the subsequent war.

"There was a time when the Fallen One—Themesis—had a seat among the gods. He was the God of Knowledge." I said, tapping a picture of him. "He was also a seducer, a master manipulator, and a narcissist. He enjoyed lording over man and took great pleasure in punishing those who displeased him." I turned the page, which depicted Themesis holding a whip, ready to strike a mortal tied to a post. "He fed off mortals. Their fears. Their desires and sins. He grew stronger with every prayer he granted. He craved the power, the control he had, and wanted to be the only god worshipped. He launched a plan to make it happen, manipulating lesser gods to his side, and waged a war." I looked up at the stained-glass ceiling. Lil's eyes followed. "Lives were lost, but the gods prevailed."

"The gods can die?" Lil said, drawing my attention back.

"The lesser gods, yes, though I suppose if you were to lop the head off a deity, the chances of survival would be slim."

Lil giggled, and I continued. "They threw Themesis, and those who helped him, into the Abyss, entombed in the obsidian of Kraagswell Mountain." I turned the page. The next picture was of Themesis being dragged to the Abyss, forced into the obsidian tomb that would become his home. "Themesis' tomb was sealed with magic. The gods needed to keep him beneath the Abyss, so they blessed some humans with magic. Their procreation created more Wielders, and the life and breath of them is what kept the tomb sealed." I closed the book, placed it on the table and picked up the History of the Suppressors. "As time went on, he was forgotten. The gods became a distant memory. No one prayed to them or worshipped them," I said. I opened the book and flipped through, finding the chapter I needed.

"Why? What would make people stop?"

I looked at Lil and shrugged. "I'm not rightly sure. I suppose people no longer believed in their existence. Perhaps they felt they were abandoned. Or maybe they resented the gods because they were jealous of Wielders."

"I can understand that," she said. "I used to pray to the gods to bring my father home. In a way, I felt as though they had abandoned me when he never came back."

My heart wrenched at her admission. "I'm sorry, Lil."

She smiled weakly. "It's alright. Go on."

I looked down at the book, running my finger across the words on the page as I read. "Those with magic are bad omens. The law states that every Wielder must be hunted and turned in. Those who do not join will be executed. Every Wielder captured will be sterilized, including the children." Sadness filled me at the last words I read. At the reminder that I would never be a father. It was always a cold blow. I looked at Lil. "You are considered lucky if you survive the procedure." Though I couldn't agree.

"Why would they do that?" Lillyanna scoffed, a screwed up confused expression on her face.

"Because only Wielders can bear a Wielder. As long as one person in a union has magic, their child will be born with it too."

"But I was born."

"Yes."

"How?"

I frowned. "I... I'm not rightly sure. Perhaps he was taken after Felicity came. Or maybe the sterilization didn't work. It's not a pleasant procedure. I wouldn't exactly say those who do it are adept at the craft."

"Did it work for you?"

I laughed. "I haven't had any woman claim I'm the father of her child, so I'd say yes."

She sighed. "But what does this have to do with me and the Goddess of Nature supposedly being my mother?"

I looked back down at the book. "The more Wielders killed, the weaker the binds on the Fallen One's tomb will become," I read. "The Suppressors will bring him forth to rule the world." I looked up at Lil. "You were born to stop him."

She laughed. "Right. I forgot she popped down to make an unstoppable baby."

I rubbed my eyes. "As a Wielder, your father is a force of nature. He can manipulate the weather and use it. Call the lightning. Cause a raging storm. Harness the wind and use cold to freeze an enemy to death. Your mother—she *is* nature. A child born of such magic would be powerful." My eyes never left her face. "And dangerous. Like every Wielder, along with your own goddess given magic, you also possess that of both your parents. As long as one parent is a Wielder, the child will be born one as well. Because of who your parents are, the magic inside you replicates what they each have and there should be something more, something of your own."

She folded her arms and raised an eyebrow. "You said the gods can't meddle in the affairs of mortals."

"They can't."

"But isn't making a child with the sole purpose of defeating Themesis meddling?"

"I suppose it could be viewed that way, though the gods are adept at twisting the truth to suit their needs." *And make it so you can't say no, even if you wanted to.*

"How is it you know all of this? How do you know so much about me?"

Because I fucked your mother, and she put me in charge of you. "Felicity found me and tasked me with being your Keeper. My job is to keep you safe and take you to Kraagswell Mountain."

"Alright, so suppose this tale is true." She looked very much like she did not believe it. "Why choose you?"

To redeem myself. And because I spent time in her bed. It was her way of tormenting me. She knew I would never breathe a word of our prior relationship to Lil, so why not put me in charge of the one person who could never know? "I don't know."

She sat quietly for a while as she absorbed what I told her. "I still want to see her. How does one meet a goddess?"

I sighed and rose to my feet. "Fine," I said against my better judgment. "When we leave here, we will travel to S'aehe to see her." Abraham would not be happy about this. Though, his ire was not what I feared. Felicity might reveal our relationship and then Lil might leave. Take off again.

I locked those thoughts away and held my hand out to her, pulling her to her feet and walking toward the door.

"Thank you, Damiyun," she said. "How are we getting out of here?"

"Don't worry about that," I said, pulling the door open. "Let's go outside. I could use some air."

W E WALKED THROUGH THE halls to a door that led to the courtyard. Walking down a worn-out stone path, we took a seat beneath a tree.

"They're taking Suppressors at a young age," she said, nodding to a corner of the courtyard where a young child of about four was playing in the sun.

"That's Ghent," I said. I had run into the precocious boy when Arden took me to his torture tower. "His father was an Elder. He now sits on the High Council. His mother abandoned him, so he lives here."

"When will he become a Suppressor?"

"Thirteen or fourteen. He comes from a long line of Suppressors. His blood can be traced back to Zachariah. He'll become an Elder and sit on the High Council as well."

"I feel sorry for him being forced to live here. Not having anyone to play with."

I shrugged. "He gets to play. The others play games with him on their off time. They're like a family to him. Brothers. Other children have been in Ghent's position. They do alright."

"It's still not right." She whispered, and I couldn't rightly disagree, but what could I do?

"Why does Arden hate you?"

The change of topic surprised me, and I answered bluntly. "Because I killed our mother. She labored for a day, and after I was born, they couldn't stop the bleeding. I took her from him." I paused, watching Ghent chase after a Suppressor, his giggles drifting on the breeze. "He tortured me every chance he could get. The pain he inflicts, it's indescribable. He took great pleasure in watching our father beat me."

"Why wasn't Arden beaten as well?"

"He could hide his abilities. His magic requires physical contact. It wasn't so easy for me. Mine was difficult to control. I was very young when I discovered it. Felt the constant pulsing inside and a pull toward fire. When I got angry, it would burst out." I sighed. "It's been a long time since I have seen my brother. I have no doubt he purposely inserted himself in the search."

I stood and pulled Lil to her feet, and we made our way back to our room.

"Why did they call you a deserter?" she asked after the door was closed.

"I told you why."

She crossed the room to the window. "But you're one of them again."

"No, I'm not," I said, though in truth, despite my defection, I would always be a part of the Order. I could never truly leave. "If I didn't play my part, I would be locked away in a cell, or executed," I said, rubbing my neck. That would be a death even Abraham couldn't pull me from. "And you... You would be in far more danger than you realize." I slipped my arms around her waist, and she leaned into me. "I care about you, Lillyanna. I care far more than I should."

She turned around and pulled me close, lips brushing mine. "I care about you too." She whispered. "How are we getting out of here?"

"Abraham should be coming."

"When?"

"Hopefully not much longer."

TWENTY-ONE
LILLYANNA

I stood outside my father's study. Taking a deep breath, I knocked, then entered. He sat behind his desk, head bent over papers, but he looked up at the sound of my shoes on the floor. A smile spread across his face, and he rose gracefully to his feet.

"Lillyanna." He glided across the room and poured two drinks. He motioned to the seating area in front of the large fireplace, and I watched him with narrow eyes as I took a seat, taking the glass filled with wine he held out. I couldn't shake the nervousness, the nagging feeling of something not being right as I sat there. Damiyun was out on one of his many patrols, and I wished he could have come with me. Even if he didn't sit with us, his presence would have granted me at least a silent show of support.

"Father." I adjusted my skirts and folded my legs beneath me. As I sipped my drink, I studied my father. Though it had been ten Grand Passages since I had seen him, he hadn't changed much, and my heart ached. Memories surfaced as if from a deep pool, one of his big hand clutching mine as we walked through our village. Another of his strong arms holding me close, and the soothing warmth of his body as he cuddled me upon his lap. He was reading me *"The Story of Jayne"* for the thousandth time without complaint. I pushed the memories away and glanced around the room to ground me. "Why am I here?"

"You were never meant to be caught. You just happened to be with Damiyun, and you being a Wielder..." He shrugged.

Right.

"They were patrolling the village at times when there weren't any scheduled patrols. I was called out." My mind went back to that night, which seemed like a hundred Grand Passages ago. How they didn't go after Damiyun. How they demanded he give me over to them. The hair on the back of my neck rose. My flesh broke out in bumps.

"They saw me with Damiyun. They wanted nothing to do with him. Only me. You sent them after me."

He sighed. "No, I didn't, Lillyanna. Why would I do that? I left to protect you. They must have thought he was still an informant." He said, waving his hand.

"Bullshit."

A hurt look crossed his face. "Why would I lie to you?"

I put my glass down and crossed my arms. "Why did you leave me? Why was it imperative to protect me? Why couldn't you have kept me safe yourself?"

He refilled our glasses and sat back down, propping an ankle on a knee. "Your mother is the Goddess of Nature."

"I know. Damiyun told me about her."

His eyebrows rose in surprise.

"You didn't think he would?"

He pursed his lips and cleared his throat. "When I met her... she took a mortal form. After you were born, she disappeared. Then one day, she came back. But not in the form she took when I first met her. She appeared in her true form. When I realized how powerful you were... I knew you would be sought after. Hunted by those who would cause you harm. They'd use you—use your magic—in terrible ways. I had to protect you." He smiled, a look that better resembled a grimace.

"Am I not in a harmful place now?"

He glanced at me for a moment, then his eyes dropped to the table as he fiddled with his glass. "Of course not. You are in the safest place you can be. I will take care of you, Lillyanna."

"Like you took care of me for the past ten Grand Passages?"

He reached out and gripped my hand. "Leaving you was the only choice I had. I cloaked your magic to keep you safe. I am a Suppressor. An Elder. No one knew about you."

I pulled away. "But now they do. Why did you join? How were you allowed to leave? To not live within the walls of this place?"

"I was taken when I was very young. They came into the house, dragged me out of bed and brought me here. Though I can't be certain, I suspect they had... to encourage my mother to turn me in. And my father?" He shrugged. "I think they agreed to let him be if he let them take me. A child is far more impressionable than an adult. As to how I was able to leave, well, I am an Elder. We are not obligated to remain within the confinements of the Compound. Some choose to do so, but I did not. How do you think I kept you a secret? You don't really think I would have brought you here, do you?"

I chewed my lip, my thoughts going to my conversation with Damiyun. "How was I born if they sterilize Wielders?"

He shrugged. "It doesn't always work."

Right. He had an answer for everything. "Do you believe the garbage you spew?"

Silence.

"That's a yes."

He ran a hand over his face, fingers tapped the table. "I was young. When you're told every day your kind is bad, that you're bad, you will eventually believe it."

"You're not young any longer, Vel, yet you still believe. Do you feel I'm evil? An abomination? Do you think you're an abomination? Why aren't all Suppressors with magic just snuffing themselves out?"

He reached out to me again, and I crossed my arms, closing myself off to him. A hurt look flashed in his eyes. "I love you, Lillyanna."

"So much so, you left me."

He refused to meet my eyes. "To protect you. I kept them from finding you."

"But they did anyway. What difference would it have made if I was captured then or now? I am still in the same place."

Again, his gaze wouldn't meet mine. "That is because of Damiyun."

I shook my head. "I would have been caught if I hadn't gone with him that night. He kept me from them."

He chuckled. "Damiyun has a silver tongue. He was an informant for us."

"He told me everything about being a Suppressor."

He raised an eyebrow. "And you still don't question why he was in your village?"

I said nothing, though I believed Damiyun far more than I believed my father. While I knew Damiyun still held some secrets, he was slowly opening up to me, and I had to trust his words were the truth. He had nothing to gain by lying, but my father did.

"Whatever he told you is a lie. He is taking you to be Blood-Bound to Themesis. Once that happens, he will be free."

"And how do I know what you say isn't a lie?" I glared at him. "Why do I feel like I am a part of some game you're playing?"

"You are letting your feelings for Damiyun cloud your judgment. Do not get too wrapped up with him, Daughter. He will hurt you. He hurts everyone he's close to." It was the same thing Abraham said, and hearing it from my father upset me more than I wanted to admit.

I slammed my glass on the table. "I am quite aware of that, Father. Tell me more about my mother. What is she like? How did you meet?" With a deep breath, I steered the conversation away from Damiyun. I still couldn't quite digest the fact the Goddess of Nature was my mother. I was part god. I wanted to laugh at the thought and yet, I also felt the truth. The magic I wielded was strong, and the things Damiyun and I worked on at Pine Crest Manor. They made me believe I had some earthly power coursing through my veins.

My father sat back in his chair; a soft smile lit his lips. "Beautiful. Kind. She was coy, a seductress." He chuckled. "Gods know it was she who seduced me. I couldn't say no to her. It was as though she had cast a spell on me. Enchanted me." He shook his head. "As to how we met, she showed up on my doorstep in the middle of a raging rainstorm, soaked to the bone. Something had spooked her horse. The animal threw her and fled. She had walked for miles before happening upon my home. So, I brought her in, dried her off and, well..." His voice trailed, leaving the details of their dalliance vague. Thank my mother. I didn't need to hear it.

I sighed. When had I thought my father was so honest and good? Looking at him, he seemed cryptic and oily, a snake with a forked tongue. "Weren't you angry at her deception? She came to you in her mortal form for the sole purpose of seducing you and becoming with child."

"I was in love."

"So, it didn't matter."

"No. Regardless of what form she chose to take, I loved her."

"Weren't you angry she left you with a baby to care for?" I swallowed back the sickness that rose in my throat over the thought of being abandoned not once, but twice.

"I was hurt, yes. I admit it was difficult trying to balance my duties here while taking care of a young child, but I managed."

"Did you leave me alone then, too? You had no problem doing that when I was twelve, and you wanted to keep me hidden."

He sighed. "Lillyanna—"

"Did you even ask her to stay when she came back? Be a mother to me? A wife to you?"

His blue eyes met mine. "I did, yes. But she couldn't."

"Wouldn't," I shot back. I couldn't imagine abandoning a child I birthed. To leave as though they didn't matter. Twice. "Did she love me? Didn't she want me?" Tears pricked my eyes and I blinked them away. "Didn't you want me?"

He reached out and clasped my hand. As much as I wanted to snatch it back, I didn't. "Of course, I wanted you. How can you think I didn't? You mean everything to me. That's why I kept you a secret. That's why I hid you. I love you, Lillyanna. Felicity did too. I am happy we have been reunited. I can take care of you now. Keep you safe."

I pulled my hand back and stood. "I can take care of myself. I have for a long time, thanks to you. May I go?"

He sat back, shoulders slumping, and his face fell. "Of course."

Nodding, I marched out of the room. I strode through the halls and made my way out to the courtyard. The more I spoke with Father, the more confused I became. He answered my questions with questions, continually throwing Damiyun into the mix. Futile attempts to make me mistrust him.

I knew, despite what Father said, I wasn't safe here. He wasn't going to take care of me. I felt that knowledge deep within my bones, though what my father's true intentions were, I couldn't guess. No one leaves a child out of love, not like he had.

My mind went to what he had told me about my mother. It didn't feel right. Nothing about his story felt right. If Felicity had loved me, she would have stayed. If my father had loved me and wanted to protect me, he would have fled to another village. A Non town where Suppressors didn't often patrol. Mother and Father, did either one of them understand, care to understand what those terms meant?

Groaning, I sat beneath a tree, and watched the Suppressors train. Ghent tottered about after them, waving a stick. They laughed and playfully fought with the child, who squealed with delight. A shadow fell over me, and I looked up to see Arden looming above. My blood ran cold as he squatted down before me.

"Well, well. If it isn't Damiyun's mouthy little cunt." A cold smile crossed his face. "I do hope he decides to defect again. I have been in need of a new plaything, and you look like a joy to break."

"Leave her alone, Arden," Damiyun said, stalking up behind his brother. Arden rose to his feet, blue eyes clashing with Damiyun's gray ones.

"You can't be with her all the time, Brother. And what if an accident were to cause your untimely demise?" He glanced at me, and I shivered beneath his cold stare. "Sure, such an event would prove lucrative for me." He smiled as if ice had formed in his soul. I shuddered as he continued to speak. "Oh, I'd keep your Lillyanna here and make her my toy."

Damiyun glared at him, hand curling around the hilt of his sword.

Arden laughed. "Try it, Brother." He took a step closer. "You have never been a match for me." He glanced at me again and smiled. "See you later, Love," he said, as he sauntered away.

Damiyun folded his lean body down onto the ground beside me and sat back against the tree. "What did he say to you?"

I turned my head toward him. His face was drawn, and lines marred his eyes. Blood spattered his face and clothing. I didn't want to know whose it was. He rested his head against the trunk.

"He hopes you defect. And he wants a new plaything. What does he mean?"

He closed his eyes. "My brother likes to keep women as pets. He thrives on control and dominance and loves nothing more than to have a submissive woman to whom he can do whatever he pleases."

I shivered at his words and vowed I would kill him first. The violence of the thought surprised me, but I immediately knew I meant it.

"How did things go with your father?"

I sighed. "He told me... He told me Felicity came back once, but not in her mortal form. She told him who she was. Who I was and what I was destined to do. That's why he left. It just... doesn't add up. What did I do wrong?"

Damiyun pulled me close. "You didn't do anything wrong. Trust me. I know a thing or two about terrible fathers."

"He said he loved me but—if he did, he wouldn't have left me."

"I'm sure he did. He's... He's just not the same person you once knew." He smoothed back a lock of hair and cupped my chin. "He's a Suppressor, an Elder at that. He's so far gone, I don't even think he knows what's right anymore."

I pulled away and hugged myself, giving him a sidelong look. "He says you're taking me to Themesis to be Blood-Bound. That I'm going to free him."

"And you believe that?"

"I don't know what to believe, Damiyun. You've hardly told me anything, either. I'm supposed to stop Themesis, which seems like it should take time and training, but you seem to think I should just know what to do. My father doesn't really answer my questions, nor do you. He only tries to make me mistrust you, but I don't trust him either."

He took my chin and turned my head to look at him, gray eyes intense. "You have no reason to mistrust me, Lil. I promise you this."

I nodded, knowing that out of anyone here, Damiyun was truly the only one I could trust. Leaning back against the tree, Damiyun slipped his arm around me and pulled me close. We watched the Suppressors train, watched Ghent chase after them as we discussed how we were going to escape. Damiyun seemed to think Abraham was going to come and rescue us, but I wasn't so sure.

I needed to come up with a plan of escape. I would not just sit here waiting for things to happen to me.

W HILE WE WERE STUCK at the Compound, Damiyun and I continued working with my magic, as little as it was. We were in our room, standing out on the balcony looking over the Compound.

"Alright," Damiyun said, crossing his arms. "Make it rain."

I bit my lip. "Are you sure? What if I call the lightning?"

Yes, my queen. Call it. Strike Damiyun down and then come to me. I shook my head at the voice. At what I knew was Themesis.

"I'm here, Lil. I won't let you. Now, do it."

I took a deep, steadying breath, and exhaled slowly. I glanced at Damiyun who nodded in encouragement. The thought of calling the lightning again didn't scare me. No, it thrilled me. The feeling of immense power coursing through me. The knowledge that I could destroy everything. Though I knew Damiyun said he wouldn't let me call it, I didn't know that I would let him stop me.

Good, Themesis' voice hissed again. *Destroy him.*

I shook myself of the intruding voice and I took a deep, steadying breath, exhaling slowly. Closing my eyes, I cleared my mind of everything and focused on my surroundings. I could hear birds chirping in the trees, the whiskers of a rabbit off in the woods twitch, the sap running through the evergreens. I could smell the sweat on the recruits who trained in the yard, the metallic scent of blood from injuries inflicted with the sword curled in my nostrils. I could hear, smell, feel and even taste everything around me. I drew on my magic, something that came surprisingly easy for me. It flowed through my veins like a raging river, filling me with power that made my skin buzz. Bumps formed on my arms and the hair stood up on end. Opening my eyes, I looked around. Though my magic was weak, it was there making the colors sharper, the green of the grass like nothing I had ever seen. I could see the individual blades that covered the ground, each leaf on the trees, the sweat that ran off a recruit's nose on the other side of the Compound.

Turning my palms up, I sent out invisible tendrils of magic to the sky, probing and searching. I could feel the moisture in the clouds above and I focused on that. Pulsing more magic up, I drew the moisture out, pulling down the rain. I could see each individual drop as it fell, hear the sound resonating as they hit the ground.

"Good job, Lil." A voice said from far away. "You can stop now."

But I didn't want to. I could feel it, the pulsing energy from the lightning. I could hear the buzz and crackle as it moved closer and the sound of thunder vibrating in the distance. I watched the lightning flash, the forks lighting up the sky. My skin vibrated in time to the flashes.

"That's enough, Lil. Stop." There it was again. That annoying, nagging voice.

Yes, Lillyanna. Draw it closer. Draw it into you. End him.

I smiled at the voice inside my head. The familiarity of it, and I drew more magic, pulling the lightning closer. The light drizzle I had created turned into a steady downpour, but I didn't feel the rain. I only felt my power, the energy of the lightning as it rushed closer. Closer.

Arms grabbed my midsection, pulling me down, the hard stones jarring me as I hit. My magic blinked out, and the storm stopped. Anger flooded through me as I fought against the man who held me down. Themesis howled his displeasure.

"Calm, Lil," the man said, grabbing my wrists, stopping my assault.

"Let me go," I growled, bucking my hips.

He grasped my jaw and turned my head. "Look at me Lil."

I glared at him.

"Calm," he said again. "See me. Know me."

Gray eyes marked with fear and concern looked down at me. There was something familiar about them. Something I knew.

"Damiyun," I said.

He exhaled hard, releasing my chin and rolling off me. "I'm sorry, Lil," he said, voice soft. "I shouldn't have made you try to make it rain. I should have known. That magic, that dark magic, it's a part of you now. I should have known."

I rubbed my arms, my body still tingling, and I felt slightly drunk from the buzz. "It's alright, Damiyun. I should have pushed back harder." Though in truth, when he mentioned what he wanted to do, I knew that the lightning would come. I wanted it to come.

Standing up, he reached down and hauled me to my feet. "Let's try something less dangerous," he said.

"Like what?"

Scratching his chin, he looked around the room. Crossing over to a table, he picked up a pitcher of water and poured it into the washing bowl. "Turn that into ice." He leaned against the wall and crossed his arms.

I stepped over to where he stood and looked down at the bowl of water. Placing my hands around it, I closed my eyes, sending tendrils of my magic around the bowl, and pictured the cold. Icicles hanging from trees, the ground covered in snow, and the deep chill of the wind. Coldness seeped into me and I shivered.

"Open your eyes, Lil," Damiyun said, a hint of amusement in his voice. Opening my eyes, I looked down at the bowl. The water was a solid block of ice. Smiling, I turned to Damiyun.

"I did..." I stopped. His hair was crusted with ice. Our breath came out in a light, puff. I shivered against the chill in the room. Turning in a circle, I looked around. The entire room was frozen. Icicles hung from the sconces on the wall and furniture. A layer of ice and frost covered every surface and a light snow fell from the ceiling. I turned and looked at Damiyun whose eyes danced with amusement and a smile curled his lips.

"Well, I'd say your freezing was successful, though I only asked you to turn the water to ice." He stepped over to where I stood and looked around. "What did you do?"

Biting my lip, I rubbed my arms against the chill. "I just thought about the cold. The snow and ice. The freezing air."

"You're lucky you didn't freeze me." His face turned thoughtful. "This could be useful. We will have to work on you doing it faster."

My teeth chattered and my limbs began to grow numb. "How do I change it back?"

"The same way you did this." He gestured to the room.

I placed my hand around the bowl of ice and closed my eyes again. Taking a deep breath, I trickled magic around it, my mind conjuring up a picture of summer. Green grass swayed in the warm wind. Brilliantly colored flowers danced, their scent drifting on the breeze. My cold limbs tingled as I was wrapped in warmth. Damiyun's laughter pulled me out of my trance. Opening my eyes, I looked at him. He pointed behind me. I turned around, gasping at what I saw. Vines of roses covered the walls. A lilac bush stood in the center of the room and grass blanketed the floor like a rug.

"I told you your magic is strong." I looked up at Damiyun. His face was serious. "You have the ability to harness nature in unimaginable ways. This will help you."

I turned back to the room. Though what I had done was amazing and beautiful, I knew I had to try and turn it back to the way it was. Closing my eyes again, I took another deep breath. Trickling magic through my body and to the floor, I envisioned the way the room was before I had changed it. I slowly opened my eyes, breathing a sigh of relief at seeing the room back the way it was, though a vine of roses now covered one wall.

"Nice touch," Damiyun said, nodding to the vine.

"I thought it would add something to the otherwise dreary place." Yawning, I crossed the room to the bed and crawled up onto the soft comforter. Damiyun perched on the edge.

"You're amazing, Lil," he said, brushing a lock of hair from my forehead. "You're extremely powerful, even with what little magic you have. The more we work, the stronger you will become and that will bring you closer to defeating Themesis."

I yawned again, weariness seeping in, and Damiyun chuckled.

"Get some rest. I have to go do a quick patrol, but I'll be back," he said pressing his lips to my temple and rising. I heard his footsteps cross the room and the clink of buckles as he strapped his sword to his back. The door clicked closed, the sound of the lock snapping into place echoed in the room. I settled down into the soft comforter, closed my eyes and drifted off to sleep. The last thing I heard before darkness took me was Themesis' voice, soft and soothing in my mind.

You will be my queen. You will destroy villages. People will cower at your feet. You will unlock your full goddess potential.

I shuddered at the words. At how enticing they sounded, and I hoped I was strong enough to resist.

T HE NEXT DAY, WE picked up the training we had started at Pine Crest Manor with Damiyun teaching me more advanced lessons with hands and sword with what little alone time he was afforded.

"Ouch." I rubbed my side, glaring at Damiyun who danced back on the balls of his feet after hitting me with his wooden sword. We were in the nearly empty courtyard practicing. He was teaching me how to wield a weapon in my left hand, something of which I was very bad at. "Why do I need to wield a sword in this hand?"

Damiyun stopped bouncing around and leveled his gaze on me. "What are you going to do if your sword arm gets injured?" He crossed his arms. "You're probably going to end up dead," he said, not waiting for me to answer.

He took a fighting stance again, and I reluctantly followed. He didn't hold back with his fighting, striking fast and hard in quick succession. I did my best to block his blows as he forced me backward.

"Strike back, Lil," he snarled. His wooden sword slammed into mine. My arm vibrated in pain, and I almost dropped my weapon.

"I'm trying," I snapped as I just barely blocked a hit aimed at my head.

"Not very hard."

I glared at him. Anger seethed within my veins. *Not very hard? We'll see about that.* I ducked another blow meant for my head and shot forward, bringing my sword up hard between his legs. Damiyun fell to his knees with a curse. Swinging my sword again, I slammed it into his arm.

"Better?" I looked down at him.

Rubbing his arm, he rose to his feet. "Yes. Your anger will be your friend," he said. "Again."

We assumed the same position once more. Bolstered by my success, I appraised Damiyun, looking for the best and deadliest place to strike. Readying myself to launch an attack, the sound of a door banging against the wall filled the silence, making me jump at the startling sound. We both turned as Ghent burst out into the courtyard, squealing with delight.

"Get back here Ghent." A man called after him. His blue robes were hiked up as he went after the boy who ran to Damiyun, throwing his arms around his legs. Stooping down, he picked Ghent up in his arms, tossing him in the air and catching him. The little boy's laughter echoed off the stone building.

"Are you causing trouble?" Damiyun said with a smile, tossing the boy in the air again. Ghent squealed as Damiyun tipped him upside down then brought him back up again. Bouncing him in his arms, he tickled Ghent under the chin. The boy threw his arms around Damiyun's neck, pressed his lips to his cheek, and blew, making a buzzing sound. Damiyun ruffled his hair with a chuckle.

"It's time for the boy's bath, something he's not very fond of." The man said, striding up to us. He held his arms out and Damiyun deposited the boy to him.

"Thank you, Damiyun," he said.

Damiyun bowed his head. "You're welcome, Eminence."

The man bounced Ghent in his arms. "You're in trouble, little boy," he said. Ghent stuck his tongue out at the man who laughed. "Maybe not so much this time," he said, kissing Ghent's cheek. Damiyun watched them leave, a sad smile on his face.

My heart broke at the look. I knew Damiyun would never be a father. I never brought the subject up, though seeing him with Ghent made me wonder how he felt.

"Who was that?"

Damiyun looked at me. "Quint Farnsworth. Ghent's father and the head of the High Council," he said, looking back at the door.

I stepped closer to him. "Does it bother you? Never being a father?"

He looked down at me. "Once it did. I'm resigned to the fact that it is no longer my fate."

"I'm sorry," I said, reaching up and touching his cheek. He turned his head and kissed my palm.

"It's fine," he said, his tone heavy. "I think we're done here for today."

Tossing our sword aside, we walked back through the door that led inside the Compound.

"Brother."

"Fuck," Damiyun cursed. Stopping, he turned around. "Arden," he said, nostrils flaring.

Arden's eyes narrowed. "It's Regulator Rayne."

Damiyun laughed. "I don't owe you any honorific."

Arden clenched his fists. "You are under my supervision. You will address me proper."

"What do you want, Arden?"

He clenched his fists. "I am organizing a raid on a nearby village. You are to lead it," he said. His eyes went to me, a smile curled his lips. "Bring her with you."

Damiyun gripped my hand, and I had to stop myself from wincing.

"No. She is not a part of the Order."

"While she is here, she is. She will come on this raid. She will see what we were about," he said. His eyes went to Damiyun. "She will see what you are about."

I tossed my hair and glared at Arden. "I know what he is about. He hasn't kept anything from me," I said, ignoring the fact that I knew my words to not be completely true.

Arden's eyes narrowed on me, and I had to stop myself from looking away.

"Get your sword," he said to Damiyun and stalked away.

I followed Damiyun through the halls to our room. He strapped his sword to his back and picked up two daggers. Slipping one in his waistband he held the other out to me.

"Use this, if necessary," he said.

Taking the weapon, I slipped it in my boot. Damiyun looked down at me. He pushed a lock of hair behind my ear and cupped my chin. "If my brother tries to make you participate, I want you to run fast and run far. I will have my magic on this raid so I will be able to contact Abraham and have him find you."

I frowned. "How?"

"Through our bond."

"But... what about you?"

He took my hand and tugged me in the direction of the door. "Don't worry about me," he said, opening the door. I placed my hand on it and closed it. Damiyun turned and looked at me, eyes questioning.

"We can escape. We're going to be away from here. I'm going to be with you. You'll have your magic."

"Too risky. Arden would block my magic the instant I tried to use it and if Arden caught you, he would torture you and abuse you for his pleasure." He shook his head. "No, Lil."

His words made me wonder if perhaps he was happy to be in the Order again. The thought chilled me. "So, what then Damiyun? We go on this raid, kill innocents, come back here and just wait for Abraham?" I shook my head. "I refuse to not try." I pulled the door open and stepped into the hallway. "Stay then. It's clear you want to. I don't. I'm going to go down fighting," I said over my shoulder.

Damiyun grabbed my arm and pulled me around. "I don't want to be here anymore than you do Lil."

I pulled my arm from his grasp. "Then stand with me on this," I said, my eyes locked on his. I needed to know where his loyalty lies.

He let out a puff of air. "I will always stand with you. When my magic is fully unblocked, I will reach out to Abraham for his help. Now, let's go. Arden isn't one to let wait."

We walked outside to where Arden sat astride his black mount with a dozen other men. I swung up into the saddle of a horse with Damiyun climbing up behind. He slipped his arm around my waist, and I leaned against him. Arden heeled his mount forward, everyone fanning out behind. We rode for a few miles until we came upon the crest of a hill. Arden pulled his mount to a stop and pointed.

"That's our target," he said.

I followed his finger, looking down on the village spread out below. People bustled about; horse-drawn wagons raced through the streets. Smoke curled up from the chimneys of houses and stores, the scent drifting on the breeze. The sound of metal being pounded could be heard in the distance. It looked like a quiet village. A peaceful village that we were about to destroy. Anger roiled inside me at the thought and the memory of seeing Wielders in my own village dragged from their homes.

Damiyun gripped the reins and guided his horse next to Arden.

"The village is teeming with Wielders," Damiyun said, his voice terse.

Arden turned to us, a smile on his face as he raised his hand. Damiyun grunted, and I knew his magic had been fully restored.

"Lead the way, Brother, and let the bloodbath begin," Arden said, drawing his sword, the light of the setting sun shining off the blade. The sound of steel rang out as the group of Suppressors drew their weapons as well. I glanced up at Damiyun who reached behind and pulled his sword free.

"Let's get this over with," he said, heeling his horse into a gallop. The group roared and the sound of thundering hooves followed behind as we raced down the hill toward the village. People stopped and looked up. Though I couldn't see the fear on their faces, I knew it was there. I clenched my jaw at the thought of what was about to happen.

It wasn't right. These people were innocent. They were just going about their day, and now their blood would turn the streets red.

"This isn't right," I snarled.

Damiyun's arm tightened around me. "I know, Lil." His voice was soft in my ear. "I've reached out to Abraham. He will come."

People fled as we raced into the village. Mothers snatched up children while the men gathered shovels, lengths of iron, and various other objects to use as weapons.

"Duck," Damiyun said, roughly pushing my head down. My hair whipped as something flew over, the sound of an explosion and the scream of a horse followed behind. I peeked over our horse's head, my eyes catching a man standing off to the side. Light flickered between hands held apart. Damiyun pulled the reins in his direction.

"Forgive me," he said softly. Silver flashed, and I watched in horror as Damiyun's sword sliced the man in half. Bile rose in my throat, and I turned my head to the side, vomiting as we raced on.

The sound of screams echoed through the night and the stench of blood filled the air. I watched innocent men, women, and children be cut down with swords. Others were dragged away from families. Young women were held down and violated. The entire scene made me sick and angry. And with that anger I felt the block Abraham put in crack more. Magic surged within my body, hot, fierce, and frightening.

"Don't." Damiyun's voice was low, his breath hot in my ear.

"I can't just watch."

"I know but if either one of us tries to stop it, it will be far worse for you. And for them. Abraham is coming. Just hold out a little longer. Close your eyes," he said, lips brushing my temple.

But I wouldn't. I wouldn't be a coward. I wouldn't turn a blind eye to the atrocity against Wielders unfolding in front of me. I caught movement to the right out of the corner of my eye. The shadows darkened and swirled. Faces formed, eyes red, white teeth glinting in the rising moon. Long, boney fingers reached out. I saw a flash of steel and a Suppressor fell to the ground. Blood poured from the slit across his throat mixing with the blood-soaked dirt.

"Abraham," Damiyun said, turning our mount and racing in his direction.

I blinked as he bent to wipe his blade off on the downed man's shirt. Demons clung to him. Smoke and shadows swirled around his body. He looked menacing. A creature born from the Abyss. I shuddered at the sight. A demon flicked its talons outward and raked a Suppressor. The Suppressor yelped in surprise and dashed away in fright only to collapse on the ground a moment later. The wound festered hot and putrid, blackened from the talon marks.

Damiyun pulled the horse to a stop and jumped down. He held his hand up to me and I took it, scrambling down off the horse.

"Let's go," Damiyun said, pulling me close and moving next to Abraham. Shadows and mist swirled around us. Demons snarled and hissed, teeth snapping and claws reaching. I buried my face in Damiyun's chest.

"It's alright, Lil. They won't hurt you," he said.

The world tilted, the bloody massacre in front of us rushed by and my stomach lurched. Within moments we were in the middle of a copse of pine trees. Falling to my knees, I emptied the contents of my stomach, wiping my mouth with a shaking hand. Closing my eyes, I took a deep breath, but all I saw behind my lids was the faces of the dead and the river of blood that ran through the streets. The sound of their screams echoed in my ears. The scent of death lingered in my nose.

This was a night that would be burned into my memory forever.

TWENTY-TWO

ARDEN

Sitting astride Storm, I scanned the carnage. The metallic scent of blood and fear filled the air, and I breathed in the intoxicating erotic scent. The sound of screams played like a symphony to my ears. I watched my men hunt down Wielders, cutting them down with swords. Those they didn't kill were beaten into submission, and those who still resisted? They came around when their wives and daughters were dragged to the center of the village and forced to the ground, legs spread and violated.

Gripping my sword, I joined in the battle. I dug my heels into Storm, urging him on, racing through the village, cutting down men, women, and children. Anything that was in my way saw the edge of my blade. A river of red flowed, my uniform and face painted in it. I licked my lips. The sweet taste of blood danced on my tongue, filling me with lust. I raced on with a roar, slashing and stabbing anything in my red-hazed vision. When I was done, when I pulled my blade from the last body, I drew Storm to a halt and looked around at the carnage. At the bodies and the blood, and at the Wielders who were captured. Disgust filled me at seeing the bound men, women, and children. If I had my way, none would live. A dead Wielder was better than a captured one. At least they couldn't escape.

They couldn't defect. I looked around at my men, searching for one in particular. Shadows moved. A dark mass coalesced next to a building. A flash of red caught my eye, and a horse raced toward the mass. A horse carrying Damiyun and Lillyanna. The shadows turned solid. Turned into a man. Damiyun and the little bitch jumped off the horse and were enveloped by the shadows, and in the blink of an eye, they were gone.

Rage coursed through me. I had warned Vel against sending his daughter along. I knew she would be a reason to make Damiyun come back. He would never try to escape without her. The blood pounded in my ears. Clenching the reins, I hauled Storm into a gallop.

"We are done here. Round up the captives and head back," I snapped, racing back to the Compound.

I didn't wait to see if my men obeyed, and raced toward home. I handed Storm off to the stable hand and stalked across the courtyard. Recruits scurried at the sight of me, something that would normally give me pleasure, but not now. I was far too furious to revel in it. I quickly made my way through the corridors, glaring at any who tried to get my attention, making my way to Vel's study. Not giving the courtesy knock, I pushed open the doors and strode inside. He sat behind his grand desk of cherry decorated with vines and flowers in gold leaf around the Suppressor sigil. His head was bent over parchment. The sound of the nib scratching filled the silence. My steps were muffled by the mismatched rugs strewn across the floor as I crossed to where he sat. He glanced up briefly to dip the nib in ink, his eyes catching me standing there. He signed the document and sprinkled sand on the fresh ink. Folding it, he sealed it with wax and placed it aside. Folding his hands, he finally gave me his attention.

"How did your raid go?"

Placing my fists on his desk, I leaned forward. "It went well with the exception of my brother." I spat the word. "He escaped with your daughter."

Vel's nostrils flared. "I told you to keep her here. You insisted on forcing her to go."

I clenched my fists. "Did I? I believe it was you who forced her. You wanted her to see what sort of man my brother is."

Vel snorted. "The lies roll easily off your tongue, don't they? Nothing is ever your doing."

I narrowed my eyes. *You would just love to blame this on me, wouldn't you, Vel?*

He leaned forward, our faces inches apart. "It is clear you do not understand the importance of my daughter. Let me refresh your memory," he said, a snarl curling his lips. "She is the key to setting Themesis free. Their Blood-Binding will shatter the seals. Their union, their child, will be stronger than any god. S'aehe will crumble and Themesis will rule but you," he leaned closer, his breath warm on my face. "You let her get away. You will gather your men and leave at first light. Search for her, and do not return until she is found. Is that clear?"

"Of course," I said between gritted teeth as I stood up.

Vel sat back in his chair. Picking up the quill, he dipped it in ink and began writing, his dismissal evident.

Spinning on my heel, I stalked through the bare halls. The tapestries on the walls depicting bloody battles between Suppressors and Wielders did not give me their normal comfort. I stepped into my quarters, slamming the door behind me, and entered the stark room. A large, four-poster bed with thick blood-red curtains tied to the posts sat across the room, the bed made up with a simple blanket of the same color. An ornate wardrobe of deep cherry with carvings of snakes and vines sat against a wall to the left, a matching desk in the corner beside a large marble fireplace. A table held a washbasin, pitcher of water, carafe of wine, and glasses. Double doors were open, as were the windows letting in a soft, cool breeze.

Everything was neat, clean, and orderly, unlike Vel's study, which was a mass of chaos. Parchments covered all surfaces and floor. There was far too much furniture, making the room cramped. Stifling. My quarters, my sanctuary, had only the bare necessities and everything was in its proper place.

Pouring myself a glass of wine, I stepped out onto the balcony and looked out at the empty courtyard below. Anger surged within me as I thought about what happened today. The vision of my brother escaping formed in my mind, and I clenched the glass, pain lancing through my hand as shards pierced my palm. I watched the blood drip, making red drops on the spotless white marble floor. Bringing my hand up, I licked and sucked the blood that spilled. The taste was as sweet as candy, the scent arousing. I had to stop myself from dropping to my knees to lick up every droplet off the floor.

It calmed me, if only briefly. Cleaning up the mess, I poured a fresh glass and sat down in the only chair on the balcony, propping my feet up on the only table. Taking a healthy drink, my thoughts again went to my brother. The night my life changed forever.

To the night, I vowed to make him pay in blood and pain for taking everything away from me.

I WAS THIRTEEN WHEN he was born. I had foolishly thought after the terrible accident that befell my sister, Azani, Mother wouldn't want any more children. And it was a horrible tragedy. I had told Azani to stay away from the pond, but like any child, she was curious. She got too close, and I was too late to save her. Mother was devastated when she saw her floating face down in the water. After the tears dried, everything went back to normal.

For a brief period.

One night, as she put me to bed, she told me she was with child.

"Arden," she had said. A smile lit her ruby lips, and she smoothed my hair from my forehead. I looked up at her. She was beautiful. Goddess-like in the way the lamplight shone on her long, white hair. Her blue eyes danced with life and her touch was warm upon my skin. "I have some news for you. You are going to be a big brother again," she said, fingers touching her midsection.

The smile on her lips, the light in her eyes, for a brief moment I wanted to take it from her. I wanted to hurt her, but I loved her and her words rang in my head. The ones of comfort and love.

That I wasn't evil. I wasn't bad. I was special. Unique. And I knew I would never hurt my mother.

"I know I neglected you when Azani was born, and I am so very sorry. I love you, Arden. Never, ever doubt that. You're older now and you can help me. You can be the best brother to your new sister or brother." She grasped my hands, earnest eyes on me. "Can you do that? Will you be my helper? I promise the stories will continue, and the garden will bloom again. Just for you, Arden. Always for you."

I felt the love pouring through her, and my walls were filled with fantastic beasts prancing in a field of green. Mother leaned down and pressed her lips to my forehead.

"I love you. Never a day has gone by where I haven't thanked the gods for giving you to me. In my day of despair, you arrived in Kallen's arms. Will you be a big brother and help me?"

I looked up into her love-filled eyes, so shiny and blue, and I knew I couldn't say no. Throwing my arms around her, I held her close, breathing in her sweet scent of roses and lilies.

"Of course, Mother. I will do anything for you."

And then the day came when my brother was born. Mother's screams filled the small house. Father paced the living room, a worried look on his face.

"Go outside and play, Arden," he had said to me. My stomach clenched, but I did what he asked. Mother's screams went on for what seemed like an eternity. Finally, they stopped, replaced by the wails of a baby.

"Come, welcome your new brother, Damiyun." Father's voice came from the door. He was holding a small bundle. A bright smile lit his face.

"Can I see Mother?"

Father's smile faltered for just a moment. "She's resting."

For three days, that was Father's response and on the eve of the third day, he came into my room and sat on the edge of my bed. Lines marred his face, and he looked far older than I remembered.

"Can I see her now?"

Tears glistened in his brown eyes, and I saw wetness on his cheeks. "I'm sorry, Arden, but your mother is with the gods now."

Disbelief washed over me, and I lunged for the door. Father grabbed me and pulled me onto his lap. "I'm sorry, Arden. She's gone."

I should have been shocked. I should have wanted to cry, but instead a deep, pounding rage bubbled inside me. My brother took the life of my beautiful goddess. The woman I loved. I would never forgive him.

My life turned dark in those moments, cruelly dark, and had remained so over the years.

As he grew older, I knew it was his magic that ended her life, and I vowed to make him pay in pain and blood. I vowed to rid the world of those like him so no other child would lose a loving mother.

S HAKING THE THOUGHTS THAT tumbled inside my head, and wiping the wetness from my cheeks, I rose from my chair. Dawn was breaking. It was time to find my brother. Time to make him pay one last time.

TWENTY-THREE
DAMIYUN

"**M**AKE A COOK FIRE but keep it small," Abraham said, when we appeared in a clearing then walked off into the woods. We made a fire, and sat in silence, the pops and hisses of the flames punctuating the quiet. The flames snaked and undulated as I stared, hypnotized by the rhythm. Nature sang around me, a symphony against the fiery ballet, warming me. Magic thrummed beneath my skin.

I looked at Lillyanna who sat across from me, her arms hugged her legs as she rested her chin on her knees. I got up and sat down next to her.

"Are you alright?" It was a stupid question, really. I could tell she was not.

"How could they do that?" Her voice was soft. Tears glistened in her eyes, spilling down her cheeks. I wiped them away and pulled her close. Her body shook, and soft sobs escaped her.

"They're a horrible Organization," I said. I pulled back and looked down at her. "Now can you understand why I defected?"

She pulled away and hugged her knees again. "But you were still a part of it."

"The Fallen One grows stronger." Abraham's voice cut through the night, and any words I was going to say, as he entered our camp. "I have heard talk of wraiths and Pyragaties."

"Pyra-what?" Lillyanna asked.

"Pyragaty. Demons who steal the power of Wielders. They feed off magic and gain strength with every Wielder they kill," Abraham said, taking a seat and putting his catch on the fire.

I frowned. "Pyragaties haven't been seen nor heard of in centuries."

"As I said, he grows stronger. His reach is no longer contained to just the Abyss. He will do what he can to make sure Lillyanna doesn't reach Kraagswell Mountain."

No. You will bring her to me. She will be my queen. My slave. She will serve me in every way...

"She is far from ready," he continued.

"I worked with her at the Compound. She was impressive, Abraham. She was able to put cracks in your block. With what little magic she has...she began to call the lightning again." Abraham's eyes widened in surprise. "I asked her to make it rain, stupid, I know, and she began to harness the lightning. It's getting easier for her to do." I glanced at Lil and smiled. "She also froze the room, then turned it into a garden." I turned back to Abraham and took a deep breath. "She wishes to see her mother. I'm taking her to S'aehe for answers."

"That is a foolish detour. We will lose precious days."

Lil leveled her gaze at Abraham. "Do you know where you come from, Abraham? Does it bring you comfort to know who you are?"

Abraham pursed his lips.

"Everyone is telling me about my damn destiny, but I don't know who is telling me the truth. I need to find my mother and get it from her."

"The gods can be as deceitful as mortals. They are arrogant and self-centered. Their actions only serve them," Abraham said, scowling.

Lil glared at him. "I will take the chance." Jumping up, she stalked a few yards away and plopped down on the ground. Ignoring Abraham's glare, I made my way to where she sat, settling down beside her.

"He doesn't understand. It's easy for him to tell me what I should and shouldn't do. I wish everyone would leave me alone. I wish I could go back home," she said. She turned her head away, but I saw the tears in her eyes. Tears stained her cheeks.

I ran a hand over my face. "I know, Lil." I didn't know what else to say. I didn't have any words of encouragement for her. Even if I had them, I knew they would sound false. I could tell her I would like nothing more than to take her back to Howling Cove, or anywhere, really. It wasn't a lie. For my own selfish reasons, I would have preferred to take her anywhere besides where she had asked me to go. But how could I have said no to her? How could I deny her knowing the woman who gave her life? The gods know I would give anything to have known my own mother.

I looked over at Abraham, who was taking the meat off the fire. Rising to my feet, I held my hand down to Lil.

"Let's go eat."

She didn't take my hand. She didn't move. She sat with her knees to her chest, eyes staring off into the dark woods. I crossed the clearing to where Abraham sat. Taking his knife, I cut off chunks of meat, placing them on a flat rock.

"I will take her to S'aehe. I will train her on the way," he said.

"No. You are hardly around. She needs someone she can trust. Someone who will remain there. I will train her as we travel."

Abraham pursed his lips. I could almost hear the thoughts going through his head. His concerns were not without merit, though I didn't want to listen to him chastise me. I had been able to keep my prior relations with Felicity from her thus far, though I feared it would come out while we were in S'aehe. Ignoring Abraham's piercing gaze, I picked up the rock with the food and made my way to where Lil still sat.

"Eat," I said, settling down beside her, placing the food on the grass. She grabbed a piece of meat and idly chewed it.

"Are you sure this is what you want to do?" My eyes were on her as she ate the food. She turned her head and looked at me.

"Yes," she said.

I never would have thought one simple word. One *yes* would seal my fate.

Seal both of our fates.

TWENTY-FOUR

I WOKE A FEW hours later to the rumble of thunder and the flickering of lightning.

"Wake up, Lil," I said, shaking her lightly as big drops began to fall and plop on the ground, sending dirt flying. Her eyes slowly opened, and she sat up. A flash lit up the sky, and she shuddered.

"We need to find lodging," Abraham said as he doused the fire. We rose to our feet and climbed on Xander, heeling him out of the woods and after Abraham. The rain slashed as we rode toward the village. We could hardly see, the sign for Tergaron barely visible through the deluge.

We pulled up to an inn, stabled the horses, and entered the nearly empty tavern. After surreptitiously securing a room, we shuffled up the stairs. Upon entering, I assembled a fire to take away the chill in the room as well as the one settling in my bones from the rain. We gathered around the fire, warming ourselves for a while. Lil yawned and made her way to the bed closest and laid down to rest.

"Speak your mind, Abraham," I said as I unstrapped my weapon, took off my cloak, and settled into an old, beat-up chair, which groaned in protest beneath my weight. I felt the heat of his eyes and knew he had something to say.

"Your detour is foolish."

I closed my eyes and sighed. "So, you've said. It is what she wants to do."

"And you are indulging her like you indulged—"

"This is not an indulgence." I knew what his next words were going to be. "We have given her precious little say in where she goes and what she should do. She knows nothing about where she came from. This is the least we can give her. Besides, I will not go back on my word."

"And when she finds out what happened?"

"I will handle it when that happens."

"She will hate you."

I looked at him. "Isn't that what you want? For her to hate me?"

"Hate, not hurt."

I shook my head. "It's one or the other, Abraham. I either hurt her or she hates me. Which is it?"

His eyes lingered on me, then he shook his head and laid down on the other bed to rest. My stomach growled. I looked at Lil who was sleeping peacefully and Abraham whose body was tense and alert. Knowing she was safe, I slipped out of the room and ambled down to the tavern, which was busier than when we entered. A fire burned in the central hearth and a bard stood in the corner strumming a lute and singing a comedic tale, the words drifting through the din of chatter.

> *"—and oh. Her arse was wide,*
> *A thing of pride, and the men looked on in wonder.*
> *And as she strode about, there was no doubt*
> *Her steps rumbled like thunder—"*

I chuckled as I brought the tankard to my lips, the cold ale running down my throat quenching my thirst, and I turned my attention to the conversation going on around me.

"—Jar Stacks saw wraiths when he was hunting," the man to my left said. I cocked my head, my keen ears honing in.

"They didn't touch him, did they?" a second man said, leaning forward in his seat.

The first man guffawed. "If they had, then how would I have known he seen them, you idiot?" He roared with laughter.

The first grunted his agreement, the conversation abandoned as they appraised the neckline of the young serving wench. Bile crept up my throat. Abraham had mentioned hearing news of wraiths. The bard's voice rose as he sang a sad, soulful song, the eerie words floating above the noise in the room.

> *"—and I pulled the dagger from her breast,*
> *My b'loved she lay a-bleeding.*
> *The tears they stung my weary eyes,*
> *Her life, it was a-fleeing.*
> *I killed my love, my heart, my light because she had betrayed me.*
> *I lay the dagger on the ground and prayed the gods would save me.*
> *And then I watched her Life Force leave, her spirit soared to the sky.*
> *And as I pulled my body up, I whispered a goodbye—"*

I sighed. The song struck like a knife, and I shoved the words and melody away. No time for wallowing in the past, I had to glean whatever intel I might while in town. My ears focusing on another conversation. After the plump wench brought me my food and another ale, I sat back in my seat. The smell of the stew and freshly baked bread made my mouth water. I took a mouthful of the hot food, slowly chewing the tender beef, turning my attention back to the conversation.

"The Suppressor activity is becoming thick," one man said.

"Aye." The second nodded. "I 'ave heard the same."

"What for, do you suppose?" The first man sat back and folded his arms.

The second man shrugged. "With the presence of wraiths and seein' them Pyragaties, an other demons, I 'ssume it's ta do wit' the Fallen One," he said.

I chewed slowly, my eyes trained on the two men.

"I can't says I'm feelin' remorse for the evil Wielders. I heard for a good price you can hand 'em straight to dem demons," the first said.

The second man shook his head. "An'you think dem Sons of Themesis be obliging?" He snickered into his ale. "I know one who thought da same. Ne'er 'eard from 'im again."

Soon after, the discussion drifted to crops and their yields. I turned my attention back to the noisy tavern, the bard still singing in the corner, his voice rising above the din:

> *"—she was a force to be a-reckoned with,*
> *The men they cowered in fear.*
> *Her eyes were cold and people ran*
> *When Jayne, she drew a-near.*
> *While Jayne the Great was cold as ice*
> *A lonely heart she had.*
> *For who could love a lass like she*
> *Whose deeds were only bad?*
> *And no one knew that deep inside the emptiness she felt.*
> *No one knew except one man, her heart he tried to melt—"*

I smiled at the words the bard spoke, words taken from a book called "*The Story of Jayne*," a tale of a fierce immortal warrior whose path crossed with a mortal man who wooed her, melting her heart of ice. It was a favorite of mine. Scholars oft debated whether the legend was history, or myth. When I was a child, it helped me escape the horrors of my life and made me believe, foolishly, perhaps, that good existed somewhere in the world. It held sentimental value to me. A reminder, good things only happened to characters in books. Not in real life.

I finished my meal, ordered a bowl for Lil and Abraham, and then pulled my body out of the chair, weariness weighing down on my shoulders from lack of sleep. I took my food and new-found knowledge and made my way back to the room.

"There's talk in the tavern about the Suppressors and the demons you mentioned. One of the men I was listening to said people are handing Wielders over to them," I said to Abraham when I entered the room. Handing him the two bowls, I grabbed my sword and strapped it to my back, then threw my cloak around my shoulders.

"Where are you going?" He asked around a mouthful of food.

"To find out more about what I heard."

TWENTY-FIVE

With my weapons secured, I slipped back out of the room. Pausing for a moment in the tavern, I trained my keen ears on the chatter to see if I could glean anything else. Picking up nothing, I made my way out into the night. Slipping a hand inside my cloak, I gripped the hilt of a dagger and pulled up my hood against the rain, and to hide my face. I did not need my eyes raising any suspicion.

I scanned the town. Though it was raining, there were plenty of people who were walking about. Including a group of Suppressors and Enforcers. Though they were from a different Compound, I knew none were aware of our escape. It would take far too long to get word out to the other factions, though that did not mean I wanted to risk being caught, especially when I felt the pulse of magic from one of their Feelers.

Hiding further within the folds of my hood, I loosened the dagger I gripped and moved on silent feet through the village. It was not a poor town, though it was not as affluent as L'Ochal. And as with any town, affluent or not, there was always a seedy section. Always a place to go when you needed information, or a deed done.

For a price, of course.

Ducking into an alley, I walked slowly down the dark corridor that, to me, was light as day. A figure loomed where I knew there were shadows. Distorted with red eyes and bone-like hands. It must be one of the demons the people had mentioned in the inn. I backed against the wall, eyes on the demon at the other end. Using my magic, I cloaked myself. Movement to my right caught my attention. A man slunk into the alley.

I watched him move toward the demons. I knew nothing good would come from whatever it was he was about, but I didn't reveal myself. Even if I had, why would he listen to me?

"Speak, human," the demon snarled.

"There are Wielders here."

"Where?"

"On the outskirts. Several houses with them. They should satisfy your hunger," he said. "Now, payment?"

Reaching into a tattered cloak, the demon pulled out a pouch and tossed it to the man. The ringing sound of coin filled the silent alley. The man palmed the pouch, tucking it into his cloak, and turned to walk away. Bony hands grabbed him. The man's eyes widened in surprise. He tried to wrench himself away, but the demon held tight. Teeth snapped and bones were crushed between powerful jaws. Limbs were torn, his screams silenced. I turned away from the scene, releasing my magic and making my way back out of the alley.

"Wielder," a low, guttural voice called.

Stopping, I clutched my dagger and turned toward the demon. Blood dripped from its mouth and claws. Forked tongue flicked out to taste the air. He recoiled. A snarl curled decayed lips.

"His." He growled. A smile curled its lips. "But we will have you when he has you. You will be one of us," it hissed. A hot breeze blew, and shadows converged on the being, pulling him back to his home in the Abyss.

A chill ran down my spine at the words. I knew who he was talking about, and I knew the demons were once people. Humans who succumbed to the evil, twisting their souls further until they transformed into demons. Demons who fed on Wielders. My stomach lurched, and I swallowed bile.

I continued down the alley, averting my eyes from the decimated body, coming out into a small courtyard. Pulling my hood up, I entered the small area and looked around. It was enclosed, three sides of walls with doors to homes. A stone path led to a small fountain in the center with four benches around it. Flowers and trees grew, in the courtyard, providing a small garden. I looked about the tranquil area spying a man sitting on one of the benches at the fountain. Tentatively I reached out with my magic. I felt power coming from him, though the lack of black clothing made me believe he was not a Suppressor. Making my way down into the area, I sat beside him, crossing my ankles. I felt his magic surge, and he stiffened beside me.

"I'm not a Suppressor. I'm looking for information," I said, thanking the gods for my cloak which hid the uniform I wore.

He shifted his position, propping a leg on his knee. "Why should I trust you?"

I held out my hand, calling forth my magic. A flame danced on the palm. "Like I said, I'm not a Suppressor. I'm just like you."

He laughed. "How do you know I'm not one of them?"

I doused the flame and folded my arms. "Because I'm a Feeler."

He relaxed a bit, though not much. "Information doesn't come free."

I reached into my pocket, finding the bag of coin. Fishing around, I pulled out a silver and flipped it to the man who caught it and stowed it in his pocket.

"What do you want to know?"

"Why Nons are giving up Wielders for coin. I just saw one speaking with a demon. It didn't end well for him."

The man shrugged. "Times are tough. People will do anything to earn coin."

"What are the demons doing with the Wielders?"

The man sucked his teeth. Reaching into his pocket he pulled out a bag. Reaching in, he took out a paper wrap, filled it with leaves and rolled it up. Lighting it, the scent of the chicory root filled the air. He took a long draw on it, then exhaled, the smoke circling his head.

"Feeding on them." He held out the chicory stick to me. Taking it, I took a long draw, then handed it back.

I sighed. "I had heard as much in the tavern. What is the purpose?"

The guy looked at me out of the corner of his eye. "Does it matter? A dead Wielder is a boon to Themesis."

I sensed this man to be holding back. Reaching into my pouch, I pulled out another silver and held it up. "Tell me more," I said, handing it over.

The man shifted in his seat. Tossing the chicory stick in the fountain, he rolled another, took a deep draw, and passed it to me. "Between the Suppressors taking Wielders, and Non's telling demons where they are, or just handing them over, speeds up the process of freeing Themesis." He took the stick from me, took a long pull and exhaled, the smoke drifting up in the breeze. "Of course, word gets around and Wielders have been leaving in droves. Not that it matters. They'll get caught. Eventually."

"Where are they fleeing to?"

"Can't say, though if I were to hazard a guess, I'd say Va'l'Victorus. They'd be protected on their lands and the Wilde Elves have nothing against humans. That is, if they make it there."

"Why haven't you left?"

"This is my home. I'm not going to run scared because of Suppressors or Wielder eating demons. I've managed to avoid them. I've lived a long life. If they finally catch up with me, then so be it," he shrugged.

I rubbed my chin. This man's news was even more disturbing than I thought. Reaching into my pouch, I pulled out a copper and flipped it to him. "Thank you for the information. Stay safe," I said as I rose from the bench.

I made my way back through the alley and into the town, pulling my cloak closer. The annoying drizzle had begun to turn into a steady rain. As I walked through the village, I watched Suppressors haul Wielders from their homes and businesses. Watched as they were beaten. As their families were threatened and as I did when I was a part of the Organization, I turned a blind eye to what they did and hurried on.

After seeing the Suppressors, running into the Demon and Non, and how what I had gathered from the stranger in the courtyard, we were no longer safe here. I had to get Lillyanna as far from here as I could.

TWENTY-SIX
LILLYANNA

I OPENED MY EYES and peered about. Flashes of lightning pierced the dark, lighting up the room. My magic clawed at me, begging to come forth. It felt like a living being inside me. The sky lit up again and my magic pulsed once more. I looked down, gasping as my veins glowed silver.

Use it. A voice whispered in the back of my head. *Destroy it all.*

I shuddered at the thought. At the fact, I wanted to let my magic loose. I closed my eyes and took a deep, calming breath, willing my magic back down.

Nearby, Abraham straddled a chair, his chin rested on his arms and his eyes were on me.

"Where's Damiyun?" I swung my legs over the side of the bed and stretched. I had heard them talking as I flitted in and out of sleep, rife with nightmares.

"He went out," Abraham said. His black eyes bored through me, and I fidgeted beneath his gaze.

"What, Abraham?"

He said nothing. I slipped out of bed and stood before him, crossing my arms. "I know you have something to say. You wouldn't be here staring at me if you didn't."

The corner of his mouth quirked as he stood and went to the window.

"Damiyun cares about you far more than he should." He clasped his hands behind his back.

"Does he now?"

"Yes."

"And that's a problem?"

He turned to face me. "Yes."

I walked over beside him. The storm raged outside. Rain slashed the windows; the crash of thunder shook the glass, and lightning lit the sky as powerfully as the sun.

"I feel it," I whispered, rubbing my arms. "I feel the lightning. I want to draw it in. I crave it." A part of me wondered if I was the one creating the storm. If my emotions had manifested it. The thought was thrilling. I liked the idea, Queen of

Lightning, Daughter of Storms. My magic reigned potent, a stalking cat ready to pounce and devour the world. Tingles ran down my spine.

"He's a part of it too. Themesis. I feel like... Like what I did, let him in further." I shook my head and looked up at Abraham, who peered down at me. "What do you want from me, Abraham? Why does my relationship with Damiyun concern you?"

"Because he will hurt you."

"How?"

He ran his hand over his face. "That is not for me to disclose. He cares about you, Lillyanna."

"So you've said."

"Damiyun has a dark soul. He has done many horrible things."

I sighed. "I know all of this, Abraham. It's obvious you wish me to do something. Speak your mind." I was tired of riddles and cryptic speech. Were all men so vague? My father, Abraham, and even Damiyun at times, though I had to admit to myself he spoke with more candor than most.

He turned his attention back to the window. "I had a daughter once. She was a lot like you. Stubborn. Willful. Bratty." His mouth quirked up into a smile that faded as quickly as it came. "I spoiled her. She was my only child."

I swallowed, unsure of where this was going, and equally apprehensive since this was the most he had ever said to me. His closeness made me uncomfortable and yet... I didn't want to step away and break whatever caused him to open up.

"What happened to her?"

"She made a deal with the Fallen One. When the time came—" He turned his head, black eyes meeting mine. "I had to collect her soul."

His words hit me like a boulder and a flood of sympathy flowed through me. "I'm sorry."

"She fell in love with a Fae. He made all sorts of promises to her. I saw him for what he was, and I had warned her against him. She didn't listen. She wanted to be with him. She defied me. She went behind my back and made a deal with Themesis who granted her immortality. He held her contract and had the power to call it anytime. I was furious with her. She was young, and foolish. I suppose she thought she was in love, but she had no idea." Abraham's voice cracked like stone. He shook his head and turned his eyes back to me. Lightning lit up the sky again illuminating his figure making him look dark and menacing. The crash of thunder rattled the windows, and I jumped at the sound.

"One day, Themesis called it, and as I said, I was the one who had to collect her soul. I offered her lover a deal. His soul for hers, but being the narcissist he was, he refused. I had to deliver my only daughter's soul to the Fallen One."

I looked at him, my brow furrowing. Why was he telling me this? "What does this have to do with Damiyun?"

Abraham brushed a lock of hair behind my ear and cupped my chin. The gesture stunned me, and I resisted the urge to pull away. "He has a task that needs to be completed, and I fear his feelings for you have blinded him. I fear it will hinder his ability to do what needs to be done."

"And that's bad?" I stepped away. The closeness, the intimacy, was becoming uncomfortable.

"Yes."

"What is his task? What is my task?" I folded my arms, fingers digging into my skin. The storm still raged, and my magic still pulsed in time to it. My annoyance with Abraham was making it challenging to not let it go. I struggled against the tide, the desire to rip through everything in my path. A jolt of exhilaration coursed through me. The air buzzed around me, thick energy crackled.

"He is to bring you to the Fallen One, where you will defeat him."

I gripped my arms harder. *Let go,* the voice inside my head said. *Show him what you can do.* I shook myself. "How, Abraham? And why should I believe either of you? I have stupidly come this far with the two of you, following like a puppy dog. Obeying whatever you tell me, and still, I have no idea what exactly I am to do."

"That is for Damiyun to tell you."

I clenched my jaw. "I'm asking you. You're here now, Damiyun isn't."

He sighed, a tired sound. "It is not for me to tell you."

"It's because this is a one-way trip for me, isn't it?" His silence was deafening. "I'm tired of all of this, Abraham. Of the mystery, of not being told anything about what I'm supposed to do. Of being lied to. I want to go home." I turned and stormed toward the door. Abraham grabbed my arm, stopping me. I glared up at him.

"Let go of me."

"Talk to Damiyun. Make him tell you what your task is, and when you know?" He shrugged. "You can decide if you want to continue," he said, releasing my arm.

I opened my mouth to speak, the creak of the door opening cutting off my words. Damiyun entered the room shaking the water from his cloak. His eyes met Abraham's.

"We need to leave. Now," he said.

Abraham nodded and grabbed his things, strapping his sword to his waist and slipping daggers into his belt and boots. I slipped on my cloak and brushed past Damiyun into the hall.

I would do what Abraham said. I would demand answers from Damiyun and if he evaded me again, I would find a way to go back home.

TWENTY-SEVEN
DAMIYUN

W

E RODE THROUGH THE night and the next day, stopping to let the horses rest, veering off the path to make camp as the sun set.

"What did you see?" Abraham asked as we settled on the ground.

I scratched the stubble on my face. "What I overheard in the tavern wasn't just a rumor. I saw a demon in an alley. A man was selling it information on where to find Wielders." I looked at Abraham. "It didn't end well for him," I said. "From what I gathered, the demons are consuming the Wielders."

"Just another way to get rid of them," Abraham said, tossing wood on the fire.

"That's what a man I talked to said. Most likely, it's accelerating the process."

I watched the flames roar, my magic pulsing inside me at the sight. It always begged to break free whenever I was around fire. Begged to join in the dance. I looked back at Abraham. "There were quite a few Suppressors in the village too. I saw some of them beating up a Wielder." *And I did nothing to help.* I shook off the thought. There was really nothing I could have done. Nothing that wouldn't have given myself away, and I wouldn't risk Lillyanna's life by trying to save another.

Rubbing my eyes, I looked around the fire, noting Lillyanna was missing. "Shit." I cursed, scrambling to my feet scanning the glade looking for her, sending tendrils of my magic out. I strode out of camp and past the tree line, stepping over branches as I followed the pulse of her magic. After a bit, I spied her standing in a clearing a few yards away, eyes fearfully looking around. Her body relaxed when she saw me.

"Don't do that again. It's far too dangerous for you to be wandering off alone," I said, looking down at her.

"I needed to be alone," she said. "I'm feeling smothered. I can't—"

"Quiet," I said, silencing her.

I looked around the woods. It was deathly quiet. The silence suffocating. Not a branch moved. Not a leaf rustled.

"We need to go," I said. The hair on the back of my neck stood up, and a chill raced down my spine. I looked at Lil who rubbed her arms, her breath coming out in a puff of smoke.

"What is it?" Her voice was a whisper. She moved closer to me, threading her fingers with mine.

"I'm not sure. Let's go," I said, tugging her along. The wind picked up, howling through the trees. The woods became black as pitch.

"There's something evil out there," Lil said.

"I feel it too."

A wail pierced the quiet, a loud screeching like the scream of a child being disemboweled. It made my blood curdle.

Wraiths.

White, formless specters glided through the woods, their wails deafening. Frightening. Long, bony fingers reached out. I watched them as they circled us, their raspy voices taunting.

"Humans," one hissed.

"Tasty," another said.

Lillyanna and I stood back-to-back, slowly circling with them.

"Don't let them touch you." I cautioned, my voice low. "It will kill you."

"Smart human," a voice purred. "We will take you first."

I looked for a way out, but the wraiths made a tight circle. I was helpless to do anything. My magic was useless against them. Only light could defeat them.

"I am not going to die. You will not take me to the Abyss," Lil growled. I turned around. Her fists clenched, jaw set, eyes narrowing on the wraiths. I felt her magic surge, an awesome flow of power pulsating through her. Light surrounded—no, emanated from her. It pulsated and grew so bright I had to shield my eyes. The wraiths hissed as the glare grew until it exploded from her. She screamed as the power rushed out, the concussion hitting me and casting me to the ground. The wraiths howled and writhed in agony, disintegrating into dust.

Lillyanna collapsed to her hands and knees.

I bounded to my feet and rushed to her side.

"Lil."

Her breathing was ragged. A trickle of blood ran from her nose. Nausea crawled up my throat at the sight.

"Easy," I said as she sat back on her haunches, wiping her face with the back of her hand. Slipping my arm beneath her, I helped her to her feet, and we limped back to camp. Abraham watched as we settled down on the ground. Concern etched his face. He tore off a piece of his shirt and handed it to her, and she pressed the cloth to her nose.

"Wraiths," I said. "She used a tremendous amount of magic on them. Almost too much, though it's wonderful the things she can do without guidance," I said, glancing over at her, a wash of relief coming over me as I saw the blood had stopped. "Are you alright?"

"I'm fine," she said.

"You used a lot of magic. You should probably rest."

"I want to be alone," she said, rising to her feet.

"Leave her," Abraham said as I stood up.

"Stay out of this." I crossed to where she stood. She looked up as I approached. "What's going on, Lillyanna? Talk to me. You haven't been yourself of late."

"What exactly is myself?" She plopped down on the ground. I knelt in front of her, waiting patiently for her to continue. "I'm scared. No... I'm terrified, Damiyun. I don't know what I'm supposed to do. What I'm supposed to think. I don't even know who I am." She yanked at the grass, pulling up clumps and tossing them aside. She looked at me, eyes brimming with tears of frustration. "I want to run away and hide," she said, slipping her arms around me and resting her cheek on my chest.

She pulled back, her teary green eyes glared at me.

My heart broke. I wanted to take her sadness away. Take her away from all of this. Hide her somewhere safe.

I leaned down and kissed her lips, her cheeks, her eyes.

"Take me away, Damiyun. Let's leave all of this. So, what if I don't defeat the Fallen One?"

"He will plunge the world into darkness. Man will be enslaved by him."

She pulled back and looked up at me. My heart broke at the pain and sadness in her eyes. "But why is this my job? Why aren't the gods doing something? Why aren't they waging a war like they did thousands of Grand Passages ago?"

It was a question I had asked myself many times over, and it was one I couldn't answer. For whatever reason, it seemed as though the gods were content to sit on their thrones in S'aehe unwilling to do the job themselves. Or help Lillyanna. I didn't rightly know their reasons, and it didn't sit well with me.

"I don't know," I said. "Perhaps they fear the destruction and havoc they wreaked that time. There are many more humans, innocents, who could get killed in the war."

"There are seven of them. Surely, they can defeat him. Surely, they're stronger than I." I could hear the despondency in her voice. She bit her lip. "I'm not coming out of this, am I?"

My shoulders fell. A feeling of hopelessness fell upon me at the thought of what was to happen. At knowing, I truly couldn't help her.

I said nothing as I pulled her into my embrace and held her tight, committing the way she felt to memory. A twig snapped, and I looked up to see Abraham scowling in the shadows.

"I told you—warned you—against a physical relationship," Abraham said. "Once again you have let your cock dictate your actions and cloud your judgement."

"My judgement is fine."

"So then why this ridiculous detour to S'aehe?"

"I told you why—"

"It's frivolous. The Fallen One's binds weaken every day. He is sending his demons through."

"We will be there a short time."

"If anything happens to her—"

"Nothing will happen. I know my role. Lillyanna will be there. She will be ready and do what she must."

We made our way back to the campsite. Lillyanna stretched out on the ground, pulling her blanket and cloak tight.

Abraham sighed and tossed another log on the fire. "And you, Damiyun? Will you do what you must?"

I said nothing as I stretched out, shifting Lil so she was cradled in my arms.

Abraham's last words resonated in my head, and not for the first time did I wonder if I could take the life of this woman.

TWENTY-EIGHT
LILLYANNA

I T WAS STILL DARK out when Damiyun's voice roused me. I pulled myself off
the hard ground, working kinks and stiffness out of my body.

"It's still night," I grumbled as I swung up onto Xander and settled into the
crook of Damiyun's arm. It was cold and dreary, the weather not improving as the
morning wore on. A foggy mist settled, the droplets clinging to clothing. Around
midday, the mist turned into a steadier rain, and the sound of thunder rumbled
in the distance.

"There's a village about fifteen miles east. We need to make haste before the
storm hits." Abraham heeled his mount into a faster pace.

The sound of thunder drew closer, and the intermittent flashes of lightning
made me shudder.

"Ever since Abraham made me call the lightning, I can feel it reaching out to me
when it storms. Feel the vibration beneath my skin. I want it, Damiyun. I want to
feel the energy. More, I wish to hurl the power outward, rage as wild as a stormy
sea."

Damiyun tensed up behind me. "He never should have had you do that. The
power can topple mountains. It comes from the darkest place."

"It scares me." *And thrills me.* "The knowledge of what I can do, the harm I
can cause." I shivered. "It frightens me." And I like it.

Oh, I had no designs to destroy or kill, but the power I had was strong. I heated
with the feel of it rushing through my veins. I could let a little trickle out. Just a
thread or strike as forcefully as a gale.

"As it should," Damiyun said, bringing me back.

I turned around and looked up at him. "What scares you?"

He paused. "When I was a child, I was afraid of Arden," he said. "As I got older,
that fear turned into anger and hatred. I suppose it's how I survived his torture.
He couldn't shatter me. Rage prevented that from happening."

"Were you afraid when Abraham came?"

"No. I always knew someone like him would come to me."

"And now? Aren't you afraid of what happens when he calls the contract?"

"I welcome death's embrace and the release from my pathetic existence."

"But won't you serve Themesis?"

"I have served him all my life. Where it happens makes no difference," he said, teeth clenched. He muttered under his breath and shook his head, something I noticed him doing more often.

"How is it Abraham had a daughter?"

Damiyun looked startled at my question.

"He told me about her when you were eating. He said I remind him of her."

He chuckled softly. "I suppose that's true. To answer your question, he was mortal once. He liked to gamble. One day his luck ran out, and he sold his soul for the Luck of the Fallen One. With that gift, he couldn't lose. I don't know what Themesis promised him when his contract is called, though I know him to be deceitful and rarely deliver on his promises," he said. "Like myself, Abraham was far from a good person, although I truly believe his magic was given to him by Themesis himself. He is what is called a Shadow Walker. He can pull darkness—the shadows—around himself and move about unseen." Damiyun shifted behind me.

"What does this have to do with his daughter?"

"Like many men, he has a weakness for the fairer sex. One in particular captivated him, and he fell in love."

I snorted. The thought of Abraham—whose face rested in a perpetual scowl—falling in love was laughable.

"He is a man, Lillyanna. Even now, he is still a man with needs and desires. This woman, Lenore, bore him a child. Jaylynn foolishly sold her soul for Eternal Life."

"And he had to deliver her soul," I breathed.

"Yes."

We rode in silence for a bit as I digested what he said. Though I didn't like Abraham, I couldn't help but feel pity for him. Having to deliver your own daughter to her eternal torment would break any man. I eyed Abraham as he rode ahead of us and then glanced back at Damiyun.

"What did he promise you?"

Damiyun sighed. "Eternal Rest, though I know I won't get it. I can't say what fate he will bestow on me, nor can I say I care, as long as I am no longer a part of this world." He winced and scowled, his face turning dark.

"Are you alright?" I was too worried to ignore it this time.

"I'm fine," he said tersely, lips pursed.

"You're lying to me. You promised you wouldn't."

He rubbed his face. "It's nothing for you to concern yourself with."

"Damiyun—"

"It's Themesis," he said, his tone reluctant. "What Abraham did to me... since that day he has been in my head."

"In... in your head? You mean you hear his voice?"

"I'm not going insane," he whispered.

"I don't think—"

"Yes, you do," he said, and I closed my mouth. Indeed, a part of me thought that could be a possibility. "What Abraham did... He was taking pieces of my soul, attacking my mind, and assaulting me with pain, and somehow it allowed Themesis to slip inside." He paused. "Perhaps I am going insane."

"Karstollan," Abraham yelled back to us from up ahead, sparing me from trying to find something to say about what Damiyun had just revealed. After all, I had heard him too. We pulled up to him and beheld the town spread out below. I was happy to see it. My hair stuck to my face and my cloak dragged down my shoulders. I longed for warmth and a hot meal. "The Cave of the Gods is less than a day's ride north," he said, spurring Violet down. We made our way through the quiet and nearly deserted village. The weather no doubt kept the inhabitants inside.

I looked around, noting a few statues erected in the square. I recognized a few from pictures I had seen. One was my mother, Felicity. She stood tall and proud, long hair flowed down to her waist. A smile curled her lips. She looked down at a man kneeling in front of her, a finger tilted his head up. His eyes were wide in awe. Across from her stood a male god, dressed in armor, sword raised above his head and shield held up in protection. Sarlay, the God of War. There was one statue that was virtually destroyed. The head was missing, as were the arms. I surmised this had to be Themesis.

"I didn't think people worshipped the gods anymore," I said, nodding to the statues.

Damiyun looked around. "Many don't, though we are close to the Cave of the Gods. It makes sense some would worship here," he said.

We pulled up to a small tavern with a sign that read The Drunken Dragon Tavern and Inn.

Abraham opened the door, and we stepped inside. My blood ran cold as I took in six Suppressors sitting at a table, the only patrons in the establishment. Two of the Suppressors looked up at the sound of the door opening, eyes narrowing on Damiyun.

"Rayne." One jumped to his feet and unsheathed his sword. The others turned and looked our way, also jumping up. The sound of metal rang through the air.

Damiyun glanced at Abraham, and they shrugged out of their cloaks and pulled their swords free.

The Suppressors leaped at Damiyun and Abraham, who stepped forward, toward the middle of the room. They stood back-to-back; swords held at the ready. I watched as they fought, Abraham and Damiyun beating the Suppressors back. I winced as a blade grazed the left side of Damiyun's face, a fine line of blood forming and dripping down, while another blade caught his right forearm. I drew on my magic and leaped forward. Grabbing the nearest Suppressor by the arm, I sent out a pulse of energy. He howled in pain, jerking his arm back, the smell of burned flesh filling the room.

"You little bitch." His murderous eyes bored through me. He gripped his sword and advanced on me.

"Here." Damiyun yelled. I turned briefly in his direction. My fingers closed around the hilt of the dagger he thrust at me.

"Duck." Abraham growled. I fell to a knee, my mouth going dry as a flash of silver flew just above my head. I thrust at my assailant, blade sinking deep into soft flesh, and jerked up. Blood poured over my hand and spilled onto the floor. I yanked the blade out and sprang to my feet, eyes scanning the room. Abraham swung, slicing one man through his midsection, while Damiyun pulled his blade from another on the floor. In a matter of moments, it was over. All the Suppressors lay dead. We stood in the center of the room, surveying the carnage, only the sound of our labored breathing remained. I looked at Damiyun whose shirt was soaked with sweat and blood. He wiped his brow, then sheathed his sword.

"You're hurt." My eyes flicked from the wound on his face to the nasty-looking gash on his arm.

"It's fine." He shrugged.

"Whelp, ye shore made a mess o' me place." We turned to see a heavy-set woman in the corner, arms crossed, and her eyes leveled on the three of us. Her gray hair was piled on top of her head in a disheveled bun, and her apron was stained with food. She sighed then rummaged behind the counter, pulled out a clean rag and tossed it to Damiyun. He dabbed the blood on his cheek, revealing a four-inch cut going from cheekbone to chin, and then wrapped the rag around the wound on his arm.

"They knew ye." The comment was more a statement. "I ain't ne'er seen yas, but they 'ave."

Damiyun rubbed his eyes and opened his mouth to speak when Abraham stepped in.

"What do you need in the way of compensation?"

She laughed. "Ye don' need ta be a-worrying. Them 'pressors chase all me good customers away. We be heavy in the magic-wielding population, 'n them don' take kindly 'n that lot coming 'ere. Nay. Ye done me a favor."

The two men exchanged looks. "If you would be so kind, we would like a room and some food," Damiyun's deep voice cut in. He picked their cloaks off the floor and tossed Abraham his. Her eyes swept over the three of us and I could only imagine what she was thinking. We were a rag-tag bunch, comprised of two men and a young woman traveling together, and it was clear none of us shared a bloodline.

Abraham reached into the pocket of his cloak and pulled out a purse heavy with coin. He opened it up and tossed two pieces of gold to the woman, whose eyes widened in surprise. "That is for your trouble and to pay for the cleanup." His eyes met hers. He reached into the bag again and tossed her a silver. "And you never saw us." His deep rumbling voice was low. "And if anymore come here this eve, more coin awaits if you let us know. We will take care of them for you. Now our room? And if it is not too much trouble, we will take our meal there."

The woman smiled as she stowed the coin in a pocket. "O' course, m'lord. I 'ave fergetten wot ye be lookin' like already. I ain't gots no rooms. Ye be welcome ta' sleep in da barn."

Taking the food, we made our way back outside, and hurried to the barn. It was dark and smelled of horse piss and shit, and I covered my nose to keep from gagging. After finding an empty stall, we settled in. Damiyun removed the rag from his arm, then stripped out of his shirt. The gouge on his face didn't run very deep. The wound on his arm was a different story. It was an angry slash across his forearm, and my concern grew when I saw how deep it was and the amount of blood that soaked the rag.

"I don't know if I can heal this. The whip marks... they weren't deep. Damiyun, this is almost to the bone." I took a deep breath and drew on my magic. Trickling it through my fingers to his arm, I wrapped it around the wound in a stitch-like pattern. My effort had little effect. The wound was far deeper than what little magic I had available could fix.

"I can't. It's too deep, and I don't have enough magic."

He pulled his arm from my grasp and wrapped the bloodied rag around it again. "It's alright, Lil. I have been hurt far worse than this. This is nothing more than a scratch." He attempted a smile through a pained glance. I leaned my head against his shoulder, and he slipped his arm around me, pressing his lips to my temple.

Abraham handed us the bowls of food. The stew was flavorless. The meat, whatever it was, was dry. Given everything else, it didn't surprise me to find the bread stale, and the butter was on the verge of going rancid. I was hungry though and didn't care. I devoured the food like it was the finest feast. When we finished eating, Abraham collected the bowls and made his way toward the door.

"Abraham," I said. He turned, his dark eyes on me. "Can you see if the innkeeper has something to stitch the wound? Also, more rags and perhaps a bottle of Serpent's Venom," I requested. Nodding curtly, he stepped out the door.

"I told you. It's not bad." Damiyun's jaw clenched.

"And I told you it's deep." I snapped. "If I don't take care of it, an infection could set in," I didn't care what he thought. He just had a bad attitude because of the pain. An infection could lead to amputation, something I had witnessed when I worked for the local healer, and something I would not let happen.

Blood seeped through the rag holding the wound closed. "The bleeding needs to stop." I looked up at the sound of footsteps.

Abraham strode in carrying the items I had requested and handed them to me. He stepped back and sat down, arms crossed and eyes on us.

Threading the needle, I pulled the stopper out of the bottle and carefully unwrapped Damiyun's arm.

"This will burn," I warned, glancing up at him. He nodded, and I poured some Serpent's Venom on a rag. Carefully, I pressed it to the wound. He inhaled sharply, jerking his arm out of my grasp. Reaching over, I calmly took it again, held it firmly, and gently cleaned the gaping gash as he gritted his teeth and grunted. I handed the bottle to him.

"Drink some. The next part will hurt far worse." He grabbed the bottle and took a hefty swig. I took a deep breath and carefully slipped the needle into his skin. He winced then took another long pull off the bottle and I continued my slow and careful stitching. The sound of the horses snorting, rain slashing against the roof, and the drip of water hitting the hay punctuated his grunts of pain. When I finished, I tied off the thread, cleaned the wound once more and wrapped a clean rag around his arm again.

Damiyun sat with his back against the wall and the bottle held loosely in his hands. I took the bottle and quaffed a healthy swig, coughing and sputtering as it burned its way down my throat. After the brief encounter with the Suppressors and having to sew up his nasty wound, I needed something to calm my nerves. He took the bottle from me and set it on the ground and then rested his head against the wall.

"How does it feel now?" I looked up at him.

He glanced down. "It's a dull, throbbing ache. I have endured far worse pain." His eyes met mine, and he flashed a smile.

"I suggest we get some rest. The sooner you get Lillyanna there, the sooner she gets back, the sooner we can continue our purpose." Abraham huffed as he settled into the bed of hay. I settled down in the nest, as did Damiyun. Curling up in his arms, I yawned, my eyes closed, and I fell into a dreamless sleep.

TWENTY-NINE
DAMIYUN

THE DULL THROBBING OF my injured arm kept me awake. Every movement sent waves of pain through my flesh. I sat up, groaning at the sight of Abraham's bulky form silhouetted against the night. I was hoping he would be asleep still so I could get a few moments of peace. I pulled myself up and stood next to him. It was that odd time between dusk and dawn when it wasn't quite night and not yet morning, the sun still hunkered down in slumber.

"I wish you would reconsider." Abraham said.

I rubbed my eyes. "It will not take long." I couldn't quite understand his need for urgency. As Themesis was sending forth his demons, Abraham let me and Lil sit at the Compound for a full Moon Cycle.

A rustling behind drew my attention, and I saw Lil sitting up, stretching her arms above her head. Her hair was a tangled mess of curls and hay, and I couldn't help but notice how frail and innocent she looked.

A heaviness filled me as my mind went to the reason we were here.

The reason I was here.

She slipped over to me and wordlessly inspected my wound, cleaning and binding it with fresh linen, and for the first time I realized I didn't deserve her.

Slipping my soiled shirt over my head, I strapped my weapons on and tossed my cloak about my shoulders as we made our way out of the barn. The morning was dreary and raw, a cold mist settling on our clothes and hair, making the ride miserable.

A feeling of foreboding blanketed me as we traveled to a place I hadn't been in a good long time, to see a woman I had wished to never lay eyes on again. Maybe Abraham was right. I should have refused Lil's request. As it were, it was too late to turn back, and I could only hope my deeds would remain buried. We arrived at the cave a little after midday. We removed our cloaks, and I handed my weapons to Abraham.

"Do not linger." He pointed a finger at me.

Saying nothing, I took Lil's hand and tugged her in the direction of the rocky entrance. I lit a torch, the fire illuminating the dark, gaping hole of the cave ahead. Our shadows danced on the wall, a distorted dirge sounded somewhere in the recess of my mind. I hesitated before I took a deep breath and plunged into the dark.

"When were you last here?" Lil's voice broke the deafening quiet.

"It's been a few Grand Passages." Though I wished it had been much longer.

We continued on in silence, the sound of our feet echoing through the void.

"Where do the other passages go?" She pointed to a yawning opening on her right.

"There are several ways to enter and exit. There are also passages that will lead the traveler through a labyrinth where they will become lost and eventually perish. It is the gods' way of protecting S'aehe. The whole cave system prevents anyone of ill intent from finding their way through. Only those who have been summoned are privy to the true passages."

"What's to stop someone who knows the way from bringing others?"

"Oohlrich. He is the Keeper of the Cave, and his job is to make sure those who enter were summoned and check whether their intent is nefarious."

Except for me. I was granted access without Felicity requesting to see me.

"Oohlrich can delve into a person's mind for the truth," I continued. "He can do it in such a way he remains undetected." And in the mind, he could spread confusion and panic. The place was well guarded from any unwanted mortal interference.

We continued on in silence until silver light shone just ahead. Taking a deep breath, I squeezed Lil's hand and continued forward to the end where the light spilled through, and saw the familiar outline of Oohlrich, broad ax at the ready in his massive hands.

"Oohlrich," I said with a nod. He lowered the ax head to the ground, leaning his bulk on the butt of the handle, and scratched at his beard.

"Damiyun. Welcome back." his low, deep voice rumbled through the cave. His dark eyes narrowed on Lillyanna who stepped closer to me. Oohlrich's look of anger turned to one of surprise.

"Welcome," he said to her, bowing at the waist, then turned his attention back to me. "The Goddess of Nature lounges in her garden. I trust you remember the way?"

I nodded. We brushed past him into the brilliant light—not quite sunlight, more of a bright whiteness—of S'aehe. We stepped onto the marble path. Beautiful flowers of every color lined the sides, and a blanket of green stretched out where lesser gods and goddesses casually lounged. As we walked, someone whispered my name to a chorus of giggles. Ignoring the voices, I kept my eyes ahead and continued on to Felicity's Garden.

The garden was in full bloom. Flowers in vibrant blues, pinks and purples made a dizzying kaleidoscope of colors, and the sweet aroma was heady and intoxicating. Dragon birds and Faery flies fluttered about, the soft hum of insects a quiet symphony. The path led to a central point where a large structure of marble and oak with a high peaked roof sat. There, a woman lounged casually on a pile of thick pillows.

Felicity.

A low table with food and wine sat in front of her. We approached the structure and her eyes widened at the sight of me, lips curling into a smile as she rose gracefully to her feet. Her waist-length blond hair was loose, the sides secured with gold combs. She wore a dark-green dress that clung to her perfect hourglass form, the plunging neckline revealing an expanse of tanned skin. Her honey-colored eyes danced with amusement as she glided toward us.

"Damiyun," she purred, voice soft and silky as she clutched my hands, leaning forward to brush her soft lips on my cheek. She smelled of elderberry flowers and lilacs, a scent I was intimately familiar with, and a flicker of desire ignited inside.

"Felicity," I greeted, dropping her hand, and stepping back.

"How is it the older you get, the more handsome you become?"

"You flatter me. It is your beauty that is ageless."

She laughed, a breathless sound. "How long has it been, Damiyun?"

Evidently, not long enough. Pulling myself from her flirtatious banter, I turned to Lil. "I have brought your daughter to see you."

Felicity's eyes went to Lil, her look telling me she had just realized she was standing there. "Welcome, Lillyanna. Come. Eat and drink," she said, gesturing to the table as she settled on her mountain of pillows. I stayed where I was, my eyes on Lil as she sat down.

"Come join us, Damiyun," Felicity grasped my hands.

"Thank you, but this does not concern me. I will leave you and Lillyanna to speak in private." I pulled from her grasp.

Lillyanna's eyes looked up at me. "Please, Damiyun. I'd like you here."

"Yes, Damiyun," Felicity said. Her eyes met mine and a small smile played on her lips, fingers stroking the jewel between her breasts. Her tongue flicked out to lick her lips, and I groaned inwardly at the gesture. "Please stay. We can catch up when I am done speaking with my daughter. It has been such a long time since you visited me. I do miss your company."

I glanced at Lil whose eyes went back and forth between me and Felicity, a frown creasing her brow.

"Thank you all the same, but I believe you and your daughter should have some privacy. What she needs to talk about does not concern me."

Felicity's eyes never left mine. "Doesn't it?"

"No."

A pout formed on her sensuous lips, and I clenched my teeth at the sight. Gods, the woman could look seductive even when unhappy. "Have a drink then."

Taking a deep breath, trying to calm my racing heart—and my body, which began to betray me—I went in and took the goblet of wine she offered. My eyes flicked to Lil who chewed her lip, frown deepening. Leaving her, I made my way to a stone bench on the edge of the walkway. I sat slowly down.

Felicity was playing with me. Being close to her, the memories of her warm, smooth skin beneath my hands, her scent, drove me mad. She knew the effect she had on me. I was nothing more than an insect trapped in her spider's web waiting for her to inject me with her venom which would render me powerless to her.

I glanced over to where Lillyanna sat with her mother, who sat back, a small smile playing on her lips. While I hoped she received the answers to her questions, I doubted Felicity would cooperate. Candor didn't exist in the goddess's vocabulary.

I sipped my wine, trying to ignore the covert glances and giggles of the young women—lesser goddesses—that walked by. What happened between Felicity, and I was not a secret, but the longer we lingered the likelihood of Lillyanna hearing details increased exponentially.

"Damiyun Rayne." A voice called out.

"Sarlay," I said, watching the God of War saunter up to where I sat. He wore a long, blood-red tunic with buttons made of gold, an intricate filigree pattern stitched in gold thread lined the buttons and long cuffs. His black, leather trousers were tucked into a pair of polished, black boots, and as always, his broad ax was strapped to his back. He sat down beside me on the bench, and I resisted the urge to get up and walk away.

"It's been a long time since you've been here," he said. "I see you've brought Felicity's daughter." He looked over at her, licking his lips, lasciviously with a bit of saliva to wet his tongue. I clenched my fists at the look. "I never thought you to be a one-woman man again. Not the Damiyun Rayne I know, the one who beds women and discards them."

"I am her Keeper and nothing more," I said through clenched teeth.

Sarlay laughed. "I'm sure Themesis will be quite smitten with her. He does like a pretty face." He glanced at me. "Similar to you. I'm sure he will charm her with his wiles."

My nails bit into my palms. The urge to unleash my magic on him was strong. "What are you doing to prevent Themesis from breaking free?" I looked at Sarlay. As long as he was here, I might as well try to get answers. If not that, then maybe some insight as to what their plan was with Themesis and with Lil.

Sarlay scratched his beard. Amusement danced in his eyes. "Surely, you know." He gestured in Lil's direction.

"She can't be the only way to stop him."

Sarlay shrugged.

"You waged a war against him thousands of Grand Passages ago. You entombed him with magic."

He folded his arms and crossed his ankles. "Yes, we did, and the life and breath of Wielders kept him bound." He shook his head. "I'm sure I don't need to tell you the story."

My jaw ached from clenching my teeth so hard. "No, you don't, but you cannot send a young woman to the Abyss in the hopes that she will defeat him. Don't tell me you, the gods, aren't doing anything about the situation."

Sarlay looked at me. "This is a mortal problem."

"This is a god problem!"

"Mortals no longer worship us. It is they who have brought this on. You know we cannot meddle in their lives." He shook his head. "They see the demons roaming the lands. They hear them in the middle of the night, their screams, their thirst for blood. When the binds on Themesis' tomb are resealed, when the demons disappear, the mortals will thank us. They will praise us and subjugate themselves to us."

I sat back, stunned. I couldn't believe what he was saying. "You're resting the fate of the entire world on one young woman's shoulders? She has her whole life ahead of her."

"It is what she was born to do."

"Why? How can she be more powerful than seven gods?"

"Her mother is Felicity. Besides myself, she is the most powerful goddess in all of S'aehe," he said, as if it answered my question.

My magic flared to the surface, and I had to struggle to keep it down. *And the seven of you are far stronger.* "What will you do if she fails? What will you do if she doesn't make it?" *What will you do if I take her far away from here, someplace where we can be alone and live out the rest of our days?*

Sarlay shrugged. "Man will fall to Themesis. They never should have turned their backs on us."

"It will not only be the mortals who fall. You will fall as well."

Sarlay rose from the bench, a smile curling his lips. "No. They will realize their folly and come back, and we will graciously welcome them with open arms and right the wrong they have brought upon themselves," he said, then turned and walked back to the palace.

I shook my head and glanced at Lil. At the woman, the gods were sacrificing in the hopes to garner prayers. The narcissism among these deities ran deep. They didn't care about Lillyanna, and I doubted they cared that Themesis was slowly breaking free. Their only want was to be worshipped. Sadness and anger rolled over me as Sarlay's words bounced around in my mind. My shoulders sagged, weighted down by the knowledge I had garnered that my Lil would be sacrificed on a hope and a prayer and there was nothing I could do to stop it.

THIRTY
LILLYANNA

I LOOKED OVER AT Damiyun who settled down on a bench. It felt a little surreal being here in the place where the gods lived. Lower deities wandered casually through gardens and across stone bridges where water ran beneath them. Giggles and whispers followed Damiyun's every step.

The garden was beautiful, the air pungent with the scent of flowers, the sounds of bees and other insects buzzing. Bushes were manicured into gigantic roaring dragons, unicorns rearing up, hooves pawing the air. The figures of gods carved into marble glistened a brilliant shade of white under the sun's gaze.

Sarlay, the God of War, stood tall in armor, a broad ax strapped to his back, his hand resting on the hilt of his sword. Euphina, the Goddess of Healing, sat nearby, her long hair was pulled back in a braid. She held her skirts up with one hand, while the other held a big basket filled with herbs. Dhala, the Goddess of Fertility, held a babe in her arms. Leoatle, the God of the Sea, stood holding a trident, a huge wave looming up behind him. Vatra, the God of Fire, held his hands out, flames danced on his palms. Samanka, Goddess of Dreams held her hand out, fingers sprinkling dream dust, and of course, my mother, Felicity, the Goddess of Nature stood among them. Her hair spilled down her back in soft waves, a crown of flowers rested on her head. She wore a dress cut low in the front, and her lips were curled into a smile.

I looked over at Damiyun whose jaw was tense. More questions surfaced.

"Why was I born?" I got straight to the point. My mother leaned forward, grabbed an olive, and popped it in her mouth, chewing it slowly.

"To defeat the Fallen One and send him back into his prison."

I shook my head. "Why me? The gods were able to imprison him thousands of Grand Passages ago. Why can't you do that now?"

"Because he is stronger now. He draws his power from the Abyss." She paused. "You are a powerful Wielder, Lillyanna. You have the blood of a goddess in your veins. You have my power as well as your father's coursing through you. You will help defeat him."

"But why me? I'm not a god. How can I do what apparently none of you can? Surely seven deities are far stronger than one," I said. "And you have lesser gods behind you as well. Themesis has himself and his demons which, I'm guessing, are easy to kill."

"I told you, Daughter. You come from strong blood."

"And there are seven all-powerful gods that would be going up against one." My frustration with my mother was growing. "I'm just one person. It doesn't matter if I have the blood of a goddess in my veins or that I'm powerful. I'm one person. Not seven. How am I supposed to defeat Themesis when none of you can? Why won't any of you help me?" Realization dawned on me. I grew cold. Nausea welled up, and I fought to keep it down. "None of you want to. You lost gods and lesser deities in the War Against the Gods. You don't want to lose anymore. You're afraid."

My mother's eyes flashed with anger. "The gods are never afraid."

Right. "So why am I the sacrificial lamb?"

"Don't be so dramatic, Daughter." My mother rolled her eyes.

I snorted. "It looks like that's a trait I inherited from you." Her eyes narrowed on me. "How am I supposed to defeat him? Everyone knows except me."

She said nothing. The nagging thought, the suspicion that I would not be coming back from this, reared its ugly head once again. I wished someone would tell me the truth. If my purpose was to die to keep Themesis bound, I would rather know. I would rather be able to prepare. But once again I was kept in the dark. I clenched my fists, my anger and annoyance slowly growing. "Why did you leave me?" The hurt ran deep. My father leaving me and my mother, never raising me. She had many expectations with little to warrant it.

She adjusted her position, pulling her legs up beneath her before she spoke. "I came down in my mortal form," she started. "My intentions were to bed your father then leave. As I am sure you know, it did not happen the way I planned. Your father charmed me. He stole my heart. I dare say I fell for him." A soft smile crossed her lips, then faded just as quick. "We are only allowed in your world for one Grand Passage and one day. If we remain longer, then we are trapped in our mortal form and can no longer return. You see, Lillyanna, it wasn't that I wanted to leave, I had to."

"Would it have been so bad to remain? To be a mother to me and a wife to Vel?"

Her silence said far more than any words could have, and I remembered Abraham's warning about the gods being selfish and deceitful. My mother's actions were proving such.

"Did you even love Vel?"

She smiled, her look far away. "I did, Lillyanna. You were created through a union of love."

I snorted at her words. "Right. It was such a loving union that both of you left me."

My mother sighed. "I did what I had to do."

I glared at her. "Of course, you did. You're a goddess. You only think of yourself."

Her fingers curled around the glass she held, and her eyes flicked to Damiyun again. "So, tell me, Daughter. Has Damiyun been taking good care of you? Has he claimed you as his own?"

I felt my face heat at the question. She looked back at me. She licked her lips, gaze pinning me, and I suddenly felt like a trapped animal.

"There is no need to be embarrassed. Damiyun is a very handsome and virile man, and he has a weakness for beautiful women."

"What does he have to do with where I came from? With why, you decided to leave me, not once coming back to see how I was?"

"I was always watching you, Daughter. And I knew you were in good hands with Damiyun." Another secret smile curled her lips as her eyes went to Damiyun, then back to me.

Unease settled over me. "Watching isn't the same thing as being there. You could have come back."

She didn't blink. She didn't say a word.

"You didn't want to, did you? You didn't want me."

My mother sipped her wine with a sigh. "Of course I wanted you. It's complicated, Lillyanna."

I glared at her. "It doesn't seem complicated," I said, refilling my glass. "You came down to have a child with Vel. You could have just as easily come down to see the same child you birthed. Instead, you stayed here." I gestured around with my glass.

She pursed her lips, and an angry look flashed across her face. Just as soon as it came, it was gone, a smile replacing it. "Damiyun. Come join us." She called out.

Damiyun turned and looked in our direction, draining his glass as he rose to his feet.

The conversation was clearly over. For now, anyway.

THIRTY-ONE
DAMIYUN

Taking a deep breath, I made my way back to the pavilion and sat down.

"Tell me. How have you been? It has been so long since you have been here." A small teasing smile lit Felicity's lips as she drank her wine.

"I am the same. Nothing much changes with me."

"Oh, come now. Surely taking care of my daughter keeps you on your toes."

I glanced at Lil. A slow flush crept up her face, and I wondered how much of our relationship she had revealed.

"Lillyanna takes care of herself. My job is only to keep her safe. Nothing more."

Felicity laughed again as she refilled her glass. "Why don't you show my daughter to her room? Take the one you are familiar with. I am sure she wishes to rest."

Nodding, we both rose and made our way to the exit.

"Oh, and Damiyun?" I turned. "Come see me when you have her settled. We have so much to catch up on," she said, her look sultry.

Shit.

"Of course, Felicity." I bowed slightly. Placing my hand on Lil's back, I guided her in the direction of the palace. We said nothing as we walked through the halls to her room. Servants scurried about the corridors, muttering apologies as they pushed by. I looked around the richly decorated halls. Rich and heavy furniture made of cherry, oak, and marble adorned each corridor. High-backed, uncomfortable looking chairs, tall cabinets, and sturdy tables. Bright rugs covered the white and black marble floor. Sunlight spilled in through the stained glassed windows, casting a kaleidoscope of colors on the floor. Bright paintings of nature adorned the walls and statues of the gods were scattered about, undeniable proof of their narcissistic nature.

We stopped at a heavy oak door with a willow tree carved into the wood. I had stayed here before, sharing Felicity's bed.

We stepped inside. A warm flower-scented breeze blew in from the open patio doors. Lil crossed the room and stepped out onto the balcony, which overlooked a vast courtyard with a large marble fountain depicting a naked nymph teasing a mortal man.

"Maybe coming here was a mistake," Lillyanna said softly, turning her green eyes to me. "Perhaps we should leave."

"I can't tell you what to do. If you wish to leave, we can do so."

And my secret will remain safe.

She shook her head. "I'm sure my coming here was a shock. No, I will speak to her again in the morning. Her answers were cryptic at best. I will push her for more."

"Why don't you get some rest?" I suggested, giving her a gentle push into the room. She crossed to the bed and crawled onto the soft comforter, head sinking into the pile of pillows. "I will make my visit with your mother short." I promised, though I doubted she'd allow me to leave so easily. I only hoped Lil would be fast asleep when I returned. Leaning down, I kissed her, watched her close her eyes and then exited the room.

I walked through the halls feeling like a man going to his execution. Everything inside me screamed to stop. To go back to Lillyanna. Grab her and flee. Had the order not come from Felicity, I would have heeded the words and the tugging.

The voice telling me this was an infinitely bad idea. That I was indeed hammering the nail in my coffin.

But I couldn't snub her and as such, I found myself outside her quarters.

T AKING A DEEP BREATH, I rapped sharply on the door.

"Come," her voice called from within. Exhaling, I turned the handle and entered.

Her room hadn't changed since my last visit, long ago. The large antechamber with its glittering, diamond-encrusted chandelier, its tapestries adorning the walls and rugs strewn about the floor. The doors to her balcony were open, and a soft, fragrant breeze stirred the sheer curtains.

Felicity lounged casually on a couch, holding a drink in each hand. Gliding smoothly to her feet, she walked in my direction, a smile curling her lips. My eyes swept over her as she advanced like a cat who had cornered her prey. She had changed into a loose, flowing dress, the trailing hem making her look as though she were floating. The neckline plunged obscenely, and the light blue material was so thin it barely existed. The outline of her naked body showed quite visibly. I again cursed the flames of desire inside as memories flashed in my mind. Memories of her naked, sweaty skin beneath mine. Of her flowery scent and her sweet taste on my lips.

"I trust Serpent's Venom is still your drink of choice?" She held out a glass.

"Thank you." My hand closed around the drink, and I took a hefty sip as I followed her to the seating area and took a comfortable chair across from her.

"How have you been?" Her eyes appraised me over the rim of her glass.

"I told you. I am the same as I was."

She laughed, the sound like bells tinkling upon the wind.

"Why did you ask me here?"

"I told you. I wanted to catch up. Why have you waited so long to come see me?" Her mouth turned down into a sultry pout. I avoided her seductive look.

"I had other things to tend to."

Her mouth twitched and her eyes danced. "Ah yes. I forgot about the wicked witch. Zenith, was it?" She rose and took my glass, fingers lightly stroking my hand as she removed it from my grasp. "Did she at least tell you where she kept your balls before you killed her?"

I clenched my teeth and stood. "Thank you for the drink, Felicity. If you don't mind, I am going to go check on Lil."

"Sit down. My daughter is quite safe here."

But am I?

I slowly lowered myself back into my chair. She walked over, handing my drink back, then settled down on my knee.

"Such a shame to mar such a handsome face." She tsked, fingertips tracing the fresh wound. "Though it does lend a dark and menacing appearance."

"Felicity—"

"What's wrong, Damiyun? Are you growing soft?" She slipped her hand between my legs. "Definitely not soft." Her voice was husky. Taking my drink, she placed both glasses on the table and straddled me. I groaned. The warmth of her pressed into my lap.

Go back to Lil. Seek your pleasure with her, my mind screamed.

"I've missed you, Damiyun." Those lips of her lingered close to my ears, her breath warm. "My bed has been so cold and lonely without you." Her tongue caressed my lobe, lips brushing my cheek then my mouth. My fingers grasped her long, silky hair as our tongues danced. She ground herself against me and I tore my mouth from hers, picked her up, strode into her bedroom and tossed her on the bed. I pulled my shirt over my head. She slipped off the bed and ran her hands up my chest, tongue and lips trailing from my neck down to my navel and down further still.

Sinking to her knees, she undid my trousers. I sighed at the feel of her mouth on me, her soft lips and tongue brushing my skin. I grabbed her hair, thrusting as she moved, pulling her to her feet before I lost myself. In one swift move, she removed her dress and lay back down on the bed. Kicking off my boots, I slipped out of my trousers and went to her, kissing her roughly, hands sliding down soft skin, fingers gently probing, pleasing. Mouth searching. Tongue tasting. She moaned in ecstasy, a sound that fueled my desire to please and satisfy myself. I kissed her hard, driving myself deep inside her. Legs locked around my waist, and nails raked down my back as I took her with a fevered urgency, spending myself as I felt her shudder beneath me, her teeth piercing my neck as she climaxed.

I rolled off her and sat up.

You foolish, selfish man, I chastised myself. Maybe she wouldn't know. Maybe I could keep it hidden. I held my head, guilt crashing over me and making me feel nauseous.

"You can't deny you missed me," Felicity purred, warm lips pressing against my shoulder, arms slipping around my waist.

"What have I done?" I held my head in my hands, pressure building inside me. Why? Repeating every mistake I've ever made again and again, it was madness. Pain lanced a place deep within my chest. I could hardly breathe.

"What you always do, Damiyun. Think only of yourself. Do only what gratifies you." She smiled. "We're not that different."

I shook my head at her words, at the painful truth, and disentangled myself from her arms.

I said nothing as I pulled my clothes on. Guilt and shame constricted my chest.

"Do you love her?"

"I am her Keeper and nothing more." Another lie. They came so easily.

"Yet you have claimed her." Amusement tinged her tone.

"I am a man with needs. You cannot expect me to be in the presence of a beautiful woman and not desire her."

A wicked smile crossed her features, making her look—just for an instant—ugly and evil.

I turned my back on her. "This never would have happened if you hadn't—"

"If I hadn't what, Damiyun? I did not make you do anything you didn't already want to," she said, coming up behind me and slipping her arms around me again. "I never heard you say no," she whispered softly in my ear.

I pulled away and hurried out of her bedroom toward the exit. The air felt thick. I couldn't breathe. All I wanted to do was escape this room. Escape the web. The Goddess of Nature, I scoffed. She was a cat, and I was a toy.

"Don't be such a stranger, darling. You are always welcome in my bed." Her voice and laughter followed me out of the room.

I shut the door and leaned against it.

"What have I done?"

You never said no.

The words damned me.

I slowly made my way back to the room, praying Lil was fast asleep. I pushed the door open into darkness, my eyes going to the lump beneath the covers, red hair fanned out across the pillow. I slipped quietly across the room out onto the balcony. The air was cool on my hot skin, and I breathed deeply. The scent of elderberries and lilacs drifted on the breeze, the smell making my stomach lurch.

What have I done?

"Damiyun?" Lil's soft voice came from behind. I gripped the railing hard and closed my eyes. I swallowed against the lump in my throat. A giant, painful lump that choked me when I tried to breathe. Guilt and sickness flooded me.

"Damiyun? What's wrong?"

I turned around and looked at her. She was standing in a pool of moonlight. The silver rays shining on her skin made her look Faery-like.

And innocent.

"Lillyanna." My voice was a strangled cross between a sob and a whisper.

I willed my legs to move. To go to her and gather her in my arms. To hold her tight and try to pretend I didn't betray her.

But they would not heed my thoughts.

She frowned and took a few tentative steps toward me. "Are you alright? You look like you're going to be sick."

More steps brought her closer still.

"Did something happen?"

Feet took her the final steps to where I stood. Her eyes searched mine, and she reached a hand to me.

I couldn't move.

"Something happened." She snatched her hand back.

"I'm sorry."

"What?" Her look was confused. Her eyes searched my face, widening as realization set in. My head snapped to the side, my face burning from the sting of her slap. "You bastard," she hissed, slapping me again. "How could you?"

Her eyes were furious, hands clenched, and I could feel her magic pulsing as it gathered within her.

"I'm sorry."

"You're sorry? You bed my mother and all you can say is you're sorry?"

"I can—"

"What? Explain? Weave lies that roll effortlessly off your tongue? Make me believe you're a victim and then what, Damiyun? Take me to bed to make me forget? You are nothing more than a whore."

My head snapped back at her words. Words that hurt far worse than any blow.

"You're a selfish, self-serving bastard."

I reached a hand for her, wincing when she recoiled, her face filled with disgust.

I opened my mouth to speak, but everything that I wanted to say vanished. What could I say? I'm selfish? I care only about my own pleasure? Both claims were true and still, I cared about Lillyanna. But why should she believe me when what I had done was such a grievous offense? Words failed me.

"This wasn't the first time, was it? You took her a long time before this night."

"Yes," I whispered, eyes on the stone floor of the balcony. I lifted my eyes back to her face. "I'm sorry, Lil. I'm so sorry I hurt—betrayed—you."

"So you've said. Perhaps if you had a modicum of self-control, we would not be having this conversation. You disgust me, Damiyun Rayne. Get out," she said, eyes furious and hands clenched.

I couldn't move.

"I said get out."

I opened my mouth to speak, then shut it. Nothing I could say—no explanation I could give—would pacify her. She was livid, rightfully so, and I knew she needed time.

My legs finally obeyed, and I nodded as I left the room. I closed the door, and leaned against it, shutting my eyes against her guttural shrieks of rage. I felt her power surge, heard glass breaking, the crack of wood splintering. The loud crashes as she destroyed the room. All the while screaming and cursing my name.

I pulled away from the door, from her fury, and made my way through the halls to another room to rest, though I was certain sleep would not come easily.

I would leave her to unleash her wrath. To tire out.

Hopefully in the morning, when she had settled down, I would be able to speak to her. I would explain what happened and apologize.

And hopefully have her forgive me.

I never should have come here. I should have let Abraham take her. Sighing, I stretched my tired body out on the bed. As always, it was too late for regret. As always, I would reap what I had sown.

THIRTY-TWO
LILLYANNA

I PICKED UP A vase and hurled it at the door as it closed. The sound of glass shattering broke the silence. I reached for anything I could find, glasses, a decanter, a mirror, and threw the items at the wall. A scream tore through me, raw and guttural. My chest constricted. It felt as though a hand was slowly closing around my shattered heart. My magic surged within me, and I let loose a torrent of power. Wood shattered and glass broke. The walls were singed black. I let my fury consume me, let it out in a fantastic burst of magic that destroyed anything in its path until my legs shook and my tears stopped. I stood in the middle of the room, looking around at the damage I had done, batting away the feathers floating about.

I didn't care that I had destroyed this room. I was furious with Damiyun, my magic pulsing at the thought of what he'd done, and I had to calm myself to contain it, lest I topple the entire palace.

I should have listened to Abraham. I should never have let him get close to me. And I should have known there was something amiss. I should have known by the way my mother acted. By the way he acted. By how evasive he was when it came to her. How he didn't want to be a part of our conversation, when I really needed him at my side if only to give silent support.

Magic rippled under the surface of my mind and body. It raged for release. I tried to keep it back, but I didn't know if I could. So, I slipped on my boots, grabbed my cloak, and slowly cracked open the door. Relief washed over me as I looked about the empty corridors, grateful, Damiyun was nowhere to be seen.

Closing the door, I slipped down the hall, eyes alert and ears listening for footsteps. I walked quickly through the quiet palace, through the empty gardens to the entrance to the cave.

To my escape.

I rushed toward the cave but stopped in my tracks when I realized Oohlrich would be guarding the entrance.

Shit.

I wouldn't let him stop me, though. I would leave this place no matter what. So, I drew on my power, holding it tight, and continued my departure. I would use my magic if he tried to stop me. I wasn't going to stay here another moment.

I was not going to listen to Damiyun's apology, his pathetic excuses. Ignoring the voice in the back of my head telling me this was a bad idea, I tiptoed through the entrance.

Strange, the place seemed so oppressive despite it serving as the entrance to the realm of the gods. Sure, it protected the gods but from what, exactly? In my short time there, all I'd seen was decadence and frivolity. Were they not concerned about Themesis, the demons? Had I not been created to defeat him and yet, I was entirely on my own? Damiyun was it, my defender, my aid and torment. It was no wonder we had given up any faith in the gods. I saw nothing of substance where my mother reigned. Damiyun was no better. The lot of them could rot in the Abyss. Fury rippled deep within me.

Taking a deep breath, I continued on, the cave entrance coming into view. I almost cried with relief when I saw Oohlrich wasn't there. I picked up my pace and hurried, holding my breath until I made it inside, only to have defeat fill me when I saw the unlit torch. I walked a few paces into the cavern. It was black as pitch. There was no way I would be able to navigate through without light.

Going back wasn't an option. I needed light, and I needed it fast. There was only one way I was going to get it, so I took a deep breath and closed my eyes. My magic pulsed as I thought about light, pictured the cave growing bright with it. But it wasn't just in my mind. I saw a light growing through my closed eyes. I slowly opened them, an orb of blue light hovered above my right palm, illuminating the cave ahead. Holding on to my magic, I stepped down the corridor. I walked cautiously on, trying to remember the way Damiyun had picked through to avoid the endless caverns. I traveled in a straight line, refusing to take too many turns, until I came upon a crossroads with one cave to the right and one to the left. I didn't remember a crossroads from the journey in.

Damn the gods. Damn Damiyun. I was lost.

I didn't want to turn around. I couldn't go back. My feet ached. I was exhausted and tired of the cold, dark caverns. Taking a deep breath, I chose the tunnel on the left and trudged on. I walked for what seemed like hours. My calves burned, and keeping the orb lit consumed more and more energy with each passing moment. Its brightness dimmed the more I grew tired. Just as I was about to give up, to douse the light, lie down and go to sleep, ready to acknowledge I was hopelessly lost and let the caverns consume me, I saw a sliver of light up ahead. My heart leaped at the sight, and I dug deep and raced toward it. Elation filled me and I almost cried at the sight of an end to the darkness. I burst out, lifting my face to the warm sunshine, breathing in the fresh air cooling my sweaty skin.

I looked around my unfamiliar surroundings, pushing down the rising panic. This was not where we entered. I began trudging across the vast, green field spread out before me, hoping I would eventually find a road leading to a town and some people.

I hadn't gone far when something sharp hit me in the shoulder. Stopping, I looked at my left shoulder, where a small arrow was sticking out.

"What in the world…?" The terrain spun, and the ground rushed up to greet me. The last thing I saw before plunging into darkness were dozens of tall figures in bright clothing advancing in my direction.

I AWOKE SOMETIME LATER, eyes adjusting to the dim light. I sat up and my head spun. Nausea welled up in my throat and I vomited on the floor. Wiping my mouth on my sleeve, I looked around. Icy fingers of fear gripped me as I took in the small window up high in the rock wall. Water dripped, the sound echoing through the corridor. I shivered against the cold, dampness seeping into my skin and bones.

I was in a cell.

"Esna dago." A voice called out in a language foreign to me. Blue eyes peered through the bars, and footsteps echoed off the walls beyond. A key scraped in the lock and the door opened. I stood up, my legs unsteady, and I braced myself against the cold stone wall to keep from collapsing.

A tall, slightly muscular man, with broad shoulders, stood in the doorway. His skin was pale. Bright-blue eyes peered at me from a furrowed brow, and pointed ears peeked out from under his long, white hair.

I had been captured by Elves.

He leaned casually against the door frame and crossed his arms. He was finely dressed, though garishly, in a bright purple shirt tucked into red trousers with a set of boots perfectly matching his shirt sheathing his calves.

Instinctively, I reached for my magic, only to scream as agonizing pain tore through me. A thousand knives pierced and cut, tearing, and slashing my insides to pieces. My knees buckled, and I retched.

"I am glad I took the precaution and put the Sigaa'Lean on you," he said in my language. I looked down at my right arm, seeing black obsidian glinting in the lamplight. "I don't suggest using your magic again. Or trying to remove the bracelet. If you thought the pain you just felt was bad, it gets much, much worse. And it can kill you." He reached into his pocket, pulled out a small knife, and casually began cleaning his nails as if this were a normal, everyday conversation.

"Who are you?" I stood back up, catching myself on the wall when my knees buckled.

He looked up with a smile, perfect, white teeth glinting in the light. "I am Phabian Trounde," he said, his voice proud as he stowed the knife in his pocket.

"Where am I?"

"Trounde Castle. You have trespassed on the Shadow Elf Lands."

Shadow Elves? I had heard them mentioned before... Damiyun. Damiyun had mentioned them when I asked about the passages. He had said they were dangerous but—

"Trespassers are executed when found here." His blue eyes locked on mine. I grew cold. My legs shook, and my heart pounded like it meant to beat right out of my chest.

No, no, no. This couldn't be happening. Curse the gods for my foolishness. I should have stayed put. I cursed Damiyun again for making me run.

"The king, however, has decided to stay your execution. For now, anyway," Phabian said.

I almost wept with relief at his words.

"Now, if you would follow me, please. He wishes to see you."

Taking a deep breath—and willing my legs not to shake—I followed him out of the cell. We walked through the dim halls. The smell of smoke from the torches burned my nostrils. The light danced on the walls, making our shadows look long and menacing. I shivered against the damp, wrapping my arms around myself. I trained my attention on Phabian's back, my mind reeling with what he had said.

I'm not going to die. I'm not going to die. The thought rolled over and over in my head, only to freeze when I remembered I was being brought to the king.

What if this was a trial of sorts? What if Phabian lied? He could have. Why be truthful with me? Perhaps this was a game. My stomach clenched at the thought. I felt sick again, and I bent over and vomited. Phabian turned, a look of disgust on his handsome face, then continued on.

If this were a trial, then I would plead my case. Beg for mercy. Throw myself at his feet and promise to be his servant—his slave—whatever he wished of me, so long as he spared my life. At least I would have more time to plan an escape.

"Am I to stand trial?"

Phabian glanced at me. "It's possible."

"But... you said you kill trespassers."

"We do."

I chewed my lip. "So why go through this charade? Why not just take my head?"

"My king has his reasons." Phabian said, picking up the pace. I scurried to keep up with his long strides, while trying to keep down the nausea. I glanced around as we walked, noting the blinding white marble floors and walls. Gold sconces hung on the walls and diamond chandeliers hung from the ceiling. Ornately carved ebony adorned the corridor, and brightly colored rugs lined the floor. It was clear the ostentatious king liked the finer things.

Finally, we stopped at a set of closed doors on which Phabian knocked. After a beat, he pushed them open and strode through. I dragged my feet behind, heart hammering in my chest.

The room we entered was richly furnished with dark, oak furniture. Bright tapestries hung on the walls and despite that the room was far from cozy. A lithe man sat behind a desk carved from obsidian.

"My king," Phabian said, head lowering in a bow. The man paused in his writing and looked up. He was attractive, eyes so light blue, they seemed almost colorless. His long, white hair was tied back in a low ponytail, and a few tendrils framed his angular face. He put the quill down and rubbed his close-cut beard. After a moment, he pushed away from the desk and moved around front, casually leaning against it. I took in his brightly colored clothes—yellow shirt, bright-blue trousers, and black leather boots—and had my situation not been dire I would have laughed at the tackiness of it.

"Please have a room made up for our... guest... a bath and clean clothes too." He ordered. I almost collapsed at his words.

Guest? Apparently, I was going to keep my head after all.

"My king?" Phabian frowned.

"Is there a problem, Phabian?"

"Of course not. I will see to it immediately," he said, bowing his head and exiting the room.

"Please. Have a seat. You look quite weary." The king gestured to a chair in front of the desk, the large diamond and ruby rings adorning his fingers glinted in the lamplight. Moonlight spilled through the many windows, illuminating the bright white marble floor. I sat gingerly down on the edge of the high-backed seat, all senses alert, ready to bolt if need be.

"I am Allendaire Trounde, king of the Shadow Elves." He inclined his head. "Who might you be?"

"Lillyanna."

"And why were you on my land?"

I hesitated, my mind reeling with the question.

Think, think, think.

In no way was I going to tell him the truth of where I had come from.

Damn it. Think.

He crossed his arms and leveled his gaze on me.

"I... my father is a tinker," I said slowly, the story forming in my mind. "We were on our way to Karstollan." Not a complete lie. We did stop in that village.

"We were attacked by bandits." Half-truth yes. As long as I tried to stick to some facts, I didn't think I would give away my lie. I looked down at my hands. "I fled and... I am not familiar with this place. I became lost and the next thing I know I'm waking up in a cell."

"Do you understand what happens to trespassers?"

Swallowing, I slowly looked at the king. "Phabian told me they were executed."

"That is correct."

I swallowed hard. Sweat trickled down my back.

I'm going to die.

"You did not seem to be a threat. You were alone and unarmed, though we took a precaution with the Sigaa'Lean. Were we correct in our assumption?"

I winced at the memory of pain and managed a nod.

He chuckled. "Since, as I said, I did not deem you a threat, we have stayed your execution, for now," he said, and I sank into the chair at his words. "You will remain here as my... guest... until further notice."

I chewed my lip and nodded. I had a feeling I might not be walking out of here—alive or otherwise—but at least I wouldn't die tonight.

A sharp knock on the door made me jump.

Phabian peeked his head in. "The room is ready."

"Thank you, Phabian. If you would, please escort my guest to her room," he said, then turned back to me. "I will see you tomorrow at the morning meal."

Not a request. An order.

"Of course." I muttered as I rose to my feet and followed Phabian out of the room. He walked with purpose, and I almost had to run to keep up with his long strides.

We drew up to a door. Phabian opened it and stepped to the side to let me through.

"Your bath is ready and the clean clothes on the bed should fit, though you are a bit thicker." I bristled at his remark but kept it to myself. "I will gather you in the morning. Apparently, I am to be your guard and escort as though I have no other duties apart from being a nanny to a human." He muttered as he backed out of the room and closed the door.

I looked around the room. A big, comfortable-looking bed dominated the center. To my right sat a tall wardrobe. A fire blazed in the fireplace where a couch, table, and chairs sat alongside a copper tub, the steam of hot water hovering above. Doors led to a vast balcony. Crossing the room, I pushed them open and stepped outside.

Damn it.

Though it was dark out, the moonlight allowed me to see that my room was high above the ground. Far too high to jump without breaking a leg. Or worse.

Nor was there any way to climb down, as the smooth marble offered no hand or foothold.

I would have to find some other way out.

Sighing, I went back inside and stripped off my clothes. Sinking into the hot bath, I leaned back. Thoughts of what led me here entered my mind. Thoughts that threatened to take over and drag me down. Shaking myself, I closed my eyes, allowing the warmth of the water to envelop me. A warmth that reminded me of Damiyun.

Damn the gods.

I cursed. I quickly washed and then pulled myself out of the tub and crossed over to the bed. Pushing the rose-colored gown aside, I climbed beneath the luxurious covers.

I couldn't say I believed my mother's words. If she had loved my father—loved me—she would have stayed and lived out her life as a mortal.

Rubbing my eyes, I thought about my current situation, reluctantly admitting it was entirely my fault. While Damiyun had hurt me, I had been rash—and foolish—when I decided to flee. I was a fool for lying with him, for believing he cared for me. I was a fool for trusting him in the first place.

To him, I was just another pretty face. A body to warm his bed and satisfy his desires. And now my actions had landed me in a situation I wasn't sure I could escape from. "Good fucking job, Lillyanna," I muttered to myself as I settled down into the soft bed and briefly wondered if Damiyun and Abraham would ever find me.

If they came here, they would be executed.

The thought frightened me, and I realized I had to find a way to escape on my own.

Find my way back to Howling Cove.

THIRTY-THREE

I WOKE THE NEXT morning groggy and weary. I had a restless sleep with horrifying nightmares lingering. I extracted myself from the sheets, which had tangled around my sweaty body. Slipping out of the bed, I pulled on the dress set out for me. The buttons at the bodice strained, and the sleeves constricted around my arms. No doubt I looked ridiculous.

I stepped out onto the balcony, the bright orange and yellow painting the sky in brilliance. I looked around, taking mental notes of my surroundings. My room overlooked a beautiful garden, with stone paths winding their way through shrubs and beds of brilliantly colored flowers. The pathway led to a wall of green that opened to what was probably a labyrinth. I scanned the area beyond, my heart sinking when I saw the entire palace was surrounded by a wall at least ten feet high.

Someone knocked on the door, and I wearily opened it. Phabian stood on the other side, eyes sweeping over me.

"It looks like we will have to have clothes made for you," he snorted, a nasty smirk on his face. I glared at him from behind as I followed him through the halls. He stopped at a set of open doors and gestured for me to enter, then strode away without a word. I hesitated a moment, unsure of what awaited me. Glancing down the hall to my right, for a brief moment the thought of bolting entered my mind.

"Come, Lillyanna," the king's voice called out.

Taking a deep breath, I entered the dining room. The room was no less ostentatious than the halls I had walked through. Marble, gold, diamond, and ebony were everywhere. A long table was the centerpiece. Trays of food graced the top and my stomach growled at the smell of it. Allendaire sat at the head, a dour-faced woman sat to his right. She was tall and thin, white hair piled atop her head in a severe bun. She was a homely woman, with a pinched face, beak-like nose, and pale, thin lips. Unlike the other Elves, her attire was dark and drab, the gray high-necked dress more suited for a death ceremony.

"Come. Sit." Allendaire's voice boomed. His eyes crinkled at the corners as he smiled and gestured to the chair on his left. The dull thud of my boots echoed off the walls as I walked to the chair and took a seat.

He waved his hand. "Eat."

I grabbed a small plate and piled it with food, happy to follow that particular order.

"Lillyanna, this is the queen, Mouranda," he said, motioning to the woman whose disdainful eyes appraised me.

I almost choked on the piece of bread I had been eating.

This ugly woman was his wife? Apparently, the king's lack of taste wasn't just reserved for the tacky clothes he wore.

"Allendaire tells me you were traveling with your father when you were... attacked... by bandits?" she asked. Her tone was sharp, voice regal. I swallowed my food and put down my fork.

"That is correct."

"And where is home, provided you even have one?"

"Howling Cove."

"Never heard of it." She sniffed. "Are you not concerned about your father?"

I clenched my fists beneath the table. "Of course, I am. He was the one who told me to run. I did what he asked and saved myself."

She sat up straighter and looked down her nose at me. "I want you to be aware, despite my husband's decision to stay your execution," she glared at him, then turned her attention back to me, "you are far from a guest. Let it be clear that should I—or my husband—have a change of mind for any reason, you will be quickly and swiftly executed. Do you understand me, girl?"

"Of course. I am an unwanted prisoner. A foolish human who unknowingly wandered onto your lands. I appreciate the leniency I have been offered and the accommodations provided. I am grateful to be keeping my head." I smiled sweetly. "For the time being, anyway."

Mouranda's eyes narrowed, and she pursed her lips. "I am glad we are clear," she said in a clipped tone as she pushed her chair away and stood. Allendaire rose as well. Mouranda nodded curtly to him then floated out of the room, the long train of her dress sweeping the floor in a soft rustle of fabric. When the queen had exited, Allendaire turned his blue eyes which were dancing with amusement on me.

"That went well." The words flew out of my mouth before I realized. "I mean—"

The king laughed. "You're right. It went as expected." He paused a moment. "Would you like to see more of my palace?"

Why not? Maybe I could find some way to escape. "That sounds nice," I said, forcing a smile as I pushed back from the table and rose. His eyes swept over the ill-fitting dress as I fell in step beside him.

"I will have a new wardrobe made for you."

"You're too kind."

He smiled as we walked through the halls. For the next half hour or so, he showed me around the vast palace, one room being a cozy library, which I made a mental note to visit. As we walked, I noted the portraits lining the walls, one of them catching my eye. The man's long white hair flowed about his shoulders. Ice-blue eyes stared coldly at the artist. He was seated on a throne, a gold scepter in his right hand. His clothes were vibrant, green shirt, orange trousers, bright-pink cape tossed casually about his shoulders and sky-blue boots. I wanted to laugh at his ridiculously clashing attire.

I couldn't help but notice the similarities between this man and Allendaire.

"That is Karrinian Trounde. The first Shadow Elf to travel and settle here." He paused, eyes going to the portrait, a look of reverence on his face. "All the Shadow Elves' blood can be traced back to the first king. Our blood is pure."

"So that's why you execute any who fall on your lands."

"Yes."

I laughed. "So why am I here? Why isn't my head sitting atop a spike as a warning?"

Allendaire's blue eyes bored into me, and I shifted under his scrutiny. "I told you. You were alone and unarmed. You posed no threat."

Right. I couldn't help feeling there was more to his reason. To my being allowed to live. I doubted I was the only one ever to arrive unarmed.

I didn't voice my thoughts but continued on. "So, how do you keep your own from procreating outside your race? Surely, your people are allowed to come and go as they like?"

Allendaire said nothing, and I almost wondered if he was ignoring my question. We walked out of the palace to the courtyard my room overlooked. Stopping at a stone bench, we sat down.

"My Elves are free to come and go as they please. I cannot stop them from traveling, nor can I stop them from seeking pleasure with other races." His blue eyes locked on mine. "I am quite aware of what goes on in my kingdom. If there is chatter of a half-breed being born and if it were one of mine who created it, the child is killed. The same fate awaits a human child born by an Elf."

I frowned. "One of yours? So, there are other kingdoms of Elves?"

A dark look crossed his face, then left just as quickly. "We are not like the Wilde Elves, who care nothing of their blood. Shadow Elves are pure, and I do what must be done to keep it that way."

"You're inbred." I kicked myself internally for letting my words get ahead of me again.

His head cocked to the side. "You feel that is wrong?" A smile played about his lips. "Humans are interesting. You care not where you come from, where your bloodline can be traced to. You copulate and produce children with anyone. My Elves will always know from whom they came. Who their ancestors are." he paused; eyes amused. "Can you tell me where you come from, Lillyanna? Who are your ancestors?"

"If the gods had intended for us to have one blood, one ancestor, then they would not have created so many races."

Allendaire threw his head back and laughed. "The gods?" he spat. "You believe there is a group of deities sitting in the clouds judging—guiding—your actions? You pray to them asking for things. When they don't deliver, when something happens, you damn them. When you get what you want, you praise them. When a tragedy strikes, you blame them." He shook his head. "Believing has taken away your own accountability. It has made you inculpable for your own actions. Tell me, Lillyanna. If something bad were to befall you, whose fault is it?"

I swallowed hard, thinking of my current situation. "Mine."

His eyes danced. I feared he knew more about me than what I had revealed.

"You humans rely on these... gods... too much. It removes your ability to accept the consequences of your actions. Everything that happens—good or bad—is due to the decisions we make. The results are because of our actions, not because some deity deemed it so."

I clenched my fists, knowing full well how real the gods were.

"We do not believe in your falsehoods," he said imperiously.

"Falsehoods? What is wrong with giving people hope? Something to believe in? An idea that there is more when our Life Force is done?" I waved my hand as I spoke.

"But there isn't." an amused smile curled his lips.

"You think your race is superior because you're inbred, but you won't even give another race a chance. You view us humans, mortals, whatever the fuck you want to call us," I jammed my finger into my chest, "as lesser because you don't—no, you won't—take the time to understand." I clenched my teeth.

He stood and began to walk, and I reluctantly followed. "Why should we?"

I stopped. He paused and turned, eyes amused and appraising. "What happens if there's a problem that makes your women unable to produce children?" I asked. "Your race dies?"

"Yes."

"And you would let it? Just... die?" I didn't want to believe what I was hearing.

He looked at me then began walking again. "It will already die. Mouranda cannot have children, so in a sense, the race dies with me." He glanced over at me. "Do you have someone? Perhaps someone whose child you will bear?"

"No," I scoffed, thinking how fortunate it was Damiyun had been sterilized.

He smiled, his eyes flicking to Phabian who stood off to the side. "I enjoyed our time, Lillyanna."

"I enjoyed it as well," I said, surprising myself it wasn't a complete lie.

"I hope to have more... intriguing... conversations in the future."

I smiled. "Thank you, my... your highness."

He laughed. "Allendaire will do just fine," he said, giving a slight bow before he left.

"I can take you to the library," Phabian's voice said from over my shoulder, startling me. "I saw it piqued your curiosity."

I said nothing and eagerly followed him back through the palace to the library. It was interesting he knew that was where I wanted to be. It was almost like he was inside my head. Something was off about him. I was determined to find out what it was.

"Enjoy," he said, stepping aside at the doorway. I brushed past him into the room, the musty scent of the books filling me with memories of my father. Of the bookstore he often took me to. He would hand me a book and sit me down, then go off with the proprietor. He would always come back with a stack of thick books, which he paid a hefty price for. He always let me walk the aisles and choose a book to buy with the coin I earned from chores.

I always wondered what the books he bought contained, never laying eyes on them again. Not even after he left. I wondered if he had taken them with him, though now I assumed he took them to the Suppressors' Compound.

Maybe they contained dark magic. Perhaps spells to bring Themesis back?

I shook myself of the thoughts and looked about the cozy room, and at the bookshelves lining the wall. A tall ladder on rails allowed access to even the highest books. Large windows faced a garden, intricately woven rugs were strewn about the floor and plush velvet chairs and sofas sat around an unlit fireplace. I crossed the room to a bookshelf, examining the books standing at attention in neat rows like soldiers. I ran a hand down the spine, feeling the rough bindings beneath my fingertips. While many titles were in Elvish, a fair number were in my language as well. My eyes fell upon one book in particular. It was large and heavy. So much so, I had to grasp it with both hands as I pulled it down. The cover was made from gold, and a design of branches wound around all four sides. In the center was an emblem of a serpent wrapped around the thorny stem of a rose made of obsidian against a background of a flaming crown. The serpent was colored in fine emeralds. The ruby eyes and the amber flames glinted in the sunlight; the title written at the bottom in flowing Elvish script.

"That is the Tome of the Kings." I jumped at the sound of Phabian's voice. I didn't realize he had been standing there the entire time.

"Don't you have anything better to do than hover around me?"

He laughed as he strode into the room and held out his hands. I placed the heavy book in them, and his long fingers caressed the cover reverently. "All the kings write their story within these pages. It is a memoir of their reign, our history, and culture." He strode to a chair and sat down. Sunlight spilled over him, glinting on his white hair, making him look angelic. "Would you like me to read some?" he asked as he undid the clasp and opened the book.

"Yes, I would," I said as I sat down in a wing back chair opposite him, the soft leather hugging me. Allendaire had piqued my interest in his brief telling of their history. Though I didn't agree with their ways, perhaps I would be able to understand it. Folding my legs beneath me, I settled back in the chair and listened to him read, his sweet, melodic voice filling the room.

It started with the first Shadow Elf king, Karrinian Trounde. The story was about how he and a few hundred Elves left their homeland of Naar'Glon and traveled in a fleet of ships across the Calgonian Sea to Il'Ekhester. With him traveled his young bride to be, his sister Arybelle who was Blood-Bound to him when she was eighteen, days after arriving at their new home.

Arybelle's story saddened me. Forced to leave a home she loved with a man she despised. She was made to produce children—ten in total. Eventually, she took her life and that of the only daughter she bore. Phabian stopped reading and looked up, blue eyes on mine.

"Did Arybelle even have a say in what happened?" I asked.

He cocked his head to the side, as if confused. "She belonged to the king. Her place was to do what he asked. Once a man lays claim to a woman, she is his."

"Like property." I fought back the bile rising in my throat at the thought.

"I suppose, if you want to view it as such." He paused. "Forgive me, for I am young and do not have much knowledge in regard to your kind. Do you not belong to your mate?"

"Not in the sense your women do. We are free to do as we wish. We are not forced to obey, nor are we forced to churn out babies," I said, trying hard to control my tone as I realized the Shadow Elves were nothing more than savages who viewed women as their property.

"Your unions are not for procreation?"

"That is not the only reason we join. We choose our... mates... based on attraction and love. Do you not love your wife?" I looked at Phabian.

He shrugged. "My Anya is a smart and cunning woman. Our children will serve the king well with their sharp minds. I suspect my first son will make a formidable captain of the king's army."

"What is considered young in your kind?"

"Your age," he said.

Wait. How did he know how old I was? The secrets surrounding Phabian grow ever deep. "How old are you?"

Phabian smiled. "I stopped counting after one hundred. Shall I continue?"

I nodded, and he shifted the book on his lap and turned the page.

The next story was of Bodwin Trounde, first son to Karrinian, who laid claim to his cousin Kaayleigh. She provided him with seven children throughout her short life.

"There you are," Allendaire's voice interrupted Phabian. I looked up in his direction. He lounged casually against the door, arms and legs crossed. His hair was loose and flowed about his shoulders, blue eyes going to Phabian, a smile lighting his face.

"Reading some of our history?"

Phabian closed and latched the book then placed it back on the shelf, fingers caressing the spine the way one would a lover. "Yes."

"And what is your opinion?" The king's eyes met mine.

"Your ways are quite interesting," I hedged, not wanting to argue again with the man who could order my execution.

The king chuckled, and I unfolded myself from the comfortable chair and followed him out, with Phabian strolling casually behind.

"Somehow I knew I would find you in the library."

I blushed. "My father loved books. He taught me how to read and write at an early age. I found a love for them as well."

We walked through the palace, stopping outside the door to my room.

"I had some of the clothing in the wardrobe altered. The ones being made will be delivered in a few days. Try to relax. Phabian will gather you for the evening meal," he said, bowing slightly then striding away.

I slipped inside the room and went to the wardrobe. Pulling the doors open, I reached in and selected a velvet dress in a deep, forest green. I slipped out of my clothes and pulled it on, fastening the tiny pearl buttons on the bodice. It was low-cut and off the shoulder with a lace-trimmed neckline. The garment was narrow at the waist, flowing to the floor with panels of light green breaking up the fabric. The sleeves were long and bell shaped, coming to a point at my fingertips. Kicking off my worn boots, I chose a pair of silver shoes, with a black opal rose adorned on the toe. I slipped them on, the soft leather cushioning my feet, and appraised myself in the mirror. The color of the dress brought out my eyes, and

I wondered if the king would approve. The glint of the Sigaa'Lean on my right wrist reminded me I was not a guest.

I sat in a chair before the unlit fireplace, sinking into the plush cushions. Pouring myself a glass of wine from the decanter on the table, I sat back and mulled over my plight. While my concern wasn't as high as the day prior, I still didn't know what the king had in store for me.

The thought that I might still be executed remained in the forefront of my mind. And while the king and Phabian had been cordial, I refused to trust them.

Especially Phabian who was always hovering for some reason. Cold sensations often flowed through me in his presence and the way he always watched, it was as though he knew every thought in my head.

Rubbing my eyes, I got up and stood out on the balcony. The evening was warm, and a soft breeze blew, carrying with it the sweet scent of flowers. I stared down at the meticulously manicured lawn where a few Elves wandered about. I sipped the wine as I again pondered my predicament.

I knew the possibility of my being rescued was slim. I had to plan my own escape. Perhaps I could return to my home in Howling Cove. I was tired of traveling. Tired of being lied to by Damiyun and my mother. Both had said the world would fall to Themesis if I failed to make it to Kraagswell Mountain, but neither had told me what my role was. Both my mother and Abraham had told me to ask Damiyun yet he refused to answer me.

Damiyun.

I sighed, hollow loneliness washing over me as I thought about him. As I pictured his face above mine, the smiles that were as rare as his laughter.

His warmth.

His hands and lips on my skin.

As angry as I was, as much as I wanted to hate him and as hard as I tried to deny it, I missed him.

The sound of knocking pulled me from my thoughts, and I brushed the tears I hadn't realized I'd shed from my cheeks. Then I walked to the door where Phabian waited to escort me to dinner.

I FOLLOWED PHABIAN AS he strode down the halls which were becoming familiar to me. Once we came upon the dining room, he left me. I stepped inside, groaning inwardly at the sight of Mouranda sitting to Allendaire's right, the dour look on her face matching her depressing black dress.

I thought about Phabian telling me how they chose their mates based on compatibility but looking at the queen I didn't understand why the king would have claimed her. Allendaire was admittedly a very attractive man. The queen, however, was quite homely. I wondered what attribute she possessed that would have made him lay claim to her.

"Thank you for joining us," he said, eyes slowly sweeping over me, something that did not escape Mouranda. Her eyes narrowed.

"So," she snapped, her tone cracking like a whip as I sat down. "I hear Phabian has read from the Tome. Tell me, girl, what is your opinion of our race?"

"You have a very... interesting... history. It amazes me there is not more illness among your race."

She looked down her nose at me. "Children who are less than perfect are disposed of."

My mouth went dry, and I lost whatever appetite I had. "You mean murdered."

"We do what we must to keep our race pure and perfect. I can't expect a primitive and sullied species such as yours to understand the importance of purity. Of heritage."

I shook my head and laughed.

"Did I say something amusing?" Her eyes narrowed to slits. "Need I remind you of your place here?"

"Of course not. Please forgive my insolence. As a primitive species I know nothing of the decorum of one as high as the Shadow Elves." I bowed my head. I glanced at Allendaire, whose face held a hint of amusement, something which angered Mouranda more.

She opened her mouth to speak but closed it when the servants breezed in carrying plates of food. We ate the meal in silence, the sound of chewing and the scrape of silverware on plates deafening. When the meal was done and plates removed, Mouranda stood and exited in a swish of skirts gliding across the floor.

Allendaire reached forward, grasping a decanter filled with rich, red liquid and poured two glasses. He raised his in a toast, and I lifted mine in return, watching him settle back in his chair, long fingers drumming idly on the armrest.

"You must forgive the queen. Having a guest is out of the norm."

I said nothing as I lifted the glass, inhaling the sweet scent of figs. The warm liquid tasted of strawberries and plums. The wine was delicious and warming as it hit my stomach. I glanced at Allendaire as he sipped his drink. The front of his hair was pulled back and braided; his beard neatly trimmed. As I appraised him, I couldn't help but notice similarities between him and Damiyun. The strong jawline, and light eyes. The thought occurred to me that perhaps Damiyun was part Elf, and perhaps his mother was one of the Wilde Elves.

"Tell me about the Wilde Elves," I said, reaching forward and refilling our glasses.

"There was a time we were one, united in blood and beliefs," Allendaire said. "As time went on, some Elves disagreed with our ways. They began claiming and procreating outside of our race. We became divided, and a war ensued. Those who went against us were banished. They formed their own tribe and called themselves the Wilde Elves."

I sipped my wine. The possibility Damiyun was part Elf was becoming more believable.

"Who rules the Wilde Elves?"

Allendaire shrugged. "I suspect they have their own king or governance. As far as I am concerned that race does not exist."

I shook my head and placed my empty glass on the table. This race was a confusing and despicable lot. "If you don't mind, I think I will retire," I said, standing up. Allendaire rose to his feet as well.

"Of course. Sleep well," he said, taking my hand and pressing his lips to the back.

I slipped out of the room and walked through the quiet corridors, surprised Phabian wasn't flanking me. I entered my room and again wondered why I was here. Why my head wasn't sitting on a spike outside as a warning. What were Allendaire's intentions for me? No doubt there was a reason he kept me here.

As I pulled off my dress and hung it in the wardrobe, I realized I was alone in this. I could only rely on myself. The thought comforted me. Ever since meeting Damiyun and Abraham, I had been pulled in all directions by them. I had no choice in where I went. No choice in what happened. I felt as though I didn't really matter. Though I was far from a guest in this palace, and though I knew I could possibly lose my head at any time, for now, I was done running. For now, I can heal from the tragedies of my past.

I realized perhaps Damiyun's poor decision in S'aehe was a blessing in disguise.

THIRTY-FOUR
DAMIYUN

S LEEP ELUDED ME THAT night. The throbbing pain in my arm, coupled with oppressive guilt, made it impossible. At least a dozen times I went to the door, intent on leaving and going to her room, but I stopped myself when my hand closed around the handle.

As dawn approached and the sun crested the horizon, I pulled my weary body out of the chair. I paused at the mirror as I passed by, running a hand over the annoying stubble on my face. The lack of sleep had left me exhausted. The shadow of a beard and hard lines that creased my face made me look ancient, and my tired body made me feel far older than I was.

I exited the room, making my way down the hall to Lillyanna. I lifted my hand and knocked softly. No answer, I frowned. When there was still no answer to my second, more persistent knock, I became concerned. I pushed open the door and crossed the threshold into the dimly lit room and scanned the area.

She had completely destroyed it.

Shards of glass, splintered wood, feathers, and torn fabric littered the floor. Black scorch marks ran up the stone walls. The door leading to the balcony was shattered, splintered wood hanging from a hinge.

Lillyanna was not there.

"Damn it," I cursed, quickly leaving the room. I should have known she would leave. I should have stayed outside her door, just in case. If she were to take one wrong turn in the cave...

No. Oohlrich would never let her leave. If she had used her magic against him, he would have alerted Felicity.

She had to still be here somewhere.

I held on to that hope as I hurried through the halls to find the Keeper of the Cave.

She's gone, Damiyun. You failed. She is forever lost in the caves to starve and die. And I will be free. You will serve me. Do my bidding. You will cause pain to those you care about. Just like you did to Lillyanna...

I shook the voice and the guilt from myself as I burst out into the light of the garden and hurried toward the cave.

"Damiyun," Felicity's voice trilled behind me.

I paused, turning my head in her direction. She smiled as she gracefully floated toward me, a long pink dress swirling about her legs.

"Lil left," I said, turning back and walking again.

"She probably got up early to do some exploring," she said, falling in step beside me.

"She destroyed her room. She... she found out what happened." I reached my hand up to my neck, to the mark Felicity left.

The mark Lillyanna saw.

"You did that on purpose." I stopped and turned to face her. "You wanted her to know."

"I told you, darling. She will not be yours forever. It's not as though you love her." Her lips curled up in a cruel smile.

"If she left... if she becomes lost in the cave—"

Felicity waved her hand in dismissal. "Oohlrich would never let her leave. She's probably off somewhere sulking."

I began walking again, the mouth of the cave and Oohlrich's outline coming into view.

"Did you allow Lillyanna to leave?"

He looked from me to Felicity. I took a step closer. "Did you?" My voice was low and threatening.

"I... I allowed no one to leave," he stammered.

Felicity placed her hand on my arm. "See, Damiyun? She is off sulking somewhere. Come join me for the morning meal."

I shrugged her hand off. "No, she's not. She would have wanted to get as far away from here—from us—as she could." My eyes remained trained on Oohlrich who shifted from foot to foot. "How long were you gone?"

"I don't know. A few hours. Maybe more."

"You left your post?" Felicity's voice was cold with anger.

"I didn't think—"

"No, you didn't." I shook with fury, clenching my fists to keep back the magic that ached to burst free and burn him to cinders. "You have no idea what you have done." I shouldered him out of the way and entered the cave.

"Damiyun, wait," Felicity said. "You're being rash. Come back with me. We can talk about this and figure out a rational course of action." She pouted, a sultry glint in her eye.

"The only course of action is to find her." I walked swiftly through the passages, stopping occasionally to search with my magic. If she was here, lost somewhere, perhaps I would feel her.

As it were, each time I felt nothing.

She's gone. Themesis laughed. I clenched my teeth against the voice.

Finally, I saw a sliver of light pouring through the mouth of the cave. I walked toward it, pausing a moment to gather some courage, then strode through. The horses were grazing, and the scent of a burning fire drifted on the morning breeze.

I stood rooted to the spot.

Coward. You did this. Take your punishment like a man, I chastised myself, forcing my legs to move. Abraham lounged casually against a rock, arms crossed and eyes watching the orange flames undulate and swirl. A branch snapped beneath my weight and his head whipped in my direction, dagger appearing in his hand.

"That was quick," he said, sheathing his weapon. A frown creased his face when I walked into the camp alone.

"She ran off," I said before he could ask.

"What did you do?"

I sat down on the ground with a sigh. "Does it matter? She's gone, and we need to find her."

"She could be lost in the caves."

"She's not. I didn't feel her."

"If she ends up in Shadow Elf territory—"

I clenched my fists. "Do you think I don't know the consequences?"

He snorted. "If you did, then Lillyanna would be here."

"I made a mistake."

"You always seem to be making mistakes."

I couldn't rightly deny his words, though I would not give him the satisfaction of agreeing with him.

I stared into the fire, watching the flames dance in a hypnotic rhythm. The performance calmed me. My connection to the flame filled me with warmth, wrapping me in a soothing embrace. I let my lust consume me and I betrayed her in one of the worst ways a man could betray a woman. She was sweet and innocent, and I had taken advantage of that. Of her. Lillyanna had woven her way under my skin and caused me to do the one thing I vowed to never do.

The one thing that would forever be my downfall.

She caused me to care.

"I'm sorry."

Abraham laughed. "Are you? You knew exactly what you were doing. You are a selfish man."

I laughed without mirth. "Are you not as well? You, whose greed—whose love for coin—caused you to sell your soul to the Fallen One? You, who only cared about what you could buy with your never-ending riches? Your own actions drove your daughter—your only child—into the arms of a Fae. Themesis knew what he was doing when he had you deliver her soul, but that didn't matter, did it?"

Abraham said nothing for a long time, and I braced myself for an onslaught of torture for my punishment. Surprisingly, however, he just said, "How do you propose we go about finding her?"

"We search," I said, shrugging. "The Faery lands are closest, so we will start there." I rose to my feet, signaling the conversation was over. Making my way to where the horses stood, I strapped my sword to my back, sheathed my dagger, saddled Xander and swung up onto him, waiting as Abraham readied Violet and then turned east toward Willowshire.

The land of the Fae.

WE TRAVELED IN SILENCE for miles. Finally, Abraham broke it.

"You are right, Damiyun. I was selfish, but I loved my Jaylynn. I may not have been the best man, but I tried to be the best father to her. I provided her with things other children could only dream of having. She was taken by Arias. Perhaps in him, she found what was missing in her life."

I said nothing. I knew the subject of his daughter to be something he rarely, if ever, disclosed. He blamed himself for what happened and since I only knew what happened from him, I couldn't disagree, though I kept those thoughts to myself.

"You don't know what it is like to have a child ripped from you. To be the one to deliver her soul to the Fallen One." He shook his head, his voice trailing off. "I did the best I could, Damiyun," he whispered, head hung low, tears glistening on his cheeks.

Averting my eyes, I trained them on the horizon and the rapidly ascending sun. There was nothing I could say to Abraham, and nothing I wanted to offer. Instead, I turned my thoughts inward and thought about Lil. I was a fool. I thought of everything I could have done differently when it came to her, but I realized I wouldn't have if given another chance.

We rode through the day, stopping occasionally to rest the horses and have a quick meal. We stuck to the woods as much as possible. While we were thick in magic territory, that did not mean we wouldn't run into Suppressors. Neither one of us spoke, and I was grateful for the silence. I had no doubt he had more to say to me. I just didn't want to hear it. The guilt I felt over what I did was heavy on my shoulders, and I did not need Abraham adding to the weight of it.

I again thought about Lillyanna. I was concerned about her welfare. Her survival skills were negligible. She hadn't been forced to hunt game for food, as a market with all she needed laid in the center of her village. Furthermore, she carried no coin so she would be unable to find shelter at an inn and would be forced to sleep in the woods, which would leave her vulnerable. While she knew about some of her magic, I did not think her knowledge adequate enough to protect her from danger.

My horse reared up, jerking me from my thoughts, and I struggled to gain control.

"Easy, Xander," I soothed, patting his neck. Abraham reined Violet in, and we both scanned the surrounding woods, which grew dark with the setting sun. I heard a tittering to my left and Xander snorted, tossing his head, and pawing the ground in irritation. Speaking softly, I tried to calm him again while I scanned the forest.

"Faeries," Abraham said.

Something moved in the brush ahead, and a beautiful woman stepped out into the fiery rays cast from the setting sun. She was slight and petite, the orange rays glinting off the golden hair cascading down her back in soft ringlets, the right side shaved short. A ring in her right nostril glinted in the sun. A long chain connected it to a silver cuff that covered her ear. Her dewy skin shone in the light cast upon her, and large blue eyes curiously looked at us from a childlike face. Her red lips curled in a bemused smile. She wore a long gown of white so pure it appeared luminescent.

"Greetings, travelers. Are you lost?" Her light sing-song voice floated on the Midsummer's Eve breeze.

I opened my mouth to speak, but a sharp look from Abraham silenced me.

"Greetings, Naleigha. We are not lost, but a companion of ours might be."

The woman blinked and glanced at Abraham, whose gaze never wavered. "You know me?"

"I know of you," he stated, face blank.

Looking from me back to Abraham, her face was confused. "We have had no travelers here," she stated. "It is late," she continued. "The forest can be dangerous. Please join me for our Solstice Celebration." She smiled as she turned and beckoned us in the direction she had come.

Glancing at Abraham, I felt a prickle of unease creep up the back of my neck. "Thank you but—"

"We accept your generous offer. It is quite a ride back to our camp," Abraham cut in.

I said nothing as I tried to push my concern to the back of my mind. I knew we could camp anywhere. The forest wasn't as dangerous as the woman wished us to believe. Nonetheless, I swung down from my mount and followed Abraham and the Faery, guiding Xander, who was still skittish. I couldn't say why Abraham agreed to join Naleigha in their celebration, only assuming it had to do with his daughter and the Fae she fell in love with. We followed Naleigha through the woods, which quickly grew dark. Soft music and laughter drifted through the night.

"Do not eat or drink anything offered," Abraham said, his low voice pulling me from my thoughts as he fell in step next to me.

I laughed. "Do you honestly believe that tall tale?"

He glared at me. "It is not a tale. You will be bound to the one who fed you for eternity, and what they choose to do with you will not be pleasant. You forget I know much about this race."

I wondered at his words. "Why are we doing this, Abraham? Naleigha said they have had no lost traveler," I hissed. "If this has to do with your daughter—"

"If one refuses an invitation from the Fae, they will live a life of poor luck and sorrow," he stated, then turned his dark eyes to me. "The less you know, the better off you are, Damiyun," he said brusquely, dismissing my thoughts before I even got a word out.

Clenching my teeth, I bit back the retort on the tip of my tongue. I should have realized he had an agenda when he did not challenge me on my decision to travel to these lands. We continued on in silence, the sound of festivities growing louder as we drew close to the end of the woods, which gave way to a large field surrounded by dense forest on all sides. Torches illuminated the area, and jars filled with Faery flies strung between trees lit the border. A long table packed with food and drink stretched down one side of the field. Situated in the middle was a raised platform where half a dozen Faeries played lutes, drums and wind instruments. Their cheerful music filled the night air. Scanning the area, I observed hundreds of Faeries dancing, feasting, and indulging in lustful acts.

"You will not need your weapons here. We are a peaceful folk and mean no harm," Naleigha said.

Looking at Abraham, who nodded, I reluctantly surrendered my sword and dagger, my unease growing.

Naleigha smiled and gestured to the celebration. "Please feel free to satiate all of your desires." Her soft, melodic voice turned husky. Tethering the horses, I glanced at Abraham. His eyes scanned the crowd as we stepped out onto the field. I watched the joyful party, drawn in by the upbeat music and laughter, moving in the direction where the bulk of the party was taking place.

"Greetings, strange one," a high-pitched voice interrupted my thoughts. Looking to my right, I found myself staring into a pair of inquisitive violet eyes. "They call me Ayelay." She pulled her green skirt out as she executed a low curtsy. Her short brown hair formed a curtain around her bowed face. "What do they call you?" She stood up and cocked her head to one side, hands folded in front of her. Like Naleigha, the right side of her hair was shaved, and a long silver chain connected the ring in her nose, to the cuff on her ear.

"Damiyun."

"Come join the merriment." She smiled, slipping her warm hand in mine, and tugging me farther into the crowd. "Drink." She handed me a cup that had been passed. I declined the offer, and she laughed, a soft, breathless sound. "Do not believe the tales told about us. Our food and drink are no different from yours."

I laughed, shaking my head in refusal.

"Well, if you will not satisfy your thirst and hunger, perhaps you will satiate your deepest desires?" Gesturing in the direction of the throng of sexual activity, she stepped forward, face inches from mine, her breath warm.

"Thank you, but no," I said, taking a step back. I scanned the darkness for Abraham.

Where are you?

"You needn't worry about your friend. Come dance with me." She slipped her hand into mine and tugged me in the direction of the dais and the group of Faeries who were moving to the jaunty beat. Glancing around one more time, I followed Ayelay and let the music draw me in. Taking her hands in mine, I joined the others. The merriment of the festivities swept over me. I smiled down at her, spinning her away then pulling her back into my arms. Her hips swayed to the rhythm, and she smiled as our hands clasped and we parted, coming together once again, side to side, one arm behind each other's neck.

I admitted I was enjoying myself and had pushed Abraham out of my mind.

That was until a scream pierced the night.

The music came to an abrupt stop, as did everything else. Scanning the area, which was dimly lit by torches and jars of Faery flies, I saw Abraham wiping a bloodied dagger off on his pant leg as he slowly stood. Ayelay bolted toward the commotion and I followed. Slowing down, my eyes went to the pair of black, motionless boots protruding from the gathering crowd. I sidled up to Ayelay, my eyes meeting her frightened ones, her warm hand slipping in my own, fingers interlacing. She gasped as we shouldered our way through the crowd, hand going to her mouth. The metallic smell of blood assaulted me, and my eyes went to the body of a man who lay motionless in the rays of silver moonlight. The bright-green shirt he wore was soaked with blood from countless stab wounds and clung to his torso. A stream of dark red spilled from the ear-to-ear slice across his neck, soaking the ground and the long, black hair fanned out beneath. Golden eyes quickly turning a milky white, stared lifelessly up into the starlit sky, mouth open in a silent plea for mercy.

Damn it, Abraham.

"What have you done?" Naleigha screamed; her voice filled with fury.

"I have served justice. The love my daughter bore for Arias cost her her life. I have returned the favor." He stood up, arms crossed, and head inclined.

"You are no god. Life is not yours to take," Naleigha's body was tense, eyes narrowing in anger. She motioned to a group of Faeries who seemed to have materialized out of thin air. They fanned out, forming a half circle around us, holding sharpened staffs, the points covered in a thick, black substance.

Ayelay released my hand and stepped back behind the armed Faeries. My eyes met hers briefly then went to Naleigha who dropped to her knees, drawing Arias' head onto her lap. She smoothed his black hair from his ash-gray face.

"No. I am not a god, but that does not stop me from serving justice. He tricked my daughter. She sold her soul for immortality and when the time came, he refused to trade his life for hers," Abraham spat on the corpse.

"Why should he?" Her blue eyes flashed with fury.

"Because he loved her."

Naleigha laughed harshly. Closing Arias' eyes and placing a kiss on his forehead, she laid him gently on the ground, and crossed his arms over his chest. She rose gracefully to her feet. "Love," she scoffed. "Do you think a species as superior as ours would stoop so low as to waste that emotion on a mortal? She got what she deserved for her foolishness."

"She was my daughter!" Abraham shouted, hands clenched, veins pulsing in his broad neck.

"And he was my son."

"Then we are even."

Naleigha smiled, a look that made my blood run cold. "No. We are not." She backed away, eyes on the guards. Their silver armor glinted in the moonlight. The long, pointed ears of their helmets looked like antennae, and I almost laughed at how bug-like they appeared. Naleigha gave a small nod. They advanced, closing their crescent formation around us. Abraham glanced at me then pulled the darkness around him, disappearing into the night, and slipping away.

Leaving me where I stood.

The guards stumbled, confused looks on their faces. I took that chance, however small, to call upon my power. My gaze locked on Ayelay's wide and frightened eyes as I called forth the flame. The heat of the fire filled me with warmth and exploded out of my hands incinerating the four guards before me. I watched as the blaze consumed them, screams erupting from all sides as they burned. My eyes jumped to the remaining ranks which pulled tight and advanced on me.

"You will pay for what has happened here. You will pay with your life for that of my son's." Naleigha's voice quivered, and her body shook, veins popping on her temples.

I pulled my magic close, though a quick glance at Ayelay made me release it. Sighing, I raised my hands in submission. Two Faeries behind me grabbed my arms and jerked them behind my back. I winced at the pain that flared through my wound as they secured my wrists.

A look of satisfaction fell on Naleigha's face. "Well, I am glad we agree." She gestured to the warriors that surrounded me. "Lock him up in the dungeon." Her eyes met mine. "I am a fair and just queen. I will afford you a trial before I take your head."

Anger coursed through me at her words. Fucking Abraham and his revenge. His actions delayed our mission, and our search for Lillyanna, even further.

Part of me hoped Themesis would break free. Perhaps then Abraham would see how foolish his actions were.

The warriors stepped forward and shoved me in the direction of a path leading into the woods. I dutifully marched alongside my captors, having no idea what was going on. The thought I could lose my head, a death that would be permanent, crossed my mind. I didn't want to think of the consequences. Pushing the thoughts away, I marched on through the woods and then down into the bowels of the palace into a cold, damp cell. The sound of rusty hinges closing, the finality of it, caused my heart to sink to the pit of my stomach.

THIRTY-FIVE
ABRAHAM

I LOOKED AT DAMIYUN as I pulled the cloak of darkness around me, the cold seeping into my bones as I drifted through the wood, and the land of the Fae. Shaking the darkness off, I walked the remainder of the way. I spied our mounts and swung up onto Violet, leaving Xander behind. There was no sense bringing him along.

Heeling my horse, I guided him back to Karstollan. After stabling him, I entered The Drunken Dragon, securing a room and a bottle of Faery's Blood.

In light of the situation, I thought the latter appropriate.

I discarded my weapons as I entered my room. Kicking off my boots, I sat back on the bed. Pulling the cork from the bottle, I took a long drink. The liquid burned its way down my throat, filling me with warmth.

I thought about what had happened. I knew Damiyun would be furious with me for fleeing, but I did not feel it prudent for both of us to be sitting in a cell facing possible execution.

I had served justice for my daughter. Though I knew my actions would not bring her back, it was satisfying to watch Arias' Life Force leave his body.

I rubbed my eyes as I thought about my Jaylynn.

Not the mindless servant who knelt at Themesis' side.

No, I thought about the vibrant and beautiful child my Lenore had blessed me with. She had all of her mother's beauty and grace. She was mischievous and sweet innocence wrapped up in one. She was impetuous and stubborn, and she had me wrapped around her finger. There was nothing I wouldn't do for her. Nothing I would say no to.

Except for her budding relationship with Arias.

When she brought him to our home, I had been furious. It was the only time I ever lost my temper with her.

"I will not allow this." I had yelled, hands clenched.

Jaylynn thrusted her chin out and crossed her arms. "We love each other. You have no say in this."

"Love." I glared at her. "What do you know of such emotion? What does he? He is Fae. They are narcissistic creatures. The only thing they love is themselves."

Jaylynn tossed her hair with a sniff. "He wants to marry me. I have given up my soul, so I may spend eternity with him."

My throat went dry, and the room closed in on me. My heart pounded in my ears.

"What did you say?"

She stood up straighter, her chocolate eyes on me. "I am going to spend eternity with him."

My hands shook, and I flushed with heat. "Please tell me what you have said is false." I hoped she was lying. Goading me. She sniffed in response, the look on her face confirming the truth.

"You have no idea what you have done. How could you be so foolish, Jaylynn? The gods be damned, what have you done?" My body shook, and it took everything I had to control myself.

"I love him," she said, her tone less sure.

I could do nothing. Even if I went to the Fallen One to plead for her release, he would not grant it. Once a name was signed, the contract was binding. The only way around it was to find another to take one's place. And so, when Themesis called Jaylynn's contract, I paid a visit to Arias.

I scoured the Faery lands until I found him. He sat on a pillow beneath an open tent. A female Faery massaged his feet while another fed him from a platter of food she held. My anger rose as I watched him sensuously lick her fingers clean after taking the food.

"Arias."

"Abraham. Jaylynn isn't here."

"I know," I stepped into the tent. I glared at the two women, and they quickly fled.

"Then why are you?" His tone was bored as he popped an olive into his mouth and chewed.

"My daughter sold her soul to be with you," I said. "She foolishly fell in love with you and thought you felt the same."

Arias laughed. "That was her mistake. Thinking I would fall for a human." He wrinkled his nose. "As if I would stoop so low."

I clenched my jaw at his words.

"What does this have to do with me?" He yawned, and I had to resist the urge to snap his neck.

"The Fallen One has called the contract. I want you to take her place."

Arias' eyes danced with amusement. "Why would I do that?"

"Because your deception led her to make a rash decision."

"My deception? In what way did I deceive her?"

"I told you how."

"Ah yes. That silly love thing." He waved his hand. "I suppose that was my fault for being intimate with her. I am a Faery and have insatiable desires. I cannot say no when a beautiful woman throws herself at me."

I glared at him. I knew it was he who had seduced Jaylynn.

He shook his head. "I will not give up my life for what a foolish child did."

"She was foolish because she loved you."

Arias shrugged. "That is hardly my fault. I regret you have wasted both of our time here." He rose and walked away in dismissal.

Clenching my fists, I pulled the shadows around and drifted back to my home, where I would be forced to bring my daughter to the Fallen One.

When I brought her to Themesis, I shamefully pleaded with him to forgive her mistake and allow her to live.

"Why should I do that?" He rubbed his chin.

"She is my only child. She didn't know what she was doing."

He cocked his head to the side, blue eyes on me. "Yes. It does hurt when your child makes dreadful decisions and is nothing short of a disappointment."

I flushed at his words.

He continued. "Like everyone else, she knew the terms. I will not alter them just because she is your daughter. If I were to be accused of growing soft..." He shook his head, "Everyone would beseech me to let them out. No. Give me Jaylynn."

The box felt heavier than any of the others. I could hardly breathe, and it took all my power to stop myself from crying. The last thing I wanted was for Themesis to see how much this hurt me. I brought it forward, my hands shaking, and opened the lid. Her soul poured out, and she appeared in front of us.

"Papa?" Her eyes went to me, her voice shaking as she looked around, fear crossing her face when she saw where she was.

Themesis slipped down from his throne and stood in front of her. He ran a finger down her cheek, and she shrank back at his touch.

He made me watch as he stripped her of her clothes and forced her into the dress of a slave. It was sheer, cut low, with slits on the side that went up to the hip. I turned away, bile welling in my throat at the sight of my daughter dressed like that.

He erased her memories, and then clasped the diamond-encrusted collar around her neck, making her his slave for eternity.

It was shortly after that my Lenore left me. She blamed me for what happened, and she wasn't entirely wrong. I blamed myself, too.

I had indulged Jaylynn, allowed her to get away with far too much. And I had not prepared her enough for the dangers of the world. The dangers involving love and evil out there. I had known of evil.

Perhaps that was why she turned from me and leaped into Arias' arms. Perhaps the love I showed her, the things I gave her, weren't what she needed.

As it stood, my life fell apart the day Jaylynn went to Themesis and I no longer cared much about anything.

I put the empty bottle on the bedside table. My mood was dark, and I wasn't quite ready for sleep. Slipping on my boots, I exited the room and wandered out into the still-bustling village.

I needed to relax and knew just the brothel to provide that.

THOUGH I SATISFIED MY needs, my thoughts still drifted to the day's events prior.

I should have dissuaded Damiyun from searching the Faery lands, but my want for revenge—the need to make things right—drove me.

All the memories I had tried to bury rose like a creature clawing its way out of the Abyss. I had reopened an old wound. Grabbing the fresh bottle of Faery's Blood, I pulled the cork and took a long drink, letting the memories fill me. Memories I planned to lock away forever.

THIRTY-SIX
DAMIYUN

I SAT ON THE cold, dirt floor, hands secured behind my back. The position made me ache, and any movement sent shooting pains up my injured arm. The small cell had no windows, a lone torch providing scant lighting. A bed, or more accurately a pile of straw covered with a moth-eaten blanket, sat against the wall to my left. In the corner sat a chamber pot. Shifting my position on the hard floor, I gritted my teeth at the painful fullness of my bladder. I turned my head at the sound of a metal key scraping inside the door lock, and Ayelay stepped into the small room carrying a tray with a bowl of food and water. Two guards flanked the doorway, blocking it, poisoned spears crossed, and angry eyes on me. Ayelay squatted down beside me, placing the tray on the ground. I was ravenous, and the bland mush in the bowl looked and smelled delicious. Picking up the bowl, she held a spoonful out to me.

"Eat, Damiyun."

"I need to relieve myself. If you could please untie my wrists?" Ayelay hesitated. "It will be rather difficult for me without the use of my hands. Unless you want to help?"

Pursing her lips, she placed the bowl on the floor. Shifting my position, I held my bound hands out to her, and she untied them. Rubbing my wrists, I crossed the small room to where the chamber pot sat. The two guards followed and stood behind me. Closing my eyes, I sighed as my bladder was emptied, then went back to where Ayelay stood, glancing at the guards who resumed their post.

"Hands behind your back." She snapped her fingers and motioned with the rope.

"Is that really necessary?" I sighed.

"You incinerated four warriors."

"That is a natural reaction when I am threatened. I give you my word I will not harm you." Ayelay crossed her arms. "It is not the most comfortable position," I gestured to my injury, gritting my teeth against the hot, pulsing pain radiating up my arm. Ayelay glanced at it, a look of concern crossing her pretty face at the sight of the blood that had seeped through the bandage. Even now, it kept turning my shirt sleeve crimson. She wound the rope up, I sat back down, wiping the sweat from my brow. Despite Abraham's warning, I picked up the bowl of mush and dug in, my mouth closing around the spoonful of cold, flavorless paste. Ayelay stood, arms crossed, eyes watching me as I hungrily devoured the food and drink.

"Did you have anything to do with what happened the night prior?"

Wiping my mouth off on my sleeve, I placed the bowl on the tray and looked up at her.

"I assure you, I did not." It wasn't a lie, not exactly, as I did not know Abraham's agenda and therefore, I wasn't involved with what he had intended to do. "You must understand, Ayelay, she was his only daughter. She had been deceived by a man she loved and who she believed loved her in return."

Ayelay's violet eyes flashed angrily. "So, you approve of his actions?"

Shrugging, I folded my arms and leaned back against the stone wall, which jabbed daggers of ice into my hot body. "Do you agree with Arias' deception?" I threw the question back at her.

Her eyes narrowed into slits and her hands gripped the rope tight, knuckles whitening. "Men are deceitful by nature."

I shook my head and chuckled. "Are women not as well?" I raised an eyebrow at her. "Do you not use what the gods have given you to entice men? Do you not make them want you? Beg them to take you, then deny them the very thing you offered?"

She bowed her head. "He was my brother, Damiyun. He was full of life. We were as close as twins. He protected me when we were children, and he was the only one who truly understood me. He was going to be king one day."

"Do you think Abraham took lightly what happened?"

She raised her head, eyes searching mine. "What if it were your brother?" Her voice was soft.

"I would have been the one to slit my brother's throat." Her face held a look of shock at my blunt statement. "There is no love lost between him and me. I suspect he would have killed me long ago if he did not derive pleasure in torturing me. What you fail to understand is Abraham was the one who had to deliver Jaylynn's soul to the Fallen One."

"And that makes it right?"

I shrugged. "It is not for me to decide what is right or what is wrong. I am hardly one to condemn a man's actions, especially those committed in a fit of passion."

"My mother will execute her own justice. Your blood will spill for your actions."

I laughed. "Do you think me afraid of death? I welcome the cold embrace. I have done things you would never believe. My time is coming to an end, and if this is how it must happen, then so be it." Regardless of what my task was, my fate now lay in Naleigha's hands. I wasn't ignorant enough to think Abraham would save me from my fate. He had left me here to take the fall for him. I could do nothing except hope Abraham found Lillyanna and completed my task alone.

Ayelay sighed, a weary sound, and her shoulders sagged. "I believe you, Damiyun. But I can make you no promises. My mother is the queen."

"I request nothing from you, Ayelay." My eyes met hers as she knelt beside me.

"Why would your friend have left you?"

Because he's a prick.

"Let me see your arm," she sighed, voice soft, the conversation forgotten. I lifted my injured limb, and she gently pushed the sleeve up over my elbow. Inhaling sharply, I clenched my fist as she undid the bandage. Her brow furrowed as she inspected the wound. A few days had passed since Lil had cleaned and dressed it. The heat burning my arm and the sweat I felt on my brow told me it was becoming infected.

Ayelay's voice wavered as she spoke. "The stitching has come undone in some places. I fear an infection is setting in. Stitched the way it was, the wound should have been healing, but it is not. It is deep, Damiyun."

"Well, perhaps the queen won't have to execute me after all." I pulled my arm from her grasp.

Ayelay's nostrils flared. "This is not funny, Damiyun." She wrapped the soiled dressing back around my arm. "I am a healer. I will be back shortly to see what I can do before the infection gets worse." She rose to her feet and nodded to the guards. Her exit was punctuated with the clang of the door and the scrape of the key in the lock.

Leaning my head against the wall, I closed my eyes, violent shivers racking my body as I let darkness take me.

THIRTY-SEVEN
LILLYANNA

I STARED AT THE book that lay open in my lap, *"The Story of Jayne,"* not really seeing the words. It had rained for what seemed like weeks. Today, while still gloomy, seemed to be the most promising. The sky seemed a bit brighter, and the constant drizzle had become a soft mist streaking the window.

I had been a captive—a guest, as Allendaire would say—for almost four Moon Cycles. Despite the luxury of not being locked in a dark, dank cell, I would hardly have called what I had freedom. Phabian never drifted more than a few paces away, nor did another Elf named Lazaro who shared his guard duties. Phabian's brother Krall, too, often lurked in the shadows, blue eyes watching. I spent most of my time wandering the labyrinth, reading and avoiding the queen. Allendaire took up a good portion of my time, mostly requesting my presence to join him at mealtime or reading from the Tome at my request. He was, admittedly, a very handsome man, and I couldn't say I disliked the attention.

Despite that, and my comfort here, my mind never strayed from escape. Though it was difficult to contemplate such a thing with Phabian and Lazaro always close by. Whenever I thought of my mother or father, I shifted my attention to the library. I wandered the rows of books. Perhaps I'd learn to read the language of the Elves. Perhaps. If my captors stopped watching me long enough to learn. They were ever present.

Watching.

"Reading again?" Lazaro's deep voice pulled me from my thoughts. I looked up to see him lounging against the door frame, arms crossed, deep-blue eyes on me. The scabbard strapped to his body glinted in the light, and I had no doubt he could slit my throat faster than I could blink.

"There's not much else I can do. It's not like I'm allowed outside these walls."

He crossed the room and picked up the book in my lap. *"The Story of Jayne?"* Don't you know how to read anything else?"

I snatched the book back and glared at him. "No. My ignorant human self only knows what my father read to me."

"Was he a good man?"

"He was as good a man as any," I said, rising and placing my book back on the shelf. Lazaro constantly badgered me with questions about my father—my past—in what I knew was an attempt to trip me up.

Catch me in my lie.

"And your mother?"

"I don't know who she is."

He smiled; a look quite similar to a snarl. "It doesn't sound as though your father were as good a man as you thought." He paused. "I requested the king send some Elves out to find him. I trust you are concerned and wish to be reunited?"

My blood ran cold, and I clenched my fists.

"Anyone would be overjoyed to be reunited with their parent," he said, blue eyes locked on mine. "Unless your story was a lie? You don't seem to be oozing with joy at my suggestion."

"Because he is probably dead. And if he isn't, why would I want him trapped here as well? Would you execute him for trespassing, even though you forced him to be here?" I shrugged.

Lazaro's eyes narrowed. "It doesn't matter. The king feels it would be a wasted and foolish journey. Yet, he does not see how wasteful and foolish keeping you here is."

I brushed past him, and he grabbed my arm. "I will find out the truth about you. Make no mistake. When I do, when the king finds out who you are, what you were doing on our lands, I am sure his accommodating nature will end." He ran a finger down my cheek, and I jerked my head back from his touch. "Your head will look quite pretty on a spike."

I yanked my arm from his grasp and pushed him out of the way. Lazaro was an intense and imposing Elf. His laughter echoed off the walls and chased me down the hall.

"Lillyanna." Allendaire's voice made me jump. I turned to see him striding down the hall in my direction.

"Allendaire." I forced a smile as he fell in step beside me

"Fancy a ride? The weather broke and I'm a bit antsy. I'm sure you are as well."

I nodded. The thought of getting out—really getting out—delighted me. We walked through the palace and ventured outside to a cobble path where a horse was saddled and waiting. The mist had stopped, and the sun began to peek through the clouds. Allendaire gracefully mounted the horse, then held his hand down and hoisted me up behind. I wrapped my arms around his slender waist as he clicked his tongue, urging the animal into a walk.

"How is it the Suppressors have not infiltrated your lands?" The question had been burning on my mind.

"We provide them with the Sigaa'Lean." He touched the bracelet on my wrist. "We have an agreement... a contract... where we provide that, among other things, and they let us be."

I said nothing. Part of me thought it a clever way to keep safe. But another part was appalled they would provide the Suppressors with a device made to inhibit the use of magic. Inhibit magic the Elves also possessed, they had as much to lose as anyone.

Allendaire guided the horse through the streets. Elves stopped and bowed to their king, curious eyes on me as we traveled through the town. He steered the beast to the edge of the town and followed a faint path through the woods which opened up to a large clearing. He reined the horse in, and I slipped off its back, taking in the beauty of my surroundings. A large lake spread out before us, where a twenty-foot waterfall poured into the water below. The sun dappled through the canopy of leaves, lending an air of enchantment.

"It's beautiful," I said, my voice just above a whisper. I was afraid if I spoke loudly, my voice would break the magic cast before me. Afraid of shattering the serenity.

Allendaire stood beside me and slipped his arm about my waist, hand resting on my hip.

"This is my sacred spot. A place I go when I wish to be alone with my thoughts." He looked down at me. "No one comes here, nor do I bring anyone to this place."

I flushed and pulled away, suddenly uncomfortable in his loose embrace. I wandered the few feet to the edge of the water and sat down, kicking my shoes off, the grass cool on my bare feet.

Allendaire sat beside me, arm propped on his bent leg. He was uncomfortably close, and I resisted the urge to move away.

I listened to the roar of the water as it cascaded down the rocky cliff, the birds chirping in the trees and the soft whisper of leaves in the breeze. I could see why Allendaire would come here to think. It was peaceful and magical. "If no one comes here, why did you bring me?" Was this a ploy? Was I lured here to be disposed of?

He glanced at me. "I thought you would like it, and I thought some time out of the palace would do you some good."

Did he? I bit my lip. It felt strange being here alone with the Shadow Elf king. I wondered if anyone would talk, and if they did, what did that mean for me?

I turned my attention to him. "Why have I kept my head?"

"You were alone and unarmed."

"No. I want the truth, Allendaire. Your kind executes trespassers to keep your blood pure. Why did I live?"

Silence.

"Why don't you just let me go?"

"We should head back," he said. He stood in one graceful move and strode over to the horse.

I stood as well, brushing grass and leaves from my fine silk dress, and slipped on my shoes. I climbed behind him, and he stiffened at my touch.

We rode in silence back to the palace, where he handed the reins over to a stable hand and hurried across the small courtyard.

"I have work to attend to," he said, striding away.

I wandered back into the palace. I was at a loss as to what to do. Our brief outing had made me long for freedom. The palace walls now felt like a prison. I was bored with the library, the garden, even the labyrinth where neither Phabian nor Lazaro followed.

I even felt stifled inside my own room.

I needed freedom.

Sighing, I made my way through the halls back to the insufferable confines of my room.

"Lillyanna," Phabian's voice called out from behind. I stopped and turned in his direction. "Where are you headed? Surely, not the library again?"

My face heated. "No. I was going back to my room."

"Aren't you tired of being inside?"

"I..." I hesitated. Phabian didn't see me leave with Allendaire, and I wasn't sure I should tell him. "I don't stay inside all the time. I go out to the labyrinth."

He rolled his eyes. "That's hardly going out."

I folded my arms. "Tell me, Phabian. Where am I supposed to go when I can't even leave the walls?"

"If you want to go somewhere, just say the word and I'll take you anywhere you wish."

"Home?"

He sighed. "Of course not."

"Why am I here, Phabian? Why have I not been set free? For what purpose am I being kept prisoner?" Allendaire hadn't answered my question, and though I doubted Phabian would, it was worth a shot. The longer I was kept, the more concerned I grew about what the Elves had in store for me.

Phabian opened his mouth to speak.

"Phabian." Lazaro's voice cut off any words he was about to say, and I cursed his arrival. He glared at me as he sauntered up to where we stood.

Phabian's features softened at the sight of the other man, and a smile curled his lips. "Laz."

"Have you forgotten about patrol duty?"

"Of course not."

"So then why have I been waiting for half an hour? Let's go."

Phabian crossed his arms and quirked an eyebrow. "Are you ordering me, Lazaro?"

Lazaro's cheeks turned red, and he dropped his eyes. "Of course not, sir."

"I didn't think so. I will finish up with Lillyanna and meet you at the gates," Phabian said. Lazaro nodded, then turned to leave. "Oh, and Laz?" Lazaro paused and looked back. "We will have a discussion about your insolence."

"Of course, sir," he said. With a small bow of his head, he whirled back around and scurried away.

"I don't like him. I wish he wasn't one of my guards," I said.

Phabian chuckled. "He's not all bad. Once you get to know him, you'll find he's quite sweet and caring," he said, a look of fondness on his face. He turned back to me. "Well. It looks like duty calls. If you ever want to leave the grounds, Lillyanna, just ask me," he said, striding off after Lazaro.

I want to go home. I sighed at the thought and made my way through the halls toward my room.

The luxurious accommodation I was afforded did nothing to hide the fact that this was my prison. I was still a captive, albeit a well-fed, well clothed one. I rolled my shoulders. I felt stifled. The blazing fire in the hearth made the room too hot. The walls felt too close. Opening the double doors, I stepped outside. The air cooled my burning skin. I took several deep, cleansing breaths.

I wanted out of here. Even if I couldn't find my way home, I would find a village to live. Some place far away from these people. Some place where no one would find me. Not even Damiyun. I looked around the sprawling lawn, my eyes going to the labyrinth. The thought of wandering those passages again did not appeal to me, nor did going back to the library. No matter how many times I lost myself within the pages of a book, when I lifted my head, my reality hit me like a bucket of frozen water.

My eyes caught sight of Phabian, Lazaro, Krall and a few others. Their bright clothing peeked out from beneath their cloaks. They carried swords strapped to their sides or backs, quivers of arrows secured to their mounts, and bows in protective leather cases hung on slender shoulders. Lazaro said something, and the others laughed as they guided their horses down the cobblestone drive toward the exit off the palace grounds. I watched them depart past the guard towers and out the open gates until they disappeared around a bend.

My eyes went back to the gates that still stood open. I stared at the open entrance. No guards came out to close the heavy, iron gates. Nor did any greet the party that exited, I realized. My heart hammered in my chest, my temples pulsing to the beat. Phabian and Lazaro, my two guards, were gone, along with Krall who was nothing but a thorn in my side. Sweat slicked my hands and my mouth went dry.

There was no one watching me. The gates stood wide open and unguarded, inviting me out. Urging me to freedom. I swallowed hard. A light breeze blew a lock of hair in my eyes, and I swept it away with a shaking hand. I didn't know how long Phabian and the others would be out on patrol, and I didn't want to miss my chance. Bolting back into the room, I kicked off my slippers and stripped out of my dress. Throwing open the wardrobe, I fished around inside, pulling out the clothes I had arrived in. Shoving my feet into my boots, I grabbed a royal blue cloak, threw it on and raced to the door. Taking a deep breath, I slowly pulled it open and stepped into the hall. A few messenger Elves and other royals milled about. Though some snarled and hissed, spitting out words in their foreign tongue, many more paid me no heed, giving me not so much as a glance or a smile. Good. The less attention I was paid, the easier it would be for me to slip outside. And with Phabian and Lazaro gone, there was no chance of being called back.

Quickening my steps, I hurried down the stairs. Though I knew the chance to be slim, if stopped by someone I would just explain I was going out to the labyrinth as usual. My feet hit the floor and I had to stop myself from shooting down the hall. I held my breath as I walked, balling my fists to keep from shaking and trained my eyes on the ground, the white marble rushing beneath my feet as I walked. I risked a look up, my heart pounding and my breath quickening as I entered the atrium, the solid oak doors that bore the Shadow Elf crest several paces away. The scuff of my boots echoed off the walls, and I winced at the loud sound, though no one called out. No feet gave chase. No hands seized me to bring me back. To toss me in a cell to await execution.

After what felt like an eternity, I reached the massive doors. Grasping the brass handle, I pushed the heavy door open, sighing in relief as it slowly swung on silent hinges. I stepped outside, the blazing sun above reflected off the white marble steps, almost blinding me. It took everything within me to not run.

Easy, Lillyanna. You're just going for a walk around the grounds. You can do this.

Lifting my head and keeping my eyes on the gates, I continued on casually, though my body was coiled like a spring, ready to launch in an instant. After moments that felt longer than an eternity, I crossed through the gates. No one called out my name. No one raised an alarm. No one stopped me. I let go of the breath I held and ran.

THIRTY-EIGHT

Taking a left out of the gates, I bolted across a vast field. I didn't want to stick to the road, knowing it led to the city proper, and most likely there would be Elves traveling the path. Or worse. Phabian and his party coming back.

Digging in deep, I raced across the meadow, not knowing where I was going or what awaited me. The sun beat down, and a wind whipped my cloak around. I kept my head down, lifting only on occasion to check my surroundings. I was too exposed. I clenched my fists. My heart pounded in my ears. I didn't want to think about what would happen if I was caught. Digging in deeper, I gathered my strength and surged on.

My lungs burned, and my legs ached, begging me to stop. I looked up, my eyes catching the tree line and a dense forest beyond. I cried with joy at the sight. I didn't breathe. Didn't blink. Didn't dare to look around until I crossed into the forest, and even then, I didn't stop. I ran blind through the dense woods. My cloak snagged on branches. Roots reached up to grab my feet, causing me to stumble. Finally, my weak legs gave out, and I tumbled to the forest floor, scraping my hands on sharp rocks and sticks, my head slamming into the hard ground. I lay there stunned and panting. Sweat soaked my shirt, a breeze blew, and I pulled my cloak closer against the chill.

Pulling twigs from my hair, I slowly sat up, wiping my bloodied palms off on my trousers, and took in the surroundings. The thick canopy of trees above blocked out most of the sun, only a few rays breaking through to cast wan light. I couldn't see the meadow I had crossed. If I could no longer see the meadow, perhaps I was also out of sight. Perhaps I was safe. I searched for traces of a hunting party, listened for the bay of dogs, the call of the Elves. I heard nothing, saw nothing. Had I evaded them or were they lurking silently in the shadows?

Not wanting to find out, I rose to my feet. Glancing around, I chose a direction and began picking my way through the woods. I walked for what felt like hours, resting at intervals, when I needed it. My feet and legs ached. What paltry light the sun had afforded was slowly dying and with the darkness, came cold. Wrapping my cloak around myself, I pulled on the hood and shoved my hands into my pockets, trying to create as much body heat as possible. I was sore and tired. My throat was dry, and my stomach growled.

"Stupid," I cursed, the sound of my voice startling in the quiet. In my want for freedom, I neglected to consider how long I would be wandering and didn't think to pack a snack. Or water. I just wanted out, and now I was tired, hungry, thirsty and.... Lost. I was lost.

I blinked back the tears that stung my eyes. "Stupid. Stupid Lillyanna. You couldn't stay where you were. Was it so bad? Having a warm, soft bed to sleep in, a hot bath when you desired, rich food and drink. Was keeping the king company that much of a chore? Was being trailed by guards that much of a burden?" I plopped down on the ground, crossing my legs and rubbed away the tears as they trailed my cheeks. "And now you're crying like a child." I snatched up a rock and flung it at a tree.

Once again, my actions had landed me in trouble, though this time it was a bit worse than the last. I was lost in Shadow Elf lands. Or was I someplace else? My stomach gurgled; my throat felt like parchment. I trembled; the cold of night had come.

I should have paid more attention when Damiyun made a fire. I should have asked questions about hunting, and cooking game. Instead, I foolishly relied on their knowledge. With the lack of magic, it made my situation much worse. And dangerous. Darkness quickly descended, black and suffocating. It was too dark to travel. I could barely see my hand in front of my face, and I was exhausted. Lying down on the ground, I curled up into a ball for warmth. I would try to sleep. Try to regain the energy I had lost when I fled. In the morning, I would reassess my predicament with fresh eyes, a clear head, and hopefully a plan.

*P*ULLING THE BLANKETS CLOSE, *I burrowed deeper into the soft, feather mattress. The pops and crackles of the warm fire blazing in the hearth filled the silence. A hand, soft and warm, slid up my thigh, resting on my hip. Opening my eyes, I looked into a pair of dark blue ones. I brushed a lock of black hair off the man's brow. Grabbing my wrist, he pressed his warm lips to my palm.*

White teeth flashed in a menacing smile. "They are coming," Themesis said, his voice low.

I pulled back. "What?"

He cupped my cheek. "They will bring you to me. You will set me free."

A screech filled my mind, and I bolted awake. Confusion filled me, though only briefly. Another screech pierced the night, shrill and haunting. It made the hair on the back of my neck rise, and a cold stone formed in the pit of my stomach. A snarling growl came from my right. Red eyes peered at me from the darkness. The beast—the demon, I realized—was close. Too close. Another demon screeched again, two more answering, drawing closer. The red-eyed beast took a step forward, a low growl rumbled deep in its throat.

They will bring you to me, Themesis had said. I took a step back, away from the demon. My heel snagged on a root; my arms flailed as I tried to regain my balance. Failing at that, I landed hard on my backside. The red-eyed demon moved closer, sharp teeth bared, saliva dripping from deadly, sharp, canines. It leaped into the air, lethal claws curling from its massive paws. I watched as it flew toward me. I skittered backward, utterly helpless.

Stupid. This is what you get, I chastised. The beast yelped, dropping from the air mere feet away from me. A blue-fletched arrow protruded from its eye.

What in the world?

Blinding flashes lit up the dark, shrieks echoed through the woods, then died. Darkness once again descended. What was going on? Rising to my feet, I looked around, straining my eyes to see, gasping at the figures advancing from between the trees. I took a shaking step back. My eyes widened as a man stepped forward. His long white hair blew about his face in the breeze. Bright clothing winked out from beneath his dark cloak, and ice-blue eyes held cold anger. His slender fingers held a long tube, which he raised to his lips and blew. Sound burst forth.

"Phabian." Relief flooded through me as I recognized the man who stood in front of me. I took a step forward. Something stung my neck. Reaching up, I pulled out a small, feathered dart. The woods pitched, and I tumbled to the forest floor.

"Shit."

I SLOWLY OPENED MY eyes, the canopy above coming into focus. A soft surface supported me, familiar pillows and blankets scented the air around me. I was in my own bed and not a cell. This fact did not mean I wouldn't lose my head. I knew all too well. Mouranda never let me forget it.

I sat up, the room pitched, and I closed my eyes and swallowed back the sickness that rose. Opening my eyes, I looked around the dimly lit room, seeing Allendaire sitting in a chair beside the fireplace. His clothes were wrinkled, and tiredness creased his eyes. Rising, he made his way to the bed and sat on the edge.

"You are fortunate to be here, Lillyanna," he said. Though his voice held no anger, I flinched, nonetheless. "Someone saw you leaving and sent word to

Phabian. Had he not found you when he did…" he shook his head. I didn't need for him to finish his words. I knew exactly what would have happened to me.

I looked down at my hands. "I'm sorry."

Allendaire hooked a finger beneath my chin and tipped my head up. "Why did you flee?"

Why do you think? Pulling away, I slipped out of bed and crossed the room to the window. It was still dark outside, though I wasn't sure if it was the same day or not.

"I only wanted to explore," I said. "I am tired of being a prisoner."

"You are not a prisoner."

I laughed. "Right. So, then why can't I go outside these walls? Why must I be trailed by Phabian or Lazaro? You might as well lock me in a cell."

Allendaire's clothes rustled as he rose and crossed the room. I could feel his heat, hear his breath as he stood behind me. "Is that what you want? To be locked in a cell?"

"Is it any different from my current situation?"

"Why did you really run?" He turned me around to face him. "Were you trying to find Damiyun?"

I blinked. "What? How do you know about him?" The words flew out of my mouth before I could stop them.

"There is a reason Phabian is my adviser," Allendaire said.

I recalled the odd way Phabian would look at me. The cold sensation blanketing me as he did so. Fragments, wisps of memories swirling through my mind so fast I wasn't sure they were there. He had delved into my mind at some point and discovered the truth. But how much of it? I was afraid to ask.

"I know all about you, Lillyanna and though the tale is unbelievable, memories never lie," he said.

"You allowed Phabian to probe my mind?" My body heated at the thought. Clenching my jaw, I pushed Allendaire out of the way. I stalked the room, running my hand through my hair. The nerve of Phabian. How dare he invade my most private place. I felt naked. Violated. He would be getting a tongue lashing.

"I did what was necessary to protect my kingdom."

I stopped pacing and glared at him. "That doesn't make it right. I shouldn't even be here. Why am I here?"

"I told you. You were—"

"Unarmed and alone. I know. How many trespassers are unarmed and alone?"

Allendaire said nothing.

I shook my head. "I want to go home. That's why I fled."

"And this, Damiyun? He had nothing to do with your rash decision?"

I glared at him. "No, he did not."

Allendaire cocked his head to the side. "You still love him, despite what he did."

I flushed at his words and clenched my fists. "For the love of the god-damned gods, is nothing about me sacred?"

"Lillyanna—"

"I want to be alone," I said, wrapping my arms around myself.

Allendaire nodded, then crossed the room, closing the door softly behind him. My blood boiled in my veins. How dare Phabian. How dare he pry around in my mind! I raged as I poured water into the basin and washed up. Pulling on a long sleeve dress of purple silk, I shoved my feet into a pair of shoes and stalked out of the room.

I would find Phabian, and when I did, he would get a piece of my mind that he hadn't yet probed.

THIRTY-NINE
PHABIAN

"**M**Y POINT," I CALLED over my shoulder to Krall as I pulled my blue-fletched arrow and his green-fletched one out of the target. "That makes it six to two." I walked across the archery range to where my brother stood, handing him his arrow.

"Cheater," he said with a scowl.

I laughed. "Perhaps if you spent less time wetting your cock and more time practicing your skills, you might win."

"Let's switch to swords."

I opened my mouth to speak, the sound of a door banging against the wall stopping my words. I turned to see Lillyanna stalking in our direction. Her hair swirled around her head in a mass of red curls that looked like fire. Fury flashed in the depths of her green eyes.

"Stupid human," Krall hissed.

I clenched my jaw. "She is not stupid."

Krall laughed. "She ran away and almost got eaten by a demon. You should have let it happen."

I glared at him. "And our king would have taken my head for it."

Krall rolled his eyes. "Doubtful. She's just taking up space."

I said nothing as I watched Lillyanna stalk across the ground to where we stood. "How dare you," she snarled, planting herself in front of me, hands on her hips. Anger rolled off her in waves, and I had to stop myself from shrinking back. "How dare you invade my mind! How dare you poke around in my private thoughts!"

Krall's eyes widened, and he laughed. "You did what now? You should know better than to slip into a human mind. Who knows what lurks there. You could come out as deaf and as dumb as they are."

Lillyanna glared at him.

"I needed to find out the truth. I needed to know if you were a threat to my king."

Krall grinned. "What did you discover? Clearly, she is not High Born. Peasant? Serf?" His eyes swept over her, a lascivious look in them. "Whore?"

I gave my brother a sharp look. He shut his mouth and stalked back to the palace. I looked down at Lillyanna who was still steaming. "I am the king's adviser. My job is to ensure his safety and to find out what is not being told in words. You wandered onto our lands, and he quite foolishly let you live. Just because you were alone and unarmed did not mean you were not a threat. You could have been sent here. There could have been an army waiting to attack."

"So, you just decided to poke around in my head at your leisure?"

"Something like that. I admit what I found out was quite interesting, though your lie was far more believable." Unstringing my bow, I began walking back toward the palace.

"It's true. All of it," she said, her voice quiet.

"And this Damiyun?" I glanced down at her. "Quite the roguish cad, though I suppose I could see the attraction."

Her jaw clenched, and her face turned red. "Just how much did you gather?"

"Enough." The red deepened, and I laughed. "I am sorry you feel my—truth gathering—was done in a nefarious way. I assure you it wasn't, and I apologize for breaching your trust, if you had any. I like you, Lillyanna. You have grown on me over these past Moon Cycles, and I enjoy your company."

She sighed, her shoulders relaxing a little at my words, though her eyes still flashed with anger. "I like you too, Phabian. That's why your betrayal... well, it hurt." She said, her voice soft.

"I'm sorry." I pulled open the door and stepped into the hall. Lillyanna fell in step beside me. "As I said, my job is to protect the king, one way I am able to protect him is through delving. It may be a foreign ability to a Wielder such as yourself, but it has proven useful from time to time."

Lillyanna said nothing as we strolled down the halls. Elves rushed by, many greeting me with words or bowing their heads. Some hissed at Lillyanna calling her crude names in Elvish.

"What are they saying?" She looked up at me.

I scratched my chin. The words hissed weren't nice. Some called her a filthy, sullied blooded human. A few called her a whore, and still others called for her head. "Nothing nice, but you already know this."

She nodded, her eyes on the floor. Slowing my steps, I came to a stop. She drew up beside me. "Next time you want to leave, tell me and I will take you on an outing." I folded my arms and looked down at her. "I know your plan was to escape."

"Is it so wrong to want to go back home?" Her sorrow filled green eyes met mine. "Why am I here? Why wasn't I executed? Why can't I go home?"

I ran a hand over my face. I wanted to give her something, but her questions weren't easy to answer. At least not truthfully. I took a deep breath. "If you went home and people knew you were here... well, I'm sure you can understand why that would be a problem." It wasn't a straight out lie.

She chewed her lip. "I wouldn't say anything."

Even though I could feel the truth in her words, it wasn't that easy. "It was my king's decision," I said.

Lillyanna huffed, and continued walking. Grabbing her arm, I stopped her and pulled her around. "I meant what I said, Lillyanna. If you wish to go further than these walls, come to me. I will take you wherever you wish to go. Except home," I said.

"Thank you," she said, and I watched her stride down the hall. I continued slowly on, making my way back to my room to change and ready for the evening meal. I didn't like deceiving Lillyanna. I liked her and felt we could be friends one day, lying to her struck a kind of guilt within me I hadn't felt in some time. Yet, my loyalty and duty was to the king, my king. I did what he asked even when I didn't agree.

But whatever happened, I would be there for Lillyanna. I would be her ally. Her friend. The only one who understood, and I would do what I could for her while pushing down my guilt and doing what my status required, despite how I felt about it.

FORTY

LILLYANNA

P HABIAN DIDN'T RETRIEVE ME for the evening meal, so I took it to my room. When I finished, and with not much else to do, I readied for bed. As I slipped my nightdress over my head, I heard a soft knock on the door. When I opened it, I was surprised to see Allendaire standing on the other side. His eyes devoured me as he crossed the threshold, closing the door behind him, and I felt self-conscious and naked in my flimsy nightdress.

"Allen—" My words were cut off by powerful hands that grabbed me and pushed me against the wall, his mouth crushed mine.

He pulled away briefly, eyes dark with desire. And I knew I would not say no. Hands pulled at my nightdress, the flimsy cotton giving way and tearing. Lips and tongue tasted skin, and soft hands—the type never used for labor—explored my body. I reacted to his touch, and though my mind screamed it was wrong, he was the king. My fate rested in his hands. I would do whatever it took to keep my head. Even if it meant lying with him.

My fingers fumbled with his belt and laces, freeing him from the confines. He lifted me up, and I locked my legs around his waist, gasping when he entered me, taking me hard and fast against the wall, clutching me tight, body shuddering as he spent himself.

He pulled back, and I unlocked my legs from around him. His hands gripped my waist.

"What are you doing to me?" His voice was soft, eyes searching mine.

"I—"

His mouth caught mine again, and he lazily kissed me. "Vixen." He hissed, a small smile forming. His eyes swept over my naked body as he slipped out of his finery and crossed to the bed, slipping beneath the covers, and moving over to make room. I crawled in beside him, his arms closed around me, and I nestled into his embrace.

"What have you done to me?" he murmured again. "What spell have you cast? I don't understand what I am feeling. I want to run from you, yet you intrigue me." He paused. "Is this what you call love?"

"I don't know."

Allendaire pulled back and looked down at me. "Did you not love Damiyun? Tell me about him."

"I'd rather not."

Allendaire sat up, propping his head on his hand and looked down at me. "He hurt you."

I glared at him. "Why don't you ask Phabian about him? He seems to know everything about me." I snapped.

"He put the sadness in your eyes," he said, brushing my hair back from my face.

"Yes," I sighed.

Allendaire rolled over, bracing himself above me. "I will do my best to take your sadness away," he said, lips softly brushing mine. His hands slid down my body, stroking and caressing, finding those places that gave me pleasure. Lips teased my breasts, my skin, my mouth. Fingers gently probed.

His tongue flicked over a nipple, a hand caressed between my legs, and I burned with desire. *Curse my body for betraying me.*

I writhed beneath his weight, pressing against his hand, fire surging through me as teeth grazed a nipple, tongue flicking over to sooth the injury. I clutched the sheets as desire filled me. I grabbed his head and drew him close, kissing him. "Please," I begged, stroking him. He was painfully close. I needed to have him. Needed him in me before I went crazy.

He bent his head, teeth nipping at my neck, lips trailing kisses.

"Allendaire, please."

"Please what?" he breathed.

"I need you," I panted, releasing him. He was close. So close. He pulled away, grabbed my wrists, and pinned them to the bed. His free hand slid between my legs again, and I wanted to weep with frustration.

"Like this?" he breathed, lips against my ear.

I struggled against the hand that held, wanted to kick him off me, to take what I wanted.

"The more you fight me, the less inclined I will be to give you what you want," he said, a wicked look in his eyes.

I stopped my fight. "Please."

"That's much better, though I can't entirely say you're begging enough."

He slid a finger inside me. I moaned, closing my eyes and squirming against him.

He pulled away. My eyes snapped open at the sudden stop. "I think I have paperwork to attend to."

"No. Please, Allendaire. Don't—don't leave me like this. Please?" I shamefully begged. At the moment, I would have done absolutely anything to keep him here. To have him.

"That's a little better."

"Please, Allendaire?" I pleaded, trying hard not to squirm. Not to wrap my legs around him and force him inside me.

"I like the sound of that word. Beg me again."

I grit my teeth. "Please, Allendaire."

He entered me with a sigh, eyes on mine as we moved together. I locked my legs around him, pulling him close, drawing him deeper, and meeting his thrusts and tempo. I clutched him, fingernails digging into his back. My body buzzed with desire, flushed with heat. I let myself go, giving in to the pleasure he gave me, writhing beneath him, shuddering as waves of bliss coursed through me. His mouth caught mine, lips hungrily devouring. He clutched me tight, a feral growl escaping as he spent himself again.

He flopped onto his back, and I curled up alongside him, my head on his chest, hand idly exploring the hard muscles and planes of his body. His lips brushed the top of my head, fingers softly stroking my shoulder.

"Won't Mouranda wonder where you are?" I asked. Or anyone else for that matter. The thought someone—Lazaro perhaps—had seen him enter my room without leaving crossed my mind.

"We stopped sharing a bed a long time ago. Once she discovered her fertility issues, she did not find it necessary to perform her wifely duties."

I shifted my position, propping myself up on my elbow, so I could look at him.

"No one saw me come here, Lillyanna. You needn't worry. And if they did?" He shrugged. "I am their king. They know better than to spread gossip." He reached up, fingers toying with a curl.

"If Mouranda can't have children, what happens when you are gone? Who will become king?"

"No one."

"But—" I bit my lip and frowned. "Won't you appoint someone to rule? Phabian perhaps? Are you not all Troundes?"

"Yes, however, the heir must be a direct descendant of the king."

"Can't you choose another to have your child?"

He shrugged. "I suppose, as there are no laws preventing such. Though, it wouldn't be fair to the mother to see her child being reared by another. And it would also pose a threat to the throne. She may very well feel she has a claim to it and could try to overthrow me."

"Do you really think that would happen? Your Elves love and respect you."

"I can't take any chances."

"So, what happens then? To your kingdom? To your Elves when you are gone?" I paused. "Are you immortal?"

He laughed. "No. My Life Force will eventually fade, as will I, though not for many Grand Passages."

"How old are you?"

"I will be two hundred and forty-seven in three days' time."

"Is that considered old?"

He laughed. "Two hundred and forty-seven is hardly old. Karrinian was seven hundred and sixteen when he passed. My father, Terrin, had he not been poisoned by my sister Rahina, would have no doubt surpassed that age."

I wondered why his sister would have poisoned their father but thought it better not to ask. Perhaps I would ask Phabian the next time I saw him. I was beginning to find the Shadow Elves an interesting—and terrifying—race.

"So, what happens when you're gone?" I asked instead.

"My Elves will have to figure it out."

I blinked. "You truly have no plan for them? No order on what to do?"

"They can set up another monarchy if they choose, though there is the potential to divide."

"But—"

He pulled me down, silencing me with a kiss. "No more questions," he said, pushing me back and positioning himself above me. "I have a hunger to satisfy," he growled, and I let him use me again. If this is what it would take for me to keep my head, then I would give myself over to the king until I figured out a way to escape. Though, it occurred to me with Phabian roaming my mind, would I ever have a chance to leave?

FORTY-ONE

I woke early. The world beyond still rested in darkness. The bed was empty, but I caught Allendaire pulling on his clothes in the soft glow of the candlelight. I yawned, and he turned at the sound, a smile crinkling his eyes.

"Did I wake you?" He crossed the room to the bed and sat down on the edge. He pushed the covers aside, dipping his head to kiss me, his hands sliding down my body. "Mmm.... I regret I have to leave you." He murmured, fingers softly stroking between my legs, teeth biting my neck.

"Where are you going?" I squirmed against his touch.

"The annual Name Day hunt," he said, pulling away, fingers still probing. Pleasing. "It's really just an excuse for my Elves to have three days of drinking and whoring."

I gripped the sheets, body shuddering as he brought me to climax.

"Don't worry, though. I promise to abstain and save myself for you." He leaned down and kissed me again. "I would much rather spend the time in bed with you."

"So don't go." I suggested, trying to be coy.

He sighed. "It's tradition. My Elves look forward to it, though I can't say I ever really have. Maybe this time I will actually hunt and catch something." He grinned.

I laughed. "Well, have a good time. I will see you when you return."

His eyes swept longingly over my naked body. He spread my legs wide. "This is how I want to find you when I come back," he said, voice husky as he rose gracefully to his feet and padded out.

I pulled the blanket back over myself, the feel of his touch lingering, heating my body. A small twinge of guilt crept in over my body's betrayal. Sharing a bed with Allendaire seemed a betrayal to Damiyun. It shouldn't. Still, I had to survive. Still, the pang of guilt hit like knives.

This is for survival, I told myself again.

My mind went to Allendaire and his upcoming Name Day. Sadness filled me when I realized my own Name Day had come and gone four Moon Cycles ago. Up to the age of twelve, my father would buy me a trinket, a book and a sweet cake. After he left, I celebrated alone, keeping up the tradition in what meager way I could.

I pushed back the tears as I settled back beneath the blankets and slipped back into sleep.

IT WAS ALMOST MIDDAY when I woke, and the sun sat high in the sky. I slipped out of bed, shivering against the chill in the room. Winter was fast approaching, and soon the land would be covered in a blanket of white. I quickly washed and pulled on a warm, blue woolen dress and headed out to the hall. I wandered aimlessly about, slipping into the sanctuary of the library. A fire roared, warming the room, and I examined the shelves I had gazed upon hundreds of times. I was tired of reading. Tired of wandering aimlessly about.

I felt stifled.

"I never have to wonder where you are. Perhaps the king can put a bed in here, so you don't have to leave." I looked over to see Phabian standing casually in the doorway, a broad grin on his face.

"You didn't go on the hunt?"

He shook his head as he walked into the room. "When the king is gone, it is up to me to take care of his affairs."

Interesting. Allendaire had appointed Phabian as regent when he was not here, but couldn't—or wouldn't—appoint another king when he was gone.

"Does that mean you will rule when the king dies?"

"That is not how my appointment is. When the king passes, another governmental structure will be put in place."

"Another monarchy?"

He shrugged. "It's possible, though it will be a long time before anything needs to be done," he said, waving his hand in dismissal. "Anyway, I came to see if you wished to join me for a brief outing. I need to pick up the king's gift, and I am sure you are bored with these walls."

"Yes," I said, excitement filling me.

Phabian laughed at my eagerness. "We will meet in the entryway in an hour. We can make an afternoon out of it if you wish."

"I'd like that."

He smiled, giving a slight bow, and slipped out of the room.

I couldn't help but feel a sense of giddiness at the thought of going out again. The trip to Allendaire's sacred place made me want more. And perhaps it would be fun. I enjoyed Phabian's company and the thought of spending an afternoon with him was appealing. Perhaps I would learn more about him.

Smiling, my body buzzing with anticipation, I left the room to find something to wear, eager to escape the palace, if only for a little while.

W E NEVER ENDED UP going into town.

As we stood in the entryway and readied to go, the door burst open. Two bloodied Elves hurried through, supporting an injured Allendaire between them. His left arm hung limply, and his right hand held his side. My eyes widened at his blood soaking his shirt.

The blood that flowed beneath his hand.

"What happened?" Phabian rushed forward. My eyes went to the door where more injured Elves poured through. One staggered, swaying on his feet, then collapsed on the floor, sightless eyes staring at the ceiling. Blood pooled around him.

On and on they came.

Injured. Dead. Dying.

"What happened?" Phabian grabbed the arm of an Elf who rushed by.

"An ambush by an unknown assailant." The man said, eyes wild.

Phabian frowned. "What do you mean, unknown?"

"Their faces were covered. All we could see were white eyes. They were fast and struck hard." He shook his head. "We fought as hard as we could, but they... They were so fast. One moment they were there, and the next they were gone, and appeared elsewhere. It was mass confusion. The king—we did our best to protect him."

"Get the injured to the infirmary," Phabian pointed down the hall. "Sound the alarms. Lock the city down. Light the warning fires for all to see." His orders sent Elves scattering.

"What happened? Where is Allendaire?" Mouranda whipped through the entryway, black skirts swirling, and had I not known any better I would have thought she were flying.

"Ambushed by an unknown assailant. The king has been injured and is being cared for in the infirmary. The alarm will be sounded, and the fires lit," Phabian said, and as if on cue the sound of a bell clanged loudly. Mouranda's lips pursed, and she whirled out of the room.

Phabian turned to an Elf on his right. "Take care of the bodies. Notify their kin." His eyes swept around, a look of surprise crossing his face at seeing me.

"Go to your room and stay there." His head turned as more injured and dying Elves burst through.

There was so much blood.

The floor was covered in it. The sharp metallic stench filled the air. The hand of death hovered, suffocated.

My head spun at the sight, and my stomach lurched at the smell.

And still, they came. Snapping out of my shock, I moved to help.

"Lillyanna." Phabian's voice cracked like a whip as he stalked over to me. "Get to your room. Now. Do not—under any circumstance—leave."

"I worked with a healer. I can help your wounded."

"I have it under control. You will only be in the way. The king will have my head if something happens to you," he said, his voice softening a bit.

I took one last look at the chaos and stepped from the scene, Phabian's authoritative voice barking orders and commands behind me. Frustrated at being told what to do yet again, I hurried through the halls, dodging Elves armed to the teeth hurrying to battle. My eyes scanned the stony faces of the women behind them, scurrying over to see if their mates were among the dying or the dead.

I all but ran through the halls to my room, slamming and locking the door behind. I leaned against it, the still quiet of the place almost deafening. I rushed to the double doors and threw them open. Stumbling out onto the balcony, I breathed the crisp, cold air in deep, filling my nose and lungs, cleansing them of the stench of blood and death.

The bell still clanged in the distance, and I could see fires burning in towers that loomed high in the sky. Below, armed Elves amassed, bows slung around shoulders, quivers at the hip. They carried dozens of knives strapped to their bodies, the hilts glinting in the sunlight.

Voices drifted up, urgent and commanding. Thundering hooves shook the ground as Elves sped off to battle, Phabian leading them, and I offered a silent prayer up for his safe return.

FORTY-TWO
DAMIYUN

DARKNESS SURROUNDED ME AND I felt as though I were falling from the sky. A voice drifted up from the Abyss.

His voice.

Calling me.

Coaxing me down, down, down.

Come, Damiyun. Come to where you belong. To where you always knew was your home.

A searing heat filled the void.

Filled me.

Flames licked and teased flesh, drawing me down. I embraced the heat and let myself go. Let my body fall toward it.

Closer and closer into the void.

Into the Abyss.

A hand grabbed my shoulder, stopping my descent. A rough jerk pulled me back.

"Not today, Damiyun," Abraham's voice growled in my ear, and I felt myself rising up.

No.

I fought against him.

Against the pull. Trying hard to go back.

Back to the Abyss.

Back to my home.

Sensations returned. The sound of voices grew louder as my Life Force was restored. I opened my eyes and found myself staring up at a wood-paneled ceiling.

My stomach clenched, and my body felt heavy at being brought back to this insufferable life.

To my pathetic existence.

"Welcome back, Damiyun."

I turned my head and found myself looking into a pair of violet eyes filled with relief.

Ayelay's eyes.

She stood beside the bed holding a tray. I breathed in the sweet cinnamon scent, the pungent spices taunting my stomach. I shifted to a seated position on the cot, scratching where the stiff wool blanket had irritated bare skin. She handed me the tray, and I dug into my meal of porridge and a cup of tea, the hot, spice-flavored grains warming me and sating my hunger.

"The infection spread. It was almost more than I could handle," she said. Her eyes met mine. "You're fortunate to be alive."

"Why did you bother saving me?"

"I am a healer. I swore an oath to do everything possible to save someone."

Though she may have used her abilities, I knew it was more Abraham's doing than hers.

"It's going to take a while for the wound to heal properly," she said.

I laughed. "Why bother? Am I not to be executed?"

"You are being allowed to plead your case in front of a panel," she said.

I shook my head. "Plead my case in front of a panel of Faeries? You might as well take my head now. Save yourselves the charade."

She pursed her lips and took a seat beside the bed, smoothing her skirts. "We are a fair race. We will allow you your time in front of our panel."

I snorted, as I dug back into my bowl, all but licking it clean.

"You're a Suppressor," she said.

Wiping my mouth, I put the tray on the table beside me and crossed my arms. "No."

"You bear their sign." She pointed to the brand on the left side of my chest.

"This is true, though I am not a part of that anymore. If I were, your brother's death wouldn't have been the only one."

She folded her arms and cocked her head to the side. "Since you have been here, they have been spotted on the outskirts of our lands. We have done well with keeping our kind hidden. Perhaps they are searching for you?"

"They are searching for Wielders. Your kind may have been able to keep hidden thus far; however, they are becoming more aggressive," I said. "You will be taken like all the others."

"Our magic keeps us hidden."

"Your magic is what attracts them."

She laughed. "They have come close to our lands, yes, but they have never entered them. If they did, they would not survive."

I said nothing. Clearly, Ayelay didn't know the Organization like I did. Wielders never stand a chance against them.

"When am I to be executed?"

"Tried, Damiyun. You will be tried."

I shook my head with a chuckle. "Tried, executed. It's all the same to me. I'd rather get it over with."

"Why do you wish to die?"

I sighed. "This life has done me no favors. If anything, it has made me realize how bad I want it to end."

"Why? Why do you wish so badly to die when life has so much to offer?"

My eyes met hers. "Because I have made choices that have hurt others. Because even in the darkest sleep, the voices of those I have hurt, killed, and betrayed, haunt me. In death, I will no longer be reminded of the person I am. In death, I will be no more than a servant of Themesis."

She sighed. "Your past does not weigh upon your present."

I thought about Abraham and the soul—my soul—he held, and the reason he had it. I laughed. "You know nothing about me, Ayelay."

"Then tell me so I might understand."

"For what purpose? Understanding me will not change the circumstances."

Ayelay rose to her feet and crossed to the door.

"When is my trial?"

"When you are healed."

Silence enveloped me as soon as the door closed. As tempting as escape seemed, I had no doubt they had posted Faeries in the hall brandishing poisoned pikes. I also knew incinerating them would do nothing to help my case.

So, I waited. The thought of this possibly being the only time I had left in this world was sobering.

And at the same time, a quiet comfort.

I T TOOK FOUR MOON Cycles for my wound to heal properly. When Ayelay came for me, I was mentally ready, and at peace with the fate that awaited me. I was given fresh clothes to wear, a light blue shirt made of silk and a fresh pair of black trousers. My arms were bound behind. Guards flanked me, as Ayelay led the way through the halls. We drew up to a door, which she pushed open, and I followed her inside.

The room was plain, a long table spanning its length. Thirteen Faeries dressed in green robes made up the panel I was to face. Naleigha sat in the middle, hands folded, a crown sat atop her head, branches of gold and silver with emerald leaves sparkled in the lamplight.

Twenty-six eyes watched as the guards led me to the center of the room.

"Mother, please," Ayelay folded her hands beneath her chin. "He had every opportunity to kill me—to kill you—but he hasn't. I don't think—"

"Thank you, Daughter," Naleigha's ice-cold voice hadn't changed from that day. Ayelay's shoulders sagged, and she followed the guards to a corner of the room and sat down on the floor.

"State your name," Naleigha's voice cracked like a whip.

"Damiyun Rayne."

"And what were you doing in our lands?"

"We were searching for a lost companion."

"And what made you think they would be here?"

"She left when we were in Karstollan. This was the most logical place to search first."

"What is your relationship to the one who killed our future king?"

I turned my attention to the petite Faery who had posed the question. She sat three seats to the right of the queen. "What does it matter? He is gone. Am I not the one standing trial? A trial for a crime I did not commit?"

"You were with the one who murdered my son. That makes you just as guilty."

I looked back at Naleigha. "I did not wield the knife that killed him. I surrendered my weapons. Your daughter can attest to the fact that I was unarmed. I had no knowledge of what Abraham was about." Though I should have guessed when he didn't protest the journey. "When Abraham spoke your name, did you not wonder how he knew you?"

"I am not the one on trial."

"Yet you still invited us to your celebration without further question."

Naleigha slammed her hand down on the table. "I am not the one on trial. You have no right to question me."

"And I shouldn't be on trial for something I did not do."

"Someone has to pay for my son's death. Vengeance must be served."

"Vengeance was served for Abraham's daughter. A child who foolishly fell in love with your son and thought he returned her affection. A child who sold her soul to spend eternity with him. Abraham's only child, whose soul he had to deliver to the Fallen One."

"Arias did not deserve his fate."

"And Jaylynn did?" I raised an eyebrow.

"She made her choice. He had none."

I laughed. "He was given a choice."

"Abraham is no god. It is not for him to decide who lives and who dies."

I shrugged. "And yet here I am having my fate decided by those who are not gods."

"Where were you when the incident happened?"

"I was in the company of your daughter, Ayelay. Had I wished to harm anyone, I could have used my magic, but I did not."

"You incinerated four guards."

"A natural reaction when poisoned spears are leveled on me and my life is at risk," I said. "Did I not surrender upon request?"

Naleigha pursed her lips.

"Have I harmed you or your daughter while here? While my hands were unbound?"

Naleigha said nothing. I saw a movement out of the corner of my eye. It was Ayelay making her way toward me. Pulling out a knife, she sliced through the rope that bound my wrists. The room was filled with gasps and murmurs. I rubbed my wrists and glanced at her, then folded my hands in front of me.

"What are you doing?" Naleigha clenched her fists.

"Proving Damiyun is not a foe. He means us no harm, Mother. I know this to be true."

"The future king is dead," A deep voice from the panel said.

"He killed four guards." Another voice.

Ayelay sighed. "As he said already, he was being attacked. Arias," she took a deep, shaking breath. Tears swirled in her violet eyes. "Arias was my brother. I loved him, but this man isn't the one responsible for his death."

Naleigha's jaw clenched. "We will vote on the fate of Damiyun Rayne," she said, her voice cold. "All those who feel this man should pay for the death of your king with his blood raise a hand and say 'aye.'"

Naleigha, not surprisingly, raised her hand with an "aye." A muscular and imposing male Fae on the end raised a hand, his bright-green eyes locked on mine as he spoke his affirmation. A petite Faerie to the queen's right raised her hand and spoke her affirmation, her eyes narrowed on me. And that was it. Even I was surprised at how many kept their hands down.

Naleigha's eyes flashed at the other ten Faeries, who did not raise their hands. "Your future king is dead. Do you not want justice?"

"Forgive me, my queen, but I cannot condemn one man for the actions of another," a sweet voice said. I looked at the tall, thin, male who spoke.

"Nor can I," another said, while the rest nodded their agreement.

"Your king is dead," Naleigha said again, her eyes going to each member at the table. "Do you not want justice for him?"

"Of course, justice is warranted, my queen, but we are not barbarians. We do not kill innocents. We will be no better than the Suppressors if we take this man's life." I glanced in the direction of the man who spoke. A pair of hazel eyes met mine, and he gave me a small nod.

Naleigha's eyes went to Ayelay. "Do you not care that your brother is dead?"

Ayelay sighed. "Of course, I care, mother, but what will taking Damiyun's life do? It isn't going to bring Arias back," she said. "You can appoint another king."

Naleigha's jaw clenched. "That is not the point." She slammed a fist on the table.

"Then what is? Spilling Damiyun's blood will not raise the dead. It will not bring you peace."

Naleigha glared at Ayelay. "Very well," she stated, her tone clipped. She inclined her head and looked down her nose at me. Ayelay placed her hand on my arm. "Damiyun Rayne. I consider myself to be a fair and just queen. The panel has spoken, though I have the final say."

I held my breath. Her eyes shot to Ayelay. "You could have easily killed us all when my daughter unbound your hands, but you did not. The majority has ruled in your favor, and as such, I will abide by it. Consider yourself lucky," she said with a scowl.

I exhaled, and it took everything I had in me to remain upright. The panel of thirteen was dismissed, leaving me and Ayelay alone in the room.

"For someone who wishes to die, you worked hard to plead your case. Your relief at my mother's decision was strong," she said. "Perhaps you truly wish to live."

I said nothing, though I couldn't rightly disagree with her words. Maybe I had prepared myself to die, but that didn't mean I was eagerly awaiting the feel of an ax biting into my neck. The thought of truly losing my head was enough to make me ponder my fate.

My life.

"I owe you a debt of gratitude for what you did."

A smile played about her lips and her violet eyes danced. "I am quite aware of the debt you owe me. The debt began when you ate our food."

"I was hungry. What choice did I have?"

She laughed. "You know nothing of our ways. If you did, you would have known the words to speak that would release the enchantment."

I sighed. "What is my debt to you?"

"You must return every Grand Passage for no more and no less than four days."

"And if I do not?"

"If you choose not to, the food you eat will smell foul and become ash on your tongue. Your drink will not fulfill your thirst. You will try to satiate your needs only to die of starvation. A slow and painful death."

I rubbed my eyes. While the thought of seeing Ayelay again wasn't terrible, I had hoped I would be done with the Faery folk after this day.

"Time to go, Damiyun," Naleigha's voice snapped from the doorway. I turned to see her holding my weapons and cloak, jaw clenched. Her cold eyes held anger, and sadness. We left the palace and hiked to the edge of the woods Abraham and I had entered four Moon Cycles prior. A stable hand stood off to the side, holding Xander's reins. I sighed with relief at seeing him. Naleigha handed me my weapons, and I strapped my sword to my back and slipped the dagger in my belt.

"Fare thee well, Damiyun and know the gods favored you this day," she said, turning and striding away.

I snorted, knowing her words to be false. The gods never favored me.

No, it was Ayelay who favored me. It was her actions that allowed me to keep my head.

"Goodbye, and thank you, Ayelay."

She smiled. "I look forward to seeing you again, Damiyun. I have much to teach you about our kind," she said, offering a small wave as I slipped into the woods. The sun's rays dappled on the ground as I guided Xander through the forest on silent feet, the scent of pine and wet leaves drifting on the fall breeze.

Exiting the woods, I swung up onto Xander and heeled him toward Karstollan.

To where Abraham surely was.

He would feel my wrath for what he did and for what almost happened to me.

FORTY-THREE

T HE SUN HUNG LOW in the sky as I drew closer to the village.

I dug my heels into Xander, snapping the reins, urging him to race faster.

The village came into view, and I slowed to a trot, then a walk. I led him down the small hill that led to the village, pulling up in front of The Drunken Dragon. I led Xander to the stables and flipped the stable hand two coppers.

"Rest, friend," I said, scratching Xander's nose.

I turned to enter the tavern. Music and laughter drifted through the door as it opened and closed, growing louder and then muffling. Striding up the stone steps, I reached for the door, jumping back when it opened, a tall man glaring at me beneath his thick brow.

"Watch it," he shouldered me out of the way. I gripped my dagger and entered the tavern.

The room was packed and stifling. The stench of sweat and unwashed bodies mixed with vomit made me gag. The bard's cheerful music grated on my nerves, and I had to resist the urge to incinerate him. Drunken patrons stumbled past, falling into me as they staggered.

"Hi, handsome," a voice purred. "In need of some company?" An arm wrapped around mine and I looked down at a heavily made-up woman.

I pulled my arm out of her grasp. "No."

"I can put a smile on your face."

"Off with you, hag." I shoved her away. She glared at me, giving a rude gesture, then disappeared into the crowd.

Scanning the room, my eyes lit on Abraham. There he sat, legs splayed in front, fingers laced behind his head, looking as if he hadn't a care in the world. I clenched my jaw so hard it hurt. Plowing through the crowd, I reached his table and shoved it into him. Ale spilled, darkening the front of his trousers.

"You son of a bitch. You left me there."

"Hello, Damiyun," he said calmly, black eyes lighting on me as he casually pushed the table back and stood, drying his trousers with a rag.

"I almost lost my fucking head."

"It appears you kept it." His lips twitched up. The bastard was amused.

I lunged across the table, grabbed him by the shirt and yanked him forward. Abraham easily jerked out of my grasp and sauntered around the table. He crossed his arms, eyes narrowed on me.

"Watch yourself."

"You fled like the fucking coward you are. My neck was on the line."

"And yet here you stand."

"That's not the point." I slammed a fist on the table. "You were blinded by your pointless revenge. You didn't even think about the consequences. You didn't even give a fuck."

"I served justice."

I laughed. "Justice for something that happened Grand Passages ago."

"She was my daughter."

"And this was my life."

"You, who always begs me to let you go? You're suddenly repentant because you almost lost your head?" He laughed. "How touching."

White-hot anger surged through me. I swung at him, fist cracking into his jaw. His head snapped to the side.

"Watch yourself, Damiyun," he growled, rubbing where I hit

I swung at him a second time. He grabbed my fist and twisted my arm hard behind my back and slammed me face down onto the table. "You know you will never beat me in a fight. Now sit down and stop making a fool of yourself," he snarled in my ear, then released me. I rubbed my arm with a glare and took the seat opposite him. He waved a serving wench over, and she placed two tankards of ale on the table.

"The Fallen One is getting stronger, Damiyun. He is sending forth beings that reside deep within the Abyss. They are coming forward to claim their place in our world," Abraham said as he sipped his drink. "We are running out of time."

"We would have been four Moon Cycles ahead if you didn't leave me with the Fae."

"And we would have been nearly there had you not fucked Felicity."

I winced at the truth in his words. "I take full responsibility for my actions. I can't change what happened. I can only hope we find her." I drained my ale and stood up. Abraham rose as well, and I followed him to a small room with two beds, a table with a washbasin and a cracked mirror. I lit the lamps and went to the table. Pouring water into the basin, I washed my face. I looked at my reflection, running my hand over the white hair on my jaw. It made me look ancient. Pulling out my dagger, I went to the task of shaving it off. When I finished, I stretched out on the bed and closed my eyes.

I hadn't been asleep long when a commotion outside the door roused me. I looked around the room, spotting Abraham standing in a corner, the shadows pulled around him making him invisible to all but me. I swiftly leaped from the bed to a corner opposite him and cloaked myself with my magic. The door swung open, and four Suppressors stood on the threshold.

"Are you sure this is their room?" a blond man with a crooked nose spoke.

"I can feel them." A short man peered around the room. "Look. Rayne's sword is here."

Shit.

I clenched my teeth and slowly brought my hand to my dagger, gripping the hilt.

"They're probably at a brothel. You know how Damiyun likes to fuck," the blond man said. "We'll wait for them to return." He shut the door, and the four settled into the room.

Fuck.

I glanced at Abraham, then released the cloak.

"What—?" The men jumped to their feet, and the sound of metal filled the silence as they drew swords. I called forth my magic, the heat of the fire spreading through my body like a warm embrace. I unleashed it, enveloping the men—and the room—in flames. I threw open the window and slipped out, jumping the few feet to the ground, Abraham following. We took off down the alley, skidding to a halt at the end.

"Shit. At least a dozen or more," I relayed to Abraham, noting the pockets of Suppressors milling about, hands on hilts. Abraham pulled his sword, and I drew my dagger and my magic. Nodding at Abraham, we stepped out of the alley and broke into a run. The sound of steel rang out, and footsteps pounded as Suppressors ran toward us. I sent out a wall of flame, burning men, their agonized screams piercing the night. Abraham slashed through Suppressors, the moonlight glinting off his blade made it look as though it were glowing.

We reached the stables with barely enough time to saddle up, and took off out of the village, the sound of thundering hooves following. I dug my heels into Xander's sides, urging him to go faster.

I would not be caught again. I would kill every last Suppressor before I let them take me.

We raced on, riding blindly through woods, horses leaping over logs and brambles. Something flew by my ear. Someone behind cried out, and I turned to see a Suppressor fall from his horse, followed by several others. The brush ahead rustled, and we slowed our mounts. I held on to my magic and the hilt of my dagger, watching three figures astride horses slip out of the shadows, each carrying a bow with quivers on their hip. They stood tall, and the points of ears peeked out beneath golden hair.

Elves.

I drew my dagger and Abraham drew his sword.

"Peace, traveler," the one in the middle said, shouldering his bow and raising his hands. "We mean you no harm."

I looked at the two who flanked him, who also raised their hands. I relaxed the grip on my dagger, though I still held my magic.

"How can, we, be sure? You're Elves."

The Elf cocked his head to the side. "This is true, though did we not kill the Suppressors pursuing you?"

"I suppose," I said, sheathing my weapon.

"Forgive my rudeness," he said, turning to Abraham. "I am Barlack Satow, King of the Wilde Elves. These are my brothers, Ingle and Flint." He nodded to the Elves to his right and left. "Am I right to assume more Suppressors will be coming?"

"That is a correct assumption," I said.

Barlack smiled. "I thought so. If you would follow us to Oaken Leaf Castle." He quirked an eyebrow. "Unless you wish to go back to those who own you?"

I glared at him. "No one owns me."

Barlack laughed. "Whatever you say," he said, turning his horse. I urged Xander behind, ignoring Abraham's intense stare.

"How did you know what they were saying?"

I frowned. "What do you mean?"

"They were speaking Elvish. You responded in kind."

I laughed. "Perhaps your ale has gone to your head."

"I know what I heard."

Barlack glanced over his shoulder, a smile on his face, but said nothing. We rode for a while, until Barlack finally pulled his horse to a halt.

"Welcome to Va'l'Victorus. You will find a tavern with spirits and beds for sleep," he said, pulling his horse back around. "Tomorrow we will speak, Damiyun."

"What—?"

Barlack laughed as he heeled his mount in the opposite direction, Flint and Ingle following behind. We walked our horses in the direction of town, and I tried hard to ignore Abraham's penetrating gaze.

"He has me confused with another."

Abraham glanced at me. "Another human who knows Elvish?"

I didn't say anything. How could I when I didn't understand it myself?

We entered the village, walking through the streets, passing the occasional whore and staggering drunk, and pulled up to an inn and tavern with a sign dangling from a chain. The Naked Nymph, it read. Tethering our horses, we went inside and shouldered our way through the crowd, taking a seat at the only vacant table. The place teemed with Wilde Elves. Eyes and heads turned in our direction as we walked through, and voices whispered, "*Damiyun*."

I clenched my teeth. "Let's get a fucking room."

"We have one waiting," a pretty Elf who came out of nowhere said. She bowed low then turned and led us to a room. "Sleep well, Damiyun."

I followed Abraham into our room to bed down for the night.

That night, for the very first time since I was a small child, I dreamed.

FORTY-FOUR

I SLOWLY CAME AWAKE, the last vestiges of my dream disappearing like smoke in the wind. I tried to grasp the fringes, but it dissipated. I stared up at the blue brocade canopy above the bed. One thing I knew, that I felt deep down inside, was the dream was about my mother.

"We are leaving." Abraham's voice was startling in the silence. I glanced over at him. He strapped his sword about his waist.

I sat up. "No."

Abraham paused as I slowly stumbled out of bed. "There is something strange, yet familiar, here. I know this place even though I have never been here."

I stood at the window and gazed down at the town slowly awakening below. A light snow had fallen overnight, dusting the ground with white. Flakes blew and swirled in the light wind. "You said I spoke Elvish, yet I don't know how that could be possible."

"We are leaving," he growled, hand reaching for the door.

"I need to know how I knew what they were saying. What if... what if my mother was one of them?"

"And how will that serve you?" Abraham whirled around. "You still have a task to complete. The longer Lillyanna remains missing, the worse the situation becomes. Finding her is far more important than knowing who you are."

I glared at him. "And your revenge on Arias? Your murder cost us precious time."

"This is foolish."

"Two days."

Abraham grumbled as he unstrapped his sword and tossed it on his bed.

There wasn't any way to rightly explain to him my sudden need. I had always wanted to know who my mother was. Who I was. My father never spoke of her, never uttered her name. I only knew she died days after I was born. Being here had turned my want into an aching desire for knowledge.

"My mother was a whore." I jumped at the sound of Abraham's voice. "Her father lost a gambling bet, and so he sold her to a brothel to pay it. She was only twelve." He came and stood beside me, eyes on the snow falling outside the window. I said nothing, allowing him to gather his thoughts and tell his story, though why he chose to share this now, I couldn't say. Abraham was a private person, and though we had been companions for a long time, I couldn't say I knew everything about him.

"I didn't know my father. My mother never spoke of him. When I asked, her answer was vague or nothing at all. The only thing I knew about him was he was a... client of hers."

"Why are you telling me this?"

"Do you think knowing who he was would have changed anything? Will knowing if these are your mother's people change your future? Your past?"

I looked back out the window, the snow fell harder, rapidly whitening the landscape. "No, but you don't bear the guilt of your birth. You didn't bear it with every strike of the whip. Every sleepless night waiting for your brother to come and hurt you. I need to know who she was. Maybe it will help me... forgive myself."

Even if no one else will.

A knock on the door ended any further conversation, and I crossed the room to answer.

It was Barlack in the doorway. "Good morning. Did you sleep well?"

"Yes, thank you."

"I hope you weren't thinking of leaving. It appears a bad storm is due to hit. Travel will be nearly impossible. If you don't mind, I ask that you join me for a moment. We have much to discuss, yes?"

I nodded and followed him out of the room. We walked down to the empty tavern and settled into a table in the corner. I looked around the room. The tavern was far richer than any I had been in. A large marble fireplace sat along the wall to the right. The floor was made of rich walnut with a cherry inlay in a crisscrossed pattern. In the center was a black stag with golden antlers and red eyes. Sturdy tables and chairs with intricately carved flowers and vines were scattered around the room. An ornate bar made of marble and cherry graced one wall, high-backed chairs with plush cushions beckoned to be sat in.

I turned my attention to Barlack. "What do you wish to discuss? I find it difficult to believe you have anything of importance to talk over with a stranger."

He looked at me curiously. "Do you think yourself one? A stranger?"

"I have never been to your lands before this."

"Yet you speak our language."

"Do I?"

Barlack laughed. "We have been conversing in Elvish."

I rubbed my temple, a dull ache forming in my head. I wanted to reject his words, call them out for the lies they were, and yet I couldn't dismiss the feeling.

The feeling of home.

The door to the tavern flew open and Flint rushed in, eyes going to Barlack who shot to his feet.

"Twenty Suppressors are heading in our direction."

"Gather your men. Get them ready to strike. Make it clear to the Suppressors they are breaking the treaty if they enter, and we will show no mercy."

"They are here because of me," I said. "I will not allow bloodshed. I will surrender."

"You will do no such thing. Go to your room," Barlack barked over his shoulder as he hurried after Flint. Clenching my jaw, I strode after the two men.

"Get back inside." Barlack said, clearly used to being obeyed.

"Unless I am a prisoner, you cannot stop me. I will have none of your people's blood spilled for me."

Flint drew his sword, and two others readied their bows. I drew on my magic. "I do not wish to harm you. Let me go in peace," I said, pulling more of the fire and wrapping it around myself, feeling the flames swirl about my fists.

"If that is how it must be," Barlack said, jerking his head. I heard a sound behind, felt something sharp hit my shoulder. The world spun, a blanket of white rushed toward me, and I tumbled into darkness before I hit the ground.

"WHERE ARE WE?" I asked when my eyes opened, and Abraham came into view. Sitting up, I swallowed against the rising nausea. Wind howled violently outside, and a draft funneled down the chimney, fanning the flames that danced. Beyond the window was an impenetrable wall of white.

"We were given a room in the palace," his gruff voice said. "I don't suggest trying to leave. They have placed guards outside the door. I tried to stop them from taking your dagger and putting the Sigaa'Lean on you, but seeing as you were ready to incinerate them, they felt it a necessity."

Tossing the covers off, I swung my legs over the side of the bed, steeling myself against the dizziness. I slowly staggered to my feet, legs shaking under my weight. "What of the Suppressors?"

"I don't know. They have not told me anything."

The sound of the door handle rattling drew my attention. The door opened and the silhouette of Barlack filled the void.

"I apologize for the treatment, but you left me no choice." He said.

"So, we are prisoners," I said, pointing to the bracelet.

"Of course not. That was done as a precaution. You may leave when you wish, though I do not suggest leaving in this storm," he said. "Come. It is time to learn about who you are."

Glancing at Abraham, I crossed the room to the door. Anticipation and fear filled me as Barlack led me through the empty halls. The palace was grandly furnished, though not ostentatious, with marble floors the color of blood, walnut and cherry wood panels on the walls. Stained-glass windows depicting scenes of nature, Elves and a crest: a black stag with antlers made of gold and eyes of rubies. Elves filled the hallways, nodding at Barlack and me. Smiles curled some lips as we walked by. Eyes followed, and I heard whispers behind hands.

Perhaps I should have let it lie. Should have left when Abraham wanted to, but the want to know who my mother was—who I was—burned within. Barlack led me to a library with walls packed with books, a cozy fire offering warmth in the room. Taking a seat, I accepted a glass of wine and settled in to listen as he spoke.

The tale was not one I expected.

Nor one I wanted.

FORTY-FIVE
ABRAHAM

THE DOOR CLOSED BEHIND Damiyun, and I pursed my lips. Though a storm raged outside, it was evident he had no intentions of talking about Lillyanna, or how to find her. Perhaps I should have taken them, but that would have been too easy. I admit a part of me wanted to protect the girl. Wanted to figure out a way to make it not have to be, though I knew there was nothing I could do to stop it. I felt pity for the girl, she deserved better in life, but to have a chance at freeing Jaylynn, of freeing myself... she had to die. There was nothing I wanted more than to keep Themesis secured in his tomb.

Pulling the shadows around me, I decided to continue the search on my own, as I had for several Moon Cycles. I drifted to various towns and taverns, where I listened to several conversations, seeing if perhaps there was mention of her. Or if I would see her. I inquired to patrons and the tavern keeper to no avail.

After spending hours searching and coming up empty, my last stop was Duenney, the area closest to the Shadow Elf Lands. An area where I knew those Elves tended to frequent.

Releasing the darkness, I watched the demons retreat to the shadows, and looked up at the sign that boasted the establishment to be The Golden Griffin. Grasping the handles, I pulled the doors open, warmth hitting me like a wall, the loud chatter and music unbearably loud. The place was packed, and I made my way to the only available table in a secluded back corner of the establishment. Removing my cloak, I took a seat and flagged the serving wench. I ordered a tankard of ale and some real food. The meals the Elves served, while flavorful, were a bit too rich and fancy for my taste. I much preferred the simplicity of a stew or fish, simply cured with salt. I looked up as the tankard was placed in front of me, my eyes appraising the pretty, young woman who served me. She gave me a smile and a wink before turning away, and I made a mental note to tip her proper later this evening.

Sipping my ale, I looked about the tavern. It was filled with Elves and humans alike. The sound of the bard playing in the corner rose above the din of voices and laughter. My eyes took in two male Elves seated at the table to my right. They were finely dressed, bright colors denoting them as holding high positions among the Shadow Elves. They sat casually in their chairs, elbows on the table and mugs of ale before them. Their conversation drifted to my ears.

"Come on, Lazaro. Let's join the others," one Elf said to the other. His face held a smile, and his eyes were bright with drink.

"Why can't we just sit here alone?" Lazaro reached over and grasped the other's hand. "I hardly ever see you, Phabian, let alone spend time with you." Lazaro's voice betrayed a tinge of whining. The Elf named Phabian winced and pulled his hand from Lazaro's grasp.

"I can't exactly tell the king no when he requests my presence," Phabian rolled his eyes. "It's been far too long since I've been out for some fun."

Lazaro's face darkened as he took a healthy drink. "You mean the King's Whore takes up your time."

"I'd watch my tongue if I were you. If the king heard you call her that—"

"It's what she is. You know, as well as I do, she's warming his bed. That bitch should have been executed."

I lowered my tankard at the words and trained my attention on them.

"But she wasn't," Phabian inclined his head. "The king is fond of her, as am I. It would serve you best to watch your words, lest it's your head on a spike."

Could the woman they spoke of be Lillyanna? My mind reeled at the thought. If it was, why would they have let her live? For what purpose?

"I don't believe the tale she has spun. She does nothing but take up space within the palace," Lazaro said.

Phabian said nothing as he finished his drink. "She makes the king happy."

Lazaro snorted. "I didn't know our king wasn't."

Phabian looked at him. His eyes were glassy from the drink. "You know he hasn't been happy for a long time. If she fills a void in his life, then what's the harm?"

"Nothing good can come of her being here." Lazaro glowered into his mug. "And don't you find it curious that he was attacked on his Name Day hunt? Don't you wonder if she had something to do with it?" He shook his head. "Her head should have been taken when he was healing."

"How dare you even speak such words, Laz." Phabian rose to his feet. He swayed a bit and gripped the table. "If anything happens to her on your watch..."

"Do you think me a fool, Phabian? The king would have my head if she were harmed," he said, eyes on Phabian. "Where are you going?"

"I should be heading back."

Lazaro rose as well. "I thought you wanted to join the others?"

Phabian glanced in the direction of the merriment. The crowd was getting rowdy. Trays of tankards were being passed around, and I smelled the distinct scent of Sal'va smoke. Made of the dried leaves of a plant with the same name, it caused calmness, heightened arousal, and intensified sexual pleasure.

"Not if you don't want to. Besides, it's getting late. I have had far too much to drink, and I know what happens when I have Sal'va," he said. "Plus, my Anya is fertile. Duty calls."

Lazaro smiled. "Oh, I do know what happens when you smoke that," he said. He took a step closer and linked his arms around Phabian's neck. "I'll go get some from Krall and you and I can get a room. It's been so long since we've been together."

Phabian's face softened, and he brushed his knuckles on Lazaro's cheek. "I know, Laz," He leaned forward and pressed his lips to Lazaro's. He whispered something that elicited a soft laugh from the other man, then pulled away and left the tavern. I sighed. The conversation was over. I had hoped to glean more information surrounding who this mystery woman was. I shook my head at the thoughts—the questions—which churned within. A mysterious woman was found on the Shadow Elf Lands, and she wasn't executed, which I thought highly suspicious.

It was too much of a coincidence. I looked about the tavern, my eyes going to the voluptuous wench who had made sure my tankard never ran dry. Disappointment fell over me at knowing I wouldn't get the chance to thank her properly.

Tossing a handful of coin onto the table, I rose and pushed my way out of the tavern. I surrounded myself in shadow and returned to Va'l'Victorus.

Though I would have preferred to visit the Shadow Elf Lands to investigate, I didn't dare, knowing what my fate would be. There was the possibility Damiyun wouldn't be turned away. He was half Elf and knew their language. And though there was a chance we would be locked in a cell, I hoped we would keep our heads long enough to find out who this woman was, and if it was Lillyanna.

I would tell Damiyun of my findings upon the morrow, and we would journey to Il'Ekhester.

FORTY-SIX
LILLYANNA

Every time I went to leave, Krall or someone else stopped me.

For four days I was sequestered.

For four days I didn't know of the fate of Allendaire, or myself.

The sinking feeling, the sickening thought, I was truly a prisoner, that I would be executed some time, never left me. I couldn't eat. Nightmares of an ax kept me from sleep.

On the fifth day, I saw Phabian leading troops back through the gate. That evening, there was a knock on my door.

"Allendaire." Relief washed over me at the sight of him. I threw my arms around him, not caring that Krall was there. He clutched me tight.

"Lillyanna," he breathed, lips brushing my ear.

I pulled away, eyes assessing him, searching for missing or maimed parts. Aside from a wound on his face, he looked perfect. He shut the door and pulled me close, lips finding mine.

"I was worried about you," I said breathlessly when he pulled away. "No one would tell me anything."

"It will take more than a few stabs and slices to kill me." His eyes swept over me, taking in the dress I wore, and he frowned. "This isn't how I told you to greet me upon my return."

I laughed. "I am just pleased you returned." And it was for my own selfish reasons. This was the second time I had managed to keep my head. I wasn't sure the gods would grant me a third. He crossed the room to a chair and sat down, holding his arms out to me. I curled up on his lap, warm and secure in his embrace. The flames in the fireplace danced, casting yellow and orange hues on his face. The wind howled outside, rattling the glass panes as a snowstorm raged.

"Tell me what happened."

"It was an ambush by an unknown group."

I pulled back and looked at him. "Will you find out who they are?"

"Phabian sent a group out to search the area." He loosened his arms, and I slid off his lap. "I wish to rest." He stood and tugged me in the direction of the bed.

Slipping out of my clothes, I curled up beside him, my head on his chest, the constant thrumming of his heart soothing, his body and blankets warm.

We lay in each other's embrace, the silence enveloping us. His presence soothed me. A reminder he lived.

And so did I.

I WAS DREAMING ABOUT Damiyun.

About being with him.

The memory of his presence—his spicy scent, the way he felt, the warmth of his body and wisps of his breath on my skin—was strong. I moved with him, gripping him tight.

"You're mine, Lil. You always were," he whispered, looking down at me as we moved.

I let myself go, waves of pleasure washing over as he slowly claimed me.

I woke with a sigh, holding on to the dream. To the feeling of being with Damiyun again.

"You love him."

I turned and looked at Allendaire. Shock and shame washed over me. I must have spoken his name in my sleep.

"I can let you be with him."

"No," was all I said, though to what, I couldn't be sure.

"Do you wish to go back? I will let you." His eyes searched mine.

"No, Allendaire. I wish to stay here with you." I didn't care about whatever it was I was supposed to do. Especially since neither Abraham nor Damiyun told me. What would be wrong with staying here? So, I had to warm the king's bed. If it meant keeping my head, it was what I would do.

"Do you?"

I pulled him close. "Yes."

He pulled away again and slipped out of bed, crossing the room to gaze out into the night. The wind howled outside. The hiss of snow hitting the window filled the silence, a slight breeze making the lamp on the table dance. I got up and slipped my arms around him. He stiffened at my touch.

"He betrayed me. That's why I ran. Perhaps what I felt for him was love, I don't know."

He turned around and looked at me. "I can have Phabian find him."

"No."

"Why? He must be worried about you."

"That doesn't matter. I want to stay here with you."

No, no, no. Why would you say such a thing? Go back. Go back to Damiyun. He's offering to let you leave. To be free. To go back to—to what? I stopped the voice from going further. To a long journey to a place where I was somehow supposed to defeat the Fallen One? Back to a man who I knew, I felt, deep down inside, I would never see again after my task was complete?

I was safe here. Content.

"I am pleased you wish to stay with me. If you want to leave at any time, say the word. I will send Phabian to find your Damiyun and bring you to him."

I felt the truth in his words. He was willing to let me go. And despite the voice in my head urging me to say yes, to let myself be free—the voice that spoke of danger forming on the horizon—I rejected his offer.

"No more talk. I have a hunger that needs to be satisfied." he said, tugging me toward the bed. I obediently followed. If this was the game, I needed to play to keep my head, then so be it.

He braced his hands on either side of me. Dipping his head, he caught my mouth with his. His musky scent filled my nose, salty sweet with a hint of honey, the smell arousing me. I slid my hand between us and gently stroked him. He groaned, teeth biting my neck, breath warm on my skin. He slipped a finger inside me, teasing me. I ground against him as he pleased me, lips trailing kisses down my body, tongue licking skin, mouth sucking nipples. My arousal peaked, and I climaxed quickly. I grabbed his head and kissed him hard.

"Take me now, Allendaire. Please. I need you. Don't make me beg. Not tonight."

He slipped inside with a growl, going deeper, and deeper, filling me. I locked my legs around him, drawing him deeper still and meeting his furious thrusts. He took me hard and fast, clutching me to him, body shuddering as he spent himself. His lips grazed my temple before he flopped onto his back. I propped myself up and looked at him, my eyes sweeping over his taut, muscled body.

"Where is your wound?" I was perplexed at the absence of a single mark from the attack.

"My magic healed me, though I did need a bit of extra help," he said. He reached up and tucked a lock of hair behind my ear. "Like I said, it would take a lot more than a stab and a few slashes to kill me."

"No one would tell me what was going on. I didn't know if you were dead. I couldn't leave my room, and for the first time—in all the time I have been here—I felt like a prisoner."

"I'm sorry. Phabian was only looking out for your safety."

Was he? While it was true, I thought him a friend, I doubted he would put his neck on the line to save mine. Even if he did, I knew the queen would issue the order to take my head as soon as she could. She might even do it herself. Phabian had subtly hinted at something going on between Allendaire and me. While he wasn't invading my mind, he knew. Whether it was from the king himself, I couldn't say. Now Krall knew.

And undoubtedly, so would the queen.

"Speak, Lillyanna," Allendaire said, finger caressing my cheek.

"What would be my fate should something happen to you?"

His silence spoke volumes. Though I didn't know what my actual task at Kraagswell Mountain was, something told me it wouldn't end well, and I might not come back. I grew cold, recoiling from the thought. As long as Allendaire lived, I was safe. I had a comfortable home. And I knew not to take that for granted after all my Grand Passages, scrounging on my own just to stay alive.

And that voice inside my head admonished my choice. *You're being foolish. Find out how to escape this place. The Elves, the king. Nothing good can come from you staying here. You may keep your head, but your fate will be far worse than death.*

I pushed the thought aside and kissed Allendaire who smiled and pushed me on my back.

Again, and again, and again he took me until I had to beg him to stop.

And as his arms slipped around me, as I settled beside him and closed my eyes, I heard him whisper words.

Words that drifted on the fingers of sleep.

Words I wasn't quite sure I heard.

Words that sealed my fate.

"You will bear my heir."

FORTY-SEVEN
DAMIYUN

"No." I rejected what he told me. Barlack sat in his chair, blue eyes dancing with amusement.

"You lie. Why do I not have the distinct markings of an Elf? Why are my ears not pointed?"

"They were clipped at birth."

"For what purpose?" I resisted the urge to touch them.

"To protect who you are. Ears are clipped for many reasons. For example, if a whore bore an Elf, the ears would be clipped so as not to associate our race with such filth."

Reaching forward, I picked up the glass on the table, looking around the room as I sipped the dry wine. Barlack had brought me to the library. It was a cozy room. Dark rugs dotted the marble floor. Shelves made of deep cherry crammed with books lined three walls. Comfortable chairs sat around low tables. Low windows broke up the shelving on one side. The wind howled. Snow and ice pinged against the glass, that shook with another cold gust of air. Barlack and I sat in front of a fire that blazed in the stone and black marble fireplace. The room was warm and the soft leather chair comfortable. The wing back embraced me, making me feel secure.

"Your mother had to protect you," Barlack said, bringing me back.

I sighed. "Why? Is my brother, Arden, Elf born too?"

"He does not share the same blood. Kallen found him wandering in the woods. He was eight. Dehydrated and confused. He took the boy home, and he and Rahina raised him as their own."

I watched Barlack rise and cross the room to a shelf. Reaching up, he pulled out a thick book and placed it on my lap. It was heavy and richly made. Bound in red velvet, a stag made of obsidian with antlers of pure gold and eyes of ruby graced the front.

"What is this?" I looked at Barlack who sat back down.

"It's the Wilde Elf Tome of the Kings. Every king since Karrinian has written their stories within the pages of a book. This is the story of the Wilde Elves."

I ran my hand over the cover, fingers caressing the crest on the front.

"Some of the answers you seek are within those pages."

I glanced up at Barlack, then opened the book. A picture of Barlack stared at me from the first page. He was dressed in finery, a black coat with a golden pattern down the arms that resembled antlers over a crisp white shirt. A crown of vines sat atop his head, golden antlers curling up from the sides. His white hair flowed about his shoulders, and his right hand clasped a scepter with a large diamond on top. Blue eyes peered at whoever painted the picture. Cold. Calculating. I shivered at the look. *King Barlack Satow, First King of the Wilde Elves,* was printed in flowing script at the base of the picture.

I turned the page, running my hand down the thick paper, feeling the words written in gold. Barlack refilled our glasses and sat back in his chair. Adjusting my position, I sank deeper into the cushions and began to read.

IT TOOK US FOUR Moon Cycles, but we finally found a place to call home. Those of us who were able to escape. Those of us who lived. We called our lands Va'l'Victorus for valor and victorious, something I felt we were when it came to this fight.

I was not the only one who did not believe Allendaire's claim that his sister Rahina poisoned King Terrin. Though it was unheard of for a woman to be chosen as heir, she was. I knew she would be as strong leader, that our king had made the right choice. And she quietly agreed with those of us who procreated outside our race in secret. She saw what was happening. She attended the Death Ceremonies of the women who took their lives and that of their daughters. And perhaps Allendaire did as well, and that was why he sought to silence her. Why he poisoned his father and blamed Rahina.

It was mass chaos after. Rahina was thrown into a cell and Allendaire proclaimed himself king. He called out all of those who went outside our race. He rounded up their secret families and brought them to the courtyard and executed them in front of all. The blood of innocent men, women, and children soaked the ground in red.

It was wrong. All of it. I was fortunate to have been able to get my own family away. I secured them in a secret place. A place I would never be able to visit and though it pained me, knowing they were safe was all that mattered.

We banded together. Those who lost their families and who would never see them again, and we fought back. Many lives were lost on each side and finally Allendaire called an end to the massacre, and we were cast out. Banished from our homes, but we rose above and became one. We cast off the Trounde name, each Elf choosing their own surnames in a Cleansing Ceremony.

We called ourselves Wilde Elves, for we were free. We were let loose into the wild and we embraced it. And we flourished and survived. We lived in peace and harmony and the past was forgotten, our future rewritten.

I had kept spies in the castle to keep an eye on Allendaire and what was happening. Spies who sent reports back to me and when one claimed that Rahina had escaped, that those loyal to her helped her get out, I had to see for myself if it was true. And though it took me a while, I finally found her living a quiet life on the outskirts of a village. She had a family, and her stomach was swollen.

And when a Moon Cycle had passed, I learned Rahina had given birth and though she died later, the son she bore survived. The news elated me.

I knew he was the one who was the heir.

Damiyun would unite us all.

C LOSING THE BOOK, I rubbed my eyes then looked at Barlack. I couldn't rightly say that I believed the words, but my name was written upon the page. I knew their language.

"I never thought my mother could have been a Wilder. How, when my father hated me for what I am? Did he know?"

Barlack nodded. "She never hid that she was an Elf from him. Only that she was royalty. She had to protect herself. Protect you. If any Shadow Elf had discovered she lived and had a child, you both would have been terminated."

Grasping the glass of wine, I took a long drink. My head spun from what I read. I glanced out the window. Though the snow still fell, the sky was becoming brighter, a sign that the storm was almost over.

Good. I wanted to be away from this place. Away from Barlack. I distrusted him. I knew there was an ulterior motive to us being here and though I wondered how he truly found me, I knew his words would be laced with half-truths and mystery. Finishing my drink, I rose from the chair, holding the book out to Barlack.

"Thank you for your entertaining tale. I regret that we will be leaving on the morrow. I expect the Sigaa'Lean to be removed, and my weapons returned this eve," I said.

Barlack took the book with a sigh. "Damiyun—"

"This eve, Barlack," I said, holding up my wrist. He nodded and I crossed the room and exited. I walked through the halls, ignoring those who greeted me or bowed their head in respect, and made my way back to the room.

"What news, Damiyun? What did Barlack want?" Abraham reclined in a chair in front of the fire.

"To tell me I am the heir to the Elvish throne." I sat down next to him.

He raised an eyebrow. "You don't believe it." He pushed a bottle of Serpent's Venom across the table. I snatched it and took a long pull, the fiery warmth spreading through me.

"I don't know. He knew my father's name. He said my mother was the true heir of the Shadow Elves, and her brother took the throne by nefarious means." I took another long pull and slid the bottle back across the table. "He said my ears were clipped to protect me." I absently rubbed an ear. "Forget this nonsense, though. We leave on the morrow."

"Your weapons—"

"Will be brought this eve and the Sigaa'Lean will be removed."

"You believe his words?"

I looked at Abraham, his face and the room swirling from the alcohol I had consumed. "He will do as I ask." I closed my eyes and rested my head against the back of the chair. "After all, he believes I am a prince."

FORTY-EIGHT

S LEEP DID NOT COME. The words I read swirled behind my closed eyes. I saw my name over and over again written into the Wilde Elf history. Rubbing my eyes, I slipped out of bed and padded over to the window. Dawn was breaking, the sky was bright, and no snow fell.

That was good.

"I told you Barlack would not heed your request," Abraham's voice grumbled from across the room. Though I still wore the Sigaa'Lean and lacked weapons, I knew he would not keep us here. There was no reason to. There was no more that he could tell me.

The creaking of hinges pulled me from my thoughts, and I turned to see Barlack standing in the doorway.

"Your weapons," he said softly, holding out my daggers. I crossed the room and slipped them into my waistband. Barlack grabbed my right arm, fingers resting on the Sigaa'Lean. He muttered a few words. The bracelet fell open, and I felt the rush of my magic filling me. The warmth of the flame spread through my body.

"This belongs to you as well," he said, holding out a sword. "It belonged to Karrinian. And then Terrin. It is high time the next heir wielded it."

I gripped the hilt adorned with rubies, sapphires, and diamonds. A thrumming of power pulsed and beat like a heart. I pulled it from the scabbard and gazed upon the snow-white blade forged out of bone.

"That's the Shadow Elf Crest," Barlack said, fingers tracing the serpent wrapped around a rose etched into the blade's fuller. "It's forged from the bone of a Pyragaty. The sword absorbs the Life Force of the one you kill. In the case of a Wielder, it absorbs their magic."

Interesting.

"Thank you, Barlack," I said, sheathing the magnificent blade.

"Are you sure you will not stay? There is much for you to learn. Your Elven magic should have been unlocked when you entered our lands."

Elven magic? I shook my head. Of course, I would have that, being as my mother was a Shadow Elf. And though this revelation of this new power intrigued me, we had stayed here long enough. I glanced at Abraham. He crossed his arms, his black eyes boring through me.

"We must leave. It is imperative that we find our missing companion."

Barlack pursed his lips. "Very well then. Complete your task, then I ask that you come back here. There is much you must learn about yourself and your magic. Much you must know before you sit upon the throne."

I laughed as I strapped the sword to my back and slid daggers into my belt and boot. "I have no intentions of sitting on any throne."

Barlack folded his arms. "It is your birthright."

I raised an eyebrow. "Is it? My mother was thought to have died in the war. She did die birthing me. I have no claim. I was not chosen."

"I am choosing you. You are a half-breed. That makes you a Wilde Elf. As the king, I am appointing you as heir."

"I don't want it."

"Damiyun—"

"I don't want it." I clenched my fists. Flames came to life in the fireplace and candles. Energy cracked around me. I looked down, gasping at the tendrils of light that cracked around my fingertips.

"That is your mother's magic. You need to learn how to harness and control it."

"Goodbye, Barlack," I said, nodding to Abraham.

"When you are done with your task, come back here."

"No." I brushed past him, following Abraham out.

Barlack grabbed my arm. "You will come back, Damiyun. On this, you cannot say no. On this, you must promise," he said.

I felt a surge of power flow through me. "I promise." The words flew out of my mouth before I could think, and I felt the grip of magic inside me. It felt like another presence within, binding me to my promise.

Fuck it all. First, I am bound to Themesis by my own deeds and death, bound to Abraham, bound to the Fae and now the Wilde Elves? Will no one let me be?

"See you soon," Barlack snickered as Abraham and I exited the room. We made our way to the stables, saddled the horses and heeled them along.

The sun was rising higher, the reflection off the virgin snow blinding. The cold began to seep in, and I pulled my magic close, letting the warmth envelop me. We rode out of Va'l'Victorous, the crunch of snow beneath hooves the only sound.

"What was that about?"

Abraham's voice startled me. "A fucking binding promise," I spat. "I have to come back when my task is finished."

Abraham shook his head with a chuckle. "The holes you dig keep getting deeper," he said.

Ignoring his comment, I pulled Xander to a halt.

"What say you, Abraham? Where do we go?" I looked down the empty road.

"When you were off playing with Barlack, I took it upon myself to continue the search for Lillyanna. I went to Duenney since it is closer to the Shadow Elf Lands, and overheard a conversation between two Elves," Abraham said, eyes on me. "There is a woman, a human, who was found on their lands."

"Do you think it's Lillyanna?" The thought was mind-blowing.

"I don't know. It is possible. It is too much of a coincidence that this woman arrived there, and Lillyanna went missing."

"But if it's her... Why was she not executed?"

Abraham shook his head. "I don't know. One of them was not happy about her presence. We will ride to their lands and see. If she is there, we will bring her back."

I shook my head. "How, Abraham? How are we going to bring her back when we can't enter?"

Abraham raised an eyebrow. "Are you not half Shadow Elf? A prince at that?"

I clenched my teeth and gripped the reins. Xander, feeling my agitation, snorted, and pawed at the ground. I patted his neck and clicked my tongue to sooth him.

Abraham grunted, and heeled Violet ahead, and I followed. As the sun slipped below the horizon, we came upon a village.

"We will rest here for the night," he said.

We made our way down the narrow, muddy road. A sign announced the town as Erador, where we stopped at The Whispering Pines Inn. Dismounting, we handed the horses to the stable hand and entered the establishment. It was crowded and rowdy. A small fight broke out in a corner and the two men were unceremoniously tossed out the door. The stench of sweat, unwashed bodies and dung made me gag. We pushed our way through, finding a table in the back, and sat down. I sipped the ale a serving wench placed before of me, listening to the bard strum a lonely song from *"The Story of Jayne."*

"... but her beauty was more
Than I ever bared,
And she is gone.
The fault is mine,
A burden I'll bear
'Till the end of time.
And I loved her
Though she didn't know,
And I loved her,

And I hurt her so…"

I shook my head of the words. Words that cut me to the core. I glanced around the tavern, noting the streamers of gold, silver and green that hung from the ceiling. Sprigs of evergreen hung above the door, and tables with offerings of food and drink sat in the corners.

Godsday neared.

With everything going on, I had forgotten about this holy day, a day I hadn't celebrated since I was with Zenith.

I had always thrown an elaborate party for it.

For her.

Thinking back now, I realized how blatant her infidelity was. How she would make her way through the crowd, touching and flirting with various men, and often disappearing for lengths of time.

"Damiyun," a voice called, bringing me back. Raising my head, I found myself looking into a pair of ice-blue eyes.

"Arden," I said, kicking out a chair to him. "Sit. Have a drink. I don't feel violence is necessary right now, do you?"

I watched my brother lower himself into the chair.

"How did you find me again?" I asked, signaling the bar wench to bring two bottles of Faery's Blood.

"It was the Luck of the Fallen One." He smiled. "Pure happenstance the first time. When we found the men hit with the Elven arrows, we knew where you were. The storm may have been a minor inconvenience, but we knew you weren't going anywhere anytime soon, so we waited at the inn, sending scouts to make sure you hadn't left. As I said, it was the Luck of the Fallen One that brought you there, right into our lap."

"And then you sent a raiding party onto their lands. You do know that could have broken the treaty."

Arden shrugged. "The treaty is ancient. It's about time we pulled some of them into our ranks."

"They provide the Sigaa'Lean. I'm sure Vel wouldn't be too pleased to lose the bracelet." I took a long pull on the bottle, then slid it across the table to Arden, who took a drink.

"I couldn't care less what Vel thinks," he spat. "He's getting on in age. He should step down."

Of course, he should, so you can take his place. "You would enslave our mother's people?"

He slammed the bottle down, eyes narrowing. "How dare you bring her up? What do you think you know of her? If it weren't for you, she'd still be alive."

I reached across the table and took the bottle back. "I know she was an Elf."

"You know nothing about her. She was sweet and kind. Everyone loved her. Father doted on her. She always made time for me no matter what." He paused, a soft smile forming. "At night, she would crawl into bed with me and hold me in her arms as she told me bedtime stories. Tales about unicorns and griffins. Phoenixes and giants. Fantastic stories woven with magic, she would send images to dance around my room, and when the story was through, she always sent me off to sleep with a lullaby. I can still hear her sweet voice every night." His eyes closed, and he hummed a soft tune, the haunting music causing me to shiver.

"She was the most beautiful woman I had ever seen. Her skin was so soft and smooth. Long, flowing hair the color of snow and eyes that matched the sky." His tone softened. Disgust rolled over me as I listened to him. I took a long pull from the bottle, then sent it back to Arden.

"Why are you telling me this?"

His blue eyes turned cold. "Because you need to know what you did. What you took from me." His hands clenched around the bottle. Taking another pull, he slammed it down onto the table. "She was absolutely perfect in every way. I can still remember how she smelled. A sweet scent of lilies and roses. She knew how much I loved both, so she used her magic to keep them blooming through the dead of winter."

"She always used her magic to make me happy. She would make lights dance in the night sky. She could make flowers bloom out of nothing. She would do anything to make me smile. I used to love to curl up on her lap and feel her warmth. Breathe in her sweetness." His voice caught and tears glistened in his eyes. "There was no place I would rather be than in her arms, cradled against her breast." His tone was quiet, and his face held a look of longing, and I realized Arden's love for her was not one of a son.

No.

It was one of a man.

"She had another child when I was ten. She was born three Grand Passages before you. After that, Mother had no time for me. She was always with Aznai. After she came, the stories stopped. The roses died." He clenched his fists. "It was such a tragic accident." He clicked his tongue and shook his head. "Aznai was a curious child. Always wandering away. It's a pity she didn't know how to swim." He flashed a smile, and I knew what he had done. The smile slid from his face and his eyes turned angry. "Then you came along, and you took her from me."

"And you would enslave her people. That doesn't sound like a son who loved his mother," I said. He glared at me as he reached across the table and snatched the bottle back. "Why didn't you kill me, too?"

"Because torture is far more fun." His lips curled up into a smile.

"What do you want, Arden?" I sighed.

"Where is she?"

"Fuck if I know."

"What is that supposed to mean?"

I leaned forward, eyes on his. "It means I don't know where Lillyanna is."

"You were her Keeper."

I laughed. "Yes. And apparently a shit one."

Arden slammed his fist on the table, and the two Suppressors who entered with him clenched the hilts of their swords. "Don't fuck with me, Brother. Where is she?"

"I don't know. She left me." I tossed back my drink, waved the serving wench over and ordered another bottle of Faery's Blood. "What does Vel want with her?" I took another swig and sent the bottle across the table to Arden.

"Your bitch will free Themesis."

"What?" I nearly choked.

Laughter echoed in my head. *Fool. Bring her to me and set me free.* I clenched my fists and shook my head.

"Are you alright, Brother?" Arden asked as I grabbed the bottle and took a healthy pull.

"I'm fine." I slammed the bottle down. "What makes you think that?"

"Brother," he said, leaning forward, elbows on the table. "I already told you. That's why she was born. Whatever you were told was a lie. She will be Blood-Bound to him. Their union will secure his place above man. Nations will crumble and all will serve him."

"Including you."

"I will kneel before him, and he will grant me a place by his side for giving him what he desires."

I laughed. "You are a fool. You will serve him like everyone else. Her blood will secure his binds."

I drained my drink and pushed away from the table. "Let's go."

Arden smiled. "I am feeling generous since Godsday is nigh. I won't take you this eve. In fact, I will give you a head start and allow you to leave at first light. If I catch up with you, you will come with me. If I don't?" He shrugged, spreading his hands wide. "You're free. For now."

"How benevolent of you."

Arden grinned as he stood. "This time always brings out my giving side, Brother." He laughed, jerking his head to his companions as he crossed the room to another table. I watched him eye a petite serving girl. He grabbed her wrist and said something that made his companions laugh. With her free hand, she slapped him across the face. His face turned dark, and his eyes narrowed. Rising to his feet, he grabbed a fistful of her hair and dragged her out the door, his companions following.

"I would strongly suggest you don't get involved," Abraham said when I started to stand.

"They are going to rape her," I gripped the hilt of my dagger.

"Yes. And so will you at sword point."

I glanced out the window, clenching my fists as I watched the men violate the helpless woman, my brother standing watch.

"Sit down, Damiyun," Abraham pointed to the chair, and I slowly sank down.

I knew he was right, and as always, I turned a blind eye to the actions of the Suppressors.

"Where are we heading?"

"To the Shadow Elf Lands. Like I said."

I rubbed the back of my neck with a sigh. "What if it's not her, Abraham?"

He drained his mug. "Who else could it be?"

Tossing some coins on the table, I rose to my feet. "I am going to get some rest. I wish to leave well before dawn," I said. Abraham nodded, and we secured a room.

I would do everything I could to put as much distance between me and my brother as possible.

I would not let myself be caught again.

FORTY-NINE
ARDEN

"Enough," I said, my eyes on the woman who lay in the mud. The man on top of her looked over his shoulder at me, eyes questioning. I was tired of hearing her pathetic cries. Normally, they were a symphony to my ears, but not this night. Grabbing the man by the hair, I wrenched him off her.

"I said enough," I snarled. He cried out in pain as my boot connected with his balls. I knelt beside the woman. Her wide, frightened eyes met mine. "It's alright, love," I soothed. "Normally, I would slit your throat or take you as my plaything," I flashed a smile. She whimpered. "But it is the week of the Holy Day, and I am feeling so very generous. I will allow you to go back to your family." I pulled away, and she scrambled to her feet.

"You think because you wear the uniform of the Suppressor that you can do what you want? Hunt who you want? You are no more than opportunistic bastards." Spit hit my face. I reached out and grabbed a fistful of her hair. Yanking her head back, I pressed my dagger to her exposed neck.

"Oh, love," I said, pressing the blade harder. "We are law. We are order. We keep the stinking filth from corrupting your children. We keep you safe."

She glared up at me. "You kill innocents."

I pressed the blade closer still, nicking her neck. She winced as red bubbled from the small wound. Leaning down, I licked the blood, the taste of fear and dread filled my mouth. She shuddered at the feel of my tongue. I gripped her hair harder. She mewled in pain, and I inhaled the scent.

"We protect the innocent. We protect your children from having abominations. We protect the world from their infestation." I released her with a shove. "Run, love. Go back home before I change my mind and cut you into pieces," I said, licking the remnants of her blood off my blade. She scrambled back and took off. I laughed as she tripped over her skirts, falling to the ground.

"Hurry, love, before we catch you again." She pulled herself to her feet and raced off through the night.

My mirth turned sour as I thought of my brother and how he had lost Lillyanna. I could only imagine what he had done to make her flee, and the thought of her gone filled me with rage. Vel would be furious with me over this, but I knew how to fix it. I knew how to find her. I knew about the demons roaming the streets looking for Wielders to feast on. I knew I would find one in the dark recesses of an alley. Pulling my cloak close, I made my way through the dark streets. A soft snow began to fall again, and I pulled my hood up. Coldness seeped in and I cursed it. Tried to ignore it, but I couldn't stop the chills that racked my body. Quickening my steps, I walked through the dark and nearly empty streets, stopping periodically and peering out from the folds of my hood to gather my bearings.

"Are you lost? Human. Wielder."

Found him.

I turned in the direction, my eyes falling upon a dark alley. Deep down in the depths, I saw a figure looming.

"Come, child," the voice hissed.

Coldness washed over me and for a moment, I was paralyzed.

"Arden," the voice hissed again. It was one I knew. One that made my legs weak and almost made my bowels loosen.

It was a trick, I knew. This was how they lured people to their demise. A trick of the eyes, and of the ears. It was a trick, but the voice still chilled me. Still sickened me. Closing my eyes, I took a deep breath. The cold air froze my lungs and grounded me.

"Arden," the voice purred. "Come give your father a hug."

Fear clutched me and I almost fell to the ground. This wasn't real. Why did it feel so real? I steeled myself against the onslaught of emotions. Feelings made you weak. Emotions are for women, I told myself as I made my way down the dark corridor. Teeth snapped, and I heard a growl. I looked up at the imposing figure. Saliva dripped from sharp teeth. Black eyes bored into me. Sharp talons dug into the cobblestone beneath. I pushed back the fear that dared to raise its ugly head. The beast's head swung from side to side. Steam billowed from its nose and mouth.

"What do you want, Wielder?" His voice made my body vibrate. Jaws snapped, and a forked tongue flicked out to lick the air inches in front of me. I had to stop myself from recoiling. "You will make a tasty snack."

I pulled out a pouch filled with coin, tossing it in the air and catching it again. The beast's eyes followed the bag.

"I see I have your attention," I said.

Eyes flicked to me. "What do you need?"

"A Wielder killed and another captured. Alive."

"I'm listening," he said.

Smiling, I tossed him the bag of coin that he caught in his big claw. "I thought so," I said.

My brother would regret escaping again. He would pay with his blood, and though it saddened me to not be the one to make him pay, his death would still cause me joy.

As for the little bitch? I had something special planned for her. Something that I will enjoy far more than her.

FIFTY

LILLYANNA

I HAD BEEN SICK for what seemed like forever. I hadn't been able to keep anything down. Just the smell, the thought of food, made me rush to grab the chamber pot and empty my stomach. I heaved and sweated. Allendaire wet my brow with a damp cloth. I leaned over and heaved again. The bile sloshed in the pot and my stomach turned. I sipped on a bit of water to wash my mouth.

"It is time I sent for the healer," Allendaire said.

"I'm fine." I wiped my mouth on the sleeve of my nightdress.

"You are not fine. You have been ill far too long," he said, tone stern. "You can barely eat and when you do, it comes back up. Get back into bed. I will have the healer here shortly."

I slipped beneath the warm covers, willing my sickness to stay at bay. A short time later, the door opened and a woman with a kind face entered. Allendaire's worried eyes met mine before he closed the door.

"The king tells me you are ill?" She crossed the room to the bed.

"A bit," I said, sitting up and resting against the headboard.

"I see. And what are your symptoms?"

"Mostly nausea and vomiting. When I eat it comes back up and the thought and smell of food..." I swallowed hard. Saliva flooded in my mouth.

"When was your last bleeding?"

I frowned. "I—I'm not sure exactly. Three Moon Cycles ago? Maybe four?"

As I said it, realization hit. The room spun as my blood drained to my feet and my stomach dropped. I had always been regular but with everything that had happened, I didn't pay attention to my cycle.

And now it was late.

Four Moon Cycles late. A sour taste filled my mouth and dread set in.

No, no, no, no. I can't be. Please. No.

The healer smiled. "It appears you are with child, Lillyanna."

Tears burned behind my eyes, and I swallowed against the painful lump in my throat. I sagged against the headboard. I rested my hand on my stomach.

I was carrying Allendaire's child, his heir. Another wave of nausea hit.

The healer patted my hand. "The sickness will subside in a few Moon Cycles," she said, backing away and exiting the room.

I stared out the window, not seeing anything, the healer's words resonated in my head.

With child. With child. Allendaire's child.

I glanced up at the sound of the door opening. "You carry the heir," Allendaire said, his tone pleased as he sat on the edge of the bed and took my hand.

"So, it would seem."

"You are not happy?"

I sighed. Captive to the Shadow Elves, a prisoner to the king, and he thought our relationship was happy, the child would be a happy boon? Another tear formed in the corner of my eye. "Happy? What will the queen think?" I turned to look at him. "And what will happen to me once the child is born?"

I knew he hadn't thought about it.

"I want to be alone," I said. Allendaire nodded. Kissing my forehead, he stood and slipped out of the room. When the door closed behind him, I let out a torrent of tears.

His words months before rang in my head. *You will bear my heir.* And I was, and there was nothing I could do about it. Gods' damn it, but I was a fool to run off on Damiyun. Though his betrayal still smarted, the Elves were not a people I wanted to join. Would I even be allowed? I never pretended I wouldn't leave these lands, though the hope was always there, but now my fate was sealed.

Now I was truly a prisoner.

T HE WIND HOWLED OUTSIDE, shaking the panes of glass in the window, and a violent down draft made the fire roar. I pulled the blanket close against the chill sweeping through the gaps. I tried to keep to myself as much as possible, seeking sanctuary in the library often.

Phabian had taught me a bit of their language and while I struggled with translation, I could understand some words. I tried to read Elven. The script flowed on the page. An Elf, a servant it seemed by their livery, skulked down an aisle of books. Under her breath, I heard her whisper, "King's Whore." Oh yes, I understood some of their language.

I closed the book in my lap, a children's book that had easy Elvish to help with my learning, and watched the snow blow and swirl outside.

"Lillyanna." Mouranda's voice cracked like a whip. I jumped at the sound, turning my attention to the tall woman whose figure filled the doorway. Her dour face looked down on me and she crossed her arms.

"Allendaire has apprised me of your condition," she snarled. "And while half-breeds are not tolerated, you are carrying the heir and therefore your child will be allowed to be born." She paused. "My husband foolishly thought you would be allowed to stay on as his whore. I assured him that would not happen. After you give birth, you will give me the child and be sent on your way. If you even think of returning—if it is known you are meeting my husband in secret—and if you so much as place a foot on our lands, you will be executed. Is that understood?"

I lifted my chin and met her eyes. "Yes."

Lips pursed, she whirled around and floated out.

I sat in my chair, a chill washing over me that had nothing to do with the weather outside.

I should have tried to flee again, while the palace was in chaos after the attack. No one would have seen me leave. I would be free right now.

You tried that once. How did that work out for you? Even if you made it to a town, you have no coin. How would you pay for shelter? Would you sell your body for a warm bed and meal? You already proved you know nothing about survival in the wild.

I pushed the thoughts away and swallowed past the lump in my throat, while the weight of my predicament pressed down on me. Sighing, I got up and replaced the book on the shelf and hurried to my room, trying to block out the snarls, the hisses of "King's Whore."

I entered my room, quickly shutting the door. A fire roared, making the room uncomfortably warm. The walls pressed in on me—the walls of my prison. My hands shook. Sweat broke out over my body. The walls continued to press in on me. I needed air. I rushed across the room, pushed the window open, and leaned out. The rush of cold and the sting of crystallized snow hit my hot skin, freezing me. I gulped in the cold air, gasping and coughing as my lungs froze.

I was trapped.

The words beat like a drum inside my head.

I stood in front of the window, the bitter cold freezing my exposed skin, and watched the gray sky turn to night.

"Lillyanna," Allendaire's voice cried. Hands seized my shoulders, pulling me from the window, which he quickly closed. He dragged me to the fire and threw a blanket around my shoulders. I pulled it close, shivering against the cold that had seeped into my body, stepping closer to the heat, feeling the stinging of needles as my frozen flesh thawed. I hadn't realized how long I had been standing there, mind racing.

"What were you doing? You could have caught your death."

And so, death seemed a far better fate. I had little control over my life and journey of late. The days of stealing food and wondering if my father were alive or dead were so distant and a comfort. I had freedom then and hope.

Allendaire cupped my chin, tilting my head up. "What's wrong?"

I swallowed. "You know what's wrong. I am to give up my child and leave."

Allendaire ran a hand through his hair with a sigh. "I tried to reason with her, but she is adamant."

I laughed. "For a race who looks down on your women, you seem quick to obey the queen. Tell her your word is law."

"You know I want nothing more than to have you stay here but doing so—it would cause conflict."

I pulled my chin from his grasp. "Right. I can see how having the King's Whore stay on would be a problem."

Allendaire winced. "Lillyanna—"

"Isn't that what I am? Your whore? At least that's what your Elves call me."

Allendaire gripped my chin again and jerked my head up. "No, that is not what you are. I care about you, and I dare say what I feel, is love. It's a confusing feeling. One I have never felt before. If there was anything I could do, I would."

I pulled away again. "Would you? You are the king. This is your child." I glared up at him. "After all, I am nothing more than a body to satisfy your desires. I could see how keeping the King's Whore on would cause a problem," I spat.

His jaw clenched, and his eyes flashed with anger for a brief moment. "Enough talk about this. Do you play 'Capture the Pegasus'?" He crossed the room and picked up a box from a table.

"I have never heard of it," I said, watching as he placed it on the table before the fireplace. Sitting down in a chair, he lifted the lid and pulled out a game board and pieces. Taking the chair across from him, I sat down and watched as he arranged the pieces on the white granite board. The board had a background of small squares with larger squares of black and white placed in what seemed like a random order. It was divided up in circles, the smallest in the middle growing larger as they radiated out, with a series of lines cutting the circles into small pie shapes. Allendaire placed the intricately carved ivory pieces on the board, sixteen black and sixteen white, and then sat back, with his hands on his knees.

"Capture the Pegasus is a game of strategy," he started. "The goal is to get your Pegasus," he picked up the figure of the winged horse, "to the center." His long, ringed finger tapped the center circle. "Now, the pieces can only move on the lines," he continued, tracing the straight lines that cut the circles, and the lines of the circles themselves. "The black and white squares must be avoided. If a black piece lands on white, the piece is out of play, and vice versa. However, if, say, a white piece lands on a white square, the piece is deemed safe and still playable. To get rid of your opponent, you must try and occupy the same space as them or force them onto a square of the opposite color, rendering them out of play," he said, demonstrating his words with pieces on the board. "Now, this row," he pointed to the first row of pieces which were carved in the shape of wolves, "they are the hunters. They can only move one space at a time, be it forward or diagonal. Their main job is to protect the Pegasus and hunt down the opponent's pieces. They are the sacrificial lambs, so to speak." He said. Moving to the second row, he picked up an end piece. "This is the crow. This piece can move forward or sideways. The serpent," he picked up the next piece, "moves in an 'S' pattern. The fox is the only piece that moves backward after its initial move and the Pegasus, the most important piece, can move in any direction. As I said, the end goal is to get the Pegasus to the center to win. However, if your piece is blocked in by the opponent's piece," he placed pieces on the board, "or is forced onto a square of opposite color, you lose the game." He smiled at me as he replaced the pieces he was demonstrating with. "Do you wish to play?"

"Yes, of course." Anything to distract me at the moment would be useful.

"I will let you make the first move."

Studying the board, I moved my third hunter forward a space, then Allendaire moved one of his into position. Smiling, I moved my piece diagonal, capturing his. Allendaire's mouth twitched, as he moved another hunter, capturing mine.

The sound of a high-pitched, screeching wail echoed outside. Bumps pricked my skin and the hair on my arms stood up.

"What was that?"

Allendaire looked up from the board. "Demons," he said in an offhanded manner.

I swallowed hard, glancing out the window. "What do you mean, demons?"

"They have been roaming the woods at night recently," he said. He reached out and touched my cheek. "You're safe, Lillyanna. They never venture far from the dark woods. Now, it's your turn to move."

I glanced out the window again, as another shriek pierced the air. Shaking myself of the dread that clenched my stomach, I put my attention back to the game. Chewing my lip, I chose the crow and placed it on its space. Allendaire chuckled softly, picking up his serpent and taking yet another one of my pieces.

We played on and on. Allendaire defeated me every time, finally calling the gameplay to a halt after his fourth win.

"You are a fast learner, Lillyanna. Your strategy is... interesting, and I am sure you will beat me in time," he said as he packed up the game and stood. "Mouranda does not care for the game, and my Elves hold back for fear of beating me." He chuckled, and I rose to my feet. "Did you enjoy it?"

"I did. Thank you, I look forward to playing again soon," I said, vowing to get better and beat him at least once. I would ask Phabian in the morning if he played, and if he would allow me to practice my skill with him.

He reached down and pulled me out of my chair and embraced me. I obediently slipped my arms around his waist and stood stiffly in his embrace.

"I regret I cannot stay longer," he said. He pressed his lips to the top of my head, then pulled away. "I promise I will be here when you wake. And you have my word that I will deal with the ones who call you the King's Whore." His jaw clenched, and his eyes were angry.

I said nothing, and he pulled away.

Picking up the box that held the game, he crossed the room and exited.

I tossed some wood on the fire, then began undressing for bed. Slipping beneath the warm covers, I sank into the soft mattress.

I placed my hands on my abdomen, on the child growing inside, and offered a silent prayer up to the gods.

A prayer asking them to take my child from me.

To free me from my prison.

From my fate.

FIFTY-ONE

I DIDN'T LEAVE MY room for over a week.

I feared what the Elves would do to me, the ones who had called me the King's Whore.

Allendaire didn't visit. My shoulders relaxed. Knots loosened along my back.

Phabian had told me Allendaire was collecting the tax from his lands, and I had to admit the reprieve from him—from his constant, sometimes suffocating attention and needs—was a blessing. I relished my time, wallowing away in the bed for hours on end.

My sickness had subsided somewhat. The healer had given me something to take for it, and it helped me keep some food down. Phabian brought me food and books, and in the evening, we played Capture the Pegasus. One night I was sitting in front of the fire when I heard a knock followed by the door opening.

"You can't stay in your room forever," Phabian's deep, lilting voice said as he came around to where I was sitting and placed the tray of food and books on the table. "You needn't worry, Lillyanna. Nothing will happen to you. The king made his intentions very clear to those who called you names."

"Yes, well, I suppose nothing will happen to someone whose throat is slit."

Phabian settled into a chair with a sigh. Long, elegant fingers strummed on the armrest. "I know your... condition... is not something we condone, but you bear the heir. No one would dare hurt you."

I leaned forward and grasped the mug of warm goat's milk. "And what are your thoughts, Phabian?" I took a sip of the disgusting drink, suppressing a gag. While we were friendly, and I did consider him a friend, I didn't know how he felt about my condition.

He shrugged. "You carry the heir. Half-breed or not, your child will rule."

I laughed. "That doesn't answer my question."

Phabian leaned forward and grasped my hands. "You have made my king happy. You will give birth to the heir. You will save the kingdom."

I looked away, blinking back the tears that stung my eyes. "And I will never know my child." I looked back at him. "Promise me something? Promise you will look after her and keep her safe? I know her life will be difficult, and I want you to make it less so.”

He squeezed my hands in quiet reassurance. Quiet solidarity. “I will look after your child like she was my own.”

“Promise me... Promise me she won’t be treated like the other women?”

Phabian bowed his head and placed a fist over his heart. “You have my word. I will protect her with my life. She will never be abused, and I will kill any who seeks to harm her.”

I smiled, knowing he would.

“The king will return this eve. Will you receive him?” He rose to his feet.

“Is refusing an option?”

He sighed. “I can tell him you aren’t feeling well, but that will only hasten his visit.”

“That’s what I thought.”

“I will have someone prepare a bath for you. Good day, Lillyanna,” he said, giving me a sad smile, and leaving the room.

I settled back in my chair, sipping the awful goat’s milk I was forced to drink, wishing for a glass of wine. I placed my hand on the small bulge forming beneath my tight dress.

“At least you will have one ally in a kingdom of enemies,” I whispered, stroking my stomach. I leaned my head back against the chair and closed my eyes.

I shouldn’t have fled. I should have waited, let my anger cool enough to make a rational decision. None of that mattered now. My fate was sealed with the child I carried. Any hope of escape had long ago faded, and I had made my choice.

Sighing, I settled back into the chair and waited for the servants to bring the water up for my bath in preparation for dinner with the king.

I SAT IN FRONT of the fire, relishing in the warmth when the door opened, startling me. I rose to see several Elves striding through, arms loaded down with garments that they placed on the bed. Allendaire strolled casually in carrying a box with Capture the Pegasus and placed it on a table.

“What is all this?” I watched as the Elves replaced the clothing in the wardrobe with the new ones they had brought in.

“Clothes to accommodate your condition,” he said, striding across the room to where I stood. He leaned down and kissed me. “I had them made while I was collecting the tax.”

The door closed and Allendaire sat in a chair and pulled me onto his lap. I obediently let myself be pulled down.

"I missed you terribly while I was away," he said, nuzzling my neck. "I wanted to invite you to join me, but I thought better of it in your condition. Collecting the tax is so tedious. At least you would have broken up the monotony."

I didn't say anything. It wasn't exactly a compliment. And I couldn't exactly say whether I missed him, as the reprieve had been welcome.

"How are you feeling?"

I shrugged. How was I feeling? Though the sickness had subsided some, I couldn't stop the feeling of doom that blanketed me. "The healer gave me something for the sickness. I have been able to keep some food down."

"Good," he said, lips brushing my cheek. "Would you enjoy playing a game of Capture the Pegasus?"

I nodded and slipped off his lap, eyes following him to where he had left the box, an idea forming in my mind. I knew if my child were to be a female, she would rule in name only. Whoever laid claim to her would be the true ruler of the kingdom. Her place would be like all the other women. She would be forced to produce children to keep the race alive.

I wouldn't have that for her. My child would be the queen.

"How about a friendly wager?" I asked as he sat down and removed the lid.

"Go on." He glanced up as he set up the board.

I licked my lips and rubbed my hands on my legs. "If the child I bear is a female, she will rule as queen. Not in name. She will be the queen. She will choose her mate, and you will have no power to confirm or deny her choice. She will decide how many children she has," I said. "If it's a male, then our bet is void."

The corner of his mouth quirked up. "And if you lose?"

I shrugged. "Then you do what you will."

He smiled. "I believe we have an agreement," he said, nodding for me to start.

I studied the board, selecting a hunter and moving it into play. The game had begun.

I took my time making my moves and selecting my pieces carefully. Too much rested on this game, and I wasn't about to lose easily, though I was forced to sacrifice some key pieces, wincing when Allendaire joyfully took them.

The game played on for what seemed like hours. Finally, when I thought all was lost, as Allendaire had a good portion of my strong pieces, I trapped his Pegasus on his safe spot.

I had won the game.

Allendaire sat back in his chair, a look of shock on his face. "You won."

I smiled in similar shock. "So, it would seem."

"You have been practicing."

My smile widened. "Phabian has been playing with me."

Allendaire laughed. "A worthy teacher and opponent."

"So, you will honor the agreement?" I held my breath, eyes locked on him. My heart hammered in my chest as I waited for his answer, though I didn't know what I would do if he said no.

"Of course. I am a man of my word, and you won fair."

I let out the breath I held, relief washing over me, and I sagged in my chair. I watched as he returned the pieces to the box, then rose to his feet. I stood as well. He pulled me into his arms, mouth finding mine.

"Will you join me for the evening meal?"

I forced a smile. "Of course."

He smiled, kissed me, and then exited the room.

I sat in my chair, relief flooding through my body.

At the least, my daughter would have Phabian's protection, and if the king was truly a man of his word, she would be queen.

I smiled at the thought and stroked my stomach. I looked around the bedroom. I was tired of staying here. It was several hours before my obligatory meal with Allendaire. I didn't want to sit here staring at the walls, nor was I tired enough to rest. Phabian had told me if I wanted to get out, all I had to do was tell him. With that thought in my mind, I slipped out of the room, hoping to find him, and hoping he would take me out for a bit.

FIFTY-TWO

PHABIAN

"Phabian," a voice called out. I turned in the direction, smiling at Lillyanna, who stood in the doorway to the sitting room.

"Lillyanna," I said as she entered. She looked radiant, dressed in an emerald long-sleeved gown of velvet. Her red hair flowed about her shoulders like fire. A black cloak was draped over her arm. Untangling myself from Lazaro, I gently pushed him off my lap and rose.

"I wish to leave the castle for a bit. You said I only had to ask," she said.

"Of course."

"She cannot leave the grounds, Phabian," Lazaro snarled, eyes narrowed on Lillyanna.

"I told her I would take her out if she wished."

"She will try to escape."

Lillyanna laughed. "Where would I go and in my condition?"

"Wha'mo," Lazaro spat.

Lillyanna's head snapped to the side as if she had been slapped. My blood boiled at Lazaro's words. Grabbing him around the neck, I pulled him forward, our faces inches apart. "Need I remind you what happened to the others that called her a whore?" I released him with a shove. He stumbled back with a glare. "I happen to like your head and would like for you to keep it."

I crossed the room to where Lillyanna stood. "I will meet you in the atrium," I said, then turned back to Lazaro. "You and I will have a talk when I return."

He clenched his jaw but said nothing, and I followed Lillyanna out into the hall.

"Thank you," she said.

I glanced down at her. "He should know better."

We entered the atrium and after running to my quarters to grab my cloak, we headed out to the stable.

"Saddle Maximilian and a horse for Lillyanna," I said to the stable girl, who ran off to do as I asked.

"I don't know how to ride."

I looked down at Lillyanna. "You don't?"

She shook her head. "I never needed to, and I rode with Damiyun."

"Well then. I will teach you how to ride."

I took Max's reins and Lillyanna swung up into the saddle, with me following behind. Clicking my tongue, I heeled him toward town. The air was crisp, our breath coming out in puffs, and Max's hooves crunched on the snow. I glanced at the sky. It was mid-afternoon, which gave us plenty of time to explore before I had to take her back.

"What do you think of my situation?"

Lillyanna's voice was startling in the crisp silence.

What did I think? She was a sweet young woman and I admit I was fond of her. We had grown close in the time she had been here, and I considered her to be a friend.

I shifted in the saddle. "I don't agree with it," I said.

"So let me go."

I sighed. "You know I can't do that. Where would you go in your condition? Most will shun you, being an unwed woman with child," I said gently.

"I would go back home."

"Which would take several Moon Cycles. What will you do when you're alone and the child decides to come?" She had no response for that. "I am truly sorry for what happened to you."

The worst thing about this all was I took it up on myself to find Damiyun. When I delved into her mind and got the truth, I made note of where Damiyun was and struck out to search, finding him on the outskirts of Fae land. Though I should have shown myself, should have told him where Lillyanna was, I had no desire to tangle with the Faerie Folk. They were a deceitful lot and though they could not lie, they had their way of twisting the truth, so it was neither true, nor was it false. And they had their ways of binding unsuspecting people to their lands, be it with drink or a veiled promise.

At least when we made a binding promise, we knew what it meant. But I didn't wish to tangle with them, so I slipped away and when I came back, I told Allendaire.

"Keep it to yourself," he had said, and though his words bothered me, I was not about to go against my king, so I kept quiet. Even knowing Lillyanna's fate, I said nothing.

We entered the town in silence. It was packed with Elves, the high ones standing out with their bright clothing among the lower ones dressed in muted colors. While some bowed their heads in respect, and others smiled and greeted me by name, all looked at Lillyanna with hate streaming from their eyes, but they knew better than to utter a word. They knew better than to call her the King's Whore.

The scent of food, meat and fish, the sweet, pungent smell of pastries and wood burning filled the cold air. Festive music drifted on the light breezes, and I smiled. Pulling Max to a halt, I swung down, Lillyanna following.

"What's going on?" She looked around and fell in step beside me as I guided Max through the crowd.

"Winter solstice is coming in a few weeks' time. Small celebrations start about now. As the weeks progress, they move closer to the palace, culminating there for a grand gala on the day of the solstice."

"Can we go?" Lillyanna's eyes sparkled, and a look of wonder and joy spread across her face. "We had small festivals in my village. My father took me to a few when I was small." Her smile faded. "I felt close to him in those times. Safe. Loved."

My heart broke for her. I took her hand in mine and smiled down at her. "Let us celebrate," I said, tugging her toward where the merriment was.

"Sir," a voice to my left said.

I looked over at a young Elf and stopped.

"Let me take Max to the stables, if I may?" His eyes met mine and immediately dropped to the ground. I gave the reins over to him.

"Of course," I said. I reached into my pocket and tossed him a silver. His eyes lit up. "Take good care of him, and you get two more."

The young Elf nodded and led Max away.

"You are kind," Lillyanna said.

I stopped. "What?"

"You gave that boy a silver to take your horse, and you promised more. You knew he would be taken care of, and you will give him two more, regardless."

I snorted. I was far from kind. If I were, she would be long gone, back with Damiyun, but I could not go against my king. I tugged her along. She pulled her hand from mine.

"Lillyanna?"

She bit her lip, eyes on the ground. "I'm not a whore," she said, voice quiet.

"What?" I turned her toward me and cupped her chin. "I never thought that of you."

"Others do. I didn't... I did whatever Allendaire wanted to survive."

My heart broke. I knew her not to be a willing participant. I knew what the king wanted, but what was I supposed to do? How could I go against his order? I shook myself of the thoughts.

"No more talk of that. Let us have a pleasant night of celebration and fun," I said. Releasing her chin, I took her hand again, tugging her back toward the merriment, smiling when she followed. We pushed through the crowd. People stopped and parted when they saw us. Some snarled at Lillyanna.

"Maybe we should go back," she said.

I gripped her hand tighter. "No. It is a festival you have never seen. I want you to experience it."

I tugged her on, and she followed with a reluctant sigh. The merriment grew louder the closer we got to the square, and I pulled her close to the front. The square was festively decorated. A dozen or more colorful ribbons were strung between the tall, black marble pillars that marked the square. More streamers hung across the entablature, creating a colorful canopy above. They also decorated the large white marble statue of Allendaire with ribbons. A crown of purple roses sat atop his head.

Performers filled the square. One male Elf, naked from the waist up, swallowed fire. Another stood ten feet tall atop stilts, juggling six balls. People danced to lively music, and I felt myself tapping a toe to the beat. I glanced down at Lillyanna, whose eyes were wide as she took it all in, a look of joy on her face.

"This is far grander than any festival in Howling Cove," she said, awe painting her voice.

"I admit, the Elves tend to go overboard."

"No. It's magical." She looked around. "How do you keep the Suppressors from coming here? Do they come here?"

It was an odd question, though I could understand why it was asked. Our lands pulsed with magic, powerful enough for a Feeler to sense miles away. "We have a treaty with them. We make the Sigaa'Lean, and in turn, they let us live in peace."

"If only everyone could do that," she said.

"This is a celebration. No more talk of depressing topics. Come," I said, tugging her through the crowd again. "I want to introduce you to my favorite food."

We made our way to the other side of the street, where a food vendor was set up.

"Phabian," the proprietor greeted with a smile. "I was wondering if you would show up to eat me out of my food."

I laughed. "You know, it's my guilty pleasure."

I watched him insert a wooden stick into two large sausages. He then dipped it in a batter, rolled it in cornmeal and dropped it in a pot of boiling oil for a minute. Pulling them out, he handed one to me and the other to Lillyanna.

"What is this?"

"Only the most delicious food in all of Il'Ekhester. It's a pity I can only get it on solstice celebrations." I bit into the hot, battered sausage, closing my eyes for a second and relishing the taste.

"This... this is delicious," Lillyanna said around her food.

"I told you."

We finished our treat, and I took Lillyanna's hand again, and we strolled idly through the fair. Merchant booths were set up along with booths where one could play games of chance for a trinket. Lillyanna and I competed against each other in a few games, giving up when we both realized neither one of us was any good.

"Are you enjoying yourself?"

The smile that split her face at my question all but tore me apart.

"I am. Thank you for taking me here."

We casually wandered on, following the sound of music playing. Groups of people clapped their hands, bodies spun and whirled to the music.

"Care to dance?"

Lillyanna nodded eagerly. I pulled her into my arms, and we spun and jumped, clapped our hands and stomped our feet. We danced until our feet ached, and our breathing became labored with exertion. I looked up at the sky, noting that the sun was quickly dipping below the horizon, and sighed.

"I regret I must get you back to the castle to prepare for dinner with the king."

The smile faded from Lillyanna's lips and the light in her eyes dulled. My heart cracked for her. Pushing our way back through the crowd, I gathered Maximillion, and we rode back to the palace in silence.

"Thank you for taking me to the festival," she said when we entered the atrium. "I had an enjoyable time."

"I am glad you enjoyed it. I will take you out again any time you ask," I said. I pushed a lock of hair behind her ear. "I am a friend, Lillyanna. I will do what I can to make your stay here tolerable."

"Thank you, Phabian." She rose on her toes and kissed my cheek. "I appreciate having you as a friend." She stepped away and made her way back to her room.

Watching her retreat, a heaviness filled my heart. I would keep my promise and do what I could to keep her mind off the situation and when her child was born, a child whose life I knew would be hard, I would protect them from harm. I would make sure they knew about the strong, beautiful woman who had no choice with what she did.

FIFTY-THREE

LILLYANNA

Closing the door behind me, I leaned against it with a sigh, relieved to be back in my room.

Relieved at being alone.

Dinner was pleasant but the hours afterward—satisfying his wants, his needs, his insatiable desires—exhausted me. Crossing the room, I changed into my nightdress and slipped beneath the warm covers, the weight a snug embrace. I thought about my afternoon with Phabian at the festival. The feeling of joy and freedom that filled me then left my body the moment he said we had to return. I enjoyed my time with Phabian. I felt comfortable and at ease around him and when he called me a friend, that warmed my soul. It was nice to know that someone within these walls liked me. The way he relaxed around me and wouldn't let me dwell on my situation if only for a few hours, truly showed he cared. The tension eased from my body as my head sank into the soft down pillow, weariness weighing down on me as I closed my eyes.

Sleep, however, was restless, my mind hovering between wakefulness and dreams.

Dreams about Allendaire and Damiyun.

A sound within the room pulled me from my fitful slumber. Sitting up, I scanned the semi-darkness, ears straining to hear. A soft shuffle came from across the room. A quiet whisper of clothing.

Shadows moved, slowly advancing toward the bed. A glint of silver flashed in the dim light. My chest tightened, and my breathing grew ragged. Sweat broke out on my body, and I vaulted from the bed, heading toward the door that seemed so very far away. My heart pounded in my chest as I slipped past two figures. My eyes focused on the door, which seemed to get farther away the closer I got. My mind could only think of escape.

Hands closed around my hair, jerking me back. I screamed and fought as I was dragged back to the bed. One of them roughly picked me up and tossed me onto my back. I kicked and clawed against the hands that grabbed.

"Keep the bitch still," the one who held the knife snapped in Elvish.

I screamed, the sound cut short by a swift and painful backhand to my cheek. My eyes watered, and I fought against the hands that pinned my arms and legs to the bed. I bucked and struggled against my assailants. My will to survive surged through me.

I will not die. I will not die.

Another sharp slap hit my cheek, and the metallic taste of blood filled my mouth. My nightdress was shoved roughly up. The cold feeling of metal pressed against my skin as the blade holder lazily ran the tip back and forth across my abdomen, pressing harder with each pass.

I will not die.

I screamed again. Hands closed around my neck, slowly squeezing.

"Let's have some fun with her first." One man slipped his hand between my legs.

I gasped for air, trying to kick the violating hand away.

No, no, no. Not like this. Not like this. I will not die.

"She is quite pretty," the man whose hand circled my neck said. "We can put her mouth to good use and shut her up at the same time." His free hand fumbled with the laces on his trousers.

I gasped for air, spots forming in front of my eyes as darkness—as death—threatened to take me.

"We don't have time for that." The blade holder snapped. "Keep the bitch awake. She needs to feel the pain. She needs to know what we do to half-breeds and whores who bear them."

I screamed over and over again. My heart pounded in my ears and pain—horrible, searing pain—enveloped me as the blade sliced flesh.

"Shut her up."

Hands clamped down over my mouth. I whimpered, tears flowed from my eyes, my body going numb as the blade continued to cut. The room began to close in on me. Darkness crept in on the fringes of my vision, closing. Closing. I was looking down a dark tunnel. I fought with my last bit of strength. My ears rang, and the tunnel began to grow darker.

I was dying.

Sounds were muffled as the ringing in my ears grew louder. Shouts, and the sound of steel ringing as blades clashed. With the last bits of strength—of life—I had inside, I struggled to sit up.

"Easy, Lillyanna." A voice floated to me as hands gently pushed me back down.

My vision swam, the room spun about me, and I tried to focus on the shadowed face that briefly loomed above. The sound of angry curses and the ring of steel continued in the room beyond.

Blue eyes scanned my body, and I lifted myself a bit to look as well. My nightdress and bed linens were soaked with blood. A river of red flowed over the hands pressed on the deep knife wound.

"Stay with me, Lillyanna," he urged, his voice a quiet whisper beneath the loud noise roaring in my ears. I tried to focus on him, vision blurry as he tightly wrapped the sheets around me and lifted me in his arms. My eyes focused on his face briefly.

"Lazaro?" My voice was weak to my ears as I recognized the face of the last person I thought would rescue me, before darkness consumed me.

Voices pierced the darkness, sharply spoken words that quickly drifted away.

I was floating down, down.

Come to me, my queen. Come.

Hands grabbed and clawed at me, dragging me back down, and I succumbed. I let myself be dragged to the Abyss. The heat was scorching. Sweat trickled down my back. I looked around and saw a man. His long, black hair flowed about his shoulders. Ice-blue eyes appraised me. He wore a tailcoat of deep, blue velvet, crisp white shirt and black trousers. Boots sheathed his legs. He sat upon a large throne. Carved griffins made up the legs and armrests. Delicate flowers curled around the base, the purple petals bright against the black. Fingers strummed on the griffin heads, the rubies, emeralds, and diamond rings on his fingers glinted in the torchlight.

He was handsome. And dangerous. He crooked a finger in my direction, and my feet moved on their own volition. I knelt before the throne and looked up at him.

"You're mine," Themesis' silky-smooth voice purred. "You belong to me. Come take your seat by my side." He waved his hand, and a matching throne appeared beside him. Rising, I started toward it. What would be so bad about spending eternity here? I would feel no pain. I would not be with the Shadow Elves. I would be safe.

But then I was pulled back. I screamed as I struggled against the grasping hands that held, kicking and clawing my way back to the Abyss. The voices became louder, and I fought harder.

"Hold her."

"Easy now. She's waking."

"I need more time. Put her back out."

And I was cast back into the darkness. Into the claws that grabbed and held. Into Themesis' grasp.

You're home, his voice hissed in my mind as the void enveloped me.

"SHE'S WAKING," A VOICE said as I opened my eyes, the dimly lit room came into focus. Eerie shadows danced on the wall. A pair of blue eyes stared down at me. My heart raced as visions of the terror I had endured flashed in my mind. I struggled to sit up, crying out as waves of excruciating pain washed over me, making the room spin. Hands grabbed my shoulders, and I screamed.

"Easy, Lillyanna. You're alright. You're safe," Phabian's voice was soothing. I relaxed at the sound, and he gently guided me back down on the bed and sat on the edge.

"What happened?" The visions flitting through my mind were jumbled, though I remembered the eyes peering out beneath a hood, and the pain.

The horrible, excruciating pain.

"You were attacked close to ten nights ago. Your assailants attempted to cut the child from your womb."

A face floated in my memory. "Lazaro—"

"Saved you. He heard your screams and put an end to the assault. Had he not been where he was, we would not be having this conversation. You and your child are very fortunate."

I said nothing. Based on my situation, I couldn't fully agree I was fortunate. Death would have been a better option.

I shivered as fingers of cold slipped down my spine.

"Do not dare think those words again," Phabian gripped my shoulders hard.

I glared at him. "Had I not been carrying Allendaire's child, your kind would have gleefully let me die."

"And risk the wrath of the king? The ones who attacked you were swiftly executed by his hand to send a strong message that he will not tolerate ill feelings toward you."

I wasn't completely convinced.

It was my child who had saved my life.

The door opened and Allendaire entered the infirmary. His eyes looked tired, and his face was haggard. The brightly colored clothes appeared out of place on his visibly weary body. He took the spot quickly vacated by Phabian and I could see fine lines around his eyes and brow, which made him look far older than when I had last seen him.

"I thought I was going to lose you," he whispered after Phabian left. He took my hand in his and brushed his lips on the back, fingers caressing my cheek as he pushed a lock of hair behind my ear. "I have not slept since this happened. When

I was told you were awake, seeing you—seeing for myself if it was true—was all that mattered to me."

"You can rest assured your child will be born," I said, pulling my hand from his and crossing my arms over my chest.

"Lillyanna—"

"Isn't that why I live? So I can have the heir who saves your kingdom?" I glared at him. "If I were not carrying your child—our child—would your Elves, would you, have been so quick to save me?"

Allendaire flinched, his hand brushing imaginary lint from his coat. "Of course, your life would have been saved. How can you think otherwise? What do I need to do to show you how I feel?"

Tell the queen I am to stay.

"You mean a great deal to me," he said. "The ones that hurt you, I personally and publicly executed them. No one will dare harm you again."

I reached out and touched his cheek. The coarse stubble felt like sand beneath my fingertips. "I know. I just..." I shook my head with a sigh.

"What?"

I forced a smile. "Nothing. I'm tired."

He took my hand and kissed the palm. "Of course. I will see you on the morrow," he said. Rising to his feet, he softly kissed me, and his hand softly caressed my abdomen. I watched him leave, blinking back the tears of self-pity that stung my eyes. I placed my hands over the bump, feeling a slight flutter of movement, like a Faery fly fluttering beneath my hands.

We were alive, this was true, though I couldn't help but think perhaps death would have been better for both of us. I certainly wouldn't have been the first woman in this kingdom to believe that.

FIFTY-FOUR

"**H**ow are you feeling?" Phabian's melodic voice spoke from the door.

I looked up from the book I was reading aloud to my child and smiled at him as he crossed the room and took a chair next to me. The baby turned and kicked at the sound of his voice, and I placed his hand on my bulging stomach.

"She is very fond of you, Phabian," I said, smiling at the look of delight on his face as she kicked his hand.

"Why do you call the child she?"

I shrugged. "I can't really say. It's just a feeling. Does Anya not feel what her child will be?"

He shrugged. "I don't know. She tends to stay away from me when she is with child."

I wasn't surprised by his words but thought it was best to not say anything.

"How are you feeling?" He asked again.

"Uncomfortable. She moves a lot," I said, keeping the fact I was occasionally hit with sharp pains to myself. I needed to keep my child inside for as long as possible.

"Do you need anything?"

I shook my head. He rose to his feet, placing his hand on my stomach again, a grin splitting his face as the baby kicked him. "Let me know if there's anything I can do for you," he said as he left the library.

I closed my eyes and rested my hands on my stomach. "I hope your father tells you about me, Serafin," I said, speaking the name I gave her. As the child grew, as Serafin became a part of me, I realized how much I wanted her. While I would never know her, I felt, I hoped, she would do something great for this race.

Allendaire spent all his leisure time with me, showering me and our child with gifts. Despite his attention and affection, I rarely left my room, and when I did, I wandered the halls like a ghost staring out the windows and avoiding the Elves who passed.

Though I would be turned out after I gave birth, and though the thought of being alone in an unknown place frightened me, staying here terrified me even more. Leaving S'aehe was a mistake, I knew. I should have let Damiyun explain.

Let my mother explain, but I let my emotions get the better of me. I blinked back the tears at the thought of Damiyun. The thought that I might never see him again. Never hear him whisper my name. Never feel his lips on mine, his hands caressing my body. I missed him more than I thought I would. Missed his dour face that rarely smiled and his gruff voice.

Standing, I started to cross the room to put my book away. A pain hit me, sharp and debilitating. It took my breath away and almost brought me to my knees. I staggered out into the hall, holding on to the wall and stumbling at another wave of agony. I grit my teeth against it, eyes searching the nearly empty corridor.

Phabian. I needed Phabian.

I walked down the hall, pausing, and gritting my teeth every now and again when another pain hit.

"What's wrong?" An Elf who was passing by asked, brow furrowed with concern.

"The baby. She's coming." His eyes widened, and he scurried off, calling out for help. I saw Phabian run toward me.

"She's coming, Phabian. Serafin is coming," I panted, leaning against him as he slipped an arm about my shoulders. I grasped his hand, squeezing hard as another contraction hit. The sounds of voices and footsteps racing down the hall drew closer, the most prominent voice being Mouranda's.

"Get her to the infirmary," she barked. Phabian nodded, and I was all but carried through the halls, back to the place where they took me after the attack. I was hoisted on to a soft bed.

"You're in good hands, Lillyanna," Phabian said, extracting his hand from mine and stepping away.

Pillows were shoved behind me, forcing me into a seated position. My knees were pulled up, and I felt fingers roughly enter me.

"Two fingers. Still quite a ways to go," a female voice said.

"Let me know when it is time," Mouranda said, cold blue eyes glowering at me before she spun around and left.

I glanced about the sparsely furnished room. A fire blazed, keeping it warm, and shadows from the lamps danced on the walls.

"The first one is the hardest." The healer I recognized from my previous time here said as she applied a cold compress to my forehead.

I grit my teeth as another wave of agony hit. A warm liquid spilled from me, soaking the linens I lay on. "Sorry."

The healer laughed. "Don't apologize. What's happening is natural. I suspect your child will be appearing soon."

Several moments, and hard contractions, after I felt her put her fingers inside me again.

"Four fingers. It appears the prince will be born."

She called out names in a loud voice, and two women entered, followed by a sour-faced queen. One woman held me up, another held my knees apart, and the healer barked orders.

I did as I was commanded, pushing when the pain hit, which seemed nearly constant now. On and on the pain ripped through me and I bore down as instructed. The pain was intense and like nothing I had ever experienced. I felt like my insides were being torn apart.

"No more. Please," I begged when the healer ordered to push again.

"I see the head," the healer cried excitedly. "Just a few more and you're done. Now push."

Once more, I grit my teeth and bore down, pushing as hard as I could over and over again. Then I felt something slip from me and I felt a hollowness. A piercing scream broke the quiet. I looked at my child, who was covered in blood, tiny fists clenched as she wailed and cursed the world.

"A girl." The healer declared, wrapping her in a blanket and handing her off to the queen. The baby stopped screaming and if I didn't know any better, I would have sworn she glared at Mouranda. The queen cradled the tiny being in her arms and looked sternly down at her.

Another wave of pain hit, leaving me breathless. "I thought I was done."

The healer chuckled. "You're passing the afterbirth. Try to be still. I still need to stitch you up when it's over."

I grimaced as more pain hit, and something slipped from me.

"You're done, Lillyanna. You did great." The healer patted my hand, and I collapsed back against the pillows, exhausted and soaked in sweat. My eyes went to Mouranda, who held my swaddled child, a look of disdain on her face as she looked upon the girl.

"Can I hold her? Just for a moment?"

Mouranda turned cold eyes on me. "Absolutely not."

"She is my child." I clenched my fists and blinked back the tears burning behind my eyes.

"Not anymore, she's not. She is my child now. You knew what would happen after you gave birth. If I were to let you hold her, she would bond with you, and I cannot have that happen." She turned and began walking toward the door.

"Serafin," I called out. My voice shook with tears, and I wasn't sure she heard me.

"Excuse me?" She turned back in my direction. Blue eyes pierced my soul.

"If I can't have my child, if I can't know her, at least allow me to name her. Is that too much to ask?"

Mouranda pursed her lips and looked down at the tiny screaming bundle whose fists waved in the air.

"I will allow you this request," she said, eyes meeting mine, and for a brief moment, I thought I saw pity flash in them. "The child will be known as Serafin Trounde."

"Thank you," I said to her retreating back. I sagged against the pillows. My body ached, and I was exhausted. Closing my eyes, I welcomed the darkness of sleep.

THE HEALERS BROUGHT ME to my room to recover. I lay in my bed, hands resting on my empty stomach. Tears of self-pity burned my eyes. The door handle jiggled, and I glanced in its direction. Icy fingers of fear ran down my spine. Relief washed over me at the sight of Allendaire.

Relief it wasn't Phabian coming to take me away.

"Allendaire," I sat up as he perched on the side of the bed. He took my hand and pressed his lips to the back.

"How are you feeling?"

"Empty. She was a part of me for so long. It's odd not feeling her kicking and turning inside me."

He pushed a lock of hair behind my ear. "I am deeply sorry, Lillyanna."

"I just wish I could have held her. Even for just a moment." Tears burned behind my eyes. Allendaire looked away. "How is she?"

"She is perfect in every way. Quite vocal too. She screams like a banshee when Mouranda so much as goes near her."

No doubt she knows that is not her mother.

"She seems quite fond of Phabian. If I didn't know better, I would say she is smitten with him."

I smiled, remembering how she would calm at the sound of his voice and kick his hand when placed on my stomach.

"I hope you tell her about me," I said softly.

"Of course, I will. She will know all about the woman I loved." He paused. "You know I would bring her to you if I could."

I said nothing. I couldn't say whether I believed his words or not. The silence stretched between us.

"I'm scared, Allendaire," I said softly. "When I leave—I don't know where I am going to go or what I am going to do." The reality of my not-so-distant situation settled in. Not for the first time.

I cursed myself for not leaving when he offered to let me. This was never my home. Had I left when he offered, I wouldn't be in the situation I was in. I wouldn't have been forced to have a child.

"I'm tired," I said. Allendaire kissed me softly. I heard the rustle of his clothes, boots scuffing across the floor, and the click of the door as it closed. Once I was alone—once the silence descended—I let loose the tears I had held back and cried.

For myself.

For Damiyun.

But mostly for Serafin.

WEEKS LATER, WITH THE help of magic, the healer proclaimed me well enough to leave.

"Lillyanna."

I turned at the voice, eyes going to Allendaire as he crossed the room. He made to pull me into his arms, sadness filling his eyes when I stepped away, crossing my arms over my chest.

"I'm sorry," he said, voice cracking.

I wanted to laugh at his words. "If you are so sorry, then let me have my child."

"I can't do that."

"Won't."

"It's time," Phabian's voice said from the doorway. I was happy to hear it.

I walked past Allendaire who grabbed my arm. "Lillyanna, please. Don't leave like this. I love you."

"Goodbye, Allendaire," I said, yanking my arm from his grasp. I walked out to where Phabian stood waiting in the hall and, without a backward glance, I followed him through the corridors outside to the waiting horse. I swung up behind him, slipping my arms around his waist, and rested my cheek on his back, letting his warmth fill me.

We rode out of town, the soft crunch of hooves on snow punctuating the silence.

"I am sorry, Lillyanna," he said after a bit.

I clenched my jaw. "It would have been better had you executed me."

He said nothing, and we traveled in silence. While I would have preferred conversation as a distraction, I knew no words could ease my mind.

Finally, well after midday, he reined the horse to a stop at the crest of a hill that overlooked a dirt road. We swung down from the horse, Phabian landing lightly in the snow beside me.

"This is where we part. You will find an inn five or so miles up the road. The town is a bit rough, though. We go on occasion, though the king prefers Duenney. If you can make the journey there instead, it would be best and far safer," he said. He took the arm with the Sigaa'Lean, lips moving as he spoke a spell. The bracelet sprang open, and I felt my magic flow freely through my veins. He then reached into his cloak and pressed a bag heavy with coin into my hand.

"Goodbye, Lillyanna. Be well, and perhaps our paths will cross again."

I rose up on my toes and pressed my lips to his cheek. "Goodbye, Phabian. Thank you for being a friend in a house filled with enemies."

He offered a half-hearted smile, then swung onto Max and guided him back down the same road we had just come.

Stowing the coin inside my cloak, I set off down the road toward the village. I looked down the lonely and empty street. Birds chirped, woodland animals scampered, and bare branches clicked as they blew against each other.

Loneliness consumed me as I walked. An ache spread deep inside, and my eyes stung with tears. I was alone in an unknown land. My isolation only highlighted just how much I had relied upon Damiyun. The thought of him brought sorrow and longing. A tightness enveloped my chest and my legs felt heavy and weak. The air felt thick as honey. A deep need and desire filled me. I loved him—Damiyun. I had long since forgiven him and I wanted nothing more than to see him, to feel him and smell him. His touch. I shuddered.

I would never tell him where I had gone or of the child I had borne.

No. That was a secret I would take to my grave. The name Serafin would never pass my lips. I would lock her deep within the recesses of my heart. My eyes burned with tears, and I brushed them away, along with the memory of my daughter.

Breathing the cold air deep into my lungs, I stared down the road edging into view. The sun had lowered as I walked, so I quickened my pace, glancing at the weathered sign proclaiming the place as Theonaus. Once I passed the first few houses and shops, I found myself walking along bustling streets. A wagon careened past, and I just barely managed to jump clear. The driver cursed and offered a rude gesture.

The village was poor.

Rundown buildings lined the streets. Shabbily dressed people hurried about. Mangy horses pulled rickety carts with people hawking their wares. I glanced in one cart, my stomach turned at the sight of rotting fruit covered in maggots. The stench of animal dung, urine, and human feces drifted on the cold breeze. I gagged and buried my nose in my sleeve. As I continued on, I glanced down dark alleyways, seeing ominous figures outlined in the fading light. In one, I caught sight of a woman kneeling in front of a man. His hands were entangled in her hair, hips thrusting as she pleasured him with her mouth. He turned my way, tongue flicking out. He slowly licked his lips.

"Ya wanna taste?" he called out, laughter following as I hurried away.

This was no place to be outdoors when the sun disappeared. Hurrying on, I breathed a sigh of relief as the sign for an inn—The Broken Wench—came into view. Drunk people staggered out, the sound of music and voices rising and muffling as the door swung behind. I hesitated a moment, then marched up the two shallow steps to the door. I pushed my way inside the stifling hot tavern. A blazing fire made the tavern uncomfortably warm, and my frozen extremities tingled and burned. The stench of sweat, body odor and wet dog hung in the air. I gagged, swallowing back the bile threatening to push its way through my lips.

"Watch it," a voice snapped, and someone forcefully shouldered me out of the way. My retort died on my lips, my heart raced, and my hair stood on end as three Suppressors pushed past me, heading to a table in the corner occupied by two others. My mouth went dry, and the room spun. I pushed my way out of the tavern, ignoring the angry growls and curses following my violent exit.

I didn't know if those men knew me—or if they had a Feeler with them—and I wasn't about to stay long enough to find out.

I hastened my steps down the road. The sun was gone and darkness was descending fast as I hurried on, ignoring lewd calls from black alleys.

I should have continued on to Duenney like Phabian said, but I didn't know how far I would have to go, and being a woman, I doubted traveling alone at night would bode well for me. Ignoring the voice urging me on, begging me to find the next town, I decided to spend the night in the woods and continue on to Duenney in the morning.

FIFTY-FIVE

I AWOKE TO A sharp kick to the ribs. I gasped for breath and started to sit up when rough hands grabbed my shoulders and held me down. A foul-smelling rag was shoved into my mouth. Yellow eyes peered down at me from a disfigured face. He leaned down, and I recoiled from his fetid breath.

I reached for my magic and as if sensing what I was doing, my attacker raised his hand and struck. Laughter echoed in my ears as darkness surrounded me.

"WAKE UP."

A wave of cold water hit me, jolting me awake. I coughed and sputtered as the water flooded my nose and spilled into my throat. I sat up and looked around. My head spun; my vision wavered. Nausea rose inside, and I vomited on the floor. Wiping my mouth, I squinted and peered around. My chest tightened as I saw the cold, stone, windowless walls.

I was in a cell. My ankles and wrists were cuffed, chains secured to rings on the wall. My eyes went to the one who held the bucket. He was tall and thin, limbs long and bony. His face was drawn, and his eyes bulged out of their sockets. Thin leathery skin covered his emaciated frame, making him look like a skeleton whose skin had been painted on. I drew on my magic, but it was weak. Barely a flicker pulsed within.

What had they done to me?

"Did I do good, Ton'Yana?" a voice hissed, and I recognized it as belonging to the one who attacked me at my camp.

A smile formed on Ton'Yana's lips. "Yes, K'Risgenl," he purred, and the other man beamed.

Ton'Yana set the bucket down and squatted in front of me. He raised a hand, and I recoiled as he pushed a lock of wet hair off my face with a chuckle.

"You should have stayed at the inn," he said.

The blood drained to my feet at his words.

They had been watching me. Following me.

"A pretty thing like you shouldn't be traveling alone in these parts. It's not safe." His lips curled back into a smile, and he rose to his feet. "Of course, it appears you are already beginning to find that out." He picked up the bucket and turned for the door, K'Risgenl following.

"Who are you? What do you want from me? What have you done to me?" I yelled as the door closed, and plunged me into darkness.

"You will find out soon enough," his silky voice floated from the other side.

Shivering with cold, I sat back against the wall, suffocating in the pitch-blackness, and the deafening silence. I yanked the chains holding me, which served only to hurt and cut my skin.

Closing my eyes, I let the tears fall, and offered up a prayer to the gods Damiyun and Abraham found me before it was too late.

I WAS LEFT IN the cold, dark cell. My wrists bloodied and raw from the shackles. From me trying to pull the chains from the wall. Though I couldn't see through the solid metal door, I knew they were there, K'Risgenl and Ton'Yana. They watched me through the eye slit, waiting for me to close my eyes. To drift off to sleep, and when I did? When darkness claimed me, freezing water jolted me awake. Time and time again I was drenched, teeth chattering and body racked with shivers as I sat in my cold, soaked clothes.

Every few days, or what I suspected was a few days, it was difficult to judge the passage of time, Ton'Yana would come in with food and drink, placing it just out of reach and propositioning me to steal. And when I said no, he would dump the tray on the floor. I was cold, exhausted, and hungry. I drank the dirty water from the puddles and my own urine when the water dried, but it did not satiate my thirst.

Tears pricked my eyes, but I was too exhausted to even let them fall. The worst part of this nightmare was the darkness. The silence. The voice in my head that taunted me.

Foolish girl, the voice hissed. It was female. Was it me? I didn't know. *What did you think to accomplish by running? Look at what you have done. Look at the mess you are in. Who do you think will save you?*

Pulling my knees to my chest, I buried my face in my legs and clamped my hands over my ears.

"Damiyun will find me."

She laughed. *He's probably between your mother's legs. He has no thoughts of you. He doesn't care about you.*

Clenching my fists, I banged them on the ground. "Shut up," I screamed, the sound muffled by the darkness that pressed in.

Does the truth hurt?

"You speak lies. He will find me. He—"

Loves you? Laughter echoed in my head. *He loves pleasure. Sexual gratification. Why do you think he couldn't help himself with Felicity? I'm sure he was sorry,* the voice purred. *Sorry, he got caught.*

Clamping my hands over my ears, I screamed until my throat burned, and when she was gone? When the voice was gone? That was the loneliest time.

"Come back," I whispered when my companion had been silent for days. "Please? I'm sorry. I didn't mean to yell. You're right. He doesn't love me. He doesn't love anyone. I know he has forgotten me."

But the voice didn't respond, and the silence and darkness pressed in on me. I curled up on my side, clutching my knees to my chest. Loneliness crashed down on me.

"Please," I whispered. "Please come back. I can't fall asleep. Please keep me awake."

So you agree I am right.

"Yes."

He never loved you.

"No, he didn't."

Then you must forget him. He won't help you. He can't find you.

I stifled the sob at the thought. At the truth in the words. At knowing Damiyun would never find me.

Do what they say, Lillyanna, she said.

I frowned. How did the voice know my name? Perhaps it was my subconscious.

You will get food. Water. Maybe even sleep.

My stomach growled at the mention of food. It was hollow and empty. I was weak. Exhausted from trying to stay awake. Cold from the water when I couldn't.

"Yes. I will. Please, just stay with me until they come again?"

I didn't know who I was talking to, if anyone. I didn't know if maybe the voice was my own, or perhaps I was going insane. It didn't matter. Whoever it was had become a comfort. A friend. It beat the silence.

The sound of her laughter rang in my head. *I will be here. I am always here, Lillyanna. Close your eyes. Pretend to sleep and when they come in, make your deal.*

And so I did. It didn't take long for the door to open. I sat up at the sound of rusted hinges opening.

"Stop," I held my hands up, waiting for the cold douse that would come, but it didn't.

"Yes?" Ton'Yana's voice said. I heard the slosh of water. The scent of meat, vegetables and potatoes hit my nostrils. My stomach clenched.

"I will do what you ask," I said.

Ton'Yana chuckled. "I thought you would," he said. He placed the tray down in front of me and my mouth watered at the smell. A blanket was placed beside the tray.

"Eat. Sleep. I will wake you when it is time to clean you for your task." He closed the door and I didn't hesitate, digging into the food. When my hunger was as satiated as the meager food allowed, I pulled the hole riddled blanket around me, I laid down and closed my eyes. Within seconds, darkness took me.

The sound of laughter echoed in my head as I drifted off.

I have you. You are mine.

FIFTY-SIX

I WAS SCRUBBED RAW, and my hair washed. Powdered and primed, I was shoved into a dress, the corset bodice pulled uncomfortably tight. Rouge was applied to my lips and cheeks. Kohl lined my eyes. I looked like a whore.

"You will serve my guests spirits and small plates. I will show you which of those stole from me. You will do whatever it takes to get my money. The others?" He shrugged, a lascivious smile curled his cracked lips, revealing yellow teeth. I had to stop myself from flinching at the sight. "You will oblige them in any way they ask." Bone-like fingers grabbed my chin. "If you wish to eat, you will do this."

I knew what he meant, but I would rather die than do what he asked. But I nodded, knowing full well I would not debase myself in that way for a scrap of food.

It's easy, Lillyanna, my friend, my comfort whispered in my head. *Just close your eyes and pretend you're with Damiyun.*

I clenched my jaw. "I will not do that. I am not a whore," I said, voice low.

She laughed. *You let Damiyun use you for his pleasure. What is the difference? I will be here with you, Lillyanna.*

I took a deep breath, calm with the knowledge I wasn't alone, and followed Ton'Yana   through the halls. The sound of music grew louder as we walked on. He stopped outside an open doorway, motioning for me to step forward. I stood beside him and looked into the room. It was a large sitting room, the only furniture being two long tables pushed against a wall. Bottles of spirits and wine sat atop, along with trays of food. The scent hit my nostrils and my stomach clenched. At least three dozen finely dressed people milled about. Men in expensive tailcoats, women in elegant dresses, jewels glittering at necks, ears and fingers. A quartet was set up in a corner beside a blazing fireplace, jaunty music being played.

"Everyone here has stolen from me," he said.

I swallowed hard and looked at the people who helped themselves to the drink and food. A bony hand gripped my bare shoulder. Skeletal fingers dug into my flesh, and I had to stop myself from recoiling.

Do what he says, the voice said. *It can only benefit you. You can live like a queen.*

"You will circle the crowd with trays of food and drink and pick the pockets of my friends."

I said nothing. He gestured toward the room. My muscles tensed and, taking a deep breath, I crossed the threshold, my feet feeling heavy. How in the name of the gods was I supposed to rob these people? What if they don't have coin on them? What if I get caught?

It's easy. Just sidle up next to someone. Offer them food and slip your hand in a pocket.

I snorted. "Right. So easy."

I glanced at Ton'Yana who leaned against a wall talking to a young man. His eyes flicked to me, lips pursed. I looked away and scanned the room. No one paid me any heed. No one even looked my way.

"I can flee."

Don't.

I glanced over my shoulder again. Ton'Yana was deep in conversation with three men.

"I can do it."

Lillyanna, don't, the voice warned again.

But why? Why wouldn't she want me to flee? I didn't voice the question. Glancing around the room, I moved slowly toward the other side. To the open door. To freedom. Voices rose and fell around me. Laughter pealed, glasses clinked. I remained focused on my goal, checking over my shoulder to see what Ton'Yana was doing. He was still in conversation. Good.

The door came closer, and my body buzzed. My heart raced as the doorway came closer. Closer. Finally, not being able to take it anymore, I broke into a run, pushing people out of the way, ignoring their angry shouts and growls. I burst into a long hallway and didn't stop. I raced through the dark corridor. Heavy footsteps and shouts followed behind. I risked a glance over my shoulder. My heart flew into my throat at seeing Ton'Yana chasing after me. Murder flashed in his eyes. His long legs ate up the distance. He was surprisingly agile for someone who looked like the dead.

The hallway turned left, and I raced on. My heart pounded and my legs shook. I was weak, but I dug in deep, finding the strength to surge on. Hands grabbed my hair, jerking me to a painful halt.

"You stupid little bitch," Ton'Yana hissed. His fetid breath hit my nose, and I gagged. He pulled harder on my hair. I winced, fingers clawing at the hand that held. "You will regret this."

The sound of footsteps echoed off the wall. Ton'Yana pulled me around, thrusting me at K'Risgenl.

"Take her to her cell and teach her a lesson."

K'Risgenl's lips pulled back into a smile, showing rotted teeth. "With pleasure," he purred.

I struggled in his grasp as he half carried and half dragged me back to my cell.

"Please," I begged. "Don't do this. Let me go. I promise I won't tell anyone."

He said nothing as the door slammed behind him. The sound of his belt clearing loops filled me with fear. There was a whoosh, and then the leather bit into my flesh. I screamed at the feel. Over and over, the belt bit into my skin. Blood oozed from wounds, pain radiated through my entire body. A boot connected with my midsection, taking the air from my lungs. K'Risgenl grabbed my hair and yanked my head back.

"You will learn," he hissed, spittle hitting me in the face. "You will do what you are told." He released me with a shove, and I collapsed to the ground, wincing as the door closed with a slam.

The scent of blood and urine filled my nose. I pulled my knees to my chest. Tears ran down my cheeks. I was trapped. Completely trapped. The only way out of my predicament was death. I gave a silent prayer up to the gods that they would take me.

I WASN'T THAT LUCKY.

Even with the festering wounds, the lack of food and sleep, the rations of water, despite all of that, I lived.

Every night I prayed, no, begged, to die, but the blast of cold water that woke me when I closed my eyes reminded me I still lived. I lay on the cold, wet floor, my body racked with chills. The voice in my head sang a song. It was a sweet tune meant to comfort me, I knew.

"That was nice," I said when it was over. "Sing it again."

And so she did.

I reveled in my companion. My friend. Without her, I surely would have gone mad. Or maybe I had. I didn't know. I just knew I drew comfort from this person, this voice, that kept me company in the dark.

I don't know how long they left me this time. The aching hunger was a forgotten memory. The pain from the whipping, the wounds that opened, the wounds that festered and stunk, replaced any other feeling I might have had. I was weak, barely having the strength to lift my head, and I was tired. So damn tired.

The sound of the door opening broke the silence. The voice stopped singing, and we braced for frigid water. But it never came. The scent of food, beneath the smell of antiseptic, filled the room. My stomach clenched and my mouth watered.

Feet scuffed, the door shut. The clang of a tray being set on the floor echoed. I heard a flint striking and blocked my eyes from the harsh light as a torch flamed to life. Ton'Yana squatted down in front of me. He wrinkled his nose.

"You smell foul," he said.

I said nothing.

"You can have food and a bath. I will tend to your wounds. In return, you will do everything that I say. You will not try to run away again. If you do, I will break your legs. Is that clear?"

Closing my eyes, I took a deep, shuddering breath. "Yes. I will do whatever you want, Ton'Yana," I said, my voice barely above a whisper.

"That's what I thought."

I blinked back the tears as he tended my wounds. As my plight crashed down around me. I ate my food and when he left, when I was plunged back into darkness, I pulled myself against the wall. When my tears had dried, when I had no more pity to give, I took a deep breath.

"I accept my fate," I said out loud. "I am no longer Lillyanna Castille. I have no name. I am no one. My life belongs to my master."

The voice in my head chuckled. *Good girl. Forget the past. Forget it all. You are no one.*

"I am no one."

Over and over again, I said the words, "I am no one. I have no past" until it became truth. Until my name was forgotten. Until everything was forgotten.

Until all I knew was this cell. And Ton'Yana.

FIFTY-SEVEN
DAMIYUN

WE LEFT WELL BEFORE the sun woke. I wanted to put as much distance between me and Erador—between me and my brother—as I could. I would not allow myself to get caught again.

We stuck to the shadows, carefully walking—occasionally running—the horses out of the village. As the sun began to wake, we paused periodically, my keen ears listening. There were no signs of Suppressors, though we remained vigilant. As the miles stretched and the sun rose higher above the horizon, I felt safer, more secure.

For now.

We rode for hours, though it would be at least three Moon Cycles to get where we needed to be. The place we rightfully should have started. We journeyed in silence, finally pulling over to a clearing to rest. After unsaddling the horses, Abraham stalked off to find food, while I made a fire. I kept the flames high, the sound of wolves howling and wraiths screeching in the distance made me extra vigilant. And aware.

Settling back against a tree, I watched the flames. I could feel Abraham's disapproval through the bond. Not that I needed it. The way he glowered at me said enough. If I could go back and change what happened, the gods knew I would. Regardless of the consequences of refusing an invitation from the Goddess of Nature, I would have pleaded—no, begged—Lil to let us leave that night. I would have ignored the invitation and instead held my Lil in my arms and comforted her.

But I didn't.

Instead, I let my selfishness—my lust—dictate my actions, and I feared for my Lil. Feared my salvation was forever lost to me. I didn't want to admit it, but I feared a horrible fate had befallen her while I stayed with the Wilde Elves. My selfish need to learn more about my mother had sealed her fate.

A noise pulled my attention, the sound like water being poured over hot coals. Pulling my sword, I rose, scanning the woods beyond, my vision clear as day despite the darkness. A massive figure at least ten feet high stood on hooved feet. Sharp spikes protruded from its back; huge dragon-like head with red eyes swung in my direction. Decaying lips pulled back in a smile revealing razor sharp teeth. I gripped my sword, feeling the power of the jewels and pulled my magic.

"Damiyun Rayne," the beast snarled. I stumbled at hearing it speak my name. None ever did. The fact this demon did gave me pause.

"How do you know my name?"

A low rumble vibrated through his chest. "I have been sent to find you."

I frowned. Themesis wouldn't have sent a demon to find me. He'd just have Abraham call my contract. "Who sent you?"

The beast took a step forward, lowering its head, eyes on me. "Oh, Brother. Do you think you can best me? You will never win against me." Arden's voice flowed from the demon's mouth and my blood ran cold. What had he done? Gripping my sword tight, I pulsed my magic through. The blade came alight with fire.

"I don't know what it is Arden sent you to do, but I can assure you, you will die before you complete your task."

The demon chuckled as he took another step closer. I held my sword aloft and fought the urge to turn and run. "You will make a tasty snack," he said.

"Not likely."

My eyes tracked the beast as he slowly circled me, his tongue flicking out to taste the air. "Where is the girl?"

I clenched my jaw. What was Arden playing at? "Some place safe. You will not touch her."

The beast snorted and stopped his circling. "I am an amicable demon. I am willing to forget this encounter. For a price, of course." His sharp teeth flashed in the moonlight.

I laughed. "Of course, and I am sure my life will be spared." I shook my head. "I do not negotiate with demons."

The beast snarled, jaws snapping in anger. Twirling my sword, I got into a fighting stance, pulsing my Elven magic to entwine with the flame. The jewels in the hilt buzzed and glowed. Tendrils of red, blue, and white wrapped around the flaming blade. "Shall we dance?"

I leaped at the demon, slashing the glowing blade. The beast howled in pain as it cut through an arm as though cutting through butter.

The beast pulled back, taking a deep breath it fired a plume of fire at me, singing my shirt and hair.

I laughed. "Do you think you can kill me with fire? I am the flame." I leaped forward, slashing with the glowing blade in quick succession, slicing limbs, slashing flesh, and finally plunging my blade into the beast's heart. The demon collapsed to the ground. Releasing my magic, I pulled my blade from the beast, and sheathed it. What was Arden playing at?

"What happened?"

Abraham's voice drew my attention. He strode into the clearing carrying a rabbit. His eyes went to the dead beast in the ground.

"Arden sent this demon after me and Lil. Its intent was to kill me and capture her." I glanced at the body. "Obviously that didn't happen."

Abraham grunted as he prepared the rabbit, placing it in a spit and securing it above the fire. We sat down in the ground, watching the meat cook. The sounds of wraiths, wolves, and other monsters echoed through the night. Rising, I gathered sturdy logs, brush, and twigs, lighting them in the fire and securing a perimeter around the camp, then settled down to eat. We consumed our meal in silence. My thoughts were on the demon encounter. I admit I was surprised the demon did not kill Arden like the one in the alley,

After so many nights on the road, I was travel worn. My body ached from sleeping on the ground, and I knew Xander had grown tired of the brief rests. Finally, after two-and-a-half Moon Cycles, a town with a worn sign that read Theonaus came into view.

The land was half a day's ride from Shadow Elf territory.

We guided our horses through the muddied streets, my eyes scanning the village. It was a shabby place, rough and downtrodden. I felt the nefarious eyes of bandits sizing me and Abraham up. I loosened my dagger and glared at those faces looking for an easy mark as we trotted through.

I held my magic close, and we continued through the village in search of an inn. We found one after a bit and pulled our horses up to a place called "The Broken Wench." We slipped off our mounts, slipped the bits loose, and let them go. I had no doubt they would be missing come morning if we tied them out front, but I knew Xander would stay close.

We entered the stifling hot tavern filled with rowdy and rough-looking clientele. A bard played a lively and bawdy tune that had the men clapping and stamping their feet. Pushing our way through the crowd, we took the last empty table in the place and sat. Abraham ordered a bottle of Serpent's Venom, and we settled back in our seats. I turned my attention to the rowdy crowd and the bard whose song had the men hollering:

She's not one to bring home to your mother
Watch out. Or she'll fuck your brother,
Her cunny is sweet
A delight to eat
And she'd be the best you'll have (you'll have).
Her legs will spread for a copper
Though some might think her improper
She'll drop to her knees

Eager to please
And she'd be the best you'll have (you'll have.).
And she struts and she struts
Like a cat who's in heat
And she has something delightful
A decadent treat
And your coin it will pay
For her cunny to lay
And she is the best you'll have (you'll have.)

My eyes went to the woman dancing on the table, who was pulled off her perch, and passed around the men. This was a rowdy and despicable town indeed. Turning back to my drink, a flash of red hair caught my eye. I watched a young woman weave around the crowd. She bumped into customers, slipping her hand into their pockets and relieving them of coin. She looked around, and though she was thin, painfully so, I recognized her eyes and the matted red hair. I would never forget the face of the woman I loved. The woman I betrayed.

"Lillyanna," I said. I rose from my seat, eyes on Lil as she wove her way through the crowd.

"Where?" Abraham's voice pulled my attention.

Shit. I lost sight of her. I scanned the crowd, seeing a flash of red. "There." I pointed. She stood beside a tall, thin man who spoke in her ear. She nodded and dove back into the crowd. I moved to follow her: Abraham's hand clamped on my arm.

"Wait."

I glared down at him. "For what? She's here. We have her."

He shook his head. "She's not the same, Damiyun. Sit down, and we will figure out a rational way to get her."

I snorted. "You have been chastising me for what happened, for losing her, and now that we have found her you want to take more time to discuss this?" I pulled my arm from his grasp. "No, Abraham. I am going to get her."

"Damiyun—"

"Fuck off, Abraham. I am doing this my way."

Stepping around the table, I pushed through the crowd searching for a flash of red, catching it out of the corner of my eye. I tracked her as she pushed through people to the other side of the tavern. I watched her bump into a patron. Watched her slip a hand in the pocket and extract a pouch of coin, stowing it in her cloak. She glanced around, then pushed deeper into the throng. I pushed my way toward her, ignoring the angry grumbles, clutching the hilt of my dagger, ready to cut anyone who got in my way.

I kept my eyes on the matted hair of red that darted around the patrons, catching up with her in moments. I grabbed her arm, she whirled around, eyes wide, fear flashing in the green depths.

"Lillyanna," I said.

She jerked her arm, but I held tight. "Who are you?"

My heart dropped at her words. "I am Damiyun."

"I don't know anyone by that name."

My heart sank further, and I swallowed past the lump that formed in my throat. "Lillyanna—"

Her eyes flashed with anger, and she jerked her arm again. "Why do you call me that? I know not that name," she said. Her eyes darted around, then met mine. "Please, let me go. My father... he will hurt me."

Father?

"If you will not give me coin, let me go." Her eyes darted about wild and strained.

I gripped her arm tighter. I was not going to let her go. Not when I had her in my grasp. "Lil, please. Come with me—"

My words were cut off by a sharp knee to my groin.

"Fuck," I let her go, falling to my knees as pain radiated through my groin and sickness welled within my stomach. I watched the swatch of red fly through the crowd moving toward the door. Toward outside.

I would not let her go.

Gritting my teeth, I rose to my feet, biting back the pain and nausea, stumbling through the crowd toward the door. I burst out into the cold, dark night, my cat vision letting me see as though it were midday. Scanning the streets, I caught Lillyanna running toward a grove of trees. I took off after her, my long legs quickly eating up the distance. She looked over her shoulder, eyes widening with fear as I drew closer. She stumbled, a root catching her boot, and tumbled to the ground. Skidding to a halt, I dropped to my knees beside her. Fear marked her face and she scrambled to her feet.

"Lillyanna," I said softly, looking up at her. Dead, green eyes showed no recognition. She only had fear. I saw it in her stiff muscles, her shortened breath and the strain in her countenance. "I don't know who you think I am, but I am not her," she said, voice soft. Her face screwed up in thought. She nodded, then muttered something under her breath.

Though I was loath to admit it, Abraham was right. This wasn't my Lil. While she looked like her, she was nothing more than a shell. Her skin on someone I didn't know. Someone who didn't know me, and it hurt me to see her dead eyes. The lack of recognition. It hurt me to see her terrified of me.

I rose to my feet and looked down at her. "You're right," I said, swallowing past the lump in my throat. "You aren't who I thought you were." I reached a hand out and though she flinched, I cupped her chin. "I will bring you back, Lillyanna. I will find a way."

"Go," she said. "Please?" Fearful eyes met mine. "He will hurt me."

I looked over my shoulder and saw the same man she was speaking to earlier stepping out of the tavern. He was tall and thin. His clothes hung on his skeletal frame. Milky white eyes scanned the night. My heart pounded in my ears and my magic burned beneath my skin. I knew this was the man who hurt my Lil. This man had wiped her memory, made her forget herself.

Forget who I was. My blood roiled.

I pulled my magic close. I could get rid of him. Burn him to ash but... My eyes took in the people, the innocents that were in the way, and I released my hold.

"Please." Lil's voice pulled me back, and I looked at her. "Give me coin. It doesn't have to be all you have, just... something." She looked over my shoulder. Her body tensed.

"I can save you."

"You can't."

"I can. I know who you are."

She stiffened. "I am no one."

She started to walk away. I grabbed her arm and pulled her back. She looked frantically over my shoulder again, and I looked up, my eyes on the man she had called father. His gaze narrowed on me, and he pushed his way through the small crowd to where I stood with Lil.

"Run."

"No."

She looked up at me. "He will kill you."

I snorted. "Not likely."

"Let me go."

I glanced down at her. "No."

She pulled away from me. A smile curled her lips. "No. Stop. Please," she cried. Heads turned in my direction, eyes locked on me.

"Lil—" my words were cut off as her knee came up and connected with my groin again. This time harder. It took my breath. I dropped to my knees, gasping for air. Through my pain haze, I saw Lillyanna run to the man, and I marked him. Through my pain, I saw him. My heart pounded. Heat radiated through me, and I saw nothing but red. Nothing but his blood flowing, his head at my feet, and I vowed to destroy him.

"Damiyun," Abraham's voice cut through my rage. I massaged between my legs and grit my teeth against the pain and grabbed the hand he held down. "She's not who you thought she was," he said, hauling me to my feet.

I took a deep breath, closed my eyes and let it out. "No, she's not." I opened my eyes and followed Abraham back to the tavern, taking our seats at the table. Abraham ordered another round of spirits.

"Drink," he said, pushing the bottle into my hand.

I took a long pull. The heat of the spirits warmed me. I will drink until my pain is gone. I will get my Lil back, and I will make the ones who broke her regret the day they were born.

FIFTY-EIGHT
ARDEN

V EL WAS LESS THAN pleased my brother escaped, but he was livid when I told him the bitch had gone missing.

"You fucking idiot," he snarled. He slammed his fists on the desk and rose from his chair. His eyes flashed with anger. Patches of red tinted his cheeks. The chords on his neck stood out. I sipped my wine and propped a leg on my knee.

"You let her go," he fumed. Spittle hit my face. I wiped it off and took another sip of my drink, my eyes on him as he sat back down.

Oh, Vel. Look at how pathetic you are. You think this was my fault? I chuckled. Was the old man starting to lose his composure? The possibility deserved attention.

"What is so funny, Arden?"

You.

Rising from my chair, I crossed the room, refilling my glass from the decanter on the sideboard. I could feel Vel's eyes on me. Feel the anger rolling off him. I sat back down and took a sip, eyes on Vel, my fingers drumming on the armrest.

"You're the one who let her roam free. You let my brother stay with her. She should have been locked in a cell chained to the wall." A picture of her flashed through my mind. A look of fear in her eyes as I approached, ready to cause her pain. I closed my eyes and took a deep, calming breath, adjusting my position to ease the ache between my legs. "This is your fault, not mine," I gestured with my glass.

His nostrils flared and his jaw tensed. "Do not try to place the blame on me for your incompetence."

I snorted into my glass. *You are the incompetent one here, Vel.*

"You will be punished for this," he said.

I chuckled to myself as I thought about the whipping. It was meant to keep me in line. To show me who was in charge, I knew, but the biting pain, the scent of my blood, gave me pleasure. It reminded me I was strong. No one could break me. Not my father, and certainly not Vel.

I walked through the halls. The sound of my boots on the polished black marble floor echoed off the stone walls. The silver light of the moon poured through the windows, casting shadows. I glanced at the portraits adorning the walls and stopped to genuflect at the painting of Zachariah Farnsworth. His dark eyes stared coldly at the artist who had captured his likeness. Blond hair fell in waves about his shoulders. The crimson robe he wore over the uniform of the Suppressors looked like a waterfall of blood pouring over him.

The blood of Wielders.

He was a god to me. I devoured his teachings like a starving dog. His words were gospel. They were the foundation of which I lived. Zachariah would have been proud of his devout disciple. Proud of the one who remembered what the Suppressors were about. Why they were formed. Kissing my fingertips, I placed them on the painting. Genuflecting again, I continued my way through the Compound to Vel's den, pushing the door open and striding through. Vel sat behind his desk, head bent over papers. He looked up at the creak of the hinges, a look of annoyance flitted across his face.

"What do you want, Arden? I am very busy."

I sat in a chair, crossing my arms. Vel sighed, placing the quill in the pot of ink. Folding his hands on the desk, he leveled his gaze on me.

"Recent events have made me think about the Order and what we stand for," I said. "Recite the five principles of the Order."

Vel's jaw clenched, and I knew he didn't know them.

"One. Wielders are a plague on this world. Two. Magic is a taint that infects others. Three. Magic is an evil born from the Abyss. Four. All magic must be eradicated. Five. A dead Wielder is better than a captured Wielder." I recited the words, the mantra, that I lived my life by.

Vel's eyes narrowed. "What is your point, Arden?"

I leaned forward in my chair. "What sort of leader are you that you can't even recite the Five Principles that formed the Order? Do you know any of the articles? I would be happy to recite them for you. Especially Article Seventy-two," I paused. "The Suppressors are a righteous organization. Those who join will uphold the principles and laws. They will seek out Wielders and rid the world of them through any means necessary. A dead Wielder is better than a captured Wielder."

Vel's jaw clenched. "What is your point?" he asked again.

Standing, I placed my fists on his desk and looked down at him. "My point is that neither you nor Quint seem to be adhering to the principles and articles contained within the Suppressor Doctrine," I said. "If all Wielders must be eradicated, why do the Elves get a pass?"

"You know why. They provide the Sigaa'Lean. It is in the treaty we have with them."

I snorted. "Aren't they Wielders?"

Vel's nostrils flared. "As are you and I."

I scoffed. Sometimes upholding the Five Principles meant breaking a few. "You know as well as I that the treaty is antiquated. They only drew it up to protect themselves," I continued. I stood and crossed my arms. "And the Fae?"

"You think you know what you are talking about, but you don't," he said. "We are done here." He shuffled the papers on his desk and picked up the quill, his dismissal evident.

He might be done with me, but I was not done with upholding Zachariah's principles and laws. Striding out of the room, I headed to the building that housed the Suppressors. I would gather a dozen of my best men and head out.

It was high time we paid a visit to the Shadow Elves.

FIFTY-NINE
PHABIAN

IT HAD BEEN FOUR Moon Cycles since Lillyanna was turned out. Her departure left a surprising hole inside me. I would often find myself walking toward the library, expecting to see her in her favorite chair, reading *"The Story of Jayne"* for the umpteenth time. I would catch myself before I got to the door, my chest constricting and eyes burning when I realized she wasn't there. That she would never be there again.

I had grown fond of Lillyanna. I considered her a friend, and she opened up to me in ways I didn't imagine, and I kept what she told me a secret.

"Phabian." Allendaire's voice broke my reverie.

"Forgive me, my king. I drifted off. Say it again," I said, dipping my quill in ink, holding it above the tax ledger.

Allendaire was reciting the payments from his recent collection, and I was checking the numbers in the ledger. He closed his book with a thud.

"I know you cared about her, Phabian," he said. He didn't need to tell me who he had on his mind. "I loved Lillyanna."

No, you didn't. She was just a vessel to give you an heir. I knew his thoughts. Knew his feelings. I had delved into his mind while he slept. He felt no love for anyone but himself.

Clearing my throat, I dipped my quill back in the ink. "Where were we?"

Allendaire opened his book with a sigh. Long fingers ran down the page, the lamplight glinting off the jewels of his rings. "Drakus Trounde, full payment. Vindie Trounde, no payment. Tomorrow, he will bring me his deed."

On and on it went. My back hurt from being hunched over the ledger. Fingers ached from holding the quill, and a headache threatened to manifest. Finally, after three hours, we were done. Closing the ledger, I pulled my body out of the chair, stretching the kinks out. I was drained. There was only one place that would wake me up. One place that would make me feel better, and so I headed to the nursery.

I heard the screams of Serafin as I entered the wing. The sound somehow broke through the room, filling the hall. I couldn't help but laugh. She was an ornery girl. A princess in her own right. I nodded to the two men who guarded the door, my cousin, Narl, and my third brother, Stanz. Though Allendaire had made it clear what would happen if any harm came to Serafin, he posted the guards as an added precaution.

"She's quite vocal today," Narl said. Stanz winced as Serafin shrieked again. Laughing, I opened the door to the nursery, seeing why she screamed like a banshee.

Mouranda held her.

The queen bounced her and cooed nonsense, but Serafin wailed, her face purple, fists punching the sky.

"My queen," I said, bowing my head to her. I looked up at her, trying to keep a straight face. I would not deny that it gave me a bit of pleasure knowing my Little Princess did not like the queen. Serafin turned my way, her screams stopping. Blue-green eyes looked at me.

"Phabian," Mouranda said.

Serafin squirmed in her arms. Tiny hands reached out to me, and a smile lit the small child's face.

Mouranda sighed. "Take her then. She seems to like you more than me," she said, handing the child over. I cradled Serafin in my arms. She giggled and settled against me.

"What am I doing wrong?" Mouranda's blue eyes flashed with envy as I cradled the princess. Serafin grabbed my hair and pulled. I stuck my tongue out at her, and she laughed with glee.

"I don't know," I said, bouncing my Little Princess in my arms. *She knows you are not her mother. You never tried to bond with her.*

"What can I do?" She took a step closer. Serafin looked at the queen and a loud wail pierced the room. She buried her face in my chest, her body shaking with fear. I rubbed her back and made soothing sounds. Mouranda's thin shoulders slumped, and she turned toward the door.

"You wish to know what to do?"

She paused and turned to look at me. "Be a mother to her. Show her you love her." I looked down at my Little Princess, smoothing a tuft of white hair streaked with red. I looked back at Mouranda. "Be a mother," I said again.

"I'm trying."

"Try harder."

"She hates me."

Rightfully so. "Read to her. *"The Story of Jayne"* is a book Lillyanna would read to Serafin when she was a babe in the womb." Serafin looked up at the mention of the book. Such a precocious child she was at such a young age. "Perhaps if the wet nurse were to pump her breasts, it could allow you to feed her. Perhaps that will forge a bond."

Mouranda nodded. "I will talk to her. Thank you," she said, then left the room.

Sitting down in a rocking chair, I adjusted Serafin in my arms. Her blue-green eyes looked at me, clear and alert.

"My Little Princess. I will tell you all about your mother when you can understand," I said. Sadness filled me and not for the first time did I think of bundling the princess up, sneaking her out of the palace and finding Lillyanna. But where would I start my search? How would I find her, and if I did, what sort of life would she have? I shook off the thoughts as I did hundreds of times before, telling myself Serafin was better off where she was. She would be pampered and never know an empty stomach.

A tiny hand pulled my hair, and I turned my attention back to the babe in my arms.

"What?" I pinched a chubby cheek. She cooed, fingers clutching mine, pulling it into her mouth. Slowly, I rocked the chair and sang an Elven lullaby that mothers would sing to their children at bedtime.

"Hush my child
Close your small eyes
Fall to sleep
Let darkness rise
Hid in shade
Wants you to come
Fall to him
You will succumb
Do not fight
You cannot win
Razor claws
Tears off your skin
Sharp teeth glint
From his large maw
Crushing bones
In mighty jaws
Hush my child
It's just a dream
Hush my child
Hush your loud screams
Wake my child
Today anew
See my child
The beast is you."

I looked down at Serafin whose eyes were closed, thumb stuck in her mouth. Rising from the chair, careful to not disturb the sleeping princess, I crossed the room to the crib and, kissing her forehead, I placed her in it, and tucked the blanket around her.

"Sleep well, my Little Princess," I said.

The sound of the door opening pulled my attention. I turned, seeing Krall enter the nursery. A look of disgust crossed his face.

"How can you stand to spend so much time with it? It stinks and drools. Its piercing wails are enough to make me plunge a dagger into its chest."

My nostrils flared at his words. I stalked across the room to him. "You'd best watch your mouth. I would hate to see my favorite eldest brother's head on a spike. Her name is Serafin, and she is your future queen." I jabbed him in the chest with my finger.

Krall's eyes narrowed. "I will never kneel before a filthy half breed cunt. The child of the King's Whore."

My blood boiled at his words, but I said nothing. He wasn't the only one to profess his sentiment. I knew her birth would be under contention, but who was I to disagree? To go against my king? But as many as there were who hated Serafin, there were those who found joy in my Little Princess, though they rarely and quietly voiced it.

"What do you want, Krall?" I said, following him out of the room.

"I spotted about a dozen Suppressors at our eastern borders.

I frowned. "What would they be doing here? And why so many?"

Krall rolled his eyes. "That's what we're going to find out. I've readied Max-amillian's saddle. I will see you out front."

Nodding, I hurried to my room, strapped on my sword, quiver of arrows, and slung my bow over my shoulder. I also slid a dagger in my boot and belt for good measure, then met Krall, Lazaro, his brother, Emory, and my eldest brother, Garson. They sat astride their mounts, heavily armed. A few new recruits had joined them. Erglen, Traln, and Myrdd shifted in their saddles, eyes wide. Erglen scratched the tip of his nose and jumped the moment an owl hooted. Patrol duty would season them sooner than mere practice in the yard.

"Does the king know?" I looked at Krall as I swung up into the saddle. Max danced on his feet, and I patted his neck.

"No. I thought it best to find out what they want before burdening him with a frivolity."

Nodding, I heeled Max to the east. Krall fell in step to my right, Laz to my left, with Emory, Garson and the others following behind. We rode in silence, the horses' hooves crunching on the snow the only sound. As we neared the border, Laz and I nocked an arrow while the others drew swords. I looked around. The bare trees made it easier to see, and I spotted a swatch of black several yards into the woods.

"There." I pointed my arrow in the direction. "You are trespassing on Shadow Elf Lands," I said, raising my voice and guiding Max forward. "I am sure you are aware of what happens to strangers on our lands."

A man sitting astride a black mount walked his horse forward. Four other men flanked him. The sign of the Suppressor, two swords crossed over a scarlet "S" was embroidered on his cloak.

"Come now. You wouldn't start a war with the Suppressors, would you?"

Lazaro and I raised our bows, leveling arrows at his head. "Do you wish to find out?"

"Don't you want to know why we are here?"

"Not particularly," Laz said.

I snorted. The man guided his horse closer. "I wish to discuss the Sigaa'Lean."

"And you needed a dozen of you to do that?" Krall said.

The man waved his hand. "Just a precaution. I know how you Shadow Elves can be."

I sighed, growing bored with the conversation. "State your business and then leave." I lowered my bow, but only slightly.

"I wish to know how to make the bracelet."

I frowned.

"It must be tiresome sending Elves out to deliver them to us, especially in these dark times, demons and other creatures prowling the lands. And we run out fast," he said.

"You wish to nullify the treaty," I said. "You should know it has been in place for thousands of Grand Passages."

Blue eyes narrowed on me. "And you should know the Order's job is to eradicate those with magic."

"We are aware of what you do. Just as you are aware, the treaty gives us immunity."

His nostrils flared. I raised my arrow back up. Krall, Emory, and Garson raised their swords, guiding their mounts a few steps closer. We were outnumbered, we knew, but Lazaro and I were deft and accurate with the bow and could fell this group before they drew swords and charge. The newer recruits held back. Smart. They had yet to see a battle. Myrdd, feeling a bit bolder, moved closer to Lazaro and I.

"I will, of course, raise your request with the king, but do not expect an answer different from mine." I pulled the string on the bow back to my ear, Lazaro doing the same. "Now. Take your men and leave our lands. My king will send his answer via a letter.

"I look forward to hearing from your king," he snapped, pulling his mount around. "Let's go," he said to his men.

I released the string, keeping my arrow nocked and ready, and watched them leave.

"Follow them. Make sure they exit completely. Be quick about it. Dark is falling," I ordered Garson. Nodding, he guided his horse behind.

I put my arrow back in the quiver and slung the bow around my shoulder. "We will wait until Garson comes back. We leave no one behind at night. I want you all to hold your magic close."

They would obey. Sure enough, as soon as darkness fell, foul shapes with eyes of fire and sharpened claws emerged from between the trees. I steadied my bow. Specters struck, several surrounded Erglen, who had wandered a bit too far from the group. He fought to return, but his green eyes wide with terror, mouth open, went down in a silent howl. The ghosts, wispy thin, devoured him. His skin shrank and rippled, dried to a prune-like husk. Screams pierced the void of darkness as shrill as a child. The veterans lit torches to ward off the spirits and the demons.

I let loose an arrow. One demon took it in the shoulder. Another tried to pounce on Lazaro, but he swept his blade through the horned creature's throat.

We had ceased border patrol because of the demons and ghosts. But the Suppressors, they did not belong on our lands. We had an agreement, much as I didn't like it.

With fire and swords, we finished off another demon. The specters fled from the fire and the fight was over. "Let's get Erglen back to his family." I motioned to Myrdd and Traln. Better to keep their minds on a task. The way they shivered; I knew it was not from any chill. I snapped, "Come on. Get to it." They moved and quickly.

I was never a believer in the gods. None of the Shadow Elves were. It was laughable to think there were deities sitting around determining the fate of all, but what comes out in the dark gave me pause and what I had observed in Lillyanna's mind—her mother. It made me think, though not entirely believe, there possibly was more than us.

I eyed the sky, noting the rapidly descending sun, sighing in relief when Garson's horse stepped out of the woods.

"They're gone," he said.

I nodded, turning Max around, I said, "Let's go." Not waiting for a response, I heeled him back toward the palace. We had our mounts stabled and were tucked away safe and secure inside the palace walls when the wails of more monsters pierced the night. I urged Traln and Myrdd to go drink off the experience and to sleep. No reason to dwell on what could not be changed.

I made my way back to the nursery. Opening the door, I saw Allendaire sitting in the rocking chair, reading to Serafin. Not wishing to disturb him with the trivial encounter, I quietly withdrew and made my way to my room. Lazaro lounged in a chair in front of the marble fireplace, the flames roaring, warming the room.

"Make yourself at home, Laz," I said, as I removed my weapons and cloak.

He flashed a smile, then rose to his feet, slipping his arms around me and pressing his lips to mine. He tasted like candy as he kissed me in a slow, sensual way. I groaned against his mouth. "It's been a while since we've had time alone," he said, his breath soft on my face.

"I know. Allendaire keeps me busy," I said. Taking his hand, I sat down in a chair, sinking into the soft cushions. I pulled him onto my lap, teasing him with my mouth.

"I wish the king didn't keep you so busy," he murmured.

My teeth grazed his ear, and he shivered. "I'm here now."

He pulled back, blue eyes filled with desire, looked at me. "You are very much here," he said, slipping a hand between my legs and massaging my hardness. I groaned.

"Did you speak to the king about the Suppressors?"

I brushed a lock of hair behind his ear and nipped his chin with my teeth. "No. He was in the nursery reading to Serafin."

Lazaro's hand stopped. His jaw clenched and eyes flashed with anger. He opened his mouth to speak. I gripped his chin, my fingers digging into his skin. "Say one thing about my Little Princess, and I will tie you to a tree in the woods and leave you for the demons."

He jerked his face out of my grip. "You wouldn't."

I pushed him off my lap and rose, any desire I had for him evaporating. "Try me," I said, stalking across the room. I yanked the doors to the balcony open and stepped out. The cold air was refreshing after the heat of the room. The scrape of Lazaro's shoe on the stone told me he had followed.

"You know how I feel about Serafin just as well as you know how I felt about Lillyanna," I said without turning. "Say one word against either one, and my threat will become a promise, despite however I may feel about you."

He stepped up beside me and slipped an arm around my waist in a quiet apology. I looked around the grounds. My eyes caught the misty wisps of ghosts and the fire eyes of the demons in the shadows of the woods. The hair on the back of my neck stood up, and my legs became weak at the disembodied scream echoing through the night.

"Something is coming, Laz. Something dark and evil." Much worse than what we had encountered earlier. I knew it in my bones. My ears twitched, and a tightness settled in my chest.

"I feel it too," he said.

Another wail pierced the night, and Lazaro shivered. "Let's get inside," he said, stepping away and quickly going into the room. I followed, closing the doors and pulling the curtains tight.

I stepped up behind where Lazaro stood in front of the fire, warming his hands. "Are you scared?" I whispered in his ear, wrapping my arms around him, pulling him close.

"It's a bit disconcerting."

I pulled away with a laugh. "Come," I said, slipping a hand in his and tugging him toward the bed. "Let us ease each other's fears."

He smiled as he followed me across the room, where we fell to the bed in a tangled mass of limbs. The wails continued, and I tried to ignore the screams that rose and fell like wind.

Something was coming indeed, and I feared it would devour and destroy us all.

SIXTY

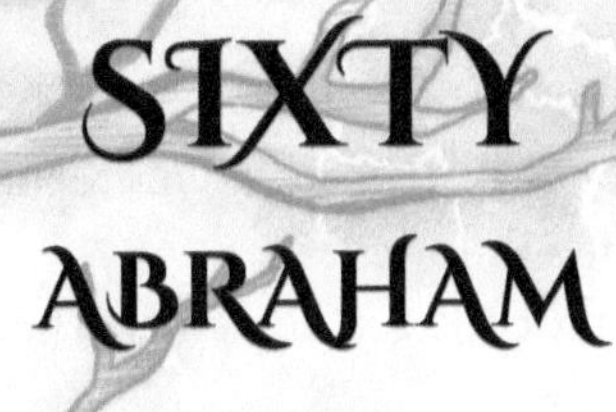

ABRAHAM

Exiting the tavern, I slipped out into the streets, while the light faded to dusk. I wandered around for a bit, searching for any sign of Lillyanna, or that man.

I wandered through the streets to a tavern seedier than The Broken Wench, The Barbarian's Creed.

The candles in the lanterns burned low, blanketing corners in ominous and ghostly shadows. Glinting eyes and knives caught the flickering light. A haze of smoke hung in the air, burning my eyes, and making the room shimmer from the tears.

It looked rough enough, the name described perfectly the patrons within. Dark eyes peered out from beneath cautious brows.

It was an odious bunch, a menacing lot.

A few whores weaved their way through the crowd, happy to accept a copper for a feel. Maybe two for a bounce on a lap.

My eyes scanned the crowd, falling on a woman bustling about cleaning tables. Her face was tired, and she seemed oblivious to the hands grabbing at her as she pushed her way through, carrying a tray laden with mugs and plates.

"Yarnnalay," I said, stopping a few feet from her as she bent over, grabbing glasses and plates, and balancing them on the full tray.

"No, I am not a whore. Get your rocks off on the other girls," she said, not even looking back as she wiped down the table with a dirty rag.

"That is not what I am looking for."

"Well, whatever it is, I am not interested. They need your coin more than I do," she said, hoisting the tray onto her shoulder.

"Yarnnalay," I said again, my tone sharp.

She sighed and swung her head in my direction. "I told you I—" Her face turned white and the tray she held crashed to the floor. Plates and glasses broke, and the tavern went silent for a moment. The ring of blades being drawn pierced the brief silence, but the weapons were once again sheathed when it was clear there was not a brawl to partake in.

"No. Please. It can't be," she said. Her voice shook, and she held one hand out as if to ward me off. She pressed the other to her chest.

"You knew the terms."

"Yes but—but I thought—"

"That I would forget? Or perhaps give you more time?"

Her throat bobbed as she swallowed.

"You put your name on the contract. You knew what you were getting yourself into."

"But—my son Micah. I can't leave him."

I frowned. "Was your husband not cured when you made the deal? Does he not live?"

She wrung her hands and shifted on her feet. "Yes, to all of that, but... He left me when he found out Micah wasn't his."

I shrugged. "That's not my problem. Let's get this over with." I turned to leave, her hand on my arm stopped me.

"Please. I can't leave him."

"So, send him to live with a relative. I will give you time to write and send a letter off."

"They won't take the bastard son of a whore. There must be something you can do."

I rubbed my eyes and sighed. While I shouldn't have cared—should just have done my job—the father I once was, would not allow me to abandon a child, allow him to die in the rough streets, or worse, an orphanage.

I stepped toward her and put a hand on her shoulder. She shrank back at my touch.

"I can make you no promises, but I will see if there is anything I can do, if only for the boy."

"Thank you," she said, turning her tear-stained face to me.

Don't thank me yet.

I strode out of the tavern, pulling the darkness around me as I made my way down the streets and slipped into the Abyss, pulling the door open and entering Themesis' tomb.

He was sitting upon Nightshade, the unsightly monstrosity of a throne. My eyes darted to his side.

To Jaylynn kneeling next to him, his hand idly scratching her head.

My blood boiled at the sight. At my daughter, who smiled up at him.

"What do you have for me?" he asked, turning in my direction at the sound of my boots on the polished obsidian floor.

I stood in front of the throne and crossed my arms. I looked up at him, despising the subjugating position.

"A problem."

He raised an eyebrow. "Oh?"

"The woman has a son."

"And that's my problem, why?"

I sighed. "Because if I take her, he will have no one to look after him."

Themesis laughed, and I clenched my fists to keep my hands still. "Do you think I care? Do you think this story might pull on any fatherly heartstrings you think I have?" His eyes locked on mine, and I clenched my jaw.

"Of course not. Why would I think you had any fatherly inclination?" My eyes never left his.

He laughed again, and I wanted to pummel him for it. A soft growl vibrated beneath my beard. I reached up and patted Bel's head, stroking softly, which settled his nerves.

"Perhaps you should take the boy in. After all, you have experience raising a child." He looked down at Jaylynn, tilting her chin, so her rapturous face beamed up at him. She closed her eyes as he caressed her bottom lip with his thumb. "Though I can't say you are the best at keeping children."

"Fuck you."

"Bring the bitch to me. I don't care if they rape the son in an orphanage or if he kills for a living. Her contract has been called, and she must pay the price."

"Hers was not for herself. It was for her husband."

"She signed her name all the same."

Heat flushed my skin. "As a living person."

"You presented her with the contract. She gave over her soul." He leaned forward on his throne.

"There should be rules," I said.

Themesis' eyes narrowed, and he clenched the griffin heads that made up the armrests on his throne. "There are rules. My rules. A person in desperate need prays to me for help, and I send a Soul Collector to them to make them an offer. Those are the rules."

I clenched my fists. "The living shouldn't be able to sell their souls. The dying... they're desperate. They're scared. They would rather not leave."

Themesis' waved his hand. "The living are desperate and scared too. Was this woman, Yarnnalay, not desperate enough to sell her soul to save her husband's life?"

"She has a son."

"I don't care."

"But—"

He leaned forward in his throne, angry blue eyes on me. "I don't care if she has a brood of sniveling brats. She knew what she was doing, and your job is to collect the souls whose contracts I have called."

"I never asked for this job.

His eyes narrowed on me. "As long as you belong to me, you will do my bidding. Now bring me her soul."

"Of course, master," I said, mocking him with a bow. Pulling the shadows around me, I slipped out of the Abyss and back to the world of the living.

NIGHT HAD DESCENDED, AND I made my way through streets rife with drunkards and cutpurses, back to the tavern I had left. I looked around the room, and my eyes found Yarnnalay seated at a table, with a boy of about six sitting next to her. I made my way over and stood before her. Sad eyes met mine, and I stamped down any bit of feeling that crept up. I looked at the boy—Micah—who played with a pile of mashed potatoes on his plate.

A fond memory of Jaylynn entered my mind, and I shook myself of it. No doubt Themesis had put it there in an attempt to make me weak. It was working.

I reached into my pocket and pulled out her contract.

The piece of paper she signed in blood in exchange for her husband's life.

She looked at Micah, smoothing his hair and kissing his forehead before rising to her feet. "I'm ready."

I looked from her to Micah. There had to be a way. The father within would not allow this boy to be abandoned. I unrolled the contract and looked at it. At her blood signature.

At the words I had scrawled in my own blood: *Contract Fulfilled*.

But what if—?

My mind raced, and I pulled the golden quill from my pocket, and drew more of my blood into it. I looked at Yarnnalay and then Micah. Taking a deep breath, I wrote two words across the paper: *Null and Void*.

I had barely pulled the quill back when the words I wrote lit up, flames burning them and enveloping the parchment which combusted and disappeared, leaving nothing behind. Not even a pile of ash.

Themesis' howl reverberated in my mind, but I didn't care.

I had saved an innocent, something I had never done, nor thought I could do.

Yarnnalay's tear-filled eyes looked at me. "Thank you. I swear to you, I will never forget this. I will someday repay what you did."

I said nothing. Turning, I made my way out of the tavern, and back to The Broken Wench.

The tavern was full, though not as it had been before. I scanned the crowd, finding Damiyun where I had left him. Crossing the floor to where he sat, I stood beside the table. He swung his head in my direction, glassy, unfocused eyes on me. I looked down at him. At the pathetic mess sitting at the table with three empty bottles of Serpent's Venom lined up in front of him. I couldn't be completely disgusted with him, not when I knew what he was going through.

Not when I felt his overwhelming guilt and shame through the bond.

Not when I knew he would rather die than see her in the situation she was in again.

"Let's go back, Damiyun," I said.

He tipped back his bottle, finished the remains, then stood up. He swayed on his feet and fell back into the chair.

"Fuck," he cursed, standing again. He took an unsteady step, staggering sideways into the table, knocking the bottles off. Glass shattered and scattered across the floor. I slipped an arm about him, he sagged against me, and I half dragged, half carried him to the room. He fell onto the bed, and I grabbed a blanket and covered him as he settled back against the pillow.

"We will get her back, Damiyun."

I stepped back and glanced outside. Though it was late, I wasn't quite ready to rest.

Reaching into my beard, I pulled out Bel. I held him in my hand, raising him to eye level.

"Keep an eye on him," I instructed. "Don't let him leave. He is in no shape to do anything rash."

Bel's tongue flicked out and licked my cheek, then he scampered down. Hopping up on the bed, he curled up on the pillow next to Damiyun. Turning, I slipped out of the room and back into the night.

SIXTY-ONE

The conversation with Themesis rose my ire. I wandered the dark streets, anger roiling through my veins. It was not up to me to question those who sold their souls. I could understand Yarnnalay's reasons. Though, why a living person would sign a contract binding them to a life in the Abyss serving Themesis was something I couldn't comprehend. She was the first live soul Themesis sent me to with a contract. I did not like doing it, but I served him. It was not until I had to collect, until I saw her child, that I had regrets.

That I second-guessed the rule he had come up with at that moment.

I walked through the nearly empty streets, making my way back to The Screaming Banshee. Opening the door, I stepped into the establishment again. It was nearly empty. My eyes swept the place, finding Yarnnalay placing glasses on a tray. Her son, Micah, sat at the same table in the corner, drawing on a piece of parchment. Various pots of paint sat in front of him, most of which was on the small boy's face and hands. I chuckled, thinking of my Jaylynn and how she would paint, getting more on herself and the table than the parchment.

Shaking off the thought, I walked toward Yarnnalay. My boots clunked on the floor, drawing her attention. Her eyes met mine, and the color drained from her face.

"You...You voided it." Her voice was loud and accusatory.

I held up my hand as I approached the table where she stood. "I did. It is done. There is no contract," I said. "Please. Sit. I wish to talk to you." I gestured to a chair. She cast a glance at Micah who was oblivious, brush flowing across the paper, tongue stuck out in concentration.

"Sit," I said again. I pulled out a chair, and she slumped in it with a defeated sigh.

"What do you want...?" Her eyes questioned me as I lowered my bulk into a chair opposite.

"Abraham."

She took a half full bottle of spirits off the tray and sent it across the table to me. "What do you want, Abraham?"

I took a long pull on the bottle, setting it down with a thud. "I want to know how one of the livings can sell their soul."

I didn't know it was possible, though I knew my Jaylynn had gone to Themesis directly. Her magic was like mine, and she could move about the shadows. She was able to enter the Abyss. But before Yarnnalay, all those who sold their souls were either dead or dying.

Then I was sent to give a living person a contract.

She laughed into the bottle. "You tell me. You gave me the contract."

She sent the bottle back, and I finished it. Rising, she went behind the bar and pulled out another. Settling into her seat, she took another drink. "So?"

I sat back, the chair creaking beneath my weight. "You prayed to the gods. So? How did it happen?"

"The gods," she spat, eyes flashing with anger. "Yes, I prayed to them, but they did nothing." She slammed her fists on the table. "In my dreams, he came." A smile flitted across her lips. I turned at the look. "He said he could help me heal my husband. He was beautiful and charming. Oh, so charming." A wistful look crossed her face.

Of course, he was. You were in need. He only preys on the forsaken. He knew.

"Go on," I said, taking another drink and handing the bottle back.

She took a deep breath. "He said if I were to exchange my soul for him..." she shook her head, and took another drink.

"What did he say? What did he promise?"

Brown eyes met mine. "He said my husband, Demming, would live."

I clenched my fists. "And you agreed."

Her shoulders slumped. "What choice did I have?"

"More choices than that."

"He was my husband."

I glanced over at the table where her son sat happily painting another picture. Yarnnalay's gaze followed mine.

"You think me a whore, like his family does."

I pulled my attention back to her. "No," I said. It wasn't my place to judge. Not when my own mother was a whore. "I think you're a woman who loved her husband. Someone who was desperate." Her eyes met mine. "A woman who found solace in another's arms when all was thought to be lost."

Tears glistened in her eyes. "Yes."

"So why sell your soul? Why give yourself to Themesis? You knew what would happen when you signed the contract I gave you."

I could understand the dead, but not the living.

She took a deep breath, her hands clenched on the table. "Because I loved him. I did." Tear-filled eyes met mine. "There was no way of knowing what was going to happen and after... after you came, after Demming lived..." She closed her eyes.

I didn't need her to continue. I knew what she felt. Reaching across the table, I clasped her hand. I had a better understanding of why the living would sell their souls. Though I understood, it didn't mean I agreed with it. It didn't mean I would enjoy taking another. If I could have done something for my Jaylynn, the gods know I would have. "Yarnnalay." Her eyes opened, and she looked at me. "I understand far better than any other could. I understand why you did what you did. You have no worries," I said. "Your contract is gone. You are free."

Nodding, she rose from the chair and made her way to where Micah sat. Pulling him into her arms, she buried her face in his neck and cried.

I felt a pull. A tug from the Abyss deep inside me. Themesis wasn't happy. Sighing, I left the tavern, walking into the night, and pulled the surrounding shadows. The shadows that would take me back to the Abyss.

Back to my home.

"WHO THE FUCK DO you think you are?" He leaped off the throne when I entered the room, stalking across the floor to where I stood. "That soul was mine."

I wiped the spittle that flew off my face. "That soul is her sons."

Themesis laughed. "Since when did you get morals and a conscious?" He turned his head, glancing at Jaylynn, who knelt on the floor, eyes wide and frightened by his outburst. "You had no qualms with bringing your daughter."

I clenched my fists, fighting the urge to pummel him.

He turned back around. "You didn't even beg for her life like you did with this woman. Her soul belongs to me, just as yours does. And now I will never get it."

"She was innocent," I said through clenched teeth. "Hers was not done out of greed. It was done out of love."

Themesis' eyes darkened. Snapping his fingers, a long whip with barbs on the end appeared in his hand. "Get on your knees and remove your shirt," he ordered.

"Jaylynn, go to your room," I called out to my daughter as I unbuttoned my shirt.

A smile curled Themesis' lip. "No," he drawled over his shoulder. "Stay, darling. Stay and see what happens to disobedient dogs."

Turning around, I dropped to my knees and braced myself for the whip.

"Thirty lashes should do it. You will call out the number. Miss one, and I will start over again. Is that clear?"

"Of course, master," I bit out.

I heard the rustle of his clothes and the whistle of the whip slicing through the air. Gritting my teeth, I braced myself. Barbs struck my back, deep cuts forming as he jerked the weapon. Pain blossomed, burning and searing. My vision wavered and I willed myself to not succumb. Willed myself to not scream.

I would not give him the satisfaction.

"One," I called out. I would call out every number. I would not give him the glory of hurting me more.

Over and over the whip bit and tore flesh. A river of red flowed across the obsidian floor. I was numb to the pain. Numb to everything. I tried to block out the sound of Jaylynn's whimpers. The sound of her retching on the floor. Finally, after what felt like an agonizingly long time, the beating was over. I collapsed onto my hands. Sweat and blood poured onto the floor. Taking a deep breath, I rose to my feet, turning to face Themesis. My eyes went to Jaylynn, who covered her face, body racked with sobs. Her quiet whimpers filled the room.

Gods, but I wanted to go to her. Comfort her and tell her I was alright, but it wouldn't matter. She doesn't know me.

"Never disobey me," Themesis spat, turning and stalking to where Jaylynn sat. Bending down, he whispered something in her ear and pulled her to her feet. Wrapping an arm around her, he led her out of the throne room.

I watched them go. Anger lit a flame inside me. Rage flickered like a wildfire. I would try to do everything in my power to make sure Themesis never escaped this wretched place, and if I couldn't?

Then I would plunge a dagger into his heart, ending his life myself.

SIXTY-TWO
DAMIYUN

I DIDN'T SLEEP.

I couldn't.

Not with the knowledge that Lillyanna was some place, possibly locked up. Possibly being beaten.

I committed to memory the face of the man who sat smiling at the table. I let my anger flow through me. I held it close and locked it deep inside.

He would feel my wrath.

He would pay for hurting my Lil.

I lay awake, staring at the ceiling until the rays of sun brightened the room. Only then did I pull my weary body off the bed. There was no need to rouse Abraham. I knew he wasn't in his bed, as the bond—though I had learned how to block much of it out—let me know he had spent a good part of the night with a whore.

My thoughts darkened as they turned back to Lillyanna and what she was doing to pay that man.

He freed her from her binds. From your *shackles.*

"She had no shackles."

You wouldn't let her be. You wouldn't let her be free.

An image of Lil flitted through my mind. Her eyes wide and scared. She backed away from me. *"No!"* She cried. *"Please. Don't."* She held up her hands. Her wrists bound with iron.

My jaw clenched, and I fisted my hands. "I never bound her. She could do what she wished."

But you didn't let her. It wasn't until your betrayal did she see. See who you are. See you are not her savior but her demise. I am her savior. I will *save her.*

"You will imprison her. Enslave her. I will not let that happen."

Laughter echoed in my head. *You will see. She will beg me to make her mine.*

Another image entered my mind. Lillyanna, dressed in a long, blood-red gown, made her way across the floor of a grand room. Torchlight glinted off the obsidian walls and the diamonds in the ten-tiered chandelier above. Themesis stood on the other side of the room, dressed in a blood-red tailcoat over a crisp, white shirt. Black trousers sheathed his legs, and polished boots came below the knee. A fine sword was strapped at his waist, the many jewels glinting in the light. His long, black hair flowed about his shoulders. He beckoned Lillyanna forward. She glided across the room to him. A smile curled her lips as she sank to her knees. Themesis placed a thorny obsidian crown on her head, rubies and diamonds decorating the points. She rose to her feet, and he pulled her into his embrace. *"Welcome home, my queen,"* he said, his lips brushing hers.

I shook the vision from my mind and leaped off the bed. "No. She will never be yours."

Laughter echoed in my head. *She already is mine. I was her comfort in that dark cell. I was the one she turned to when loneliness choked her. You were nowhere. You drove her to me.*

"She will never be yours," I snarled, drawing my sword, which Abraham had rested against the wall earlier that night. The jewels felt warm beneath my hand, pulsing faintly, and the blade—Shadow Blade—glowed, power flowing through it as I gripped the hilt tight. Wielding it, I stood ready, eyes searching the small room for Themesis. I lowered the sword and shook my head. I was talking to a voice intent on driving me mad, and drawing my sword made me wonder if perhaps I already was.

I sheathed the blade, and I strapped it to my back, then left the room searching for Lil, and in search of the man who hurt her.

I slipped out of the inn, eyes scanning the street that gained more and more traffic. Carriages raced by. People hustled. Hollering voices—merchants trying to entice customers—rose above the din. I moved through the crowd, eyes alert and hand on my dagger.

"Fruit. Fresh fruit. The best there is," a voice called out.

"Fresh baked bread. I've got pies—mincemeat and apple—and pastries for everyone," another bellowed. I moved through the market, weaving my way around people. If Lillyanna's job was to get money, this was the perfect place for a pickpocket.

For a pretty and stealthy thief who was trying to survive.

Trying to please the one she served to avoid a beating.

To avoid starvation.

"Have you seen her?" Abraham appeared on my right and fell in step beside me.

"No, but since I interrupted her activities the night prior, this seemed like the place for her to steal."

Abraham grunted his agreement and as if on cue, a voice yelled out in the crowd.

"Thief. Thief. Get that little bitch. Don't let her get away."

I peered through the crowd, watching a hooded figure dart and weave, tendrils of fiery red hair blowing out from the sides. I darted through the crowd without hesitation. The sound of pounding boots behind told me Abraham was in close pursuit.

I pushed my way through the crowded street, shouldering and shoving bodies out of the way, ignoring angry curses and threats. I kept my eyes trained on her back, on the trail of red hair blowing in the breeze.

She looked over her shoulder, eyes narrowing on me as we closed the distance. I almost lost her when she dove into a group of men. But soon, my eyes once again caught sight of a figure darting down an alley. I surged on, determined not to lose her.

As I reached the corner, I skidded to a halt.

It was a dead-end.

We had her trapped.

Abraham drew up next to me, and we formed a formidable wall blocking her escape.

"Come to take my pickings?" she snapped, hatred filling her emerald eyes trained on me.

"I have come to take you home."

"I told you. This is my home. I don't even know who you are."

My heart shattered at her words.

"Get the fuck out of the way and let me give my pickings to him."

"Lillyanna—"

"I'd prefer not to be beaten tonight."

"Please—"

Lillyanna sighed. "Foolish man. Just know you brought this upon yourself," she said. A cold, evil smile crossed her lips.

A smile that chilled me to the bone.

She turned her palms up to the sky. The wind whipped. Thunder rumbled in the distance and the sky lit up.

She was calling the lightning.

"Stop her, Abraham," I yelled, though I didn't need to say anything.

He had pulled the shadows around himself. Smoky darkness swirled in her direction. Her eyes widened as the mist weaved around her. The darkness slowly dissipated to reveal Abraham, who had her secured in his arms.

Or so I thought.

She struggled against the strong grip. Eyes narrowing, she opened her mouth and screamed.

It was a shriek similar to the wraiths but far more piercing.

My knees buckled, and I clamped my hands over my ears, trying to block the horrific sound out. Abraham released her, and he dropped to the ground as well.

She stopped for a moment and laughed, a sadistic and evil sound. Shadows moved. Red eyes peered out from the darkness. Teeth glinted in the moonlight. Demons drifted to her. Surrounded her. Her skin was ghostly against the darkness. Evil poured out of her haunted eyes.

"How is she doing this?" I glanced at Abraham, who shook his head.

She has given herself to me. She has surrendered to her true self. She will be mine. She will set me free, and we will rule.

I clenched my teeth at the voice. At the taunt. *She is mine.*

Themesis' laughter echoed in my head. I steeled myself against him and concentrated on Lillyanna. Bony arms pulled her close. Darkness surrounded her, and then she was gone.

"How did she do that?" I asked again.

"She's tapped into the darker side of her magic. Let's go," Abraham said, striding out of the alley and into the market. I took one last look around, peering into the shadows in the hopes that I would see her. Sighing, I followed him to the tavern.

It was fairly crowded for the time of day. We pushed our way through and found a table in the corner. After ordering up two bottles of spirits, I rubbed my eyes and folded my arms on the table.

I sighed. "What are we going to do, Abraham? The magic she used—it's frightening."

"Whatever those men have gotten her into, she's found and used the dark side of her power."

I swigged from the bottle in front of me, eyes scanning the room, ears picking up conversation. I was tracking down the man who Lil worked for. Listening for any mention of him.

Or of her.

But all about was mundane chatter about failing crops. Dried-up profits.

"We need to catch her," I said, turning my attention back to Abraham.

He snorted. "You saw how successful that was."

"It would have been easier if you had blocked her magic. Why didn't you?"

"I wasn't thinking. My only goal was to get her." He sipped his drink. "What makes you think it will work this time?"

"She's a picker."

"And?"

"And we will go out. Set her up."

"And you think you will find her?"

"The market is busy. She has plenty of marks. My guess, she wasn't careful before, which is why she almost got caught. Regardless, we know she is here."

Abraham sighed. "What do you propose then, Damiyun?"

I took another swig from the bottle, capped it, then stowed it in my cloak.

"We go back to the market. I will hide myself as much as I can and get close to her. With any luck, she will try to pick me. When she does, I will grab her. And you," I said, rising to my feet and pulling my hood over my head, "you will put her in a forced sleep state so we can bring her here."

"And if this doesn't work? If she sees you and flees? Or uses magic on us? Then what?" He reluctantly pushed back from the table and stood.

"You will block her magic, and we keep trying until we have her. Or until I find the man who did this to her and make him pay."

Turning, we pushed our way through the tavern back out into the street, making our way back to the crowded market. My eyes scanned the throng as we pushed our way through, and I spied her sliding away from a man who was looking at trinkets—children's toys—at a booth. She swiftly skirted around people, coming up to another man at a booth selling baked goods. I pulled the hood of my cloak up, and sidled up beside her, looking like I was inspecting the food.

"Whaddaya want?" the burly man on the other side growled.

I pointed to a pastry. I reached into my pocket, bumping Lil as I did and making a point to jingle the bag as I fished out the few coppers for the day-old sweet.

I could feel her eyes on me as I pocketed the bag. Thanking the proprietor, I took my purchase and wandered away.

I didn't have to look to know she followed.

I could hear her soft footsteps, feel her eyes burning through my back.

My eyes flicked to Abraham who stood against a wall all but invisible in the shadows, his eyes tracking me. I went up to another booth and scanned the fruits.

I felt a bump. A hand slipped into a pocket. I snatched the offender's wrist, turning her around. Green eyes looked up in surprise. Surprise that turned to anger and annoyance.

"Fuck it all. You again?" she snapped, trying to wrench free, but I held tight.

"Yes. Me again." My eyes flicked to Abraham, who quickly advanced.

"It's apparent you have failed to learn your lesson," she growled.

A surge of power came from her, and a bolt of energy snapped through my hand. "Fuck," I released her. She shoved me and I stumbled. I reached for her, fingers skimming her cloak as she ran away.

"I got her," Abraham growled, taking off in pursuit, with me behind. She deftly wove her way through the crowd, casting a glance over her shoulder now and then, eyes filling with panic as we closed in. She turned down another dead-end alley.

"What do you want with me?" she yelled, angry eyes on us.

"Calm, Lil," I said, holding up my hands. Something flickered within her eyes and for a brief instant, I felt she knew me.

But then it evaporated, replaced with bared teeth and fiery eyes.

"I told you what we want. We want to take you home."

"And I have told you this is my home."

I took a step toward her.

"No, it's not, Lil. Please. Listen to me."

She glared at me, spreading her arms wide, palms facing the ground. There was a low rumble. The ground shook then heaved violently up, knocking me and Abraham on our backs. Dust and debris filled my lungs, choking me and making my eyes water, but through the haze I saw a flash of red as she ran by.

"Abraham," I scrambled to my feet.

He held up his hand. She gasped and stumbled, surprise flitting across her face, which turned to a scowl.

"What did you do to me, you fucking beast?" she snarled, leaping forward, teeth bared. Abraham sprung on her like a hound, long strides quickly closing the distance. Powerful arms closed around her.

"Let me go, you uncouth bastard." She kicked and clawed at him, desperate to break free, but he held tight, tackling her to the ground. Her head hit the stone with a sickening thud. Her eyes closed, her body went slack, and I sagged in wary relief.

Relief that we finally had her.

Though what we were going to do with her, I didn't know. Pulling his body up, Abraham lifted her and cradled her in his arms. Saying nothing, we made our way back to our room.

We had her.

We had my Lil.

SIXTY-THREE

I SWALLOWED HARD PAST the lump in my throat. I felt numb as I cut strips of cloth from the bedsheets. My hands shook and twice I almost sliced myself. I took a deep, shaking breath. My chest tightened as I grasped her wrists and tied restraints around them, making sure they weren't too tight.

Though she had knocked herself out, Abraham put her in a forced sleep state as well, just to keep her in check until we figured out what to do.

"She needs a bath," I said, pushing a crusty lock of hair from her eye. She sighed. A small smile tugged at the corner of her mouth at my touch, and for a moment, a spark of hope flared within.

"I will see what I can do," Abraham said, exiting the room.

"Lil, Lil. My Lil. What happened to you? Where did you go?" I blinked back tears, smoothing her matted hair. "I am so sorry for hurting you. For betraying you. Please. If you come back to me, I promise—I promise—" I swallowed hard and wiped the tears that wetted my cheeks.

Promise what? You won't hurt her again? That is a lie. Tell her all the lies. Bring her back, only to bring her to me. She will never forgive you. If she even remembers you.

I shook my head. "She will know me, and she will never be yours," I shook my head of the laughter that echoed.

I wasn't mad.

I wasn't mad.

I would never let him drive me mad.

The door opened, and I looked up, watching as tavern wenches brought in a washtub and placed it in front of the cold fireplace. The help went in and out bringing buckets of warm water and when the tub was full, I nodded to Abraham who—with hesitant reluctance—brought Lillyanna out of her sleep. She stirred, eyes opening, fear and panic flashing in them as they darted frantically around the room. She sat up, eyes narrowing on me, confusion crossing her features.

"What—?"

"Your magic has been blocked."

She glared at me.

"It's for our safety. We're not going to harm you."

Her jaw clenched. "Then give me back my magic."

"No."

She vaulted off the bed, shouldering me out of the way. She charged at Abraham, who caught her and restrained her in his strong arms. She screamed and thrashed. My heart constricted at the sight of her, looking like a wild and trapped animal. Tears burned my eyes, but I would not let them fall.

"Calm, Lil," I whispered, standing in front of her, holding my hands out as if trying to calm a skittish horse. She paused. A look flashed in her eyes and again, for an instant—just a moment—there was recognition. She jerked in Abraham's arms and her green, hate-filled eyes focused on me.

I chose another tactic. "How about a bath and some food? I am sure you are hungry, and a nice soak will make you feel better," I offered in a soothing tone. She stopped thrashing, eyes looking past me to the washtub. I nodded to Abraham, who cautiously released her.

"Let me heat the water up some more," I said, crossing the room, sighing in relief at the sound of footsteps following. Using my magic, I warmed the water. Steam rose from the tub, and then I made a fire. I cut her binds with my dagger, and she began stripping off her clothes, eyes on the steam. I backed up toward Abraham, clenching my fists at the sight of bruises covering her. At the bones jutting from her painfully thin frame.

"Get her some food and clean clothes," I said.

"Are you sure you can handle her?"

I glanced over to where she lay in the tub, slowly washing the dirt and grime from her body.

"She's not going anywhere," I said softly.

"If she tries to flee..."

"She won't."

Abraham grunted his response and slipped out of the room. I rubbed my eyes and sank down on the edge of the bed.

"What happened to you, Lil?" I whispered softly, watching her lean back in the tub.

"Can you heat the water again?" Her soft voice drifted to me.

I crossed the room and did as she asked, then tossed another log onto the fire.

"Feel better?"

"Yes. Thank you...?"

"Damiyun. My name is Damiyun," I said, chest constricting over having to tell her who I was.

She smiled faintly, then leaned back in the tub and closed her eyes. I let her soak for a while, occasionally heating the water back up. When Abraham returned, I reluctantly woke her, wrapped her in a blanket and sat her down in front of the fire. Abraham tossed a sack to me, then placed a tray that held several bowls of stew on the table.

Lil's eyes never left the food.

"Go on. Eat," I said. She licked her lips but didn't move.

I picked up a bowl and held it out to her. She hesitated, her gaze going from my face back to the bowl. Uncertainty shone in her eyes, though her hunger eventually won, and she snatched the food from me, hungrily shoveling hot stew into her mouth. When she finished, she eyed another bowl.

"Go on," I encouraged, and she picked it up and ate some more. While she feasted, I grabbed a brush Abraham had bought and began working it through her hair. While she had washed it, the locks were still a tangled mess. I could have used my dagger to remove all the knots, but I didn't. I couldn't bring myself to cut one piece of the once silky hair I loved to feel in my hands. Feel the caress of it on my face and body.

The blazing pile of red that was soft beneath my cheek on the pillow.

I couldn't cut that which defined her.

Which I loved. Instead, I carefully and meticulously undid every knot, every snarl and every tangle until her hair was free and as beautiful as I remembered.

I will make the men who did this to her pay in blood.

When I finished, she pulled on the fresh clothes Abraham had bought.

"Get some rest," I said.

She did as I asked and slipped beneath the blankets. Her eyes closed and within seconds she was asleep.

"We should bind her again," Abraham said, his gruff voice startling me. I had forgotten he was there.

"There is no need for that. She didn't hurt me."

"No, but we don't know what her state of mind will be when she wakes."

I shook my head. "No, Abraham. If she's wild—I will take full responsibility. I refuse to bind her. Not when there is a glimmer of trust in her."

Abraham said nothing more about it. "There are clean clothes for you as well. I suggest that you perhaps bathe while you can," he said, and I couldn't disagree, I required a good soak. I sank into the hot water, which enveloped me like a blanket. I leaned back.

I was bone tired.

I glanced over at Lil who slept fitfully. I was grateful to have her back. I just prayed she would remember me.

After I washed the grit and grime from myself, I pulled my tired body out of the tub. I slipped on fresh clothes, then shaved the scratchy and bothersome beard.

"Get some rest. You look like Death," Abraham said. "I will watch over Lillyanna."

I looked at her sleeping form again, calm for the time being, then slipped beneath the blankets of the other bed, darkness consuming me before my head sank into the pillow.

S CREAMS JOLTED ME AWAKE.

It was Lillyanna.

I threw off the covers and leaped out of bed. She was thrashing and kicking in Abraham's grasp.

"Let me go."

"She tried to flee," Abraham glared at me.

"Why are you keeping me here?" She fought against Abraham; teeth clenched in anger.

"Calm, Lil," I said, standing in front of her. "You're safe."

She glared and spit at me. "The fuck I am."

"You are," I said.

She yanked her arms which Abraham held trying to pull free from his grasp, then slumped in defeat. "Please let me go. I don't want to be here anymore."

I reached out and brushed my knuckles on her cheek. She didn't flinch, and she didn't try to pull away. "I'm so deeply sorry, Lil. This is all my fault." I dropped my hand and swallowed against the lump that once again lodged itself in my throat. "We are not the enemy." *Though I am.* "We are trying to help you. Once...once you knew us. Knew me."

"I've only known Father."

My jaw clenched, and my blood boiled at her words. "I will fix this." I looked at Abraham. "Can you handle her for a bit?" Crossing the room, I pulled the door open.

"Yes, but where are you going?" His voice made me pause.

My eyes met Lil's depthless ones. Everything I had done to her, my actions that made her flee, flashed in my mind. I was the reason she was in this state, and I would make it right. "To seek justice." I said, then left the room and stepped into the hall. It was early, and I was surprised to see the tavern still crowded. As I took a seat and glanced around, I wondered if any of the patrons ever actually left. Faces looked so similar to those I had seen before. I ordered my meal and sat back in my chair, scanning the room, my ears picking up on idle conversation. Most of which was talk about dark things happening. Demons were walking the night.

I turned my attention to the food on the table, slowly chewing as I looked around the crowded room. I scraped the last bits of stew out of the bowl and pushed away from the table, ready to head back to the room, when I saw two figures pushing their way through the crowd toward the door.

I recognized the man who had stood in the street. The one Lillyanna ran to. The one she called father. My pulse raced, and I grew hot as rage filled me.

Keeping them in my sight, I tossed coins onto the table and pushed my way through the crowd. Exiting the tavern, I stepped out into the street. Last night's rain had washed the town clean. The fresh-smelling air was something I knew wouldn't last. I scanned the street, catching sight of the two men hurrying down an alley. I took off on light feet after them. Making sure to keep my distance, I stayed as silent as possible as I trailed them. They weaved through the maze of alleys, finally stopping at a large building that faced a forest. It wasn't like the others in town. It wasn't rundown and dilapidated, rather it was made of brick and stone. The large door the tall man stood at was ornate, the home much finer than those closer to town's center. Based on the man's shabby appearance, it was quite obvious he had come by his wealth through ill-gotten means. I used my magic to cloak myself for a moment, watching the man make his way up the steps to the large door. As I stepped part way out into the light of the moon, the sound of my boot scraping on cobblestones drew their attention.

"May I help you?" The tall man's raspy voice broke the silence.

I took a few steps forward, keeping my face shadowed. "Yes," I said slowly, baring my teeth in a grin. "I'm looking for a young woman."

"You've come to the wrong place, then. I do not deal with that sort of thing. There are plenty available in any alley. Good night," he said, turning and pulling a key from his cloak.

Fuck it all, you don't.

"You misunderstand," I said, taking another step forward, my eyes never leaving him. Dropping his hand with a sigh, he turned in my direction again. "This young woman was no whore. Or thief. In fact, she's been quite lost." I paused for a moment, watching as he crossed his arms, face filled with annoyance. "Perhaps you have seen her or possibly know her? She had green eyes? Red hair? She was a petite woman and innocent in many ways," I said, watching his face. Eyes momentarily widening in fear before he turned his back on me, shaking hands attempting to insert the key in the lock.

"Oh. The pretty girl," the hunchbacked man who had been quiet, spoke up, earning him a sharp kick from the tall one.

"So, you do know her," I said calmly. Anger surged inside, the tingle of the Elven power coursing through my body.

I clenched my fists.

"I have no recollection of such a woman," the man said, glaring at his companion.

"You know exactly who I am talking about." My grip tightened so hard my knuckles turned white and the Elven magic begged to be released.

And I obliged.

I opened myself to the power pulsing within, eyes on the two men.

"I've got you," I said to the tall one who fumbled with the keys. I released the magic I held, letting out a concussion of power. I stumbled backward as it left, catching myself before I hit the ground. But my eyes never left the duo. A rippling wave of amber moved swiftly toward them, and their eyes widened in fear. The air undulated as the force rushed forward, their bodies slamming against the building and crumpling to the ground.

"You will regret ever hurting what is mine." I made my way to the still forms. Grabbing them by their shirts, I dragged their limp bodies behind as I made my way to the forest beyond. I whistled, elation filling me at the thought of what was to happen. While I could easily take care of them using my magic, I wasn't going to do that.

No.

The torture they would suffer would come by my own hand.

I stripped them naked, tearing pieces of cloth from their shirts into strips and binding their wrists. Then I strung them up from a branch, their feet barely touching the ground. I hung them in such a way they faced each other. I wanted them each to see what I was going to do. I wanted them to be terrified as they anticipated being next. Checking to make sure the binds were secured, I ventured back to the village to gather supplies for my task. I wasn't concerned about anyone coming upon these two, and if they did, no one in this town would bat an eye. When I returned, I made a fire, placed the iron rod I had bought in the flames and settled in on the ground, opening the bottle of Serpent's Venom I had also picked up. I sipped the liquid while I waited. I kept the fire low. I didn't start it for warmth, rather for the hot coals. I kept my eye on the two men as I tended the fire, rising when I saw the taller one stirring.

"What in the name of the Fallen One is going on? Who are you?" He was an ugly man. Tall and thin, gaunt face and white lips pulled back into a snarl. I was disgusted just looking at him, my heart pounded, and my body tensed at the thought of Lillyanna being subjected to whatever horrors he inflicted on her.

I leveled my gaze on him and crossed my arms. "Who I am is not relevant, for you will never see me again after this night." I smiled coldly as a thought entered my mind. Tearing off two more pieces of cloth, I stepped toward the hanging men. Turning to the small, fat one, I shoved the cloth into his mouth, gagging him.

"What's your name?" I asked the tall one. His name didn't matter much to me, though knowing it made what I was going to do much more personal.

"Ton'Yana."

Reaching into the fire, I pulled out the rod, the hot tip glowing orange. I walked over to where they were suspended, holding the heated implement close to Ton'Yana's face. I laughed as he pulled back at, feeling the heat radiating from the tip.

"Please," he begged. "I'll give you anything you want. Coin. I have lots of coin."

"Your coin will not fix the damage you have done to what is mine. What I want, is answers. If you give me what I wish to my satisfaction, then I will let you live," I lied, as I lifted the hot iron up. I brought the tip close to his face, then slowly pressed it to his cheek. I smiled as he screamed in pain, the scent of burned flesh reaching my nostrils. A feeling of euphoria settled over me. I put the weapon back into the hot embers of the fire and turned back to the one before me. Tears ran down his cheeks and he continued to howl in pain.

"That was just a starter," I growled. Pulling my dagger, I grabbed him between the legs, placing the blade against his penis.

"No. Please," he gasped.

"You're right. It's not time. Yet," I said, smiling wickedly as I brought the weapon up and deftly sliced off one of his nipples, the sound of his screams, music to my ears.

"What did you do to her?"

"I don't... I don't know what you're talking about," he gasped.

"No? Well then let me see what he has to say," I said, turning to the fat man. I removed the gag and shoved it roughly into Ton'Yana's mouth.

"What's your name?"

He licked his lips. "K'Risgenl."

I pulled the rod out of the fire. The length that was in the heat glowed yellow. The end I gripped was hot, but I ignored the discomfort. "What did you do to her?"

K'Risgenl looked at the thin man.

"He's not going to help you. You can only help yourself by telling me what you did to her."

K'Risgenl licked his lips. "I—nothing. I didn't do anything to her."

"Wrong answer." His eyes widened in fear as I brought the glowing metal close to his face, his agonized screams a sweet symphony as I pressed it to his cheek. I tossed the rod back into the fire then grabbed the sack and emptied the contents, carefully arranging the items I had bought on the ground: a length of chain, a hammer, a metal tipped knout whip, pliers and my dagger. Pulling the weapon free of its sheath, I ran my thumb along the blade, noting its dullness. I could have sharpened it, but I didn't. I didn't want the cuts to be easy, rather jagged, and painful. I smiled at the flicker of fear that crossed both their faces as they watched me. Placing my dagger on the ground next to the whip, I made a show of pondering which instrument I was going to use, choosing the length of chain. Wrapping it around my hand, I turned my attention back to K'Risgenl.

"She doesn't know who I am. She is like a feral animal," I said, my face inches from his. "What did you do to her?"

He said nothing, no doubt thinking his silence would save him from pain. He was right, in a sense. I slowly unraveled the chain, my eyes on him as I did so, watching him flinch as the links clinked when I drew my hand back. I didn't hit him with it, rather I turned and struck the unsuspecting Ton'Yana. The metal clinked as it hit his skin with a thud, the sound of bone cracking deliciously satisfying. He whimpered in pain, tears spilling from his eyes. I pulled the rag out of his mouth and shoved it into K'Risgenl's.

"She came to us," he cried before I had the chance to ask my question.

Sighing, I tossed the chain on the ground and picked up the dull blade. I leaned casually against the tree and cleaned my nails with the tip. "Do you think me a fool?" I broke the intentional uncomfortable silence. I sauntered back over to Ton'Yana. "You could make this so much easier if you would just tell me what you did to her," I said, though my words were a lie. He kept silent, and I shook my head, clucking my tongue in disappointment.

"You think your silence will save you. I can assure you it won't," I said, grabbing his foot. He kicked and struggled in protest, and I grasped his ankle securely under my arm. Grasping my dagger, I sliced off his big toe, making his screams pierce the night. Dropping his foot, I faced him, casually tossing the bloodied severed digit in the air and catching it. K'Risgenl squeezed his eyes shut with a whimper.

"She was vibrant and full of life, something which you took from her." I turned my attention to K'Risgenl whose eyes were squeezed shut, eyes that snapped open when I pulled the gag from his mouth and tossed it aside. I *wanted* to hear the one not being hurt beg and plead while the other screamed in agony. Turning my attention back to the array of devices on the ground, I dropped the dagger and picked up the knout whip.

"We found her in an alley. She... she was looking for sex." Ton'Yana's words tumbled out in a rush.

Sighing in aggravation, I gripped the handle of the whip. Moving behind him, I raised my hand.

"Why." *Crack.* "Must." *Crack.* "You." *Crack.* "Lie?" *Crack.* I closed my eyes and relished in the agonized howls he let loose. Blood flowed from the wounds, dripping down his legs and soaking the ground. "She was a sweet woman." I gripped the handle in my hand. "You broke her. She doesn't know who I am. She is like a wild beast." The knowledge Lillyanna didn't even recognize me hurt in a way I never thought possible. I banged the handle of the whip against my leg, hot anger surging through my body. The jangling sound of the metal tips made him wince, adding to my pleasure. "Now—" My words were cut off by the sound of howling close by, the call answered by barks and bays surrounding us.

Wolves had smelled the blood.

"Shit." I stood still, eyes scanning the woods, seeing the massive forms of wolves just outside the perimeter. Looking around, I grabbed a hefty branch. Removing my shirt, I wrapped it around the stick and held it in the fire until the material caught. I stood at the edge of the clearing, holding the torch out. I saw the glint of dozens of eyes and heard low growls. Looking around, I picked up a large rock and hurled it in the direction of the dogs. A high-pitched yip signaled I had hit one.

"Get out of here," I stomped forward while waving my quickly dying torch, and hurled rocks in their direction. The pack slowly backed away.

It wasn't time for the wolves to feed. Yet.

I tossed the makeshift torch that was dead into the fire and pondered over the array of weapons I had, selecting the pliers, briefly heating them in the flames. Pulling them back out, I turned toward K'Risgenl.

"Please," he whimpered, kicking, and thrashing as I grabbed hold of his leg and secured his foot in the crook of my arm and grasped the nail on his big toe.

"What. Did. You. Do. To. Her?" Each word was punctuated with the removal of a nail. He howled in pain, tears running down his face. I didn't give him a reprieve. Picking up the length of chain, I slammed it hard into his back, my nose wrinkling in disgust at the smell of his bowels emptying.

"You're pathetic."

"It wasn't me. It was Ton'Yana," he cried. "It was him. It was all his idea."

I stepped back, looking at Ton'Yana, whose eyes narrowed angrily. "Go on," I said, turning my attention back to K'Risgenl. He licked his lips, frightened eyes on me. The silence stretched, which only fueled my anger. Sighing, I wrapped the chain around his member and jerked it tight. "Tell me what you did, and I will offer leniency."

"We found her in an alley. Ton'Yana... he offered her some food and a place to sleep if she helped us."

"Wrong," I said, tossing the chain on the ground and grabbing my go-to weapon of choice: the hot length of iron.

His eyes widened in fear as I brandished the hot metal implement. "You're right. You're right. She—she—wasn't in the alley."

"Too late." I slid the hot iron between his legs, my eyes never leaving his as I slowly pressed it against his genitals, smiling as he twitched and howled. His screams died off as his eyes closed, and he slipped into unconsciousness. "No," I growled, pulling back and striking him across the cheek with the iron, the sound of bone crunching making me giddy. His eyes snapped open, and he sobbed pathetically. "You are a poor excuse for a human being," I hissed. My face was inches from his, and he turned his head as my spittle hit his face. "What did you think you were going to accomplish, hurting an innocent young girl like her?" I pulled away, putting the iron back in its resting spot, and picked up the hammer. I casually slapped it on my palm as I turned to address Ton'Yana, my ears perking up at the sound of howling.

The wolves had returned.

"Do you hear that?" I whispered softly; my lips close to his ear. "They smell blood. Your blood. They are famished and would like nothing more than to devour you." I pulled back, smiling at the look of terror in his eyes. "Sadly, for them, it's not quite time," I said, walking away to again drive the hungry pack animals back, noticing they had ventured closer this time. Then I turned my attention back to my victims.

"Where were we?" I tossed the hammer from hand-to-hand. Ton'Yana's eyes were glued to the weapon, as if hypnotized by the movement. "Right," I said, standing in front of the man. "You were just about to tell me how you found her."

He licked his lips. "She came into the tavern. She was alone. Something... something made her leave. I don't know what it was, but she did. I could tell she wasn't from here. She... she was too pretty." He paused for a long moment. I slapped the hammer against my hand, and he jumped. "K'Risgenl. He... he followed her." He continued in a hurried manner, licking his lips. "She went to the woods, and he followed."

"And then what?"

"He kicked her awake. Hit her in the head with a rock, then brought her to me. I had no idea—"

"No." I leaned forward, my face inches from his. I pulled back and smashed the hammer into his ribs. The cracking sound of bone breaking, deliciously satisfying. He screamed in agony, gasping for breath. Then he went silent, head hanging limp.

"You're not getting out of this that easily," I snapped, slamming the hammer into his knee, the excruciating pain pulling him awake. The cords on his neck stood out as he screamed and thrashed about in pain. The sound of K'Risgenl whimpering made me turn. I had briefly forgotten about the other man. Tears flowed down his cheeks, and a stream of urine ran down his legs. His eyes were on the hammer I held. I looked at the hammer, then at him.

"Don't worry. I'm not going to use this on you. No. I'm going to get my pound of flesh another way," I said, chuckling at the look on his face as I made my way back to where my tools lay. I grabbed the dull dagger and sauntered back to K'Risgenl. I casually ran the blade up and down his chest, increasing the pressure with each pass.

"Tell me what you did to her." I was getting tired of asking the same question. After all I had done to them thus far, I would have thought one would have opened up with the truth. As it was, they did not, and I was forced to continue. The blade of the dagger dug into tender flesh, forming a trail of blood. I increased the pressure, my eyes never leaving his face as the blade sunk deeper into his chest.

"I didn't do much," he cried, and I paused.

"Go on."

He swallowed hard, his eyes darting to Ton'Yana, who was flitting in and out of consciousness. Turning to the other man, I made a quick slashing motion, the blade cutting across his stomach, pain rousing him.

"Go on," I turned to K'Risgenl.

He licked his lips. "We saw her come into the village. She... she was alone. She didn't fit in. He... he saw her and knew she wasn't from here."

"And?"

He licked his lips. "And he used her. He made her steal. He had her go into the market and lift coins from people."

Anger surged within me. "Wrong answer," I snapped, smiling at the tears falling from his eyes as I grabbed him between the legs, slicing the blade across his member. "You did more to her than just have her lift coin, didn't you?" I stood back and silently watched him. He licked his lips and yanked on the binds that held him.

"I am feeling generous. This is your last chance to answer my question. What did you do to her?"

"Please..."

"Not the answer I was looking for," I said, as I slowly sawed through his penis. He thrashed about, something that only made the task last that much longer. His screams pierced the night, and I knew the scent of blood would draw the wolves again, and this time I might not drive them away.

"She didn't want to do what I asked," Ton'Yana's desperate voice cried. I finished my cutting, then turned to him. Crossing my arms, I stood back and listened. "We needed her. She was small. No one knew her, so it would have been easy for her to do what we... what I required. She was locked in a small, lightless cell. I withheld food and rationed her water for weeks. She was left completely isolated during her captivity. I... I would torment her by slipping in food, leaving it far enough away so she couldn't reach it but close enough so she could smell it, and it worked. She agreed to steal coins upon the promise of a hot meal after each venture," he said. He licked his lips and continued. "She... she stole coins. Sometimes it wasn't enough, so she... she was beaten for it and left alone again." He hesitated.

I felt myself grow cold at his words. "Continue." I growled, though I wasn't completely sure I wanted to know.

"Please..."

"What else?" I raged, grabbing the hammer, and slamming it into his shin, shattering the bone.

After his agony subsided, he continued. "There were people... men who had double-crossed me. I wanted to get back at them, so I—she—was tasked with taking care of them. Sometimes it was poison, other times she used her magic," he said.

My stomach turned at his words, and I had to stop myself from vomiting. I had listened to enough. "You will wish you had never seen her."

"Please. I'm sorry. Please," he begged in a pathetic tone. I was tired of hearing his voice, and so I cut his tongue out, his scream turning into a gargle as the blood gushed down his throat.

Then I grabbed him between the legs, painfully grasping his bloodied member, quickly slicing it off.

Turning to the other man, who was barely conscious, I picked up the dull dagger and began slicing off pieces of skin.

I took my time, drawing out each wound I inflicted, taking turns on each one until the early hours of the morning.

I didn't kill them. No, that would have been far too easy and a mercy I was not going to give. They were barely alive, skin stripped when I cut them down from where they hung, bodies falling to the ground in a bloody heap. I felt a hand claw at my pant leg and glanced at Ton'Yana's disfigured face looking up at me.

I kicked his hand away and tossed the bag containing fresh clothes for myself over my shoulder. "You had better pray to Themesis to take your soul before the wolves get you." I spat, smiling when I heard howls, this time far closer than they were before. I walked in the direction of the cries and tossed their bloody members to the dogs, laughing when I heard the growls and snaps as they attacked what I offered. I knew it wouldn't be long before they descended on the battered and bloodied bodies I left behind. I made my way through the empty streets back to the inn, whistling a tune I had heard earlier. I slipped in the room, closing the door behind, eyes going to Abraham who stood in front of the window.

"It's done," I said. I quickly washed the blood from my skin and changed into the fresh clothes I had bought. Grabbing my cloak, I threw it around my shoulders. Abraham turned as I was strapping my sword to my back.

"Let's go. I want to get Lil as far away from here as possible." I went to the bed and looked down at Lil, pursing my lips when I saw Abraham had bound her.

"I did it as a precaution," he said.

"Wake up, Lil," I said softly. Her eyes flew open and darted around in fear. "You're safe," I said in a soothing tone. She looked at me, relaxing slightly, and I took that as a small win.

"What's this?" she jerked her bound arms and gestured to her bound ankles.

I rubbed my eyes with a sigh. "Abraham bound you."

She glared at him. I undid her ankles and pulled her to her feet. "We have to go," I said, guiding her out of the room. Exiting the inn, we made our way through the waking town. When we got to the edge of the woods, I let out a loud hoot, smiling when I heard hooves and saw the silver coat of Xander followed by Abraham's mount. I helped Lil into the saddle, then swung up behind her, holding her close. She leaned against me as I heeled Xander on. Within seconds, I felt the steady rise and fall of her chest as she slipped into sleep. Knowing she had fallen asleep, I felt, was a small step of trust.

"Come back to me, Lil," I whispered, kissing the top of her head. "Come back home."

SIXTY-FOUR

W E RODE UNTIL DUSK, only stopping to water and rest the horses. Lillyanna slept peacefully in my arms, occasionally becoming restless. At those times, I spoke softly to her, and she calmed at the sound of my voice, making me think—making me hope—somewhere in the dark and broken recesses of her mind there remained a memory of me.

And as we traveled, Themesis' voice—his laughter—taunted me inside my head, trying to make me go mad.

You have failed, Damiyun. She will never know you. She will only know me. The darkness that resides in her heart, in her soul, is mine. You don't even know what she did. She murdered. She gave her body to men and slit their throats in their sleep. She gave her body to the man she calls Father.

I grit my teeth. "You are wrong. She will never be yours. She will know me," I snarled.

Lil stirred in my arms. "My king. I am here," she sighed.

Themesis laughed. *She already knows me. She knows who she belongs to. She will be my queen. She will birth the heir of my realm.*

"That will never happen."

His laughter faded, but I knew he was still there. He never leaves. He is always in the dark recess of my mind. A dark presence weighing on me.

As the sun slipped lower, we navigated through the woods, and found a clearing suitable for camp.

"Lil," I said, gently shaking her. She bolted up, head turning, frightened eyes darting about. "It's alright. You're safe." She looked up at me, and I smiled.

Swinging down from Xander, I helped her off. I unloaded him and went to the task of making a fire while Abraham went searching for food. I glanced at Lil who sat down against a rock. Pulling out the length of sheet that I had cut from her ankles, I moved to where she sat. Pulling her ankles together, I began to bind them.

"I'm not going to flee," she said. I hesitated. "Where would I go? I don't even know where we are."

The snap of a twig pulled my attention, and I saw Abraham, who entered the camp bearing two good-sized fish. Lil's eyes went to him as well, her look hungry as she stared at the fish he put over the fire to cook. We sat in silence as the food was cooked and when it was done, I took a hefty piece and placed it on a flat rock. Grabbing my water skin, I went back to where Lil sat. I pulled a chunk of flaky white meat off the bone and held it out to her. She took the proffered food, hungrily eating it. She ate until her hunger was satiated, and after taking a long drink of water, she sat back against the rock and watched me finish what little was left.

After a while, she slipped down to the ground, body curled up in a ball, and closed her eyes. I unfolded a blanket and tucked it around her, watching as her breathing became slow and even.

"We can't keep her bound forever, Abraham," I said, turning my eyes to the orange and yellow flames that undulated and danced.

"We will keep her bound for however long we have to."

I pulled my gaze from the fire and looked at him. The firelight flickered eerily on his face.

"If we do, then we are no better than them." I said.

"If we unbind her, she will try to escape."

"She is not our prisoner." I rubbed my face. "We need her to trust us."

"We need her to stay with us. We cannot afford her leaving. We will travel to Kraagswell Mountain and if she has to remain bound then so be it."

I said nothing, knowing the folly of arguing with him. I did not feel like having another painful lesson delivered by him. Wrapping my cloak around myself, I stretched out beside Lil. I slipped my hand beneath the blanket, finding hers.

Just before I slipped into darkness, I felt her fingers curl around mine and a soft sigh carried on the breeze to my ears:

Damiyun.

THE SOUND OF SHRIEKS pulled me from my sleep. Pulling my sword, I jumped to my feet, eyes scanning the woods. Abraham rose, hands grasping his own sword.

Translucent figures drifted through the woods. Long claws scraped the bark of trees. Another long scream shattered the silence. The hair on my arms rose, and I shuddered at the sound.

"What is that?" Lillyanna's frightened voice asked. I glanced down at her. Her wide eyes looked around.

"Wraiths." I turned my attention to Abraham. "We need to set a perimeter."

Nodding, he went to the task of cutting thick branches and saplings, while I searched around scavenging for twigs and brush. Abraham drove the poles into the loose dirt and using pieces of blanket that I cut up, I attached the twigs to the top, stuffing them with brush. Using my magic, I set them on fire. The wraiths screamed at the sight of the light and retreated into the darkness.

Another sound pierced the dark. Guttural. Evil. Fiery eyes glinted in the dark. Jaws snapped.

"Demons," Abraham said.

A movement drew my attention. I looked to my left, seeing Lil struggling to her feet. I went to her and, using my dagger, I undid the binds around her ankles and wrists.

"Are you sure that is wise?" Abraham snarled.

"Would you rather I throw her to the wraiths?"

He clenched his jaw.

"What do we do about the demons?"

"I'll handle it," Abraham said. Reaching into his beard, he pulled out Bel. Bringing him to eye level, he spoke in a language both guttural and foreign. The little demon scampered down, shooting off into the woods. A roar shook the ground and echoed through the night.

Bel.

Demons screeched, his roars reverberated and crashed through the trees.

"Are we safe?" Lillyanna's voice drew my attention. She had pulled herself closer to my side. Her green eyes were wide and frightened.

I wanted to pull her close. Pull her into my arms. The urge to do so overwhelmed me. I took a small step to the side. "As long as you're with me and Abraham, you're safe."

We spent most of the night keeping the torches lit and the wraiths at bay. Abraham and Lillyanna were vigilant at gathering sticks and brush. I kept the fires stoked. Finally, when the first rays of sun poked over the horizon, the wraiths retreated slowly on air, and then we were able to settle for rest.

Hours later, a painful tingling in my arm drew me from slumber. A warm weight was on my chest and a tickling feeling on my nose made it itch. I opened my eyes to see Lillyanna curled up on her side beside me, her head on my chest. I softly brushed her hair from her face, and she sighed my name, a small smile forming on her sleeping lips.

Though I was at an awkward angle, I remained still for fear of waking her. I didn't know when we would be like this again, and I wanted to stay in this moment. I lay with her in my arms, watching the first crimson rays of dawn paint the sky. She stirred, eyes slowly fluttering open.

"I'm sorry. I was still frightened. You felt safe. And warm," she said, wiggling about in an attempt to move away.

"Don't," I said. She stopped, green eyes on mine. I beckoned her. "Don't move. It's alright."

Her eyes searched mine, then she slowly settled back down. I adjusted my position, slipping my arm beneath her, cradling her neck.

"Thank you, for what you did last night. For keeping me safe." She paused. "What was I to you?" she asked, pulling away and looking at me. "I believe this is right yet... not. Being next to you, I... I had flashes of memories. They came and went so fast but the feeling... I feel safe with you, and I don't know why."

"We were lovers once."

"What happened?"

I closed my eyes for a moment. *I fucked up. I hurt you. I betrayed you. I made you leave.*

"I lost you," I said, opening my eyes and looking at her. "But I found you. You're back where you belong, and I promise I won't lose you again."

She wiggled away from me, and I felt a pang of regret. Having her beside me, in my arms, I could pretend she wasn't lost. Though, when she whispered my name, hope surged in my chest, making me think my Lil was in there somewhere.

"Let's move." Abraham's voice barked as he strode through camp.

Sighing, I rose to my feet, reaching down a hand and pulling Lil up, holding on for just a moment, before bending down and picking up the blanket. Gearing up with my weapons, I made my way to Xander, Lil following beside me.

"Are you, his prisoner?" she asked as I secured my belongings on the back of the horse.

I gritted my teeth, eyes going to Abraham, who sat astride Violet.

"Yes," I said, helping her up onto Xander, then swinging up behind.

"I'm sorry. I know how it feels," she said softly. "I don't like him."

I chuckled. "You never did," I said, heeling Xander after Abraham.

Lil leaned back against me, eyes closing, long lashes brushing her cheeks as she settled to rest. I slipped my arm about her and held her close, her warmth a much needed—and much missed—comfort.

"Welcome home, Lil." I whispered, softly kissing the top of her head, following Abraham, our journey taking us that much closer to Kraagswell Mountain.

SIXTY-FIVE
ABRAHAM

THE DEMONS AND WRAITHS faded as the sky brightened. Damiyun and Lilyanna stretched out on the ground to rest. Though I did not agree with her being unbound, she helped keep the torches alight and did not flee, and I put my reluctant trust in that.

I heard a rustle of leaves and a soft whimper to my right. Looking down, I saw Bel limping to where I stood. I carefully picked him up. One of his wings was torn. Deep cuts and scratches marred his little body. His tongue flicked out, licking an open wound on his front foot. He made a few chirping noises, followed by clicks and a growl. The demons from the night prior were far bigger and stronger than what we had seen before. If Themesis can send them through, then his binds were weaker than I thought.

Carefully tucking Bel beneath my beard, I stepped out into the woods and pulled the shadows close.

It was time I visited S'aehe to find out what the gods were doing to stop this.

Or if they were preparing for a war.

"WHAT ARE YOU DOING here?" Oohlrich demanded when I stepped to the mouth of the cave. He clutched his battle ax in his hands, eyes on me. "You know you are not welcome in this place."

I knew my appearance would not be met with warmth, but I didn't care. "I seek a council with the gods."

"You would have better luck seeking council with a dragon who has a thorn in its paw." Oohlrich hefted his ax threateningly.

I crossed my arms. "What is happening in the human realm will affect them, and you. Especially if Themesis breaks free."

Oohlrich pursed his lips and lowered his weapon. "I will see if they will receive you. Do not move from this spot. If they decide to turn you away, you will leave."

"Of course," I said with a bow.

The Keeper of the Caves hurried off, returning a scant few moments later. "They will listen to what you have to say, and then you will leave."

I nodded and followed him down the path toward the palace. The light, I couldn't call it sun, as it radiated from nowhere, was warm and bright. Birds trilled in the trees. The pungent aroma of flowers filled my nostrils, and the sound of bees gathering nectar vibrated in the petals. S'aehe was a breath of fresh air compared to the stifling hot of the Abyss. The beauty here was breathtaking. I knew it was Felicity who cultivated it. She would not have herself surrounded by anything ugly. I knew the gardens only enhanced her beauty.

I followed Oohlrich through the palace, noting the white marble floors and fine furniture. It appeared every single god fancied the finer things. I now knew where the coin left as offerings went. He stopped at a set of double doors made of oak. Pictures of the six gods were carved into the thick wood. The Keeper of the Caves stepped aside. Grasping the solid gold handles, I pushed the doors open.

The council chambers were the size of an amphitheater. The rows of benches were empty, except for the first. Seven gods occupied seven seats.

Sarlay, the God of War. Leoatle, the God of the Sea. Valtra, the God of Fire. Euphina, the Goddess of Healing. Dhala, the Goddess of Fertility, Samanka, the Goddess of Dreams and in the middle, sat Felicity, the Goddess of Nature.

I stepped across the room to the center, my boots scuffing the floor of the polished white marble. My eyes met those of each god.

Felicity leaned forward, green eyes on me. "You are on limited time. Though your presence here is forbidden, I have allowed you council. Now speak."

I snorted at her words. It was just like the narcissistic cunt to think she ruled over the others. I knew Sarlay to be far stronger than Felicity. But then again, she probably had him in her bed.

Clearing my throat, I clasped my hands behind my back. "I thank you for your generosity in granting me council," I said.

Felicity's eyes narrowed. "Get to the point. What is this about?"

I locked eyes with hers. "You know what this is about. This discussion has been long overdue. Themesis grows stronger. With every Wielder, the Suppressors capture or kill, his binds grow weaker. You know this." I scanned the panel of gods, my eyes settling back on Felicity.

"You know what will happen if he is set free." I looked at Sarlay. "Are you prepared for a war? Do you want the blood of innocents on your hands?" My eyes went back to Felicity. "What are you doing to prevent his escape? His rebirth?"

Her jaw clenched. Green eyes glared at me, and she gripped her skirt. "My daughter will seal his binds. Is that not what you are about? Making sure she gets there? Guiding her there?"

I shook my head and laughed.

"Do not mock me," she snarled. "I—we—have granted you council despite the fact you are not allowed here."

"I mock no one," I said. My eyes met each god that sat silent. "He grows stronger. The demons he sends grow stronger. The girl is just a child. She is not strong enough to defeat him."

"She is my daughter. My blood runs through her veins. You know he expects a god to make the attempt on his existence. He will never suspect a mere mortal capable of the job," Felicity said, her tone cold as ice.

Except he already knows. Though I didn't voice the thought. "And what will you do if he breaks free before the girl gets there? Drag her to him? Slay her yourself?" I shook my head. "Once free, he will be stronger than any of you."

Euphina's blue eyes met mine. She licked her lips and pushed a lock of white hair off her forehead. "He raises a good point, Goddess." Her voice was soft and sweet. "He would know better than any of us what Themesis is up to."

"Yes, he would, wouldn't he?" Felicity pursed her lips. "My daughter was created to stop him. This is her purpose, and yours is to get her there," she said, her tone like ice. I did not miss Sarlay's surreptitious glance at her.

What were the two of them about?

"Goddess," Valtra's deep voice echoed off the walls. "Perhaps it would be wise to have a plan. Themesis will destroy S'aehe. Destroy man," he said, stroking his beard.

Felicity's jaw clenched. I could tell she was not pleased two gods had spoken against her. Questioned her authority.

She rose gracefully from her seat. "This council is over. You are dismissed. Do not ever dare enter S'aehe again." She turned and stalked out of the room, her skirts flowing about her feet. Sarlay rose and followed, confirming my suspicions about him warming her bed.

"Our apologies for having wasted your time," Dhala said, her voice husky and seductive.

I gave a small bow. In reality, I didn't know what to expect. I found it troubling the gods had no plan besides the girl. And it was equally troubling Felicity would not listen to me or the others.

"You do understand what is happening."

"Yes," Leoatle said.

"Then whatever happens is on you." I turned and left, making my way back to the cave and into darkness. Oohlrich gripped his ax but let me pass.

Once in the cave, I pulled the shadows close. The demons, my familiars that hid, lying in wait, clawed their way toward me. Long arms embraced, pulling me into the darkness. Back to the campsite.

With the information I gleaned from the gods, such as it was, the urgency to get the girl to Kraagswell Mountain increased. Whether her memories returned was irrelevant. The fate of the world rested on hers and Damiyun's shoulders, and I would make damn sure Themesis didn't escape.

Ever.

SIXTY-SIX
LILLYANNA

*D*ARKNESS AND WARMTH ENVELOPED *me like a lover's embrace.*

He stood at the end of the hall. He was finely dressed in a deep purple tailcoat, white shirt, snug, black trousers, and boots that came to the knee. His black hair was pulled back, a few tendrils framed his angular features. Ice-blue eyes met mine, and a slow, sexy smile curled his lips. My heart skipped a beat at the look.

I walked toward him. He pulled me into his embrace. His hot and hungry mouth claimed mine. Warmth shot to my core at the feel of his want. Of his need.

"Come, my queen," he whispered, breath hot in my ear. His fingers softly traced my jaw. My body hummed at his touch, want and desire flowed through me. Slipping his hand in mine, I followed him through a door that opened to a bedroom occupied by a large bed with blood-red curtains tied back on the posts. He led me to it, pulling me down onto the soft comforter with him. Mouth, hot and demanding, claimed skin. Hands sought the places that gave me pleasure.

Closing my eyes, I succumbed to his touch. Succumbed to him.

"You belong to me," he whispered as he claimed me again and again.

*"L*IL, WAKE UP." A*N urgent and concerned voice pierced the darkness.*

I began to rise. The darkness, the pleasure, faded. I was being pulled from my king. From my salvation. I fought against it. Clung to him, but I was yanked back to this insufferable life. Back to horror and pain. Opening my eyes, I looked around, momentarily disoriented. I was astride a horse at the edge of the woods. A man's arm was secured around my waist.

Where was I? And more importantly, how did I get here?

The lack of recollection terrified me.

You're alright. You're alright. Think, Lillyanna. Think.

But I couldn't. I inhaled deeply, trying to control my breathing.

Escape. I needed to escape.

I struggled in my captor's grasp, thrashing around in his tight grip. Throwing myself back against him, I slammed my head into his chin.

"Fuck," he cursed, his grip loosening just enough for me to wiggle free and spring from the horse. The sound of a gurgling river beyond urged me on, and I dug in deep, racing in its direction. Curses and footsteps followed as I sprinted.

"I told you she would try to escape."

"Fuck off, Abraham. I got her."

I looked over my shoulder, panic hitting as a white-haired man quickly closed the distance. I pumped my legs as hard as I could, pushing through the trees, branches scratching my face, catching hair and snagging clothes.

His footsteps drew closer still, and an arm hooked around my midsection, pulling me to the ground. I kicked at vulnerable parts and clawed at his face and eyes as we rolled around and around. His arms closed around me as we came to a halt, his heavy weight holding me down, his grip tight. I screamed and struggled, trying desperately to get free.

"Calm, Lil," he said, ragged breath in my ear. "It's alright. You're alright. You're safe."

I struggled, but I couldn't free myself from his embrace.

"Look at me, Lil. Remember me. Know me," he said. He rolled to the side and pushed up to a seated position, pulling me with him.

"Let me go."

"Look at me, Lillyanna," he said again, taking my chin and lifting my head back.

I found myself looking into a pair of gray eyes that glowed lightly in the shadowed woods. Tired eyes and a haggard face.

I knew that face.

My body sagged as I recognized the man who held me.

"Damiyun."

He sighed and relaxed his grip slightly, though he still held fast.

"Yes."

"I—I didn't know where I was. I got scared and panicked."

"You're safe now. No one is going to hurt you." He relaxed his grip completely, and I sank against him.

"I warned you, Damiyun," a gruff voice snapped. Damiyun sighed, rising to his feet, pulling me with him. I stood beside him, my eyes going to the other man. Abraham.

"She was scared and confused for a moment. She's fine now."

Abraham's eyes narrowed on me. I lifted my chin and glared at him. "Forgive me for being scared when I woke up somewhere unknown in the arms of a stranger."

He turned his attention back to Damiyun. "You will bind her again."

"No."

"Then I will."

"You will not touch her," Damiyun clenched his fists.

I watched the two men bicker, completely oblivious to me standing there. Slowly and quietly, I backed away in the river's direction, coming out into a small clearing. A mist hung over the water, drifting out across the grass. The late morning sun dappled through the leaves, the rays sparkling on the mist, giving the place a magical and mystical feel.

Sitting down on a large rock at the water's edge, I pulled my knees to my chest. Damiyun and Abraham's angry voices drifted on the soft breeze.

"... want to believe it to be true."

"Because it is."

"... feelings for her dictating your actions."

I trained my attention on the sound of the river, blocking out the angry voices. I turned my face up to the sun, feeling the warmth of the rays on my skin. I reveled in the warmth.

In the feeling of freedom. I wasn't chained to a wall. I wasn't being constantly watched.

I wasn't being beaten and starved or forced to do Ton'Yana's bidding.

Damiyun had undone my bonds.

I was free.

I felt dizzy at the thought and laughed. Free. Not bound. Not a prisoner.

Free.

I laughed again, tipping my head back and closing my eyes. I breathed in the scent of pine sap, the crisp, early spring air filling my lungs, reminding me I was alive.

I was safe.

And I would heal.

The sound of a twig snapping drew my attention, and I turned to see Damiyun entering the little sanctuary. Smiling at him, I moved over on the rock. He hesitated a second, then slowly sat down next to me.

"I'm free," I breathed, looking at him. He sat still, one leg up, arm resting on his knee. His eyes were focused on the river, his profile illuminated in the sunlight. A breeze blew a lock of hair in his eyes, and he pushed it away.

"You are," he said softly, turning to look at me.

"I'm sorry about before."

He smiled. "Don't be. You've been hurt in unimaginable ways. I can't expect you to... to..." He shook his head and looked back out at the water.

"To remember?" I looked at him.

He closed his eyes briefly then nodded.

"I will, Damiyun. I know, I will. I want to know you. To remember you."

He exhaled hard, shoulders sagging. "I don't know you will feel that way when you do."

"Why?"

"Let's go. We have lingered here long enough," Abraham's brusque voice barked.

We pulled ourselves off the rock and I followed him back to the horses. I climbed, and Damiyun slipped his arm around my waist and urged his mount on after Abraham. As we rode through the afternoon, I hoped—no, prayed—my memories would return. The black nothingness came whenever I tried to recall anything. It terrified me, and I feared it would consume me. Erase everything.

Including who I was, and that terrified me more than anything. Part of me wanted to go back to Ton'Yana, yet something deep down inside told me I was safe with Damiyun and Abraham. Damiyun had unbound me, he hadn't hurt me, and I had a feeling he was something to me.

I would hold on to the feeling of his safety and hope he helped me discover who I was.

WE RODE UNTIL EVENING, entering the town of Duenney and stopping at The Golden Griffin, where we dismounted and went inside.

It was crowded with humans and Elves; the deafening din of people talking and laughing overwhelmed me. Serving wenches bustled about, trays laden with plates of food and tankards of ale. The smell of roasting meat wafted from the kitchen, making my mouth water and stomach growl.

We took a seat in the back corner, Damiyun and Abraham with their backs to the wall, eyes scanning the crowd, bodies tense and alert. Damiyun stroked the hilt of his dagger. The two men talked idly, their voices a soft murmur beneath the loud conversations. A wench set down a meal of lamb and vegetables, and I devoured it. The succulent and tender meat melted on my tongue. I half listened to Damiyun and Abraham, and half listened to the conversations floating about as I ate my meal.

"... dark times a comin'," a voice to my left said. I glanced in his direction, training my ears on the conversation.

"Aye," his companion responded, slamming his tankard on the table. "Dark times fer sure. I 'eard tell of demons roamin.' Dark nasty creatures. Da tings nightmares be made o'."

The first man grunted his agreement. "Themesis be callin' 'em forth. Kin only mean one ting."

The second man shrugged. "They defeated him once."

The first man laughed into his mug. "If ye tink da gods be comin' ta save us..." He shook his head, the conversation over as their meals arrived.

I turned my attention back to the busy tavern, watching patrons enter and leave, the volume within rising the more people drank.

I sipped my wine, growing bored with sitting there. I contemplated asking Damiyun if I could go back to the room, he had secured, though I knew I wouldn't be allowed to go alone.

But alone was all I wanted to be right now.

Settling back in my seat with a sigh, I went back to watching the patrons. My eyes drifted to the front door. It opened, and three Elves walked in, pushing their way through the crowd to a table across the room. They were dressed brightly, the vibrant colors a sharp contrast to the muted greens and browns of the other people. My eyes followed the tall man leading them. He was handsome. White hair spilled about his shoulders. His close-cut white beard made him look distinguished. He had a commanding presence. Almost regal.

Some patrons nodded or bowed slightly as he passed to the table, sitting with his back to the wall, the other two Elves on each side. One Elf said something, and he laughed, a robust sound carried above the din.

I froze and slowly set my glass down.

I knew that laugh. The sound sparked a memory, and the face—the blue eyes sparkling with amusement. I looked at the Elf to his left and I knew him too. I felt it deep inside, but I couldn't remember either one's name. The Elf to the left turned, his eyes locking with mine. He blinked; an incredulous look crossed his face for a moment, and then he grinned broadly.

No. My mind screamed as he turned to the first man. I saw his lips move, head nodding in my direction. Something deep inside me told me to run. Told me to leave this place before the truth was revealed. The room grew hot. Nausea rose inside me and the room spun. My chest constricted and I couldn't breathe.

I had to get out of here.

I leaped up, jarring the table, and knocking over glasses. I sprinted for the door, ignoring Damiyun and Abraham's voices yelling for me to stop.

I had to get out. I had to get away from those Elves.

I burst out, running into the night, the air cold on my hot skin. I ran blindly through the streets, my vision blurred by tears. I didn't know where I was going.

I just knew I needed to get away. I ran until my legs ached, and my lungs felt like bursting. Collapsing to my knees, I let my tears loose. Sobbing, I embraced myself, rocking back and forth.

I was in the woods, the moonlight dappled through the pine trees. Leaves wet with snow soaked through my pants. I heard rapid footsteps through my wailing and saw the blurry figure of the Elf I had seen in the tavern.

"Lillyanna. What's wrong? What happened?" He dropped to his knees beside me.

I brushed the tears from my cheeks and wiped my nose. "Who are you? How do you know me? I feel like I should know you, but... I don't."

"I'm Phabian. You spent a good deal of time with me. What happened to you?" Blue eyes searched mine.

"I... I don't know." Tears burned behind my eyes. "I was with these men and... I can't remember anything that happened before then."

"Let me help you," Phabian said, his voice soft. He placed his hands on either side of my head. "Close your eyes."

I did as he commanded. A rush of energy pulsed through me, and with it came pictures flashing in rapid succession behind my eyes. Memories flooded my mind.

Pictures of me as a child sitting on my father's lap as he read a story, his strong arms holding me close. I could feel his warmth. His scent—wood smoke, spirits, and snow—surrounded me. I could feel his love as he held me close.

Then I was twelve. He sat me on his knee and told me he had to leave me. The pain, the feeling of loss and abandonment, filled me. My chest tightened and my eyes burned. Memories of being alone, of struggling to put food in my stomach, came next. The pain of being hungry. The fear of being caught stealing. Of being caught by the Suppressors. Fear twisted my stomach at the thought. Images of Damiyun flashed. His spicy woodsy scent. His rough hands and soft lips. The warmth of his body as I lay cradled in his embrace. Knowing I was safe with him.

More images of my father, who, I thought, was dead. My body flushed at the knowledge he sent the Suppressors after me.

The barrage continued. My mother. Her cold disinterest in me. The flirtatious way she spoke to Damiyun. He flashed in my mind again. His betrayal. Rage flowed through my veins. My magic leaped in response.

"Lillyanna." A distant voice tainted with concern called to me. I ignored it and let the memories continue.

The Elves flashed in my mind. Tall and regal, their bright clothes blinding. Memories of my imprisonment, of Phabian's kindness and friendship. Of Allendaire and complying with him, warming his bed to keep my head. Of becoming pregnant.

Oh, gods. Serafin. The child I was forced to have and forced to give up. I clutched my stomach, a phantom kick fluttered beneath my hand. Sobs racked my body. I felt empty.

"Lillyanna, come back to me." That distant voice called to me again, and the memories continued to come in a tidal wave.

Being taken by the two men. Beaten. Starved. Chained to a wall.

And again, of Damiyun. The hurt in his eyes when I didn't recognize him. The kindness he showed me. The way he combed my hair, the tenderness, the hurt and guilt flowing through him as he worked each matted knot.

Through it all I heard a wail. A keening scream sounding in my ears.

It was me. I was screaming.

My body convulsed as the onslaught finally halted.

And still, I screamed. That voice, louder and more concerned, rose above my wail.

"Lillyanna. It's alright. You're alright."

I lifted my head and looked at Phabian. "I remember. I remember it all."

He pulled me into his arms. The familiarity of his embrace almost undid me. "It's alright," he pulled away and looked at me.

"I—after I left I...went to Theonaus. I didn't..." I took a deep breath. "I should have gone to Duenney. I had not wanted to run into any Elves, but there were Suppressors there, and I went in the woods and..." I shook my head and pulled away.

"I know what happened, Lillyanna." He brushed the tears from my cheeks.

I took a deep breath. "Serafin. How... How is she?"

A smile curled his lips and his eyes lit up. "She is beautiful, precocious, and very alert." he said. "I don't think she likes the queen much. She screams whenever she's around."

I laughed. "Please tell her about me when she's older."

Phabian cupped my chin. "Of course I will. She will know how much you loved her. How hard it was for you to give her up." He dropped his hands, his eyes locked on mine. "I can't tell you how many times I've wanted to bundle Serafin up and sneak her out of the castle. How many times I've thought about just running away to find you." His gaze dropped to his lap. "I should have." He swallowed hard.

I gripped his hands, and he looked back at me. Tears glistened in his blue eyes. "I'm glad you didn't, Phabian," I said. His eyes widened in surprise. "What kind of life would she have with me? I...I don't even know how much longer I'll be around." I swallowed hard around the truth of the words I spoke. "By your laws, Serafin should not have been born, and yet, she was. I feel she will do great things for your race. Please take care of her. She will need an ally in a harsh and difficult environment."

Phabian pulled me into his arms again. "I will. She will know nothing but love and equality from me."

"Lil." A voice called out. I pulled away, looking over Phabian's shoulder to see Damiyun striding toward us. His eyes went to Phabian who let me go and glided gracefully to his feet.

"Who are you?" Damiyun's eyes narrowed on him.

"I am Phabian."

"What were you doing to her?" Damiyun took a threatening step forward.

"Nothing. Lil—"

"It's fine, Damiyun. This Elf, Phabian, he only came to see if I was alright."

I glanced at Phabian. Understanding and sadness flashed in his eyes. He gave a small bow, and then turned back in the direction of the tavern.

"Are you alright?" Damiyun's eyes searched mine.

I took a deep breath. "I remember," I said, my voice hoarse, "My memories. They're back."

Damiyun's head bowed, and he dropped to his knees. "Lil." His voice was barely a whisper.

"I should have stayed. I never should have left," I said, knowing that—while Damiyun had betrayed me—what happened after was arguably my fault.

"Lil," Damiyun said again. "I'm sorry. I never meant to hurt you—to betray you. I am a weak and pathetic man. If only we had left. If only I hadn't gone to her." He swallowed hard, eyes never leaving my face. "I knew what would happen and yet—and yet, I still went, and I hurt you in the worst way possible." His hand shook as he rubbed his face. "Ah, Lil. My Lil. I can never make up for what I did to you." His voice cracked and tears glistened in his eyes.

"It doesn't matter. We are both to blame."

Damiyun lowered his head. "No, we're not." He looked back at me. "What happened... it's my fault, Lil. You know it is. I should never have left you. I should never have gone to your mother."

"Damiyun—"

"No, Lil." He grasped my chin. "You know I'm right."

"You are right." I jerked out of his grasp. Anger welled inside me. The hurt of what he did. Of what happened to me because of it filled me.

"Hurt me then. Make me feel the pain I gave you." He put his arms behind his back. His gray eyes bored into me.

And I wanted to. I wanted to hurt him. To cause him pain. Bring him to agony, but the only way I knew how, was the one thing I wanted to keep from him. It was the one memory I wish I hadn't been given back.

I reached up to touch his cheek. He flinched at the movement. "No," I said. He looked at me, his eyes questioning. "Hurting you won't erase what happened."

"I don't deserve you, Lillyanna. I never did," he whispered, tears falling and wetting his hands, folded in his lap.

The sound of footsteps drew our attention. Damiyun wiped the wetness from his cheeks. I looked at Abraham, whose enormous frame loomed above.

"What news?" Damiyun looked up at him.

"All seems quiet. Almost too quiet," Abraham said. "I suggest you get back to the room and get some rest." His eyes focused on me. "We have a long journey ahead and as it is; we have wasted far too much time."

Damiyun rose and pulled me to my feet. We made our way back to our room and slipped into bed.

"You're safe, Lil," he said softly, his arms slipping around me and pulling me close. "I know what those men did," he continued, his tone hard. "They will never hurt anyone again. They paid for their actions in pain and blood."

A chill ran down my spine at his words. At the coldness and lack of feeling behind them. I remembered he was a cold-blooded killer, and he had killed for me. And a new, cruel spot in my heart rejoiced at it.

"Thank you."

"I would give my life for you, Lil," he said, lips softly pressing on the top of my head.

I felt the truth in his words.

And somewhere deep inside I felt this truth would be tested at Kraagswell Mountain.

SIXTY-SEVEN

ARMS SLIPPED AROUND MY waist, resting his hand on the bump that formed. His warm lips brushed my ear.

"Our prince grows strong," Themesis said.

I leaned against him. Turning my head, I caught his mouth with mine, kissing him in a slow, teasing way.

"He does," I said. Themesis chuckled as the child fluttered beneath his hand, as though in response to our words.

"You are where you should be, my love."

"Lil. Lil? Wake up. Come on now."

A voice came from far away.

"Ignore it," Themesis said, turning me around in his arms. His mouth captured mine, hot and demanding. Hands slipped beneath the shift I wore, soft and warm upon my skin. I moaned against his mouth as his fingers brushed my erect nipples. Slipping my shift off, he pushed me down on the bed, spreading my legs, his hands stopping at the apex of my thighs. His blue eyes were filled with lust and desire as he looked down at me.

"Lil. Lillyanna."

That voice came again. Closer now. I closed my ears to it, ignoring it, focusing on Themesis whose hands and mouth found the places that gave me pleasure, bringing me to climax. He loomed above me, positioning himself between my legs. Reaching up, I ran a hand through his dark hair. He turned his head, mouth sucking my fingertips. I craved him. Craved his touch, his mouth on my skin. Craved to have him inside me. I bucked my hips against him, and a smile curled his lips.

"Eager, are we?"

"Lillyann, wake up." That voice came again. Louder. More insistent.

"Ignore it," Themesis growled. "You are my queen. You are where you should be."

"Yes," I sighed. I knew the words to be true. I felt at home in this place. With him. My magic woke when I was here, responding to the darkness. Pulling from the darkness. I was Themesis' queen. Mankind would kneel at my feet. Cower in fear before me. I would be their god.

Hands grabbed me. It wasn't Themesis. I thrashed and struggled against the one intent on bringing me back.

"Lil, come on. Come back to me," the voice pleaded.

"Damiyun," I said. Themesis pulled back, a look of rage crossed his handsome features. I struggled against the hands that pulled. Against Damiyun trying to bring me back to misery. Back to pain.

"No!" Themesis screamed in rage, lunging at me as I was pulled away.

My eyes snapped open, and I found myself looking into a pair of gray ones filled with concern that quickly turned to relief.

"Hello," Damiyun said, a small smile playing on his lips. A smile that didn't hide the fear and concern reflected in his weary eyes.

"Hello." I sat up and stretched my arms over my head.

"You were having a nightmare."

I swung my legs over the edge of the bed. Nightmare? No. It was a reality I wanted desperately to go back to. "It's nothing to be concerned about." I touched his cheek. His eyes bore a hint of skepticism, though he stepped back and allowed me to get out of bed. I could still feel the heat of Themesis' lips and hands on my skin. Desire pulsed in my core.

It was still dark out. The stars twinkled in the black sky, and a waxing crescent moon hung high. I didn't know what time it was, though based on my exhaustion I could only guess it was very early, and I had only slept a scant few hours. Abraham stood in the doorway with arms crossed, fingers tapping impatiently, watching as we gathered our things, and I followed him out.

The stormy downpour overnight had slowed to a mist, the annoying wetness clinging to our hair and clothing. A dense fog hovered above the ground and an ominous feeling settled over me as we made our way out of Duenney. I leaned into Damiyun, feeling his familiar warmth, a comfort I had missed deep within my soul.

Having my memories back came as a relief, though I wished some could have remained hidden. Damiyun's lips brushed my cheek.

"Tell me about your nightmares."

"It's nothing."

Damiyun sighed. "It's him, isn't it. Themesis."

Tell him. Tell him all about me. Tell him how you want me. Crave me. You yearn for my touch. My kiss. My cock. A jolt of desire hit me at the sound of his voice.

"Lil?"

"Yes, the dreams are about him." I couldn't call them nightmares. They weren't frightening, rather they were comforting. I took a deep breath. "I can feel his want. His desire for me and I want to be with him. I don't want to come back," I whispered.

Damiyun exhaled sharply. "The magic Ton'Yana made you use is very dark and draws, pulls you to the Abyss. It has brought you closer to him."

You belong to me. I will have you.

I shuddered against the voice. Against the urge to close my eyes. To go to sleep, so I could be with him again.

"Are you alright?" Damiyun's voice filled with concern.

I turned and looked up at him, forcing a smile. My fingers softly caressed his jaw. "I'm fine," I lied, kissing his chin. His mouth captured mine, and he kissed me softly. He pulled back for a moment, but I reached up and brought his mouth back and teased him with my lips. When I drew away, he pulled Xander to a halt, eyes searching mine. I didn't have to say a word. He knew what I was asking and guided the horse off the road and into the woods. Damiyun carefully led him through the brush, coming to a small clearing. Pulling to a stop, he slipped off his back then lifted me off, hands circling my waist, eyes searching my face.

"Are you sure about this, Lil?" he asked, brushing a piece of damp hair from my face, hand gently cupping my chin.

I rose onto my toes and pressed my lips to his. "I need you, Damiyun. Please?" I said. I needed to feel normal. I needed to get back to myself. I had to get away from Themesis.

I stepped back, removed my cloak, and spread it out on the ground, then turned back in his direction. He had slipped out of his shirt and held it in his hands. He seemed shy, almost unsure of what to do.

I pulled the shirt from his grasp, dropped it to the ground, then grabbed his waistband and tugged him closer. Pressing my lips to his warm skin, I trailed kisses across his chest as I undid his trousers, slipping a hand inside to grasp and gently stroke him as I sank to my knees.

"Wait," he said, stopping me.

I looked up at him. "What's wrong?"

Pulling me to my feet, he cupped my chin. "I... I'm unsure about this. It feels wrong." His voice was soft.

I pulled away. "You don't want me anymore?"

He knows you're damaged.

"Gods no, Lil. Of course, I still want you."

Lies. He doesn't want you. He will never want you, but I always will.

"Then show me, Damiyun. I need you." I ran a hand up his chest. He caught it and pressed his lips to the palm.

"I know you do. I need you too, but this doesn't feel right, Lil. You've been through a lot. I want to help you, but this? This isn't the way." He shook his head.

Tears stung my eyes. I bit my lip. "Am I ... am I still yours?"

Damiyun pulled me into his arms and held me tight. "By the gods, yes, Lil. You will always be mine. No matter what happens, you will always belong to me," he said, kissing the top of my head. He pulled away and looked down at me. "You need to heal. We need to heal. Even if it means taking it slow. Just holding each other. Getting to know each other once more."

His words undid me. Burying my face in his chest, the flood gates opened and I sobbed. He held me, gently rubbing my back while I cried, speaking soft words of comfort. When I had no more tears to shed, I pulled away.

"We'll get through this, Lil," he said, wiping away my tears.

We pulled on our discarded garments, mounted Xander, and made our way out of the woods.

Though, what greeted us on the other side was not an angry Abraham.

SIXTY-EIGHT

X ANDER REARED UP AND danced on his back legs, snorting and huffing, hooves pawing at the air. Damiyun did his best to control him, but after a few bucks, he tossed us unceremoniously to the ground. Stars danced in front of my eyes, and I gasped for breath.

"Get up," Damiyun leaped to his feet and drew his sword strapped to Xander's saddle. He peered about, eyes glowing faintly in the shadows, walking cautiously toward the edge of the woods, his sword at the ready. I scrambled to my feet and followed closely behind.

"What—?"

"Shhh," he hissed, eyes still scanning.

I heard a deep growl that vibrated deep within my chest, followed by a loud hiss like water pouring over red-hot metal. Before us on the road stood the most terrifying creature I had ever seen. My heart thrashed in my ears and my mouth went dry as I stared at the monster.

It was a massive creature, at least ten feet tall. Its bulk filled the clearing. A tattered cloak billowed behind. The beast stood on hooves; its long claw-like fingers clutched a sword with a curved blade. A large jewel on the pommel pulsed with a red light. The beast swung its head in our direction. Large horns protruded from its skull; flames flickered in empty eye sockets.

My blood ran cold, and I couldn't tear my gaze from the huge and terrifying beast.

"Pyragaty. Run," Damiyun ordered, sheathing his sword.

Fear had locked me in place. I couldn't move.

"Let's go, Lil," Damiyun growled, hand closing around my arm and yanking me after him. I stumbled, almost falling. Damiyun caught me, and half dragged me behind until I got my feet beneath and sprinted after him.

The sounds of heavy feet, crashing trees and brush closed in behind us. Damiyun skidded to a halt, eyes searching the dense foliage in front of us, the sound of the beast growing ever closer.

"Damiyun—"

"Fuck. There's no way we're going to lose it." He swung around to face me. "Stay behind me and whatever you do, do not use your magic," he commanded, moving out in front of me and holding his sword out. I watched as the demon broke through the foliage, maw dripping with saliva, fiery eyes surveying the area.

"Come on, you bastard," Damiyun yelled. The beast scowled at him, pulled back its weapon and struck. Damiyun deftly—though just barely—dodged the blow. He slipped beneath its arm then spun around, striking its back with his blade. The beast shrugged his blow off like it was nothing more than an insect bite. It swung out again, and grazed Damiyun's thigh, the blade hissing as it sliced through flesh. Damiyun fell to his knees. Head whipped around, and he raised his sword to block another killing blow. Sparks flew as the beast's weapon crashed into Damiyun's blade. He scrambled to his feet, limping out of the way, just barely avoiding another blow from the sword.

But not from its brutal claws.

Drawing back its massive hand, it slashed Damiyun across the chest, razors tearing through his skin. He stumbled back, his face a mask of shock as he stared down at the blood soaking his shirt.

"No," I cried, watching him crumple to the ground. The beast swung its head in my direction, a chilling grin splitting its face. It pointed the hilt of its weapon at me. The crystal pulsed white, the light growing blindingly bright until it shot forth, lancing me in the chest. White-hot pain seared through me. My body convulsed, as I was wrenched backward, almost bending in half. Tears coursed down my cheeks, and I gasped for breath as the beast ripped my magic—my Life Force—from my body. My lungs burned. I tried to get air. There was none. My vision wavered as darkness crept in, the canopy of leaves above growing smaller and smaller as it pulled away my life.

Themesis had won.

The world would fall to him.

As the last bits of trees winked out of existence, something grabbed me and pulled me from beyond.

From death.

I crumpled to the ground, coughing, and gasping for air, gulping and gulping, filling my lungs. My body ached, and I could hardly move. I knelt in the dirt and glanced around. Through my tears, I saw the figure of a man standing before the Pyragaty. I wiped away my tears, eyes widening at the sight of Abraham, his arms out to the sides, a black smoking mist swirling from his body and surrounding the demon.

"Zedekiah," the beast's rumbling voice snapped.

What?

"Still a disgrace to your father. A sorry excuse for a man," it hissed. "Still trying to hold on to your wretched humanity. Helping ill-fated and wretched humans. He should have killed you when he saw you for what you are."

"Not a day goes by when I don't wish he had," Abraham growled.

The beast hissed and lunged at him, but the smoky mist held it in place. It thrashed about, howling into the night.

"For such a formidable beast of my father's creation, you are quite pathetic. Go back to your hole and tell him he must do better than this," Abraham said, pulling his sword and hacking the demon's head off. The beast crumpled to the ground, its body crumbling to ashen dust. The crystal at the end of its sword went dull, and I gasped as my magic came rushing back within me.

"Damiyun," I cried, pulling myself to my feet. My legs buckled. Abraham caught me under the arm before I collapsed.

"Easy, Lillyanna," he said, as he slipped his arm about my shoulders, and guided me across the clearing to where Damiyun lay in a crumpled heap, his blood soaking the ground.

"He's not—"

"No," Abraham said, removing his arm from around me and kneeling on the ground. I sank to my knees, watching Damiyun's back rise and fall sporadically. Every exhale he took ran the risk of being his last.

Abraham glanced at me. "I own him. He does not die unless I allow it," he said, rolling Damiyun onto his back.

"Lil," he gasped, eyes opening as he struggled to sit up, Abraham's hands pinned him to the ground.

"She's right beside me."

Damiyun's body relaxed, eyes closing again as he slipped back into unconsciousness. Abraham tore open Damiyun's shirt, revealing deep wounds oozing blood. Digging into the blood-soaked ground, he packed mud on the injury, then lifted Damiyun's limp body.

"Can you walk?"

I nodded, though I wasn't completely sure. My legs shook as I stood, but I managed to keep my balance. Abraham nodded then strode purposefully out of the woods with me ambling after, breaking through to where the horses stood. He swung himself up onto his mount, securing Damiyun's limp body in his arms. I stumbled to Xander and heaved my tired and aching body up into the saddle. Clicking my tongue, I spoke softly to the beast who danced nervously beneath me. Abraham frowned but held his tongue as he heeled his horse into a trot. I followed behind, my mind on Damiyun.

And also, on Abraham.

The beast had called him Zedekiah.

It also called Themesis his father.

Pushing the thoughts from my mind—though making a note to get an explanation later—I watched his back as we made our way down the road, hoping the next village wasn't too far away.

W E RODE WITHOUT STOPPING, Damiyun's grunts of pain almost more than I could bear. Finally, as afternoon descended, we entered a town named Marney-Faire, a tiny fishing village on the coast of the Calgonian Sea. The distant sound of waves crashing against the shore echoed throughout the town, and the breeze carried the scent of salt and fish. It smelled clean and reminded me of the one time my father took me to the sea.

I was a small child, and I was taken by the sheer magnitude of it. Even now, I couldn't believe how far the water stretched beyond, of the terrifying power of the giant waves, the roar they made when they hit the shore shaking the ground.

I had forgotten about that time, but the soothing scents brought it all back to me. My chest constricted, and I hugged myself, an overwhelming loneliness washing over me.

A want to go back to a time when everything was simple. A time when I still had my father, and I didn't know who I was.

"Lillyanna." Abraham's voice pulled me from my thoughts, and I looked at him. He had stopped in front of a building called The Kraken Tavern and Inn. I reined Xander in beside him and dismounted, gathering Damiyun's sword from Xander's back. Abraham climbed down from his mount and helped Damiyun off, securing him beneath his arm. After packing up the saddlebags, we made our way into the building. The tavern was nearly empty. A few patrons graced the tables and serving wenches bustled about, one of whose eyes lit on us. She frowned then scurried off to the back. I could only imagine what we looked like, especially Damiyun whose torn shirt revealed a mud- and blood-caked wound.

"Whaddaya want?" A man wiped his hands off on his apron as he walked toward us. He was short and balding, with a stomach that protruded over a belt cinched too tight. His round face was red, and he breathed as though he had run a distance. "We don't need no trouble. We be a peaceful town," he said, eyes going from Damiyun to Abraham.

"We need a room and a healer," Abraham said. "We encountered a Pyragaty. As you can see, it has gravely injured my companion."

The man's eyes widened and the dull chatter in the room ceased. "Where?"

"A few miles outside Duenney," Abraham said, shifting Damiyun who leaned heavily into him. "We don't have time to dally. A room and a healer. Now."

The man jumped at Abraham's tone, yelling toward the back for someone to rouse the healer, then led us up a set of rickety stairs to a room. Abraham pushed open the door, shouldering his way in and depositing Damiyun onto a bed.

"I'll git da healer an send 'er up," the man said, shutting the door and plunging the room into darkness. Abraham lit some candles, then stood beside the bed, looking down on Damiyun as he struggled to sit up.

"Lie down," Abraham said gruffly, placing hands on Damiyun's shoulders and pressing him back down on the bed.

"I'm fine," Damiyun snapped between gritted teeth, face contorting in pain. Sweat dotted his brow, and I wiped it away, concern twisting my gut at the burning heat.

"He has a fever."

Abraham scowled, whirling around at the sound of a sharp knock. The door opened, and a woman bustled into the small room, shouldering past us, eyes on Damiyun.

"Leave me." She placed a leather bag on the night table and opened it. Abraham slipped out the door, but I hesitated a second. I couldn't look away from Damiyun. His chest rose and fell in a ragged rhythm.

"He's in the best hands possible. I promise," the healer said, squeezing my hand. She offered a kind smile. "Go now. I cannot do my work with distractions." She released my hand and rummaged through her bag. I took one more look at Damiyun—hoping it wasn't my last—then left the room.

I made my way down the stairs, eyes finding Abraham sitting at a table in the corner. A bottle of Serpent's Venom and two glasses sat in the center. I crossed the room and took the seat across from him, watching the tavern fill with people—mostly fishermen who had finished their day. A bard tuning his lute on a small platform, and the smell of fresh bread and fish wafted through the room.

Pulling my attention back to the table, I picked up one of the glasses and sipped, the liquid burning down my throat and warming me. Abraham tossed his drink back and refilled it as I slowly sipped mine. The silence between us stretched, the sound of his glass tapping on the table grating on my nerves.

"I suppose you seek an explanation," he finally said just as I was about to grab his glass and hurl it against the wall.

"Who are you? Why did the demon call you Zedekiah?" I asked, settling back into my chair.

"Zedekiah is my given name. It is one I haven't heard spoken in a very long time." He paused, raising his eyes to mine. "Themesis is my father, though I suspect you gathered as much."

Though I did dimly remember the reference, the news rocked me, and I almost dropped my glass. Liquid sloshed on my trousers as it tilted to the side. Abraham handed me a linen, and I wiped up the mess as he continued.

"My mother was a whore. Her father sold her when she was a child to pay a debt. She was also a mighty Wielder, much like you. Her magic was white and pure," he said, knocking back his drink. "She was also breathtakingly beautiful. That coupled with her young age made her quite desirable."

I said nothing, though I felt for the poor young woman. No one should be forced into that sort of life.

"Themesis was drawn to her beauty and power. He seduced her. Enticed her to his bed. He took her away from the life she lived. He showered her with gifts. Made her empty promises to get her to agree to be his queen. To join him and overthrow the gods and rule man by his side." He paused, finishing the bottle and ordering another, hands idly toying with his glass again as he collected his thoughts.

"She, of course, rejected his offer. The war between the gods raged, and they tossed him to the Abyss. It was during that time my mother discovered she was with child. She was carrying Themesis' heir."

"I'm sorry, Abraham."

A sad smile formed on his lips. "As am I. I don't understand why she kept me. Why she didn't rid herself of a Child of Darkness. She never answered when I inquired about my father. I got vague answers at best. It wasn't until my magic manifested I knew something was wrong with me."

I frowned. "How can you be certain Themesis is your father? Your mother was a whore and if she never told you, perhaps, she herself didn't know."

"I was experimenting with my magic. Learning how to use it. I pulled the shadows around me and wound up in the Abyss. In Themesis' throne room. That was when he told me who I was. That he was my father."

I reached across the table, grabbed the bottle of spirits, and took a healthy pull. I couldn't believe Abraham's tale. For the first time, my heart went out to the gruff and fearsome man.

"I wasn't a bad person, Lillyanna. Though Themesis' magic and blood courses through my veins, I never wanted to be who I am. I rejected him. Rejected myself. After finding out the truth, I did my best to not touch my magic. To not let it—him—draw me in." He rubbed his eyes, took another long drink, then sent the bottle over to me.

"How did you become a Soul Collector? If you were trying to not be like him, why did you become what you are?"

He stared at his hands splayed on the table. "He made me what I am. I tried to be a good person, but he wouldn't let me. No matter what I did, it turned out bad and I... I hurt people. He took my soul to teach me a lesson. To show me who I really am. To make me enslave those pathetic beings I cherished so much. Delivering Jaylynn was his attempt to break me. To steal whatever humanity I foolishly held on to, and it worked. Once my daughter was gone, once I watched him turn her into his mindless servant," he spat, clenching his fists, and pounding the table, "I no longer cared. I became the person he wanted me to be."

"Why did you change your name?"

"No one knew my name. When I was with my mother, she rarely used it. I suspect she did not want the reminder. I ran odd errands for the other women in the brothel and in town, and no one called me anything besides boy. My name didn't matter to them. After my mother was murdered, and I was taken as a slave, I was given a number. That became my name. Abraham was the name of another slave boy. We shared the same master and became friends of sorts. He was killed when my master's... perversion went too far. When I killed the master, I fled. I called myself Abraham. A show of respect, I suppose, and maybe to free him as well. If people had known who I was, they would have hunted me and tossed me to the Abyss. Lock me in the same tomb as Themesis," he said.

"Damiyun doesn't know this," I said. It was more of a statement rather than a question.

"No. Nor will he. The only one who has ever known the truth was my wife, Lenore," he said, dark eyes boring through me.

"Why haven't you told him?"

"What would that accomplish? He despises me. If he knew the truth, he would think I was helping Themesis."

"Are you?"

Abraham's eyes pinned mine. "No."

"So then, why are you the one taking us there?"

"I am the only one who can. Mortals cannot enter the Abyss alone, let alone gain access to Themesis' tomb. Even though you have the blood of a goddess, you are not immortal."

"What is my task, Abraham? Don't tell me to ask Damiyun. I want—no, I need—to know. Neither one of you have been forthright with me. It's time one of you was."

"You will use your magic to defeat him."

"How? And then what?"

"The binds on his tomb will be sealed once again."

I rubbed my eyes. I knew he was lying to me, avoiding my question once again. There had to be more to my task than simply using my magic on Themesis. Somewhere deep inside, I felt I wouldn't be returning. Thoughts of running went through my head but for what purpose? There was nowhere I could go, nor would I escape my fate by fleeing.

"Will this be a one-way trip to Kraagswell Mountain for me?"

Abraham looked away. "It might be for all of us."

My eyes went to the window, noting the darkness beyond, and I wondered how long we had sat here.

And what was happening with Damiyun.

"Don't worry about Damiyun," Abraham said, sitting back in his seat. "Tell me, Lillyanna. Where have you been? I know you were not with those men the entire time."

"How can you be so sure?" I asked hesitantly.

"I know you were with the Shadow Elves."

My eyes widened. "How... How did you know?" I didn't even attempt to lie about it.

"I was in the tavern at Duenney when you were missing. I overheard two Elves, Phabian, and Lazaro, talking about a woman, a human, who was found on their lands around the time you fled S'aehe," Abraham said. "How did that come to be? They execute trespassers on sight."

"I was alone and unarmed. When I came out of the cave, I didn't know where I was. An Elf shot knocked me out, and I woke up in a cell."

"So, you were a prisoner."

"Of sorts. A prisoner with luxurious accommodations, hot meals, and tailor-made clothes. Despite this, though, my freedom was limited. They kept guards on me at all times, and I could not venture outside the walls without an escort. And I always wore the Sigaa'Lean."

"How long were you there?"

I took a deep breath. "A bit over a Grand Passage."

"And how is it you were allowed to leave?"

"Allendaire, the king, he ...initiated... a relationship. I was a prisoner. I didn't know what would happen if I refused, so I allowed him to warm my bed. I... I became with child. After my daughter—Serafin—was born, I had to hand her over to the queen. I never even got a chance to hold her." I took a deep, shaking breath at the thought. "Weeks later, I was escorted off their lands. Forced to leave the first home I had known since my father abandoned me as a child." I looked at Abraham, whose face was expressionless. "Damiyun can't know. Promise me you won't tell him. I fear... I fear he will go search for her. She's something I want to keep to myself. She's better off with the Elves. I feel she will do something great. Possibly bridge the racial divide and have peace among them."

Abraham nodded. "You have my word. And I trust I have yours?"

I agreed. A shadow fell over the table, and I looked up.

"I am done with your friend," the healer said. "He must be in favor with the gods. By all counts, he should be dead. I stitched him up and applied a poultice. I left you the ingredients and instructions. Keep the wound clean lest he get an infection. He is resting comfortably. I suggest you do not disturb him," she said, her tone formal.

"Thank you," Abraham rose to his feet, pulled out some gold pieces, and handed them to her. Saying nothing further, he tossed a coin on the table then made his way out of the tavern, leaving me to digest our conversation. An icy chill fell over me as I thought about what he had told me.

About the truth of who he was, and I couldn't shake the feeling—the possibility—he was leading Damiyun and me to our slaughter.

SIXTY-NINE
ABRAHAM

I WANDERED OUT INTO the night, gathered the horses, and stabled them, and tossed the stable boy an extra silver to ensure they would be there when we came back. I kept my hand on my dagger as I made my way through the tiny fishing village. The darkness hid the rundown buildings with peeling paint and nefarious figures who skulked in alleys. As I walked, my thoughts went to what had happened.

I never intended to reveal my identity. Zedekiah was a name long discarded and forgotten. It was a name I had hoped would never be spoken again.

Themesis never used it. Long ago, he had dismissed the son who was only a disappointment. Nor did he call me Abraham, a name that told him I rejected who I was.

Dragging myself up from the dark thoughts, I looked up at the sign above the tavern by the docks. A sign so worn by salt and weather the name was unreadable.

It didn't matter. I knew Raymous would be here.

Pulling open the door, I stepped inside. It was a rough establishment made up mostly of sailors, some of which were pirates. A handful of whores sashayed through the crowd, looking for someone to take them up on an offer for a good time. Some sat on the knee of potential customers, smiling as hands wandered and groped. If the potentials didn't take them to bed, then they would be plied with drinks and robbed of coin.

My eyes scanned the crowd, lighting on the finely dressed man sitting at a table in the corner, Captain Raymous.

My mind went back to the first time I had met Raymous.

After my time as a slave, I vowed that I would do everything I could to save those who had the unfortunate luck of being in the same situation. I encountered difficulty in finding a captain who was willing to do as I asked. Most didn't have ships big enough, and they weren't battle ready. Others all but admitted they traded for extra coin. It was Raymous who approached me in this very tavern.

A shadow fell over me. I looked up and saw a man dressed in a fine blue velvet coat, black trousers, and polished boots that went below the knee, cuffs turned down.

His brown skin was weathered, black hair pulled back in a low ponytail. Dark eyes peered at me.

"Word around here is you're looking for a captain." His voice was deep.

"I am," I said, motioning to the chair opposite.

Sitting, the man waved a serving wench over and ordered an ale. "I'm Raymous Zeln, captain of The Sea Witch. What do you need?"

"A ship to take me to Myn'onys."

The man took a sip of his ale and stood. "I'm not a slaving ship."

I eyed him over the rim of my mug. "I never suggested you were."

"Myn'onys is slave territory," he said, but he didn't leave.

"I'm well aware of what it is." I unconsciously rubbed the numbers burned into my chest. Four two four. My slave number.

"Why do you want to go there?"

"It's personal."

The man laughed. "Good luck to you, then," he said, turning and walking away. I pulled out my pouch of coin and tossed it on the table. The sound of gold jingling brought his attention back. I kicked the chair out, and he lowered himself down.

"I trust I have your attention?" I raised an eyebrow.

He took a sip of ale and hefted the pouch. "I'm listening."

"I was a slave," I said. It wasn't something I talked about with many people. I needed a captain and if that meant an explanation, then so be it. "I escaped when I killed my master." Just saying that word, master, turned my stomach. "I've heard that there's been an increase in children missing. I can only assume they're being taken to Myn'onys."

"And?"

"I want to go there and rescue some."

The man laughed. "That's a bold idea."

Reaching across the table, I grabbed the pouch of coin back and rose. "Thank you for your time. I'm sure I will find someone willing."

"You haven't yet," he said, finishing his drink. He waved down a serving wench and ordered two more. "And I haven't said no."

Sitting back down, I picked up the fresh mug of ale.

"When do you wish to leave?"

"Whenever you're ready," I said. I had wasted enough time, enough Grand Passages, in my attempt to gather enough coin to pay for my voyage.

Raymous took a long drink. "I can have The Sea Witch ready to set off tomorrow evening." He eyed the pouch of coin on the table. "It's a long trip."

I pushed the pouch of coin back over to him. "I'm sure you won't complain about the compensation." Raymous picked up the pouch and stowed it in his cloak pocket. "So, we have a deal, then?"

Unfortunately, my plan had not gone as anticipated, and we found ourselves in a battle in the middle of the Calgonian Sea. We prevailed, but the cost was heavy damage to Raymous' ship, but at least two dozen young boys and girls had been rescued and returned to their families.

I shook my head of the thoughts. Those were the days. I had done some good. Part of me had forgotten. Pushing my way through the crowd, I pulled out a chair

"Abe." Raymous smiled as I settled into the small chair that groaned beneath my weight. "Your being here can only mean you need a favor."

I laughed. "That obvious, eh?"

Raymous chuckled. "Been a long time since I've seen you," he said, signaling a serving wench who dropped a tankard of ale in front of me. "Back to saving slaves?" He shook his head. "Those were the times. Being chased by angry traders. Almost getting our heads cut off. I almost miss them." He chuckled into his mug.

"No," I said, taking a sip of ale. "I need passage to Varnalay."

Raymous frowned. "I'd much rather fight an entire fleet of slavers. Whatever for?"

My eyes locked on his over the rim of my mug. "You know better than to question me."

"Yes but—Varnalay?" He rubbed the stubble on his chin. "With everything that's been going on—demon sightings, talk about the Fallen One breaking free..." He shook his head. "It's a dangerous journey. At least give me some idea of what I'm getting myself into."

"Thank you for your time, Raymous. I am sure I can find another willing to take me without question," I said, rising from the chair.

"Yes, as long as you're willing to bend over and be fucked."

I shrugged. "I've got the coin."

"Which they will relieve you of as soon as you go to sleep."

"It was nice seeing you, Raymous." I moved away from the table.

"Sit down, Abe," he sighed. "I didn't say I wasn't willing to take you."

I looked down at him. "You didn't need to."

"I said sit down, Abe."

I raised an eyebrow at him. "Telling me what to do, eh?" I chuckled, settling my bulk back into the chair.

I had no intentions of leaving. Raymous was a trusted friend who made himself available to me upon request. I understood his hesitance at taking us where we needed to go. Few people ventured to Varnalay and for good reason. The shadow of the mountain—of Themesis—was oppressive. Both bore down on the depressed town. The blight cast upon the land also fell on the people.

"What's your business there, Abe?" he asked again, holding up his hand to stave off any comment I had. "You don't have to divulge all of it. Like I said, I just want to know what I am getting myself into. No one in their right mind would travel to that place without good reason."

"When have you known me to be in my right mind?"

Raymous laughed shortly, but his face turned grave. "I'm serious, Abe. It's a long and dangerous trip."

"When have you ever shied from danger?"

"When it comes in the form of demons."

I sighed. "There will be three passengers including myself and since you are insistent on knowing, once we get to Varnalay my companions and I will be making the journey to Kraagswell Mountain. There will be no need for you to wait for me once we are off your ship."

Raymous opened his mouth, then closed it with a shake of his head. "Gods, Abe. That's the Abyss. You are most definitely not in your right mind. Why anyone would willingly go there..." He shook his head and picked up the fresh mug off the table. "Can't you just do your shadow thing and take these people there?"

"No. Mortals cannot enter the Abyss on their own. I am the only one who can get them there. If you would rather not do this..."

He shook his head. "The price will be steep."

"That's not an issue."

He sighed. "When do we leave?"

SEVENTY

LILLYANNA

BRAHAM HADN'T HEEDED THE healer's words, I didn't expect him to, but he roused us before the sun rose. Bastard.

"The healer said he needs to rest," I snapped, folding my arms over my chest, watching as he shook Damiyun awake.

"We don't have time to waste."

"What's a few more days? By the gods, Abraham. He was gravely injured last night. If not for you, he would be dead. Let him rest."

"He can rest on the ship. Get up, Damiyun."

"Ship?" I took a step back.

"Kraagswell Mountain is across the Calgonian Sea on Varnalay. The journey is long and we cannot linger here. Damiyun can rest and heal on the journey."

I swallowed hard. I had never been on a ship, and the thought of being in the middle of the sea—the middle of nowhere with water as far as the eye could see—made me queasy.

Damiyun grunted as he struggled to sit up, drawing my attention, and I rushed to his side to tend to his wounds.

"You don't have to do this," I said, voice low, as I applied the poultice and bound the wound in fresh linen.

"Abraham is right. We need to get going." He grimaced as he rose. I gripped his shoulder and gently pushed him back onto the bed.

"He owns your soul, not your will. You almost died."

Damiyun gave me a wan smile, taking my hand, and pressing his lips to the palm. "But I didn't. Abraham brought me back. I owe him—"

"Nothing," I jumped to my feet, locking eyes with Abraham. "He owes you nothing. You owe it to him to let him be. Let him heal."

Abraham pushed himself off the wall with a snort and grabbed a burlap sack on the table. "Get dressed. It's time to go," he said, tossing the bundle to Damiyun who pulled out clothes and changed. He wrenched the door open and stepped out into the hall.

I looked at Damiyun as he rose to his feet, face contorted in pain, sweat dotting his brow. Sighing—and knowing my protests would continue to go unheard—I followed Damiyun out of the room, walking on silent feet down the stairs and out of the empty inn to where Abraham stood. We followed him through the quiet village. The sky was painted in a kaleidoscope of color as it woke from its night's rest. As we walked down to the docks, the pungent smell of rotting fish guts turned my stomach.

Abraham guided us past the curious eyes of fishermen readying their nets, and we stopped before the gangplank leading to a large vessel called The Sea Witch. A tall man ambled down the plank, brown skin wrinkled like worn leather, black hair blew in the breeze and dark eyes peered at us from beneath a heavy brow. He wore a crisp white shirt beneath a blue coat piped with gold threading, and black trousers tucked into boots. Abraham stepped forward, and the two men clasped arms.

"It's about damn time," the man said, mouth twisting into a smile showing brilliant white teeth. "Had you not paid me half already, I would still be warm beneath the covers of my blanket."

"And I would have found you and dragged your sorry ass to your rickety ship. Are you sure this pile of junk is seaworthy?" I gawked at the smile that curled Abraham's lips.

The man laughed, clapping Abraham on the back, and then turned his attention to Damiyun and me.

"Who do we have here?"

Abraham glanced at us. "This is Damiyun and Lillyanna."

The finely dressed man nodded. "I am Captain Raymous Zeln. Welcome aboard The Sea Witch," he said, stepping aside and gesturing up the gangplank leading up to the deck. I hesitated a second, fighting back the dread and foreboding itching between my shoulders. But ultimately, I followed Damiyun and Abraham onto the ship. Striding across the deck, Captain Raymous opened a door leading below. We followed him down, and he showed us to a cabin. It was small, with a bed on each side and just enough room to squeeze between.

Damiyun lowered himself onto one bed. "I'm fine," he snarled through gritted teeth when I made to help him. He stretched out, and I perched on the bedside, pushing his hair off his face.

"You don't have to be strong for me, Damiyun. That beast... You should be dead right now. I know you're in pain. It's alright."

"I don't deserve you, Lillyanna," he whispered, taking my hand and kissing each fingertip. "You're too good for me. Perhaps it would have been better if you stayed away. If I never found you—"

"Hush. You're talking nonsense. You still have a fever. Rest, Damiyun." I leaned down and pressed my lips to his. He closed his eyes, and only when I saw the steady rise and fall of his chest did, I slip out of the room and go above deck.

Raymous was barking orders, sending deckhands scattering about tossing ropes and pushing the large boat out onto the water. I watched in awe as the breeze caught the sails, which billowed out with an audible snap. The ship lurched forward, causing me to stumble.

I looked about the deck, my eyes going to Abe's massive figure standing at the rail. His white shirt sleeves were rolled up, revealing massive arms covered with eerie tattoos of skulls and faces. His black hair billowed in the breeze. I crossed the deck and stood beside him.

"You still don't believe he can't die."

"Did I say that?"

Abraham chuckled. "There is no need to. I can read the doubt in your eyes. I have pulled him from the Abyss many times. I assure you, his time here is not over."

"And when will it be over for him?"

"When I deem it so," he said, turning his dark eyes to me. "All Damiyun wants is his Eternal Rest. To serve his master—Themesis—forever. What he fails to realize—or acknowledge—is that this life, as horrible and painful as it may be, is far better than anything my father will inflict on him. I know what the Abyss holds and what is in store for him."

"And what is that? What does the Abyss hold for him?"

"Torment and pain. Worse than anything he has ever felt in this world. Everything he has done will come back to him a thousand-fold," he said. "He is not the righteous man he pretends to be. His deeds were dark long before I came to him. He may say it was for survival—that death wasn't an option—but I know better. Damiyun relishes in the power he holds. The control he has over others. Knowing he can let a person live or die."

"Don't all Wielders feel that? A superiority over the Non?" I asked, the words my father often spoke ringing in my head. About how we were better than Nons.

"Do you? Do you take pleasure in knowing you could end a Non's life in mere seconds?"

I said nothing. Though I had done exactly that, I didn't enjoy it.

"That's what I thought," he said, turning his attention back to the sea.

We stood next to each other, the silence stretching. I looked out at the sea of blue, at the waves pushing out from the boat as it slipped through the water, the spray cool and refreshing on my face. Deckhands shouted as they scurried about. The sound of sails snapping tight as ropes were pulled and wind caught fabric punctuated the silence.

"What is my task, Abraham?" I asked, pulling my wind-blown hair out of my eyes.

"That is a question for Damiyun."

I clenched my fists at his answer. Stepping away, I crossed the deck, staggering as the surging waves made the boat heave. Fortunately, I caught myself before I tumbled, much to the amusement of the sailors.

"Dat's why lassies should no be 'bove deck. Dey be too damn top 'eavy," a man called out.

My face heated at the guffaws that followed. Stumbling down the steps, I made my way to the cabin where Damiyun was struggling to sit up.

"Easy, Damiyun," I said, rushing over to help him.

"I'm fine." He pushed me away.

"Gods. You are anything but fine. If you don't rest, you won't heal. I won't... I won't..." I turned away. Damiyun reached out and turned my head back to him.

"You'll never lose me, Lil," he whispered, resting his back against the wall.

"What is my task, Damiyun? What is it I am supposed to do when we get to Kraagswell Mountain?"

Damiyun closed his eyes. "I'm tired, Lil."

Sighing, I moved to the other bed and stretched out. All I wanted was for him to tell me what I was supposed to do. I couldn't shake the feeling I wasn't going to make it back.

That I was going to die there.

I clenched my teeth. All I wanted—all I ever wanted—was for Damiyun to be truthful with me.

His silence—his avoidance—only served to confirm what I already feared.

SEVENTY-ONE
ABRAHAM

"Come," Raymous called to me from the other side of the captain's quarters. Turning the handle, I pushed the door open.

The room took up the entire stern. Windows lined the back, granting a breathtaking view of the sea. Chairs, a lounging couch, and a table were situated at the front. A large ornate desk of mahogany sat in the corner, parchment maps and navigational tools on top. A large table split the room in half, with intricately carved high-back chairs tucked neatly beneath. Against one wall stood an ornate cabinet that held copper plates and cups, and next to it there was a matching sideboard with two crystal decanters, one filled with a red liquid, the other amber—with matching glasses. To my right was a heavy oak door leading to his ostentatious bedroom.

I scanned the large room, eyes going to Raymous who rose from a chair, pulling up his trousers as he did so. A plump, young woman with long dark hair stood, a smile on her face as she looked at Raymous.

"Go to the bedroom. I will have a meal sent to you," he said, kissing her cheek and smacking her backside as she scurried away from him. I watched the woman as she crossed the room to the closed door. Brown eyes appraised me, and she winked, hips swaying provocatively as she slipped into the bedroom. I raised an eyebrow at Raymous as he sauntered to the sideboard and poured two glasses from the decanter with red liquid. Handing me a glass, he motioned to the chairs. Choosing one, I sat down and propped an ankle on my knee. Raymous pulled out a game board, setting up the pieces for Capture the Pegasus.

"You bring your own whore?" I sipped the glass of sweet wine.

Raymous laughed. "It's a long journey and unlike the majority of my crew, fucking a man does not appeal to me," he said, taking a sip of his drink. "You are welcome to her. Unless the girl you brought—"

"No," I snapped. "She is not like that. She belongs to Damiyun."

Though I tried my best to keep them away from each other, their wills were far stronger than I had thought. I could readily admit my attempts to keep Damiyun focused as the girls Keeper to be selfish. She was a sweet and innocent woman. She reminded me much of my Jaylynn and in that respect, I felt as though she had allowed someone like Arias to take her. Allowed herself to believe the man she was with loved her. I only wanted to save her from the hurt that would come from being involved with Damiyun.

And of course, I had to make sure Damiyun would remain focused and do what needed to be done, but I could only do so much to stop the inevitable. I could only hope the dark side residing in him—the unfeeling, uncaring side—would ignore whatever feelings he had for her. We needed the Damiyun who murdered his father in cold blood and plunged the dagger into his wife's heart. Love was not a luxury we could afford.

Though, I knew nothing ever went according to plan.

Raymous drew my attention. "So, you haven't—"

I picked up a hunter and moved it into position. "Your turn, Raymous. And if you ever suggest again—"

Raymous held his hands up. "I get it, Abe," he said, moving a piece into play. "I know you didn't want to tell me anything other than that you needed passage to Varnalay, but money has exchanged hands, and you are now on my ship." He sat back in his chair. "What's your business, Abe?"

I chose a serpent and moved it into position. It was a losing spot I knew, but that didn't matter. I would win all the same.

I rubbed my eyes with a sigh. I was weary.

The presence of my father and the position he thought I would gleefully take weighed heavily on my shoulders. Raymous' eyes burned into me and though I didn't think he needed to know, he was a trusted friend. He had brought me places no other would, including this trip to Varnalay.

"The girl," I sighed, watching him move another piece. "She was born to stop Themesis from breaking free. I will take her to the Abyss and stop the darkness."

Raymous exhaled sharply. "Fuck, Abe. Why would you do this? She's so young."

Yes, she is. I shook any fatherly feelings that tried to seep in and turned my attention back to the board.

"You know as well as I what will happen if Themesis breaks free. The demons you have heard of... It's just the beginning and a small taste." I said, watching Raymous make a move. "Damiyun and Lillyanna encountered a Pyragaty. Had I not got there when I did..." I shook my head at the thought.

"But the girl. Gods." Raymous shook his head. "The thought of the world's fate resting on her shoulders—it's mad. How do you know she's the one?"

"I know."

"But—"

I sighed. "Her mother is Felicity. Lillyanna was born to do this."

Raymous rubbed his eyes. "You're crazy, Abe. Why you would ever agree—?"

"I had no choice," I said, making my final move, trapping his Pegasus on its safe spot.

"You and that damned Luck of the Fallen One. It will get you into trouble one day," Raymous chuckled. I laughed and tossed back the rest of my drink.

"So, your whore?"

Raymous grinned. "Are you looking for some fun?"

I stood up and tossed some coins on the board.

"My bed is yours for however long you need," he said, laughing. I made my way around the table and walked back to the closed door. To Raymous' bedroom and the whore who waited. Pushing the door open, I smiled at the woman who lay on the bed covers. Closing the door behind, I crossed the room, pulling my shirt off as I did so.

I looked at the woman who lay naked and ready, and descended on the whore who would do my bidding for however long I wanted.

And who would make me forget about the journey.

About my father and about my role in this.

About Jaylynn, Lillyanna and Damiyun.

If only for a little while.

SEVENTY-TWO

W E HAD BEEN SAILING for three days. The skies and wind favored us and the boat flew through the water, though I suspected some speed was due to Raymous' magic, the hard lines on his face and the constant look of exhaustion telling me as much.

"The winds are in our favor, Raymous. There is no need to use your magic."

"The faster we sail, the faster I get you to Varnalay."

"At what cost?" I shook my head. "Spare your magic and your energy. You cannot know when you will need it."

Raymous nodded, and the ship jerked beneath my feet as he released his hold, and the vessel came under wind power.

I looked about the deck, eyes going to Lillyanna as she doubled over the railing, heaving into the sea. Damiyun stood beside her, holding her hair back, and stroking her back as she got sick.

After supper on the first day, she became ill, and she had not stopped since. The sailors found her plight amusing, placing bets on when and how often she would be sick. They even composed a song at her expense, which they sang now, their loud voices carrying across the ship on the breeze:

> *"Lil, Lil.*
> *The lass is ill.*
> *She's gonna be sick,*
> *Oh, she's gonna spill.*
> *Lil, Lil.*
> *The coin you fill.*
> *I'll pay a copper,*
> *Oh, will she spill?*
> *Lil, Lil.*
> *Toss your fill.*
> *The boat, it heaves,*
> *Oh, so you will.*
> *Lil, Lil.*

Take a nap.
Come back in the 'morrow.
Oh, we'll be back.
Coin. Coin.
Toss a coin.
When she's sick,
Oh, you earned that coin. "

I chuckled at the song, hand slipping into my pocket and touching the pouch of coins I had won the day prior. Pulling out four coppers, I tossed them to a sailor who was walking by.

"Three more times within the hour and another upon smelling dinner," I said, watching as he carefully marked down my bet with a grin.

I crossed the deck to where Lillyanna stood wrapped in Damiyun's embrace. Her skin was ghostly white, beads of sweat dotted her brow and tendrils of hair stuck to her face. She breathed heavily, disentangling herself from Damiyun, then turned and dry-heaved over the side. I glanced at the sailor who I had given coin to.

"It's gotta be solid, Abe. Dry heaving don't count," he called out.

"You're betting on her?" Damiyun growled, eyes angry.

"I need to pass the time."

"Bastard," Damiyun pulled Lillyanna back into his arms.

"I'm glad you are taking pleasure in my misery," she said, voice muffled by Damiyun's shirt.

"I had all intentions of sharing my winnings with you."

"How caring."

I chuckled, my laugh cut short by an ear-splitting screech and the loud flap of wings above. I looked up, shielding my eyes from the sun, only to see a large, winged beast circle the ship. An alarm sounded—bells clanged on the mast—and deckhands scurried about.

"What is it?" Raymous' voice came from beside me.

"Demon, though I don't know what sort," I said, frowning up at the creature.

Most monsters of my father's creation were made from darkness. Light destroyed them. The fact this beast was impervious to the sun concerned me.

The beast screeched again and dove toward the ship, red eyes darting rapidly within their sockets.

Scanning.

Searching.

"Get Lillyanna below deck," I snapped to Damiyun who stood still, watching the beast. "Now, Damiyun." I shoved him toward the door leading below.

Shaking himself, he grabbed Lillyanna's hand and dragged her across the ship, disappearing behind the door.

A growl came from beneath my beard. Reaching in, I pulled out Bel. A bandage kept his left wing at his side, and a sling held his forefoot.

"No, Bel," I said. He growled in disappointment, red eyes looked at the demon in the sky. He let out a high-pitched screech, front foot pawed at my hand, red eyes glared at me. "You're hurt. I will not risk you getting injured further. I might need you later," I said. Bel sighed, his good wing drooped, and I tucked him back beneath my beard.

"Now would be a good time to use your magic. That is, if you aren't already spent?" I said to Raymous, eyes on the beast as it dipped and swooped. There was nothing I could do to stop it. There were no shadows for me to call. No darkness for me to use. The only thing we could do was try to out sail it.

"I have enough energy," Raymous said.

The sails snapped, cloth billowing out, and I stumbled as the boat surged forward, picking up speed.

"I can try to kill it with my magic," Damiyun's voice said to my right.

"And set the entire ship on fire? No." I shook my head.

"You know I have other magic."

"Which may or may not work."

"It won't hurt to try. We can't possibly outrun it."

"No," Raymous cut in. "But we might be able to lose it in a storm." I followed where he pointed, noting the dark clouds and rain far off on the horizon.

"Are you sure?" I asked, not keeping the concern out of my voice. The last thing I wanted—the last thing we needed—was for Raymous to expend his magic and burn himself out.

"What are our other options? I've got this, Abe. Haven't I gotten us out of worse situations?" He grinned, a look more like a grimace, and then hurried off toward the helm. Grasping the wheel in both hands, he gave a hard turn to starboard. His teeth clenched, his face a mask of concentration as he steered the vessel toward the advancing storm with the winged demon still hot on our tail.

R AIN SLASHED, STINGING, AND biting flesh, and the waves heaved, tossing the ship about like flotsam. Raymous yelled instructions to the deckhands, his voice almost lost in the howling wind. Sailors ran about the ship pulling and securing lines, desperately trying to keep it under control. A gust caught the main sail, which snapped violently and caused a sailor to lose his grip on the line. The boom swung around, catching two men, throwing them overboard.

"Fuck." Raymous swore. He held tight to the wheel, desperately steering the ship, as the sailors fought to control the main sail.

And above it all, above the noise and ruckus, was the sound of the pursuing demon. A ball of white light flew into the sky, followed by two more. The explosions lit up the dark, and the demon screamed as they hit their mark. I looked over at Damiyun as he launched another ball at the beast. Again, it hit its mark, and though it knocked the beast back, it didn't seem injured.

"Its scales are too thick," I yelled to Damiyun, my voice just audible over the wind.

"But it's getting knocked back. If I can just knock it out of the sky, or far enough away, it could give us a better chance," Damiyun yelled back, launching two more balls at it.

I glanced over at Raymous, who had a tight grip on the wheel. He gritted his teeth, his face a mask of concentration as he struggled to keep the boat from capsizing. The sound of flapping wings came closer, and the demon swooped down. Claws grabbed a sailor, tearing him in half and dropping the body on the deck. It shot upward, turned around, and came flying back down toward us. Damiyun threw another ball and knocked it back a few feet. The beast shrieked. Burning red eyes locked on him as it dove. I bolted forward, pulling the shadows around as I ran, and launched myself at the beast, wrapping it in darkness. The beast screamed and struggled as I wrapped myself around it, pulling the darkness closer and closer. Crushing and suffocating until it stilled. Releasing the darkness, I dropped the lifeless body onto the deck. It was a big beast with a dragon-like appearance. Thick, black scales covered its body. A serpentine tail wielded sharp barbs at the end. Barbs that I knew to be venomous. Its long snout boasted wicked teeth, and it had razor-sharp talons at the end of curled feet.

"What in the Abyss is that thing?" one sailor pointed at the corpse.

"A nasty demon of Themesis' creation," I said. "Toss it overboard, but take care of the barbs on the tail. They're venomous." The man nodded and gathered five other sailors.

"He's trying to keep us from getting there," I said to Damiyun.

"Us, or me? We both know he wants Lillyanna. He's in her nightmares. He calls her his queen. He speaks of being Blood-Bound to her," Damiyun said. "Her father spoke of it too. He thinks she will submit and free him. There would be nothing stopping that from happening if I was gone."

"There's me. I would never let that happen to her. And you know I will not let you die."

We stood in silence in the middle of the storm, watching the men drag the demon across the deck then toss it in the ocean. After a while, Damiyun turned and made his way below deck, and I went and stood beside Raymous, who struggled at the helm.

"Need help?"

"I got this, Abe. For now. Just pray the storm breaks soon."

For two days, the vessel tossed around in the turbulent sea.

For two days, the boat rocked and heaved, and I struggled to keep my stomach calm.

Finally, on the dawn of the third morning the winds ceased, and the slashing rain slowed to a drizzle and at midday the clouds parted, and the sun cast its golden rays onto the deck.

I stood at the rail, Lillyanna and Damiyun silent by my side, and watched as the outline of a mass of land came into view. A giant mountain rose high into the clouds. The dim sunlight glinted off the smooth glass-like surface, flashing like a beacon.

Like a warning. I rolled my shoulders. The oppression of the mountain—of my father—sat heavily between them.

The land mass grew close, and the mountain rose larger as we drifted toward the port of Bogy Hatch. Deckhands scurried about, lowering sails, tossing lines, and they soon hauled in and tied the ship. Damiyun held Lillyanna in his arms, their eyes fixed on the distant mountain.

"Let's go," I turned on my heel as soon as they lowered the gangplank, and stepped off the boat.

A somber pall descended upon us, and for the first time I was unsure of myself—of what was to be done. And I hoped that when the binds on Themesis' tomb were once again secured, Damiyun would understand and forgive me for the role I had played.

SEVENTY-THREE
DAMIYUN

I grasped Lillyanna's hand as we staggered off the ship.

I didn't want to be here.

As it were, fate and the damned gods had brought me to this place, and now the inevitable loomed above.

The obsidian wall known as Kraagswell Mountain.

We made our way through the dreary streets of Bogy Hatch, where nefarious eyes tracked our movements, assessing the sort of target we were. I loosened the dagger in my belt and pulled Lil closer to my side. Shadows flickered and moved, sharp teeth glinting in the dim sunlight. Eyes flashed in shapeless faces. Evil beings wandering the streets looking to prey on the weary and unobservant. I clutched my dagger tight as we stopped in front of a tavern and inn. The stone exterior was crumbling. Boards covered broken windows, and the door just barely clung to its rusted hinges.

Pulling the door open, Lil and I stepped into the dim establishment. Eyes peered out from beneath untrusting brows, glints of light flashing off deadly steel. The tension in the room was palpable. This was not an area I wanted to linger. Leaving Abraham in the tavern, I secured a room for me and Lil. I quickly closed and locked the door behind, propping a chair beneath the handle.

I crossed the small room to the window, opening it to clear the enclosure of the fetid stench of body odor, waste, and semen. The window looked out at the mountain, an ominous presence in the distance, and my heart ached at the thought of what was to come. Lil came up beside me and I slipped my arm about her waist and drew her close, pressing my lips to the top of her head.

"I don't want to do this, Damiyun," she said, her soft voice piercing the quiet. I pulled back and looked down at her.

At her sad, water-filled eyes. My heart broke.

"I know, Lil."

She rested her cheek on my chest, and I held her close. I held her tight. I counted the seconds and then stopped, just breathing in her scent, her sound. Stepping away, I took her hand and tugged her to the bed. Pulling her into my embrace again, my mouth caught hers. We kissed slowly at first, the intensity and need increasing. Slipping my hands beneath her shirt, I cupped her breasts, running my thumbs across nipples that quickly became erect, and she moaned in pleasure. Releasing her for a moment, my eyes searched hers. She slipped her shirt over her head and dropped it on the floor.

I gazed upon her. Her smooth white skin. The curve of her breasts. She sank to her knees, eyes locked on mine as she pulled my belt free, fingers undoing the laces to my trousers and easing them over my hips, taking me in her mouth. I groaned as the soft warmth of her mouth enveloped me. I thrust, meeting her pace, my fingers entwining in her hair as she pleasured me. Stopping her before I lost myself, I drew back and pulled her to her feet, then pushed her onto the bed. Quickly stepping out of my trousers, I relieved her of the rest of her clothing. Trailing kisses up her legs, I stopped at her apex, fingers lightly massaging her thighs, eyes locked on hers as I flicked my tongue between her legs. She moaned in pleasure, back arching and fingers tangling in my hair. Slowly I gave her pleasure.

She writhed beneath my tongue, soft gasps escaping her parted lips. I pulled away, stopping just short of her climaxing, and a look of frustrated desire flashed in her eyes. Moving up her body, I kissed her, sighing as her soft hands gently stroked me. I pulled back to look down into eyes dark with lust and need, and I paused.

I needed her. I needed to be inside her, feel her soft warmth, her breath on my skin, but I wasn't ready yet.

No. What I wanted most was to hold her in my arms. To prolong this moment for as long as possible.

"What's wrong?" Her face a mask of concern when I stretched out next to her.

"Nothing. I just want to hold you for a while," I said, pushing a lock of hair behind her ear. I gave her what, I hoped, was a convincing smile. She curled up in my arms, head resting on my chest and fingers idly tracing the brand. We lay in silence, the only sound that of our breathing. Her skin was soft and warm, and she felt good in my arms.

"I wish we could run away," she said, her soft voice breaking the silence. "I wish we could go someplace where no one knows us. Build a cabin in the woods. Live a meager life and grow old together."

I swallowed hard past the burning lump lodged in my throat. What Lil said ... I would kill to have. Once, I had thought to have such a life with Zenith and now what I desperately wanted with Lillyanna. As it were, the gods delighted in toying with me. Giving me a taste of what could be, only to snatch it away. I had often wondered if this was their way of punishing me for the atrocities I had committed throughout my life. If denying me true happiness was their idea of a game. Give me just enough to believe I could have what I had always wanted, only to rip it away.

I admit, I had spent many a night trying to think of a way to outsmart Themesis. To trick him into thinking I had fulfilled the prophecy. Perhaps implore Abraham to bring her back. To take her soul so she could live, but I knew he would not do that. Just as I knew, Themesis could not be fooled.

"What happens when this is over?" she asked, sitting up to look at me.

The burning in my throat and the sting of tears behind my eyes was almost more than I could handle.

I forced a smile. "We do exactly what you just said." Reaching up, I pulled her toward me, mouth devouring hers. "No more talk," I said, pushing her onto her back. She wiggled out from beneath me.

She opened her mouth to speak, and I kissed her again, then closed my eyes and leaned my forehead upon hers.

"Not tonight, Lil." I pulled back and looked down at her. "Tonight, is for us." Her eyes searched mine for a moment, then she pulled my face close and kissed me softly. I slipped inside her soft wetness, sighing at the feel of her as I slowly thrust. Lil wrapped her arms around me, drawing me close. Her legs locked around my waist, and she lifted her hips in rhythm to my thrusts.

"I love you, Damiyun Rayne," she whispered.

Swallowing hard, I held her close and let free the tears burning behind my eyes, naming each one as they fell:

Shame.

Deceit.

Pity.

Love.

I wished she had never spoken those words. Words I could not bring myself to say, even though I knew them to be true deep within my soulless body.

I loved Lillyanna. I loved her with every fiber of my being. But I couldn't say it. I couldn't say the words that would bind us for eternity. Words that would keep me from doing what needed to be done.

Instead, I held her close and wept a lifetime of tears. I held her in my arms, and I could feel her own hot tears on my skin, as we silently mourned together.

I took her three more times until we finally fell together, exhausted with desires fulfilled. Arms and legs entwined; we lay on the dirty bed cover speaking not a word. Finally, I felt the even breaths as she fell into sleep. But me? No, I couldn't sleep. I stayed awake holding my Lil, my love, close until the dim light filled the room, marking the start of a new day.

The start of our journey to reseal the binds on the Fallen One's tomb.

WE SET OUT EARLY the next day. Abraham waited outside the inn, sitting astride one of the two horses he procured for the journey. The air was chilly. A heavy mist cleansed my face of the tears that fell. Pulling my hood up, I boosted Lil onto the horse and swung up behind, slipping my arm about her and holding her close.

The streets were empty, and we rode through the sleepy town in silence, aside from the sucking noise of the horses' hooves in the mud.

I was exhausted. I had watched Lil as she slumbered. It was a fitful sleep. She thrashed around, calling out my name, only temporarily calming when I offered my soft voice and gentle touch. Once, her eyes flew open and darted around the room, fear, and panic on her face. She threw herself into my arms upon seeing me, body racked with sobs and her hot tears raining upon my skin.

At that moment, whatever strength I had inside fractured just a bit, and I wanted to pick her up and carry her out of the inn. Out of Bogy Hatch to hide her away.

"I don't want to do this." Her voice pulled me from my thoughts. She reached up, fingers brushing the tears from my cheeks. I leaned down and kissed her.

"Rest, Lil," I said, and she settled back against my chest with a sigh. I smoothed a lock of hair from her forehead and kissed her softly. I didn't deserve Lillyanna didn't deserve this situation. She deserved a real life with someone far better than me.

Not for the first time did I wonder why I was chosen, and once again I could only surmise it was a test of my will and my strength, both of which were close to breaking.

We traveled on, stopping well after dusk to make camp in a wooded clearing. We were in dangerous territory. Being so close to Kraagswell Mountain meant demons freely roamed the area. As such, I made a large fire, lined the perimeter with torches and held my magic close. Abraham unloaded the horses and divided our meager meal of dried fruit, meat, cheese and stale bread between us. We said nothing as we ate, the popping of the fire punctuating the deafening silence beyond.

It didn't feel right, this lack of noise. There were no night sounds. No creature's footsteps on dry leaves. No wolves calling to each other. I pulled my magic closer still and rose to my feet, as did Abraham.

I scanned the darkness beyond, eyes picking up a flash that darted between trees. My hair blew as the wind picked up, and the figures drifted out from the dark. Shrill, screeching wails pierced the quiet.

Wraiths.

Lil jumped to her feet, and I felt her draw on her magic.

"No," I said, glancing at her. "We cannot afford to have you spend yourself. I will take care of this."

"But—"

"Let Damiyun handle this." Abraham said. "You stay close to me."

I crossed the camp to just outside the lit perimeter, eyes watching the ghostly specters float closer and closer, their ear-splitting shrieks making me cringe.

I grit my teeth and drew my magic, the Elven power which resided inside. Holding my hands apart, I let the magic surge. The energy cracked and hissed as it flowed through my fingertips, forming a swirling ball of light. I heaved it out at the specters, a blinding flash briefly illuminating the dark. The sound of wraiths screaming echoed through the night as they disintegrated.

A movement to my right drew my attention. I turned to see Lillyanna standing a few feet away, her back to me. I could feel the raw power she wielded as she drew on it. We worked side by side. I threw orbs of light out into the night. Abraham lit the dry grass with his torch. Lillyanna, gods, she was the most impressive. Light emanated from her, surrounded her, and she sent it out in a terrific and powerful pulse. The wails of the dying specters pierced the air.

Over and over again we fought the beasts until at last a final scream rose and died. The silence was startling, though my ears still rang.

I was exhausted and drenched with sweat. My legs were weak, and I collapsed to the ground. I had completely spent myself from using my magic, and the lack of sleep the night prior only made it worse. Abraham hauled me to my feet, supporting me beneath his left arm, Lil beneath his right. We leaned heavily into him as he carried us both back to the campfire, where we collapsed next to each other.

"Where did that magic come from?" Lil asked.

"I am half Shadow Elf," I said wearily.

An odd look crossed her face, a mixture of longing and sadness, but I was too tired to ask. I closed my eyes, relaxing beneath the soothing stroke of her hand through my hair.

I could only hope no other beasts visited the camp this night.

If they forced me to use that much power again, I would be incapacitated, if not burned out, and I would not let Lil spend herself by using her magic.

And I would not let Themesis win.

Not when we had come so far and were so close.

Themesis' voice resounded in my head, telling me we had already lost. It was the last thing I heard before the darkness embraced me.

SEVENTY-FOUR

The journey was slow and arduous, the rocky terrain forcing us to travel much slower lest a horse break its leg.

The closer we drew to the mountain, the sparser the forest became. It became difficult to seek any sort of shelter beneath the trees, let alone construct something to protect us.

To hide us.

Every night the wraiths came, and I had run myself ragged with the effort of keeping them at bay.

"We can't keep doing this, Damiyun. You can't keep doing this. You've been using the most magic of all of us." Lil chastised when we collapsed to the ground, clothes soaked in sweat.

I removed my sweat-soaked shirt, reveling in the cool air caressing my skin. "I just need to rest."

She reached up and wiped beneath my nose, her finger red with blood. "You're killing yourself, Damiyun. You're weak and you barely sleep. Let me take care of them. You need to rest, if only just for a night."

"I'm fine, Lil." I forced a smile and ran my hand through her hair. The thick, fiery mane that I loved.

She opened her mouth to speak, and I silenced her protest with a kiss, my arms slipping around her and pulling her close as I stretched out on the ground. She curled into me, head resting on my chest, tears flowing upon my skin.

Her eyes turned to the fire that crackled and spat. "I'm not coming out of this alive, am I?"

My chest constricted. Of course, she knew. "I'm sorry, Lil." I choked, tears stinging my eyes.

She turned and looked at me, the firelight reflecting off the water that filled her emerald eyes. "Why did you not tell me? All those times I asked, you... You said nothing."

"What could I have said? What would my telling your fate change? What would you have done if you knew?"

"I don't know. It would have given me a choice. Since I've met you and Abraham, every decision that's been made has been made by the both of you."

"I'm sorry, but there was no choice. We could have run. We could have gone somewhere to try and hide. Gods, I've sat up at night trying to think of a way to outsmart Themesis. Have Abraham bring you back, if only to make Themesis think it happened, but I know he is not one who is easily fooled. It never would have worked, and I didn't tell you..." I reached out and took her chin in my hand. "I didn't tell you because I'm selfish. I didn't want to lose you. I didn't want you to hate me."

She buried her face in my chest, body shaking with sobs and hot tears raining upon my skin.

"I think someplace, deep down inside, I've always known it. I just wish you had told me when I asked. At least I would have been prepared," she said, voice cracking.

I kissed the top of her head. "I'm sorry. I love you, Lillyanna. The gods be damned, I didn't want to, but I do."

I swallowed hard, my eyes stinging with tears. The gods who had damned me for my life had given me what I had always searched for.

My Lil. My life. My light. My missing piece.

"Sleep, Lil," I whispered, lips brushing her brow.

"Damiyun—"

"Sleep, Lil. You needn't worry about me. I will be here when you wake, like I always am," I said softly.

Her green eyes met mine, and I looked away, unable to take the hurt—the love—shining in them. And only when I felt her relax—felt her fold into my embrace again—did I look back at her.

And only then—gazing upon her sleeping face, at the peacefulness in it as her body curled into mine—did I let my heart break.

Let the hard stone shatter into a thousand pieces. Let the love I felt for her wash over me.

And I held her close and wept a lifetime of tears. And when it was done? When I had no more tears to shed, I closed my heart—myself—up against another who might make me feel or care again. I'd close myself off, harden myself against feeling anything for another again. I locked Lil deep within my mind. Never again—when my task was done—would her name cross my lips. Soon, I would never see her eyes, her face, feel her hair and skin on mine. Soon, I'd never smell her or hear the way she laughed. She would be gone forever from this life. And from me.

No matter who I touched, I drove them to a dreadful end. My darkness destroyed.

I settled back against the cold, hard ground with my Lil in my arms, as my eyes met those of Abraham as he looked upon me—upon Lil—with sadness, as weariness descended, I finally succumbed to darkness.

To torment and torture.

To what awaited me on the other side when Lil was gone, when I had nothing left to live for.

To when Themesis finally had me.

To when he finally won.

SEVENTY-FIVE

NO ONE SPOKE AS we traveled. Even the horses stepped lightly, hooves barely making noise on the rocks. Even they were afraid of waking the beast below.

Themesis

We traveled on through the morning, the landscape becoming bleaker as we traversed. There were no trees. No grass. No flowers. No birds flew above. Only the crushing silence, the muddy road, and the shining wall of black looming beyond.

We finally came upon that wall—Kraagswell Mountain—sometime late in the afternoon. We pulled our horses to a stop, and I looked up at the massive rock face that disappeared into the misty clouds. Themesis' presence was thick here, and I could feel him, his power, his control.

His evil.

I rolled my shoulders and hopped down from the horse, then reached up and pulled Lil off.

"What now?" I turned my attention to Abraham.

"We go in."

I looked at the mountain of black. An impenetrable fortress that stretched high. My eyes went to Abraham, who strode forward toward the wall with purpose.

Taking a deep breath, I stepped forward, following Abraham, and pulling Lil along. She looked up at me, eyes brimming with tears. Wiping them away, she took a deep, shaking breath and gave a small nod. We walked several feet then stopped at a crevasse, a slim crack in the otherwise pristine mountain. I watched as Abraham strode forward and slipped through the jagged opening. Closing my eyes and gripping Lil's hand, I stepped toward the crack.

A wall of heat engulfed us. Lil inhaled sharply, and I gripped her hand, pulling her against my side.

It was cramped. The only way to slip through the opening was to walk side-ways, and even then, the wall of sharp rock pressed into my chest and back. The ceiling was low, just mere inches above my head, and I tried hard to steady my breathing and calm my racing heart as the walls closed in, suffocating me.

When we had somehow made our way through the small crack, I looked at Abraham, whose back was to me.

"Themesis knows I am coming. Move or I will do it for you." His deep voice growled, his words not quite registering as the huge demon guards with gnarled claws moved aside.

The hair on the back of my neck rose, and a cold sweat trickled down my back. Slowly we followed Abraham, past the guards, down another corridor, and I fought the urge to turn and run. He stopped in front of a set of massive stone doors. Taking a deep breath, he pushed them open and strode through. Lillyanna and I reluctantly followed.

Tapestries lined the walls, depictions of the war that raged between the gods when they tossed Themesis to the Abyss. Multicolored rugs were strewn across the floor. Carved in the middle of the floor was a large triangle within a circle, surrounded by odd words and pictures. Four channels ran from there across the room to the walls, where several chairs sat in a line.

But then my eyes went to Themesis.

He sat upon his throne; the garish monstrosity known as Nightshade. He was smartly dressed, ebony jacket over a crisp white shirt, black trousers tucked into knee-high leather boots polished to a mirror shine. His jet-black hair flowed about his shoulders, and his ice-blue eyes regarded us. As he looked us up and down, he idly scratched the head of a young woman who knelt beside him, cheek pressed against his thigh and a rapturous look on her face. She wore a green dress with a neckline that plunged to her navel, the sides cut up to the hip, her naked body outlined through the transparent material. Raven-colored hair spilled over her breasts, and a diamond collar glinted at her throat.

Abraham's face tightened, and I knew the young woman was Jaylynn. Themesis leaned down and whispered to her, lips brushing hers as she rose to her feet and exited through a door to the right and just behind the throne.

Themesis turned his attention back to us, his eyes narrowing slightly when they looked at me.

"The bastard son returns. Welcome home, Zedekiah," his voice boomed as he looked at Abraham.

"Father." Abraham dropped to a knee and bowed before the throne.

"And you have brought me my desire," he said. His blue eyes raked Lil's figure. He flicked his tongue out, lust clear in the hazy expression on his face.

"Did you doubt my loyalty?"

Themesis chuckled. "I admit your actions deceived me, though I suppose one must do what they must when playing a role," he said, sliding off the throne. He crossed the floor to where a solid gold sideboard sat. The light from the dozens of lit candles in the many tiered black diamond chandelier that hung from the center of the ceiling glinted off the polished gold. Vines and leaves of obsidian wound around the legs of the piece. A crystal decanter filled with red liquid and four crystal glasses sat on top of the gaudy piece.

I watched him move, frozen, the words echoing in my head.

Father.

The realization of what Abraham had done hit me like a ton of bricks and I staggered back.

"You son of a bitch. You lied. You betrayed us," I snarled, pulling my magic close.

"And that surprises you?" Abraham said casually, raising an eyebrow. He waved his hand, and I cursed as my magic disappeared behind a wall. Lil gasped, and I knew he had blocked her as well.

Abraham chuckled as he sipped the wine Themesis handed him. "You are so pathetic, Damiyun. So, trusting." He clucked his tongue and shook his head.

I clenched my fists at his words, wanting nothing more than to wrap my hands around his neck and choke the life out of him.

"Try it, Damiyun. I will snap your neck like a twig before you even raise your hands," Abraham snorted, which only fueled my rage.

Themesis' manicured fingers curled around the glass; his eyes danced with amusement.

"What are your plans?" Abraham turned to his father.

"I shall take my queen and free myself from this insufferable place. Damiyun will serve as my lap dog. And you, Zedekiah, you will take your rightful place by my side," he said, gesturing to the golden throne that sat to his right. His eyes went to Lillyanna. "Bring her to me."

Abraham strode over to where we stood.

"Don't do this, Abraham."

Ignoring me, he jerked his head to Lil, who followed him across the floor to the throne. Themesis motioned to her to come forward. She hesitated, and Abraham grasped her by the back of the neck and shoved her closer.

Themesis' eyes swept over her. "You're mine, Lillyanna. I feel your hunger. Your want. Your lust." His hand cupped her breast, thumb lightly stroking a nipple. She pulled back, though Abraham's grip kept her in place. "I will give you all you desire. I will make you mine," he said, leaning forward and pressing his lips upon hers. She jerked back, turned her head, and spat on the ground, angry eyes on Themesis as he chuckled. "Feisty little bitch. This will make breaking you all the more enjoyable. Take them to a cell." He waved his hand in dismissal and sat back on the throne, leg propped on his knee and chin resting on his fist. "You will call Damiyun's contract." His icy stare locked on me. Abraham nodded, grasping Lil by the arm and dragging her behind him.

"Let's go, lapdog." He grabbed my arm and pulled me along as well. I glanced at Lillyanna whose face held no expression, though she held her head high as she marched beside Abraham. We exited through the door Jaylynn had gone through, stumbling down a dimly lit corridor, then a flight of stairs leading to the bowels of the tomb. Huge, hunchbacked creatures with ugly, twisted faces and towering demons, with long, jagged teeth glinting in the lamplight scattered beneath Abraham's scowl as he marched by. He stopped at a metal door that he pushed open, the hinges moaning in protest, and shoved us inside the small, dark cell.

"You son of a bitch." I launched myself at him. He grabbed me by the neck and tossed me back. "You betrayed us. How could you? I trusted you, Abraham. Or do I now grovel at your feet and call you Zedekiah?"

Abraham chuckled as he snapped his fingers. A rolled-up piece of parchment appeared in his hand, along with a golden quill.

"All it takes are two words—Contract Fulfilled. With those two words, you will be Themesis' dog. His handsome slave who will obey his every word and command," he said, rolling up the contract—the piece of paper that had my name signed in my blood—and slipped it up his sleeve. "I won't write those words. Not yet anyway. There is much more for you to witness before your eternity of torment begins. And Abraham will do just fine." He flashed a quick smile and then turned his attention to Lil.

"I suggest you try to get some rest. My father is having a banquet, and you are the guest of honor. You will need every ounce of energy for what is in store for you," he said, turning away and striding out the door, plunging us into darkness. The scrape of the key doomed us to whatever fate Themesis felt ready to deal.

I reached out blindly for Lil in the suffocating darkness. My hand found hers and I pulled her into my arms. Her body shook with silent sobs, her hot tears seeping through the thin fabric of my shirt.

I was helpless. Completely useless.

I cursed myself for trusting Abraham. Though we often fought, I had believed in him, and now Lillyanna and I were locked beneath Themesis' tomb awaiting... what? I didn't know.

Sighing, my shoulders heavy, I sank to the cold, hard floor, pulling Lil with me, and leaned up against the wall to wait for Abraham.

SEVENTY-SIX
ABRAHAM

Closing the door to the cell, I stalked through the halls back to the throne room.

I was furious with Themesis for addressing me by name. In all the times I had been to the Abyss, he had never called me Zedekiah or Abraham.

Nor did he ever acknowledge I was his son. He would rather have pretended the disappointment like me wasn't his spawn. Damiyun was furious, and I couldn't say his feelings were wrong, but I was unable to concern myself with that. I had too much riding on this.

"Welcome home, Zedekiah," Themesis said again, a proud smile splitting his face. He handed me a glass of wine and motioned to the chair to the right of his throne.

The coveted position of honor was mine to take and rule from beside him.

"I admit you had me fooled," he said, sitting on his throne and propping his foot on his knee.

I hesitated a second, then took the chair he offered. "It seems they were as well."

Themesis laughed. "Here's to us." He raised his cup in a toast.

"What are your real plans?"

"I will take Lillyanna as my queen. Servant, really." He paused, taking a sip of wine. "The power she wields astonishes even me. Once we are Blood-Bound, the binds holding me will crumble, and together we will wage a war on the gods who damned me to this insufferable place."

"Her mother is Felicity. I doubt she will want to destroy her."

He laughed. "Yes, she loved her so much she abandoned her daughter shortly after she was born," he said. I acknowledged the fact with a nod. "The girl wasn't created to destroy me. They created her to join me."

I frowned at his words. He saw my look and chuckled.

"Felicity is a vixen. I dare say I graced her bed more than once. Do you think she chose Damiyun by accident?" He shook his head. "He can't resist a pretty face and an enigmatic woman. Pleasure is his vice. She knew this and knew he would satisfy his lust. She did it to torture him for leaving her." He took a sip of his drink.

"So then, why entomb you here?"

His eyes narrowed. "Because some gods envied me. Coveted the power I hold."

I shook my head. "If all of this were true, then why did you not just have a child with Felicity? Why would she have gone through the trouble of claiming a mortal? A child born of the two of you would be far more powerful than Lillyanna is now."

Themesis smiled. "Who says I didn't?"

I frowned at his words. If there was another child of his, a full god… I didn't want to think about the consequences. "Damiyun won't give her up without a fight, and Lillyanna isn't going to willingly submit."

"Willingly? No, though there are things that can be done to force her to," he said, smiling over the rim of his glass. He snapped his fingers, and my heart sank at seeing Jaylynn appear. In her hands she carried a tray that held a metal container, a brush used for painting and a slave dress. Themesis jerked his head in my direction, and my daughter walked the short distance to me and held out the tray. I looked down at what it held, stomach churning at the metal container holding paint infused with magic.

Magic that would make the wearer do whatever Themesis wanted against their will. I hesitated but a second. Feeling my father's eyes upon me, I gathered the items and rose to my feet.

"There will be a banquet in Lillyanna's honor. Make sure she is ready for it," Themesis said, turning his attention back to Jaylynn as she curled up at his side, all but purring like a kitten as his hand stroked her hair.

Clenching my jaw, I exited the throne room and made my way back to the cell where Lillyanna and Damiyun waited.

SEVENTY-SEVEN
DAMIYUN

THE SOUND OF THE key turning in the door jerked me to attention. Lil stirred in my arms, slowly waking, and sitting up. The door opened, and I shielded my eyes from the bright light of the torch Abraham secured in a holder on the wall. He left the room for a moment, returning with a gold container and a brush. A crimson-colored garment draped on his arm, which he hung on a nail secured in the stone wall.

The garment was a flimsy piece of cloth—if one could call it that, as thin as it was—cut high on the sides, neckline plunging obscenely in the front and back. It was a dress like the one Jaylynn wore.

"Take off your clothes," he snapped in Lil's direction as he removed the top of the gold container and placed it on the ground.

Lil curled up tighter in my arms, burying her face in my chest. Abraham sighed loudly.

"I have no patience for these—theatrics." He crossed his arms.

"Leave her alone, Abraham."

He glared at me then reached down and grabbed Lillyanna by her hair, wrenching her out of my arms and hauling her to her feet.

"Either you remove your clothes, or I will do it for you, and believe me when I say you do not want that."

"Leave her alone." I leaped to my feet.

Abraham glared at me.

Shadows moved swiftly toward me. Red eyes peered out, and sharp teeth snapped. Bony arms grabbed me, holding me in place. Putrid breath coated my neck, heat from their bodies crowded me. I had no ability to move or fight. I was frozen. "Don't do this." I struggled against the beast that held me.

He turned his attention back to Lillyanna. "Take off your clothes."

She glared up at him. "Fuck you," she said, spitting in his face. Had the situation not been as dire as it was, I would have been proud of her.

Abraham's jaw clenched. "The hard way it is." He grabbed Lillyanna's shirt and tore it open. She crossed her arms over her naked breasts. Grabbing the waistband of her trousers, he undid the laces and yanked them to her ankles. Tears spilled down her cheeks.

"Why are you doing this?" Her voice was barely above a whisper. "You said you weren't helping Themesis."

Abraham laughed. "I said a lot of things. You fools believed me."

I watched as shadows moved toward Lil. Hands grabbed her arms, pulling them behind her back. Abraham stooped down and picked up a jar from the gold box and opened it. Dipping the brush, he stepped toward Lil who struggled against the beasts that held her and began applying it to her skin, the metallic liquid covering vulnerable parts. The beasts released her. Abraham took the dress off the nail, pulling it forcefully over her head.

"Let's go. My father does not like to be left waiting," he barked, pulling the torch from its sconce with one hand, the other closed around Lillyanna's arm as he strode out of the cell. The beasts that held me dissipated, and I followed Abraham, who dragged a sobbing Lil through the halls.

Back to Themesis' throne room.

THE SOUND OF MUSIC drifted down the hall, growing louder the closer we came to the door to the throne room. Abraham reached out, grasped the handle, and pulled the door open. I gripped Lil's hand, giving what I had hoped was a reassuring squeeze as we crossed the threshold into the room.

A long table piled high with food—platters of fruits and vegetables, plates of pastries and bread and a large boar with an apple in its mouth—cut the room in half. Chatter rose above the music played by a quartet of beasts. Devilish creatures with horns and fiery eyes strummed instruments, their hooves kept time to the music.

"Abe, you lying fucker," a voice called out as we entered the room. I followed Abraham's eyes to a man of average height and build with close-cut auburn hair and hazel eyes dancing with amusement.

"All this time." He shook his head with a laugh. "All this time, you never let out your secret. I suppose I could understand. No one would want to think Daddy was playing favorites."

Abraham's jaw clenched. "Lucas," was all he said, tone tight. Lucas turned to Lil, a lascivious grin crossing his lips as his eyes swept over her.

"Well, well, well. What's this?" He took a step in her direction.

"Nothing," Themesis' voice called out from his throne across the room. Silence descended, and all eyes went to him. "At least not yet." His lips curled up in a smile, and he held out his hand. "Come to me, Lillyanna. My queen. My love." His voice was soft and kind. His tone coaxing.

I watched the gold paint glow bright. Her eyelids drooped, and a seductive smile curled her lips as she crossed the room in Themesis' direction, hips swaying provocatively.

"Lil—" My words were cut off by magic. I glared at Abraham, whose power bound my arms and legs, so I couldn't move.

Themesis' hands roved Lil's body. She shivered in pleasure, responding to his touch. He leaned forward and bit her neck, her breast. I couldn't do anything but watch as Lillyanna, spellbound, controlled by the paint, knelt in front of Themesis. She took him in her mouth. I choked back the urge to vomit. He used her in every way and when he was done, he invited his guests to have their fun. The other Soul Collectors and half-men, the beasts all surrounded her. The noises, and she went along, blindly and unable to fight it.

Fury burned within me. I could not unleash my fire. This was my punishment. My torment. I would never forgive Abraham for this betrayal. Never.

A tug came through the bond between Abraham and me. A feeling of dread. And two words: *I'm sorry.*

EVERY NIGHT, WHEN WE were brought back to the cell, the magic faded as soon as the door closed the paint was removed.

Every night I held Lillyanna, who wept in despair and shame.

Every night I reassured her she wasn't dirty.

She wasn't a whore.

That I still cared, and she was still mine.

And no matter how many times I told her I was bound and under Abraham's control. I couldn't do anything to help, I saw the mistrust build in the pools of her green eyes.

She whimpered at the sound of the key in the lock. Shook at seeing Abraham enter with a slave dress and paint. Cried as he applied the gold to her skin.

I pleaded with him. Begged him to not do this and all but threw myself at his feet, clutching at his coat tails and begging him to stop.

"Call my contract," I said one evening when he came, holding a shaking Lil to my chest. "Let Themesis do what he will to me but, please. Please, Abraham. Leave Lillyanna alone. Let me suffer his torment."

He turned his back and busied himself with the paint. "Are you not tormented? Does watching not hurt you?"

And with those words, I knew—I understood what Themesis was trying to do.

He failed to drive me mad with his taunts.

He failed to break me with his nightmares, but this? With what he was doing, I feared he would succeed.

That he would shatter me.

"You are doing to me what your father has done to you."

The muscles in his jaw tightened, but he said nothing as he finished up with Lil.

"Let's go," he barked, striding out of the cell, leading us back to the throne room.

To Themesis.

And to where I would again watch the magic in the paint control my Lil.

SEVENTY-EIGHT
LILLYANNA

THE DOOR TO THE cell opened and Abraham strode in holding the tray with the gold paint and a fuchsia slave dress draped over his arm. Casually, he hung the dress on the peg, then turned toward me.

"Clothes."

I glared at him. Damiyun slipped an arm around my waist and pulled me close. Any other time, I'd find comfort in his embrace. But not now. Not when he stood back and watched as I danced. As I fucked. As I was debased.

I shoved him away, ignoring the hurt look, the pained look that crossed his face. Ignoring my want to curl up in his arms and cry. This was my fate. This was what I was drawn to. With my eyes on Abraham, I took off the shirt he ripped, slipped out of my trousers, and stood naked in front of him.

"Paint me."

Black eyes met mine and for a brief moment, I saw sadness and pity.

For only a brief moment.

"Unless you want to fuck me too? You haven't yet. Why is that?" I slipped a hand between my legs, eyes pinning Abraham. "Taste?" I brought my hand up.

Arms grabbed me, pulling me against a firm chest. Hands covered my naked parts.

Damiyun. "Stop this, Lil," he said.

Wrenching out of his grasp, I sauntered to where Abraham stood. Spreading my arms wide, I slowly turned in a circle. "You like?" Dropping to my knees, I knelt before him.

"Stop." Damiyun said again, grabbing my arm to pull me up.

I yanked free. "Fuck you, Damiyun. Don't act like you don't enjoy this. You stand there and watch me get used. You do nothing to stop it."

His jaw clenched and nostrils flared. "Zedekiah binds me. He forces me to watch."

I laughed. "Well, then, since you enjoy it so much, I will give you a private showing."

I looked up at Abraham through lowered lashes, His jaw clenched and un-clenched. Reaching up, I hooked my fingers in the waistband of his trousers and licked my lips. He grabbed my wrists and roughly hauled me to my feet.

"Enough, Lillyanna," he said. His tone was gruff and held an edge.

"What's wrong, Abraham? Don't I turn you on?"

His nostrils flared and, again, pity flickered in his eyes for a moment. "Let's get this over with. Themesis despises being kept waiting."

I stood still as Abraham applied the paint. I didn't even wince. The pain I endured. My body throbbed with bruises and aches all over. When it was happening, when I was being used, I was far away, but after... I felt it all.

"Don't make her do this again," Damiyun said.

I glance over my shoulder at him. "Oh, but I enjoy it," I said, forcing a smile.

"Stop it, Lil. I know you don't."

I whirled around to face him. "You know nothing, Damiyun. You brought me here. For all I know, this has been your plan."

His jaw clenched. Hurt and anger flashed in his gray eyes. Good. I wanted him to hurt the way I've been hurt. He said nothing, but what could he say? Nothing would make me believe his words. Words felt hollow to my ears.

Abraham held out the dress and I laughed. "What's the point? It only gets torn off me anyway," I said. Tossing my hair over my shoulder, I straightened my back. "Let's get this over with. The party can't start without the guest of honor."

Abraham turned and opened the door. We followed him out into the hall. Damiyun came up beside me and slipped his hand in mine.

"Don't," I said. I jerked out of his grasp, ignoring the hurt look that once again crossed his face. A part of me wanted to believe he had no part in this. I wanted him to wrap me in his arms and tell me it's alright, but he just stands there. Watches. Does nothing to stop it.

As we walked to the throne room, I felt the eyes of the demon guards on me. Bony hands reach out to grab and touch. I swallowed back the bile that rose. At least when the magic in the paint came to life, I didn't know who I was with. I was detached. Not until it was over. Not until we were back in our cell and the magic dissipated. The knowledge of what had been done to me made me want to vomit.

We entered the throne room that was again packed with demons and Soul Collectors. Themesis lounged on his throne, a goblet of wine held loosely in one hand. His ice-blue eyes met mine and a slow smile curled his lips.

"Come to me, my queen," he said, crooking a finger in my direction.

Taking a deep breath, I crossed the room to where he sat and knelt at the base of the throne. "My love," I said, as I looked up at him.

Leaning forward, he pressed his mouth to mine. Slipping his tongue between my lips, he claimed my mouth. His warm, soft hands roamed my body as he kissed me.

"My pet. My queen. Mine," he whispered, breath hot in my ear. I closed my eyes and swallowed past the sickness.

"The guest of honor is here. Let the festivities begin," he said.

My body heated. A soft yellow glow emanated from the paint. Desire and want wrapped around me. My core pulsed with lust. Music began to play and Themesis rose gracefully to his feet.

"Come. Dance," he said, holding his hand down to me. Taking it, he pulled me up, wrapping me in his warm embrace. His scent, a musky mixture of sweat and sulfur, surrounded me. He held me close as he whirled me around the room. Hungry eyes watched. Tongues flicked out to lick lips as they waited for the dance to end. Waited for the fun to start.

When the song ended, Themesis smiled at me. His lips brushed my cheek. "Go, my love. They're waiting for you."

The paint flared at his words, glowing brighter, the desire, want, and lust all but consuming me. My vision became hazy, my body detached as I looked around the room at the men and demons who waited to get a piece of me. I turned back to Themesis.

"You first. Always, you first." I sank to my knees, my eyes locked on him as I undid the laces on his trousers and grasped his length. His head rolled back as I took him in my mouth, hands grasping my hair as he thrust. Then he laid me on my back and claimed me hard and fast. I shuddered in climax beneath him.

"Now go," he said, pulling his heavy body off me. Adjusting his trousers, he sat back on the throne. Sipping his wine, he watched me dance. Watched me be used. The magic of the paint made my desire insatiable. All I wanted was satisfaction. The only thing I wanted was to satisfy my insatiable appetite for pleasure.

I didn't care who—or what—was providing it, as long as I was satisfied.

And though it was all a hazy blur of being passed around—hands touching, grabbing, and prodding—the one thing that stood out in my mind, the one thing I saw over and over again, was Damiyun.

The man I had loved and who was supposed to protect me did nothing to stop what was happening. While I was being used, while I debased myself, while I crawled and groveled on the floor to Themesis, begging him to take me again, Damiyun did nothing.

He just stood there silent. Eyes watching.

And Abraham, too, stood back watching the show I put on.

Though his betrayal was sharp, Damiyun's cut me deep to my soul.

I didn't believe his words when he told me Abraham had bound him. That he couldn't do anything to help me. How could I when he had kept my fate a secret until the end?

And so, I gave in to the magic. Into the pleasure. The need. The want. I let it consume me. Flow through me. And I did whatever was requested and let them do whatever they wanted to me.

But when it was done, when we were brought back to the cell and the magic had worn off, that was far worse.

The memory of what I had done—what was done to me—came flooding back, and I felt dirty.

Ashamed.

A whore.

And the one I had trusted, the one I had loved, held me, and whispered over and over again I wasn't bad. But his words always rang false. Always, he did nothing when I was again forced to do what another wanted.

And knowing, he stood back and watched. Knowing he did nothing to stop it...

It was the end for me.

It was when Themesis broke me.

It was when I knew I was his.

SEVENTY-NINE
DAMIYUN

TIME STRETCHED.

Abraham didn't come for Lillyanna and the only things distinguishing one day from the next were the guard changes and the meager meals they provided us. Lillyanna lay in a ball on her pallet, oblivious to the rancid food slid through the opening beneath the door.

Oblivious to even me.

"You need to eat, Lillyanna. Please," I held her hands in mine.

"Why? Am I not going to die, anyway? Isn't this the end for me?" She lifted her head. Her tone was flat and dejected, but her eyes pleaded with me.

They begged me to tell her the truth and as I looked into those eyes—as I gazed upon the woman I loved, who I had sworn to protect and yet failed—I wanted to tell her the truth. Everything inside me screamed—begged—to come out, and like the coward I was, the pathetic person that I was, I said nothing.

She rolled back over and retreated deeper inside herself, and I was helpless to do anything.

Finally, when fifteen days had passed, when I had just about given up hope myself, did the door to the cell open, Abraham's bulk filling the doorway. There was no canister of paint, only the slave dress draped over his arm, which he tossed at Lil.

"Get dressed. Themesis waits."

Lillyanna didn't move, and I couldn't say I blamed her.

"The longer you make him wait, the more severe the punishment becomes. I doubt you would like to have the flesh peeled from your back."

Lillyanna grabbed the dress and sat up.

"I'll be with you, Lil," I said.

Hate-filled eyes turned in my direction. "Like you were when I was forced to perform? You did nothing to stop it."

I jerked back at her words. Had she struck me, it wouldn't have hurt half as much as what she said.

"I'm sorry, Lil. He bound me. I couldn't speak. Couldn't move."

"Save me your pathetic excuses," she spat as she slipped the obscene dress over her head.

"Take me to him," she said to Abraham, who gave a curt nod and led the way out of the cell. We followed him out. Lil's back was straight, and she held her head high. No words were spoken as we walked the familiar halls. My senses were elevated, and I kept myself alert. A foreboding feeling nagged at me, and I couldn't help but fear for what was in store for us.

For Lillyanna.

Abraham pushed open the door to the throne room. Aside from Themesis who sat on his chair—face tight, chin propped on his right fist, the fingers of his left hand drumming on the head of a griffin—the room was empty. There were no monsters, or demon guards, which I found curious. No doubt, he arrogantly assumed things would go smoothly. They had taken away the long table and everything was as it had been when we first entered his chamber what seemed like a Grand Passage ago.

Themesis rose to his feet when we entered, eyes cold.

"I told you to not keep me waiting."

"Lillyanna was being difficult, as usual," Abraham said, turning to glare at Lil whose chin jutted out in defiance. "I told her the punishment would be severe. Apparently, that means nothing. Perhaps she enjoys pain."

Themesis chuckled. "I will enjoy finding out," he said, eyes sweeping over Lil. I lunged in his direction only to be bound by Abraham once again.

"Why are you doing this?" I shouted at him.

He said nothing, though his jaw clenched, as did his hands.

"Bring her to me," Themesis said. Abraham grabbed Lil's arm. She glared up at him, wrenching it free, then made her way to where Themesis stood.

"What do you wish of me, my liege?" She bowed her head and executed a low curtsy. Then she fell onto her knees.

Themesis laughed softly. He stepped forward, cupping her chin, and tilting her head to look at him.

"You know what I wish." His voice was low. Lil closed her eyes, mouth opening slightly as his thumb caressed her bottom lip.

I opened my mouth to speak—to protest—frowning when a warning shot through the bond I held with Abraham. I turned my eyes in his direction, but he stood stoically, hands clasped behind his back, eyes watching Lil and Themesis.

"Now to take my queen," he said, releasing her chin. Lillyanna gazed up at him as he smiled. "Zedekiah." His eyes went to Abraham, who stepped forward. His hand grasped the dagger in his belt and unsheathed it. Themesis held his hand out. I watched as Abraham sliced his palm. Lillyanna turned her hand up, and Abraham sliced hers.

"No."

Abraham cast a glance at me at my outburst, and I watched as they grasped hands. As words were spoken, and as they marked each other's forehead with their blood, binding them together for eternity. Themesis then reached into the pocket of the red plush velvet coat he wore and pulled out a box. Sickness roiled inside me as he opened it, and I swallowed back the bile that burned the back of my throat as I gazed upon the emerald-encrusted collar nestled against the cream fabric.

"Once I put this collar on you, you will truly belong to me. My servant. The one who will give me a strong and worthy heir. A daughter who will produce the strongest son with the strongest son," he said, eyes resting on Abraham, who smiled.

"Is that not why I'm here? To carry on your legacy? To secure your presence in the world of the living?" Abraham said, head cocked to the side.

Themesis laughed. "I always knew you had not forsaken me."

"Why would I?"

Themesis chuckled, turning around and placing the box holding the collar on his throne.

The binds holding me loosened.

Do nothing. I blinked at the words filling my head. It wasn't Themesis' voice, but Abraham's. I looked at him as the binds fell away completely.

Stay still. Do not let him know, was the next message, and I clenched my fists, stifling a grunt as I felt my magic fill me.

I frowned and looked over at Abraham, whose eyes were trained on Themesis.

Trust me.

EIGHTY

I DID AS HE said, though I struggled to do nothing. To just stand there. I watched him stride to where Lillyanna knelt. He casually leaned down, brushing dirt off his boot. His big hand gripped her shoulder, and I felt her magic return as well.

What was going on?

Abraham stood back up as Themesis turned around holding the slave necklace, the beautiful emeralds glinting in the low lamplight.

Beautiful and dangerous.

I clenched my fists as he stepped off the dais to where she knelt.

Trust me. Wait.

Wait? Wait for what? I sent back.

Trust me.

Themesis held the necklace high. "Once I put this on you, it will bind you to me for eternity."

Lil bowed her head and peered up at him through lowered lashes, her look seductive.

"I look forward to serving you, my lord," she said, voice husky. "I know it will be enjoyable, and I will do whatever it takes to please you."

Themesis smiled, and his fingers caressed her cheek. "I know you will."

He leaned down and brought the necklace closer, closer.

I clenched my fists as I watched, letting my magic fill me.

Do nothing. Not yet. Abraham's message was urgent.

He will enslave her, I sent back angrily.

Trust me.

Trust a betrayer? I realized this could be a ruse.

He sighed. *I did what I had to. I am no betrayer.*

Right, Zedekiah.

Abraham shot me a quick look over his shoulder and then in one quick motion he picked Lillyanna up and tossed her in my direction. I caught her in my arms and held her tight.

Themesis blinked, momentarily confused. Abraham threw his hands out, and Themesis flew backward, crashing into Nightshade.

"You ungrateful, useless son of a whore!" He raged, slowly rising.

"Did you think I would let you win? Let you spread your darkness—your perversion—upon the land?"

"You would have ruled beside me. You would have had mankind—these pathetic, weak beings—serve you. You would have been all powerful," he spat. "You cannot turn your back on who you are, Zedekiah. They have trapped me in this insufferable place for thousands of Grand Passages. It is time the gods—and man—pay for what they did to me."

Lil thrashed in my arms. "Let me go," she snarled.

"No," I said, gripping her tighter. Pain sliced through my arm as teeth clamped down. She bit hard, drawing blood, and I released her. Spinning around, she kneed me in the groin.

"Fuck," I cursed, falling to my knees. "What are you doing?"

I felt her draw her magic. Scrambling to my feet, I bit back the pain and launched myself at her. My arms encircled her, and we crashed to the ground.

"Get off me," she snarled.

Themesis laughed. "Come, my pet," he said, brushing dust off his fine velvet coat.

I pulled Lil even closer. "Don't," I said, my lips close to her ear. "He's controlling you. Fight it, Lil."

Though she no longer wore the paint, I knew what she did brought her closer to him. Made her closer to being his. Despite the hatred she showed, I knew my Lil was still in there. I hadn't rescued her from those men only to lose her to Themesis.

"I am his," she hissed. Silver swam in the green depths of her eyes. Her veins glowed bright. Shit. She was calling the lightning.

But how?

"Abraham," I called out. His eyes met mine and then went to Lil's.

Run. His voice echoed in my head.

No, I said, gripping Lil tighter.

"Stupid fool. Do you think you can defeat me? Defeat us?"

Her veins glowed brighter. And hot. It was different from fire. From the flame, that had no effect on me. It was white and searing. The obsidian ceiling rumbled.

"Damn it, Abraham. She's calling the lightning," I called out.

Themesis laughed. "Yes, she is." His blue eyes pierced me. "She will destroy you. She will destroy all." His eyes went to Lil. "She is mine."

I couldn't hold her any longer. The heat, the burning fire she radiated was more than I could take. I had to release her. She spun around and looked at me.

Darkness and silver swirled in her empty, emotionless eyes. The obsidian above rumbled like thunder. Light crackled around her.

I would not lose her again.

Abraham.

His eyes snapped to me.

She will kill us all, I said.

"Who shall meet their demise first, my queen?" Themesis' voice was filled with amusement. Lil's eyes met mine. A slow smile curled her lips. The silver in her veins pulsed. The bolts of lightning curled around her like a serpent. Her hair stood up and the ceiling trembled.

"Him," she said, pointing at me. "He hurt me the most."

"Did he?" Themesis drawled. Fingers tapped his lips and a small smile formed. "Hurt him. Make him suffer."

"I will, my king." She turned to me. Hatred curled her lips, and her depthless eyes pinned me. The walls and ceiling shook more. Sparks danced around the obsidian.

Shit. She was going to kill me, I knew.

Do something. I sent through the bond.

Abraham clenched his fists. The floor rumbled beneath my feet. His eyes were on Lil.

"Wait. No!"

The ground heaved beneath us. For a moment, a painfully slow moment, we were airborne before crashing back down to the ground. The air rushed out of my lungs, and I gasped for breath. Black dust obscured my vision. Shards of obsidian sliced into my back. I shook off the pain and leaped to my feet. My eyes found Lil through the dust and debris. She lay in a pile of rubble, her body twisted unnaturally. I rushed to her side, ignoring the throbbing pain that coursed through my body. Ignoring the blood that dripped down my back.

The room shook and rumbled. Dust rose and rock rained down, pelting my head and back as Abraham and Themesis engaged in battle.

"Lil?" I carefully turned her head. Pressing my fingers to her neck, I felt for a pulse, sighing with relief when I felt her heart flutter beneath my fingertips. Her eyes opened and she looked at me. Recognition flickered in her eyes.

"Damiyun?"

"I'm here. You're alright," I said, brushing a lock of hair out of her eyes.

"What's happening?" She tried to sit up, and I gently pushed her back down.

"It's fine, Lil. Don't worry about it."

The battle raged behind us. Flashes of light lit up the room. Loud booms and crashes vibrated off the walls. I had to get the dagger from Abraham. I had to end this now.

"End him." Themesis' angry voice called out. "Kill the bastards who hurt you. Kill the bastards keeping you from me. Kill them both."

Any recognition Lil had faded from her eyes, replaced with black emptiness. Pushing me away, she leaped to her feet and drew her magic. What I felt from her was dark and strong. I knew she was feeding from the Abyss.

From Themesis.

"Lil, don't. Please. Come back to me."

"I am his," she snarled. "You will not keep me from him."

Turning, she focused across the room. "You will die, Zedekiah."

A blast of light raced across the room. Abraham's eyes widened in shock as it hit him in the chest, throwing him against the wall.

"Lil, please. Stop," I begged again.

She turned toward me. An ugly and twisted snarl curled her lips as she let loose another blast.

EIGHTY-ONE
ABRAHAM

M Y BODY HIT THE wall hard, knocking the breath out of me.

Fuck. She was stronger than I thought. She should have been knocked out. I heard Damiyun's thoughts. His want for my dagger, but then... then Themesis called to her.

And the girl answered.

"You will pay for this, Zedekiah." Hands gripped my hair bringing me back.

"Pathetic. Useless. The best part of you ran down your whore of a mother's leg," he snarled, jerking me to my feet.

"I wish all of me had," I retorted.

I heard a hiss and felt a stirring in my beard. Bel launched himself at Themesis, tiny claws scratching his face. Themesis roared, releasing his hold on me. Grasping Bel, he tossed him to the side. I heard a thud, followed by a whimper, but I didn't have time to worry about him. I scanned the rubble. Damiyun lay heaped among the rock and debris.

Get up, I snapped through the bond. There was no response. The girl stood over him, a smile on her face. Taking a step back, she turned to me. Dark eyes that swam with silver met mine.

"Your turn," she said.

The throne room shook. More rocks fell from the ceiling and the ground rumbled beneath my feet.

"That's right, my queen. My pet. Show him who you are. Show him who he could have been," Themesis crooned.

Darkness enveloped her. Tendrils of shadows crawled to where she stood. Her silver eyes looked up at me. A shudder shook my body. She looked dark. Evil.

A shell of the girl she was.

The Abyss, Themesis, was claiming her. I could not let that happen. Smoke curled and snaked its way toward me. Red eyes formed as it curled into a massive demon, its wickedly sharp teeth and claws glinting in the lamplight, saliva dripping from its massive maw. And just as soon as the beast formed, there was a blinding flash of light and it disintegrated.

Themesis' laughter echoed. "How cute. Your loyal puppy has decided to help." He clucked his tongue. "You could have had everything, Zedekiah. Everything. Riches beyond compare. Slaves kneeling at your feet." A wicked grin split his face. "I would have even given you Jaylynn back."

I hesitated. His grin widened.

"I would have returned all of her memories. She would have known her father again. Is that not what you want?"

I shook my head. "No. I am not easily manipulated like the mortals are. I am no fool," I growled. I pulled the shadows closer to me, and the darkness moved, creeping along the floor, swirling and undulating, forming four massive dog-like beasts. With lips curled back in snarls, their yellow eyes peered at my father, and smoke drifted from nose and mouth as they breathed. Their backs were hunched, with wiry hair that stood up in sharp points, and a low growl rumbled in their chests.

I flicked my hand, and they tore off across the room in his direction, leaping in the air and descending upon him. Jaws latched onto limbs, bones snapped and Themesis screamed. The cavern rumbled, and an explosion tore through, the concussion throwing me backward. The shadow dogs yelped as Themesis tossed them away, and they slithered back into the shadows from whence they came. Themesis rose to his feet. His fine coat was torn, his hair was tangled, mess, and dirt and blood marred his face.

"That was not very nice, Zedekiah," he said, rolling his shoulders.

Movement to my right caught my attention. I saw Lillyanna making her way to where Damiyun stood. Pain flashed through the bond. He had broken some bones when he was thrown. Lillyanna held up her hands. Light sparked between them.

"Lil," Damiyun said, holding his hands up in supplication. "Please. Don't. You know me. I know you do."

She hesitated a second, a soft look flickering across her face. The light that she held dimmed just briefly. "Damiyun," she sighed.

He relaxed, taking a step in her direction.

Don't, I warned.

"End him," Themesis hissed.

The darkness fell back upon her. Lillyanna snarled and sent a blast of magic at Damiyun. He flew back, slamming hard against the wall, right leg twisted in an unnatural position.

"Your turn." Lillyanna's voice pulled my attention.

She stood with her hands out. The room rumbled. Rocks fell from the ceiling and walls. I called the shadows. Twisted figures rolled out from the darkness. Red eyes peered out. Jaws snapped and bony fingers grabbed. Smoke billowed from empty sockets with a hiss. They flowed across the floor, but... not to me. To Themesis.

The figures curled around him, draping him in darkness. A ghastly skull settled upon his head.

"I own the Abyss, Zedekiah. I own the darkness. The demons. Not you," he said. He turned his attention back to Lillyanna. "Finish him," he said.

A rolling mountain of black and rubble came at me, slamming me in the chest, throwing me to the ground, and partially burying me. I blinked my eyes against the pain and nausea and through the haze of darkness and dust, I watched Lillyanna glide across the room to Themesis and drop to her knees.

"Now, where were we?" He pulled out the necklace again. Lillyanna swept her hair up, and, tilting her head back, locked her eyes on him.

Pushing the pain and agony aside, I pulled myself out from beneath the rubble and stood up.

EIGHTY-TWO
DAMIYUN

No. This couldn't be happening.

Gritting my teeth against the rolling pain and swallowing back the bile and nausea, I pulled my body up, and glanced at Abraham, who stood as well.

I pulled my magic close, drawing on the Elven power. Feeling the vibration move through my hands and out my fingertips, hissing and snapping as the orb formed.

"Forgive me, Lillyanna," I whispered, then hurled it at her at the same time Abraham launched another attack on his father.

The orb hit Lil in the back, exploding in a flash of light, and she crumpled to the floor. Abraham's pulse hit Themesis. The necklace fell from his hand as he flew across the room. Ignoring the excruciating pain radiating through my leg, I rushed to Lil. My eyes went to the necklace lying on the floor. I pocketed it, then rolled Lillyanna over. Her eyes opened. For a moment, recognition fluttered within. A look quickly replaced with hatred.

And I knew it was this room—this place—that had gotten to her. That it was sinking its claws into her and bringing her to the darkness.

"Lil—"

She snarled at me and placed her hands on the floor. A low rumbling filled the room, and the rock beneath me vibrated then heaved up, tossing me into the air and back down in a mass of rubble and pain. I picked myself up, eyes watering and coughing from the dust and debris. I looked at Abraham who was embroiled in a fight and at Lil who stood with her arms out to the side, palms up. The cavern rumbled and shook, and I knew she was going to bring the entire place—the entire mountain—down upon us. Again, I drew my magic—far more than before—and launched it at her, watching as it hit her again, tossing her into the air and across the room. She slammed into the floor; body motionless.

"Do what needs to be done, Damiyun. Do it while she is unconscious," Abraham grabbed my attention, and I looked in his direction. He had Themesis pinned to the wall with his magic. Dark tendrils of shadow and smoke held him. Abraham's jaw clenched, his face a mask of concentration, and sweat rolled down his temple. He reached into his belt and pulled out a dagger, which he dropped on the ground and kicked to the center of the room.

"Now, Damiyun. I can't hold him much longer."

His words registered in the dark recesses of my brain and, pulling myself up with a strength I didn't know I had, I ran across the room to where Lil lay. Picking up her limp body, I cradled her in my arms and limped to the center of the room.

To the circle where the dagger lay.

I placed her on the ground and brushed a curl from her forehead. Her eyes fluttered open, and she looked at me.

And it was her who looked at me.

It was my Lil.

"Do it, Damiyun. Please. Do what needs to be done. End this. End him." Her eyes brimmed with tears. "Do it before this place claims me. Before I'm forever lost to you."

"I'm sorry, Lillyanna," I said, brushing the wetness from her cheeks. I swallowed against the lump in my throat. "Lil. My Lil. Always and forever, you will be mine. You were my savior and my torment. The only one who ever saw good in me. The only one who saved me from myself. My Lil. My light. My life." I leaned down and pressed my lips to her as my right hand clutched the dagger beside her. "Part of me wished you never returned. Part of me hoped you were in a better place, with one far better than me. And when you came back, when your memories returned, when you knew all I had done, despite my betrayal, the way I hurt you, you still loved me. You still stood by me." Tears flowed from my eyes, dripping on to her face.

"I love you, Lillyanna. I love you far more than I ever thought possible. I will never love another like I loved you. Please forgive me once again," I whispered, pulling back. With eyes on hers, I plunged the dagger into her heart. She gasped, eyes widening, and her hands gripped mine as she drove the weapon deeper and jerked up.

"I love you, Damiyun Rayne. Thank you." She whispered before her body went limp, and her Life Force left her, sightless eyes staring at the ceiling.

I watched the blood flow out onto the triangle, the odd symbols and words glowing as the river of red flowed over and into the channels.

"No," Themesis screamed. "What have you done?"

A loud rumble tore through the chamber, shaking the walls and floor. Rocks fell from the ceiling and crashed around us. Themesis clutched his head and fell to his knees, howling in anguish and pain.

"Let's go," Abraham jerked his head.

I gazed down at Lillyanna, whose face was peaceful, and kissed her one last time before hurrying after Abraham, running through the dark caverns back to the entrance of the cave.

Themesis' howling faded, but the voice in my head—his voice—did not.

You will pay for what you have done. I will torment you ten-thousand-fold and you will go mad. I will own you, Damiyun Rayne.

I shuddered at the voice. At the words I knew were true.

And a part of me didn't care, as I knew I deserved it.

I knew I deserved whatever torment he inflicted, for nothing could be worse than the torment of a life without Lillyanna.

IT WAS NIGHT WHEN we emerged from the Abyss. Abraham pulled the shadows around us, and we appeared in Marney-Faire, the village where our horses were stabled. It felt odd not having Lillyanna with me. It was as though a piece of myself were gone.

The knowledge I would never look into her green eyes, hear her voice, feel her soft skin and lips upon me hurt my soul. My vision wavered, and I refused to wipe the tears wetting my cheeks as I readied Xander for the trip back to L'Ochal.

"Damiyun—"

"Do not speak to me, Zedekiah." I tightened the straps on the harness.

"I had my reasons for not telling you."

"I trusted you."

"You wouldn't have if you knew the truth."

I shook my head, clenching my hands at his words. Visions of what happened to Lillyanna—what I was forced to watch—flashed through my mind.

"You betrayed us. Betrayed Lillyanna."

"Did you think we would just walk in there, do what needed to be done and walk out? My father is no fool, and you would have been dead before you could draw on your magic. I had to play my part. I knew what I was doing."

"You hurt Lillyanna. You let her become Blood-Bound to Themesis. How could you have done that to her? How could you stand by and watch? Make me watch?"

"I told you. I was playing a part. It was the only way, Damiyun. Once they were bound, his power would be restored. Her blood flowed within him. Had you just killed her, it would have done nothing. She had to become a part of him. Her blood ran through his veins after the ceremony. Binding them and then killing her was the only way to destroy him. To secure his binds once again," he said.

My body flushed at his words. At the casual way he said them. "You truly believe you did no wrong."

"What did you expect me to do, Damiyun? Had I not done what I did—had I not got him to trust me—"

"Save me your excuses, Zedekiah. You are no different from your father." I winced as I pulled my broken and bruised body onto Xander. "Do not come near me. If I feel your traitorous presence, I will cut your head off. May you rot in the Abyss and suffer an eternity of torment," I said, heeling Xander out of the stable, leaving Abraham, Lillyanna and all that happened in the Abyss forever behind.

EIGHTY-THREE

I SAT OUT ON the back terrace of Pine Crest Manor, drinking from a bottle of Serpent's Venom as the hazy sun slipped below the horizon.

Four Moon Cycles had gone by since I killed the woman I loved, and even though the house was thick with memories, I wanted the quiet countryside of L'Ochal.

And I wanted to be reminded of what I had done.

The hurt I felt when my thoughts turned to her—when I thought I saw a glimpse of her ghost, a flash of red hair out of the corner of my eye—was as strong as when it happened, and I let the hurt—the guilt—consume me.

The evening was quiet and hot. Not a leaf stirred on the trees. My shirt clung to me and sweat trickled down my back. Though it was fall—a time when there should have been a chill to the air—the days were hotter than the peak of summer and the darkness of night offered only a brief reprieve.

Not for the first time did I wonder about the heat or the wailing sound of wraiths in the distance at night. The talk that I heard at the tavern in town was equally disturbing. Livestock found mutilated beyond recognition. Wielders being consumed by Pyragaties. Glimpses of dark, hooded figures with red eyes and bone hands roaming the earth.

Dark demons of Themesis' creation.

The thought that what I had done, what we had done, had not yielded the desired effect...my Lil had died for nothing, echoed in my head every day. And I let the guilt and pain consume me.

Shaking myself from the thoughts and draining the bottle I held, I rose to my feet, steadying myself with a hand on the chair back as the world spun then righted. I limped back into the house, wincing at the throbbing ache in my right leg from the injury sustained in the Abyss. Though it had healed somewhat, it still punished me from time to time. I tossed the bottle onto the floor with the others, grabbed a fresh one, and stretched out on the couch. Pulling the cork out, I took a long drink. The liquid fire burned down my throat and warmed me. I reached into my pocket and pulled out the emerald necklace I had taken from the Abyss, and ran my fingers over the gems as I drank the spirits.

Drank myself into darkness.

It was the only way I could sleep. The only thing that helped me forget and the only thing keeping my nightmares at bay. Or at least let me forget them when they came. Let me not wake up screaming in agony and pain.

Themesis was true to his word—not that I thought he wouldn't be. His voice, his taunts, tormented me in the waking hours and his nightmares—the pain, the torture—tormented me in my sleep. I couldn't get away from him, save for drinking myself into oblivion, and I feared he had long since succeeded in driving me mad.

I feared I was too weak—too pathetic—to fight him, and I didn't have the strength to let it bother me. Perhaps in my madness I would finally find peace.

Rubbing my eyes, I slipped the necklace back into my pocket and lifted the bottle to my lips, pausing and lowering it again as I looked around the room.

Looked at the empty bottles littering the floor.

At the sorry, pathetic state I had let myself slip into, and I felt awash with shame at what had happened to me.

With what I had allowed to happen.

I had no excuse for the state I was in.

Lillyanna was gone, and though becoming blindingly drunk saved me from the torment, it couldn't erase what happened.

It wouldn't bring my Lil back. And it wouldn't absolve me of what I had done.

And knowing I had become a weak and pathetic person sickened me.

I rubbed my eyes and pulled myself off the couch, dumping the contents of the bottle I held outside. I then grabbed a bucket and dunked it into the nearly empty rain barrel sitting below a rafter and dumped the contents over my head. The freezing water was as startling as it was refreshing and sobered me up if only just a little.

I made my way back to the house and went to task, picking up the discarded bottles and debris littering the room. As I cleaned up, I realized I couldn't go back to the state I was in. I couldn't allow my sorrow to consume me. That was not who I was, and I formulated a plan and clung to it.

In the morning, I was going to leave this place again and travel back to Va'l'Victorus.

Back to see Barlack like I had promised.

And on my way, I would find a way to put my Lil to rest. To right the wrong that I had done to her.

Maybe then, she would forgive me, and I could finally forgive myself.

EPILOGUE
MOURANDA

STANDING BESIDE THE CRIB, I looked down at Serafin. Her eyes were closed, lashes brushing her cheeks. Her left thumb was stuck in her mouth, and her other hand clutched the arm of a ragdoll with white hair streaked with red and blue-green eyes. Just like her.

A gift from Phabian. He was constantly showering the child with useless gifts.

She looked peaceful as she slept. Quiet. I knew the child hated me. She screamed until her face turned purple when I was around. Screamed until Phabian or Allendaire took her from me. Or until I left the room.

Perhaps it was the fact I knew nothing about being a mother. Or perhaps the wee child knew the truth. I couldn't take her screams. Her insufferable wails. And when Phabian or Allendaire took the child, when she settled into their arms and giggled, smiled, and cooed, it only served to show my inadequacy.

My flaw.

I would never be a mother to this child. She wasn't mine, and she knew it.

I resented that fact. Resented Allendaire and Phabian for their relationship with her. I hadn't thought of the consequences of my actions. Hadn't thought I would be jealous of my husband. I hadn't thought I would grow to resent a wee child.

A babe who showed me everything I wasn't. Everything I would never be. A babe who showed me who my husband truly loved.

Lillyanna should have been executed, but after Phabian delved into her mind, I saw an opportunity and a way to save my people. I made sure to remind her she was a prisoner, keeping the threat of execution in the forefront of her mind. I knew she would do whatever it took to live.

Including allowing Allendaire to warm her bed. With the threat of losing her head looming over her, I knew she would not reject his advances.

Though the child was a half-breed, she was allowed as she was the heir. And Lillyanna? I knew she would never speak of her time here. Never speak of the child she gave up. But I did not think of what Serafin represented.

I looked down at the sleeping child who held the ragdoll. Her mouth moved as she suckled her thumb, soft sighs escaping her. She looked sweet. Serene.

It would be so easy.

I carefully picked up the doll that looked like the child. It would be such a sad accident. So horrible for Serafin to suffocate on a toy Phabian had gifted. A toy inappropriate for a baby only eight Moon Cycles old. There would be no crowning on her twenty-first Name Day. No lands bestowed. No title to give. The Shadow Elf monarchy would end with her death. As delightful as her demise sounded, I could not bring myself to harm a child. A babe who was innocent in all of this deceit.

Sighing, I put the doll back. But still, I could not let her rule.

The child stirred in her sleep; eyes cracking open ever so slightly as though she had heard my thoughts. Backing away, I slipped out of the nursery on silent feet, quietly closing the door.

I walked down the halls, the only light available came from the moon through the windows. My night dress made soft swishing sounds as I walked. My slippers scuffed against the marble floors in the silent night. I made my way through the halls. The quiet was peaceful. There were no servants rushing about. No Elves to come to me with petty grievances to settle, Allendaire sending those who had squabbles to me. I saw the disdain in their eyes for what it was, a lack of respect, a lack of trust. I was no true queen. I was a simple woman, broken, unable to bear children. The amusement in their eyes as I settled their disagreements. Their looks telling me I was nothing more than a child playing at being a grownup.

As the Grand Passages past and I failed to produce an heir, women began to avoid me, the other Elves whispered their scorn, thinking I could not hear. Queen Mouranda, Queen Pariah. The Barren Queen. An icicle formed within the cage of my chest. My heart fluttered, cold fury.

Turning a corner, I stopped outside the door to my quarters. Grasping the handles, I pushed them open. The room glowed orange and yellow from the fire in the hearth, the warmth enveloping me like a blanket. Striding across the room, I lit the lamps, then settled in a seat in front of my desk. Taking the key I wore around my neck; I unlocked a drawer and pulled it open. My eyes rested on the thick book inside.

Picking it up, I ran my hand over the cover. My fingers traced the crest in the center. The dragon with scales made of emeralds. Ruby and citrine plumes of fire pouring from its mouth. Obsidian eye looked at me, and the diamond talons glinted in the lamplight.

It was the Dark Elf crest. I had found the centuries old book in the back of the library, buried within the stacks. I found it curious the Shadow Elves would possess a Dark Elf book, and that curiosity made me eager to know what lay within the pages. When I figured out how to open it, when I read what the book contained, I brought it back to my room, locking it in a drawer.

Pulling out a dagger, I sliced my hand and squeezed the blood on the solid gold lock. It sprang open. More blood spilled onto the pages. Letters swirled and moved, forming words written in the Old Tongue. Flipping through the pages, I found what I was looking for.

It was a spell. A dark spell, but one that would give me what I needed. I read the words and though they made my stomach lurch, I knew it had to be done. It would ensure the daughter of a whore, the filthy half-breed, would not remain on these lands.

It would ensure Serafin would never sit upon the throne.